CW01044030

OBLIVION

A native of California's San Joaquin Valley, Dean de la Motte has degrees in comparative literature from the University of California, Santa Barbara and the University of North Carolina, Chapel Hill; he studied French and German at the Université de Poitiers (France) and the Deutsche Schule of Middlebury College (Vermont), respectively. The co-editor of *Making the News: Modernity and the Mass Press in Nineteenth-Century France* (with Jeannene Przyblyski) and *Approaches to Teaching Stendhal's The Red and the Black* (with Stirling Haig), he has published a wide range of articles on nineteenth-century French literature and culture and numerous essays on the teaching of literature.

Oblivion

The Lost Diaries of Branwell Brontë

A NOVEL IN THREE VOLUMES

DEAN DE LA MOTTE

Valley Press

First published in 2022 by Valley Press
Woodend, The Crescent, Scarborough, YO11 2PW
www.valleypressuk.com

ISBN 978-1-912436-78-1
Cat. no. VP0195

A CIP record for this book is available from the British Library.

Text and cover design by Peter Barnfather.
Cover artwork by Lindsey Tyson.
Edited by Sarah Meaney.

Printed and bound in Great Britain
by Clays Ltd, Elcograf S.p.A.

for Maria and William

VOLUME ONE

VOLUME TWO

VOLUME THREE

AFTERWORD

Volume One

Of one, too, I have heard,
A brother – sleeps he here?
Of all that gifted race
Not the least gifted; young,
Unhappy, eloquent – the child
Of many hopes, of many tears.
O boy, if here thou sleep'st, sleep well!
On thee too did the Muse
Bright in thy cradle smile;
But some dark shadow came
(I know not what) and interposed.

– Matthew Arnold, 'Haworth Churchyard'

I've watched and sought my life-time long;
Sought him in heaven, hell, earth, and air –
An endless search, and always wrong!
Had I but seen his glorious eye
Once *light the clouds that wilder me*
I ne'er had raised this coward cry
To cease to think, and cease to be;
I ne'er had called oblivion blest ...

– Emily Brontë, 'The Philosopher'

Ah corpse! [...] in exchange for thy untroubled calm,
Thy gift of cold oblivion's healing balm,
I'd give my youth, my health, my life to come,
And share thy slumbers in thy ocean tomb.

– Patrick Branwell Brontë, 'Real Rest'

I.

A New Beginning

New Year's Day, 1840 ·
High Syke House, Broughton-in-Furness

Here I am at last, arrived in Broughton, and settled in just enough to begin my new life and, suitably enough, a new journal. Like the shirts that my sisters have sewn for me, Papa's gift of a diary and wallet mark a change in the material world to correspond to a new post, a new condition, a new beginning, a new year: *annus novus.*

How very odd, it occurs to me, that – though from an early age I have spilt more ink than many a published poet – I have never yet attempted to write what appeared to me simple, and true, and real in the world, as those appearances pass through the prism of my own mind. I therefore make a New Year's resolution of it: *this* journal is not a notebook of ideas for future development, but the homely narrative of my progress in this world.

This, then, is me, unadorned, as I perceive myself; my intended audience – if any – is my future self, just as Anne and Emily write diary papers to be read, by themselves alone, several years hence. It is only fit that I should do so, as I have now vowed both to Papa and to myself after much thrashing about and subsequent soul-searching, to earn my daily bread as a tutor here on the wild borders of the Lake District.

I have tried my hand at painting portraits for a living, but I confess here and to no other that I lack the talent – the genius – to pursue that profession. My friend Leyland was encouraging, but I fear his friendship and our frequent indulgence in drink has ultimately distorted his view of the matter; or, more likely, his affection for me has prevented him from telling me the truth. Even my painting of my sisters and myself is so deeply flawed that we all bear too much of a family resemblance, like the nearly identical figures of a mediaeval fresco.

What has painfully dawned on me is this: my sisters and I – and all those like us – are in a particularly vexing position: raised as gentlefolk, the children of a Cambridge-educated clergyman, we have through books and newspapers and conversation gained the sense of a greater world, of distant horizons, and our desires are thus constantly stoked, like a fire roaring in the Parsonage kitchen. There is an indescribable yearning, so strong that it almost resembles a wound desperately requiring either surgery or amputation. The nature of this yearning? Power, glory, love – nice abstractions, all. But also a yearning to be something other than the precocious children of a poor clergyman – to be great, to be famous, and yes, to be rich.

My sisters, at least, have the excuse of the limitations placed upon the fairer sex – I have no such pretext for failure. Papa once enquired of an acquaintance in Liverpool about procuring a situation for me as a clerk in a bank, but when I learnt of it, I promptly scotched the idea. I can imagine no drearier profession than the hard-headed business of counting filthy lucre day in and day out. I think it more likely to glimpse a fire-breathing dragon skimming over the surface of Duddon Channel than to discover an accountant or bank clerk who has not been stripped of his natural wit or imagination, whose vision has not been irreparably blinded to anything beyond the endless columns of figures marching drearily across a ledger.

II.

The Fairer Sex

February 7th, 1840 · Broughton

I am now fully settled in my lodgings, have the lie of the land and have come to know my landlord and his family, and of course my employer and my charges, and so can at last give some accounting of these. High Syke House is a long farmhouse built in the last century, and as such lies on the edge of the town, close upon the brow of the hill, within view of St Mary Magdalene's Church below. My landlord, Edward Fish, is a surgeon, and if his behaviour this week and last is a proper indication, he spends two days out of every seven as drunk as a lord. His wife Ann is a bustling, chattering, kind-hearted soul, and the children are blooming, lively things all three. The eldest, Margaret, is eighteen, and a wonder to behold – dark ringlets framing an alabaster brow, eyes wide and blue and almost shockingly frank when she looks at me, a sensual mouth that knows only three attitudes beyond speaking and eating: a pucker as if she were kissing one's cheek, a biting of her lower lip when lost in reflection, and a flashing smile that borders on laughter, the last leaving me forever wondering whether she is laughing at me or begging me to join in her mirth.

My intercourse with Miss Fish is, of course, verbal and minimal. Her physical attractions aside, she and her younger siblings, John and Harriet, form a lively trio in contrast to my own plain and studious sisters, and one could imagine sharing a roof with far less pleasant young creatures. From the windows of High Syke House I look across the fields to the church, and beyond it can just glimpse the sea. With the first hint of spring I will set out to explore the area, and perhaps even make my way into the Lake District. For now, however, the cold keeps me largely indoors, shuttling from my lodgings to the home of my employers, the Postlethwaites: Broughton House, three imposing stories of stone, is the grandest house in town.

Mr Robert Postlethwaite, the patriarch of the clan, is about fifty years old, a retired county magistrate, a large landowner, and of a right hearty and generous disposition. Mrs Agnes Postlethwaite is a quiet, silent and amiable woman, while my charges, John and William, are two fine, spirited lads. My 'work' is more pleasure than toil, except when the boys determine, as they do on occasion, that they are averse to doing their lessons. I do fear that such obstinacy may increase as the weeks pass, both through familiarity with their tutor and the advent of the warmer months. We shall see.

March 13th, 1840 · Broughton

All in all, my life here has far exceeded my expectations. I am determined to succeed and believe I have made a good impression on my employers: punctual, polite and pious, I have not missed a lesson from either illness or neglect; I am as regular as clockwork in the fulfilment of my duties. I attend church routinely as well, but can confide to this journal that I do so only to keep tongues from wagging: it is already well known by all in such a small town that my father is a clergyman, and so flouting my Sunday obligation here simply will not do. Indeed, it sometimes makes me laugh to hear the character people give me. Oh, the falsehood and hypocrisy of this world!

Well, what am I? That is, what do they *think* I am? A calm, sedate, sober, abstemious, patient, mild-hearted, virtuous, gentlemanly philosopher – the picture of good works, and the treasure house of righteous thoughts. Cards are shuffled under the tablecloth and glasses are thrust into the cupboard if I enter the room. I take neither spirits, wine nor malt liquors; I dress in black and smile like a saint or martyr. Everybody says, 'what a good young gentleman is Mr Postlethwaite's tutor!'

Meanwhile, I ride to the banker's at Ulverston with Mr Postlethwaite and sit drinking tea and talking scandal with the old ladies. As to the young ones, well, I've already mentioned Miss Margaret Fish – fair-faced, blue-eyed, dark-haired sweet eighteen – she little thought the devil was so near her as I sat penning a letter to John Brown near the fire today!

Aside from the ladies, there are several fine young girls and women of the servant class who, despite their lowly station and simple manners, dress and speech, are capable of stoking the fires of carnal desire. Eleanor Nelson, just eighteen, is a servant at Broughton House, where I see her nearly every day, and our paths cross frequently in the sloping lane between the great house and my lodgings, as she lives with her brother in cottages situated midway between. Her beauty overwhelms her simple dress and aspect, for she has brilliantly flaming-red hair, even redder than my own, and large, soulful green eyes as deep and warm as a tropical sea. While slight in figure, like Anne or Emily, she exudes a primitive, almost animal sensuality, despite her downcast eyes whenever we meet. 'Mornin', Sir' is all she can muster, but her rapid glances, when she thinks I am not looking, announce an easy conquest if I wished to risk my position with so foolish a capitulation to vague, base desires. Her brother John, three years her junior, is a strapping stable boy, whose countenance seems forever cast in an odd scowl of fear and contempt, like a cur who has been repeatedly kicked and is thus ever ready to bite as repayment for his sufferings. I am certainly afraid to appreciate her beauty when he is present, lest he spring at me in fury.

Serving us tea as I write these lines is yet another fine specimen, a certain Frances Atkinson, a mere sixteen, but whose gracefully formed person is every bit the match of her employer's elder daughter. With her unusual combination of plaited blonde hair,

Roman nose, laughing brown eyes and the ruddy complexion of her class, she could be the fruit of the union of a Scandinavian princess and an Italian nobleman. Unlike Eleanor Nelson, she is bolder in her attentions to me, but with a hypocrisy that must be more innate than learnt – for society's brand of this vice she will never need – as she cunningly shields her flirtations from everyone but me.

Indeed, this small town seems almost bursting with feminine charms. Is it simply because at twenty-three years of age I have never yet felt a woman's embrace that I am thoroughly racked with an aimless and yet overwhelming desire, and I thus find in nearly every young member of the fair sex, regardless of rank or appearance, of intelligence or bearing, a potential lover? Is this inferno of lust entirely of my own making, and these girls and young ladies as oblivious to my yearnings as they are to the finer points of Latin grammar or the geography of Africa? Quite likely so.

III.

A Letter from Home

March 25th, 1840 · Broughton

Ah, news from home! My eldest sister writes of the comings and goings of the great metropolis of Haworth, and in her narrative is most prominently featured Papa's curate, one William Weightman, who arrived last summer. Her friend Ellen Nussey – her 'dear Nell' – has come to visit, and together with the other ladies of the neighbourhood, they seem positively smitten by the young man. Charlotte's bantering tone, calling him Miss Celia Amelia, does not fool me: this is the betrayal of an incipient infatuation, for she would no more tease someone whom she disliked than she would marry a missionary and move to India. No, no – stony indifference is what Mr Weightman would have received in such a case, I would wager my life on it. Already in autumn I noticed her pale efforts at nonchalance, but her flushed cheeks announced his presence more readily than our old servant Tabby's Broad Yorkshire ever could.

Anne, whose cold is better, grows restless, and is determined to find another situation as governess. She seems bent upon proving herself independent and making her way in the world. I cannot blame her, for Papa and Charlotte – and, I suppose, I am guilty of this as well – have always treated her as not just *the* baby, but *a* baby, if not a complete cipher. And yet beneath her calm regard and seeming docility, I have glimpsed iron strength and determination; qualities I wish I shared. She *will* prove that she is the baby no more. I have no doubt that her dismissal from her first post at Blake Hall was less a result of her inexperience than it was the inevitable end to *anyone*'s attempt to subdue and instruct those wretched Ingham children – nasty little monkeys from all accounts – without due authority to check their excesses.

Governesses and tutors are stuck in a most incommodious in-between place. Of course, at once considered the very persons to make ladies and gentlemen of the wild cubs of the aristocratic, and increasingly, the mercantile classes, as the latter acquire not just money but land and even titles, but remain – and this is the cold reality of it – simply upper-servants, who can be sent packing at the slightest whim and on a moment's notice. How fortunate am I to have Mr Postlethwaite as my employer! It is hard to imagine how I might lose my place with *him*, for he is jolly, generous and forbearing, with family and servants alike.

No word about our Emily, and that is hardly a surprise: the girl is an enigma, a bundle of contradictions. She says little but writes prolifically. There seems to abide in her heart not only great feeling and compassion, but also a selfishness, a haughtiness, a coldness. To a certain extent we Brontës all have these last qualities, and to compound the matter, our innate shyness – when it comes to making new acquaintances, a timidity bordering on a slow, creeping terror – is often perceived as aloofness or arrogance.

But with Emily, any small talent we might have for social niceties, such as the 'small talk' that greases the wheels of society's great engine, has been siphoned away, and she retains in adulthood a kind of petulant, childlike dislike of anything that might smack of hypocrisy. If she were a man, she would be an explorer, an inventor or a conquering general; I could also fancy her, in another age, a mediaeval mystic or a youthful Lucrezia Borgia. She is a simultaneously mesmerising and repulsive creative; sometimes I think she is a saint, a demon, a madwoman, or perhaps even a genius. One can easily imagine her running a man through with a sword for speaking ill to her dog Grasper, or any other family pet for that matter.

Yet Emily is also rooted enough in this drab world to know all too well that her eccentricities must forever lie interred beneath the pedestrian paving stones of everyday society, and her solution is to be a good, if taciturn, girl for Papa and the rest of us. I do miss the strange creature, as I do in my way Papa, Charlotte, Anne and Tabby, not to mention John Brown and the rest of the turbulent company that gathers to drink at the Black Bull, the King's Arms or the White Lion. I have come to an understanding with Mr Postlethwaite that by mid-summer I shall have a holiday, and at that time plan to return home. I am not a little pleased with how well things are proceeding for me here, and in three months' time will be able to demonstrate my triumph in person.

The days lengthen and there appear, here and there with increasing frequency, hints of spring in the air, although the fields and woods retain their solemn, wintry aspect. I have begun to explore the Duddon, and even in this drear season, as Old Man Winter tries mightily to keep his icy grip on the land, the scenery is most delightful, especially the road over High Cross to Duddon Bridge and Ulpha, which I walked yesterday with a mild southwesterly breeze at my back and a copy of Wordsworth's sonnets in my pocket.

Although my own writing has thus far been confined to this journal and letters to friends, I feel that old pull to throw everything off and *create*, as if the imminent arrival of spring were drawing forth a parallel motion in my mind and even in my person, not so much a rebirth as the arousal of a long-dormant passion, one that seeks to be consummated, but whose very consummation only enflames further desire. How infernal is this yearning that can never be fully satisfied, a thirst that will not be quenched, a void that can never be filled! How at odds with Wordsworth's *peace of heart* and *calm of mind and soul*!

IV.

Agnes Riley

April 6th, 1840 · Broughton

This morning, outside Broughton House, I came upon a most unusual, unpleasant scene. John Nelson, the stable boy, stood shouting at a young woman, who, having dropped to her knees, was sobbing over a smashed crate of eggs and a spilt jug of milk, the untidy mess oozing into the cobblestones.

'Damn thee,' cried the young man, holding not one but two horses by their reins, twisted together as one, 'thou worthless bitch, I told thee to shift and le' me pass!' Trembling with rage, he stood above the woman, not knowing how to proceed, and lacking all ability to find any other mode of expression between wrath and fear, now noticing that I was a witness to this drama.

'Is that any way to speak to a lady?', said I instinctively, but realising immediately my error – I had spent too much time in our imagery childhood worlds of Verdopolis and Angria, where ladies predominate. Or perhaps I thought myself a gallant knight-errant, rescuing a damsel in great distress.

'*La-dy?*', drawled the young rascal, 'why *she's* no *la-dy*, she's a farm 'and, almos' an ol' maid at tha', an' a dirty slut an' a whore in't bargain.'

By now I had my feet planted squarely in the real world. 'Now John,' I said, trying my utmost to remain calm, 'first, whether she be a servant or a lady, she is a member of the fairer sex, and on no account should a man address a woman thus, whether he be stable boy or gentleman. Second, I would ask that you speak to your betters with more respect. Now then, let us help her up and try to resolve the matter.'

Wordlessly, but with a flaming brow and exaggerated gestures that betrayed his inner fury, he tied the horses to a hitching post and together we lifted the poor thing to her feet. While he said nothing, I could sense his inarticulate rage, which, if translated into proper English, might be rendered as such: *You, Mr Brontë, may be considered by some a gentleman, but we are servants both of us, and may be dismissed for the slightest reason, or no reason at all, in the twinkle of an eye. Your manners, speech and learning are the only thing separating you from me – you have no riches, no name and no estates. So, you may think yourself 'my better', but you are no better than I.*

At least this is what I imagined.

The 'whore' as he called her, rose slowly to her feet. Her garments revealed her to be most certainly an agricultural labourer, even if the demolished eggs and proverbial spilt milk had not announced her station in advance. Her almost impossibly thick chestnut-coloured hair was tied back with a strip of torn cloth, and her large, exceedingly pale blue eyes were wet with tears, but the tears that had been shed in despair over her loss – for which she would surely be held responsible – now shone with scarcely hidden gratitude at my intervention. The dirty, tanned face that had collapsed in weeping now showed itself to be, if not beautiful, unusual, intriguing and most appealing: one of those faces that draws in and holds fast one's gaze, with an unlikely and unexpected power of attraction.

Her eyes were bright, and through those windows of the soul shone an intelligence that I had scarcely anticipated; her ears, mouth, nose and chin were all exquisitely small and round, as were the breasts scarcely concealed beneath her snug blouse. She had also outgrown her rough skirt, whose hem has been splashed with milk and eggs, and revealed the outline of her ample hips. This was no girl, nor was there anything ancient about her; she looked to be in her early to mid-twenties; in my three months in Broughton I had never seen her – or, more likely, I had not noticed her, as she would have been a faceless member of the constantly shifting mass of servants and country-folk whose presence is as regular and unremarkable – and necessary – as the cobblestones on which we stood.

'What is your name, then?', said I.

'Agnes Riley, sir. I lives at Sunny Bank, past Meanfield and o'er the ridge, jus' beyon' Wreaks End. D' y' know it, sir?'

'Ah, yes', I reflected. 'My rambles have taken me past it on more than one occasion.'

Agnes Riley and John Nelson shifted uncomfortably, perhaps not feeling that they should be acquainted with my personal movements about the area.

'And what brings you here, then?', I asked.

'Why … why … I comes wi' th'eggs and milk ever' market day, sir', she stammered, as though surprised I should not know this basic fact.

'Very well then … and what happened just now?'

Agnes was reluctant to speak and looked down, frowning and biting her lower lip. John had no such hesitation.

'It were like this: I telled 'er t' shift when I come down t' lane, and she would na' move aside, so I jes' ploughs through like, 'cause t' Maister has pressin' business abroad. The red'un 'ere' – he gestured to one of the horses – 'hits her fro' behin' and she goes tumblin' down, and then she sets up a flaysome wail like 'tis the judgement day, and tha's when you come along, Mr Brontë, sir.'

Whether the last word was added to show true deference to my status as one of John Nelson's 'betters' or was meant purely in sarcasm – or whether he was trying to eat his cake and have it – I can't say. Agnes simply sniffled and said, 'Bu' I did *try* to shift, bu' 'e would no' wait.'

'Well, I shall have a talk with Mr Postlethwaite and try to make all right. Let's hear no more about it. You may go.'

At this, John quickly loosened his horses and led them down the lane to Broughton House. Agnes seemed rooted to the spot, not knowing what to do, bereft of her usual agricultural goods and thus her reason for being in the village at all. Over her shoulder I could see Frances Atkinson emerging from her home up the lane, off to work at High Syke House, whence I had just come.

'Just wait a moment', said I, and dashed up to fetch Frances, whom I set to work cleaning the mess of eggs and milk in the lane. Frances clearly shared John Nelson's feelings of superiority towards her; indeed, likely vexed at having been summoned by her employer's lodger, her face mirrored the lad's annoyance. Looking the poor thing up and down and aiming her remarks more at Agnes than at me, she said, 'Mr Brontë, the dogs roamin' the town would 'ave 'ad this muck fettled up as quick as I could, surely.' She then retreated up the lane, spinning her head round with a final backward glance of dismay as she ducked through her doorway.

April 8th, 1840 · Broughton

This morning I awoke to this thought: how different, really, is Agnes Riley from Patrick Brunty, the young man Papa ceased to be when he crossed the Irish Sea and matriculated at Saint John's College, Cambridge? And if the difference *is* great, would it have been just as vast between Agnes Riley and Patrick Brunty's mother or grandmother? At what point does one's family escape the base servitude of field and factory and begin the ascent to gentility? Why can some make this climb and others not? And how much more shackled are women than men!

I was able to gain an audience with Mr Postlethwaite later on the day of the incident, when he returned from his business. As I entered his library he sat smoking a cigar, a glass of brandy before him. It occurs to me that on the one hand, Mr Postlethwaite represents everything I detest, in theory, especially the triumph of crass, if wily, commercialism over genuine feeling and erudition – of cold, hard cash over poetry. On the other hand, I cannot help but like the actual flesh-and-blood Mr Postlethwaite. He has an enviable ease of manner with all those he encounters, from the local gentry to the lowliest of servants; there is an effortless confidence and genuine bonhomie in his manner of addressing his fellow humans that makes them wish to remain in his presence.

Needless to say, he is also responsible for my livelihood: no small matter, this. He offered me a glass of brandy – which I officiously declined – and leant forward in his great leather armchair.

'Well, Mr Brontë, how goes your crusade to stamp out ignorance? Are you ready to lay down your arms and fly back to Yorkshire in retreat? Have those young rascals finally put you past your patience?'

All of this was said with a sly grin and twinkling eye. That John and William could, occasionally, be trying was in fact true, but I would no more confess this to their father than I would tell Dr Fish that I had dreamt of watching his daughter Margaret disrobe. And besides, compared to what Anne and Charlotte have told me of their experiences, I feel extraordinarily fortunate, for both lads share their father's sunny disposition, so that their occasional tricks and pranks are never meant to wound, but only to amuse and divert. In short, I feel I live a somewhat charmed life here in Broughton and have no intention of undermining the goodwill that I have endeavoured to build since my arrival in January.

I assured Mr Postlethwaite that the boys continued to be a delight – a bit of an exaggeration, perhaps, but not so far off the mark that I felt it to be a bald-faced lie – and proceeded to inform him of the incident in the lane involving Agnes Riley and John Nelson.

'Ah, well, I am not surprised. John has some sterling qualities, and though a young lad he is already strong as an ox, so I should like to keep him on. I will let him know of my displeasure anon and make restitution to Mr Tyson at Sunny Bank.'

'I hope, Sir,' said I, 'that I was not presumptuous in approaching you about such an insignificant matter, but I did not know what else to do.'

He puffed at his cigar for a moment and then said, 'No, no, Mr Brontë, you did quite right. We can't have people in our employ dashing others to the paving stones, can we? And while Agnes Riley is no grand dame, she's a child of God, is she not? I wager my grandmother – and yours, no doubt, for did you not say your father was an Irishman who was made English by the purifying waters of the River Cam? – was not much different from young Agnes. "Three generations to make a gentleman", isn't that the old saying? Well then, three to make a lady – surely it must take three, if not more.' He looked thoughtfully into the fire, puffing on his cigar. 'Are you certain you would not like some brandy?'

Although I fail to share Mr Postlethwaite's enthusiasm for the increasing fluidity of the social classes – for without boundaries surely chaos would ensue – I could not argue with the logic of his argument, and his allusion to my own lineage cut close to the bone. I could feel my face flush from my own hypocrisy, but hoped he either attributed it to the fire or took no notice.

'No, sir, but I thank you for the invitation. You are too kind,' I said and withdrew with a simple word of thanks and a bow, not too obsequious, I hope.

The following day, upon encountering John Nelson in the lane, I could tell in an instant that our master had already spoken to him, for his countenance darkened with the hatred of a demon, an infernal scowl that positively gave me gooseflesh. I heard him muttering as he walked away and can only imagine the imprecations that arose from his black heart. At the same time, I cannot tame an inner desire to see Agnes Riley once more, if only to inform her that all has been made right.

V.

Letters, Poems and Invitations

April 15th, 1840 · Broughton

A letter from Papa: Anne has promptly found herself a new place, as governess to the children of one Reverend Edmund Robinson, at Thorp Green, near York. It appears to be a grand estate, with five children and a raft of servants, all living in; I should like to see it someday. For Charlotte, nothing, and Papa appears glad of her company. I suspect she is fond of young William Weightman's proximity more than anything else. I, who know her best, can attest that once she is comfortable, she will marshal all manner of arguments to remain where she is (Papa's health, her indispensable presence for the smooth running of the Parsonage, etc., etc.); once she is unhappy and determined to fly from a situation, new arguments are adduced, and the troops once marshalled for one sort of victory reverse course and retreat towards another, to justify her own desires (she needs to be independent and no longer a burden on Papa or her siblings, etc., etc.). Although he says only that she is well, Emily is doubtless forever, eternally Emily: fierce, wild, self-contained: an inscrutable world unto herself.

April 18th, 1840 · Broughton

When I returned from Broughton House this afternoon, Mrs Fish greeted me with this: 'Well, Mr Brontë, you've had a most unusual invitation.' Miss Margaret and Frances, who were taking and serving tea, respectively, did their utmost to suppress a titter, and their eyes were filled with mischief.

Margaret could not even permit her mother to finish. 'Mr Moses Tyson of Sunny Bank called for you – and when we said you were not here, he simply said, in his rapid way, trying his best to sound like a gentleman, "Would it please you to inform Mr Brontë that I should like him to pay a visit to Sunny Bank? I should like to speak with him and show him round the place."'

With this, she sprang up from her chair and cried, 'Ah *ha*, Mr Brontë, what wonders await you at that place of song and fable, that veritable land of milk and honey, *Sunny Bank*! How thrilling to see cows milked, hens lay their eggs, or,' her face flushing slightly, 'who knows what else?'

'That is quite *enough*, Margaret', fairly shouted Mrs Fish, whose spirited daughter routinely puts her past her patience, but in this particular case, the said offspring had stretched her dainty foot dangerously close to a line never to be crossed.

'I don't know where you get such ideas,' – here looking meaningfully at Frances – 'but no *lady* speaks this way, and no young man should receive such shocking treatment at her hands. Believe you me, no true *gentleman* will ever find you attractive if you are in the habit of uttering such dreadful things.'

Whether it was keeping Dr Fish's frequent tippling confined to the house and thus largely unknown to the townsfolk (for if Frances or the other servants were to repeat *that* intelligence, they would surely be sacked), keeping a spotless house, or ensuring that Margaret's clothing, manners and speech adhered to her idea of ladylike behaviour, Mrs Fish's every effort appeared bent towards presenting her elder daughter, like a dripping roast, as the choicest possible piece of meat for the most eligible young gentleman – rich, of course – to consume someday. If she had ever had passions or yearnings of her own, these had long-since been warped and twisted in a single direction, like moorland firs bent by decades of northerly blasts. In short, this was now her life's work.

Miss Margaret, however, would have her fun at my expense. Inching closer to me, bright blue eyes laughing, she continued,

'Well, Mama, have it *your* way, I was just teasing Mr Brontë, who surely deserves it. After all, from what I hear tell, he treated a servant from Sunny Bank as an equal, even calling her a *lady*. So, if you wish to lecture someone on the proper order of things, perhaps you should speak to *him*, and not me', she concluded triumphantly, and her eyes flashed towards her mother as if to say, *Now then!*

Clearly the story of the incident in the lane had been recounted, most likely with embellishments, by John Nelson, and had made its way through the channels of rumour that surely ran, like an underground river, through and around, between and among, the houses of Broughton. I could even fancy Frances, at the first opportunity, seeking John out for a full report of the matter, and repeating every detail to Miss Fish.

'I'm afraid,' said I, struggling to rein in my own nerves as I sat down, 'that there was a bit of a misunderstanding. I saw what I felt was a wrong and tried to do right. That is all.'

'Well,' said Mrs Fish somewhat absently – for she was surely still thinking far more of Margaret's unseemly behaviour than of mine – 'if that's the case, you did quite right. At any rate, Mr Tyson has said that you are to send word if you are willing and able to pay him a call in the coming days.' So saying, she asked Margaret to step into the next room to have a word – no doubt a further expostulation of her views on the proper comportement of the fair sex – whilst Frances proceeded to clear the table. 'No tea today, Mr Brontë?', she said loudly enough so that the ladies could hear, but then, her brows knitted, she leant forward provocatively, her breasts so near that the only way I could avoid staring in their direction was to look fixedly into her eyes.

'Take care if you meet up with tha' Agnes Riley again,' she said softly and urgently, 'folk's been known t' gossip about 'er.'

'Why do you say so, Frances?', I whispered in return.

'Jes' take care', she said meaningfully, and I thought almost threateningly. I had no idea what she meant by this pronouncement, which she uttered with the gravity of the Oracle of Delphi. With that she turned and carried her tray into the kitchen.

I have sent word to Mr Tyson that I would be pleased to call at Sunny Bank four days hence.

April 20th, 1840 · Broughton

Is it truly a passion for writing or a dislike of any other occupation that drives me to continue to seek a foothold on Mount Parnassus? Do I wish to *write* poetry, or simply *be* a poet, as I imagine a poet to be? Did all of my inspiration – that wild childish fury to create, that 'scribblemania' as we called it – dry up years ago, like my long-abandoned paints? Is this what it is to be a *man of the world* – to kill off all hopes and dreams until nothing remains but a harmless cog in society's great wheel? Do I need to give over, once and for all? Does making one's life in the world require one's soul to perish?

How fortunate, in the end, are those who have a stupid, animal-like contentment with the everyday world, or happy even those brilliant men whose knowledge has a purely practical bent! For who can imagine the great engineer Brunel, as, godlike, he transforms England's landscape with tunnels, bridges and railways, chomping his cigar and bitterly weeping at the death of his childhood dreams? Nay, the tunnels and bridges, the railways and profits – those surely *are* his childhood dreams! I envy such men, for they were made for this world; they were given dreams that conform to it as snugly as a locomotive fits along the rails of the Great Western Railway.

It was in this disconsolate state of mind today that I wrote to Hartley Coleridge, the great poet's eldest son, at Nab Cottage. I explained to him that since my childhood I have devoted any spare hours to literary composition, but that I have reached a critical moment where I am about to enter active life fully. With my letter I sent a long poem, written some years ago but reworked for this purpose, whose subject was 'the fall from unguided passion into neglect, despair and death', depicting those who may be 'too near pleasure for repentance and too near death for hope'.

Too long have I sought a word – even one of discouragement – from men of letters, and not one has deigned to send the slightest response: how much worse even than rejection is such indifference! Many a day there was, especially when I was very young, that I expected a letter to arrive in the post; I was certain that Wordsworth, or at least the editor of *Blackwood's Magazine*, would write to confirm me in my chosen path, that even if my work was youthful and inexperienced, I should soldier on heroically; in short, that I held great promise. How much would such words have cost them? How little I now expect to hear from anyone, and how close I am to abandoning my writing altogether!

I have thus set myself an ultimatum: if I have no response from Coleridge, I will consider his silence definitive, a final verdict on my suit to gain entry into even the outer corridors of the pantheon of letters.

VI.

An Ecstasy Most Unexpected

April 22nd, 1840 · Broughton

How can I describe what has happened this day? My blood is racing still – my brow perspiring – my limbs tingling. I have tasted the sweet fruit of a woman's embrace, from a most unexpected place, and my world is turned upside down. The truth is this: for all of my manly bantering with John Brown and company in Haworth, or Joseph Leyland's circle, I no more knew how a woman's body would *truly* feel than I could imagine living under a blazing West Indian sun. In a recent missive Brown was his usual jesting self, writing thus: 'I should expect, young Brontë, that if it is fairly surrounded, as by all your accounts it indeed is, by a veritable *brood* of plump and ready hens, that it is high time that young cock doth get to work. Do you know that if your prick doesn't stand regularly, it could fairly drop off from want of activity? I am sure one of your philosophers or men of science has proven this beyond dispute, for it *stands* to reason.'

Once the Postlethwaite boys had finished their afternoon lessons, I made my way out of town, past the basketworks and the poorhouse at Meanfield, over to Wreaks End, and at last to Sunny Bank. A lad directed me up to the house, where I found Tyson standing on the steps, his hands thrust into his pockets. He seems to be something between a common labourer and a yeoman farmer, although the latter seems almost too refined a denomination for this roughly handsome man who seems about thirty years of age; even now, in early spring, his face and arms are embrowned from years of exposure to the sun and wind, and his hand, as it shook mine vigorously, gave proof of genuine toil in the daily operation of the farm. Whether he owns it or simply works it, I know not.

'Ah yes, Mr Brontë, welcome, welcome!'. He seemed to have very little interest in small talk, but did give me to understand that he had relations in the West Riding of Yorkshire. 'Yes, yes, I know your countryside well and even find myself in Halifax from time to time. Shall we take a turn around the farm?', he asked. Although the accents of his speech are heavily marked by this northern region, he was striving to sound the gentleman, there was no mistaking it: an ambitious young man, in a way at once similar and completely unlike myself.

'I expect,' he continued, gripping me firmly by the arm, just above the elbow, and tugging me along, 'that just about now you are wondering why I requested a visit.' Before I could respond, he continued, 'You see, Mr Postlethwaite informed me about what occurred in town the other day, and he made amends for the lost goods. He also told me about your treatment of my farm hand Agnes, and his account tallied with her own.'

Again, I tried to speak, but Tyson ploughed on to the end; a man of few words, he seemed to wish to be done with this task of explanation as quickly as possible, so that he could get back to the world of crops and livestock – the sphere of action – the silent, satisfying, finite movements of *real* work. 'It is quite simple,' he concluded, 'I just wanted to thank you and see for myself what sort of person would take the part of a poor farm hand, and over his own employer's stable boy, at that!' This last aspect of the incident is one that had never occurred to me, but as Tyson concluded, it flashed upon me that I had surely not chosen sides with my own interests in mind. No employer likes to learn that his own servants have erred, and it is in man's nature to feel more at ease in placing blame on the enemy without, rather than the foe within. Then again, for all I know, Postlethwaite himself owns Sunny Bank, so extensive are his interests and landholdings in the neighbourhood.

We walked round the farm, passing stables, a barn and a pigsty, the farmer emerging from his silence just long enough to accompany his occasional gestures with an explanatory word or two. Between this beating heart of the farming operation and the fields beyond lay a labourer's cottage. As we approached the dwellings Tyson said, 'Someone else wants to thank you'. He knocked but did not await a response, opening the door as only he would be permitted to do. A man and woman whom years of labour had aged more swiftly than those who have, like Papa, less strenuous lots in life, appeared to have just come in from the day's work.

'And where's Agnes?' said my guide. 'I thought we had agreed that she would be here to thank Mr Brontë,' he said abruptly, as though any show of kindness to his labourers might be discerned a token of weakness. The man spoke up: 'She's jes' out to fetch some water, Maister Tyson, sair.'

At that moment the door pushed slowly open and in walked Agnes with a pail of water, brought from a common well. Glancing shyly in our direction, she proceeded to set her burden down by the hearth, then turned to face her visitors. As the sun moved towards the horizon a ray passed through the open door and fell upon her face, like a lamp directed towards a stage actress.

Something was different. Had word of my visit prompted her to wash what were quite possibly nearly her only garments – for the same they appeared to be, only freshly laundered – and even bathe her person itself? The thick mane of chestnut hair seemed freshly cleansed, and was tied back not with a rag but with what appeared to be a blue ribbon – faded and frayed, but a ribbon nonetheless. Her face, too, had lost all traces of dirt; only a veneer of the slightest perspiration covered her face and neck as her chest heaved from her brisk walk uphill. I would not have thought it possible, but her eyes were bluer than I recalled, and her small features were united in a demure smile.

'Well now, Agnes, I think it only proper that you thank Mr Brontë for his kindness to you,' said Tyson almost impatiently, for he had work to do, including the unloading of a packhorse due any moment from Broughton. Already exceedingly uncomfortable as a spectator, I had now been drawn in as an actor to this scene. My nerves were strung taut and my face, I am certain, flushed crimson as Agnes's parents gaped at me. Had my host not just reached out, to put an exclamation on his comment, and again grasped my arm tightly in the palm of his powerful hand, I would fain have rushed through the door and run like a fugitive all the way back to Broughton.

'Thank ye, sir,' said Agnes, now blushing in turn, 'thank ye for your kindness to me an',' she said, then seeming to remember something she had rehearsed, 'thank ye for askin' Mr Postlethwaite to make … to make …'

'Restitution,' said Tyson shortly, but not unkindly.

'Yes … that … to Maister Tyson.' She looked down, embarrassed that she had failed to remember the word in question, and aware of the farmer's impatience, to which she was surely accustomed.

'Very well, very well, on we go then,' he exclaimed, clapping his hands and moving towards the door. 'Mr Brontë, let me show you the way out,' he said, eager to have accomplished this small gesture of obligation, which, it now occurs to me, he might well have undertaken with no other end than to remain on good terms with my employer. Oh, the hypocrisy of this world! Does self-interest lie beneath every kind gesture that we offer or receive?

As we emerged from the Riley cottage a lad came running, a dog racing along beside him, to announce that the packhorse had fallen and broken a leg as it descended the hill from Broughton. Tyson let fly a torrent of oaths, leant back into the humble dwelling and shouted, 'Agnes, show this gentleman out!', whereupon he dashed off with the boy and dog in tow, in the direction of the stables, without a further word to me.

Agnes stepped through the door and said, simply, '*Coom*,' gesturing with her head towards a path that led away from the farm buildings and main road, and towards the wooded area to the immediate south of the farm, which I later learned is locally known as Butts Wood. She walked quickly, so quickly that I found it difficult to keep pace.

'But see here, Agnes, this is not the way I came!', I exclaimed. My first instinct had been to call her 'Miss', just as I had referred to her as 'a lady', but such an appellation would only make the poor thing believe that I was mocking her.

'It's no' t'road we're takin', it's another way I know.' Soon we were through Butts Wood and onto a footpath, which crossed a ridge dotted with sheep and emerged on a lane just south of Meanfield. Agnes clutched at my arm and tugged me to the left, at which point we fairly ran until we joined another footpath, this one steeply descending a trough to the valley floor. The path was not well worn, which prompted me to enquire, 'Are you sure this is the way?', but Agnes strode forward with an animal intensity, saying only 'Aye'.

We crossed a footbridge, whereupon the path opened into a small clearing, where recent rains and sunshine had brought signs of spring all around us: the willow and hazel trees employed by the basketworks were in leaf; wild, bright green grasses had sprung up; and the first May flowers had begun to appear here and there, at which I could not help thinking of my sisters, especially Anne. After a bleak, damp and dreary winter, the past ten days had been remarkably warm, with the inevitable result that springtime was bursting forth with unusual rapidity, so that one could almost see the greening of field and forest before one's eyes. Today was the warmest day thus far, and though the sun began to approach the horizon, the valley floor retained the heat it had absorbed at midday, when the great flaming orb, unimpeded by a single branch, had rained down its nourishment to each blade of grass and every struggling marigold and bluebell.

Lost in my thoughts, I did not notice that Agnes had stopped, and I nearly knocked her down with the force of my momentum, preventing her fall only by clutching her elbow and pulling her towards me. What next transpired occurred with such intensity and rapidity that I can hardly find language to describe it. Just as she steadied herself on her feet, we heard, from the direction of the main road, a gunshot, its uniqueness underscored by its echo fading away into the early evening, like the multiple circles spreading out from a single stone dropped into the stillness of a pool. Here was no hunter's volley scattered across the sky in hopes of slaughtering a few birds – in any event impossible in this season – but a single, most purposeful bullet to the unfortunate fallen horse's temple.

At the sound, Agnes, her small but rough hands already in mine, threw herself into my arms and pressed her head against my shoulder. She was trembling like a leaf, as if a great chill had come over her. When she finally lifted her head, I saw that tears stood in her eyes and I understood why she had taken this circuitous path and the velocity with which she had sought to escape the horse's imminent destruction. It had never occurred to me that such a one – habituated as she surely was to such close contact to the farm's rough, daily cycle of animal life – could share the same tender feelings towards the lower creation as my own, more delicate, sisters.

'Now, now, then,' was all I could say, in a confused effort to comfort her, and yet extricate us both from such intimacy. I began to push her away, though our hands were still clasped firm. Agnes at first complied, and her hands loosened their grip on mine, but as our fingertips were almost parted she threw her arms round my neck with renewed vigour and tilted her ruddy countenance – wherein grief and desire, I could see now, were curiously intermingled – towards mine. The slightest hint of adorable dimples now appeared and her azure eyes caught the sun's last rays; and with the force of the sea at high tide, her peculiar, rustic beauty swept before it all considerations of rank, propriety and education. We moved our faces ever so slowly towards each other, so that our lips barely touched, and then in an instant all of the inner forces that we had exerted thus far to maintain our proper roles were unleashed in the opposite direction, like an archer letting fly his arrow, or like water bursting through a dam. It was as though we were falling from a cliff or, more precisely, were enclosed in a bubble while the world itself fell away into nothingness.

Lips, first meeting gently, were soon pressed firmly to each other. I encircled her waist with my arms and, with a single motion, pulled her entire person closer to me, joining us from head to toe. Agnes said nothing, only making low, almost desperate, moaning noises, as she guided my hands beneath her simple frock, where I touched, first one place and then another, each more arousing and aroused than the last. As I did this, Agnes's own hand, which appeared to need no such assistance or direction, loosened and plunged into my breeches.

All of the practical reasons we should not do this, all of my poetic notions of love and literary fantasies of seduction – and for that matter all of Brown and Leyland's jests about pricks and cunts – all of this dropped away with our own, very real clothing, as we fairly fell to the earth, where just enough dried, fresh grass and wildflowers made for a rough lovers' nest. I was trembling, with excitement and anticipation, with lust, surely, and quite possibly with fear, but all of this was submerged beneath the surface of sensation, for all rational, reflective capacities had fled. Just as she had guided my hand over her breasts and between her legs, Agnes now lay back, pulling me towards her and then slowly inside her, at which point my mind seemed first to collapse upon itself and then, along with every atom of my being, explode into her.

Like a flock of birds scattered by a rifle shot, but who, one by one, cautiously regain, in the ensuing silence, their various perches, my senses eventually returned to me and I lay, still trembling, next to Agnes. Although the world had fallen away, and time seemed at once to have stood still and yet been blasted to infinity, the sun told a simple – and short – story: all of this had transpired in no more than five minutes. Far from the dashing seducer or jaded, practised debauchee, I was quite unmistakably a babe in these woods, and as my mind refocused, I recalled John Nelson's drawling accusation: *She's a dirty slut and a whore.* I sat up and rubbed my eyes, as if waking from a dream. Whether it was John's words, embarrassment at the brevity of the act, shame at having traversed a forbidden barrier, or a bit of each of these, I know not; but, still trembling, I looked around the clearing and began rapidly, nervously, to utter a stream of gibberish that was equal parts apology, reproach and sermon. I was further confused by having misplaced my spectacles, victims of this bout of passion, for when I do not see clearly, somehow – or so I fancy – I fail to think properly as well. I nervously dressed, then began to search for them on my hands and knees, still babbling on about 'my apologies' and how this 'would simply not do' and how 'no one must know', etc., etc.

Agnes had never fully undressed, and now she lay on her side, with her head upon her left elbow, holding my spectacles within a few scant inches of my nose. Putting them on, I saw a woman transformed, a simple farm girl become my Venus, and as I continued to chatter on nervously, she placed her right hand over my mouth and said, simply, 'Whisht'. I did as commanded, for now her eyes were free of tears and her pert little mouth with its small but perfect teeth shone fully, her adorable dimples on full display. A wildflower had been caught in her tresses, and I plucked it out gallantly and presented it to her, saying, in spite of myself, 'For you, Miss'. She pushed me onto my back and wriggled over far enough to place her head on my breast, and after a few moments of silence pointed up to the sky, which was still bright high above despite the shadows that the trees cast upon us at this late hour. 'Look!' was all she said, her finger extended to a billowing, towering bank of clouds moving slowly eastwards.

We watched in silence as the clouds, the marvellous clouds, marched away from the declining sun. Was this not further proof that poetry resides in us all, no matter how humble our station? This same woman, who had felt so deeply the loss of a horse, had a visceral grasp of the beauty of creation more powerful than any words could express. Now, instead of standing still, time seemed to race forwards, as the shadows quickly lengthened into dusk. We did not move for what seemed a very long time, until finally, as dew began to fall, Agnes again took my hand, and – our eyes still directed skywards – she moved it slowly under her garments, first in a circular motion around each of her perfect breasts, then between her legs, in a regular motion as she arched her back and moaned softly. From the act of touching her thus, of hearing her soft groans of pleasure, I could feel myself harden once again, and by the time her hand had reached over to me I was ready, I wanted her again, my mind again went blank as all thoughts were drained away, as my entire being stiffened with a sharp, unique desire.

This time could not have been more different from the first. Agnes climbed expertly upon me, first lifting and bunching her rough woollen skirt up around her waist, then slowly loosening her smock and letting it fall from her shoulders, so that her breasts hung tantalisingly, like a pair of beautiful ripe fruits, just beyond my lips. Holding me with one hand and her skirt with the other, she took me into herself, sliding down and then rocking, at first slowly and gently, then with increasing alacrity and vigour, her moans rising in frequency and pitch. I alternately rose up on my elbows to encircle the ruby tips of her breasts with my mouth and lick them with my tongue, or lay back entirely, at times with my hands on her hips and bum, at others with arms stretched out above me, as if I were bound and could only arch my hips to meet hers, as she rocked back and forth, up and down, her insides tightening around me, as if massaging me – not just every inch of my 'cock' as old John Brown would have it – but my entire being, my soul, so that I never wanted it to end; I wanted to be inside her until the end of time, poised on the threshold of ecstasy, until finally, finally, finally I exploded – this time afterwards not trembling, but tingling with a mixture of relief and pleasure, so completely that I almost lost consciousness in a sort of oblivion that no spirit or opiate could ever procure.

Night was now falling fast, and yet still we lay together, kissing each other with nearly the same fervour as we had before, as if we both wanted this moment to stretch to eternity, or as if we had – for our respective reasons – so much buried desire that now that it had been uncovered it could not but issue forth, like an infinite subterranean spring bursting at last into the open.

Finally, Agnes pulled gently away, rose up on one elbow, and said, 'We mun go now,' and within a moment or two we were dressed and moving along the valley floor, where the path runs along a slow-moving, almost brackish creek called Eccle Riggs

Pool. Soon the marshlike valley had given way to a slope whose footpath led to a small cluster of houses.

'This is Eccle Riggs,' said Agnes simply, but still with that bewitching, dimpled smile. 'I were born here, you know.'

As we reached Eccle Riggs Lane, just above Broughton, she simply pointed down the hill and turned to go, but I clutched her forearm with one hand, and her waist with the other, and pulled her so close that I could see only her eyes, as if to read what was written there. The moon had risen sufficiently so that we could see each other perfectly. While I am far from certain that my body could have complied, my mind – my soul – already wanted her again, wanted to retrieve that feeling of – how can I describe it? – not of the ecstasy itself, but of the feeling just an instant *before* – or even, to speak truth, the imperceptible and indescribable space between, the eternal twinkling of an eye, where prolonged and seemingly infinite desire gives way to explosive, but finite, fulfilment. I opened my eyes as widely as I could, as if trying to match her pale blue orbs. I wanted to fall into those eyes, as into a sea, and somehow drown myself and yet live to drown myself again and again and again.

'I must see you again,' I said, almost desperately, 'surely there is a way.'

'Meet me at t'same place,' she said, nodding over her shoulder, 't'morrow, jes' afore nightfall.'

Save for the occasional barking dog, all was quiet as I made my way along the lane and down into Broughton in the moonlight, my limbs still trembling and my mind slowly – *very* slowly – passing from one sort of confusion to another: what had happened? Surely I did not love this woman, nor could I think of her as a mere 'whore' – to use John Nelson's appellation – whose only purpose was to gratify my animal desires. There was veritable beauty and joy there – not just in her person, not simply in her amorous enthusiasm, but also in her mind and soul, from her grief over the fallen horse to her appreciation of the passing clouds – and it was not difficult to imagine her a lady, had fate only dictated otherwise.

What to do? While far preferable to being discovered in Miss Fish's bed or, for that matter, in a compromising position with Frances Atkinson, it would simply not do to be found out with Agnes Riley, for any number of reasons, including a failure to observe proper stations and a communal unease, I have no doubt, with what would appear to be the disease of lasciviousness and a fear of its contagion.

All I know, at present, is that I will find my way to the foot-bridge again tomorrow.

April 25th, 1840 · Broughton

Three days have passed since the entry above, and each day I have found a way to see Agnes, my usual afternoon rambles abroad providing a ready explanation for my absence at the end of each day. She, in turn, has made it clear that her weary parents care not where she goes, provided that she has finished her work. While fictional rakes and debauchees may grow weary of their conquests, I can imagine no such end with Agnes, for each time we are together surpasses the last in duration and intensity and, leaving her each time just before the trail quits the woods, I pull her hips close to mine and already I desire her again, want to be engulfed by her, forever and ever, until the end of time, Amen. If this is blasphemy, what is an eternity of damnation compared to such moments of ecstasy?

Is it in the nature of hidden affairs of the heart, that lovers, themselves transformed, deem it necessary that the world around them has also observed this change, although no words or acts betray their secret? Or does the world, in fact, witness this metamorphosis? Do those around me sense that I am transformed? Or is it only that I am changed within, and coupled with a constant dread of discovery, that change has caused me to read new meaning into the words and gestures of others where none is intended? Is Miss Fish – Margaret –

changed in her attitude towards me, or is mine altered towards her? Does Frances look at me differently, somehow sensing that I am different, that I have been initiated into the great secret? Or am I imagining all of this?

What is undeniably true is that I can never see *them* in the same light. In eating from the tree of knowledge – viz., exploring each inch of Agnes's body – I now see the fairer sex anew, for I can easily imagine, beneath even the most extravagant efforts of fashion to conceal or distort a woman's figure, the real wonders that lie beneath. Do my imaginings reduce all women solely to their bodily attributes, as if they were no more than mere chattel? No more than Mrs Fish herself, who will surely auction her precious Margaret off to the highest bidder. And three sisters have I who never hesitate to remind me of the beauty and complexity of the feminine soul, or the strength of a woman's intellect and character.

VII.

A Different Kind of Invitation

April 27th, 1840 · Broughton

Hartley Coleridge has answered my letter! He has read the translations and the poem I enclosed – I am invited to spend May Day with him at Nab Cottage! How I have longed for such affirmation, for just a word, no matter how reserved, from a true man of letters – and this one no less than the great poet's son, and protégé of the great Wordsworth himself. My nerves can scarcely contain my feelings, so wild am I with excitement and anticipation. Returning last eve from my assignation with Agnes to discover Coleridge's letter, I could not conceal my joy, and I fairly leapt into the air, whooping with glee – unfortunately, my outburst took place in the small parlour, before Dr and Mrs Fish, Margaret, and the ever-present Frances, and so an explanation could not be avoided.

'Ho ho!' exclaimed the good doctor, 'To what is owed this great display of joy from the pious, sober Mr Brontë?' He had a glass of whisky before him and was already a step or two beyond sobriety himself. He took another sip, and added simply, 'Hmmmm?'.

'Yes, Mr Brontë, *do tell*,' said Margaret. 'I fairly expected you to cut a caper or dance a jig!' Frances said nothing, though from her position behind the others, she allowed her lovely brown eyes to dance above a sly smile. Abruptly reining in my enthusiasm, I gave a brief and direct explanation, trying my utmost to conserve a calm, even detached exterior.

'Indeed,' said Dr Fish, 'well then, we must raise a glass to celebrate your forthcoming journey up the road to the Lake

District, that haven of poets!' Although she stood just behind him, he fairly shouted, 'Fetch another glass, Frances,' for as with all serious tipplers, the only joy he held dearer than drinking alone was partaking with others.

'Many thanks, Dr Fish, but I must decline your offer,' said I.

'Really man, on such a propitious occasion as this? Come, come,' he said, gesturing to the chair beside his, 'sit yourself down here and let us toast your next adventure! You may try to refuse, but I simply won't hear of it. These are physician's orders and not to be trifled at!'

Before I could utter another word of protest, Frances brought the requested tumbler and my landlord poured an inch of whisky.

'See here,' he continued, pouring almost thrice as much into his own glass, 'I know you are not one to imbibe – perhaps fearing your wild Irish blood, eh? – but I can assure you that this will only do you good. Would you like me to water it down a bit, so that we have the same amount to drink?' he continued, and I assented, knowing that I myself would be far less likely to get into mischief if the better part of my glass were water. Even thus diluted, the whisky did not fail to warm me immediately, the slight burning sensation as I swallowed soon transformed into a diaphanous, multi-hued glow, like a setting sun radiating gloriously through a thin veil of clouds.

This single glass, regrettably, was just enough to loosen my tongue, so that after the ladies and Frances had retired – thanks be to God, for I should have been mercilessly teased had Margaret been present – I remained with Dr Fish, earnestly confessing my poetic ambitions, my desire to make the name Brontë known throughout England, perhaps even in the far reaches of Queen Victoria's Empire, or in the remotest corners of America, wherever kindred souls might reside.

Dr Fish is that sort of companion – at least when he is in his cups – who, rather than questioning and challenging as some might do, seeks good-naturedly to smooth his fellow's way – whether towards simple drunkenness, inane chatter, glory or damnation. He knew just enough about the Lake Poets to keep the conversation going, but seemed primarily interested in getting to the bottom of his glass. I suffered him to pour me one more, this time without water, and as the second dose of whisky spread its warming blanket upon the first, I began to question my rigid adherence to sobriety, and as I write this today – stone sober – I continue to do so. Am I not now become the man of the world I once could only imagine in my poems and tales? Have I not been with a woman – not once but repeatedly – and felt the shame of my childish innocence fall away like her blouse from her breasts? And now, to crown all, have I not been summoned to spend a day in the presence of the son of one of England's great poets – he who sat on Wordsworth's knee and toddled amidst the towers of books in his uncle Southey's library? By refusing to take anything, have I in fact given too great a dominion to drink – making its despotism nearly equal to that of perpetual drunkenness and debauchery?

April 28th, 1840 · Broughton

This afternoon I was again summoned by Mr Postlethwaite. The servant girl Eleanor Nelson knocked just as the boys were closing their books for the day. 'T'Maister wishes t' see you, sir,' she said with a somewhat detached air. She was pallid, almost sickly, in contrast to her usual appearance, that striking combination of red hair, green eyes and full lips, and I took this to mean that she was somehow privy to, and troubled by, the subject of my imminent interview with my employer. Walking behind her, I was filled with dread. Is this a condition common to all sentient beings, or is it the consequence of being a parson's son – for such a one hears about nothing but right and wrong, good and evil, sin and redemption, salvation and damnation – that causes my blood, whenever I am summoned by my superiors, to run as cold as the Duddon in spring?

My thoughts raced: what sin had I committed? Had the mischievous doctor divulged that I was indeed a hypocrite, that I was as fond of a good glass of whisky as any other Irishman? Worse, had someone followed me into the woods and witnessed Agnes and me *in flagrante delicto*? While such actions were not necessarily grounds for dismissal, I was employed at Mr Postlethwaite's pleasure, and could be sacked for any reason – or no reason – at all. Our initial agreement – that I would tutor the boys for six months, on a trial basis – would soon expire; was I being sent packing back to Haworth? All of this coursed through my mind in the few seconds it took to walk the length of the great house's central gallery. I was not prepared for what happened next.

'Ah, so there you are, Mr Brontë,' said my jovial employer, his warm manner immediately putting me at ease, whether justifiably or not. He folded the newspaper he had been perusing and crossed his legs. 'Well, well, I have just had quite a gossip with your landlord, Dr Fish' – again I felt a cold, creeping dread – 'and he shared a bit of your conversation from yesterday' – my heart pounded, so much so that I almost thought it audible to us both – 'he tells me that you have been invited to spend May Day with Samuel Taylor Coleridge. What an honour indeed! I would ask you to have a glass of brandy, but I know you do not imbibe.'

So relieved was I at the topic of conversation, so grateful for Mr Postlethwaite's congratulations, that, even if my lowly position in the household had not dictated silence, I had no temptation to smile at his confusion. I was also pleased that Dr Fish had not, evidently, mentioned that I had joined him in his evening libations. Or was my employer mocking me?

'Well, sir … uh … well, *that* Mr Coleridge has left this world, some six years since. I have been invited by his eldest son, Mr Hartley Coleridge, to Nab Cottage, at Rydal Water.'

'Yes, yes, of course,' said he, pleasantly enough, though he is clearly – like so many of his station – a man who does not fancy being corrected. I have no doubt that this particular mistake was not even considered an error as such, for his brow was untroubled: surely, to him, the difference between Coleridge *père* and *fils* could not be less significant.

‘That is the very thing I wanted to discuss. I’ve been quite pleased with the progress you have made with John and William and I’d like to offer you – as a bit of a treat – the use of my gig. Surely you know how to drive, yes?’

I answered in the affirmative, thanking him profusely for his generosity. I was about to take my leave and make my circuitous way homeward via my habitual rendezvous with Agnes, but my employer gestured to the chair next to his. As April drew to a close the weather had continued to be unseasonably warm, so that no fire blazed in the grate. The heavy winter curtains had been pulled back and the large library windows had been opened just sufficiently to permit a faint, sweet breeze to steal in, causing the gauzy sheers to tremble from time to time, while a fly bumped against the panes at irregular intervals. I sat at his command.

‘See here, Mr Brontë, I truly *am* most grateful for all that you’ve done, but’ – and here my nerves, which had finally relaxed at his offer of the gig, were yet again stretched tight: *O God, what now have I done?* I thought, with directionless but palpable feelings of guilt washing over me yet again – ‘but I want to be sure that you follow the terms of our agreement.’

I was confused, and my bewildered countenance clearly betrayed me, for before I could ask for an explanation, he continued, ‘What I mean is, you were hired to instruct the boys “in a general course in education, including the classics, with the strictest attention to grammar”. Was that not the advertisement in the *Leeds Intelligencer*, word for word? Is that not our agreement?’ Here he held the newspaper aloft.

‘Why yes – yes of course it is,’ said I, ‘are you unhappy with the results? Should I do otherwise than I have done thus far?’ My confusion deepened, and if he were not my employer I might have fairly kindled up at such an innuendo, that I had somehow not performed my duties. Had he not just said that he was pleased? The fly continued to buzz and tap, trapped as it was between the sheer curtain and the windowpane.

‘No, no, it is not that. I suppose what I mean to say is that – since you are an aspiring poet – I want to make sure that John and William receive an education that has a *practical* bent.'

Again relieved, and finally with a clearer notion of where this conversation was heading, though at the same time knowing that a certain amount of diplomacy was required in my response, I simply said 'Of course, sir,' though to myself I thought, *do you wish to equate reading the classics with keeping a bank ledger?*

Although he sat surrounded by books that he had never read and would never lift from their shelves – indeed, most of their pages had never been, and would never be, cut – and was himself a hard-headed businessman, Mr Postlethwaite was – is – no fool. As though reading my very thoughts, he continued: 'Let me be plain. I don't give a toss for the classics myself, and don't really care whether the boys do either. But the reality is this, that to make one's way in this world one needs to be able to converse with all kinds, from the labourer in the field to the lord and lady of the manor, and where the latter is concerned, a smattering of the classics and, above all, an absolute mastery of English grammar and diction is essential.'

I knew exactly what he meant, though I sat silently, appearing somewhat mystified. Truth to tell, I began to take a somewhat perverse pleasure in feigning such obtuseness that he was forced into a more explicit statement of his views. The fly, meanwhile, had freed itself from the curtain and spiralled around the library, landing occasionally near one of us before launching itself back into the air.

'What I mean to say is this: the boys, and especially William, are quite enthusiastic about their readings; John has even attempted to craft some religious poetry himself. So, while I congratulate you for having inspired the boys to such an unwonted degree, I cannot countenance the sort of enthusiasm that has carried you thus far in *your* career, so that you appear even on the threshold of making a life in letters. If you can make your way in the world by some combination of teaching and writing, I say, *good for you*, for as the son of a poor clergyman, what are you to inherit? John and William, however, are Postlethwaites, and their future has already been mapped for them. My grandfather was a shipbuilder and my father a merchant, so successful that he constructed this home with the fortune he amassed. We build fortunes, we don't squander them. This is the century of industry, of movement, of change, Mr Brontë – think of the railways, I can tell you that they are coming soon – yes, even to this remote outpost – and we will all, like it or not, be linked together in a vast web of commerce, and if you were to ask me where to apply yourself I would say *there* – and so my boys will need to seize the moment, *carpe diem*, isn't that it?'

He seemed quite pleased with himself, blissfully ignorant of the irony of this particular employment of Horace. I, on the other hand, wanted to cry out: *No, damn it, to seize the day means to lose oneself in utter ecstasy in the arms of a woman; it means having a second – or third or fourth – glass of whisky, with no regard to the duties of the following day; it means writing a poem today, when one should be planning for one's future.* It was, in fact, contrary to everything Mr Postlethwaite believed about this world.

However, by now I had resumed – as a matter of survival – my habitual cloak of hypocrisy. 'Why yes,' I said, brightening, 'that's Horace ... the very poet whose *Odes* I have translated and sent along to Mr Coleridge.'

'You see!' he replied, slapping his knee and unconsciously prolonging the irony, 'I'm sure Mr Coleridge himself would agree with me. I'm glad you do, too, Mr Brontë.' As in previous interviews, I again found that I could not dislike my employer – although I will forever find his view of the world repugnant – and I was increasingly convinced that his genuinely congenial nature was surely one of the primary factors of his success as a magistrate and the second-largest landowner in the district. I also knew that he would terminate my employment without batting an eyelid if he felt I was not the proper tutor for his sons.

Again appearing to read my thoughts, he concluded, still smiling, 'The truth of the matter is that if one of my boys were to announce his intention to be a poet or artist of some sort, I would cut him off without a shilling, and I would very likely blame you for having put father and son asunder.' Without the slightest warning, he brought the newspaper crashing down on the table before him, obliterating the fly beyond recognition. 'There now!' he cried triumphantly, and he stood to dismiss me, for it was clear that the interview had ended. As I rose from my chair to depart, Mr Postlethwaite again thanked me kindly for my service thus far and assured me that John Nelson would have the gig ready for me just after sunrise on May Day.

VIII.

Nab Cottage

May 2nd, 1840 · Broughton

My visit to Nab Cottage, home of Mr Hartley Coleridge, has filled me with an almost indescribable admixture of sentiments: exaltation and hope, but also trepidation akin to terror, if not despair at my true prospects of earning a living solely by my pen. Well might scripture say that *man shall not live by bread alone*!

Rising with excitement before dawn, I walked down to Broughton House to take possession of the gig from the ever-scowling John Nelson. If looks could kill, I would not have travelled the twenty miles to Rydal Water, which in fact I did, arriving at Nab Cottage well before noon. A lone servant showed me into the library. The odd little man – some twenty years my senior – who greeted me on the threshold could not have formed a greater contrast to the Byronesque scion of the Romantic Movement that I had anticipated. And yet here was a large and noble brow, with graying hair swept back in the old fashion, and side whiskers not unlike my own; his face showed, if not the traces of physical suffering – for little, if any, physical want has he ever known – then the deep imprint of spiritual trials, which gave him a look of well-earned sagacity.

And the library! Surrounding us were shelves and stacks of books, some more well worn than others, but all clearly intended to serve a *purpose*, unlike the decorative tomes lining Postlethwaite's walls. I laughed inwardly at this curious paradox: whilst my employer had sat expounding on the importance of practical knowledge, he was surrounded by books that served instead as pure ornament, and could easily have been replaced by factitious replicas with blank pages. A painting of my host as a young man hung on the wall, along with several landscapes, and an elegant clock stood ticking on the mantel above an unlit fire.

The high glee with which I looked about the room soon led me, in turn, to speak, in hushed, reverential tones, about his father, about Southey, and, of course, about the great Wordsworth himself, the last of whom lives just a mile away, in Rydal Village. Coleridge said nothing, a strange little creature seated in a very large armchair; he simply stared out the windows facing the lake, over which a grey heron swooped, dived spectacularly, and emerged with a fish.

I thought I heard him laugh softly, but that was all. I paused for him to respond, and hearing nothing – *horror vacui* – I rushed nervously on. I told him that I had written to Wordsworth and had never had a reply, but that Charlotte had received a letter both encouraging and sobering from Southey, the poet laureate and uncle of Coleridge – for so he insisted that I call him, dismissing my attempt to address him as 'Mr Coleridge' or 'my dear sir' with the wave of a hand and the words, 'Please, please', as though such formality could not be borne.

When finally even my own ears could no longer bear my fulsome prattling, I fell silent. Coleridge continued to gaze out at the water, and then slowly turned his large languid eyes towards me. His stare, though far from cruel, examined me as though I were the rarest of African beasts, seen for the first time in captivity: did he even know who I was, and why I was there? Still he said nothing, until finally, after what seemed like hours but was surely only a few moments, his eyes focused, then narrowed, and he leant forward in his chair.

'Brontë,' (in return, I would apparently be neither 'Mr Brontë' nor 'Branwell'), said he, 'you are young, and so retain a somewhat ideal view of the world. To you, my father and my uncle and Wordsworth – those Lake Poets as they have come to be called – are heroes. You know them for the most part only by their work, which is as it should be, but you must not envy them their *lives*, or envy me mine. Their kind of genius, which I hardly pretend to share, was often akin to madness, and to make heroes – or worse, Gods – of them can lead to no good. From my earliest memories my father was either plunged in the deepest despair or so giddy with happiness that we thought him quite mad. Later, he was in such thrall to the accursed habit of opium that it destroyed him utterly, severing every meaningful tie that remained of his prior life. He married my mother for all the wrong reasons and, in the end, despised her for it, as though the decision had been solely hers.'

Coleridge sighed heavily at the recollections he had called forth, but continued, 'As for me – well, as for me, I am afraid I share most of my father's flaws and precious little of his genius. I was so routinely and completely drunk at Oxford that I lost my fellowship at Oriel – no small achievement, I can tell you that, for the place is hardly a temperance society.'

At this I could not help but bring to mind, with a curious blend of shame and pride, my solemn adherence to the oath of Papa's quaint little Haworth Temperance Society of just a few years ago; had Coleridge's tale not been so grave I would surely have smiled outright at this thought of my former innocent self.

He pressed on, 'Indeed, I don't think it was so much the *drink* itself, but the effects it *wrought* on me: I disappeared from my tutorials and spent nearly all of my time and money in the public houses and brothels. On one occasion I awoke in my bed with a naked woman of dubious morals beside me' – here he seemed quite delighted, for his face broadened into a smile at the recollection – 'with no memory of returning to my quarters or what had transpired; on more occasions than I care to admit, I was dragged or carried through the streets of Oxford and deposited unceremoniously at my front door, in an inebriated heap. The old man' – and here he flippantly designated none other than the great Samuel Taylor Coleridge – 'the old man was crushed, of course, and he tried his utmost to have the judgement reversed. If anything, the Coleridge name kept me at Oriel longer than was appropriate, but ultimately the college had to amputate such a diseased limb as I.'

He went on to tell of his life in London and the composition of his first poems; of his failed attempts to operate a school at Ambleside and, more recently, at Sedburgh; and of his contributions to that childhood favourite of mine, *Blackwood's Magazine*, which I had repeatedly – and, I now understood at last, impetuously – assailed with letters proclaiming my poetic worth, including offering myself as its editor in place of James Hogg in 1835, when I was scarcely eighteen! I did not care to admit any of this to my host. The biographies he had written – of Yorkshire worthies and the dramatists Massinger and Ford – he had done, quite simply, for money. Now, at forty-three, he felt only what he called 'the woeful impotence of weak resolve'.

Coleridge was again silent for some time, as he sat with his hands folded on his waist, his two index fingers pointing skyward, like a church steeple. 'You see, Brontë, while of course I find no small merit in your writing – especially your translations of Horace – what drew my interest most was your letter, in which you speak of – what was it?', and here he placed a pair of spectacles on his nose and reached over to a stack of papers near his chair, seizing my letter, 'oh yes, you speak of an "hour too near those of pleasure for repentance, and too near death for hope". This above all spoke to me, for it seemed that a kindred spirit had somehow reached into my very heart and soul and understood the quiet desperation I feel.' At this I felt another strange commingling, this time of pride and disappointment – pride that Coleridge had somehow found in me, however slightly, a kindred spirit, but disappointment that my letter, not my poetry, had prompted these feelings.

His hand trembled visibly as he returned my letter to where he had found it, and again he was lost to me – his mind surely travelling to another place or time – and he once more gazed silently across the water, as the sun rose higher and higher in the cloudless azure sky and the ornate mantel clock ticked off the seconds dividing one minute from the next. I thought briefly of Papa, and his habit of winding the great clock on the Parsonage landing each night at precisely nine o'clock, on his way to bed.

Oh, to be a creature of such regular habits!

'You see,' Coleridge said finally, as though prompted by the clock's inexorable march, 'although I have no desire to end this life, I have no great desire to do anything with it – beyond the small, daily pleasures of human existence. The very notion of ambition of any kind seems to me the most alien of concepts, *vanitas vanitatum*. And yet, and yet: without the burning fire of ambition, there would be no great art or poetry, no palaces, no cathedrals – for that matter, no steam engines, viaducts or railways – would there? But is it possible to *domesticate* ambition, so that it glows gently in the grate rather than flaring up into a blazing conflagration that consumes house and inhabitants in its way?' My host sat, seemingly puzzled, whilst another heron skimmed the bright surface of Rydal Water, in search of prey.

At last, Coleridge turned his head, squinting as though again seeing me for the first time, and slapped the arms of his chair with both hands. Leaping up with surprising agility he said, 'Now, let's have a look at those translations, shall we?' Together we sat sharing each other's renderings of Horace's *Odes*, and when we had finished it was already half past three in the afternoon. His work displayed flashes of his father's genius, at times so overwhelming that I felt I should consign my own efforts to the fire. On the other hand, I could not help but wonder: had he not been raised amongst the greatest poets of their generation – and possibly of the past hundred years or more – and not benefited from all of the privileges that his favoured birth entailed, how much 'genius' would he have displayed? Here my mind wandered to Agnes, her bright, speaking eyes and deep sympathy with nature, and her intellect that – I was convinced – was limited only by her benighted condition. Just the thought of her caused my entire body to tingle with desire, and this metaphorical hunger for her brought with it the recognition that my host had not offered me so much as a glass of water or a crust of bread.

It was not long, however, before Coleridge exclaimed, 'Ah, let us dine! I am sure you must be ravenous, my friend. We'll have dinner early today, as we did in my childhood.' He showed me into a modest low-ceilinged dining room, but the meal itself betrayed the man's rarified upbringing, from the fine linens, silver and crystal to the food and wine themselves. For there were multiple courses, and the wine – he was partial to Haut-Brion, he explained – flowed prodigiously; he drank his first glass before he had lifted his fork, as though to put himself in the proper frame of mind for what was to come. Declining to join him was simply out of the question: for the poor parson's son to display such extreme temperance would be perceived, I was convinced, not only as churlish in its own right, but would smack of judgement, particularly following my host's avowal of his spirited and spirituous adventures at Oxford.

By the end of a delicious first course of pigeon in white sauce, his second glass had been emptied, and so for me to finish my first at that moment displayed just enough – but not too much – temperate restraint. Coleridge's hand, now steady, grasped the bottle and poured us each a large glass, as his lone servant brought out a splendid venison pie. His face had grown bright, his eyes sparkled, and he seemed at once more at ease and animated, as if the claret had gently rendered him unto himself. He set the bottle down and gazed into his glass.

'Once upon a time,' he began, and I half expected a fairy tale to ensue, 'Yes, once upon a time, I wrestled mightily with Old Man Bacchus, but we are now old friends.' Seeing my knitted brows, he continued, 'You see, Brontë, I once believed that a man with such appetites as mine could make only one of two choices: complete and utter abstinence from all wines and spirits – a tee-totalling temperance if you will – or a complete surrender to the 'demon drink', as our Baptist friends would say. But I finally became insistent on finding a middle way, avoiding all excess, *meden agan* as the temple of Delphi tells us. I determined that were I to give over entirely and drink no more, I would in essence show myself to be every bit as routed by the enemy as though I were to succumb entirely to drink, for I would have given Bacchus an omnipotence that he scarcely deserves, as if he were Satan himself. His power over me would be complete, so miserable would I be in my sobriety, for I would surely do nothing but *think* about drink, or the dangers of falling again into its clutches. Whereas the *via media*' – here he reached for a second bottle of claret, already uncorked, and moved it towards my glass, but seeing it still full, refilled his own – 'yes, yes, the *via media*, that middle way, that is the answer: *moderatio, moderatio*!'

Again I felt the clash of emotions that seemed to characterise my entire visit to Nab Cottage. To be in this place, sitting opposite this man of talent who had been raised in a hothouse of poetic genius, possibly unlike any England had seen, at least since the days in which Shakespeare had dwarfed the work of his own brilliant contemporaries, was an experience so unreal that I would fain pinch myself to ensure that I was not, in fact, in a dream. On the other hand, I was uneasy as I watched him drink at twice my pace, and I found most disturbing of all his precise echoing of my own recent musings about moderation, which appeared, to me, as simply a justification for being drunk for only *part* of each day. I have no doubt that Coleridge – who had all of his faculties and was now discoursing volubly on all manner of topics, with a particular genius in finding connections where none was readily apparent, and with an irreverent wit whose end was surely to leave the listener to wonder which remarks were meant in jest, and which in earnest – would be mightily offended at any accusation of drunkenness, but since he alone had already consumed nearly a bottle and a half of claret it was difficult not to reach the conclusion that here was excess of some kind.

As an assortment of sweets, pastries, nuts and fruits was brought out on a large platter, I finally dared to ask what he thought of the original poem I had sent him, one of three-hundred lines, beginning 'At dead of midnight, drearily'. I had noted the beatific glow of his countenance and knew that he would likely speak truth in such a state; *in vino, veritas* being a far more relevant phrase in this case than his *moderatio, moderatio*.

'Ah yes,' he began, 'as you can imagine, you are by no means the first or the only person who has applied to me for judgement of his writings. Indeed,' said he, laughing softly as he swallowed yet another generous mouthful of the claret, 'I smile to think that so small an asteroid as myself should have satellites.' Then, more seriously, he continued, 'I must say that you are one of only two young poets in whom I can find enough merit to comment without flattery. I was struck by the power and energy of many of the lines you sent me.'

Here he paused at great length. 'What I mean to say is that I respect your work and thus your intellectual maturity enough to be quite honest with you. The truth of the matter is that you clearly possess what Wordsworth calls "the faculty of verse" – and good for you, for how much better to have some considerable talent than little or none. The problem, however, is that many volumes of poetry are now published every year without attracting public attention, any of which, if it had appeared half a century ago, would have obtained a high reputation for its author. In short: whoever is ambitious of distinction in this way ought to be prepared for disappointment.'

I told Coleridge that these last comments were nearly identical to the counsel that Charlotte had received from his own uncle Southey, three years ago, with a particular emphasis on how the *literature could not be the business of a woman's life, and it ought not to be.*

'Ah, the old poet laureate did quite right,' he responded, 'and oft have we discussed just such matters. However, I would argue that both sexes would do well to heed his advice, not just women – his comment shows just how conventional that erstwhile revolutionary has become of late! In any event, I fear my father and his generation have made poetry so fashionable that there are more young poets living and writing in the visionary poetic world than there are potential readers in the real, all too prosaic one. From what you have intimated – and forgive me if I tread too heavily on sensitive ground – as a man of modest means, you do not have the leisure I do, and must make your own independence.'

I acknowledged the sad truth of this with a simple nod of the head.

Here he paused again, as though weighing his words carefully. 'The truth is – and I do not expect you to sympathise with me in any respect – such 'leisure to create' is, in my case, coupled with the famous name I have inherited, more curse than blessing.'

A few seconds of further reverie elapsed and he resumed, 'But to the point, to speak crassly of the matter, there is simply very little interest in poetry today, and even less in long poetry. The time and attention today's reader wishes to devote to the reading of verse – especially if such poetry is crafted so as to challenge the imagination, as indeed it should be – is minute when compared to the public's appetite for novels. *Stories*, young Brontë, and preferably stories with a happy end!'

Here he slapped the table. 'Yes, yes, Mr Richardson's virtue rewarded, Miss Austen's genteel tales tied up neatly with a marriage, like a pretty package with a bow, and now we have Mr Dickens with his band of orphans, as if Mr Fielding's *Tom Jones* has not already tapped that keg a century ago! But the reading public is insatiable, and now to read such stories one needs only a rudimentary education and access to the latest newspaper. So, do I think your poetry has merit? Absolutely. Do I think you should cast aside all other practical, *useful* pursuits to win fame as the next Wordsworth or Coleridge – and I clearly speak not of myself,' he said with a mix of bitterness and mirth, 'absolutely *not*. That way madness lies. No, in the present state of the publishing and reading world a novel is the most saleable article that exists, preferably a novel in three volumes. What do they call it in the advertisements? A *triple-decker*? Entertainment, my good man, *divertissement*! Do you know Pascal?'

Here I had to avow my mediocre knowledge of the French language and its literature, despite my childhood fascination with Napoleon – that I had focused on Greek and Latin to the detriment of modern languages, those being the province of my sisters, as in most families.

'Hmm. Well, that great philosopher and mathematician writes memorably on the purposes of entertainment or *divertissement*, by which he means primarily such activities as gambling and hunting. To those we might safely add carousing, drunkenness, dancing and novel reading. He says, *Les hommes n'ayant pu guérir la mort, la misère, l'ignorance, ils se sont avisés, pour se rendre heureux, de n'y point penser*: since men cannot eliminate death, poverty and ignorance, they have determined to make themselves happy by no longer thinking of such things. Small wonder, then, that the French have kept the same word for oblivion and forgetting: *l'oubli* – even though they really are not quite the same thing, at least in our tongue, are they, Brontë? The mass of men who know their letters want to be entertained, they want to forget, to drink from the Lethe, preferably tumbling down the rapids of an exciting story. They hardly wish to be reminded of their own sufferings and eventual mortality, let alone hear about someone else's – i.e., the poet's. No, by Jove, their desire is a slightly more wholesome cousin to drowning themselves with gin or stunning themselves with opiates, or whoring until they can whore no more. Indeed, on that note, and in all *moderatio*,' said he, reaching for the bottle with mock gravity, 'let's drink the last of this claret, and drink it to forget: *buvons pour oublier*!'

Decidedly, Coleridge was as fond of the language and letters of France as he was of its wine.

'In short, my advice to you is the same old Southey gave your sister: write poetry for its own sake, not in a spirit of emulation, and not with a view to celebrity: the less you aim at *that*, the more likely you will be to deserve and finally to obtain it. My own counsel – if counsel I dare give – is to continue in the good graces of your employer, meanwhile attempting to establish yourself as a translator, since there will always be a market for improved translations of the great works – for if such volumes appeal to a smaller, more discerning public, they are also more likely to appear in a way that is both a credit and a boon to the translator, being printed on the finest paper and bound expensively, to be sold at a considerable profit to publisher and author alike. If, however, it is fame and riches you seek, I would suggest you follow the path of Mr Dickens. Though you may pretend that you are above and beyond the pursuit of riches – that you seek only poetic 'glory' – one cannot eat or drink glory, and I have no doubt that such wealth is most desirable to you, if only because it would at last procure for you the independence you seek, and which you believe would finally permit you the leisure to *create*. As I have said, though, beware such leisure, for it can be as great a snare as misery. As Pascal also says, 'all of man's misfortunes come from his being unable to sit alone, tranquilly, in a room.'

He finished the last of his wine, and gestured to me to do the same, then abruptly stood as he said, 'Let us confirm the great Pascal's thesis, and quit this room, for it is time for my daily walk round the neighbourhood. Can you stay long enough to accompany me?' I had no other obligations, and the use of Mr Postlethwaite's gig to speed me home, and so I readily assented. We had soon donned our hats and were walking along the turnpike towards Ambleside. Apart from the occasional identification of a local landmark, my host was lost in his thoughts, which permitted me to indulge in a bit of reflection myself.

On the one hand I continued to exult in the presence of Coleridge, whose discourse had given me much food for thought, as we walked along on this brilliant May Day afternoon, a soft but constant breeze cooling us in our exertions, as the aromas, colours and movement of the bright green leaves, newly sprung after the protracted winter, delighted the senses. He had seen in my verse *power and energy*, and had encouraged me to continue to write. On the other hand, what he had said about the need to support myself and about the state of the publishing world today rang dismally true. While it was consistent with what I had resolved upon my arrival in Broughton, it now had far more weight than my own opinion: it now seemed an objective truth hallowed in its utterance by one who stood just a step away from the eternal greatness of Wordsworth and Coleridge, Shelley and Lord Byron. And yet I have no doubt that the considerable amount of wine I had consumed at dinner gave a more positive lustre to these thoughts, and for a few brief moments, all seemed possible: I *would* be both a man of the world and a poet, for the first would enable the second.

As we approached Rydal and began to pass some of the inhabitants of the neighbourhood, Coleridge greeted them heartily, doffing his hat and bowing slightly to the ladies and introducing me as 'my friend, Mr Brontë' to those he knew particularly well. Pointing to a large but simple structure on an impressive elevation overlooking both Grasmere and Windermere Lakes he stopped and thrust his walking stick repeatedly in its direction, with what seemed almost a stabbing motion. 'There lives "the Great Man" of English poetry, Wordsworth. I doubt not that he'll be poet laureate someday, when poor old Uncle Southey goes to his maker. After all, he has been sitting on his laurels for decades.'

I again mentioned that I had written to Wordsworth, the claret permitting me now to confess that it had been with a warmth that I now regretted, and that the poet had failed to respond.

'Well, although we are not on the best of terms, I must admit that the man receives more letters than he can possibly answer.'

I learned that Wordsworth and Coleridge's father had become estranged over the latter's opium use, among other things, and that soon thereafter the former had taken the position of Distributor of Stamps in Ambleside.

As he recounted this, my host seemed to brighten. 'Do you know Shelley's reprimand, his sonnet "To Wordsworth"? He takes the great poet to task for abandoning pure devotion to his poetic calling in order to procure a regular income, ending thus:

In honoured poverty thy voice did weave
Songs consecrate to truth and liberty, –
Deserting these, thou leavest me to grieve,
Thus having been, that thou shouldst cease to be.

'Is this not the very matter we discussed over dinner?' he continued. 'For let us take a tally of the best-known of this exceptional band of poets: Wordsworth sells his soul to procure a comfortable existence for himself and his family, his powers ebbing away with age, under the dreadful monotony of bureaucratic toil. Uncle Southey similarly exchanges his youthful calls for liberty for a comfortable pension as Poet Laureate and will, in all likelihood, fade into obscurity not long after his death. My father stuns himself into oblivion, becoming a mere ghost of his former self, a leech on his physician's family, whilst at the same time he severs his ties with his *actual* family and friends, dying far earlier than he should. Lord Byron and Shelley cast all decency – I do not simply mean the rigid bounds of convention, I mean any human decency at all – to the wind, breaking hearts, destroying lives, and having it off with, yes, *fucking* – forgive me Brontë, but no other word will do here, and no ladies are present – fucking, I say, anything in a skirt. Or, in Byron's case, I should say *fucking anything on two legs*.'

I must have appeared shocked, for Coleridge laughed and lectured me as he might a small child. 'Come now Brontë, surely you have heard the most proper of ladies – why, even your pious young sisters, I would venture – say they don't care a *fig*, or a *farthing*, or a *fillip* for something! What word do you believe those replace? And I'm quite certain it was that celebrated libertine, the Earl of Rochester's, favourite word – not to mention his preferred activity.'

Coleridge's face was crimson from the combined effect of the wine, our brisk walk and the subject of his discourse.

'Right then, what was I saying? Yes, Shelley drowns at twenty-nine – how poetic! – and Byron dies at thirty-six, like an imbecile, not even killed heroically but trying desperately to be something he was not in a foreign war that was none of his business, expiring from a cold and a fever, with all of the glory of a millworker's son in one of your squalid Yorkshire villages. Finally, there is young Keats, poor fellow, dead at twenty-five of consumption.

'And so, I ask you, Brontë, who is your model poet? You will say that all of these gifted men have, like shooting stars, blazed across the poetic heavens, at the same time somehow creating in their wake works of eternal beauty that now shine like the constellations, and will do so for all eternity. You might even dismiss all of the damage they did to those who surrounded them as a necessary evil, pardoning the rare exceptions – Wordsworth and Southey especially – for their embarrassing transition into a regular, almost wholesome kind of existence, for their presumptuousness in seeking to support their families as their youthful powers ebbed away, for their steady attention to others, rather than a wild careering between the immediate gratification of their every earthly desire – yes, here I am thinking of the *fucking* I mentioned a moment ago, but also all manner of appetites – and an obsession with their own immortality.'

We walked in silence for some time, after which he arrested my forward progression with the top of his cane. 'It is a question as old as the ages, I know, but still a conundrum, is it not? Must genius and contentment be sworn enemies? Must human suffering feed the flames of genius, and as those flames grow, must they, in turn, consume all that surrounds them, visiting still more suffering on the world? Can we not be both fully human and humane – compassionate, kind, considerate – at the same moment? Why can we not simultaneously obey our overpowering instincts to create and our kindest impulsions to tend and to nurture?'

The passion with which Coleridge had spoken seemed fully at odds with his self-professed *woeful impotence of weak resolve*, but it occurred to me that these questions – all various forms of the same dilemma – were of deep personal significance to him, and that he was, perhaps, less interested in the eternal questions themselves than in what had happened to *him*. He was a victim, a casualty, of the unrestrained genius he described, and stood before the blasted lives and eternal works of these poets with a toxic mixture of awe, rage and impotence. The perfect emblem of all this was Shelley and his sailing companions immolated on their makeshift funeral pyre on the beach at Viareggio: a spectacle of beauty and light, of carnage, waste and death, of oblivion and eternity.

As we turned to retrace our steps to Nab Cottage, the sun still high enough to warm our necks and shoulders, the bright leaves fluttering even more beautifully, like ten thousand green butterflies rustling their wings, my host lapsed into a quiet gloom. I fear he had reached that very place in his imagination that had prompted his feelings of weak resolve, and as the day declined, so too did the fleeting exultation I had felt from our earlier conversation and, likely, from the not insignificant quantity of wine I had consumed. By the time we had reached his dwelling, we were in that most unpleasant state where habitual tipplers often find themselves, when the effects of their drink have worn off, but it is far too early to go off to bed. Like a fork in the road, such a state demands a choice: more to drink, in an effort to regain the lost state of grace that one feels slipping away; or forging through the remainder of the day with a headache and a parched throat.

A third choice – that of a nap – was not at my disposal, but Coleridge himself had formed just such a scheme. 'Well, Brontë, this is when I have a brief *sieste* before answering my correspondence. I trust I have not been too discouraging, too saturnine. The long and short of the matter is that I am no Oracle of Delphi. I dwell in the twilight land between the world of letters and the world of action, and so may be singularly ill-suited as an adviser. If I were a true poet, I would tell you to sacrifice all, to gamble all on your writing, with little thought or care for the welfare of your sisters, your father, or anyone else, including your own person. If I were a true man of the world, I would counsel striking off in the opposing direction, to seek a useful path in this life, one where you can feed yourself, possibly a wife and offspring, and even assist your ageing parent in his declining years. If you can strike a balance between the two, you will have achieved what few men have before you.'

As I climbed upon my employer's gig and took the reins from his servant, Coleridge lifted his hand up to shake mine, but I felt it also to be a benediction of sorts. 'I suppose my advice is no different from what you yourself have confided to me: stay in the good graces of your employer and continue to write if it pleases you. Refine those translations and send them to me. Begin writing a novel, if it is really fame you seek. Try to be happy, Brontë.'

Uttering these final words, he seemed quite overcome, his eyes suddenly brimming. He gave one last wave, turned and walked slowly inside. I followed him with my own eyes before making my way homeward to Broughton, following the course of the setting sun.

IX.

Love and Treachery at Sunny Bank

May 12th, 1840 · Broughton

Great Heavens, my head is positively splitting as I scribble these lines. So much has transpired since my visit to Nab Cottage that I hardly know where to begin.

I returned with heart and mind unsettled, still incapable of reconciling my practical need for independence with my deepest desires and ambitions. Coleridge meant well, but as Mr Postlethwaite might say, *the net gain was naught*. That is, although my heart soared to hear praise of my verse, and my mind was fortified by encouragement to continue working at, and ultimately seeking a publisher for, my translations, I was sobered by the seemingly intractable dilemma of trying to make one's way practically, 'normally' in the world while achieving real success as a poet. How likely was it that I could sail between Scylla and Charybdis when even the greatest poets had foundered on the rocks? Surely teaching – or even more practical occupations – would drain away any lingering inspiration, would snuff out the vital spark of creativity.

Papa, Charlotte, Emily Jane and Anne – even our servant Tabby – have all of them every confidence in my genius and the expectation that once I have found my true path I will achieve, if not glory and fame, then at least my independence and the high regard of all who know me. But their very expectations – and my sisters' frequent reminders that as a member of the stronger sex I am free to pursue nearly anything – is more a burden than an inspiration, one that presses down upon and suffocates me, like the slab in a burial ground, or chokes me like a rope twisted about my neck.

And yet, I continue in my employer's good graces, struggling ever more mightily to perform what should be the simplest of tasks, for I am not so blind as to fail to appreciate the difference between my work and that of the Postlethwaites' other paid subordinates. But is my suffering any less real because it is unreasonable?

The only moments when I have been free of this sensation of suffocation, of drowning, is when I am with Agnes, although after today I fear I will see her no more. With her I can lose myself entirely, and in our passion I feel myself wanting to consume her entirely, to absorb her into myself, while at the same time she takes me into her, blotting us both out of existence, in a towering blaze that fades into blissful nothingness, like smoke that dissipates into purest air.

All that *fucking*, as Coleridge had said with disgust, and waiting at the end, Shelley's funeral pyre. In moments of cold reflection, I understand him, but had he ever felt such exaltation in his drunken carousing at Oxford or in London? When my lips meet Agnes's, when she eagerly, thirstily, takes me into her depths and I, in turn, move within her – slowly at first, then faster, then, at the end, very slowly, so that we can extend and savour that moment when the rising wave of anticipation crests almost imperceptibly into a deafening, blinding torrent of ecstasy – all such considerations fall away, and the entire universe vanishes around us. Like two parched desert travellers who at last arrive at a plentiful oasis, we drink wildly, madly, and the water is at once more than we can drink and yet never enough to slake our thirst.

John Nelson can go to the Devil! He whose carelessness and cruelty first introduced me to Agnes has now proved our undoing. When I returned to Broughton House with the gig on May Day, John's usual scowl was even blacker with hatred than was usual, but so unpleasant a lad is he that I thought no more of it.

The next morning I was to learn from Frances Atkinson, always a ready gossip, that John's sister Eleanor had been sacked by the Postlethwaites.

'But why, Frances?' said I, truly surprised.

She only giggled maliciously.

'Come, come, Frances, if you are going to spread gossip, pray spread it all.'

'*We*-ell,' she responded coyly, drawing out the word for dramatic effect, 'though she's go' no 'usband, she's been tupped you see – she's found herself in a *family way* to say i' a bit more polite like. Seems Mr Postlethwaite sent her packin' on the spot, once it were plain.'

Although such occurrences are far from rare, now that I myself have been with a woman – another unmarried woman of the lower orders at that – this took on greater significance. I also wondered if John's strange manner towards me was somehow related to his sister's misfortune, though I could not imagine how or why. Who, I wondered, had fathered Eleanor's child? The Postlethwaite boys were too young. Postlethwaite himself? Stranger things have happened, surely, and if his appreciation of feminine charms is anything like his appetite for good food, cigars and brandy, Eleanor's attractions cannot possibly have gone unnoticed. He held absolute dominion over his servants, after all. How many respectable gentlemen of our day, if transported in time and place to a harem, would not use their position as Sultan or Pasha to its fullest? Hypocrites! Would they shrink from the decadence of such rich and multiple carnal possibilities? Of course, it was entirely possible that the father was a fellow servant or just about any other man in Broughton, for those lovely, imploring green eyes would be hard to resist under the right circumstances. What I know is this: I am not the father, and I haven't the slightest notion of who is.

Agnes and I had long agreed that heavy rain meant that we would not meet at the footbridge, but today, after nearly a week of steady showers, we were able to do so again. We speak little when we see each other, and few words are needed. The marshy ground near Eccle Riggs Pool remained so wet that we used a table-like outcropping of rock that had dried in the sun, our clothes softening its rough surface. It was a new and thrilling posture – me standing and her with toes pointed to the sky – that caused us both to moan so loudly in ecstasy that each simultaneously reached out to cover the other's mouth; then came laughter and an embrace, the warm disinterested entwining of lovers basking in the afterglow of their passion. At that moment I heard a twig snap and birds flap out of a field nearby. I turned and thought I saw movement along the path that I had taken from Broughton, via Eccle Riggs.

'It's nowt, love,' said Agnes, kissing me hungrily; I, however, was thoroughly distracted, agitated even. The news of Eleanor's dismissal had introduced a legion of fears to my mind, and though they had politely drawn away as our passion raged, back they rushed when I heard the sharp cracking noise. Habitually, such kisses would quickly enough have led to my wanting and needing to have her again, but I rapidly dressed and told her I must go. Pressing her sweeth mouth firmly and audibly on my lips, she said with a dimpled smile and those magnificent azure eyes, 'Be off then … but come back t' me tomorrow.'

'Of course I will,' said I, and set off for the lane to town. The path was muddy from the incessant rain, and I stepped carefully from one rare dry spot to the next, using stones and roots whenever I could. A few feet into my ascent I suddenly found myself sprawled in the mud – but I had not slipped. John Nelson was on top of me, his hands fastened round my neck.

'What the deuce?' I cried, the strength and skill I had acquired from boxing and wrestling in Haworth coming to my rescue. With considerable effort, I managed to prise his fingers loose, his grip still burning in my gullet. Still, in the long term I would be no match for the hulking young man; he could crush my ribs like a rotten hazelnut if he so desired. Diplomacy was required.

'See here now, John, hold fast! What are you about?'

'I le' it pass when you took that cunt's part for them broken eggs and spilt milk, for ye seemed to be in t' maister's favour, and I'm too clever to drown a man if it means I mun go wi' 'im t' bottom of sea. But now I could fairly kill ye, for what ye done to me sister. And I jes' seen you havin' it off wi' tha' whore' –

still trembling with rage and gesturing towards the path that Agnes has taken – 'and so tha' proves it were you that got Eleanor wi' child, it do.' As he spoke, he apparently thought better of *actual* murder, for which he would surely be hanged, for his hands now dropped fully to his sides.

'Now see here, John, I swear on all that is holy – on the graves of my dead mother and sisters, and on the heads of my venerable father and my living sisters – that I have not touched *yours*.' To my shame, I did not defend Agnes against his calumny, for surely what he had witnessed qualified her – especially if I was not her first lover, as her actions seemed to suggest – for such a denomination in society's eyes.

Was it because it is well known that Papa is a clergyman that my oath seemed to seize his attention? Or perhaps, beneath his bearish exterior, he is devout, or at the very least fears for his eternal soul. He seemed, if not entirely convinced, at least willing to consider that I was not the culprit where his sister was concerned. He took a breath – almost a sigh – and looked around as if wondering what to do next. Finally, his face brightened. If he was not to punish me for Eleanor's state, he had other reasons to do so: the incident with Agnes, my reporting of it to Mr Postlethwaite, and the general dislike that people of his rank have for those of mine: tutors, governesses and suchlike, educated and refined but just as dependent as they on the good graces of their masters.

What he had in mind, of course, was extortion.

'I'll say nowt about this t' maister, but I'd take care if I were ye. Y'might be seen on yer rambles, and a body's attachment to maintaining the upright morals of this place might cause 'im to le' yer employer and landlord know about yer doin's. I'm no' so sure Mr Postlethwaite would want such a person *educatin'* 'is boys, and surely Mrs Fish would not want such a devil so near 'er precious daughters.'

'And if I were to deny such accusations, John?'

'Ah, well, tha's a chance I'm willin' to take, Mr Brontë. Ye see, I am so upse' by Eleanor's condition that I can't reliably say *what* I will say or do next. And she 'erself 'as overheard ol' Postlethwaite telling the missus that 'e 'as some serious concerns about whether you, Mr Brontë, was app … app …' Here he stumbled on the common Latinate word, which he nevertheless understood perfectly: '… abou' whether you was *fitted* for t' post of tutor to 'is boys.'

'Appropriate,' said I, my knowledge of the likely word my only remaining shred of superiority. It was now my turn to be furious – at John, certainly, but also at Postlethwaite. I had no doubt that John's animal intuition was right, and that any negative intelligence about me whatsoever would tip the balance in the direction of my dismissal.

I grudgingly nodded my understanding. At this he seemed satisfied, and turned directly around and struck out in the direction of Broughton. 'Oh, and,' he said, stopping briefly and turning to face me, 'I'd be grateful for a goo' word meseln, if y'chance upon the *appropriate*' – he drawled, *ah-PROH-pree-ut* – 'moment.' The clown seemed especially pleased with himself now, and swung back round, disappearing up the hill.

I could not bear to imagine Agnes waiting for me at the footbridge day after day, and decided that there would be no better time to inform her of what had occurred than the present. The sun was not yet down and, in any event, my clothes were already caked in mud from John Nelson's attack, so I hastily made my way back down the slope and across the footbridge, retracing the circuitous route we that had taken that first day, over the ridge footpath and through Butts Wood, to the Rileys' cottage. There would be no safer moment than the present, with John well along towards town.

Upon seeing me, Agnes was alarmed, but did her best to conceal it before her parents, slipping quickly out of doors, where we made our way back to the woods nearby. I explained, in as few words as possible, what had happened, and told her that I could not meet her until I had fashioned a plan to do so, nor could I be without her. Once there, she turned to face me, clasped her arms about my neck, pressed her head close to my breast, and wept without saying a word. As the light of the setting sun spread open into the peculiarly beautiful, kaleidoscopic shower of light that only occurs at day's end, as it filters horizontally through the woods, Agnes lifted her face to me. Those lovely eyes brimmed over with tears, each of which I hastened to kiss as they streamed down her cheeks.

To anyone who has not both felt such passion and had the liberty to act upon it as often as possible – so that it becomes a craving far greater than any other – what happened next might seem preposterous; those, however, who have lived in such an exalted state, however briefly, will find it not only plausible but *inevitable*. For there, in the mud of a week's heavy rain, we desperately engaged in amorous congress as though it were the last time, for well it might be, trying to satisfy in this act every last atom of desire. Agnes, above me as on that first day, collapsed once again onto my breast, her sobs now pouring forth in great, strangled gasps.

'I'm sorry for it,' said I, 'but until we can devise a way to see each other safely, I must stay away. I will come as soon as I can.' With that, I tore myself away from her, looking back only once, to see her grasping a tree for support, her sobs still racking her frame. For the first time, I too, began to weep as I made my way to Broughton, only regaining some control as I neared town.

To the few townsfolk I encountered I felt compelled to say, 'I have had quite a tumble in the mud on my rambles!' At High Syke House, Frances brought me water, soap and clean linens, and as she did so she seemed to treat me with even more than her usual degree of cheek. Had she already heard something of John Nelson's suspicions about me? Worse, was there a current of rumour among Broughton's servant class about me? Was it even possible that Eleanor was pregnant by Postlethwaite himself and so rather than impugn him and lose all, including her brother's post, she had hinted that I was the father? Did others know about Agnes? My mind sped through the range of possibilities.

Or, more likely, was it I who had changed? What ponderous weight we give to each passing glance, to each insignificant utterance, when we suspect that our secret has been discovered! Like blackest night, our guilt makes monsters of the habitual shapes of everyday life – or so I tried to convince myself. It was likely that Frances was no different than she had been since my arrival in Broughton, for she had always spoken to me in the same provocative, flirtatious way when unobserved by others.

And yet I struggle to sleep, so great are the twin fears of losing Agnes and my situation. I have begun having at least one glass of whisky – and often several more – with Dr Fish at day's end, for it deadens my anxiety, and eventually gives way to a shallow, disagreeable slumber. I awake each morning with a seemingly unquenchable thirst and an insufferable headache. How long can I persist in such a state?

X.

Dismissal

May 20th, 1840 · Broughton

More than a week has passed and I am no closer to devising a plan to see Agnes. I am wild with distraction, but I struggle mightily to retain the inward calm necessary to continue in my situation at Broughton House. The warming weather and lengthening days commingle with my own inattention, which makes the boys' lessons almost unbearable to tutor and pupils alike. Once, I used the excuse of Virgil's *Eclogues* to take the lads out of doors, but this reminded me too powerfully of Agnes, and I did not repeat the experiment. I fear I gaze out of the windows even more than my charges do. The truth is, I wish to keep my position at the Postlethwaites' but have no desire to do the work entailed, although easier and more suitable work I cannot imagine.

I cannot conceive that my overwrought nerves can endure this state for long: I must keep my bearing and thus my position, and yet within my soul there is nothing but tumult and torment, and I could no more sit down to write – or even translate – in my current state of mind than I could settle into that long, dull career as a bank clerk that Papa had once imagined for me. I am wild with desire and yet I cannot act. I yearn for Agnes and yet see no way forward. Perhaps I can frame a solution during the summer, for a solution there must be. Is there not always a solution, with enough will?

June 5th, 1840 · Broughton

Confound it all, my life in Broughton is finished – I am to leave this place at week's end! Home – Haworth, which was to be a brief haven – will now be a prison, though the inmates the same. It is I who will be changed. If indeed an Inferno there is, I am convinced that we, ourselves, give birth to it, nurture it, and then carry it with us wherever we might go. That this Hell is of our own making only makes the wormwood and gall the more bitter!

Two nights ago – one of the two nights a week when the good doctor permits himself to get as drunk as a lord, though he drinks nearly every night – I finally succumbed to my desire to drown myself entirely, so anxious was I that John Nelson would reveal my secret life. Dr Fish was all too willing to invite me along on his drinking bout, and we sat up many hours after the family had gone to bed. What we discussed mattered not to me; only the numbing sensation that spread from my throat to my entire body and at last to my feverish brain was of any importance.

The next morning, I awoke with a dry mouth and head pounding like a drum. As I arrived at Broughton House, none other than Mr Postlethwaite himself awaited me under the portico. I smiled as climbed the steps, feigning good spirits – after all, I became expert in such deception at Haworth, years ago. For the briefest moment I found my master's physiognomy reassuring, until he spoke.

'Well, Brontë, good morning. Please follow me, I've some things to discuss with you.' My veins ran with ice as I followed him to the library, where he motioned for me to sit. 'This is hard for me to say, but I have some bad news for you: I'm afraid I must terminate your employment here. It's my hope that you will come to feel that it is best for you as well.'

Struggling to remain calm, I asked what had prompted such a decision; I could not imagine that John Nelson had already said something.

'As we discussed, I've been concerned for some time whether your abilities and temperament were the best match or *fit* for the boys.' Here I stiffened somewhat with resentment but battled to keep it at bay. Postlethwaite might be a hard-nosed businessman, but one of his practical talents is to read the language of the human body, and he clearly perceived my inner furore.

'See here, Brontë, there is no question that your intellectual abilities are superior, and your behaviour with the boys has been beyond reproach, though they have begun to intimate that your heart appears not to be in your work – that you often sigh and look out of doors, lost in your own thoughts. The servants report that once or twice you have arrived quite late, and that you occasionally smell of drink. The boys have said no such thing, and their unwillingness to compromise you – that is, their loyalty to you despite these circumstances – is also cause for concern, for I wonder to what extremes your conduct would need to go before they would report you to their own father. That, I would rather not find out.'

He sighed with what seemed genuine regret.

'I just think it best for everyone to start afresh. I shall of course write you a glowing reference to carry with you and will send it along in a day or two. You will be paid for the work you have done; indeed, I shall make it a point of honour to pay you until midsummer' – here he tendered me an envelope – 'though I would ask you to return no more to Broughton House after today. You may say goodbye to the boys when you leave. They are waiting for you in the schoolroom.'

I was not ready to depart, however, and pressed him for a fuller explanation.

'Well, Brontë, already rumours were afoot in the village that you were not entirely the steady, abstemious, pious gentleman that we thought you at first. Although such talk is perhaps as insubstantial as the air that carries it, it can, if violent and unceasing, do great damage to a person, just as a blasting wind and constant mist erodes the mightiest cliffs along the sea.'

It appeared that Postlethwaite, in spite of himself, was a poet. Is not everyone, at some moment of his life, before putting away such childish dreams? Here was a lesson, I suppose: at some point the poet or the man of the world would need to triumph, the one slaying the other once and for all. As I gazed out the window, my mind wandered towards my conversation with Coleridge, and then what I would tell Papa and the others, and beyond that, what I would do next, when I heard my employer calling my name.

'Brontë … Mr Brontë …'

I removed my spectacles and gazed at the blurred features of Mr Postlethwaite. This is an action I habitually perform in uncomfortable circumstances, when I must look directly at a person but do not really wish to see him, whether from dislike, diffidence or trepidation.

'Yes, sir?'

'As I was saying, Mr Brontë, a fresh start for all will be just the thing. Although you leave under a bit of a cloud, I intend that you should know – and that the world should know – that you have performed your duties well, and that I am not ashamed to clasp hands with you as you go. A cloud is not the same as a storm, and I suppose what I mean to say is that it is best that you depart before the cloud bursts upon you.'

First a weather simile, now a weather metaphor. Did Postlethwaite know the difference? Did it matter? Surely not to him. Yet I continued to like him, and there was no manner in which I could deny the fairness – even kindness – that he had consistently shown me, even now.

'I understand,' said I at last, and stood to shake his hand. He accompanied me down the great corridor to say my farewells to his boys. They stood when we entered, and their father's presence no doubt dampened any warmer sentiments they might have displayed at my departure. John, a serious, golden-haired lad of eleven, seemed at war with himself, and his 'Goodbye, Mr Brontë' trembled with emotion. Had I committed the sin of opening his mind to poetry and then abandoning him to a world that had little use for such things, just as Papa had done to me – to us all? Had I cast him into the same dilemma I faced, but in miniature?

William, a year or so younger, was a less sensitive soul, all dark bushy hair and swarthy skin, a rough-and-tumble lad with a quick intelligence, particularly for the practical: he delighted in the mechanics of grammar, as though he were tearing apart machinery, and had little patience for more elevated poetic sentiments. And yet, like his father, he was eminently likeable, and I fancied him as the logical successor to the Postlethwaite empire, if not the legal one. What, meanwhile, would the pious young John do? I could not worry about it – my own life was far more than I could manage.

As I left Broughton House I encountered John Nelson, who was readying my former employer's coach. His face was oddly apprehensive. I walked directly to him and said, 'Well John, you will be glad to know that I am to be employed no more here and am to leave the neighbourhood within the week.'

Thinking perhaps that I suspected him of having divulged my secret relations with Agnes, he quickly said, 'But I said nowt, I swear it!'. Perhaps he was clever enough to know that now that I was free of his dominion, I could in turn do him harm, if I chose.

'I believe you, John, strange as it may seem. And besides, all is lost, so what does any of it matter?' I left him gaping in the street, apparently mystified at my resignation.

High Syke House was as silent as a tomb when I returned. Frances was away, Dr Fish was on his rounds, and his wife and children appeared to have gone on an errand or visit. Upon regaining my room, I lay down and curled my knees to my chest, like an unborn child in its mother's womb, exhausted by all that had occurred over the past several days: my encounter with John Nelson, my excessive drinking, and, most of all, my dismissal from Broughton House.

Could it be that I was also relieved, somehow – that the pressure, which had been building up in me like that of the boiler of a steam engine, had finally been released? This thought had scarcely begun to dawn upon me when I was overcome with sleep, which lasted well into the next morning. Is there anything so pure as the relief of such real rest?

June 10th, 1840 · Broughton

Mr Postlethwaite had his letter delivered today, and in it he recommends me heartily. He speaks no untruths, but rather brings to the fore his desire to make a change in his sons' course of study, towards the *evermore practical.* He even goes so far as to say, 'In five short months, through his excellent tuition, Mr Brontë laid the foundations of a Classical education and instructed my sons to pay the *strictest attention to grammar*,' the same language he had employed in the advertisement that had appeared in the *Intelligencer*. He even pays homage to my 'reliable, upright character'. I suppose this corresponded to his experience of me, and he chose not to acknowledge even the most plausible of rumours. With a clear conscience, then, he could both sing my praises and silence any misgivings he might have.

Around the letter of reference was wrapped another, a brief personal note from Postlethwaite. It read as follows:

My Dear Sir,

I trust that this testament to your abilities and character will be of service. Should you, however, wish to strike out in an entirely different walk of life, I enclose here the address of a Mr Wright, who is overseeing all aspects of the railway that is under construction between Leeds and Manchester. Although he currently is at work in your neighbourhood, he hails from mine – indeed, he still has his accounts with Petty and Postlethwaite in Ulverston – and the enclosed from me will suffice to put you on the best possible footing with him. I know not whether he seeks anything above navvies for his project, but I leave that to you to discover. Who knows but this may be just the fresh start you need?

Wishing you only much continued happiness and success, I am,

Yours sincerely, R. Postlethwaite, Esq.

I leave for Haworth on the morrow and thanks to my former employer can arrive home with a plausible excuse. Even my arrival would not be a surprise, as they are expecting me for summer. I hope that I, alone, will know what truly transpired here in Broughton, and can carry it to my grave.

While a weight had thus been lifted, others pressed more heavily than ever upon my breast: I must see Agnes again, but what will I say? What course must I take next to make my independence? I recall Coleridge's final words, which seemed simple enough: *continue in the good graces of your employer and continue to write if it pleases you. Refine those translations and send them to me. Begin writing a novel, if it is truly fame you seek. Try to be happy, Brontë.*

I have failed at the first of these, and since John Nelson's discovery of Agnes and me, I have also failed at the second: I have written nothing, so complete is my paralysis, so all-consuming my distraction from the fear of being discovered. As for writing a novel, while I had said nothing to the effect to Coleridge, I find the idea repellent, for I will forever associate storytelling in prose with my childish, back-and-forth scribbling with Charlotte of the tales of Verdopolis and Angria – which I put away once and for all when I left Haworth for Broughton. Perhaps I can rescue a few old poems embedded in those texts, polish *them* up. But the thought of creating anything new is sufficient to plunge me into a state of exhausted despair.

Happiness? If there exists a tame, domesticated form of happiness, perhaps more justly named contentment, is *that* what Coleridge meant? For I seem to know only two extremes: restless desperation – a kind of itch that no scratching will ever relieve – or the bliss bordering on annihilation, on unconsciousness, on death itself, such as the moments with Agnes when my entire being seemed to rush out, to explode into a million atoms as our bodies blindingly blazed and blurred and blended into one; or the rare moments – now seemingly gone forever – when, utterly immersed in my writing, I would lose all sense of time and space, in this case not an explosion but an implosion that concentrated my very existence into the creation of each word, when I would, half-consciously, feel that the entire universe was collapsing into the minute space where ink flowed rhythmically from my pen. Lacking either or both of these experiences, there was always Dr Fish's bottle of whisky, which served to deaden my desperation and provide a passing euphoria, a mirage of possibilities that rose up in a wave as I drank and then crashed to earth as the spirit ebbed from my veins, ultimately replaced by the stark reality of morning, when I awoke conscious of no sensation but a parching thirst and a sickly loathing.

I have a highly refined gift for procrastination; the more onerous the duty, the more likely I am to delay its accomplishment until the final hour: so it has been with seeing Agnes, for my heart breaks to think of saying farewell! One would think that I should be spending every possible moment with her, but alas, I find I live in denial these final days, as though keeping at a distance from her could somehow prevent our imminent separation. I have taken great rambles, including an entire, happy day spent in half-drunken conversation with that most unusual character, the owner of the public house in Ulpha, discussing my translations as I downed one whisky after another. I was able, if only for a few hours, to forget my woes and stumble numbly and contentedly home.

In short, I have sought distraction wherever I could: even this entry in my journal is an act of procrastination, for I must see Agnes before my stagecoach leaves in the morning, and yet *still* I resist. I have no idea what I will say, and yet I can no longer delay: I must set down my pen and go to her.

XI.

Farewell

June 11th, 1840 · The Inn, Kirkby Lonsdale

How strange the human organs of perception, which distort the world around them to fit the inner life of the perceiver! Our feelings rule us so that our vision of the world shifts as wildly as if we were constantly switching lenses – not just from rose-tinted to clear spectacles, but from spectacles to magnifying glass, from microscope to telescope. How oddly different is this little inn now that I am so greatly changed! When last I passed here, on the eve of this year, I was full of hope and zeal, and celebrated my new beginning by a somewhat reckless participation in a drinking bout with a crowd of strangers, including a mad Irishman and a stubborn Jew, whose riotous debate over whose people was the more persecuted caused us all – including and especially the two contestants themselves – to collapse into great gales of drunken laughter. Yet, if my life were a novel, what a perfect foreshadowing of the months to follow: mirthful hope drowned ultimately in drink.

Now the inn is quiet; no potential drinking companions are about, and that is just as well. Tomorrow I return to Haworth, and my story – given credence by my letters from my former employer – is prepared. The calm I feel in this regard, the tranquility of the inn and the fatigue I feel from the day's journey, should be sufficient to vouchsafe me slumber, but sleep I cannot, for I can think only of Agnes. What living being has not at some moment felt his heart heavy with remorse and regret, so thick that it seems to spread through the arteries to the limbs, and rise even unto his throat, threatening to choke him with unbearable sorrow?

Yesterday afternoon I at last took the back way – our way – to Sunny Bank, not wishing to be perceived by anyone, including Moses Tyson himself. A warm, steady breeze blew a handful of clouds in from the sea and bade the leaves – now exchanging their bright spring green for a deeper hue as the season progresses towards Midsummer – to dance, though to me the scene was hardly merry. All around me was a beauty that held no joy, for I knew I would not pass this way again. I passed first the spot by the wooded embankment beneath Eccle Riggs where John Nelson knocked me to the muddy ground, then the footbridge where Agnes and I had met so many times, and the nearby stone outcrop that had served as our dry refuge that last fateful day. I followed footpaths and lanes, retracing our route that first day, when Agnes had fled the imminent destruction of the horse, finally passing the place where we had last been together, paying no mind to the mud beneath us, enveloped in a blanket of fear, grief and desperate desire.

My heart rose in my throat as I approached the Riley cottage, so much did I dread this final farewell. The door opened slightly in response to my knock, and a rough, unpleasant countenance thrust itself through the opening: Mrs Riley.

'I am sorry to disturb you, ma'am,' I said somewhat absurdly, not knowing her Christian name and at a loss for what else to call her. 'But is Agnes here?'

'She's poorly, sair,' she growled, 'and can see n'one.'

I tried, ever so subtly I thought, to peer over the old crone's shoulder, but she narrowed the opening further and scowled. 'I *say* she's unwell, sair, and mun have her rest.'

'See here, Mrs Riley,' I began, but the door was slammed squarely in my face; I heard a plank lowered into place to bar it, followed by contentious but muffled conversation. The dwelling's two small windows were covered, and so despite my best efforts I could have no intelligence at all of Agnes's condition. I did not think it possible, but my anxiety rose higher still as I slowly picked my way back towards the stream, frequently glancing behind me in the fervent desire that somehow she would emerge and run after me. Instead, I saw nothing but the clouds marching eastwards and the treetops waving to and fro; I heard nothing but the occasional bleating of sheep and the scolding of the neighbourhood rooks, who circled constantly in their eternal hunt for nourishment.

Would I not be able to see her this last time, unable even to convey the dreaded news of my departure? The coward in me – he who would fain have skulked off without having to perform this awful task – was, for once, routed by a man of nobler sentiment: I loved her far too well to disappear without an explanation, without a final embrace. I lashed myself inwardly for having delayed this visit for so many days, for leaving it to the final moment.

I turned to take one last, hopeless look in the direction of her cottage, and saw, to my surprise, the figure of a woman running towards me, her thick auburn tresses flying wildly, her hands lifting her skirt high enough to enable her legs to move freely. I ran towards and embraced her, crying pitifully, as if in a wretched romance, 'Oh my Agnes, my darling girl!' Her dash along the path had her cheeks flushing, her heart racing, her breasts heaving. Those impossibly pale blue eyes were damp from crying, and I leant to kiss her, her simple beauty overwhelming me.

'No' 'ere,' she whispered urgently, taking my arm and leading me once more into the woods. We stopped in the precise spot where we had last fallen to the sodden earth, where we had desperately clung to each other and wrung a final, melancholy ecstasy from each other's flesh. Several days of sun and wind had dried the ground so completely that it was difficult to imagine that the mud had ever been, though I fancied I could read the imprint of our bodies captured in the now-solid earth. A fallen tree served as our couch.

There was hardly a gentle way to break my news, so I simply blurted out, as she caught her breath, 'Agnes, we are entirely undone … I have been sacked by Postlethwaite and must leave tomorrow for Yorkshire. I … I …', I knew not how to continue, 'I don't know if or when I can ever see you again, for I cannot remain in the neighbourhood. I … I …'

Agnes placed her hand over my mouth and simply said, as she had on our first day together in the meadow, '*Whisht.* I know, love.'

'But how could you know?'

She smiled sadly, beautifully. 'Them great society ladies ain't the only ones tha' traffic in gossip, is they?'

Of course, of course: I had been so absorbed in my own woes in the week or so since my dismissal that it hardly occurred to me that all of Broughton, from my employer to the lowliest stable boy and scullery maid, would have bustled with the news of my ignominious end.

Agnes linked her arm in mine, as we sat side by side, as if on a church pew, the chattering brook our chanting monks, the wood our cathedral walls, the sky our vaulted ceiling. She leant her head on my shoulder and I kissed her forehead, and for the first time noticed that she burned with fever.

'Great Heavens,' I said with alarm, 'you *are* unwell! You should not have come.'

'I 'ad to see ye once more … jes' once more.'

'But I have to see you again, I must!'

She seemed possessed of a preternatural calm that gave rise to an aura of wisdom, and taking both of my hands said, 'All things end … *all* things. You mun leave this place, it's spoilt for you now. And even if ye remained, and still 'ad yer post down Broughton House, and John Nelson 'ad never seen us down Eccle Riggs Pool – what then? Would you've asked for the 'and of a poor farm girl in holy matrimony? Did ye never think o' tha'?'

'No,' was all I could utter in reply, but somewhere in the deepest recesses of my being I had, of course, known that such a union was impossible. I had pushed the question out of my mind with a persistent avoidance, just as I had postponed this final encounter with Agnes herself. It is forever in my nature, after all, to avoid the most painful of realities.

Agnes could tell from my downcast eyes that I acknowledged the justice of her remarks. 'It's, it's', her heart struggled for the words it needed, 'it's like a beautiful day … i' comes and then i' goes … or when the sun goes, and gives place to rain. It's like when spring comes and then it goes … just 'cause winter comes, tha' don't mean tha' spring never *was*: tha' first day when you and me laid us down on't valley floor don't stop bein' – nay, i' lasts forever, 'ere' – she touched my forehead gently with her small hand, rough from her daily toil, a reminder of just how different she was from even the daughters of an impoverished parson – 'and 'ere' – she placed her hand gently on my breast, over my heart.

My eyes welled with tears; they do again as I write this. She had, in her simple way, said more than I ever could. If nothing but a memory, it would be a memory as durable as the eternal rocks beneath the changing seasons. There was nothing I could add, and we sat in silence, the only sound now the melancholy wind rippling through the leaves above us; even the horses and rooks seemed to have gone dumb, in reverence to her beauty and her simple wisdom.

At last, her flushed cheek and feverish brow recalled me to the reality of her illness, and I said, 'Darling, you need to rest, and I am certain your parents are displeased that you ran after me.'

'It don't matter, really, for they're already angry wi' me 'bout' – she hesitated for a moment – ''bout any number of things. I'd like fairly to run off someday!' I wanted to cry out, 'Come with *me*!' but I knew it was impossible. Imagine appearing at the Parsonage arm in arm with an unmarried farm hand, and no employment for either of us in the bargain! And even if I had ventured such an absurd idea, Agnes would, with a single penetrating glance, have disabused me of the notion.

All I could say was, 'Let me walk you home, for you are truly not well.'

We rose from our homely bench and made our way to the edge of the woods, where the path crosses the stream. 'Come no further,' said she. 'Me da' may be old and tired, but 'e's terrible cross jes' now. Leave me 'ere.'

I again embraced her, one final time, kissing first her forehead, then each tiny ear, then her eyelids, then the spots where her dimples lay hidden, at which point she smiled softly and they faintly appeared. I kissed her gently on the lips, gazing directly into the impossibly radiant blue of her own wide eyes, that warm ocean in which I had so many times drowned myself, only to be born again.

'I shall never forget you, my sweet, beautiful girl.'

'Nor I you, Mr Brontë,' she said simply, with a polite formality that signalled the end of all. At long last I released her, and as we parted she turned once more as though to say something, but thinking better of it she bowed her head and walked determinedly towards the family cottage, never looking back. I watched her – my fair forsaken one – from the edge of the woods, heard raised voices as she entered her parents' humble dwelling, and then, as the voices fell silent, made my way back to Broughton.

Now, perhaps, I can sleep, for with the morrow comes the long voyage home to Haworth, and I need the energy required to face my family and begin my life anew.

XII.

The Parsonage

June 18th, 1840 · The Parsonage, Haworth

My return to the Parsonage has been as agreeable as might be hoped, but I will surely be unable to endure remaining here much longer. I coolly recounted Mr Postlethwaite's decision to seek a different sort of tutor, playing on my family's inherent disdain of the purse-proud merchant class and framing the entire episode as an example of pearls cast before swine. Charlotte in particular, always so ready to be disappointed with me, was here entirely duped, the arrogance which springs from her own insecurities making her all too happy to join in the general round of condemnation: yes, yes, I was well rid of such a *dreary* post, in such a remote village lacking the cultured diversion of Halifax or Bradford, or even Keighley for that matter, etc., etc. Meanwhile Papa – whose indulgence for his only son always eclipses any doubts he might have, no matter how well founded, about my career – also readily accepted the explanation, and congratulated me on the fine recommendation that my former employer had provided.

As I suspected, Charlotte seeks to conceal her infatuation with Papa's curate, Mr Weightman, through jest and mockery, but I am not deceived. I say nothing, not wishing to broach the topic of affairs of the heart, for fear of being asked questions about Broughton. Would Charlotte know I was lying? Would she – could she – sense that I was forever changed, having loved a woman as passionately as I had?

What was clear was that this jeering tone had seeped into all of her communications, not just those concerning the unfortunate curate. Mr Postlethwaite's note suggesting that I might consider a career with the railway sent her into paroxysms of laughter; the same 'wit' that had been directed at William Weightman was now turned upon me.

'Oh ho,' she cried, laughing so heartily that she could with difficulty continue her raillery, 'I can picture it now! Our young poet sets off to seek his fortune, in the wild, wandering, adventurous, romantic, knight-errant-like capacity of clerk on the Manchester and Leeds Railway!' This was more than mere teasing; it was cruel derision. I conceive that it sprang from the twin sources of envy and contempt: envy that as a woman her choices were so much narrower than mine; and contempt that despite the wide berth the accident of my sex had awarded to me, I was still without a post. I sometimes think she might kill a man to be offered the opportunity to work as a railway clerk, if only then to be in a position to turn up her nose at it! Could it also be that her own inability to secure a position at present makes her mockery all the more acid in tone?

As I write these words, it dawns upon me that any unease I feel at the Parsonage springs almost entirely from Charlotte. Once my closest companion, the precocious little girl with whom I created one imaginary world after another is now a stranger, by turns censorious and sarcastic – the latter simply a gentler version of the former – towards nearly all those who come into her orbit. She at once holds herself superior to all, and yet can scarcely hide within her a deprecation of self, the two apparently opposing forces in fact feasting, cannibal-like, on each other. I conjecture that she would sell herself to Satan himself to be an admired beauty who moves with effortless grace in the highest social circles, for if she truly cared little for such matters her attitude would be one of absolute indifference, that which we display towards those things we value little. I also fear that she would abase herself in shameless adulation before the first man of quality and intellect who demonstrated any true appreciation for her.

In the first weeks away from Broughton I thought ceaselessly about Agnes, but just as I tend to delay all painful actions in life, so have I striven to place my grief at a remove, like some terrible secret locked away in an attic, or better still, like the cauterisation of a wound with a hot iron. When even that fails, I rely on her own insistence that I leave Broughton: *You mun leave this place.* Why should I feel guilt? But even as the guilt fades, my yearning for her comes, unbidden, and sometimes it is so great that I must walk out onto the moors until I find a place hidden by rocks, where I lie down and imagine myself with her until, for a brief instant, I feel a spasm of relief – shameful, paltry and transient though it be.

I can no more share what happened in Broughton than I can leap over the Pennines, but it has caused in me great disquietude when I am thrown into too close quarters with young ladies who are not my sisters – for here are three creatures I do *not*, Heaven be praised, imagine without their clothes. I was covered with utter confusion, however, when Charlotte's friend Mary Taylor, from her time at Miss Wooler's school, came to stay at the Parsonage just days after my arrival. She is a beauty, with the golden ringlets and the alabaster skin of a porcelain doll, and it was not hard to imagine – indeed it was impossible *not* to imagine – the perfectly feminine curves to match, moving beneath her dress. It was thus not surprising, then, that I paid homage to this young lady, for I cannot help but be drawn to a beautiful woman, like a moth to a flame. In this case she is also a noble, warm and generous creature: I doubt not that she would die willingly for one she loved, and her intellect and her attainments are of the very highest standard. I was hardly smitten – let alone *in love* – but like any young self-respecting gentleman, I drew myself up, peacock-like, in the most gallant manner possible, not so much to seduce as to impress.

To my surprise, I could feel her respond to my 'attentions', and I suddenly found myself baffled. Yet why should I be surprised, and why baffled? Was it because Agnes had been of the lower orders, but with Mary I felt that if a *lady* were pursued, such a chase would be harmless sport without consequence? Did I, like Charlotte, have so little regard for myself that I could not conceive of an equal – and, in truth, the Taylors are far superior to us in social standing – returning my passion?

It was quite safe to treat Mary as a real goddess, as long as she took no notice of *me*. But once she did, I knew not how to proceed, for I had known a very different kind of love from what society deems proper, with its long and tedious gradations, its tortuous paths of courtship and marriage. Any true passion for Mary, if it were to be consummated, must issue ultimately in marriage, for no other way forward was possible. Even if such a marriage were to be wished for, what business had I in marrying, I who had no employment and was, at twenty-three years old, still dependent upon my father for my food and shelter? No, no, there was no way.

As Mary's affection for me became manifest, all of these thoughts and more raced through my mind, and I recoiled in panic. Then what did I do? I confess it with shame – I shrank icily into myself, like a snail, and at every glance retired colder and farther; until, finally, the poor innocent was led to doubt her own senses. I found myself making excuses for being out of doors alone, which usually meant that I went seeking the fellowship of John Brown. Besides, the truth of the matter was that I wanted a practical man's advice on whether once and for all to cast all serious artistic ambitions aside and look into that post with the railway, regardless of what Charlotte might say.

August 1st, 1840 · The Parsonage

Yesterday I came upon John Brown where he is often to be found, in the churchyard, digging a fresh grave. It was an unusually hot day, even for late July, and the sexton was all too glad to break off his toil. He jammed his spade into the pile of dirt he had disinterred, wiped his brow on the back of one of his powerful, sunburnt forearms, and dusted his hands on the seat of his breeeches. Although he speaks with a slightly gentrified version of the rough accent of the West Riding, he is an exceedingly literate, if not a literary, man. He has read his fair share of the classics, especially Shakespeare and Milton, and he knows his Bible through and through. Indeed, the stonemason is entirely capable, for comic effect, of assuming the accent of the gentry, although with me he tends to chip off his words whenever it suits him – in other words, most of the time.

'Well, if i's no' t' poet himself!' he exclaimed heartily. 'By God, you're a sigh' for sore eyes, as I was lookin' for any excuse at all to sit on t' wall and smoke me pipe. E'en you'll do,' he said, eyes filled with their usual mischief. 'Pray tell, have you devastated the heart of tha' youn' Mary Taylor? Is she writin' you *billets doux* from afar, now she's gone 'ome?'

John is the only person to whom I have confessed my love for Agnes, and the revelation of what happened at Broughton is an endless source of mirth to him whenever we find ourselves alone, when he christens me Romeo, Don Juan, Lothario, etc. It is harmless enough when confined to our private conversations, and yesterday I was gratified that he who had initiated me into the secrets of the Freemasons, he who had taught me how to box and how to drink – for Papa was of an entirely different order of man – now acknowledged that I had forded the most important stream of all on the road into manhood, even if this recognition came through amiable mockery. It occurs to me now that I have been most fortunate to have two fathers: one of the mind and spirit and occupied with matters of the hereafter, the other with those of this world. How often are young men, through the fault of no one, born to fathers who are singularly inappropriate to their needs!

I explained what had happened with Mary Taylor while John puffed meditatively on his pipe. 'Well, surely,' he said, 'I've no doubt that the womenites over there – he nodded his head in the direction of the Parsonage – *are* upse' wi' ya, but o' course y'done the righ' thing. You erred – if any error there were – in your initial desire t' please, bu' wha' red-blooded male can be thrown into t' proximity of such a charmin' creature as tha' and *no*' wish to please? 'ad you begun icily enough, or failed to take par' in t' ladies' diversions, you'd a been condemned just as roun'ly for your *misanthropy*, would you no'? She go' t' wrong end o' t' stick, tha's all.'

He paused to reflect. 'For example, our Martha,' he said, referring to his twelve-year-old, who has just begun doing errands and other odd jobs for us, 'reports tha' Miss Brontë 'as been known to speak quite ill of our virtuous curate, Mr Weightman, callin' 'im a *shameless male flirt* and suchlike. As far as *I* know, the young fella 'as a good heart and spreads 'is charm evenly all about the neighbourhood. 'e can't help it if 'e's so devilishly good-lookin' and charmin' tha' any kindness, any eagerness to please, appears to those eager hearts – and I suspect your eldes' sister t' be one of 'em, in spite of 'erself – to be a cruel tease and nothin' more. 'e would be just as roundly censured, if no' more so, if 'e held himself back from entering into the fun: 'e would then be *cold, arrogant, proud, aloof, superior*. 'ow can such a man win?'

As was his wont, the sexton had cleared away my bewilderment as easily as if he were wiping the dust off a freshly chiselled headstone. I could only nod in agreement with his view of the situation.

'As for you, lad,' he continued in more formal tones, 'until you've made your independence you'll be thwarted from the *proper* expression of love in the sacred confines of holy matrimony.' Here Brown's eyes were again full of mischief and *double entendres*, though the shadow of the church steeple now fell across us like a condemnation from on high, and his daily contact with mortality, I thought at first, should have been a constant reminder of the ephemeral nature of the pleasures of this world and the eternity of the next. Then again, perhaps digging graves day after day had wrought the opposite effect upon him: could it be that death was so familiar to him that its attendant awe and mystery, its fear and dread, had rubbed away entirely, like the shine of a shovel-blade from constant use?

Brown's comment approached blasphemy, and it was doubly amusing – or for one truly believing in eternal damnation, doubly perilous – because he is known to stray outside the 'confines of holy matrimony' as often as he can, his appetite for women possibly the only thing greater than his thirst for strong ale. At thirty-six he has already fathered six children, with another on the way – and that's counting only those I know of, those he has had with his long-suffering Mary. He succeeds in playing the faithful husband here in Haworth, of course, for the Reverend Brontë would sack him if he had clear intelligence of his sexton's philandering, and now that his little Martha is at the Parsonage nearly every day, the bond between parson and sexton is even tighter. Of course, John is not unhappy to have a great deal of business concerning memorials, headstones and other sextonly activities, which take him regularly to Bradford or Halifax, where he can be at his ease.

While these thoughts occupied my mind, Brown puffed silently on his pipe, then continued in his habitual voice, 'And t' make your independence – for d'ya really wish to be under tha' roof any longer, with your father payin' for, and your sisters cookin', every bi' o' food ya take, havin' t' borrow money just t' join me for a glass of whisky down t' Black Bull? Settin' aside the question of the fairer sex for a moment' – and here his gaze followed, in Parsonage Lane, an especially pretty young woman just blossoming into full adulthood – 'yes, settin' that aside for a moment, d'ya no' simply need t' be gone from the neighbourhood once more, to find your independence at last? All the rest' – here he nodded in the direction of the lovely creature – 'all the rest, by which I mean *life*, will follow. But you're barred from all bu' the impotence tha'ud come from bein' a perpetual inmate of tha' Parsonage if you do no' take your destiny in hand. Even if the railway is bu' a steppin'-stone t' greater things, will it no' procure for you a livelihood tha'll once and for all free you fro' the shackles of dependency on others? What 'ave you t' lose by lookin' into t' post, eh? And what 'ave you to *gain* by failin' to do so?'

With that he knocked his extinguished pipe against the stone wall, stood up and reached for his spade. 'Ashes t' ashes, Romeo,' he laughed, and set himself to work. I left him to it, but as I passed through the churchyard gate I heard him say, as he effortlessly assumed the diction of a proper gentleman once again, 'It is *I* who shall buy *you* a drink this time; we shall toast your next adventure!' He seemed supremely confident that he had just convinced me to contact Mr Wright about the railway position, and indeed he nearly had. 'The Black Bull, nine o'clock, mind you – there will be a tumbler of whisky waiting for you there.' Without slowing the pace of his digging, he nodded downhill, past the church, in the direction of the public house.

As I returned to the Parsonage, I turned things over in my mind. I began to understand why Emily preferred performing domestic duties to taking up the life of a governess, for as she has sometimes said, this leaves her mind utterly free to wander the landscape of her imagination. Teaching, on the other hand, allows no such freedom and is, in fact, ruinous to the creative impulse. Even Charlotte has begun to see this, saying sometimes that she would rather be a scullery maid than a governess! I see what they mean. Perhaps, indeed, the railway might not be such a bad thing. Although I would not be digging tunnels like a navvy, how intellectually onerous could the duties of a railway clerk in fact be? Would I not have time to myself, to refine my translations and write my poetry? Still, I resist Coleridge's idea of a novel, for to me the form is – like the work of the tutor or governess – an unseemly mongrel, a mélange of the poetic and the everyday, and though he might justly call it the most saleable of products, I reject the idea out of hand.

Let Charlotte mock the railway, but is it not exciting, if sometimes terrifying, to watch the very future unfold, as lines are laid along the valleys, tunnels penetrate hills, and bridges are cast gracefully, like a sorceror's spell, over deep river gorges? Perhaps the choice of her words – *adventurous, romantic* – reveals, even in her mockery, her own occupations, for she obstinately craves to remain in the childhood worlds of our own creation. So, she would have me find a career that is truly adventurous and romantic? What, pray, would such a career look like in this pragmatical century? Surely teaching does not fit the bill.

And what of her? Staying at the Parsonage to receive visitors, write letters and heap sarcasm on everyone, while Emily bears the brunt of the domestic duties and Anne – our baby Anne – has already found another position at Thorp Green, in which she is, it appears, highly valued? Is she using what she has learnt any more than I am employing what I have? *No*, in a word.

In brief, the eternal, sterile sameness of life at the Parsonage – for which the perfect emblem is my sisters' circling the dining-room table each evening, reading or reciting poetry to each other – is unbearable, and so I have applied to Mr Wright for a position with the Manchester and Leeds. At the same time, I await word from Coleridge on my translations of Horace, which I revised and sent along upon my arrival here in late June. As the days drag on with no word from him, I have little hope in that direction, but as he is the only man of real intellect who has taken an interest in my work, I have at least followed his counsel in *this* respect, although I may have failed to do so in all others.

XIII.

The Dead and the Living

August 14th, 1840 · The Parsonage

What a dreadful nightmare I have had! Rarely do I dream – or perhaps my dreams are so vile that my waking self refuses to recall them? This morning, however, I awoke from the most vivid and heart-wrenching of scenes, perhaps more memory than dream – a recollection that stole upon me, like a spirit, in my slumber. And spirits indeed there were! I stood – my present self of three and twenty years – behind my four-year-old self, one of five little children standing with our nursemaid of long ago, Sarah Garrs, at the foot of a bed, the deathbed of a pale, wasting figure lying quite still.

Papa and Aunt stood on either side, and Maria, the eldest, held baby Anne, the youngest, in her arms. Mother – oh God, Mama – please do not die! We had all just emerged, somewhat miraculously, from scarlet fever, and stood quietly weeping, the sobs of grief that wrack even the stoutest hearts so much heavier a burden for the very young, though their elastic resilience quickly proves their salvation. They may be scarred forever, but the wound itself heals quickly. My present self regarded this scene at a remove, almost coolly; I was more fascinated than troubled.

Mama looked round at us all and moaned, 'Oh God my poor children – oh God my poor children!'

Papa, perhaps afraid that this constituted an oath that would offend the Almighty, said desperately, 'Shhhh … hush, my love … do not let the great enemy disturb your mind … give over … have confidence that Christ is your Saviour, and Heaven your eternal home.'

Whether with her own mind or with the fiend himself – I would prefer the former, not the latter, construction of events – she seemed to struggle mightily, as she said at last, 'My darling Patrick … you know that my heart has always been more ready to attach itself to earth than to heaven.' Tears rolled down her cheeks in silence, as once more she exclaimed, with every atom of her being concentrated in grief, 'Oh God, my children!'

It was this last outburst, her love of life, of us – not her dying or the sorry contingent of diminutive mourners that included my former self – that finally caused my chest to heave. Silence ensued, for her spirit had left her. Papa, too overcome by his own sorrow to worry, or even notice, that we had witnessed our dear Mama's final, blasphemous words, threw himself on her body and cried out, 'Oh my dear sweet Maria, God have mercy on you, my love, oh my life, how can I bear it?' At this, our own wails now rose in such a chorus that poor Sarah, herself overcome with tears, ushered us at last from the room.

Next, I stood in the damp cool near the altar at Haworth Church, as John Brown's father William lowered her coffin into the vault. Whether I was my four-year-old or current self I know not, but I was there, and my grief knew no bounds.

'Oh God, Mama, my sweet Mama, who will read to me by firelight, whose fingers will wriggle through my mass of red curls, who will kiss me on the cheek, who will call me her little Branny, her Little Angel? Oh Christ, oh sweet Jesus, God Almighty in Heaven, Mama!' I wanted to fling myself into the vault, to be covered up and blotted out for all eternity, so great was my grief. 'How will I endure sitting here listening to Papa's sermons while just below my feet I know that worms consume your sweet flesh, those soft cheeks once so close to mine? How ever will I bear it?'

I awoke this morning bathed in sweat, aching with grief. After breakfast I walked down to the church and there, on the cool flagstones covering the vault, I stretched myself out and lay silently, feeling, for just a moment, at peace. Beneath me lay not just Mama, but also my sisters, Maria and Elizabeth, both of whom died four years after her. And although Papa watched over his little bereaved flock with truly paternal solicitude and affection – for he was our constant guardian and instructor, and he took a lively interest in all our innocent amusements – my two elder sisters mothered me, Maria reading to me just as Mama had done, Elizabeth washing my ever-begrimed little face and struggling to keep my hair and clothes in order, particularly on church days.

I had always believed that *their* deaths had mattered to me far more than our mother's, but now I saw that to them I had transposed an even greater childlike grief, one that was as profound and necessary as the foundations of the church, and as deeply buried as the three coffins that lay side by side beneath its cool pavement. As I lay there, I heard not a sound, and at length drifted not into slumber, but rather a sleep-like trance, and in my reverie, I recalled first Maria's, then Elizabeth's, funeral.

Beloved, angelic girls, how I remember that dreadful hour when you – when your coffins – and that velvet pall descended – and descended – slowly – slowly – into the horrid clay, and we who remained on the earth in that dark hour were borne death-like, and wishing to die, for in that moment I thought I would never be able to enter this church again! How I ache for your kindnesses, your goodness, which Mama on her deathbed seems to have bestowed upon you both. No wonder you have died, for you were far too good for this world!

I lay thus, half-conscious, half-dreaming, half-dead, half-alive – or so it felt – but with the cool sensation of the stones against my flushed cheeks still very real indeed. Only when the bell marked the hour did I kiss each name on the vault – Maria Branwell Brontë, Maria Brontë, Elizabeth Brontë – and lift myself from the flags and escape from the church.

August 17th, 1840 · The Parsonage

Dreams mean nothing until they are interpreted by the waking.

I took my dream as a sign that I need to live, to move beyond the spiral of impotence into which I am drawn when I am here. The wellspring of childhood creativity has run dry, at least for me, and so I must turn elsewhere. Charlotte continues to be an interesting study, and I wonder if my dream gives some clues to her character as well. Within a month of her elder sisters' deaths, she went from being an unremarkable, if headstrong, middle child who worshipped her sisters as I did, to the unchallenged leader of our sad little band. We were fast friends and collaborators, yes, but more accurately we were – we are – *competitors*. Her disdain for me springs, I have no doubt, from her sentiment that I continue to cast away all the advantages that nature and the world have afforded me.

I see now – or should say I, guess – that my dream arose from two events. The first was the conversation with John Brown as he dug yet another grave, but the second was the rare treat of a visit from Mama's family: her cousin John Branwell Williams and his wife and daughter. They were a lovely trio, at once refined and dignified but natural and friendly in their manner. The daughter, Eliza, was a distant enough relation for me to appreciate her charms from head to toe, for she is quite a beauty. Upon their departure, I saw that Charlotte's sarcastic tendencies extended far beyond me, and that they in fact had fastened themselves with particular relish, like the jaws of a watchdog on an intruder's ankle, on the unsuspecting visitors.

'Well now,' she began as we sat round the table after their departure, 'they reckon to be very grand folks indeed; to my eyes there seemed to be an attempt to play the great Mogul down in Yorkshire, don't you think?' Emily did not even lift her eyes from her work. I weakly objected, 'Well, I'm not sure I agree, Charlotte –'

'Oh come now Branwell!' she said sharply, 'All right then, I will grant you that Mr Williams was much less assuming than the womenites' – she had picked up John Brown's playful term, and added it to her growing repertoire – 'he seemed a frank, sagacious kind of man. Did you see how, the moment he saw me, he exclaimed that I was the very image of my Aunt Charlotte? But the ladies … for heaven's sake: Mrs Williams set up for being a woman of great talents, tact and accomplishment, but I thought there was much more noise than work, don't you?'

A grunt from Emily, whether in assent or dissent, I could not tell.

'As for that simpering girl, Cousin Eliza,' she continued, particularly animated by now, 'she may have been intended by nature to be a bouncing, good-looking girl, but *Art* has trained her to be a languishing, affected piece of goods!'

I tried to appraise my sister as a man who was not her brother might do: she is almost impossibly small, and her head seems too large for her body. Despite her fine, intelligent eyes, her face is marred by the shape of the mouth and by her complexion. She has but little feminine charm about her and seems uneasily and perpetually conscious of this fact. How often do our judgements of others tell far more of ourselves than the objects of our derision or praise! Charlotte had neither Anne's outer grace and inner strength of will, nor Emily's ferocious independence and – to be candid – indifference to almost everything that lay beyond the smooth functioning of the Parsonage and the world of her imagination. Anne would have sought out, in her sweet and winning way, the most positive things she might say about the family and left the rest *unsaid*. Emily, I felt, was at once capable of dashing pretty young Eliza's empty head against the paving stones and yet was far too uninterested to pay her any regard at all.

Like all those who speak ill of others, only to find that no one joins in their mockery, Charlotte grew red in the face, for our silence was a judgement of sorts upon her unseemly behaviour. She hastened to get up, finding something else to occupy her. As she left the room, I turned to Emily.

‘Can you believe’ – but I fell silent after these three words, for the full power of Emily Jane Brontë’s gaze was suddenly turned upon me, and its meaning was as unmistakable as if she held the tip of a dagger to my throat: *If you think I am going to repeat Charlotte’s sin, and speak ill of her – who after all is my dear sister and abides under the same roof, whereas at least her harmless twaddle was visited upon the head of those we have never met and are likely never to see again – you are quite mad. Do not even think on it, Branwell!*

Yes, those piercing, hawk-like eyes said all of this, and far more: in their presence, there was nothing for me to do but shrink from any further discourse on the matter, and I too made my way out of the room, with only these pages to receive my confidences.

August 21st, 1840 · The Parsonage

How often do we fail to keep our own counsel, and how often does this failure stem from our pride or our vanity! Surely now I regret the day in June when, shortly after my arrival home, I boasted of my visit to Coleridge at Nab Cottage. Of course, I emphasised the more encouraging of his words, framing our discussion in such a way as to cast myself in the most favourable light. Is that so wrong, or so rare?

I had revised my translations and sent them off almost immediately, but thought no further of my conversation with the family. Now I learn that not only has Charlotte sent her own manuscript to Coleridge; he has answered her! She claims with great delight that he cannot decide whether the author is of the ‘soft or hard sex’, but I cannot imagine that Coleridge was unable to discern that the pseudonym concealed one of my sisters, for how many such missives can he possibly receive from the Parsonage at Haworth! I think, rather, he is toying with her. Still, how I wish he would respond to *me*! Coleridge has given her quite the same advice he offered to me: keep her expectations low and consider packaging her work for market, on the scale of a three-volume novel.

What grieves me seriously is that I cannot but feel that Charlotte has stolen my one foothold in the world of letters, just as she has so often taken my stories, filling them with swooning heroines and a superabundance of French. With due justice, though, while I do not care for her tiresome tales, I must recognise that she has made them very much her own, and that is the most frustrating part of all, for I feel at times that I have poured my very being into my work, only to have it reshaped beyond recognition in hers. More accurately, when I read her tales and poems I feel my inspiration everywhere, but my being nowhere. While I cannot truly claim that Charlotte has stolen any of my work, I sometimes feel that she has robbed me of my very soul.

Melodramatic? Unjust and untrue? Yes, perhaps. But I feel it all the same, and the *feeling* is real.

September 4th, 1840 · The Parsonage

And so, a railway man I shall be. After a languid summer, events are suddenly moving at the speed of a locomotive! Just two weeks ago I applied to Mr Wright for a position; a week later it was announced that the section from Leeds to Hebden Bridge would be open by early October. My appointment as Assistant-Clerk-in-Charge at Sowerby Bridge was confirmed in Manchester just four days ago! Charlotte may choose to mock me however she wishes, but I have employment at last, as she continues idly to receive her friends, write letters and read French novels, while Papa cares for his flock, Anne continues faithfully as governess at Thorp Green, and Emily oversees the Parsonage, for that matter. Not only do I embark on a new career, in an enterprise that can only grow in the coming years, but I am also able to leave this stifling house once again, God be praised. And to have Halifax so close at hand, with its concerts, plays and lectures – and best of all, my old friend Joe Leyland, whose marble works and studio now stand hard by the centre of town.

Yesterday, when word came of my appointment, I struck out to find John Brown rather than endure Charlotte's incessant teasing. Soon we were at our habitual table in the Bull, celebrating my good news. 'D'y' reckon,' asked Brown, 'tha' you'll be permitted to travel wherever y' please on this newfangled railway?'

'I haven't the foggiest notion,' said I, somewhat giddy at the thought of hurtling along in space, spinning about the world, as the network of railways expand to every corner of Britain. 'After all, my position ties me to a station, not a particular railway train, and after what occurred at Broughton the most essential thing of all is that I keep my post, and I suspect that means being *present*.'

'Aye, of course, of course, and I 'ave no doubt tha you'll succeed in tha'. Wha' exactly does it signify to be Assistant-Clerk-in-Charge?'

'Now John, you aren't going to skewer me as Charlotte has about this, are you?' I said with a rueful smile. He laughed and slapped his knee, then made a signal to Abe Wilkinson to refill our glasses.

'Ho ho, no indeed, I really want t' know!'

'Well, I'm not so sure myself, but from what I'm given to understand, there is a bit of everything involved: minding the books, keeping logs of arriving and departing trains and their contents, supervising the loading and unloading of freight, assuring the safety of passengers … that sort of thing.'

'Surely you'll be able to come home from time to time, or visit your friends in Halifax, will you not?' I assured him that I would have time not only for holidays, but also for that matter time to eat and sleep – and to continue writing when I could.

'Well, in tha' case I suspect my stone-carvin' will be takin' me quite regularly to see old Joe Leyland, and together we'll make an infernal threesome – though of course the more the merrier! I know some absolutely *charmin*' ladies in Halifax, and surely' – here he lowered he voice – 'your bollocks must be aching – if they haven't yet been cut off and thrown t' th'dogs by the womenites up t'parsonage!'

'Very witty, John ... though at times it feels that way. Or at least, I feel suffocated there, buried alive,' and then I thought of my recent dream, and of Mama, Maria and Elizabeth in their cold and silent vault beneath the flags, a mere stone's throw from the Bull. I shuddered, finished my glass, and this time it was I who motioned for another. 'If for no reason other than my escape from this place, the next adventure fills me with hope, a hope I have not felt in months.'

'Let us lift our glasses, then, to Lady Hope,' said Brown, assuming his more gentlemanly diction and drawing me into the warmth of his mirth, 'and let us *hope* that Hope does not let us down.' Aided by the whisky, I did indeed feel hope surge through every fibre of my being. After three glasses, I felt anything was possible, and imagined a response from Coleridge, in which he wished to attach his name and his own translations to mine, due to which, within months, I would be able to walk away from my humble post at the railway and, once and for all, devote myself entirely to letters.

I know but one thing above all, as I told Brown: *the most essential thing for now is that I keep my post*, not just to make my independence but to prove once and for all – to everyone, but especially to Charlotte – that I am capable of success.

September 13th, 1840 · The Parsonage

I am in that most delightful of periods in life, that twilight region between appointments, where one has earned the respect that comes from having secured a post, but where one is not yet required to fulfil any of its obligations. This respect – even a grudging version of the sentiment from Charlotte herself – has also won me a certain leisure, even idleness, in the days preceding my installation at Sowerby Bridge on the first of October. I am thus free to ramble about the moors, visit friends in Bradford and Halifax, write poetry, or just sit daydreaming at my ease, without the usual attendant guilt, for no one can claim that I have done nothing to make a living for myself. Ah, what bliss it is to have left behind the responsibilities of my post at Broughton, to have laid down the burden of finding a new one, and yet to feel only the anticipation and excitement of my life to come! I know that it is absurd to wish that this state might continue forever, but that recognition does not make the feeling any less real.

In rereading these pages, I have come to realise that in one way or another, all of my family, even dear Mama, Maria and Elizabeth, have found their place, with one notable exception: Papa. Why is it that I find myself unable to bring him to mind? It cannot be that he holds no importance for me, for upon Mama's death he did his best to raise us into adulthood, in a gentle but firm manner. So much of what I know I owe to him, for he has been my sole tutor and guide in the realm of the intellect. And yet, I find myself resistant to the very idea of probing this paradox further – all the more reason, in this time of unusual leisure, where I have the luxury of true reflection, to do so.

Could it be that Papa's strengths – especially those corresponding most closely to my weaknesses – are a condemnation of sorts? He, too, had literary ambitions, and still carries a passion for the written word; but his desire to make his way and to sustain his family ultimately triumphed over any dreams of glory in the world of letters. Although he rarely speaks of it, it takes no great intellect to suppose that he drinks no spirits and co-founded the temperance society in reaction to a vice that may have plagued his forebears.

Finally, and perhaps most significantly, there is the matter of his faith: it is beautiful, it is childlike, it is most earnest and sincere. At the same time, he displays a marvellous tolerance of the various sects of dissenters, unless of course they are in league to deprive him and his family of his living as perpetual curate. While I dread death and the possibility of eternal damnation, how can I *make* myself believe as Papa believes? When I think of poor Mama and my dead sisters, I cannot picture them in immutable, perfect unity with the Almighty, but only food for worms in the church vault.

Am I stronger for this ability to see death for what I believe it is, the *end of all*, or is his childlike faith the sign of a superior mind, or rather, of a *soul* touched by God, with an unshakeable faith in his redemption through Christ Our Lord? I recall Mama's dying words – or were they really *my* words, shaped by a dream? – 'my heart has always been more ready to attach itself to earth than to heaven', and I cannot help but wonder whether she passed her preference for this life over the next to her children – or at least, to *this* child. And it stands to reason that one could not possibly prefer the pains and joys of this life to everlasting bliss unless one were sceptical of the very *existence* of the latter. But such doubts could never have been – can never be – uttered in a parsonage, where not just the soul but the body daily depends upon the Church for its nourishment.

The Reverend Brontë makes a great show of being stern with us – especially when others are about – but we who were comforted by his tender paternal presence in the absence of our mother know that he would sacrifice all for our happiness, as though seeing us thrice bereft led him to make protecting us his primary obligation in this world, and I fear that this impulse has at times led us to be far too petted, so that we are ill-suited for anything required to make our way in the 'grown-up world' that we have now fully entered.

But I begin to stray again from the topic of Papa himself, and wonder if this is because I find it too painful to dwell upon the differences between us: the Reverend Patrick Brontë is selfless, abstemious, industrious, reliable and devout; Patrick Branwell Brontë is none of these things. Why, then, do I still believe that there is a place for me in this world, that I can find happiness and love, joy and fulfilment, possibly even fame? Why do I feel that the name *Brontë* will come to be known throughout England and the world, with a feeling so certain and palpable that it has an even greater reality to me than the names John Brown almost daily carves into his headstones? Am I quite mad?

XIV.

The Sculptor and the Railway Clerk

October 20th, 1840 · Sowerby Bridge

What a strangely different world is upon us with the railway! The activity is ceaseless, and even in such a humble place as this the movement of people and goods continues almost without respite. Such work – to my great surprise – is perfectly suited to the active side of my temperament, that part of my character that cannot sit still and bring my mind to bear for long on a single thing, for this post will not even allow such a state of tranquil concentration! No, here is constant 'hustle and bustle', as the common folk say, and so uniquely fitted to a mind already in a state of constant movement and distraction. I am determined to do well, to confound Charlotte in her scepticism, and believe that thus far that the head clerk and the railway hold me in the highest esteem.

The only element of the position I dislike is the keeping of the ledgers, for my old loathing of money-counting, which had prompted me to refuse even the briefest *consideration* of Papa's idea that I might make my living as a bank clerk, has only grown more intense. I cannot imagine what sort of narrow mind could delight in such work, which is at once so simple that a child can do it, and yet so stultifying as to drive an imaginative person quite mad! But I will do as I am required to fulfil my obligations to the company.

How to describe the grand opening of the railway here two weeks ago? Such a multitude! Thousands came to view the arrival of the first train, waving banners and flags, cheering the locomotive – a sight most of them had never seen before, a great ‘iron horse’ drawing behind it goods and passengers in a motley array of waggons and coaches. The Sowerby Bridge station has not even been completed, but bunting nevertheless decorated our temporary outpost, and banners were strung gaily from lamps and bridges along the way. A small orchestra had been assembled to play music to herald the train’s arrival. I, lover of the ancients, felt, in spite of myself, my chest swell with pride at the unrelenting march of progress, now come even to this remote place!

The head clerk, Mr George Duncan, and I stood proudly at the front of the assembled multitude to watch the beast puff slowly into the makeshift station. That day there was nothing but a communal glee mingled with national fervour, for no other power in the world comes near to the pace at which the iron rails currently unspool through Britain’s hills and dales, so that perhaps even little Haworth will soon hear the shrill whistle and thundering rattle of engines. The public houses overflowed, and at the end of the long day even the sober Mr Duncan and I were able to lift a single, moderate glass to the railway’s successful arrival.

All of this excitement is but *nothing*, however, when compared to a ride on the railway itself! As an employee I am permitted to travel at no cost, and within days of the grand opening I was able to take my first journey, and was invited to stand with the driver in the locomotive itself, so that rather than viewing the countryside speed vertiginously beside me, I was at the very tip of the engine as it penetrated into the wilderness, banking along the hills and moving beside the River Calder. I felt I was on a flying carpet, like Prince Husain in the *Arabian Nights*! The engineer bade me lean my head out of the locomotive itself, and I could feel the exhilaration of the wind moving like a stream about my face and neck, my hair swept back from my forehead as though I had plunged into the Calder itself. The wind was like a balm, for it was a perfect early autumn day, clear skies and brilliant sunshine illuminating the turning, falling leaves with a thousand different shades, the kind of day that causes lovers of this season of sweet, gentle decay to cherish it even more.

The driver, a Matthews by name – for he had introduced himself with a hearty handshake, after doing his utmost to wipe his hand clean of grease – assured me that the age of rail had just begun, and that unimaginable speeds would be reached in the future. It was a race of sorts, with all the world's great powers feverishly erecting railway lines, stations and increasingly powerful engines to carry freight and passengers more and more quickly, and the latter in greater and greater luxury. Matthews was a practical philosopher of sorts, for he added thoughtfully, 'Think on't, Mr Brontë, we've depended on horses fer thousands o' years, bu' soon I reckon they'll be used only for sport and show!' While I find such an assertion far-fetched indeed, I cannot but wonder, having glided along those rails with the wind in my face so powerful that I had to remove my spectacles: what an age of change we inhabit! Where will it all end?

Up at the Summit Tunnel, the workers toil away and hope to lay the last brick by December. We shall see, for such projects always cost more in time and labour than imagined. Still, the work advances. Until it is completed, we have only three trains a day, but soon there will be many times more than that – possibly as many as twelve each way – once the link with Manchester is complete. If I believe myself occupied at present, what shall I do with eight times as many trains?! Well, I suppose there is security in such activity, and it may be that the railway determines that more clerks are needed to assist us. Until then, Mr Duncan and I shall manage. Take each day as it comes, I tell myself, and do each thing necessary to continue in good stead with the railway. Or, as Papa might say, *Sufficient unto the day is the evil thereof.*

It occurs to me that a career – like the Summit Tunnel itself – must be built brick by brick in just this way, in increments, through steady application. Of course, I already know that Rome was not built in a day, but what a difference there is between a stale epigram and one's life experience! How vast the gulf between *knowing* that something is true and putting it into daily *practice*, especially with a nature as restless and variable as mine!

All Saints' Day, 1840 · Sowerby Bridge

Well now, that illustrious sculptor, Joseph Bentley Leyland, has been to visit at last, and since the trip from Halifax is less than three-and-a-half miles, it was high time! I forgive him, though, for he says his commissions are coming faster than he can execute them. Where at times I am guilty of the cardinal sin of envy when I encounter successful artists, Joe Leyland is one of such genial good humour and effortless talent that he is impossible to dislike, despite – or perhaps even partly because of – his streak of playful cruelty.

He is of that company of men who attract other men of genius – real or pretended – and women. Oh God in his Heaven, does he attract women, so many that sometimes I think I could be sated simply by eating the crumbs that fall from his table. But I'm running on too fast, seduced to distraction by the very thought of being with a woman, who inevitably assumes the shape of Agnes, whose lips I again feel pressed to my own, whose breasts sway above me, who surrounds and massages me with her love until our bodies are a single ecstatic blur of being.

As I said, I'm running on too fast …

Joe arrived with a new acquaintance to me, his brother Francis, who operates a circulating library that I have already promised to visit. He is a gentler, far more sweet-tempered version of Joe, and seemed to view me as a curiosity of sorts, as if he were a novelist looking for characters for his next tale, so carefully did he observe all about him, so attentively did he listen to our conversation, though without adding much at all to it himself.

I showed my guests about the station, now nearly complete, and Sowerby Bridge itself, including the unremarkable rooms that I have taken with a most unremarkable family, the Wilsons. The ageing, childless couple has just two ageing servants, themselves a childless couple. Here I will find no garrulous Dr Fish, no flirtatious Margaret, no seductive Frances. In short, a proper place to sleep and take my meals, and stay out of mischief.

We settled into a public house, *The Mermaid*, for a drink.

'I daresay,' began Leyland, with significantly less sarcasm than Charlotte on the matter, though with a bantering mockery all the same, 'Patrick Branwell Brontë is just about the last person in Yorkshire – nay, in all of Great Britain herself – that I would have expected to see employed as a clerk on the *railway*. But Frank here claims that it is the way of the future, and utopian philosopher that he is, he has set you up in his mind as a hero of the industrial age!'

'Well,' said I, smiling and bowing my head slightly in the direction of Francis – for who cannot pardon the jest that comes from such a one as Leyland, whose only wish was to enliven us with his mirth whilst we awaited the effects of our first drink to do the same – 'that is most generous. And I confess to an unexpected enthusiasm for the railway, for I do believe it will change – is changing – everything, especially how we see time and space, for they are collapsing, being bent to man's will like a white-hot iron under a blacksmith's hammer.'

Joe beamed across the table at his brother and brought his heavy right hand down upon the table, slapping it with an open palm, his large dark almond-shaped eyes laughing.

'You see? How often have I told you of young Brontë's poetical gifts? With him, even the railway is transformed, like a train going through a tunnel: it enters his mind as just so much wood and iron and smoke, but emerges from his mouth as song, a mechanised chariot of the Gods!' At this he paused, and said, more seriously, 'And what of your poetry? Writing anything? What of those translations you sent along to Coleridge *fils*?'

I told them that I had yet to hear from Coleridge, but that yes, in odd moments, I continued to write now that I was free of the oppressive atmosphere of the Parsonage. What I lacked, I said, were men of true intellect who could read and critique my writing. In the childhood days of secret composition, only my sisters read my work, but I now realised how important it was to throw off my diffidence and, once and for all, seek the wisdom of fellow poets. I also comprehended that I no longer desired to share any of my writing with Charlotte, for I was certain that what she did not object to in *style* she would condemn in *substance.*

Francis remained silent, but Joe, the whisky beginning to work its magic, cried in mock indignation, 'What are you saying, that we are not men of true intellect? I have half a mind to leave you with this tab, Master Assistant-Clerk-in-Charge!'

I was in that familiar state of mind where we welcome and even wish to participate in the mirth of the moment, and yet still have a serious point to make. 'Very droll, my friend. You know what I mean … I haven't seen you in ages, and this is my first acquaintance of your brother – who, by the bye, is considerably more gentlemanly than you.'

'Well, my friend, that is the difference between the artist and the bookshop owner, is it not? His quiet, steady temperament will likely permit him to live decades beyond me, for he does nothing to excess. Which are *you* to be, Brontë? Do you wish to make a life on the railway, perhaps becoming a rich shareholder, an elegant suit stretched tightly over your plump belly, so full that it is only with great difficulty that you can extract your watch from its pocket to ascertain that the trains are running on time? Somehow, I don't picture that for you, lad – there is a beast within you, trying to claw its way out.'

Leyland, whose colossal, terrifying *Head of Satan* we had seen so many years ago when Charlotte's drawings were exhibited in Leeds, was serious now, though his ardour always retained more friendship than censure: I was certain he only meant me well. Seeing his own great head in such passionate animation gave me the thrilling, fleeting thought that his famous sculpture of the Great Deceiver was, at least in part, a self-portrait.

Joe's harangue was far from finished.

'I suppose what I mean is that it is hard to find those in this life who manage to live a temperate, steady, wholesome life and at the same time create art. Find me the functionary or bank clerk' – he had purposely, and I thought, for him, sensitively, avoided 'railway clerk' – 'yes, find me such a man who is also, consistently, creating great and passionate works of art. Perhaps such a creature exists, but I have yet to encounter him in my travels.'

Francis remained unaffected at what other men might have considered a genuine affront to his character. He was surely used to Joe's meditations on the topic, and like so many of us, he allowed the genius and affability of his brother to wash away the sins of his arrogance. The conversation was following the same channel as my earlier dialogue with Hartley Coleridge, but in a new and improved version, with examples of flesh and blood: Francis served as the steady, wholesome man of business and Joe the Byronic hero, given to excess of all kinds, to be practised – or at least excused – in the name of artistic and existential freedom. My place in this drama? Why, apparently, to choose between these extremes. Was there, in fact, no middle way?

'As you might imagine, my dear sir, I have wrestled with such thoughts since I abandoned the career of painter. For I cannot burden the good Reverend Brontë any longer. I agree with you that it is with a difficulty akin to impossibility that I continue to pursue my writing and my mundane occupation on the railway, but I see no other way at present. I must make and keep my independence, and to do so I must give the better part of myself – my energy, my attention, my time – to that which sustains me.'

'You see!' cried Joe, again slamming his huge sculptor's hand on the table, this time so loudly that several other patrons looked up. Then, more softly, 'That's the key to this puzzle! What sustains you! Did not the Reverend Brontë ever tell you that man does not live by bread alone? Damn it, little man' – this is another of his favourite epithets for me – 'do you wish to let *the world*, as it is called, slash your wrists, so that the passionate beating of that noble heart ebbs slowly away into nothingness?'

I was indeed growing weary of this debate: it was, in fact, a topic that had occupied my sisters and me almost since childhood; Papa had made it clear that he had vanquished the extreme temptations of literary activity, channelling his erudition and desire to write into his sermons, his letters to the newspapers, and his other occasional compositions. And yet, despite his own moderation in this matter – as in all others – he could not help but bestow his passion for letters upon his children. Again. it was the same topic I had discussed with Coleridge – who seemed to have no real solution to it – and with Mr Postlethwaite, for that matter. *The bottom line*, to use a favourite expression of the latter, was that man could not live on unpublished poetry alone, either.

Joe signalled for another round of whisky. Meanwhile, I would hardly let him, of all people, beat a parson's son at the scripture game.

'I believe the Reverend Brontë would say that you are forgetting the rest of the verse – whether you are quoting Matthew or Luke – which Matthew gives as: "not by bread alone, *but by every word that proceedeth out of the mouth of God*."'

But he waved his hand dismissively. 'Please, Brontë, are you one of those ignorant blockheads, like your father's Baptist foes in Haworth, who take scripture as literal truth, believing you should gouge out eyes and pluck off limbs, and that the earth is only five thousand years old?'

'Which means?'

'Which means that *the mouth of God* doesn't refer to an old man with a white beard who floats up on the clouds – a chap who, after all, is nothing but a pale version of Zeus, without the lightning bolt or any of the rollicking fun, for that matter. Think of how many goddesses *he* had it off with – even his own sister Hera!'

I thought of my own three sisters, my mind's eye briefly, weirdly – against my will – trying to disrobe them, and then failing, revulsion coming so quickly that my throat and mouth seemed to fill with bile, so that I had to take an especially large swallow of whisky.

There was no stopping Leyland, who could never resist displaying his erudition, although it was always in such mirthful good humour that one could hardly accuse him of pedantry.

'And his progeny! Apollo, Hermes, Artemis, the nine Muses, the three Graces, the list goes on and on and on, *ad infinitum*.'

The Three Graces. It was the name of the Masonic Lodge in Haworth, but I thought instead again of Charlotte, Emily and Anne, but this time pictured them circling the table in the Parsonage dining room, reading to one another, a chaste, cerebral dance of virgins. I could hardly imagine them presiding over banquets and representing *beauty*, *charm* and *joy*. No, I suspect Leyland's *fêtes* – for I would be invited to them, now that I had returned to the neighbourhood – would feature young women far more palpably, even unabashedly, committed to those qualities.

'What exactly,' said I at last, as Leyland stopped to take a long draught from his glass, 'is your point? Is there one?' The three of us exchanged smiles, for we were still sober enough to recognise that phenomenon of enthusiastic storytelling under the influence of strong drink, when digressions proliferate, whilst the original topic recedes from view so quickly as to become nearly irretrievable.

Leyland himself laughed aloud. 'I may need to implore Zeus' own granddaughter, Ariadne, to help me follow this particular thread back to its beginning!'

He mused for a moment, then drew himself up, puffing out his chest and pronouncing sententiously, 'My point, dear Brontë, is this: the *Mouth of God*, like the mouth of the Oracle of Delphi, simply means the truth transcendent, whatever nourishes our mind and our soul, like those eternal qualities of great art and literature and all other things that distinguish man from beast. *Bread alone* is just what it appears to be, the nourishment of man's animal nature only.'

'And my point is this,' riposted I, confronting in my own mind the justice of his words in the abstract with the dreary realities of the workaday world I inhabited, 'that as much as I would tend to agree with you, let us take a concrete example, a page from the life of one Patrick Branwell Brontë: I cannot continue to be dependent upon my father and currently have no other way to make my living than to be an "Assistant-Clerk-in-Charge" for the Manchester and Leeds Railway. What to do? Quit my post, and eat the pages of my unpublished poetry? Plead with Papa to allow me to live in the Parsonage and spend my days writing – or more likely, unable to create in that oppressive place? Crush my desire to write once and for all and, as Saint Paul wrote to the Corinthians, *become a man and put away childish things*?'

How fitting, I thought, that Paul had sent his epistle to the Greeks. Zeus indeed. Was Leyland – was I – no more than an overgrown child? Was that, ultimately, the problem?

While there was no anger in my words, a desperate seriousness had crept into our conversation and an awkward silence ensued. Francis Leyland had been a mere spectator to all of this, but an attentive one. He looked down at the table, while his brother matched my warmth with his own, though it was that of a kindred spirit.

'Damn it to Hell, Brontë, of course you are right – but so am I! I suppose that the best we can both do is to keep at it, and hope that something breaks in our favour.'

I looked at him quizzically, for he had blazed onto the art scene long ago, and when I first met him he could scarcely keep abreast of his commissions. What was *his* struggle in this arena, compared to *mine*? I had always imagined the grass to be quite green in his pasture, and could not imagine his needing a 'break' of any kind. I said nothing, but Joe read my confusion correctly.

'Yes, yes, you might call me a great success, but you would be surprised at how little profit such work yields, and how often I have had to seek advances from my family.'

Francis simply smiled mildly and said, 'This is true.'

Joe continued, 'Notoriety, even fame of a minor sort – none of this puts much bread on the table.'

All it took was a look from me, and Joe burst into laughter. 'Very well, you have me there – I am again vanquished by that great philosopher of the railway age, PBB,' he said, using the initials by which I sign my letters to him. 'Let us agree, then – nay, let us even toast with another round of drinks – that we have wrestled with this intractable problem and that it will *not* give over, indeed, that it will never yield a satisfactory answer, for it is somehow linked to that paradox of mankind: a yearning for the eternal, the transcendent, the sublime, joined to a body that begins to decay the moment it reaches its full maturity, and that shares all of the appetites of the animal kingdom.'

Francis declined the third whisky, but I gladly accepted mine.

'Please do not call me the great philosopher after that final flourish,' said I, grateful to have turned the page on this conversation. I could bear dwelling so directly on my condition for only so long. 'Pray, tell, good man, when am I to be invited to one of your famous – or should I say infamous – soirées in Halifax?'

Joe grinned. 'I assume that all this talk of animal appetites has whetted yours, then?' In keeping with the theme of our conversation, he pronounced sacrilegiously, and with great dramatic flair: 'Fear not: for, behold, I bring ye good tidings of great joy, but in this case it shall not, alas, be to all people, but only the elect, which of course will include yourself: for unto you is born – or *borne* with an "e" if you prefer – this day an invitation to my next *fête*, a regular jollification – for let us say here and now that next Saturday, in the ensnaring town of Halifax, that Devil's Cauldron, I shall expect the honour of your worship's presence at half-past seven o'clock – that is, if you are able to tear yourself away from your enchanting little railway station here in Sowerby Bridge.'

As we parted company that afternoon, I agreed to try my best.

XV.

Une Soirée chez Leyland

November 12th, 1840 · Sowerby Bridge

Although I have sat before my coffee for an hour on this quiet Sunday, then splashed my face with the ice-cold water of my ewer, I am still unable to wake myself suitably after last evening's excesses.

Leyland did indeed hold the promised banquet at his studio in The Square, and what a *fête* we had! What a band of stout-hearted artists were gathered round Joe! Some I knew from my days of portrait painting in Bradford, but others were new acquaintances, all devoted in one shape or another to a love for the sublime and the beautiful.

John Frobisher, the musical impresario, was there, as were William Dearden (the 'Bard of Caldene'), John Nicholson (the 'Airedale Poet') and Thomas Crossley (the 'Bard of Ovenden'). Joe's brother Francis ('Mr Frank') was there as well, standing a bit beyond the orbit of the rest of us, observing. Finally, there were others present who appeared to be members of a more businesslike subspecies of *homo sapiens*: Joe's patrons, perhaps?

Last, but far from least, I was pleased to see present a number of young women of indeterminate social standing – for they were neither ladies nor servant girls. Their connection to the sculptor was unclear, but their sole purpose appeared to be to add female companionship to our festive gathering. As I entered the studio Joe eagerly waved for me to join the cluster of people gathered around a large sculpture. He thrust a glass of brandy into my hand and announced, so that all could hear over the rising din of voices, 'All hail the Bard of Haworth, Lord Patrick Branwell Brontë!' There was much laughter, followed by curious – though hardly timid – smiles from the women, introductions to new acquaintances and warm greetings and claps on the back from friends of yore.

The sculpture that stood before us was a seated nude, a beautiful young woman. Her hair, adorned with flowers, is twisted into ringlets, some of which fall forward onto her lovely bare shoulders, just above her perfect naked breasts. She leans to the right, her arm supporting her weight as her legs extend out to her left, the right tucked under the left at the knee. Her hips are broad and perfectly proportioned, and one can even see the muscles of her torso reflecting her posture, which is that of a beloved who has just raised herself from her pillows at the approach of her lover. The fingertips of her right hand rest gently on a support, while her wrist lifts away from it; she draws her left arm towards her face, as though to brush away a stray ringlet. The lifelikeness of Joe's sculpture is almost disquieting, for one could easily imagine this creature springing up to meet her lover or pulling him down onto her couch of stone.

'If I had to wager,' said Joe, drawing me aside, 'I would say that the same quality that has caused you to lose yourself in Kilmeny's beauty' – for such is the sculpture's name – 'is that which has prevented me from selling her.'

'What do you mean?'

'You tell *me*, friend. You're the philosopher. Why did you just stare at her in this way? Surely you have seen statues of nudes before. I know you have, in my own studio. Whence this current fascination?'

'It – she – appears to be so real, she looks as though she could come to life at any moment, as if she could throw that beautiful body of hers into the arms of the viewer.'

'*Precisely*. Do you wish to hear my tale of woe?'

'Of course,' said I, nodding eagerly. Leyland refilled our glasses and drew me far from the crowd that had formed around Kilmeny, indicating two chairs at the other end of the studio.

Thus installed with large tumblers of brandy and fresh cigars, we leant back in unison as Joe sighed.

'Well then, what happened is this: some years ago I received a commission to create a sculpture based on James Hogg's poem "Kilmeny" – you know it, of course you do, even those who scarcely know their letters do: "Kilmeny, the Sinless Maiden" – but once I had finished, the good gentleman and his pious wife rejected the lovely creature, and thus refused to pay what was due. I was left with their initial deposit and a statue with no home. They – especially the lady – called it vulgar and obscene, the representation of a harlot, the very opposite of the "sinless maiden" of the poem!'

'Because you sculpted what looks like a real woman?' Here I lowered my voice. 'It is not as if you had depicted her spreading her legs, or in the throes of congress.'

'I know, I know,' he said bitterly, 'but since good Victoria – God save her! – became Queen three years ago, the notion of what is *proper*, what is *wholesome*, or even what is *beautiful* is becoming more and more restricted, like a noose tightening about the neck of artistic liberty. My erstwhile patrons – along with the rest of this island nation – are increasingly ashamed of their own bodies, and to see a sculpture that reminds them of this is surely what caused them to reject it. That's my learned hypothesis, anyway. And to think, young Victoria hadn't even ascended to the throne then, but already this blasted virus of prudishness was circulating in the body politic!'

Here Leyland smiled ruefully. '*You*, on the other hand, seem positively captivated by Kilmeny.'

'It reminds me of someone I once knew.'

'Truly now?' Joe seemed distracted and was looking past me. 'Why lad, the lovely Kilmeny herself, surrounded by a band of hopeless sinners, is just there!'

He leapt up, seized my elbow, and towed me across the studio, towards one of the young women I had seen earlier. Her *décolletage*, elongated bodice and ample skirts were scarcely necessary to accentuate her perfect face and form; her flaxen hair was twisted into braids, not unlike those of the statue before her. Had this young woman posed as a true model, or had the wicked Leyland seduced her and simply used his memory of her pretty face and exquisite form to create *Kilmeny*?

She blushed as we approached, and yet smiled bravely at Joe, saying nothing. He, meanwhile, took one hand of each of us and brought us together. Addressing the young woman, he said, 'This, Miss Margaret, is Patrick Branwell Brontë, otherwise known as the young Bard of Haworth. Brontë, this is Maggie Heaton, the *true* Sinless Maiden.' Maggie wrinkled her brow, and both the form and substance of her first sentence immediately betrayed her origins, for she spoke with an only slightly polished version of the rough accent of the neighbourhood. She seemed puzzled at my occupation.

''ow do?' said she, attempting a curtsy. Following a pause, she asked, 'What *does* a bard do?' Joe, whose streak of cruelty far surpasses mine, and which he immediately lays bare to the world when in his cups, laughed loudly, and so I drew Maggie away towards another corner of the studio. 'I am watching you both,' shouted Leyland after us, wagging his finger, 'so take care!', but he was soon deep in conversation with our mutual friend, Frobisher, who gesticulated as feverishly as if he were conducting one of his frequent Halifax performances.

Leyland, as he often did, had exhausted me with his energy and enthusiasm, his good humour and incessant teasing. I was, moreover, warm from drink and from the overcrowded studio, for my friend had invited at least seventy-five people to his soirée, and the party was beginning to reach its zenith, where the maximum number of people present collides exactly with the highest level of general inebriation. One could not hear oneself, let alone one's neighbour, speak. I fairly shouted in Maggie's ear, 'Do you want to take some air?' then smiling, 'I can tell you what a bard does, then.' She nodded assent.

Strangers to each other, we did not walk far, for truly my only desire as we quitted the studio was to breathe in the cool air of late autumn. As I looked at Maggie – Kilmeny, the sinless maiden, as Joe called her, for reasons still unclear – in the light of a full moon, I was nevertheless especially pleased to be with this lovely young woman, whose hair caught the moonlight almost like a mirror; it seemed to illuminate us both. For the first time I noticed how similar her eyes were in shape and colour to Agnes's.

'Are you any relation to the Heatons of Stanbury? Ponden House? That's just a stone's throw from Haworth – my home – you know.'

'Oh, by 'eck, no!' she laughed. 'Y' can't swing a cat round these parts without you'll hit a Heaton.'

'What of young William Heaton, the poet, then? He's one of Joe's friends – see, he's right over there.' I pointed through the window at our mutual friend Billy, who stood speaking in great earnest to Frobisher and Dearden; Joe was now whispering in the ear of a raven-haired beauty. 'Is *he* one of your family?'

She laughed even harder. 'I don't have much t' do with them types of folk.'

'Well then, it's time to introduce you to one: me.'

I bowed, and she giggled. 'A *bard*,' said I, 'is an old-fashioned word for poet. Shakespeare is called *the Bard of Avon*, or oft-times merely *the Bard*.'

'So you wri' verses and such,' said she. 'Don't fancy there be much of a livin' in *tha*'.'

I could not restrain my laughter, whereupon she somehow managed an adorable expression halfway between a smile and a pout.

'So, now yer laughin' at me *too*, Mr Bronte?'

'No, Maggie, I am laughing at myself. You see, I am not really a poet at all. I like to write poetry, but as you say – and that is why I laughed, because you immediately struck the proverbial nail on the head – it is no way to make a living, particularly at this time and place. So, a more accurate description of me is that I am a railway clerk who dabbles in verse, when the time permits.'

Maggie immediately, and unexpectedly, grew so excited that I thought she might well throw herself into my arms. Instead, she contented herself with facing me and clutching both of my elbows, trembling with enthusiasm. 'The *railway*, you work for the *railway*? 'ow thrillin' tha' mus' be! So y'been on th'train when she's movin' up the tracks?'

'I have indeed.'

They's say it's like you might fairly fly apart, they do. But folks don't, do they?'

'No, no,' I smiled, 'no one flies apart, and one only feels faint by looking sideways, at the world racing by. One must gaze straight ahead.'

Maggie bit her lip – one of creation's great gifts to man, a lovely woman biting a full, red lip, is it not? – and was silent for a moment, her eyes gazing far into the distance. '*I'd* like to ride on th'railway someday.' Clearly there was no practical reason for her to spend her scanty income – whatever it was – on railway travel.

'What *if*,' said I, looking deeply into her eyes, which though they could never match those of Agnes, were exceedingly large and pretty, with irises that sparkled like perpetual fireworks, 'what if I were to arrange an excursion for you from my station at Sowerby Bridge to Manchester, when the Summit Tunnel is complete? Do you know it will be the longest tunnel in the world?'

Although I would have thought it impossible, her eyes widened even further, and I believe it was all she could do to restrain herself from giving me a kiss. Instead, her hands slid down from my elbows to my hands, which she shook vigorously up and down.

'Oh, *would* you? *Could* you?'

'Of course, my dear, I wield enormous power as Assistant-Clerk-in-Charge at the Sowerby Bridge Station of the Manchester and Leeds Railroad. Your wish is my command.'

'Now you *are* teasin' me,' she said, but without any trace of hurt, and the earlier pout – as adorable as it had been – was here supplanted by a dazzling smile.

'No, as I told you before, I am mocking *myself*. And now that our conversation has appeared to come full circle, we should probably rejoin the soirée.'

'I think,' said she, with a sincerity that would melt the iciest of hearts, 'that you're a good man, you are, and that there is much good not only 'ere' – she placed a warm palm on my forehead – but 'ere' – moving her hand to my heart.

The memory of my last meeting with Agnes washed over and through me with such a force of mingled sadness and longing that I felt torn between, on the one hand, wildly embracing this girl whose eyes so recalled those in which I had bathed myself so many times and, on the other, falling to the ground in a convulsion of grief.

Not knowing how to reply, I simply said, 'Now then, shall we find old Joe Leyland, the devil himself?'

She smiled again and walked before me, turning as we approached the threshold. 'I know 'e teases me cruelly, but I can't 'elp but like 'im, Mr Leyland.'

'I know just what you mean, Maggie.'

We agreed that I would send word about the railway excursion through Leyland, whose relationship with her remained a mystery.

The sculptor did not fail to notice us as we entered the studio, and shouted, 'Oh ho, there are the lovers! I trust that the maiden is still free of stain in both mind and body?' He then leapt onto a chair, raised his glass, and drunkenly declaimed a snatch of Hogg's own 'Kilmeny' – much to our genuine and mutual mortification:

Never, since the banquet of time,
Found I a virgin in her prime,
Till late this bonnie maiden I saw
As spotless as the morning snaw:
Full twenty years she has lived as free
As the spirits that soujourn in this countrye
I have brought her away frae the snares of men,
That sin or death she never may ken. –

Some of the gathering began to applaud, but Leyland motioned for silence. 'Wait, wait … come now, everyone, take a moment to recharge your glasses and join me in the final verses of Hogg's touching portrayal of this exception to all of Eve's daughters, through all of man's history, that Presbyterian Virgin Mary' – there was great laughter at this deft blow to Scots and Papists alike – 'Kilmeny, the Sinless Maiden!'

'Ready?' shouted Leyland after a moment, 'Here we go!' The poem was known by nearly everyone, and following Joe's lead, the gathering fairly sang in unison:

It was like an eve in a sinless world!
When a month and a day had come and gane.
Kilmeny sought the green-wood wene;
There laid her down on the leaves sae green,
And Kilmeny on earth was never mair seen.
But O, the words that fell from her mouth
Were words of wonder, and words of truth!
But all the land were in fear and dread,
For they kendna whether she was living or dead.
It wasna her hame, and she couldna remain;
She left this world of sorrow and pain,
And return'd to the land of thought again.

The communal recital ended in thunderous laughter and applause, with still more drinking – considerably more. I looked round the studio for Maggie. Despite his advanced state of inebriation, Joe, ever the observant artist, said to me, 'You seek Kilmeny? The sinless maiden is gone, little man – she is gone, *never mair seen ... she has left this world of sorrow and pain, and return'd to the land of thought again*!'

Leyland was where he most liked to be, surrounded by friends, talking about art and literature and women, but taking nothing in earnest, eventually drinking himself thoroughly and quite happily into a stupor. With Maggie gone, I decided to join him in his descent, as the party lurched along to its inevitable collapse. I haven't the slightest notion of how I got back to Sowerby Bridge and into my bed.

I awoke to find myself fully dressed, except for my boots, my coat and hat missing. In one pocket I found a small piece of paper, reading only this: *Franz Listz, Halifax, January 29* – written in what I recognised to be John Frobisher's elegant, almost feminine hand. Slowly, like Hansel and Gretel picking their way home with breadcrumbs, I began to remember the end of the evening. Frobisher had been in a state of high excitement, for he had succeeded in including Halifax in the tour of the great virtuoso, Franz Listz. There were no bounds to his enthusiasm; it seemed he would positively explode with joy and was spreading the good news through the studio. Perhaps realising I could drink no more, I took my leave of Leyland and have the vaguest notion of stumbling the three miles or so home. It is a miracle that I did not fall into the Calder, or onto the railway line, though fall I clearly did, for my trousers bear the dirt and grass of at least one tumble, and my right shinbone aches as I finish this entry. I either lost my hat and coat *en route* or left them at my host's. If the latter is the case, I suppose I will find out soon enough.

Thank Heaven I do not work today, for it is all I can do simply to move about: penning this entry has drained me of every atom of energy I was able to summon this morning. I know I should not drink to the same excess as Leyland – if only because his far greater mass can support it – but I doubt quite seriously that I will be able to make it through this day without at least *one* drink – surely the only way to soothe my splitting head.

November 15th, 1840 · Sowerby Bridge

No sooner had the ink of the last sentence dried than I heard a loud rapping on my windowpane, which might as well have been an iron stake driven through my skull. There stood Leyland, prepared to rap again with his walking stick. He held my missing hat and coat and gestured for me to meet him outside, clearly not wishing to disturb my landlord. Still dressed, I pulled on my boots and was outside in an instant. This time he had not brought Francis with him.

'So, we made it home, did we, little man?' His voice – at least to my hearing – boomed. With mock gravity, like an obsequious tailor, he held my coat out so that I could slip my arms into the sleeves, and then planted my hat squarely – and I thought altogether too roughly – on my head.

'Oh, blast you, Leyland, that's a nasty trick! Confound it, must you shout so? Softly, eh?'

Although he obeyed, he tried to convince me that it was an excess of drink – not himself – that was to blame. 'And, my friend,' said he, his voice rising enthusiastically in spite of himself, and my head throbbing accordingly, 'I believe you know that there is but one solution to such an ailment, and it is homeopathic in nature – *similia similibus curantur* as the great physician Hahnemann dictates. Or as our good Mr Hogg, the celebrated author of *Kilmeny* himself – what a coincidence, eh? – says, "If this dog do you bite, soon as out of your bed, take a hair of the tail the next day!"'

Soon we sat at the same table of *The Mermaid* that we had occupied with Francis a few days before, a glass of whisky before us. 'Drink this one quickly,' said Joe, 'it will soothe your nerves.' I obeyed my friend, and almost immediately felt much improved. He ordered two more and we then settled comfortably into what now seemed our personal corner of the establishment, with no desire to move. Morning had brought a steady rain, the kind that, in this season, seems far colder than snow. The amber liquids before us danced like jewels in the light of a fire blazing in the nearby grate, and soon my friend's features had taken on a similar glow.

'Now *that*,' said he, 'was a soirée, was it not? I half wonder how you made it home, Brontë, for you seemed to have had a bit of difficulty simply walking by evening's end.'

I gestured to the knees of my trousers. 'Indeed I did – I *did* have trouble walking but I made it home all the same. I'm surprised you noticed my state, Leyland, for yours was rather exalted!'

Joe laughed. 'I'm nearly twice your size, little man' – this is an exaggeration, but yes, he is easily five inches taller, and significantly broader – 'and the only reason you can drink as much as you can, I am quite convinced, is that you're an Irishman in disguise.'

Here he tousled my bright red hair, as a father would his son's, and added, 'Well, not much of a disguise … ha ha! I hope you say a prayer each day, thanking the Good Lord for that half of your lineage!'

My mind, at last fully awake, flew briefly to Haworth and Papa, and then to poor Mama.

'Say, Joe, where was His Excellency John Brown last night? I'm surprised that he didn't journey the ten miles to Halifax. Or did you not vouchsafe him an invitation because he somehow does not conform to your notions of proper society?'

'No, don't be daft – I think Brown a capital fellow, the most learned sexton I've ever met and a first-rate stone-carver into the bargain. He can dig your grave for you, carve your headstone, and I fancy could even say the requisite prayers as he shovels you under, if the Good Reverend Brontë or his curate are otherwise occupied! Most of all, though, he is a lively companion in deviltry! What an appetite for wine, women and song! Had he been here he would surely have been standing on a bench singing at the top of his lungs, with his arm around one of those pretty, not-so-sinless maidens.'

'So why, then, was he not present?'

'He sent a note of regret and stated simply that he is could not be away from Haworth. This means either that the residents of your little village continue to die at an unseemly pace, damn them – which, by the way, must be most inconvenient not only to poor John but also to your good father and Mr Weightman – *or* that Mrs Brown has finally put our dear friend on a rather short leash. Or, perhaps, both. But you know him far better than I, Brontë. What do you think?'

I did know John Brown better. He had arrived in Haworth with his father when he was sixteen, and is a dozen years or so years my elder. As we both grew older and he eventually assumed the duties of sexton at his father's death, I idolised him, for he was everything Papa was not: stout and hearty; plain-spoken to just shy of obscenity and irreverent to the point of blasphemy; a lover of food and drink and women and song. He knew how things worked – how the world worked. He could repair nearly anything, and from all appearances knew all of the intricacies of women, too, for they were immoderately fond of him. He had taught me to box and had ushered me into the mysteries of the Masons, which I joined not so much from any enthusiasm for freemasonry as from my blind worship of anything that Brown himself did.

'I'm sure if John were here he would tell us with his usual candour, but I would guess that it is a bit of both. And he does love his Mary, even if he might stray on occasion.'

'On *occasion*?' Leyland laughed heartily, the second tumbler of whisky having its desired effect. 'That rascal – he's such a hearty, good-looking devil that women positively swoon when he's about, so he fairly has his pick of the lot.'

'Some people might say exactly the same thing about you, Joe.'

Leyland bowed his head in acknowledgment of the compliment. 'Well, thank you kindly for that, but the truth is that I'm a bit too rough and unpleasant – at times even cruel, as astonishing as that may seem to you, little man – whereas our friend Brown, despite his humble origins, knows how to concoct just the right admixture of pleasant raillery and sweet nothings, as if sprinkling so much fairy dust over his conquests.'

I finally hazarded the question that had been on my lips since I'd seen Leyland standing outside my window.

'And what of that lovely girl, that Maggie Heaton, and why do you call her Kilmeny?'

'Oh ho, the immaculate Kilmeny! Taken a fancy to that one, have we, Brontë? What a thoroughly exquisite creature, from her flaxen tresses to the tips of those little toes – and everything in-between of course.'

'I am in earnest, Joe. Who is she?'

'Becalm yourself, little man. Maggie's the daughter of a Halifax innkeeper. She lives with her parents there and serves in various capacities: kitchen-girl, housemaid, book-keeper – for she can read and write and tally accounts, far better than her worthy parents, I'm quite sure. I suppose you guessed that she posed for Kilmeny, eh?'

I sat quietly for a few seconds, and Leyland, who is one of those beings who cannot abide doing so, read my mind as only a close friend can.

'I can see those wheels turning, my railway friend. Indeed, I can almost see smoke puffing out of those ears of yours. Let me put you at ease: here is the story of how Maggie came to be Kilmeny; or, if you will, how Kilmeny came to be Maggie. I'm surprised I've never told you of her in all these years, but then, you've never resided in the Devil's Cauldron. Just think what discoveries await you, little man!'

Leyland leant back, crossed one leg over the other, and began.

XVI.

Leyland's Tale: Maggie Heaton, or the Sinless Kilmeny

'I had just received my commission for the sculpture of Kilmeny, and had the great ambition to execute it *from life*; I had not even really begun to consider how I might approach this, when I went to take my dinner at the White Swan, and who should appear but this lovely creature. I had seen her before, certainly, but she had just fully blossomed into womanhood within the last year or so, and it was at this most fortuitous meeting that I first saw her as such. The thought struck me immediately. But how could I convince her to disrobe and be my model?

'Indeed, I had no small work to convince her and her parents, because I determined that given her young age – for she was then just sixteen – and, more importantly, given the bearish physique of her papa, who is considerably more imposing than I, it would be folly to pursue my intent without their permission.

'Do you know how I did it? Well, I was as sly and calculating as old Mephistopheles himself. I made certain to dine at the inn at least twice a week, and showed far more interest in Maggies' parents than in her own person. I was temperate in all things except for my gratuities, which I showered on them as liberally as if I were a prince. I made myself wait nearly a month before I took even the first step towards the subject, and I did so by mentioning in a most offhanded manner that I had received an important commission, but that I had met a seemingly insuperable barrier to creating the kind of lifelike sculpture I had imagined; I then pulled out my watch and claimed that I was terribly late. I left them hanging from a cliff as I dashed out the door. Ha!'

I was at once fascinated and somewhat repelled by Leyland's account of these proceedings. I simply said, 'It is well that you, yourself, recognise that you can be cruel, for this seems cruel indeed.'

'Bollocks!' said he, 'what harm was done? A local artist was showing them great respect, and, far more importantly, was filling their coffers with his liberality. If this was a crime, I would ask you to seek the victim.'

'The truth?'

'Tut tut, Brontë … the end justified the means, or as the great Bentham might say, the pleasure outweighed the pain. As for *your* truth, it is always open to debate, is it not? Whose truth? Tablets handed down from Mount Sinai? Mahomet scribbling down whatever the Angel Gabriel supposedly whispered in his ear? The Pope issuing preposterous edicts from the chair of Saint Peter? Or would you prefer the Bishop of York, or perhaps the brainless, Bible-thumping Baptists at the bottom of the hill in Haworth? All Beauty, Truth, God are one, and they are as resident in this' – he lifted his glass of whisky – 'and that' – he pointed to the rainclouds scudding past the window beside us – 'as they are in all creation, especially in the transcendence of *Love*. Which brings us back to your love, Miss Kilmeny.'

'She is not my love, Leyland.' I had heard such speeches from Joe on countless occasions and was glad he had returned to the topic at hand.

He laughed. 'The wee lad doth protest too much, methinks,' said he, and continued his tale.

'In any event, what next transpired was this: I returned two or three days later for my usual repast, and let *them* approach *me*. I studiously avoided the topic until the innkeeper could bear it no longer – he must know what it was I had meant by *an insuperable barrier to my creation*. The moment had come to land this big fish. I gestured to him to join me, and insisted that he have a drink with me – by now his expectation of my munificence made him, I am sure, loathe to contradict me in any way. Once he had settled in across from me, I leant over conspiratorially, my voice low, and told him that I needed to sculpt from *life*, which meant that I needed a beautiful young woman to pose as Kilmeny, and that although such modelling was perfectly acceptable in Paris or Rome, the accursed prudery of this island made it almost impossible to secure such services. How maddening, I said, thumping the table theatrically, to think that three hundred years ago the Duchess of Ferrara – a woman of the same social standing as our own upstanding aristocratic ladies – had considered it the highest honour to pose in the nude for the great Titian!

'I would not, as some artists might, employ a woman of ill-repute, especially when I sought to create *Kilmeny, the Sinless Maiden*. Heavens no! Nor would I, as others might, cover my model's face with a mask, for it was the marriage of an innocent countenance with the beauty of the whole person that would convey the very *essence* of Kilmeny's purity. Her innocence would only signify, I insisted, if she were as beautiful as she was sinless – for what virtue would there be in an *ugly* sinless maiden? No, it was the unity of bodily perfection – the kind, I thought to myself, but did not tell the innkeeper, that positively invites one to sin – with blameless conduct that I sought. In short, I was seeking a young girl or woman of just this appearance and character, and – here I brought down the *coup de grâce* – was willing to pay her very handsomely indeed for her modelling, as I was desperate at this point, for the commission needed to be fulfilled. I pretended not to see his eyes travel over to his daughter, and simply leant back and sighed.

'Well, Brontë, you can imagine well enough what ensued. I left an especially large gratuity, saying somewhat wistfully, "That's for listening to my sad tale, my friend", and I made a point of all but ignoring Maggie as I put on hat and coat, leaving the rascal to think things over. It was *he* who took the next step, appearing at my studio the following morning. I feigned surprise and asked whether I had forgotten something at the inn. Nay, he had come with a possible solution to my dilemma. He had spoken to his wife, and together they had approached Maggie.

At first, she had recoiled at the thought of removing her clothing before a man, until they explained to her that great ladies of all sorts did this, and that though *some* people did not think it proper, they were just ignorant folks who did not know the true ways of the world – is it not delicious to think of the simple innkeeper castigating others for their lack of sophistication, Brontë? ha ha! – and that her mother would always be present in the artist's studio, for it was only on that condition that they would consider this. They even told her that she could have a portion of the money to buy whatever she liked. She would be helping Mr Leyland, who after all was Yorkshire's greatest young artist, thereby helping her parents. No one would know about this, they assured her.

'Though I do not ever like to be observed while creating, I thought for a moment about these simple souls, and quickly concluded that having her mother present would be no more distracting than being kept company by my dog Dionysus, so I readily assented. Once the wily fellow had negotiated Maggie's fee – which was nearly twice what I had hoped – I regretted having agreed so quickly, as I now wished I could get more in the bargain, if you know what I mean. But I was now so enamoured of the idea of sculpting Kilmeny from life, and – don't be cross, Brontë – so thirsty to see, after such a protracted process, the young lady as God had made her, for she truly is magnificent, that I was nearly ready to agree to anything, and we shook hands on the bargain.

'The purpose of the initial sitting was to allow me to roughly outline Kilmeny's position, and so Maggie was to recline on a couch in various attitudes until I found just the one that suited me. She arrived that morning with her mother, who seemed more nervous than she, and who helped her disrobe behind a screen. I had provided a dressing gown for her to wear, which she wore as she emerged into the full light of the studio, her mother trailing awkwardly behind her, not knowing quite what to do. The girl's face was nearly crimson with embarrassment, but I tried to assure her by assuming a businesslike air.

'"Just hand the gown to your mother," said I, turning my back on her nonchalantly, "and recline on the couch, on your back please, with your feet facing me. You mother may sit just there" – I motioned to a chair just a few feet to the side – "Today I shall be determining the position of Kilmeny, and making a preliminary sketch." I turned towards her and by all that's holy, Brontë, how I kept from crying out or rushing towards her I know not, for what a perfect exemplum of the female form! There was not a freckle, not a birthmark, not a single flaw on that lovely little body. I struggled mightily not to react, I tell you, but cannot say whether my eyes betrayed me or not. Only a fool or a miss nancy would have been unaffected. Indeed, not to feel the urges that the sight of such a beautiful woman prompts would make me a cold *savant*, don't you think? Besides, what would give meaning to Kilmeny's purity would be her beauty, her desirousness. For her to appear, *herself*, tempted by sin, and in her attitude to tempt a man to sin – but not to give way – that was what I hoped to capture. What is virtue if it is not tested, eh lad?

'I walked up to the divan. Maggie averted her gaze and her mother stiffened in her chair. I explained to them both: "Now, it is essential that I be able to touch Maggie to indicate how she should move, and what position she should maintain. Do not be alarmed." Both women nodded vaguely, and so I drew beside the couch and surveyed the young woman from head to toe.

'Truth to tell, I did make her assume a number of different positions before asking her to return to the initial one. I did, I confess, move her legs in diverse directions before tucking her right leg under her left, as you see in the sculpture. I placed my hand on her hips, then her abdomen, to twist her just slightly, in such a way that her ribs and muscles were visible, so that she seemed a creature of flesh and blood, the subject of the real desires of real men. I found a support for her right hand, posing it delicately by its fingertips, and bent her left arm at the elbow, bringing her fingers towards her face so that the viewer could not tell whether she was beckoning a lover or showing apprehension, as she appears to reach to pull her ringlets from her shoulder. I held her left hand in various positions near her face, and as I moved it about, I grazed her soft cheek and lips with the back of my hand. What a goddess!

'Would you be surprised to hear that by this point in the modelling session I began to be aroused? No? Well, nevertheless, you should know that I was the very image of saintly virtue: as the back of my hand rested for a moment upon her glowing cheek, I made a grand show of being all business, and finally stepped briskly away from her, back to my drawing table, asking her to hold that position as long as she could. Slowly her blushing subsided, her mother finally relaxed into her chair, as I set to sketching, and within just a few moments I was lost in my work. Is it not a wonder how times flies by – or disappears entirely – as the world seems to fall away, when we are truly immersed in creation?

'In any event, once I had finished my initial sketch, I sent her and her mother away with an assurance that I would send word once the sculpture had been sufficiently roughed out as I would need her for the final sculpting. When they returned a few weeks later, Maggie seemed almost eager to get to work, and her shyness seemed to have dissipated: no doubt my *virtue* had made its desired impression. Perhaps, upon reflection and with an absence of several weeks, Maggie determined that posing for me had not been all that bad. Her mother also seemed more at ease, and this time they needed no direction. The girl was undressed and lying on the couch almost immediately.

'"Do you remember the precise pose you held last time?" said I, and though she then resumed nearly the identical position I could not help but use this excuse to touch her as I had before. Without changing much at all of her attitude, I placed my hands successively on her calves, knee, thighs and hips, and as I went to position her left hand again near her face, I confess that it took a supreme effort of control not to brush the back of my right hand lightly across both of her breasts.

'From day to day, my sculpture came closer to completion, and from day to day, Maggie seemed more comfortable in her modelling. I no longer even needed to position her, so thoroughly had she memorised exactly where to lie, and how to position her limbs, pose her fingertips and tilt her head. Her mother grew positively bored with the monotony of the final sessions, and when I announced that the next day would be the last, she seemed overjoyed. I am sure she was also relieved that her daughter's questionable employment had almost come to an end – with no harm to any party. Maggie, on the other hand, seemed almost downcast. I am convinced that she had come to enjoy posing and was especially proud of the nearly completed statue itself.

'The next and final day Maggie appeared without her mother. "Where is your dear mama? Is she unwell?" said I, the nascent hope that mother might not appear at all that day kindling a desire I had thus far successfully crushed.

'"No," the girl replied, "me mum's a mess o' work to do, and tol' me that she *trusts Mr Leyland, as 'e's a proper gentleman, to be sure.*"

'I was not surprised that by now her mother trusted me, and that, between her boredom and her enterprising nature, she could not bear to sit still for one more day, especially with the end in full sight. I shuddered, though, to be alone with Maggie, and realised that the presence of Mrs Heaton had hitherto protected me – and her – from myself.

'She climbed upon her couch and assumed her position, by now nearly an identical twin of the sculpture I caressed before her. At length we were finished, and I fetched her dressing gown, handing it to her and saying, "Well miss, that is that. You have been a splendid model for *Kilmeny*." I wanted her to leave quickly, so little did I trust myself alone with her.

'Instead, she pulled the sash around her gown tightly and walked softly, in her lovely little naked feet, up to her replica, standing just beside me. She placed her hands on the shoulders of her likeness and raised herself up on the tips of her toes.

"Do I really look that that?" she asked.

"Well, I hope so!" I laughed. "Otherwise I have wasted my money and we *both* have wasted our time!"

"It's jes' – this might soun' vain – she's jes' so beautiful. No, no … I'm sure I don' look like tha'," she said, lifting up to me those immense blue eyes that have already enslaved *you*, Brontë.

'I am sure you can guess what happened next. I could not help myself. I turned to her and placed my hands on her cheeks. "Hmmm. Now let me see … let's have one last look to make sure, since you are questioning my craftsmanship." I loosened her sash and opened the front of her gown, thinking that her innocent question had a deeper meaning. As her gown fell away, I was overcome with lust. I fairly quivered as I ran my right hand over her breasts and slid my left down her abdomen; I wanted to carry her back to her couch and put her in quite a different position; indeed, preferably more than one pose before the day was through.

'Instead, I was sent reeling backwards with the force of a blow I would scarcely have imagined from such a little thing; my cheek burnt doubly, both from a hearty slap and my own confusion. In a flash, she had put on her gown again, and her sudden wrath was itself replaced with concern, if only that she and her parents would not be paid their due.

"I'm sorry, I am, Mr Leyland. It's jes'… it's jes' tha' I'm a good girl, I am."

By expressing contrition, she had offered me – us – a way to salvage this situation.

"No, my dear girl, it is I who must apologise. I mistook your intentions entirely. You were quite right to do as you did. You see – for I must confess that I am not always as good as you – sometimes an artist and his model form a bond that goes beyond the work itself, and I am afraid your beauty has intoxicated me utterly."

Although flattery is always a help in such situations, I was hardly stretching the truth here.

"Y' won't tell me dad, will you?" said Maggie, and whether she was referring to my actions or hers, I assured her on the souls of my ancestors that I would not say a word. Since the hulking innkeeper is known to throw two drunks into the street at once, and could probably crush a man's throat with one hand, there was no danger in my telling her dear papa or anyone else *anything*. Of course, you don't count, Brontë – although now that I think on it, this may explain why I haven't told you this story until now. In any event, I told her to get dressed, and when she had finished, I handed her a five-pound note. "I shall pay your parents the agreed-upon amount for your work, but this is just for you – it will be our other little secret."

"You're not a bad man, Mr Leyland," she said, looking up at me with those damnably enthralling eyes, "Y' jes' wan' things you can't 'ave, like mos' folks."

'I remember laughing to myself ruefully: she had just done what I wanted my statue to convey: a maiden *to tempt a man to sin – but not to give way*.

'"And you, sinless Kilmeny, are indeed a good girl," I said, and off she went.'

Leyland peered into his glass and smiled.

'That was five years ago. Now you know the whole story, Brontë, and why, especially on an occasion such as last night, I could not but tease Maggie as the *Sinless Maiden*. And if you are wondering how she finds herself at such events, especially after my bad behaviour, the reasons are two-fold: first, I pay her worthy parents for the food and drink, and second, I think she truly likes being surrounded by different sorts of people. For all I know, her beauty has given her grand ideas about her future, for despite having a rash of suitors, she has refused them all.'

'Joe, I don't think your behaviour was so bad. You could honestly claim that you thought she was seducing *you*. What surprises me is that you gave up so easily.'

'See here, my friend. Whether it is virtue or my high opinion of myself I know not, but I could never force myself on a woman. Join to that the likelihood that Maggie's father would quite cheerfully have murdered me had he known, and there you have it. Many thanks for the high praise, however. Coming from the son of a clergyman of the Holy Church of England it means a great deal!'

I was growing weary of his constant references to the *Good Reverend Brontë*, and so simply ignored him.

'I told Maggie that I would try to arrange for her to take an excursion on the railway, and that I would send word through you. I assume, then, that you make frequent appearances at the inn?'

'Yes, but not so often that Mr and Mrs Heaton grow suspicious – and after all, what could be worse than to have such suspicions aroused when I haven't even tasted the forbidden fruit!'

We have agreed that once I have secured a way for Maggie to join me on the train, I will write to Leyland and he would convey the message to her. I confess that I am pleasantly surprised by the turn his story took, and I find myself yearning to see her more than ever.

XVII.

A Magic Carpet Ride

November 23rd, 1840 · Sowerby Bridge

I have written precious little about my post here at Sowerby Bridge, for despite the bustle of activity, there is a monotony to it that can easily be condensed to this: trains come and go; passengers and goods are loaded and unloaded; figures and accounts – the bane of my existence – are kept current. Mr Duncan keeps me on my toes, and that is quite all right by me, as time passes far more quickly when I am thus occupied. I have even succeeded in concealing my dislike of keeping the accounts, so much so that – cruel irony – he has delegated all such work to me. Would that I, in turn, had an assistant to whom I could hand such tedious work! In short, beyond the idea of the railway – of a vast web connecting nearly every village in England, so that people and goods can travel at increasingly dizzying speeds – and the exhilaration of riding on an actual train itself, the everyday work of the Manchester and Leeds is no more exciting than any other dreary sort of business.

Despite the cold weather, we have just received word that the last brick will be laid on the Summit Tunnel in three weeks' time, and a grand ceremony is to be held. I have decided to take Maggie on her excursion just after that, so that we can travel all the way to Manchester and back, if both she and I can arrange to take the time away from our respective duties. I continue to think of Joe's description of her, and picture her gown falling down around her shoulders, brushing past her hips, thighs and calves to his studio floor. The other night I even dreamt of her, posed as Kilmeny, beckoning to me.

Living at such proximity to Halifax is a mixed blessing indeed. That Frobisher has arranged for Franz Listz to perform in January is but one example of what is accessible to me there. But there also resides Mephistopheles himself, as I have taken to calling Leyland. Although his soirées are infrequent, Joe finds any occasion he can to join me for a puff and a stiffener – usually several of the latter – so much so that I begin to wonder how long even *his* sturdy constitution can sustain such self-indulgence.

Meanwhile, his teasing about Maggie – whom he insists on calling *Kilmeny* – is unrelenting. Last night he walked up from Halifax, just a few moments before I would be leaving the station for the evening. He followed me about, feigning interest in the minutiae of my work, until at last all was completed but the final accounts to be tallied in the ledger.

'Come now, Brontë, surely you can do that tomorrow. I am more parched than the Israelites after their forty years in the blasted desert,' and as usual, Leyland – for like most devils he is part bully and part charmer – prevailed. I scribbled a note of what was to be completed the next day, and off we went to The Mermaid.

'Ah,' said Leyland, after his first swallow, 'that's the thing.' Although it was too soon for his libation to have had any effect, the very act of swallowing – nay, I suspect of simply having eyed the glass before him – was enough to settle his nerves. I told him about the completion of the tunnel, and asked him to communicate my invitation to Maggie. Like a schoolboy, he found the proximity of the words *tunnel* and *Maggie* in the same sentence to be a source of great amusement.

'Oh ho!' said he, 'so you think your train is the thing to gain access to that tunnel of virtue, where the "Greatest Young Artist of Yorkshire" has failed?'

'That's not at all what I am thinking,' I lied. It was a lie because I confess to having imagined how it might feel to be lost in the arms of Maggie, who resembled Agnes in so many ways that by a simple act of imagination I could blur my actual memories of one into my ideal representations of the other. It was true, however, that I was just as eager to see the look on her pretty face, to watch those bright eyes open wide, as the locomotive picked up steam and the countryside passed by. If that was all that happened, I would still count myself a happy man, just to be in her company, just to witness her delight.

'Whatever you say, little man. Besides, she has kept herself pure so long that now she's fairly a spinster – she must be twenty-one – and stale goods are not much better than damaged goods when it comes to being marriageable, in my view.'

'*Stale*?' I objected warmly, letting my feelings get the better of me. 'How can you say that of such a lovely creature? You, yourself, said she was *perfect*.'

'Calm those nerves of yours, little man. That was five years ago, remember? A woman's body is like any other ephemeral gift of nature: it reaches perfection just before it begins to decay. Think of the rose, at its most expansive, ravishing beauty the very instant before it begins to brown and wilt away. Or a fruit, whose sweetest, ripest, tastiest moment just precedes the beginning of its ultimate decline.

'In any event, listen to me: I was talking about aesthetic perfection. Five years ago, Kilmeny had just reached the full bloom of womanhood, like the aforementioned rose at the apogee of its beauty. Does she remain a lovely creature to ask round to my soirées? Absolutely! Would I like to feel those legs wrapped about me, and see those breasts heaving beneath or above me? Mmm, God in Heaven, yes!' – I frowned at this, I'm sure, and am equally certain that Leyland had said this for the express purpose of annoying me seriously – 'but if you look closely at her face, you will see that already the lines have begun to creep in about her eyes, and within a few years these will be joined by fissures on her brow, then her neck, and so on. That is all I meant to say, Brontë. It is a biologically undeniable and irreversible fact.'

There was no arguing with Leyland on this matter, and so despite – or because of – my dismay, I changed the subject.

'I imagine Frobisher is wild with excitement over the arrival of the great virtuoso in January – he was positively jumping for joy the other night.'

My friend also seemed relieved at this new topic, removed as it was from of our own experiences.

'By God, yes, he views it as a crowning achievement, I daresay!'

I confessed to knowing precious little about Liszt, except that he was, like Mozart before him, an Austro-Hungarian child prodigy, dragged by his father from one great city on the continent to the next, to perform for all manner of people, including the crowned heads of Europe. He was currently on his first tour of our Kingdom.

'Frobisher reports he is around my age,' continued Leyland. 'He says that the man is devilishly handsome, and so entrances his audience – especially the softer sex – that he is in danger of being crushed by his admirers! Frobisher told me the ladies have been known to fight over his coffee dregs and cigar stubs! Can you imagine having that sort of power over women? I'd wager that *he* could seduce the innkeeper's sinless daughter,' he added, unable to help himself.

I refused to rise to Joe's bait, instead asking him if any sort of formal reception or dinner had been planned for the great man. 'Why that is an excellent question – I believe I shall ask Frobisher himself, if for no other reason than to watch him twitch with anxiety, poor fellow! I fear his nerves put yours to shame, Brontë, for they appear at any moment ready to snap like one of Herr Liszt's piano wires!'

Joe lifted his glass to signal another, and was, uncharacteristically, at a loss for words – though not for long. Seemingly casting about for a topic, he said, 'Oh yes, Brontë, have you been doing any writing of late?'

I had not, in fact, been writing much of anything, and had quite given up on ever hearing anything from Coleridge. It had not taken long for me to learn that performing my duties at the station with the regularity required, including the dreaded account ledgers, sapped me of all creative strength, so that I could do little more than scribble the occasional thought or sketch in my notebook, or, at most, polish up old poems and translations. The creation of new work of any length was simply out of the question. I was not sure how to convey this to Leyland without triggering his usual mockery of my chosen profession. Not everyone, I thought, looking at Leyland's fine clothes and thinking of his extravagant soirées, had a brother to rescue him from creditors at regular intervals. Not wishing to quarrel with my friend, I decided to frame my dilemma more positively.

'As a matter of fact, I have readied some pieces for publication and was wondering if you and Francis could exert some influence with your father's old newspaper, the *Halifax Guardian*. It is hardly *Blackwood's*, but their poetry pages are respectable enough – far superior to the other Yorkshire papers, from what I can ascertain.

''The idea is, in theory, a sound one,' Leyland replied, 'but for God's sake man, do not mention *my* name, for when my father sold the paper three years ago, negotiations soured so much that a raft of solicitors were called in to settle the matter. The current proprietors would rather cross the street than speak to me, although with Francis they are on minimally civil terms – so you might speak to *him*.'

'If I had to guess,' said I, happy to have a rare upper hand with my friend, 'you have not helped matters at all, and have even been heard publicly speaking ill of the newspaper and its editor, whereas Francis, ever the steady, prudent businessman, has tried to make amends, given the complementary nature of his reading room.'

'Guilty as charged,' said he, 'but damn it, Brontë, they offered one price verbally – with the shake of a hand, mind you – and then changed their offer when it was time to sign the papers. They're sodding thieves, I tell you.'

'So, you fought it, and – let me guess – you ended up paying your lawyers considerably more than the difference in dispute, correct?'

'Yes, yes,' Leyland smiled ruefully, 'if you want to speak of a band of highwaymen, we can discuss my solicitors. I think Francis just paid the last of those fees a few months ago.'

'In short,' said I, 'you are going to be of no help in getting me published.'

'Alas, you are correct. I am afraid that any publication you manage to secure, Young Faustus' – for such is his response to my baptising him Mephistopheles – 'will be on your own merits alone, with no help from this particular devil. In short, the surest way to have your poems cast into the fire by the august editors of the *Halifax Guardian* is to mention our friendship – on that I would be willing to wager.'

Leyland stood and insisted on paying, though I fear I now have more steady employment than he. There was no questioning him on the matter, however, as I learned long ago. As he stepped up onto the fly that he'd hired to take him back to Halifax, I reminded him to inform Maggie of the train ride and invited him to come the previous day to the grand opening of the tunnel. I had again mentioned Maggie in too great a proximity with the word tunnel, but this time my friend simply collapsed in uncontrollable paroxysms of laughter as he bounced away, his own mirth giving his conveyance itself a kind of comic absurdity to my eyes. How could one not like him, Mephistopheles or no?

As I write these lines at day's end, I wonder whether something more profound lies buried beneath Leyland's words: *think of the rose, at its most expansive, ravishing beauty the instant before it begins to brown and wilt away. Or a fruit, whose sweetest, ripest, tastiest moment just precedes the beginning of its decline.* I think of the feeling of transcendence – ecstasy – with Agnes, that acme where mounting desire finally burst forth into glorious consummation, that wink of an eye that widened out instantly into eternity.

Indeed, is this the essence of life itself? Is it the spark – the heartbeat – separating a vital being from an inanimate corpse? Why did Mama, Maria and Elizabeth die, while we others lived on? At what moment does ambition become success, or decline forever into hopeless failure? Is Leyland's – and, I confess, my own – love of drink a sign of vitality, of a love of life, or is it merely the first step towards madness and death? When does the uphill striving of youth become the downhill march to the grave? Perhaps the walker knows not that he is on a downhill course until long, long after it is too late.

How simple it is to believe in the extremes of health and decay, or of good and evil for that matter. But what if the meaning of human existence is concentrated in those infinitesimal interstices, as transient and ineffable as the play of light and shadow in the willows, or the fleeting clouds beyond them, as Agnes moved above me, and I inside her, until my mind at last felt no more pain, though it exploded into a thousand fragments. What if the secret of life – God himself, and His promise of life eternal – is somehow resident in that instant? Does not scripture say that *in a moment, in the twinkling of an eye, the trumpet shall sound, and the dead shall be raised incorruptible, and we shall be changed*?

December 20th, 1840 · Sowerby Bridge

The Summit Tunnel has at last opened, and one may now travel on a single train from Leeds to Manchester. The grand opening was an even greater jubilee than the event in October, after which the dignitaries dined at the Summit Inn whilst the workers were regaled at long tables of planks and trestles, hastily erected after the last brick was laid and the first train had made its way successfully from one side of the mountain to the other. Massive torches stood between the makeshift tables, and a fiddler added to the festivities. Each worker was permitted a pint of ale, no more. I had no time to share in the celebration and was kept so occupied with my sundry duties at Sowerby Bridge that I could scarcely even think of seeing Maggie the next day. Indeed, so exhausted was I that I had only the strength to eat a crust of bread and a bit of cold beef, washed down with a single glass of wine.

Is there any sleep like that of a man exhausted from physical exertion, rather than from worry or drink? I awoke feeling better than I had in what seemed like months, and was soon on my way to Halifax to meet Maggie, with whom I then rode the omnibus back to our station, so that we could take a train up to the tunnel, then down the western slope of the Pennines, through Littleborough, Rochdale and, at last, into Manchester. I was able to obtain a holiday, and had arranged with my friend the engine driver, Matthews, to let us ride with him in the locomotive itself. How Maggie had convinced her parents that she needed to be away from the inn I know not, but she is now truly a grown woman, and for all I know she is still drawing on the reservoir of the debt they owe her for fairly compelling her to model for Leyland.

I met her before the White Swan, where an omnibus was preparing to take its passengers up to Sowerby Bridge – how much more convenient it will be when the railway extends a branch line to Halifax itself. Maggie was radiant in the simplest of dress, her hair wound up and knotted on top of her head, 'for I'm tol' the wind fairly lashes a person to death,' she said, those magnificent incandescent eyes wide with anticipation. We travelled the steep hill to the station, and then Matthews and I helped her aboard, doing our best not to be observed by Mr Duncan. Although I had spoken to him about taking a ride to Manchester, I had no wish to see him on this day, especially since I had failed to mention my highly unusual female companion.

We had just climbed onto the locomotive and wrapped ourselves in woollen blankets against the December cold, when Duncan called out to Matthews. I motioned for Maggie to sit down with me and placed my finger on my lips to Matthews. He is no fool, so he merely winked and smiled, then hopped down to have a chat with my supervisor, thus preventing him for climbing up onto the locomotive and discovering us there. What I was doing was not necessarily wrong, but it would most likely have been frowned upon if discovered. I had not asked whether it was permitted but had simply addressed myself directly to the good-natured engine driver. How often in life do we act in just this manner – knowing that we are quite possibly doing wrong, at least in respect to the letter of the law, and yet choosing to act rather than discovering the truth of the matter, so great is our desire to please ourselves, or others!

Soon we had left the station behind and could stand, and as the train gained speed, moving along the Calder, Maggie positively squealed with delight, thrusting her arm through mine as we banked one way and then the next, following the path of the river, upstream, towards the tunnel. Her lovely face was an amalgam of childlike joy and fear, the first eventually dominating the second as it became clear that despite our speed and the route we travelled – so different from any a horse-drawn conveyance might take – she would be safe. Her initial apprehension settled into a state of constant, bubbling excitement, like a boiling kettle moved just far enough from the flame to simmer gently, and as we rounded yet another curve she shouted to Matthews, over the noise of the engine, ''ow is it tha' we don' fly fairly off t'rails, int' river or woods, with a great crash?'

Matthews laughed, but not unkindly.

'Well, you see, Miss, them great railway engineers 'ave used all manner of learnin', like mathematics and physics and other scientific know-how, to tell just how far they can tip the iron beast 'fore it topples over. O' course, the fastest and easiest road is a straight line, and downhill at tha', you won' be surprised to learn, ha ha!

'But though *men* sometimes act that way' – here Matthews winked at me – 'tha's no' how God made the worl', is it now?' he said, gesturing across the rugged landscape. I could tell Matthews was charmed by Maggie, even wrapped as she was in a heavy cloak and the woollen blanket – and what man would not have been?

We were making our way slowly uphill along the Calder, passing the future stations of Luddenden Foot and Hebden Bridge, currently under construction. At last the train entered the dark tunnel, and it was hard to believe that just a day earlier it had been the scene of the grand ceremony led by Mr Dickinson, the tunnel's engineer, followed by a rumbustious celebration of the workers, torches blazing, blasphemous oaths flying about, and no doubt manifold toasts offered in remembrance of co-workers who had died in the construction of the tunnel, this marvel of modern engineering. I have even heard Duncan say – in the reverential tones usually reserved for saints and martrys – that the great Stephenson himself is planning to visit the tunnel soon.

Today, however, it had been stripped quite bare, and only the train's lantern illuminated the few feet in front and to either side of us as we slowly advanced into the darkness. Maggie clutched at my hand and stood close to me, and I could feel her warm cheek within an inch or two of my neck, could smell her sweetly perfumed and carefully braided hair just under my nose, and was overcome with a desire to take her in my arms, though all I did was squeeze her hand. Her hand embraced mine in return and, like a child huddling close to a parent – for there was far more fear than passion in her gesture – she pressed herself close to me. The pinprick of light we saw in the distance soon grew to reveal the tunnel's opening on the western side of the summit, and as we emerged into the precious sunshine of this fleeting December day Maggie removed her hand from mine and gazed out the side of the locomotive, so that I could only see the back of her neck, which appeared to have flushed bright red.

'You were right, Mr Brontë,' she said, now somewhat subdued, 'a person only gets dizzy by looking at the world sideways … a body must gaze straight ahead.' Her gravity was soon dispelled, however, replaced by unrestrained glee as we gained speed downhill, rounding corners that caused our bodies to fly together and then apart, together and apart, together and apart. There was something of a dance in our movements, if not more, but unlike skilled dancers or passionate lovers, we had little control over our movements, dictated as they were by every twist and turn, every rise and fall, of the railway line itself. Just over two hours later we were in Manchester, which to Maggie might just as well have been the distant shores of the Americas, for it was easily twice as far from Halifax as she had ever travelled.

Soon we were retracing our route on another train, this time riding alone in a covered first-class coach, where we sat on benches opposite each other, as was her preference, a thick woollen blanket warming us each. She was quiet for the better portion of our journey, mostly gazing out at the bleak landscape. From time to time I attempted to engage her in conversation, but her responses were generally limited to a nod or a 'yes' or 'no'.

After an especially long pause I ventured, 'Imagine how glorious this ride will be in spring, when these woods will be swathed in green and wildflowers and teeming with life!' Her lovely eyes met mine, and I imagined, if only for an instant, that we were in a meadow, loving each other – devouring each other – in utter abandon, and she was somehow at once herself and yet also Agnes.

'Perhaps,' said I, 'you might wish to make this journey then?'

She simply nodded and returned her gaze to the window, and I could not tell what was wrong. Had I said something amiss?

'Well now, you are looking at the world sideways – I surely hope it does not make you swoon,' wishing to add that her bouncing along next to me on our way to Manchester had nearly made me do the same.

Here she granted me a small laugh and replied, 'Though t'is dizzyin' indeed, I rather like the way it makes me feel, the world flyin' by, but me all safe and warm under me blanket.'

'If only *life* were like that,' said I, not thinking before I spoke.

'What d'y' mean?'

'I mean that sometimes I wish I could wrap myself in a woollen blanket and simply watch the world go by, instead of labouring at a post I do not love, merely to earn money.'

She looked puzzled. 'Why shou' you be any different from anyone else, Mr Brontë?' she said simply.

'I just *feel* different,' said I, and why I bore my soul to Maggie I do not know. Was I falling in love? 'I feel,' I continued, 'as if I were meant for higher things. All of this hustling and bustling and grubbing about to earn a few pounds seems so coarse and undignified to me.'

She said nothing, but bit her lip, as she had that night at Leyland's, but now there was only sadness in her eyes. I had wounded her, and soon grasped my blunder. She turned to me and said, with a curious blend of melancholy, reproach and affection, 'I think maybe yer jes' a little boy who wants to be taken care of, are ye not?'

I could have kindled up then, and answered sharply in my own defence – that after all I was working and doing quite well at it, thank you very much – but she was so lovely, at once so strong and so vulnerable, her cheeks red from the cold, her eyes glimmering with just the hint of tears, her golden braids catching the last rays of this brief December day, that I could only say, feigning jocularity, 'Yes, yes, I suppose you are right, Maggie. I imagine that what I *really* want to do is to read and write all day, and have someone else take over the wretched, dirty, practical business of everyday life, especially that nasty part about earning one's living. But see here! I am in the exalted post of Assistant-Clerk-in-Charge on the Manchester and Leeds Railway, heroically fighting my every slothful instinct each step of the way – not unlike this train labouring up the hill towards the Summit Tunnel – even going so far as to keep all of the dreaded ledgers for the station at Sowerby Bridge! Surely the twelve labours of Hercules were as nothing when compared to this!'

I paused for just a second or two, and added, 'So you see, I am fully a man. Indeed, let me protect you as we enter the mouth of the tunnel, for we shall be like Jonah in the belly of the whale, though our captivity shall be closer to three minutes than three days!' I moved over next to her and drew my blanket over hers as we approached the tunnel.

This silly speech had its desired effect, and she was now smiling in spite of herself. 'I see why you and Mr Leyland are friends,' said she. 'Y'not only talk the same way, yer both naugh'y boys … and like naugh'y boys who misbehave an' then smile sweetly, you confound those who'd rightly take y' t' task.'

As the train entered the obscurity of the tunnel, I could again feel her warmth and smell her breath and, most of all, her sweet perfumed hair just beneath my nose. I inhaled deeply, drew her closer, felt with my right hand for her face, cupping it in my palm as I leant to kiss her. She drew her lips away, and although we were alone in the carriage, she whispered as if not to be heard, simply, 'No'. She did not move her body away from me, however, and I could feel her soft hip move against mine as we made our way through the tunnel and back into the rapidly fading sunlight of this nearly shortest day of the year. At least she had not levelled a blow at me, as she had at Joe five years earlier.

'I *am* sorry,' I began, but without moving from her side, 'it is just that –'

She did not move away from me, but simply said, 'Hoosh', and as the train bumped its way down along the Calder and back through Hebden Bridge and Luddenden Foot, she let each jolt of the coach carry her where it would, sometimes against me for a brief instant, then away from me at another. In the final moments of our approach to Sowerby Bridge, she let her head fall back and rest on my shoulder, and I again drew a deep, hungry breath, savouring each instant of her presence while I could.

'And now who is the little child?' I said gently, wishing she would turn her head and place her lips on mine.

Instead, she gazed out the window and said, 'We're all of us children of God, aren't we? And we're never really fully growed. But we must "put away childish things", ain't that what the good book says? But you and Mr Leyland, well, y' can't do tha', can you? And it's why people hate you and why they love you and most of all why they are sad for you. They want the life you have, but don't want what comes with it, and you don't wan' the life *they* 'ave, but you wan' the *things* they 'ave.'

This was not the romantic picture I had painted of my train ride with Maggie. She must have seen my knitted brow, and even kissed me sweetly on the cheek, saying, 'You may be a naughty boy … but you're a good man. Y' jes' don't believe it yourself.'

We spoke little as the train pulled into Sowerby Bridge, or on the short omnibus ride to Halifax. As I handed her down to the driver, who should stand there but Joseph Bentley Leyland himself, waving his eternal, infernal, walking stick – and laughing.

'Ho ho, well I'll be married, buried, devilled and damned, if it's not our love birds!' said he, then bursting into appropriately seasonal song: 'Two turtle doves, and a partridge in a pear tree! I suppose that makes me the partridge, eh?'

Maggie half-curtsied and smiled politely at Leyland, but quickly and silently made her way to her father's inn, across the street. Leyland called after her, 'Now Kilmeny, don't be cross with old Joe! I'll be sending you a note soon about my next soirée! Count on it!'

Leyland insisted that I come to the studio for a celebratory drink, and he was fairly bursting with glee as we strode across The Square. Once there, he hastily removed his coat and hat and drew two chairs up to *Kilmeny*, then fairly raced over to a sideboard to secure a bottle and two glasses. Gesturing me to sit, he poured us each a generous portion of whisky with trembling hand, stoppered the bottle, and nestled its base between *Kilmeny*'s smoothe marble thighs, its neck just a hair's breadth beneath her perfect, lustrous left breast.

I feared my friend would begin a round of incessant teasing, but not today, for he had momentous news to share: after learning that the great Liszt and his entourage would have to pass the night in Halifax before making their way to London and then on to the continent, Joe had convinced the ever-worried and easily led Frobisher that it was important – nay *essential*, for the reputation of fair Halifax itself was at stake – that a celebratory event be given in the musician's honour. They had further learnt that the concert in Halifax was to be the last of his long tour of the British Isles. Joe was even paying Frobisher to transport a pianoforte to the studio – 'just in case the virtuoso wishes to play' – and there would be nothing but the finest food and drink Yorkshire could produce in honour of the great man. All of this would take place immediately after his performance, with the studio transformed into a ballroom of sorts.

I wondered how Leyland was to pay for this, and suspected his usual banker, Mr Frank, but as if reading my mind, he said, 'And the beauty of it is that I have all of the cash in hand I need to give the party. Some might say that I should pay off my other debts or place the funds in reserve for a rainy day, but *carpe diem*, my good man, right? When will Herr Liszt ever play in Halifax again? Never, I should say, and what purpose will money serve sitting inside a bank, or squirrelled away in a mattress? Only fools make an idol of their unspent gold, for does not the Holy Scripture say, *Lay not up for yourselves treasures upon earth, where moth and rust doth corrupt, and where thieves break through and steal?* Surely your righteous papa would agree, would he not?'

Leyland's special talent for picking and choosing from the Bible whatever he felt would justify his present actions was unrivalled, and I decided not to crush his good humour with any contrariness, laughing along with him rather than pointing out that he had conveniently omitted the key phrase from the same passage in Matthew: *But lay up for yourselves treasures in heaven, where neither moth nor rust doth corrupt, and where thieves do not break through nor steal. No man can serve two masters: ye cannot serve God and mammon.*

'What the Devil,' said I, 'have you at long last found yourself a wealthy patroness?'

'Alas, no,' he replied with feigned dejection, 'but you are not so far off as you might think.' He extended his glass towards his sculpture and said simply, 'I have sold my dear *Kilmeny*, and am using part of the proceeds to fund my gala event. My sole regret is that the beauty will be carried away before Liszt can see her. I should like to have seen his reaction to her, famed rake that he is.'

I stood and walked over to the sculpture, placing my tumbler next to Kilmeny's right thigh and scanning her from head to toe. 'Perhaps,' said I, wondering if I would ever see Maggie as Leyland had, 'perhaps her absence will give you even more room for entertaining your multitude of guests, especially with a piano placed amidst it all.'

At this Joe leapt up and walked over to where I stood. 'No, no, I am prideful enough – and as it will come as no surprise to you it does not amount to a true confession – to want Europe's greatest musician to see at least one work of Yorkshire's greatest young artist.' He had once been called this in an article in the *Halifax Guardian* and had never let his friends forget it.

Leyland ran his hands up the length of Kilmeny's legs and torso, over her breasts and neck, then circling around the braids and knot of her hair before heaving a great sigh. 'I will miss her, though,' said he, which finally brought him round to the conversation I had dreaded since first seeing him with Maggie.

'Say, I did not ask you, young Faustus, what transpired on your grand voyage to Manchester and back with Kilmeny, alias Margaret? Were you a great hero, a rake, a rascal, a regular Don Juan?'

'We rode with the engine driver to Manchester, then in a covered carriage on the return trip. I think she enjoyed herself thoroughly.'

'Is that all?'

'That is all, my friend.'

'Bugger me, Brontë, what a disappointment you are. Surely that was the moment – on your magic carpet ride, as you have described it to me – to take her in your arms and go to extremes. Were you never alone?'

'We were alone in the coach on the return journey.'

'Well confound it, little man, you missed your chance.'

'What would you have recommended,' said I, 'handle her as roughly as you did five years ago? I did try to kiss her and was rebuffed.'

Pausing for a moment, I remembered how twice she had called me *a good man*. I looked from Kilmeny to her creator, whose expression was fading from disappointment to mere boredom, and simply said, as we resumed our chairs, 'Well Joe, as she has told us on separate occasions, she's a good girl, isn't she?'

XVIII.

A Promotion

January 15th, 1841 · Sowerby Bridge

A new year and another new beginning! What wonderful news has come with Christmastide: I am so valued in my position here that I have been promoted to Clerk-in-Charge of the new station at Luddenden Foot, at the first of April! My salary has risen to 130 pounds a year, more than anything I have earned before, thrice Anne's annual wages, and almost a third more than Weightman, Papa's curate's.

The Reverend Brontë was overjoyed at the news, no doubt feeling that I have found my calling – or at least *a* calling – and seeing that I am capable of advancement, even in such a short period of time. He doubtless thinks that I have finally exorcised the demon goading me to seek literary fame, just as he himself did so many years ago, at precisely my age. We shall see.

Emily and Anne seemed equally pleased with the news, and congratulated me sincerely, each in her own, distinct way: the first gruffly but genuinely, the second sweetly and warmly, with a light-hearted joke or two. Only Charlotte seemed unable to welcome this news: her response was a restrained 'good for you', which seemed to take every atom of her strength to utter, and I later overheard her say to Emily, 'Let us hope that his removal to another station will turn out for the best. It *looks* like getting on at any rate.'

As I have thought on more than one occasion, could it be that my success only reminds her of her own failure? For she has yet to secure another position, though she is better trained and more seasoned than Anne, who from all acounts continues to make herself invaluable to the Robinsons. Emily – for Emily is a special case – has made herself similarly inestimable to Papa, and I cannot imagine anything prising her loose from Haworth, for she clings to her home as a starfish fastens to its reef.

Charlotte, meanwhile, continues to be more burden than help, for she is dependent without contributing much, spending her days corresponding with her childhood friends, only half-heartedly attempting to find employment, even making Miss Wooler, her old teacher, do most of her work for her. I do not even think she is writing anymore, for when I asked her for news from our imaginary land of Angria, she simply said, somewhat haughtily in fact, 'Branwell, there comes a time when the imagination should be pruned and trimmed and judgement cultivated in its place. It is time to clear away the countless illusions of our youth, is it not?' I find I no longer understand this strange creature – who not so long ago was my twin, nay perhaps even my better self – for her own judgement seems to vary according to the case at hand: as I have said before, she fits her pronouncements to the end that is most convenient to her. On the very day that she turned up her odd little nose at my advancement in the world – the real world of men, industry, railways, money – she excused her own lack of poetic activity by claiming sententiously that it was *time to clear away the countless illusions of our youth.* Really now? I begin to think that she is thoroughly impossible.

As I turn these things over in my mind and survey the year just passed, I wonder if I have been altogether too hard on myself. After all, I was a valued tutor in Broughton, and was dismissed only because of Mr Postlethwaite's lack of appreciation of a true education in the classics. The reality is that I performed my duties well and was an excellent boarder. I cannot bear to reflect at any length about Agnes, but that *too* was a good thing – it was as pure as the sky and clouds above us when we moved together as one.

I had ultimately followed Mr Postlethwaite's – and John Brown's – advice and sought work with the railway, where I have quickly proved myself more than capable. With the exception of a rare visit home and an occasional trip to Halifax, I am forever trying to anticipate the needs of Mr Duncan, and even offer to work additional hours if needed, taking over the ledgers and keeping them with an exactitude that surprises even myself, so much do I detest that dreary work. In one respect, my employment at Sowerby Bridge has been easier than writing a single poem, for the share of my mind required to perform such tasks is minimal; it requires an entirely different kind of thought and energy, and though it is not perfectly suited to my nature, I have laboured to make the adjustments required to excel.

Now then: what will the world hold for Patrick Branwell Brontë, aged twenty-three, as *Anno Domini* 1841 unfurls? Luddenden Foot is scarcely two miles up the Calder, so that except for my lodgings, little in my life need change. My salary will have risen more precipitously than I could have dreamt just months ago, almost double what I am earning now. Moreover, I will now be Clerk-in-Charge, and though such a title might draw down upon me the derision of my elder sister, it far outshines anything she has accomplished. I can see, now, how easy it would be to lose oneself in the pursuit of Mammon, for the thought of nearly twice the income for doing, I doubt not, altogether similar work, is positively intoxicating. Tempting indeed it is, to use Charlotte's own words, to *clear away the countless illusions of youth*, if this is what assiduous application yoked to just a bit of intellect can yield in such a short time! What, then, might I accomplish if I were to give over entirely, and to bury my literary ambitions once and for all?

I confess that my mind has even wandered into uncharted territory with the news of this promotion: what of marriage, and what of Maggie as my bride? Would not her good papa think highly of such an offer from a man whose salary has nearly doubled? Of course, I know what my own family would think of such a union. Charlotte would scorn to be related to such a woman – for in nowise would she stoop to call Maggie a *lady* – and would ridicule her simple manners and speech, and even rougher hands – as if Emily's hands were not just as rough, and as if our own grandparents were not Irish farmers and Cornish merchants. What a curse it is to be raised with the manners and expectations of the gentry, but to lack all means to live a genteel life! We think ourselves betters, but what makes us better? Our learning, our speech and our manners: that is all. The thought of asking for Maggie's hand unleashes a flood of contradictory emotions: passion, longing, excitement, fear and dread. In the meantime, Leyland's elaborate preparations for Herr Liszt proceed apace; even when sober, he is positively drunk with excitement over the coming event.

Although I am curious to see Liszt, as well as what Leyland has prepared for him, I am most eager of all to see Maggie. I trust and hope that she will accept Joe's invitation. Twice I have tried to see her at the White Swan, and twice her father has reported that she was away on a commission. His scowl the first time encouraged me to finish my drink promptly and be off; the second time he was friendlier to me, for I was in the company of Joe, who used the occasion to place a large order of food and drink for his *fête*. This fact, of course, made the grasping old man giddy, for he could surely already picture the sculptor's cash filling his till. He even offered, 'I suppose you'd like Maggie to be there, eh, to oversee it all?'

'Well Heavens, yes, would you please tell her? Especially in this bleak season, her beauty will be just the thing to replace the flowers we need to adorn the studio!' Leyland paused artfully, and added, 'of course you and your missus are invited as always. I do wish you would come for once. You would have all your worst fears confirmed, about just how wicked we artists can be, ha ha! And Herr Liszt will be there, *mein lieber Gott!* It will be *wunderbar*!'

The innkeeper merely laughed. 'Why, us common folks coom to *your* do? Now y' know full well, Mr Leyland, that we cannuh' so much as nip ou' of t' inn, especially if Maggie is gone,' adding meaningfully, in what must have been an allusion to her modelling sessions for Leyland, 'we trus' you, and we trus' Maggie.' Laughing, he added, 'and can y' picture suchlike as us mingling with the likes of them grand folks? Did you no' tell me last week tha' the man's lover is a countess, and that 'e's e'en played his pianoforte for kings and queens?'

'Ah, my good man, we are all God's children, are we not?' He looked over at me and, holding the paradoxical attitude of playful gravity of which he is master, nodded meaningfully. 'After all, is there much of a difference between the likes of Liszt on the one hand, and the Bard of Haworth here and myself on the other? I think not!'

Naughty Joe had once again charmed his audience, though the fat purse intended for the soirée surely did not hurt matters. After a bit of laughter all around, Maggie's father got back to work. I leant across the table to Leyland.

'Are you daft? What are you thinking of, inviting her parents?'

'Hush, hush, little man. There is always method in my madness. Have you not heard of variolation, or inoculation against smallpox?'

'Yes, yes, of course. What has that to do with this?' I was beginning to be seriously annoyed.

'Well, I've just conducted a bit of metaphorical inoculation with that rascal over there,' he said in a low, conspiratorial voice, nodding in the direction of our host.

'Meaning?'

'Meaning, young Faustus, that having invited – even insisted – that he and his wife come, we can now be thoroughly at our ease and as wild as we please – goodness, that's a rhyme, did you notice that?'

'Go on,' said I, still impatient to understand his reasoning.

'Calm yourself, Brontë. What this means is that we may conduct ourselves with reckless abandon, and you may, if you're so inclined, carry the innkeeper's daughter off into a corner, or into the cellar, under a table, into a waggon, upon the roof, or out into the street if you please, and have it off with her. Please just do it, for pity's sake, because your nerves are even more tautly strung than usual! Of course, the great pianist may have other ideas!' he laughed.

Throughout Joe's stream of foolishness, I had kept a sharp lookout for Maggie herself, but when we left half an hour later, she still had not returned.

Good God in his Heaven, how I long to see her again! How I hope she will be there!

XIX.

The Great Liszt Performs

January 31st, 1841 · Sowerby Bridge

Where to begin? The great Liszt has come and gone, and I feel almost at a loss to describe his passage. Although two days have passed since Leyland's *fête*, my head still throbs. I journeyed to Halifax by omnibus as the day declined, for Joe desired that I see the studio before the concert, which was to begin at eight o'clock that evening.

As I entered, I nearly had the sensation that I had happened into the wrong building, so transformed was the vast room. All the tools of Leyland's trade had been cleared away, extensive cleaning had been conducted and colourful bunting was draped from window to window. Carpets had been laid over the stone floor and fire already roared in the grates. Tables flanked two of the four walls and were soon to be covered with all manner of dainties, whilst two lads were just beginning to prepare an assortment of beverages – mulled wine, claret, whisky and brandy, for there would be no ale or gin at an event honouring Herr Liszt.

Joe, however, was interested in the two objects confronting each other in the centre of the studio.

'So,' he said, gesturing with a grand sweep of the arm, 'what do you think?' He was beside himself with excitement. *Kilmeny the Sinless Maiden* was no more and had been replaced by Leyland's monumental *Head of Satan*, whose ferocious, stony gaze stared directly at Frobisher's pianoforte.

'I certainly hope Herr Liszt does not take this juxtaposition amiss,' said I, adding, 'Though I must say that your Satan bears a striking resemblance to its creator.' What a lifetime ago we had seen it in Bradford! It, like Kilmeny, had languished in Leyland's studio, hidden beneath sheets in a distant corner. I was now thoroughly convinced that it was an accurate self-portrait of Joe, at the height of his youthful, sardonic arrogance.

'Lucifer himself take me, Brontë,' said Joe, who, from his breath and even more expansive mood than usual, I could tell had already begun drinking – no doubt to calm his nerves over the impending events of the evening – 'Satan's soul may be black as pitch, but surely he must be a handsome devil – ha ha! – just as the sinless Kilmeny must be a beauty worth ravishing, if her virtue is to mean anything at all. I remember casting all about me at the time and finding not a single face remotely as handsome as the one I saw peering back at me from the glass each morning! As for our distinguished guest and his band of musicians, this afternoon I met John Orlando Parry, the Welsh baritone accompanying him, and he assured me that Liszt is immoderately fond of cigars, drink and, especially, the softer sex. Ho ho! What an evening we shall have!'

Leyland circled the piano, growing thoughtful for a moment. 'I surely hope he is willing to play, for we can hardly have Frobisher or someone else of his ilk – even you, Brontë, though you're tolerably good for an amateur – hacking away at the keys with Herr Liszt in the room! And yet, we cannot *force* the poor man to play, especially after he has given a concert, now can we?' Brightening, he added, 'Ah well, enough drink and conversation will surely fill the void. I shall make it plain that there is no expectation, for that and some mulled wine or fine brandy are more likely to do the trick than any form of supplication.'

'What of Kilmeny?' I asked.

'Dost thou mean mean the sculpture or the model, pray?' he said, raising an eyebrow.

'The sculpture,' I said impatiently, 'has the buyer already taken her away?'

'Yes, alas, and I even shed a tear as the sinless maiden in all her naked splendour bumped out of the square, chained, like some nineteenth-century Andromeda, to the back of a waggon. The only thing more modern would have been to load her into a railway coach and send her over the Pennines to Manchester!'

'Speaking of the original, is Maggie scheduled to adorn your gathering tonight?'

'Ah *ha*!' he responded, clapping me on the back with such force that I had difficulty not tumbling forwards into his satanic sculpture. 'Yes, little man, I anticipate that she will grace us with her presence, or so I have been told by her august parent, the gentlemanly innkeeper. I, however, have seen not a sign of her since your infamous, mechanised magic carpet ride to Manchester and back. I wonder, have you bewitched our poor Kilmeny? Perhaps she pines for your noble brow and Roman nose?'

'Or my towering height, these fashionable spectacles or this shock of flaming hair,' I laughed. 'No, I doubt that seriously, my friend.'

In whom could I confide my secret wish that Maggie was indeed pining after me, or at least thinking of me as often as I was of her? Surely not Joe Leyland. We had that sort of manly rapport that allowed for seriousness only in questions of art, history, politics, faith or the meaning of existence, while matters of the heart were banished for all time. No, the subject of the fairer sex must be treated in a crude and bantering manner between men, with all noble feelings proscribed and elevated sentiments considered a mere instrument of seduction, especially for the Leylands of the world. Above all, women must not be treated as the yearning, thinking, feeling creatures that they are.

As for my own sisters – and three more yearning, thinking, feeling persons I can scarce imagine – I strain every thread of my imagination to picture any one of them in the arms of a man, though of course they are made of the same flesh and blood as I. How can we be so different, then? Is it nature that made us so, or has the world's different treatment of the sexes turned us, in adulthood, into utter strangers? How curious it is that we could, as little children, be as solidly united as the trunk of a single great oak, but are now split by life's storms into such different branches that we scarcely know each another!

I was still musing over these things an hour later, as Leyland and I sat in the front row at the Old Assembly Rooms, awaiting the concert. He nudged me with his elbow.

'Say, you'll never guess who is here.'

A thrill of excitement coursed through my veins, for I expected it to be Maggie, as unlikely as that now seems. I turned in the direction of Joe's nod, and saw, however, a few rows back and to our left, the Reverend Brontë, along with Charlotte and Emily, and, on the far side of my sisters, Papa's curate, William Weightman. I had hardly expected them to make this trip or spend any of Papa's scant income, but here they sat, as if summoned by my musings. I glanced at my watch and seeing that ten minutes remained, stood and made my way around to them.

'Why family, what brings you to Halifax in the depths of winter?'

As is usually the case, Charlotte spoke first, staring at me with those large watery eyes of hers, a tense smile closed over her crooked teeth. She forever seems – with me, at least – on the verge of boiling over in a fit of passion, but never quite does.

'Hello to you *too*, dear brother. Surely you do not think only railway clerks are capable of enjoying the celestial beauty wrung from the piano by Herr Liszt, do you? I hope you are not too embarrassed to see your poor relations from Haworth.'

Emily said nothing, smiling enigmatically – with just a bit of wickedness to be detected around the upper edges of her eyes, I thought. I wondered what my two sisters truly thought about the dashing Weightman next to them, especially as he was now struggling to restrain his laughter. With his fair hair swept forward and large side-whiskers, prominent nose and chin, he was a taller and far more handsome version of myself.

'Come now, Miss Brontë, you are treating poor Branwell a bit harshly, don't you think?'

'No,' she replied, 'quite the opposite: he wants a bit of unsparing treatment.'

This was said in a seemingly flippant, even playful tone, but her eyes told a different story, for they bore into my very soul.

Did she recognise that, even in jest, such a pronouncement was an indictment of Papa?

The old man himself shifted uncomfortably in his chair and spoke at last. 'We procured four tickets at a family rate, a mere 21 shillings, so how could we not make the trip from Haworth?'

Ah yes, always frugal Papa: he had realised the monumental savings of three shillings! At this it was Charlotte's turn to shift uncomfortably in her chair.

'Oh yes, and Branwell, Charlotte has some very good news to share, which she has not yet had the time to write you about,' he continued.

She rarely writes to me anymore about anything, I felt like saying, so I was not surprised that she had been too 'occupied' to do so.

'Really? Pray, tell.'

Charlotte reddened a bit, and then said, 'I've been offered a post as governess to the White family, of Upperwood House at Rawdon, to begin in March. I've not yet determined whether I shall accept, however.'

'Why would you not?' said I.

She hesitated, whilst Papa filled the silence. 'The pay is quite modest,' he said, 'only twenty pounds per annum.' I could see both sisters stiffen, and Willy Weightman made a point of studying a particularly pretty young lady sitting directly across the aisle from him, this pious man of the cloth giving her a thorough going-over, from her lovely auburn ringlets to her pretty little booted feet.

Meanwhile, the Brontë children were, for a brief instant, once again united against the world, for we all feel the public discussion of money to be vulgar, and indeed to be in unforgivably bad taste. Papa has no such scruples, but he was correct in his assessment just then: Charlotte would be earning half of what Anne was paid at Thorp Green, not even a fifth of my new salary at Luddenden Foot. And yet, rejecting the offer would appear to be churlish, whimsical, and most of all selfish, for if Charlotte did so she would continue her dependency on Papa whilst Emily managed the household and Anne and I were gainfully employed.

'I am certainly *inclined* to accept,' said she after an awkward silence, 'and at least Rawdon is a mere nine miles from Brookroyd, so I shall see dear Ellen with great regularity.'

At this moment, voices began to fall silent as Frobisher strode across the stage on the tips of his toes, so I quickly took leave of my friends and made my way back to the front row. Our local concertmaster then introduced the London impresario and conductor Lewis Lavenu, who presided over the stage at the pianoforte.

The programme was divided into two parts, the first beginning with selections from Mozart and Handel, performed by two female singers, a Miss Steele and a Miss Bassano; Richardson, the celebrated flautist; and John Orlando Parry himself. Three, four, five, six pieces were played, and still no sign of Liszt. Was he ill? Could he bear the English chill no longer? Had he left for France already, since this was to be his final performance in the Kingdom? No, no – after six pieces, the others left the stage, and Lavenu introduced not *Herr Liszt*, but *Monsieur Liszt*, pointing out that more than half of the great pianist's life had been spent in France. He was more French than German, and after that, more German than Hungarian. As I learnt later in the evening, he was even more Italian than he was Hungarian. Indeed, he had nearly obliterated his origins; I liked that about him.

Onto the stage strode a strikingly handsome man – as I also later discovered – of exactly Leyland's age, nigh-on thirty. From our seats in the front row, Leyland and I were nearly as close to him as if we had sat across from him at dinner. His thick hair was a chestnut colour, with streaks of a lighter brown here and there, and it was swept back from his large, noble brow and cut in a straight line just above his shoulders, so very different from the fashion in England. His prominent nose, lips and chin were perfectly balanced, and his cheekbones gave a hint of some remote Slavic parentage.

But it was the eyes above all that impressed. Dark expressive brows stood over a gaze so intensely mesmerising that it was easy to see why he had made a conquest of a duchess and was rumoured to have seduced all manner of women, of all stations. As I have said before, what man possessing such power of attraction would not use it? Only a saint, surely.

Two lads had, under his supervision, turned the pianoforte to the side, so that the audience could see man and instrument equally, could watch his hands move over the keyboard. Such a thing had never before been seen in Halifax, I am quite certain! Liszt sat and made his way slowly into his transcription of the overture from Rossini's *Guillaume Tell*, his hands and fingers moving faster and faster until they attained a seemingly impossible rapidity, so that what I beheld, even from my vantage point, seemed little more than a blur. Towards the middle of the piece, he again slowed before reaching the celebrated, climactic finish, and then stood and bowed as he was showered with a storm of applause, his penetrating gaze moving over the assembly like the beam of a lighthouse across the sea. Parry then sang a *buffo italiano*, after which the curtain fell for intermission. Liszt had played one piece, for only a few minutes, but the audience was in raptures as a din arose in the wake of the concert's first half.

'Let's step out for a smoke, Brontë, I can't abide the noise in here.'

'Let's exit from the other side, then,' said I, hoping to avoid further conversation with my friends, and especially Charlotte.

As we left the assembly room, Leyland handed me a cigar and reached into his pocket for a flask of whisky. 'Ha, not just a puff but a stiffener, too. That'll make that din more bearable.'

I was sure that Leyland's afternoon drinking had begun to wear off, and a headache had supplanted the agreeable numbness he had felt when we were inspecting his studio. I took a pull from his flask and then drew on the cigar as he lit it, coughing as I almost always do, for my lungs seem particularly sensitive to all manner of smoke and damp – something else I share with my sisters.

'There, there, little man, keep smoking and that cough will clear off nicely,' said Leyland. 'So, what do you make of our Herr – Monsieur – Liszt?'

'I'm struck dumb with admiration, Joe. I've never seen anything like it. He deserves all the fame heaped upon him, and more besides.'

'I concur. I'll wager that if his health holds out he is just getting started. Did you see the faces of the ladies in the audience? Methinks that devil could wade out into that sea of femininity and have his pick, that he could merely crook his finger and induce any one of them to follow him behind the curtain for a good *bang* on the pianoforte, ha ha! My only disappointment is how little he has played. I hope we'll hear more from him after the interval.'

I had not paid any attention to the playbill, but one was posted directly behind Leyland's head, by way of an advertisement for the concert. 'Look here, Joe, it says right here: Part II will include Liszt accompanying Miss Steele on the piano as she sings *The Wanderer*, and he will then play a solo of the finale of *Lucia di Lammermoor* and the *Galop chromatique*. So, I suppose we'll be treated to a bit more this time round.'

Leyland harrumphed and said, 'Well, we can always hope that he'll play for us at the studio, eh Brontë?' I scarcely heard this, for my eyes had wandered down the playbill and fastened on the following: 'MR J. PARRY will sing his celebrated song, "Wanted, a Governess"'. Ha! How curious, and how droll! I wondered if Charlotte had read the playbill – of course she had, for she reads everything, and in the minutest detail, I will give her that – and if she was eagerly anticipating this particular song. I found myself wishing I could sit next to her to observe her reactions. This solo was to be followed by a trio of Miss Steele, Miss Bassano and Mr Parry, 'Tis a Very Merry Thing', which would close the concert. One could hope for an *encore*, for surely Liszt's final concert in England should end with the great virtuoso himself!

XX.

Wanted, A Governess

Soon we were back in our seats, restlessly awaiting the second half of the concert. As it got underway, the strange coincidence of Charlotte's news of an appointment as governess with the appearance of *Wanted, a Governess* distracted me so that I scarcely heard and surely insufficiently appreciated the great Liszt himself, as he played his way through *Lucia di Lammermoor*. I did briefly think, however, how wondrous it was that our own childhood favourite, Walter Scott's *Bride of Lammermoor*, had formed the basis for Donizetti's opera, which in turn this brilliant Franco-Austro-Italo-Hungarian had effortlessly – or so it seemed – transformed into a piano piece. What a curious web was this nineteenth century, and how much more quickly would such translations and transmogrifications multiply with the advent of the railway!

Liszt's piece was scarcely longer than five minutes, and soon he had moved on to his own *Grand Galop Chromatique*, which was even shorter. But the virtuoso had packed a multitude of notes into that brief span, expressly crafting a vehicle for his own dexterity, his fingers again flying across the keys, gaining speed like a locomotive that has crested a summit and has both momentum and gravity on its side as it charges downhill. The audience erupted in applause as he finished with a flourish.

Now it was John Orlando Parry's turn to take the stage alone, with only Levenu at the pianoforte to accompany him, for the great Liszt had bowed, once again surveyed the public with that penetrating gaze of his, then disappeared. Parry looked to be about the same age as Liszt and Leyland. His features were round but in no wise heavy, his Welsh eyes glimmering, his mouth drawn back in a perpetual smile. Indeed, he almost laughed as he spoke, and his humour was infectious. 'Greetings to you, fair nobility and gentry of Yorkshire. I would like now to share part of an operetta that I wrote just this past year, and which – if I may humbly say so myself – has a little something for everyone gathered here today.'

I glanced furtively back at Charlotte, who was gazing at Parry with considerable concentration.

'I have an especial interest in newspapers and advertisements – for surely they are read more often and by a broader public than anything in the history of the world – and so I set myself the challenge of putting a "want", as they call it, to music. I must confess, in fairness, that my friend George Dubourg, Esq., is the author of most of these words, though I will take full ownership for the mischievous idea myself!'

Parry cleared his throat, nodded to Lavenu, and as the piano music began, sang in a lovely, laughing baritone the following words, as closely as I can recall them:

I know not a cure so good for the vapours,
As reading the 'wants' which appear in the papers;
There's 'wanted a husband' or 'wanted a sample',
Or 'wanted to borrow', but here's an example:

Here Parry theatrically drew a newspaper from his waistcoat pocket, and balanced a pair of spectacles on the end of his nose, all the while continuing to sing:

'Wanted a governess' – 'Wanted a governess'
  – 'A governess wanted' –
A governess wanted, well-fitted to fill
The post of tuition with competent skill,
In a gentleman's family highly genteel,
Where 'tis hoped that the lady will try to conceal

Any fanciful feelings or flights she may feel.
For this gentleman's family's so very genteel,
    they're so very genteel!

Again I turned to observe Charlotte, whose gaze had lost none of its intensity, but whose visage had gone as white as the Duddon Sands. She had so often spoken, with such gravity and even ire, of the need to crush one's feelings in the presence of one's employers, to be little more than a servant, nay, even an automaton, if one were to retain one's post. I certainly knew something of this myself, for my experience with the Postlethwaites had taught me the perils of too great an enthusiasm as well.

On sang Parry, still smiling and feigning to read:

Superior attainments are quite indispensable,
With everything, too, that's correct and ostensible;
Morals of pure unexceptionability;
Manners well-formed and of strictest gentility
The pupils are five – ages six to sixteen –
All as promising girls as ever were seen;
And besides (though 'tis scarcely worthwhile to put that in)
There are two little boys, but they only learn Latin.

I thought of my father's decision to keep me home and instruct me in Greek and Latin. No emphasis on modern languages for me – these were the province of the ladies, and besides, Papa would often say, 'if you know Greek and Latin, the modern languages are as easy to acquire on your own as A-B-C'.

I was hardly convinced of this now, and had realised that I was far more likely to employ the living languages of French or German in my current work, but how could Papa have known all those years ago that his son would lead the life of a railway clerk? Again, I glanced back at my friends, this time at the Reverend Brontë himself, who, unlike Charlotte, was by now smiling along with Parry and the rest of the assembly, oblivious to how the song might be affecting his children.

Wanted a governess, fitted to fill
The post of tuition with competent skill,
In a gentleman's family highly genteel.
Where, in order that things may go 'Toujours Tranquille',
They seldom express themselves quite as they feel.
For this gentleman's family's so very genteel,
they're so very genteel!

Must true gentility, then, forever be opposed to passionate feelings? Was the real secret of gentility then *hypocrisy*, a refusal to acknowledge man's most basic emotions and instincts? I cannot call them *animal* instincts, for the slow and delicate congress I experienced with Agnes – where we prolonged the moment of ecstasy for as long as possible, as if to spread it out over all of existence and to defy death itself – proved that Virgil was wrong, that love was not the same for all, that in fact *amor omnibus non idem*, did it not? What we had done together had no more in common with a dog in heat than that same dog's howl had with Parry's clever song, which continued thus:

The lady must teach all the several branches,
Where into polite education now launches;
She's expected to speak the French tongue like a native,
And be to her pupils of all its points dative;
Italian she must know, of course, nor needs banish
Whatever acquaintance she may have with Spanish;
Nor would there be harm in a trifle of German,
In the absence, that is, of the master, Herr Hermann.
'Wanted a governess', fitted to fill
The post of tuition with competent skill,
In a gentleman's family highly genteel,
Where the lady will find, by attention and zeal,
That she'll scarcely have time to partake of a meal,
For this gentleman's family's so very genteel,
they're so very genteel!

I thought of Charlotte's flaunting of her French and could not help but smile. Again I stole a backward glance, and again I witnessed a pale and stony gaze directed at Parry. Did Charlotte recognise that the real victim of his satire was the gentlefolk and *nouveaux riches* who employed such beings as her? On the other hand, did *they* get the joke? If so, no offence was taken, for nearly the entire assembly struggled not to laugh so loudly as to prevent themselves from hearing the singer's concluding verses:

The harp and the piano (*cela va sans dire*),
With thorough bass, too, on the plan of Logier.
In drawing in pencil and chalk, and the tinting
That's called Oriental, she must not be stint in.
She must paint upon paper, on satin and velvet,
And if she knows wax work she'll not need to shelve it.
Dancing, of course, with the newest Gambades,
The Polish Mazurka and best Gallopades;
Arithmetic, history, joined with chronology,
Heraldry, botany, writing, conchology,
Grammar and satin-stitch, netting, geography, astronomy,
Use of the globes and cosmography!

These are the principal matters (*en reste*).
Address, 'J. Z. X. Q. V., Easy Place, West'.
As the salary's very moderate, none need apply
Who more on that point than on comfort rely;
But, perhaps, 'twere as well, to make matters shorter,
To mention the terms-namely, five pounds a quarter.

At last Parry's satirical sword had fully penetrated Charlotte's armour, for when I once again turned in my chair I could see her face had turned crimson, and this time she caught my gaze, returning it with one that surely rivalled that of the Furies themselves. Parry's lyricist, in seeking the most humiliatingly paltry salary, had alighted precisely upon the Whites' offer to Charlotte of twenty pounds per annum; the only thing worse would have been a salary greater than hers. Papa was still too buoyed by the fun, it seemed, to make the connection, for he laughed uproariously: after all, he was himself, despite his years at Cambridge, not 'so very genteel'.

Parry concluded where he had begun, as he folded his newspaper and spectacles and slipped them into his coat pocket:

Wanted a governess, well fitted to fill
The post of tuition with competent skill,
Where 'tis wished that the pupils should never be still,
Nor the governess either, be she well or ill
'A governess wanted' – 'Wanted a governess'.

The assembly, now free to laugh without fear of missing a word, joined to its mirth a storm of applause. Parry laughed along with us, and took multiple bows, finally gesturing for quiet. 'And now, as a special treat, we offer you an *encore* – or perhaps more, that is entirely up to him – by the person you truly came to see and hear, Monsieur Liszt.'

Parry and Lavenu left the stage and were promptly replaced by Liszt, who, as soon as the assembly was fully silent, and without looking at a single sheet of music, launched into as many as five or six pieces, none of which I knew, save the last: a dazzling set of improvised variations of *God Save the Queen*. Was this the virtuoso's usual tactic, playing more in the *encore* than in the concert itself, a delay of his public's delight, like a dessert that eclipses the meal itself, or like the water Christ changed to wine at Cana, which far surpassed that which had been served before? Or had Liszt, more simply, just prolonged his encore in recognition that this was his final concert in Britain, hence the choice of *God Save the Queen*? Whatever the case, as he finished and stood to take a final bow, the applause was deafening, the enthusiasm unlike anything I have witnessed in all my life.

Leyland clapped me on the back, as is his wont, and exclaimed, '*Now* then, what do you think of *that*?' I turned once more to see the reactions of my friends, but they had already gone.

XXI.

The Mephisto Waltz

We did not wait for the applause to end either, but instead made our way quickly to Joe's studio at The Square, for he was eager to see for himself that all was ready for the virtuoso and his entourage. The vast room was ablaze with candelabra, their light in turn refracted and reflected by the fine table service and glassware, dancing along the walls, ceiling and floor. No guests, no music, no laughter and no drink – and yet already the décor was furnished for an evening of magic. A great pot of steaming mulled wine was kept hot over one of the two fireplaces, and a phalanx of bottles stood to attention, brave soldiers ready for deployment in the eternal war against *ennui*. Surveying all of this was Leyland's enormous *Head of Satan*, across from which stood the pianoforte, positioned so that the musician would stare directly into the eyes of the great hulking portrait of evil, which so resembled our host himself.

But another pair of eyes – great heavenly blue eyes, in which, the moment I saw them, I wanted to lose myself utterly – surveyed the scene with businesslike seriousness. For indeed, all the food and drink had been arranged through the White Swan, and so there stood Maggie – Margaret – dressed in the same attire that she had worn at Joe's soirée in autumn, but with all of her hair in ringlets, cascading onto her lovely shoulders, for the chignon she had worn – *Kilmeny*'s knot – had been undone. She was to serve, so it seemed, in the double capacity of proxy for her father and as an ornament for the evening: the first would require an effort, the second she could do wearing a simple smock – or nothing at all, I thought ruefully. My mind raced to an image of *Kilmeny*, and beyond it, to Joe's description of Maggie's very real, soft body as her dressing gown fell slowly around her shoulders, then her hips, her legs and finally her ankles.

She had not yet seen me, and yet I was already filled with desire, for all of this, fused with images of Agnes and the ghostly feeling of their respective hands, one after the other, pressed to my heart – 'You are a good man' – caused my heart to race and my throat to tighten. I could scarcely restrain my emotion as I walked over to where, her brows knitted in concentration, she stood with her armed crossed.

'Greetings, Maggie!' said I, trying to appear somewhat nonchalant – *so very genteel* – though I fear my own eyes betrayed my true feelings: utter delight and breathless excitement at seeing her again. Who has not felt his heart quicken and his spirit soar at the sight of his beloved? Even Charlotte has felt such things, I am sure of it, if only in the presence of Weightman – before disguising them with sarcasm, castrating the poor fellow as 'Miss Celia Amelia' – in short, concealing *any fanciful feelings or flights she may feel.* And even if she had felt the physical ecstasy that remains to her and my other sisters, I am quite certain, an utter mystery, what proper lady could ever give voice to it in this cold, forbidding, unfeeling, nineteenth century?

I wonder if they will ever know it. Even if they do someday marry, will they merely serve as passive recipients of some brutish oaf's fumbling passion, and afterwards a vessel for his progeny? Will they *ever* be partners in an ecstatic, angelic dance, whose ineffable joy defies all description? Also, was it just having it off, just *fucking*, as Coleridge and Brown and Leyland would have it? No, surely it was more than that – I had felt it to be more than that, and I was desperate to feel it again with the woman who stood before me. Like stones falling from a tipped waggon, or books tumbling down a staircase, so were the thoughts that cascaded through my mind in the instant during which I awaited her reply.

Maggie had been so absorbed in her work that she appeared not to recognise me. Finally, those marvellous eyes fixed upon me and she blushed slightly.

'Hello, Mr Brontë. 'Ow are you keeping? I'd like to thank ye'gain for the ride on't' railway.'

'That was some time ago, Maggie. I confess that I had a delightful day, and that I have tried to see you on more than one occasion, but you were forever from home when I called at the Swan.' No way to seduce a woman, thought I, but I could not help myself. I was at once overjoyed to see her and annoyed at how long it had been.

She coloured up again, laughing nervously, and said, 'It all comes back to t' railway, don't it? Ye see Mr Brontë, the planned branch line to Shaw Syke has created so *mooch* activity – proper rivalry, really – 'tween the inns o' Halifax tha' we scarcely fin' time to sleep. Mother and Father are no' getting' any younger, so more and more falls to me. They count on me no' only to maintain, but to increase, their income as they grow old.'

Before I could respond, the doors flew open and in strode Frobisher, followed by Lavenu, Parry and the other musicians, with Liszt arriving last of all, wearing, against the January cold, a small stylish Tyrolean hat and an elaborately decorated Polish fur coat and gloves of kid, which he hastened to remove as quickly as possible, revealing a slender but vigorous physique.

Frobisher was overcome with excitement, clearly, and was about to make a grand announcement, but before he could open his mouth the guests who had already begun to assemble spontaneously erupted in applause and acclamations. Liszt doffed his hat and announced in simple English, with an accent that betrayed his multiple origins, though surely it was more French than German, 'Ah, thank you, dear friends. This is a lovely way to finish our concerts in England.'

Frobisher then led him to Leyland, to whom Liszt bowed and gave thanks for the soirée, as he looked about the cavernous studio. Standing next to Maggie, I wondered what he made of this homely, if festive tribute to his genius, he who had from childhood played for royalty, had been surrounded by the Continent's greatest artists and poets, and had even succeeded in seducing a countess, convincing her to leave her husband and children, so magnetic were his charms. How deliciously *French* it was to place passion and genius above morals – and yes, even above money!

Leyland had done his utmost to honour the great musician, of course, but this remained a sculptor's studio, and the two fires burning in their grates on either side could not entirely chase the chill from the room, which was nearly as high and as wide, if not quite as long, as Haworth Church.

Having paid tribute to his host, the virtuoso began to sweep the room with that mesmerising gaze. Leyland supplied him with a steaming mug of mulled wine and a cigar, lighting it with a flourish. Liszt lifted his wine quizzically, but soon pronounced with satisfaction, 'Ah oui, *vin chaud, Glühwein*!' Meanwhile, the last stragglers from the concert had arrived, filling the room with voices, which, as the company partook of food and drink, rose in volume so one could scarcely hear one's closest interlocutor.

In the meantime, none other than John Brown himself, whom I had not seen since Christmas, sidled up to us, placing first his hand, then a mug of the mulled wine in my outstretched hand; as he did so, Maggie moved away to examine the state of the refreshments. 'Well now, Branwell, wha' an affair our friend Leyland 'as put on for t' grea' virtuoso, eh? I wonder 'ow 'e pays for i' all.'

Like Papa, his sexton felt no compunction about discussing money. I thought again of the sale of *Kilmeny* and pictured her bumping along, lashed to a waggon, and of Joe's decision – so typical – to spend most of the proceeds on this soirée rather than to pay his debts. But I simply said, 'I haven't the slightest idea, John'.

'Oh yes, right, I'd forgot tha' the Brontë children are averse to any discussion o' filthy lucre – except when y' need a loan from ol' Brown, eh lad?', he added, winking and nudging me good-naturedly with his elbow.

I deserved this riposte, for John has indeed paid my debts in the past, and I have never had any scruples on the topic when I am most desperately in need of cash. As much as I wanted to counter-attack on a different front – for example, asking how it was that his Mary had let him out of the house – my better self prevailed for once, and I could only laugh and raise my mug, still smoking, and say, 'You have me there, my friend, you have me there.'

He nodded his head towards Maggie. 'By the bye, who is *tha*' loovely creature?'

'That is the very person I spoke of at Christmas, she of the fabled railway excursion to Manchester and back,' said I.

'Sod it all, lad, y' didn't do 'er justice. Damn me body and soul, she's a beauty, and strangely familiar. 'appen I've seen her somewhere before.'

'She's been to Leyland's *fêtes* before, so surely it was there.'

'No, no, by God, I'd remember tha' golden hair and them blazin' blue eyes and pert li'l mouth, those lovely sloping shoulders and those perfectly formed little –'

'All right, all right, Brown,' said I.

'Ho ho, man! You really 'ave fallen for the poor thing, 'aven't you?' Then, frowning, 'But 'ow odd, I know that I've seen her, and yet *no*' seen her. How can tha' be?'

Of course: *Kilmeny*. Had we been further into the evening – and our cups – I might have said, 'Don't you remember *Kilmeny, the Sinless Maiden*? The sculpture that languished for years in Joe's studio because the patrons who had ordered it were disgusted by it. Maggie was the model, and that lucky bastard Leyland got to fix his wolfish gaze on her perfect form day after day. He even tried to seduce her, but she resisted him, sweet, virtuous girl!'

Instead, my affection and impulse to protect her triumphed over my desire to share a secret with old John Brown, and I simply said, 'I can't say, old squire. Have you never had the sensation that you have already seen something, though it is clearly unlikely or even impossible? Perhaps it is just that simple.'

Meanwhile, Liszt had wasted no time in noticing Maggie, and I saw Leyland lead him across the room to make the introductions. He may have seduced a countess, but Liszt was also rumoured to have done the same with pupils, actresses, opera singers – even housemaids and kitchen-girls – so insatiable was his appetite. It was thus safe to wager that an innkeeper's daughter or two had been among his conquests. I fairly trembled as he approached her and since I had not yet met him, I steeled myself to do so, for in my natural timidity I dislike meeting anyone new for the first time, much less this modern musical wonder. I left Brown behind me and found myself awkwardly drawing up to Maggie's side just as Leyland and Liszt arrived before her.

'This lovely young creature,' said Joe, 'is Margaret Heaton, known hereabouts as Maggie.' He clearly could not bring himself to call the innkeeper's daughter a young lady, although her valiant defeat of his own advances five years earlier surely made her one in my mind. The virtuoso simply said, 'Franz Liszt, but people call me Ferenc or François or Francesco or Francisco or Francis; that depends on where I am.' He reached for her hand, lifting it to his lips as his mesmerising gaze met her own wide, startled orbs. In just an instant or two, he seemed to have drunk in her eyes and her lips – his gaze lingered on her mouth as if imagining what it could do – and moved slowly, caressingly, down her person.

'And this young rascal,' said Leyland, 'gesturing to me, is the Bard of Haworth, Patrick Branwell Brontë, Esquire, England's greatest poetic hope since Wordsworth.'

Liszt turned his head towards me, but his eyes lingered for another moment on Maggie's. When at last he met my regard, gone was the intense gaze he seemed to reserve for the softer sex, replaced by a quizzical squint, as he said, '*Bard*? What is *bard*?'

This was the same question Maggie herself had asked, but for very different reasons.

'Poet,' smiled Joe, delighted to be able to impart something to such a genius. '*The* Bard or the *Bard of Avon* is Shakespeare, and so sometimes we call other poets by the same name.'

'But in this case,' Liszt said, pointing at me, and smiling as the joke dawned on him, 'you are mocking poor Monsieur Brontë, no?'

Joe, whose French is superior to mine, felt emboldened to say, '*Oui, un petit peu*'.

'I adore the poets,' said Liszt, 'above all the Romantics – Goethe and Schiller, Heine and Hugo and Musset and Dumas, and George Sand, though that particular "he" is a *she*, a lovely woman' – here he paused briefly, gazing into the distance – 'yes a lovely woman in her way – hardly a ravishing beauty, but full of passion, brimming with desire, the Baronne Dudevant, with eyes so impossibly large a man could nearly swim – and drown – in them: she devours men with those eyes the way men usually do women with *theirs*. Would you like to meet them?'

Liszt said this as if his illustrious friends were queuing up just outside Leyland's studio, or, like Gulliver's Lilliputians, were magically hidden within his Polish fur coat. Such are the subtle perils of speaking a language other than one's own! I did not know what to say, and quickly sensing my confusion, he added, 'What I want to say is that if ever you come in France or in Germany, I will present to you with pleasure my friends, but also the painters and composers. Do you like painting?'

Leyland interposed, 'Now *that*, Monsieur Liszt, is a sore subject.' Liszt squinted again. 'I mean, a painful subject,' he revised, and the pianist immediately brightened with understanding. 'You see, young Brontë here tried to make his independence as a painter, and that did not work out so well.'

'Ah, *l'argent*, the money! What madness and degradation because of the money! We begin our lives in the search of the beauty, of the perfection, of the ideal, and we find ourselves fighting through the freezing mud and snow of Ireland and Scotland' – I suppose he was careful not to say *England* or *Yorkshire*, so as not to offend his hosts – 'to earn some money.'

Leyland and I, not knowing what to say, were silent.

'*Ah, oui*, I know precisely what you are thinking – the great Liszt, renowned throughout Europe, living with a countess, what care could he have? Well, my friends, the Countess in question *abandoned* the Count, so I suppose you know what that means. This is the reason for which I give lessons and concerts, for gone are the days of the troubadours of Eleanor of Aquitaine or the court musicians of Louis XIV; all of that was swept away once and for all by the Revolution. Guillotined, if you like. *Non non, maintenant nous sommes tous des marchandises, n'est-ce pas*? We are all cultural *marchandises* – to be advertised and sold – as in clever Mr Parry's "wants", eh? – and no matter how great one's genius, genius alone will not pay one's debts. Those days are gone, *tout cela, c'est fini, das ist ganz kaputt*!'

During this soliloquy Parry and Lavenu had drawn up to our group, the former smiling just as he had on stage – perhaps this had become a permanent feature of his physiognomy – and the latter looking ashen, as if to confirm Liszt's grim view of the 'business' of the arts. Before the troop had even arrived in Halifax, it had been rumoured that the entire tour of the kingdom had been a financial disaster – Liszt had forfeited his fees, and Lavenu had lost a small fortune. These 'rumours' had come directly to Joe from the excitable Frobisher, who doubtless embroidered – as is his wont – on something he had heard from Lavenu or Parry.

Despite the rising tide of voices in the studio, Frobisher had decided that music, too, was needed. He began playing a harmless tune on the piano, at which Liszt's brows furrowed briefly as his raven eyes darted towards the centre of the room, where we could see Frobisher's back and, above his head, the towering *Head of Satan*, which the pianist seemed to see for the first time. He muttered something in French, then turned to his host, pointing one of his impossibility long fingers towards the sculpture, asking, 'What is *that*?'

Leyland had now had sufficient to drink that he found nearly everything amusing, and so simply began laughing. I touched the great man's sleeve meekly and said, 'That, Monsieur Liszt, is your host's most famous sculpture, his monumental *Head of Satan*.' The pianist swept his hands along either side of his chiselled countenance, pulling back his locks as if to reinforce the *coiffure* he had cultivated, moving rapidly from his proud forehead in a semi-circular motion, ending at his shoulders.

'Ah, has the rumour of my diabolical behaviour travelled until the very city of Halifax itself?' This short sentence seemed to begin with great gravity, but by its grammatically awkward end, it was clear that Liszt was attempting to make a joke.

Leyland laughed all the harder.

'I am afraid my association with Monsieur Berlioz and others – and *oui, d'accord*, some of my own questionable conduct – has led some to call me something of a devil myself.'

'No, no, it's a mere decoration, I assured him. 'My friend Joseph here was used to adorn his soirées with a beautiful reclining nude, but she was sold at last.' As I spoke, Maggie moved into my vision, as she walked from one table to the next, overseeing the food and drink and sending her lads for more as needed.

'T'is a pity,' said Liszt, 'for I would far rather gaze upon the form of a beautiful woman than the face of the Great Deceiver.' Here his gazed followed mine, until it lit again upon Maggie. Only her neck and cheek could be glimpsed beneath her swaying golden ringlets, while the hourglass shape of her shoulders, waist and hips moved gracefully from one table to the next.

'Let us take a closer look, though,' said I, with dread in my heart, and as we passed Frobisher and stopped before Joe's sculpture, I added, 'Do you not see a resemblance to someone?'

'In effect!' cried Liszt, turning to Joe, who had come up behind us, 'T'is the artist himself!'

'You see, Monsieur, it is not by chance that I have come to call Joseph here – with all the respect that is due him, of course' – and here I bowed obsequiously – 'that I have come to call him Mephistopheles.'

Joe, who had finally recovered his composure sufficiently to speak, although he sniggered still, added, 'And of course this' – he thumped me on the back so that my hot mulled wine nearly spilt – 'is young Faustus himself. Do we not make quite a pair?'

As the conversation and laughter grew, Frobisher felt it necessary to increase the volume of his own playing, until the assembled company, in turn, fairly shouted to be heard, though their heads were drawn as closely together as in a *tête-à-tête*. Soon it had become unbearable, and whilst Liszt covered his ears, Leyland strode over to the pianoforte and thumped it as loudly as he could, shouting, 'See here! See here! Quiet please! There, that's much better. This may be a congregation of artists but let us behave as ladies and gentlemen!' This last remark was said with the generous laughter that always made even the most insulting of Joe's remarks seem innocuous. 'Now that all are gathered, I wish to thank you for your attendance here tonight, and most of all to thank our assembled musicians, especially the world's greatest virtuoso, Monsieur Franz Liszt!'

Here the pianist bowed politely and was showered with applause, which Leyland promptly quieted. 'I also want to thank our own illustrious John Frobisher, without whom we would never have seen Herr Liszt – as the maestro travelled to so many other cities in the Kingdom, John felt more envy and longing than an old maid who sees her sisters married off one by one, ha ha! The only greater gift Frobisher can give us now is to desist from playing the piano.'

Joe had calculated that such an unexpected stab at his friend would elicit a mixture of laughter and cries of feigned censure from the assembly, and he again gestured for quiet and placed his hand on Frobisher's shoulder. What he next said made it clear that had just reached that moment of inebriation where all reserve and timidity had been dashed to earth, but where he retained sufficient presence of mind to know exactly what he desired, and to express it as boldly as possible.

'Now, now, good friends, I say this only because I am going to ask Herr – Monsieur – Liszt to play one more *encore*. We have not discussed this, and I am putting him into an impossible situation – terribly rude of me, I know, but then all of you know me, and so will find nothing strange in that.'

Liszt, too, had now had enough to drink to be fully at his ease, and not only was his hesitancy in English now gone; so, too, were any reservations that he might have had about resorting to the languages he spoke most often: French, German and Italian – whether anyone understood him or not. He bowed and stepped over to the piano, shaking Frobisher's hand while the latter stood and moved to the edge of the crowd that had gathered round the pianoforte.

'Thank you, Mr Leyland,' said he, pronouncing Joe's name as if it were French for *the Moors – les Landes* – 'it is a pleasure to end our tour of your beautiful kingdom with such a soirée, for what is more joyous than ladies and gentlemen thrown together, with good food and drink and conversation and yes, music. Since Mr Leyland has surprised me in this way, though it is a far more agreeable experience than that of a lover surprised by a jealous husband' – here this already joyous assembly obligingly laughed – 'I will play on only *one* condition.' He paused for dramatic effect, as if listening to the ticking of a metronome: one-two-three-four. 'Do you know what it is?'

Again, a pause. He turned round and aimed his long forefinger towards the *Head of Satan*: 'Behold the massive head of the Dark One!' He then glanced, with exaggerated theatricality, from the sculpture to its sculptor and back, a number of times, until the assembly laughed and clapped. 'I have come to learn that not only does that evil face resemble its maker's' – here the pianist was having more than his just revenge on Joe – 'but that this very man has come to be called *Mephistopheles*!'

I laughed along with everyone else, unaware that I was about to drawn into Liszt's comedy. 'And this young poet – what is it again, this bard? – is Mr Leyland's Faustus … how amusing, no? *Qu'est-ce que c'est drôle, ça!* Please, Monsieur Brontë, come forward, though you may also regret your friendship with Mephistopheles in the end,' said he, with a conspiratorial wink.

I, too, had at last imbibed just enough to set aside my natural reticence, and so walked gamely towards the piano. The virtuoso put his right hand to his chin in mock reflection. 'Hmmmm, what – or who – is lacking now?' Gazing across the room, and again extending his arm and index finger with the rapidity of an arrow, he pointed directly at Maggie: '*C'est elle!* The story cannot be complete without *her*. You see, I will only play with their participation.'

Maggie was overcome by embarrassment, but doubtless fearing to be the only person to oppose Liszt's will, and urged on by the assembly, whose laughter only heightened her confusion, she slowly made her way to the centre of the vast room. Blushing, she stood awkwardly, not knowing what to do with her hands, shifting from one foot to the other and back.

'*Voilà*, there she is. I confess,' said he, again smoothing his thick hair and looking about the room, 'that I tend to forget most names, but – *chose étrange* – when a name is united to a beautiful face, I mysteriously am able to recall it.' The men in the room sniggered at Liszt's mention of this 'strange' phenomenon, as common to ploughboys as it is to kings.

'In this case, what a perfect name for our little game, for this lovely creature is called Margaret – *Marguerite, Margot, Maggie, Margarita, Margherita, Greta, Gretchen* – yes, yes, Gretchen, too!' I did not think it possible, but Maggie coloured an even deeper shade of crimson, and if I did not blush as she did, I began to feel a creeping humiliation for us both. I found myself wanting to walk to the table along the wall, uncork a bottle of whisky, and take two or three long draughts. But Liszt talked rapidly on – for this had utterly ceased to be Joe's event – improvising as he went. On one side of the room Lavenu and Parry were deep in conversation, whilst a smiling John Brown stood to the other side with Joe's brother Francis.

'Now you all know the story of Faustus, yes? Did not even your Shakespeare – your *bard* – write about him?'

No one, including Leyland and I, dared interrupt Liszt to correct him on his misattribution; at least he had hit upon the right century.

'So, it is quite safe to say my German friends are entirely *obsédés* by this story, and of course you know about the great Goethe, but my countryman Lenau, too, wrote such a poem just a few years since. Let me tell you the story; it is the price you have to pay, because your host has been so naughty.'

More laughter here, at Joe's expense.

'Mephistopheles and Faust are passing through a village when they hear the joyful sounds – not unlike those we have been enjoying this evening – of a wedding feast coming from an inn.' Here Maggie frowned so slightly that I – or at least so I fancied – was the only person to notice. 'There is music, dancing and carousing. Yes, my proper English ladies and gentlemen,' he said, raising his steely brows with his own mock-opprobrium, 'I said *carousing*. Mephistopheles convinces Faust that they should enter and join the festivities, and the tempter soon takes the instrument from a lethargic fiddler's hands – sorry, Mr Frobisher,' said Liszt with another wink, 'and draws from the instrument the most seductive and intoxicating strains ever heard.' Here he paused to look round the room and said innocently, 'Does this sound like anyone you know?'

Still more laughter from the assembly.

Standing now before Maggie and me, he joined our hands together in a farce of holy matrimony. '*Alors*, young Faustus joins in the wedding dance, and Mephistopheles' music drives him mad with desire for the young village beauty he holds in his arms. Together they waltz in utter abandon, out of the inn and into the woods. What they do in the woods I leave up to your imagination.'

Maggie dropped my hand as soon as she was able, for she surely experienced the confusion anyone feels when made a figure of fun before a multitude. I felt the same.

Liszt would not be countermanded, however. '*Nein nein nein, das dürft ihr nicht*, you must play along to the end, *mes enfants*,' he said somewhat more softly, joining our hands once more. He grew very serious for a moment, his magnetic being now enfolding the entire gathering like a warm blanket, his eyes two glowing embers, touching one person after another as he gazed round the studio.

'How oft do we consider that the true essence of life, what holds the world together – *was die Welt im Innersten zusammenhält* – is present in each single moment, but that each moment is then gone, each tick of the metronome replaced by another. Existence is so full that we cannot bear it, we are quite overcome! Do not believe those who say we seek distraction from the emptiness and misery of life, for they lie; no, no, we cannot bear its overwhelming plenitude, its unbearable *beauty*, for it is like looking directly into the sun, or upon the face of God. We can neither grasp it in its entirely, nor stop it from disappearing, we can only sense its ephemeral fullness as it passes. Perhaps such is the meaning of Goethe's words, when he has *his* Faust say, '*verweile doch! du bist so schön!* – stay but a while, you are so beautiful!' A hushed, almost reverential silence had supplanted the assembly's mirth; the room was silent, expectant, rapt, in awe – the moment seemed to contain the very fullness he described.

At the pianist's last words my mind returned to the exaltation I had felt as a boy when, in the throes of creation, I would lose myself utterly in my writing; or the feeling of the wind whipping over me on my first railway journey; or, especially, the moments at Broughton with Agnes, when our bodies formed one, and when, in a brief instant, we found an ecstasy that eclipsed the very sun and blotted out the universe – when our souls escaped time and place and perhaps even our bodies, and when for an instant we gazed into the face of a god synonymous with ecstasy.

I looked over at Maggie, who seemed mystified by Liszt's flight into these more esoteric realms, and most of all impatient for this all to end. I squeezed her hand, but she glowered at me and even dug her fingernails into my palm.

When the silence became almost unbearable in its duration and gravity, Liszt at last brightened and said playfully, 'Let us return to Lenau's story, though, shall we? – for the great Goethe is far too serious for such a gathering as this. I pray you to excuse me to have spoken for so long.'

Turning again to Maggie and me, he put her left hand in my right palm, still smarting from her nails, and her right hand on my left shoulder, and finally, my left hand on her waist, and it became clear what the mischievous Liszt had in mind. He whispered to Maggie, on whose face was clearly written her dismay, '*Ne t'inquiète pas, ma belle, toi et ton ami, vous ne serez pas tout seuls*, you two will not be alone,' then strode around the circle with an elastic step, forming random couples wherever he could find a man and woman in close proximity to each other, fairly dragging them into the open area between the pianoforte and the *Head of Satan*. Some managed to elude his grasp and flee, laughing, to the extremities of the studio, and so Liszt was content once he had formed eight or nine couples, whom he demanded to assume the same position as us.

'Remember now,' he said, seating himself at the pianoforte, 'we are all at a village wedding feast, and the musician is none other than Mephistopheles himself.' Turning to Joe, who now stood next to Frobisher, Brown and his own brother Francis, he added, 'I am so sorry, *je suis désolé*, now I have supplanted *you* too, Monsieur Leyland, you may take a holiday from your satanic duties this evening!' Both Liszt – who under far more serious circumstances had displaced other men, such as husbands and lovers – and Leyland were having a grand time. I turned to face Maggie, who had becalmed herself somewhat as we were surrounded by other couples, though she was still clearly displeased.

'I know not 'ow t' waltz,' said she. In her wide eyes were mingled more emotions than I thought possible, but I could clearly see through the windows of her soul those of annoyance, resentment, embarrassment, confusion and fear. Did I also glimpse a drop of desire in the blue ocean of her eyes, or was this merely a shadow of my own?

'Besides,' she whispered angrily, 'why would Mr Liszt ask an innkeeper's daughter to dance wi' a gentleman?' She seemed to think the virtuoso had done this only to mock her, but I had a different theory – or theories.

'First, he doesn't know anything about you, does he? Second, you are the village beauty as far as I am concerned – and he clearly saw that too. For heaven's sake, Maggie, one would have to be blind not to see that you are the most beautiful woman here. Third, you have the same name as the character in the story! As for waltzing, I don't know how to do it either. It mostly seems that one spins like a top. The primary thing is to keep moving until the music stops. If we do not tumble down by the end of its course, I suppose we will have succeeded.'

As for Liszt, any Germanic *froideur* or French *hauteur* he might have possessed had melted away in the ambiance of the moment and with the warming qualities of the mulled wine, another tankard of which Leyland had posed on the pianoforte itself.

'*Allora, ragazzi, ascoltami per favore*,' he began, 'now my children, listen to me please: I have been known to fantasise on this instrument, to invent as I go. The French call this *l'improvisation*. I may or may not write the piece down some day – and perhaps only years from now – and it will be quite a different thing when that happens, I am certain. In a sense the real music will die, and when it is again performed by me or anyone else it will be but a pale copy of the original, just as an actor plays a role invented by the genius of another man, and then goes home to drink his wine, eat his roast beef, embrace his wife and fall asleep.

'*Mais l'improvision, mon Dieu*! It is a thrilling and terrifying thing, as if one were leaping off a great cliff without knowing where one will fall, and with only one's coat tails to float down upon! The mind reels and races, the skin tingles' – here he looked at Maggie – 'and one at last, if but for a moment, escapes the *ennui* of existence, one is alive, one is in the truth, *dans le vrai*. How bizarre, that a thing which happens only once has the most eternal of qualities! Is this the secret? Maybe even Goethe's secret, eh? In the end, it is as different from playing each note from memory, or even worse, from a written score, as embracing a new lover is from going to bed with one's spouse of many years, ha ha!'

I smiled to myself at the thought of Charlotte or Papa hearing such *shocking* language.

'But I digress,' continued he, 'for what I want simply to say is that I cannot at all predict where this will go.' Nodding at Leyland, he pronounced with mock-solemnity, 'Let us call this, in honour of our august and most generous host Mr Leyland, *The Mephisto Waltz*.' He blew on his mulled wine, sipped it to find out how hot it was, took a generous swallow, and at last turned to the keys to begin his improvisation, shouting '*Allora, allegro vivace*!'

Still holding my beautiful prize, I thought, *if this is half as genial as his fantasising on 'God Save the Queen', we should prepare for a rare treat.*

He began with a truly Satanic pounding on the keyboard, the same note repeatedly, wringing from the instrument a sound more like the valves of a steam engine, *bam-bam-bam-bam-bam-bam-bam*, on top of which he layered a second note, *bam-bam-bam-bam-bam-bam-bam*, then a third, then a fourth, all pounding along together – at a speed that made it impossible to dance even the most rapid steps imaginable.

The couples did their best for the honoured guest, but we were more successful at colliding into one another than anything else. I was delighted to see that our collective confusion had at last drawn a smile, and then laughter, from Maggie, the dancers' shared experience washing away, at least for the moment, her annoyance and her wrath: indeed, protected by the anonymity of the other dancers, she became giddy and girl-like, her eyes laughing in high glee, her body finally yielding to my touch as we did our best to spin to Liszt's diabolical strains. Was there also a yearning, an unquenched desire in her gaze? I ardently wished it to be so!

Soon the virtuoso had changed tempo, and quickly altered it again, the thumping gradually giving way to what seemed, to my untutored ear, one shower of notes after another, like bands of rain passing through a village. The piece was as mercurial as Liszt himself, as changeable as the great deceiver Mephistopheles. Dancing was impossible, and yet still the couples fought on valiantly. At last, after two minutes or so, the tempo sped up again, slowed briefly, then raced forward, and we were again dancing furiously in circles. Another minute and the pianist had, like a rushing locomotive coming finally to a halt, slowed his hands so much that only two fingers of his left moved back and forth more and more slowly, more and more softly, the final note barely audible. The dancers stood motionless, awkwardly in each other's arms; I felt more foolish than when we had begun our dance, and Maggie's consternation began to return, her face to redden once again. The music had, in essence, stopped, and Liszt whirled round on his stool. He was smiling broadly, mischievously, those bright, twin beacons flashing round the assembly.

'*Ah là là là là là là, je vous ai joué un tour*, I am afraid I have played a bit of a trick upon you! There are waltzes for dancing – smooth, clockwork things that allow you not to think at all, and no matter how much wine you drink you may whirl with your partners in elegant circles with nary a misstep. My naughty trick is this, as you have without a doubt now comprehended: my waltzes are not meant for dancing at all, my friends, they are meant for *me* to play and for *you* to listen and, especially, watch and admire, because *le piano, c'est moi!* That Liszt truly had such a grand view of himself permitted no doubt, but his self-love was tempered by an amusing dosage of self-knowledge, just sufficient to raise him even further in our esteem and, no doubt, to make him even more fascinating to the ladies, if such a thing were possible.

Here he snatched up and raised his cup, laughing, 'Let us toast our brave – or foolish, for the difference between courage and folly is always so hard to tell, *nicht wahr*? – dancers, for never in the history of music was a such a waltz invented with the express purpose of *bedeviling* those who wish to waltz – ha ha! Now it is time for them to have a drink – *richement méritée, à mon avis* – and for me to play.' Liszt drained his cup whilst we dancers, with laughter and cries of relief, faded into the crowd that encircled his piano, most of us moving quickly to obey his orders by charging our glasses afresh. To my surprise, even Maggie partook, filling a mug with mulled wine and blowing to cool it as quickly as possible.

XXII.

Verweile doch! du bist so schön!

Before I could speak, Liszt had begun again, playing in a completely different vein, a slow and languorous melody that spoke unmistakably of love. It was as if this virtuoso – more magician than musician – were taking the essence of what it is to love and wringing from it one beautiful note after another, so vividly did the next two minutes or so suggest the gaze of two lovers, of their caresses, even the slow movement of fabric over bare skin as their bodies grew closer and closer to each other, finally becoming one.

Perhaps wishing to ensure that his humble Yorkshire audience fully grasped what he was doing, he shouted, '*Allora, espressivo amoroso*!' I looked about the vast room and all was silence, the men – nearly all of an artistic temperament – lost in admiration, the women sighing with desire. And yet every two or three moments, just as the lovers seemed about to consummate their love, the devil Liszt would change direction, shouting '*Presto!*', but just as quickly returning to his languorous melody. It was as if the lovers were each time about to consummate fully their passion, and each time were chased from their lovers' retreat – by a rainstorm, by a mischievous, prying child, or by Satan's emissary Mephistopheles himself, for what is more infernal than a desire that is almost, but never, sated?

Maggie herself – all business before, and largely resentful during, our 'waltz' – was not impervious to the music and stood drinking it in as deeply as her wine. The dancing, the fire, the crowd of people, and now her steaming tankard had caused her cheeks to flush and her brow to glisten with the slightest perspiration. The strong, red mulled wine had given a sheen to her ruby lips and caused her eyes to shine with the brilliance of sapphires. I leant over her shoulder and said, 'I know you are entranced by Monsieur Liszt, but shall we take some air together? It is oppressively warm here, is it not?'

She turned to me, and her eyes continued to flash contradictory messages, as though a battle raged within her. She glanced around the room to make sure all was well with food and drink – or, perhaps, to make certain that no one observed us – and said, 'Yes, let's step outside, but only for a moment'. The January air cut into us as we left the warmth of the gathering, slicing our faces like a freezing blade; my delicate lungs felt as if they were filled with the icy waters of Sladen Beck in early springtime.

'By Heaven, it is freezing!' said I. 'Let's see if we can find some shelter from this confounded wind.' I took her by the arm and led her around the back of building, where a small, unlocked shed stood. It held discarded pieces of marble and clay, some scraps of wood, a few rusted implements, and an abandoned chair. Over the chair hung an old dressing gown, which Maggie immediately recognised.

'*Why*, this is the gown Mr Leyland bought for me to use when I – I'm sure you know – posed for his statue. How long ago that seems!'

The garment had indeed seen better days, for it was stained with dirt and clay, and seemed to have more recently served its owner as a rag or mop. It was hard to believe that it was the same gown that had covered the young girl, and that Joe had untied and watched fall slowly to the floor. Whether Maggie reddened from the memory or from the frigid temperature, I know not. Alone with her at last, and several mugs of mulled wine into the evening, I cast all caution into the wintry blast.

'I want to kiss you, Maggie. Nay, I am desperate to kiss you and to hold you, and have been since first we met. If you feel even a fraction of what I do for you, surely you will not refuse!'

She bit her lip adorably, but her eyes, filling with tears,

refused to meet mine.

'What is it?' I continued. 'Why do you say nothing, either *yes* or *no* … for Heaven's sake, why do you refuse to kiss me, and yet you do not run from me? What are you playing at?'

With Maggie I had forever felt as if I were trapped in Liszt's melody, swept forward by overwhelming waves of desire, but each time thrown back onto the bitter rocks of reality.

She would not meet my gaze, and as the tears spilt down her cheeks she began to tremble with the cold. I shook the dust off the old dressing gown and enfolded her in my own waistcoat, so that I was dressed in only a shirt; still, I did not tremble, my distracted ardour eclipsing all other concerns. 'There, there, Maggie, let me warm you,' said I, pulling her finally close to me, 'that's better, my love.'

At the words 'my love' she pushed away from me, though gently, and her tears were now joined with great wrenching sobs. 'What is it, what is it?' I said, 'Surely you can tell me what's the matter?' I sat down on the old chair and pulled her onto my lap, whilst she pressed her head against my chest so that she would not have to look at me, for doing so seemed to grieve her. This arrangement appeared to suit her, for at last she collapsed against my breast, like a little child who, after initial resistance, seeks only to be comforted.

'I'm a good girl, I am,' she began, 'and –'

'I *know* you are a good girl, and so you have proved yourself to be, again and again – no doubt remains on that score. I will not force myself upon you, Maggie.'

She laughed ruefully, but then smiled, not unkindly. 'Tha's not what I meant at all. I already know *tha*' about you.'

'What is it, then?'

She took a deep breath. ''ere I am, goin' on two an' twenty, near a spinster by all accounts, wedded, it would seem, only to the White Swan. But do y' think that jes' because I've chosen no' to give myself to a man, that I am soulless and heartless?' Still she averted my gaze, though her head pressed all the more fiercely against me.

'How is it,' she continued, at last drying her eyes and turning them to me, 'tha' I can 'ardly know you, and yet feel wha' I feel?'

'What do you feel?'

'I would rather not say, because –'

'Because?'

I felt positively driven mad, goaded by those twin demons, desire and despair. What could she possibly mean? What man with a beating heart and pulsing veins has not yielded to the temptation of drawing a woman's uplifted face to his lips? Maggie's was made all the more beautiful by the heroic struggle that seemed be taking place within her, by her flushed cheeks, by the gleaming veneer her tears had given to those enchanting cerulean eyes.

I could stand it no longer, and repeating the word 'because', I drew her head towards me and pressed my lips to hers, and she at last, at last, at last, yielded, the struggle – at least for the briefest moment – over. Soon we were embracing as hungrily as ever I had with Agnes, our ardour nearly causing us to forget the icy gale rattling the walls of our squalid retreat, the heat of intoxicating lust spreading outwards from our lips to our extremities, engulfing our entire bodies as if in a protective flame. I began to wonder – in the kind of thoroughly unreasonable, impassioned state of mind that one finds oneself in, when lust drives away all else, so that an amorous madness reigns triumphant over body, mind and soul – I began to wonder if at last I might possess Maggie *fully*, began to wonder if I might lead the sinless Kilmeny to commit the delicious, exalting sin of fornication – and is it, really, a sin at all?

'Because?' I asked again, teasingly, this time kissing Maggie's mouth deeply, as Agnes had taught me, my hands seeking, without much success, to make their way beneath her garments. She pulled away.

'It's too cold here, and we 'ave t' talk.'

She stood up and threw off my waistcoat and Leyland's gown, and I followed her out of the shed and into the night. The wind had shifted to a more temperate southerly breeze, and a light snow had begun to fall; the first of the season. Maggie ran towards the Square Chapel, shouting behind her, 'I think my church is left open, follow me.'

Knowing that the Reverend Brontë and John Brown kept Haworth Church firmly locked against the less friendly elements of Haworth society, I was sceptical, but she did, indeed, find an open door and soon we were far warmer than before, the massive, unusual red-brick walls sheltering us fully from the elements. It is said that the great John Wesley had visited the chapel, but all I could think of was finding a flat, dry place in this house of God to stretch out and love his creature, my Maggie. After weeks – nay, months – of imagining what it would feel like, aided by memories of Agnes, my every vein pulsed with yearning, my every inch strained to be one with hers, blotting out all other considerations. I did not wish to profane the house of the Lord – although I was not certain that this Dissenters' chapel merited such a holy appellation – but I would gladly incur His wrath for a moment of ecstasy in Maggie's arms. I reached to pull her close, but her earlier consternation had returned and she held me at arm's length. I was wild by this point, any higher faculties having utterly deserted me, like Faust bewitched by Mephistopheles' fiddle, although in my case the lovely innkeeper's daughter needed no such supernatural intervention.

'Sit,' she commanded, though gently, pointing to a pew in the back of the chapel, taking a seat a safe distance from me. My madness had not yet subsided, for I immediately slid down the bench seeking to embrace her again, but she moved away as I did. 'And now you mus' stop, *truly*, please stop, because –'

'Ah,' said I, sliding again towards her, '*because* is just where we left off.' Snowflakes still clung to her flaxen ringlets, but soon melted out of sight.

'Yes, precisely,' she said now deliberately, trying – but not entirely succeeding – to enunciate her words more fully and properly, like a lady, as if she had practised her speech before a mirror. 'I was goin' to say tha' we mus' stop, because it's impossible that you and I should 'ave anythin' to do with each other in future.'

'But what do you mean – what *can* you mean?' I cried, my desire almost instantly transformed into dread, tinctured with wrath.

'What I mean,' said she, looking at her hands, 'is tha', as I tried t' tell you, I'm a good girl –'

'The Devil take me, Maggie,' I swore, now quite past my patience, 'you have made that quite plain! Your virtue is as fully established as goddamned Sinless Kilmeny! Yet you continue to look at me a certain way, and what were those impassioned kisses a moment ago? You did not recoil from me *then*, did you?'

This shocking outburst, blasphemy in her own house of worship, seemed to give her the calm that she needed, and without any tears she now admonished me, as a governess would her little charges.

'Allow me to finish, Mr Brontë, and don't interrupt,' she continued in her formal speech. 'Wha' I meant to say was tha' because I'm a good girl I mus' do what me dad and me mum wish, and *they* wish me to marry Mr Benjamin Mortimer, the landlord of the Royal Hotel; by joining our fortunes we plan to build a new public house near Shaw Syke.'

Of course: the station to be built at the end of the projected branch line – the very line I had so often hoped for, to ease my travel to and from Halifax, as much to see her as anything. Maggie's father, the wily innkeeper, had looked beyond the wild scramble of horses, coaches and omnibuses from Halifax to Sowerby Bridge, to a future where they would all be supplanted by a direct railway link, and was using Maggie as a pawn to win access to the new station, with the future pub the dowry. The future, I thought bitterly, belongs to men such as this.

A crushing weight pressed down upon my chest. 'But what of our first meeting, what of the railway excursion, what of the embrace that we just shared? Do you not feel as I feel? Are you a traitor to your own sentiments? Why do you betray your own heart, Maggie? Are you nothing but a hypocrite?' I fairly shouted this last, and at last the stony fortress of her countenance gave way, and she collapsed again into tears.

'I've always done what me dad says, and are we not commanded t' honour our mother and father?'

'What if I told you,' said I desperately, 'that I have been promoted to Clerk-in-Charge of the Luddenden Foot station, and my salary doubled? Eh? What of *that*? Would that not convince your worthy parents that I am a responsible young man, making my way successfully – in the railway, no less, on which they themselves seem so reliant for their future prosperity? I would gladly sacrifice all other ambitions, put my nose to the grindstone, my shoulder to the wheel, to make you my wife!'

'I scarcely know ye, Mr Brontë, for we've seen each other but three times now.'

At this, I felt the slightest spark of hope flame up within the dying embers of my desires. 'But do you not *feel* what I felt? Surely you do – for as you say, you are *a good girl* – and so only true affection could have led you to kiss me as you have just done, not base desire.'

Again, she looked away; again tears streamed down her cheeks. 'Me dad's decided.'

'But,' said I, 'what of *my* proposal? Would not your worthy papa look kindly upon such ambition and advancement as I have already demonstrated in just these four months at Sowerby Bridge?'

She again wiped her eyes, turning solemnly towards me. 'No, me dad's firmly set 'is sights upon this marriage, an' 'e'll brook no dissent on the matter. An' –' she said, hesitating to continue.

'And what?'

Her next words tumbled out with great rapidity as well as great passion, as though they had been considered for some time, but dammed up in her mind, and could at last finally burst free: 'And I've seen the way ye look when ye talk 'bout poetry, or music, or art; it's the same way Mr Leyland looks, and Mr Liszt too, where the world seems to fall away an' yer lost in a dream, as if ye fairly walked on clouds, yer faces shining like angels in communication with God. Nothing else matters then, not even me.'

'That is not *true*,' I exclaimed, 'I *adore* you, I *worship* you! I would throw off my ridiculous poetic ambitions to earn a steady living for you and our children.'

I was again in a passion, which seemed only to confirm the wisdom of Maggie's sentiments.

'Please 'ear me now,' she said calmly, now finally past her tears, again struggling to make her diction as proper as possible. 'I believe tha' *you* sincerely believe tha' you would, truly I do. But I would no more wish to break yer spirit – it's the very thing that I am drawn to, like a moth to a flame, but also wha' I fear – than risk my future security and the love o' my parents and friends. One of these two things – or both – would 'appen if we were to wed: either your spirit would be crushed or my family lost, and I can no' endure either.'

I sat quietly for a moment, considering, remembering her words to me when first we met: *So you write verses and such. Don't fancy there be much of a livin' in tha'.* For all of the noble sentiments that we had exchanged, could it be that I simply wanted to possess Maggie? Could it equally be, despite the concern that she seemed to show for my spirit and the love of her family, that she feared, most of all – and quite understandably – being someday the repentant bride of a penniless poet?

In short, in the most unfavourable view of the matter, was I simply a man driven wild with desire, and she herself the hapless victim of commerce, sold by her parents to the young owner of the Royal Hotel? Was that all there was to this damnable existence?

Maggie stood up to take her leave, but before she could reach the door, I seized her arm.

'Are you quite certain about this?'

Again, biting her lip and refusing to meet my gaze, she replied, 'Quite certain. Now we mus' return before it's noticed tha' we've gone. Besides,' said she, now assuming her most businesslike air, 'the platters will be raided and the mulled wine and spirits drunk by the serving boys if I'm not there t' oversee matters.'

She ran ahead of me, down the chapel steps and along Square Road to Leyland's. The snow fell thickly now, as I walked, utterly dejected, around to the back of the studio, entering unnoticed only because I happened to arrive at the precise moment that Liszt's hands banged out their final notes, swallowed up by the wild applause that ensued. Only a few minutes had passed since Maggie and I had left the *fête*, which had doubtless seemed to Leyland and his guests, and Liszt at his pianoforte – none of whom seemed to have moved an inch – a mere instant. And yet in that brief time, I had felt a lifetime of emotions: desire and the exaltation of a love briefly requited; followed by hope, fear and trepidation, jealousy, betrayal and utter, final, disillusionment.

Maggie had resumed her oversight of the refreshments. I walked quickly past the mulled wine to pour myself an extremely large glass of whisky. Leyland had only seemed oblivious to my comings and goings, and as the applause died away, he sidled over to me, winking maliciously. 'Well now, Faustus, that didn't take long! I'd like to think that, had it been me, I'd have taken my time with Kilmeny, but then you are young and excitable, ha ha!'

'Lower your voice, Joe,' said I, crossly, 'it's not what you think. We only had a brief conversation, to set some matters straight.'

'I'll wager you *did* get things straight! That's just the kind intercourse you needed, Brontë. Tell me, how was it?'

The whisky had already begun its magic work as the last snowflakes disappeared from my shoulders. I was incensed, not so much at Maggie – for I see, especially as I write these words at the remove of two days – that her logic was unimpeachable, and that she was quite right about any future we might have. I can scarcely care for myself, and despite my protestations, I could no more imagine giving up my writing than dispelling my lifelong aversion to being a bank clerk. But that night I was angry at the world and loathed myself; drowning my sorrows seemed *just* the thing to do.

I looked across the room and lifted my glass in a mock toast to Maggie, who was far too occupied to notice. As I gulped the burning liquor, I felt myself falling, falling, falling into an abyss, found myself wanting to punish myself and the world, *wanting to sin*. Soon I was speaking as coarsely as Leyland, as I filled a second large tumbler with whisky.

'Sod it all, Joe, I *wanted* her, but it seems she is to marry Mortimer, the scion of the Royal Hotel. A goddamned bloody business decision, if you will.'

Leyland sighed. In a brief moment of clarity, in which he suddenly looked quite old, he said, 'Ah, yes. But really, little man, can you blame the poor thing? Sometimes I think the only people who do not compromise themselves in one manner or another generally finish in Bedlam, or in the debtor's prison, or blowing their brains out with a pistol.'

Meanwhile, after a brief pause, Liszt had been cajoled into a final encore, which he surely permitted himself – along with a great deal more to drink – because there would be no more concerts in the coming days.

'*Mesdames et Messieurs*, all good things must end, yes, yes, even my visit to Halifax,' he said with a laugh, 'and so it is only proper for me to share with you something I have been turning round in my mind' – here he tapped with mock gravity on his impressive forehead – 'for some years, *la Danse macabre, der Totentanz* – the *Dance of the Dead*, you would say?'

The virtuoso's hands began to pound out a slow, lugubrious march, and one could fairly see the Grim Reaper stalking across a barren landscape – the moors above Haworth perhaps – scythe in hand. Soon I heard the music no longer, and found myself speaking with anyone who would listen, becoming increasingly prolix as I drank my third and then fourth glass of whisky.

I am only able to call dimly to mind a few scenes from the remainder of the evening: a final burst of applause for Liszt, and his subsequent departure, where he shook hands all round and said to me, 'Remember, Herr Brontë, what Goethe says: *das Ewig-weibliche zieht uns hinan*, the Eternal Feminine draws us aloft! Ha ha!' and here he winked and nodded in the direction of Maggie; later, my shouting at her as she left the party with the servers from the inn, who carried trays, bottles and suchlike: '*Maggie, stay but a while, you are so beautiful!*'; lunging for a kiss from one of the less reputable women who remained behind, as the party staggered to its drunken, dismal close – with Frobisher back at the pianoforte – but instead pitching onto the floor, for by then I found it impossible to stand.

I have no memory of falling asleep, but apparently Leyland

had, in the end, enough presence of mind to extinguish the candles, lock the doors and find a blanket for each of us, leading me to one hearth whilst he took the other, so that each of us could be warmed, at least for a time, as the fires burned down to their dying embers.

Volume Two

I would rather give my hand than undergo again the grovelling carelessness, the malignant yet cold debauchery, the determination to find how far mind could carry body without both being chucked into hell …

– Branwell Brontë, letter to Francis Grundy, 22nd May 1845, concerning his months at Luddenden Foot

Patrick Branwell Brontë was no domestic demon – he was just a man moving in a mist, who lost his way.

– Francis Grundy, *Pictures of the Past*

I.

A Letter from Charlotte

March 25th, 1841 · Sowerby Bridge

Nearly two months have passed since last I visited these pages. The dreary weather has been surpassed only by my depressed spirits, alas. We are now in the midst of that raw season when nature seems so stripped and bereaved that one feels that life might never return, although springtime be but a few weeks distant. Even the transient beauty of an occasional snowstorm is now denied us, for as March progresses we have but glacial wind and frigid rain whipping through the bare branches, and only icy mud where once were piled high drifts as delicate and lovely as the white icing of a cake.

Still I place one foot in front of the other, and still I present myself as cheerfully as possible at work, although the knowledge that I will soon be in charge of my own station at times makes me chafe under the command of Mr Duncan, who could not be more kind or more just, in his clipped, business-like way.

Already the banns have been published for Maggie's marriage to Mortimer, and I can afford to think no more about her. As is now my habit, I have done my best to crush that unpleasant memory and look forward to Luddenden Foot – not only the liberty that the position will give me in my employments, but also the independence that the increase in salary will procure me. Nor have I given up on writing, quite to the contrary: I have begun once again to revise old poems, and even, on occasion, to write new ones. I have tried to cauterise the wound with forgetfulness, and then sterilise it with occasional doses of whisky taken with Leyland, who alternately plays the roles of tempter and saviour.

He continues to exhort me to apply the healing balm of a woman's embrace to the scar, as he so often does with his Halifax whores, but I have not yet descended to such desperation.

On the first of this month, a grand occasion presented itself to our little corner of the world: the great railway pioneer, George Stephenson himself, accompanied some of our shareholders from Manchester to Normanton to see the Summit Tunnel, and on the return trip the train made a point of stopping at each station. I stood with Mr Duncan and our porter, Smythe, and shook the hand of the great man himself. He had an almost stately, aristocratic bearing, and yet condescended to greet us all as companions in this great enterprise, which he was largely responsible for moving from an idea to a reality now spreading with hitherto unimaginable speed throughout the kingdom. Before climbing back onto the train, he embraced one young man with particular affection, as though a long-lost son. My brow doubtless betrayed my curiosity, for another young man, who stood just between the lad and me leant over to whisper, 'That's Stephenson's *nephew*; he happens to be none other than my roommate in Halifax, where we've both just arrived.'

'How do you do, Sir,' said I, introducing myself. 'I'm the Assistant-Clerk-in-Charge here, but am moving in just under a month's time up the line to Luddenden Foot.'

'Grundy,' said he, 'Francis Grundy. I am among the engineers engaged to begin work on the branch line from Sowerby Bridge into Halifax.'

Ah, yes: the damnable branch line, which Maggie's intended and her father surely believed would be a river of gold washing into the centre of Halifax in general, and into their new inn in particular, would forever be associated in my mind with her, and the choice she had made. My heart continued to be enraged with her, but my mind could hardly blame her. Do our heads and hearts ever act in perfect accord? Happy must be those who have experienced such a blessed alignment of prudence and passion!

Much remained to be done that day, but I told Grundy that I would be delighted to receive him another time, either in Sowerby

Bridge or at my new post in Luddenden Foot.

However, I must say with a broad smile as I write this, that the greatest diversion I have had of late consists of Charlotte's letters, written from her new situation at Rawdon, for she did indeed accept the post at Upperwood House. She claims that while she may have the faculty to acquire knowledge, it is quite another matter to impart it, particularly while having to repel the rude familiarity of children. I do sympathise with her when she says that, when confronted with unruly children, she finds herself wishing herself a simple housemaid or kitchen-girl.

Could it be that we all, brother and sisters alike, share this singular inability to blend the work of the mind with that of the body, particularly where children are concerned? Anne alone seems capable of this, and perhaps only the age of her charges at Thorp Green makes it possible, for was she not sent packing from her earlier post?

Emily is the fullest embodiment of this phenomenon, for moving taciturnly through her domestic employments at the Parsonage, she is free to allow her heart and mind and soul to ramble over the moors at complete liberty. I, too, on rare occasions, sometimes felt this way at Broughton, when the Postlethwaite boys would resist doing their lessons. I recall thinking that I would rather follow a plough through the fields or dig canals like a navvy than try to force the young lads to their lessons. One extreme or the other: poet or ploughman. Could we have absorbed, through our very flesh and blood, this quality from Papa, the Irish farmer purified by a Cambridge education? And yet does not the future belong to the Stephensons of the world, those who can at once employ both body and mind? So it would seem.

More enjoyable, because it touched not on one of my own weaknesses, but solely on hers, was a recent mention of her employers. 'I like Mr White *extremely*,' she writes, while 'respecting Mrs White I am for the present silent – I am trying hard to like her.' There is little doubt what is occurring here: if she is not positively in love with Mr White, she has melted before what is quite likely mere civility and good nature, in the form of a tolerably attractive older man. Having watched her closely in the presence of men, I find that she fairly swoons before one who is authoritative, older (but not so old that she cannot imagine herself in his arms), handsome (but not so handsome that she cannot conceive of a possibility of love), and, above all attentive, kind and respectful of her considerable intellect.

Were I to wager on the matter, I would say that the unwitting Mr White has simply been friendly and quick to recognise Charlotte's best qualities, her mind and her eyes, sparkling with intelligence, and has possibly even made a joke or two at his own or his children's expense, as such men often do. Even better, he is safely married, and so there is no harm in such a friendship. The only thing that could make him even more appealing would be if he were himself as learned as Charlotte. In such a case she would likely throw herself at his feet or abase herself in Heaven knows what other fashion!

As for Mrs White, she possesses everything that my sister does not: a fortune, a grand house, a husband that Charlotte likes *extremely*, and children. If, as I suspect, Mr White is a jolly, good-natured fellow, then it has doubtless fallen to his wife to manage all household affairs, including the children's nurse and governess. The distance required to conduct such a relationship properly is doubtless perceived as *froideur* by Charlotte, whose passionate soul will positively burn with a sense of (most likely imagined) injustice!

In a gentleman's family highly genteel,
Where 'tis hoped that the lady will try to conceal
Any fanciful feelings or flights she may feel.
For this gentleman's family's so very genteel,
    they're so very genteel!

I wonder, does Charlotte remember Parry's words ruefully, or does she try, as I do, to blot out all of those things that bring her pain? And then, by Heavens, if Mrs White is in the least a pretty woman it will positively seal the bargain, for Charlotte will surely despise her. Her most recent epistle contains a great many animadversions on the subject of the unsuspecting Mrs White, from her low birth and vulgarity when in a passion, to her *hauteur* in regard to 'tradesfolk', although she herself is a mere taxman's daughter; even her bad grammar and worse spelling fail to escape Charlotte's censorious gaze.

Am I being unfair to my eldest sister? I think not. For how conveniently she forgets our own humble origins – and as for spelling, only Papa's orthography has any rhyme or reason to it, thanks, no doubt, to his years at Cambridge. Ours is execrable, and I confess that I can hardly tell when 'i' should precede 'e' or *vice-versa*. Nor do I give a fig, a fillip or a farthing, in the end.

Oh, dearest Charlotte! Well might Burns speak of *man's inhumanity to man* – how much worse is woman's inhumanity to woman! I should like to get a good look at Mrs White, for I suspect her to be quite a strapping beauty to have elicited such venom; my sister, alas, has ruled out all such visits, even though the Whites themselves have invited Papa to Upperwood House. One wonders: is Charlotte ashamed of them, or us, or both?

As for me, I have found lodgings at Brearley Hall, just half a mile's walk from the Luddenden Foot station, where I shall remove just three days hence in preparation for my new post there. While doubts may sometimes cloud my brow as I prepare to take this next step up in the company, I will struggle to keep my post, whatever the cost! I cannot say the same for Charlotte, who appears *determined* to be miserable. No, no, I must not be like her, I must find what is good and fruitful in my post, I must gladly suffer what is less than agreeable – and with any luck the most onerous of tasks may be shifted to my inferiors – while not letting this work extinguish entirely the fires of poetic ambition.

I feel in the very marrow of my bones that Maggie was right, in the end: to me, *nothing else matters*.

11.

Luddenden Foot

April 10th, 1841 · Brearley Hall, Luddenden Foot

To some it may seem that I am now removed to the very ends of the earth, but Luddenden Foot is not so bad as all that, and not all that remote from Halifax. And, after all, as time permits, I may journey wherever I please, and free of charge. My lodgings at Brearley Hall are more than sufficient, and my landlords, a Mr James Clayton and his wife Rachel, are prosperous farmers whose two grown sons and their families also live on the premises. They have arranged my living quarters in such a way as I might come and go as I please without disturbing anyone, and indeed even the dogs are already used to me, so that I am greeted not with growls but with wagging tails when I approach, whatever hour of day or night. The Claytons say that the house was built some two hundred years since with riches earned in the wool trade, but that they are merely humble farmers. The fat rosy cheeks of the grandchildren, the quality of the family's clothing, the abundance of good food and drink, and the pristine state of repair of their carriage and even their farming implements, however, suggest anything but hardship: industry, yes; hardship, no.

To my relief, the Claytons have achieved that delicate balance of amiability and diffidence, where a sincerely warm greeting and enquiry after my health does not lead them to further, less discrete, interrogations. Mr Clayton is a stout, hearty gentleman farmer of some fifty-five or sixty years, and his wife Rachel is a small, birdlike creature who bustles relentlessly about the house and farm, seemingly employing each waking moment in profitable exercise of her faculties and person, for, as she often chirrups, 'There is always work to be done, Mr Brontë! It never stops, never stops!'

Knowing that I might come and go at my ease under such a roof as this is already a source of great comfort, for I may set any anxieties on this score aside as I seek further promotion with the railway and try, once again, to publish a poem or two, at the very least. My daily walk takes me downhill through open fields to the new station, which lies along the thickly wooded valley bottom. The trees are at last beginning to bud, and Mrs Clayton assures me that within just a few weeks bluebells will appear as far as the eye can see. The station itself is a humble outpost of the railway, but there is more than ample room for me, the clerk Mr Spence and the porter Mr Killiner to do our work as the trains pass through each day. I still find it difficult to believe that I am the clerk in charge or 'stationmaster' as now we are called; indeed, I cannot fathom that I am in charge of *anything*, for I can scarcely care for myself.

Yesterday, as I left the station, a delicate, warming breeze gave a foretaste of the weather to come, and not having anywhere that I needed to be, I struck out in the direction of the nearest moors. Within minutes I had climbed the summit of the closest hill, and sat atop a large stone precipice, my knees pulled up under my chin. Although the day was fading, the southerly breeze continued to warm me, gently caressing my cheeks and tousling my hair, like a lover returned after a long absence. The air was so warm and sweet, and my heart was so inexplicably and unexpectedly full, that I know not how to describe it. In a single instant I felt at once as old and weary as Methuselah and yet somehow as young and hopeful as I had in those first days at Broughton. I wanted to sob with grief: the crushing of childhood hopes, the failure of prior schemes and, most of all, the loss of Agnes and then Maggie – though I had never really possessed the latter, so how can one lose what one never had? Is being stripped of one's hopes and desires every whit as devastating as losing what one already possesses? Indeed, is it worse?

Still, my heart also fairly exploded with a love for life and wild hopes for the future. Surely one who has not felt this intoxicating blend of grief and hope, of desire and despair, is no better than a beast of burden, trudging stupidly from one day to the next, like a carthorse from field to field. I felt I had already led a thousand lives, died a thousand deaths, and yet had another thousand to live. I rose to my feet and turned on the great outcropping of rock, looking into the distance in every direction: east towards Halifax and Bradford beyond; west towards Hawksclough and Mytholmroyd; south towards Longroyd and Mill Bank, and last, northwards across the vast moors towards Haworth: *home*. How can a single human breast hold equal parts of hope and despair?

And yet so it seemed to me, and I fairly wept with the nearly insufferable feeling of being fully alive and fully aware, of great potential yoked to powerlessness, of a yearning for immortality contained within a pitiful mortal shell, and such a state was at once so exalted and so unbearable that I thought for a moment of dashing my own skull against the massive rock on which I stood. Was this what Liszt had meant when he said that *existence is so full that we cannot bear it, we are overcome*? Was this seeing *the face of God*? My heart was brimming with a multitude of sensations, and my mind was swimming with a thousand simultaneous and yet contradictory thoughts, so that I felt my heart would positively give out from exhaustion or that my mind might explode like an overheated steam engine.

I lay down on the massive rock and closed my eyes, breathing as deeply as I could, striving to calm my feverish mind, to *think of nothing*, to lose myself in the oblivion of the mass of white clouds billowing above me. Slowly, slowly, I emerged from this place – was it heaven or hell? – and looked about me. A crow circled in ever-smaller spirals, while cows lowed in a distant pasture. The sun was close to setting, but still the air was warm and pleasant, like a benediction. Hope and joy seemed to have carried the day against grief and sadness, for now I felt anything was possible. I cannot account for this change, but I was – if only for a brief moment – swept forwards once again by the comforting waves of ambition and hope that had nourished me for so many years, and felt I could conquer all by dint of hard work and sheer force of will. Had I not doubled my income just now, by sheer application – even going so far as to keep Mr Duncan's ledgers in perfect order?

I foresaw a meteoric rise in the company, perhaps managing a vast organisation of lines and stations, of goods and passengers, with all of the employees required to operate it. I confess that for an instant, I imagined myself a wealthy man, flaunting my success before a weary, ageing Maggie at her husband's new inn, but I obliterated that phantom as soon as it arose. Instead, I endeavoured to work out how I might retire with my fortune and spend the rest of my days in study and reflection, in the writing of prose and verse, in correspondence with other men of letters. For an instant, standing on that stone gazing for miles in every direction, I felt that these twin goals were as logical and inseparable as the two rails of a railway track.

As the sun finally set, the last clouds marched north and the breeze abated somewhat, although every so often I would feel a warm caress intermingled, increasingly as night fell, with the fingers of a cooler wind. Who has not felt this rare, curious blending, as if, for the briefest of moments, the four winds, the *Anemoi*, were at war – or perhaps better, were dancing – with one another? I leant back upon the rock, my coat rolled up as a pillow, to watch the stars appear one by one. The winds had blown away the smoke of the railway and of the factories of the Calder Valley, and so I was treated to a spectacle like no other, watching star upon star stealing into view as night swept forwards. I shuddered in awe at the grandeur of the scene, and felt my chest fill again with the joy of simply being *alive*. Just as these thousand worlds of light before me had been hidden by daylight, so my wish for the more exalted life as a poet had been eclipsed by my humble occupations at the station; but instead of filling me with despair, this understanding merely confirmed in me the belief that great things were not only still possible, but inevitable.

Oh God – if God there be – would that such feelings might last forever!

April 22nd, 1841 · Luddenden Foot

The railway has given me a right-hand-man *and* a left-hand-man, and I will at last have some independence in my comings and goings, for it is expected that I should shift some of my duties to them, just as Duncan did to me at Sowerby Bridge. The first of these is a Mr William Spence, my assistant, some twenty-five years of age. He lives hard by me at Brearley, with a wife and young son. He is an earnest, somewhat simple fellow, whose every action seems intended to ensure the good opinion of his employers. His hair is exceedingly fair, and his strong frame towers over me like some Scandinavian giant, but he is exceedingly kind and gentle in his manner, even if his accent on occasion bears the traces of his humble origins and limited education. As he has made quite plain, he feels it a great boon to have secured the position of clerk and will do anything to retain it. So much for my right hand; now let us turn to the left.

My other employee is a one Henry Killiner, the porter. His rough manners make Mr Spence seem as though he were a member of good Queen Victoria's court. He claims that he is a man of some thirty years, but at first view he could easily pass for forty or more. A stout man of middling height, he has dark, somewhat stringy hair and a sallow complexion, small ferretlike eyes and a turned-up nose. The contrast between Spence and Killiner could not be starker. Although a mere five years separates them, the first is a young man with a spring in his step, a family to nourish and a narrow but driving ambition to move forwards to the next station in his career; the second seems almost an old man, who is at his humble post not because he believes it can vouchsafe for him greater opportunity, but because it is a mindless occupation sufficient to earn his bread and the quantities of ale sufficient to shoulder the burden of existence.

What I have discerned in the few days that we have laboured together as a trio is the importance of each of us working to his strengths. Although Spence is a humble, plainspoken fellow with no especial gift for grammar or spelling, he appears to be wondrously talented in the matter of arithmetic, and so, as Duncan did with me, I have shifted all matters of accounting to him, though I make a desultory show of daily reviewing, and giving my benediction to, the ledgers that he keeps. As for Killiner, his strength is, well, his *strength*, and even beyond his prescribed duties as porter it is understood that when hefting of any kind is required, he will take such matters in hand. He has made it plain that such an arrangement suits him perfectly, for to him 'real work' does not exist apart from physical exertion. How like me in an odd way, although my wish is to flee any occupation that will require me to perspire or to soil my hands!

My role, then, is to supervise all things, from the arrival and departure of trains and their goods and passengers, to the condition of the station and the accurate keeping of accounts, so that in an odd way I do not do anything but am responsible for everything. Is this what it is to be in charge? If so, what an odd thing it is, *managing*! For it reposes on power and responsibility, and thus breeds both confidence and terror, for if anything should go wrong it is I who shall be held to account.

For the present, all is well, and after just a few days we have begun to operate as smoothly as a well-oiled engine, each playing the part he likes and performs best, though each assisting the others as needed, to ensure that the flow of persons and cargo is unimpeded by anything we can prevent. Already I feel that Mr Spence is more than equal to the task of overseeing the station in my absence; one hardly need a thorough knowledge of Greek and Latin for that! Soon I hope to be able to devote a portion of my time to verse, which requires so much concentration that the slightest worry about more mundane occupations is sufficient to snuff out the flame of creativity.

III.

The Leylands in the Wilderness

April 29th, 1841 · Luddenden Foot

Just yesterday, for the first time, I absented myself during work hours, when Joe and Frank Leyland arrived unexpectedly on the train from Sowerby Bridge. I had been sitting at my desk, pretending to look over the previous day's ledger, but in reality scribbling in a notebook just like this one, which I keep locked in a drawer, and which in odd moments receives my sketches, poems and other miscellanea. This diary, on the other hand, never leaves my lodgings, and is even tucked safely under my mattress each time I leave my room.

Just as I do when any train pulls in, I flung my notebook in a drawer, closed the ledger and walked officiously out to the platform to oversee Killiner's activities. Spence joined me, as is his wont, in the event that two or even three of us were needed to assist passengers or oversee the unloading of goods. I was standing, as I often do, with my hands in my pockets, surveying the busy scene, when something knocked my hat entirely off my head from behind. I turned in agitation to take to task what I assumed was some young rascal, only to see Joe balancing my hat on the end of his walking stick, and Francis standing quietly, just a step or two behind him.

'Ho ho, Brontë, I thought I'd play a little trick on the station *head*. For there you stood with your hands thrust in your pockets and your feet planted so firmly – such a towering titan of railway navigation that I could already imagine a momental sculpture larger than my *Head of Satan* of you – that I could not help but bring you down a few notches!'

He held my hat out of my reach for a moment, then at last, again laughing, allowed me to snatch it and place it back on my head. After exchanging a few pleasantries with the brothers Leyland in the time it took for the train to depart for Hebden Bridge, I introduced them to Spence and Killiner. Winking at me, Joe said to the two men, 'I am certain from the looks of you that you can easily keep things in hand for a bit in the absence of your stationmaster, for we have some important business to conduct with him. We won't go far, and you may send a lad for him at a moment's notice, I give my word.'

'Joe, I'm not sure this is wise. Perhaps we can conduct such business at my desk?'

Perhaps all subordinates are eager to see their superiors depart, for Spence and Killiner, despite their vast differences, were eagerly united in the opinion that I should benefit from my friends' rare presence and conduct our business elsewhere. In a more *fluid* environment, I was quite certain.

'Be at your ease, Mr Brontë,' said Spence, 'We have matters entirely in hand, truly we do.' Killiner grunted in agreement.

'You see, my friend? Did I not tell you so?' Turning to Spence and Killiner, he said, 'Should you need your exalted leader, you will find us at the nearest public house, wherever that is!'

At this Killiner spoke up, clearly from frequent experience. 'Ah, tha'll be the Anchor and Shuttle just yonder,' and he nodded in the direction of the handful of houses and the public house that made up the whole of Luddenden Foot. I should have liked a walk to the village of Luddenden, which was another half a mile distant, but prudence won a rare victory over preference, for I wished to stay near the station. Within an instant, I was reasoning to myself that such an absence would have to happen eventually, and Spence and Killiner should get used to it – for what if I were to fall ill or be called back to Haworth?

My conscience thus soothed, I was soon seated with my friends at the Anchor, which I had succeeded in avoiding thus far; the amount of drink I had consumed at Leyland's that fateful night, and my fervent desire to make the most of my promotion, have united to imbue me with uncharacteristic sobriety and seriousness of purpose of late. Indeed, I entered into the familiar old relationship with the Leylands with some trepidation, but at the same time I was truly happy to see Francis and Joe, and – truth to tell – thrilled with anticipation as I gripped a tumbler of whisky in my hand for the first time since the fête that the latter had given in honour of Liszt.

'Why did you not tell me you were coming?'

'What! And strip away all the wonder from the event? No, no, lad, had I tried to plan such a visit in advance you would have found manifold excuses why it could not occur until next month, or next year! No, a surprise attack is always best, hey? Besides, the competent stationmaster should be prepared for anything, practised at thinking on his feet, should he not?'

This was vintage Leyland: confounding, incorrigible and supremely likeable. Francis, usually more observer than participant in such conversations, nevertheless said, 'if the Manchester and Leeds had the electric telegraph of Cooke and Wheatstone, as the Great Western does, we could have sent you a message over the wires. Did you know it is being put along the new Blackwall Tunnel Railway as well, as we speak?'

'You seem to have missed my point entirely, dear brother,' said Joe. 'Even a telegraph message an hour in advance of our arrival would have removed the element of surprise.'

Ignoring his brother, and quite earnest on the topic of this latest marvel, Frank continued, 'As a railway man, do you think the telegraph will spread along all of the rail lines, from station to station?'

I honestly had not given the subject any thought, and had only just read about the telegraph myself, in the *Halifax Guardian*, and I said so.

'Really, Francis, you cannot expect our young bard to give a toss about such things. Isn't it enough that he has managed to keep his situation with the railway, given that his heart lies elsewhere?'

At this I protested, albeit weakly. 'Now Joe, I wouldn't say that's exactly true. I enjoy much of what I do, truly.'

'Why is it, then, that your eyes fail to meet mine as you say so? Ah ha! It is because you *lie*, my dear sir – I know your heart, and it is no more enamoured of the comings and goings of goods and passengers than mine is of the chiselling of headstones. The railway is for the Spences of the world, just as the gravestones belong to the John Browns.'

'Just a moment,' said I, 'I very much like being a part of the railway: all the movement, the excitement, the *progress* as more and more lines are built – it is the future.'

'You just don't wish to soil your *hands* with that future, correct?' said Joe, laughing. 'You like the *idea* of the railway, preferably a fictional one, or better still, an allegorical one – that huffs and puffs through a poem or story, perhaps – but not the dirty, stinking, *real* thing. Heavens, no!'

I had to laugh at his characterisation, which was not far off the mark. Although I was merely sipping it, the whisky had begun to work its old magic.

'Well, my dear sir, we do what we must, and I can think of worse occupations. And who are you to tease me, when you advertise yourself, in an almost grovelling manner, as being willing to do just about anything in stone, do you not? What does your sign say again?'

Here Francis spoke up, reciting from memory:

Halifax Marble Works,
Square Road
J.B. Leyland, Sculptor

Monuments, busts, tombs, tablets, chiffonier
slabs and all kinds of marble work used in
the upholstery business, made to order.
A variety of marble chimney pieces on
view, cleaned, repaired or set up.

Leyland clenched his teeth, his smile now more of a grimace. 'Surely, Brontë, you do not believe that such wording was *my* choice. No, it was my banker's.'

He nodded in the director of his brother.

'I will say that when Frank insisted upon such a practical approach to the marble works – for he has the nasty habit of always wishing things to be profitable – I took the idea and ran even further with it, debasing myself entirely. It was either this, or "the Great Sculptor of *Sinless Kilmeny* and the *Head of Satan*" – I could envisage no intermediate step between the two. If you're going to sell your soul, sell it entirely, eh young Faustus?'

Francis flashed his usual indulgent smile, and simply said, 'To use one's gifts to earn an honest living whilst pursuing more elevated but less remunerated activities is hardly what sets one on the road to perdition.'

'You know exactly what I mean, Frank, and so does Branwell.' He brought his fist thundering down upon the table. 'It's maddening. Even Liszt is worried by money – Frobisher told me just yesterday that Lavenu did, indeed, confirm to him that the entire tour of the Kingdom was a financial catastrophe, and the virtuoso took no fees at all for his troubles, just so the lesser musicians could be paid – though I'm sure he learned a lesson in the bargain, if only to play by himself and never to return to this accursed island!'

He was silent for a moment and then added, with a sigh that seemed to come from the deepest recesses of his soul, 'By God, I am so very weary of this topic.'

'Why, then,' I asked, 'do you continue to indulge in it?'

'You're right … of course you're right, Brontë. I would like nothing more than never to think or speak about money again. But when one is worried unto death about how to make one's living, to pay one's debts, it becomes all consuming, and can nearly drive one mad. When money worries me in this way, I can think of nothing else – and could easily sink into a paralysis of despair.'

He paused again, then brightened at last. 'Let us thank God, or Zeus, or Mother Earth, or our lucky stars, or Dionysus, also yclept Old Man Whisky – not my sweet old mastiff of that same name, of course – yes, only drink can blot out such cares,' and here he motioned for our glasses to be refilled.

I looked at Francis with sympathy and admiration. The long-suffering brother did not say what we all knew, that Joe pays no mind whatsoever to his expenditures, has prepared no budget for his living, but instead employs any additional earnings that might come his way to give grand soirées, pay his friends' drinking debts – he has paid mine more than a dozen times, easily – or procure an evening with one of his whores, although the last of these arrangements might be conceived by both parties as something slightly less sordid. At what point, I wonder, will Francis have to walk away, to *cut his losses* as those fond of the gaming table might say, leaving Joe to his own ruin? It chilled me to think about it, but the second glass of whisky soon caused such cares to melt away.

'As you suggest, Stationmaster Brontë, it is high time we speak of something else. Are you writing? If so, would you be willing to share your work with your fellow poets and artists?'

I nodded affirmatively to both questions, and Leyland continued, 'You see, your friends Dearden, Heaton, Crossley, Nicholson – even Frobisher – are thinking of getting together regularly – a sort of informal literary society, if you will, for no one wishes to be bound by silly rules or tyrannised by an official schedule – to drink and talk and drink and read and drink and criticise. Oh, and *drink*. It will be a moveable feast, if you will – why, we shall even come up here to the wilds of Luddenden Foot on occasion! What say you, little man?'

I laughed. 'First, it is not even five miles here, so it can scarcely be called *the wilds*! And we have this clever little invention called the railway – I'm not sure if you've heard of it – that can carry you hither and thither at dizzying speeds, old friend. It's the way of the future, even if it is a bit dirty. Second, I would be delighted, if time allows. For now that I am responsible for a station, I must worry about it even when I am not present.'

'Tut tut,' replied Joe, 'your good Mr Spence seems quite eager to please, and – what's his name, Killjoy? – why, he does the nasty, dirty business whether you are there or not, yes?

What is the point of being in *charge* if you cannot quit the rails from time to time, eh?'

The logic of Joe's comments was questionable: in just a few weeks as stationmaster I had indeed found that rather than providing freedom and peace of mind, my new role made it nearly impossible for me to stop thinking about my post, and if I allowed myself to consider all that might go wrong, I grew positively frozen with dread: what if there were a fire? What if a train truly derailed, or a passenger were hurt or killed? The one thing that did not worry me were the ledgers, for I had already determined that it would be best for all concerned for Spence to handle that repellent task.

'See here, Joe, it is not so easy as you might imagine. Whether I am at the station or not, I am ultimately responsible for all that transpires.' Yet as I said this, my heart fairly leapt at the thought of a regular gathering with my fellow poets, with the Leylands, and other sympathetic souls like Frobisher. Despite my initial misgivings, I found myself quickly bending towards Joe's point of view and saying, 'But we shall see – perhaps I can tear myself away, and no man can work all the time. The distraction would be a welcome one.'

'Ah! You see, Francis, there sits a reasonable man,' said Joe, beaming. 'I will charge myself with organising the first assembly, and we shall go from there. That's sufficient trouble unto the day.'

We finished our glasses and walked back to the station, for another train was to arrive in ten minutes. Already two hours had passed, and as we arrived Spence nodded – somewhat obsequiously, I thought – but Killiner was too occupied to notice. As Joe and Francis prepared to step up into their first-class carriage, I said, 'How will I know when and where we are to meet?'

'What if Francis sends you an ethereal message along some celestial telegraph lines?' said Joe, laughing and thumping the side of the coach with his cane as he ducked inside. As the train began rolling downhill towards Halifax, he leant out a window and shouted, over the din of the locomotive, 'We'll send word. Fear not, little man!'

It is my hope that my subordinates did not overhear him, for I could hardly expect them to take me seriously with such an appellation!

IV.

Who, Then, is My God?

May Day, 1841 · Luddenden Foot

To think that a year has passed since I spent that day with Coleridge! It seems at once a lifetime and only a fleeting instant. On the one hand, I have been dismissed from my post, abandoned Agnes, refined my translations of Horace and – with no response – sent them to Coleridge. I have followed Mr Postlethwaite's advice and found work on the railway, and have been promoted at twice the salary. I have again yearned for a woman, but had all hopes dashed. Anne has continued steadily in her situation, Emily has taken the up the reins of daily management of the Parsonage, and Charlotte has at last, after much resistance – how like me she is, in some ways, despite our vast differences! – found another situation as governess.

The great Liszt has come and gone, and we shall surely not see the likes of him again. I continue to write when I can – jottings here and there in my notebooks, the revision of a poem or two, and on rare occasions something new. Indeed, just yesterday I mailed something off to the *Halifax Guardian*, taking my favourite character Northangerland as a *nom de plume*: what better name for a saturnine Yorkshire poet! Odd, though, is it not, that in my thirst for glory I still hide behind this character, the descendant of a wooden soldier of childhood? Oh, such diffidence mixed with a yearning for fame is strange, but no less true for that: it is as if I were to light a flame with my right hand and yet snuff it out with the left!

Ah, but in the essential has anything changed? Still I long for a situation that allows me to devote my time to writing; still I am harried by the eternal need for money; still I go through each day in quiet fury at the world's hypocrisy, baseness and cupidity; still I feel, especially when in the company of Leyland, like blotting out all such cares until I feel nothing more. As for the softer sex, am I not far worse off than I was a year ago? For I have not only lost Agnes and failed to gain Maggie; I now have no prospects for such affection. Alas, it is far worse to have felt such bliss and have it brutally withdrawn than it is to be ignorant of its very existence, as I was before I arrived in Broughton last January, for now I have within me an aching, craving desire that often knows no bounds.

How strange that the same man, when viewed solely through his conduct, can be seen to progress on an upward arc, as if calmly and steadily climbing a hill towards his ultimate goal, while in the depths of his heart, he spirals downward into a personal Hell, one mostly of his own making! Is concordance of the two ever possible? I am certain Papa would have something to say about the matter, and he would counsel a number of things, all equally impossible for me to put into action: crush any last desires I have to make my living solely through writing; put my faith in the God and follow his teachings. I can fairly hear him now: If we love God and wish to serve Him, let us try to be like Him, to do His work, to labour for His glory, etc., etc.

Most men of faith have moments of doubt, but I am the man of doubts who occasionally has moments of faith. What I mean to say is that, to me, God is something of a trickster: although nowhere do I see demonstrable evidence of his existence, everywhere is his name loudly proclaimed, either in impious oaths or, as at the Parsonage and in Papa's clerical circles, at times with great fervour and sincerity, and at others with simpering hypocrisy. A rather impressive feat, I must admit. Indeed, doubt of His existence is not openly permitted, except by those of such wealth or renown that they can be indifferent to the usual censure of society. As I reflect, it is not that I harbour such doubts either; rather, it is that I refuse to believe in that *pale version of Zeus*, as Leyland called Him.

Meanwhile, the Reverend Paley and his ilk claim that God is a simple watchmaker, who has wound up His elegant timepiece and walked away, refusing to occupy Himself with our day-to-day affairs. Others, on the contrary, believe He is like an over-protective mother keeping watch over her young children, and that all of the good that we do and suffer must be the direct result of His divine intervention. Of course, questions of the origin of evil, free will and so forth, soon arise to muck up the works; and how silly, really, to believe that the Divine One spends his time shaping each cloud and snowflake, deciding which horse will fall and break its leg, or which child will have green eyes and which blue! Stuff and nonsense!

And what of our friends, the utterly mad Calvinists, who believe that all is preordained? Does this mean that if the doctrine of predestination so worries me that I might simply lie down and wait to die, or chuck myself into a ravine, since, after all, this too must be preordained from the creation of the universe? Fools! And do we, as Papa says, need to labour for His glory? Surely, in his omnipotence, He hardly needs our assistance on that score! If, truly, God is love, then he will let no one perish, for Hell is the invention of man – I feel that deeply in my bones, and there exists no more infernal world than the one we ourselves create and inhabit in this life.

Who, then, is *my* God? He is the one we cannot name and cannot grasp, and will only know when our life's day fades. He is not stooping over and deciding our every act, but He is *in* everything that is bright and beautiful and good: the roaring fire in the hearth on a wintry eve, a warm breeze as it shimmers through the green leaves of an oak tree on a spring day, and the ever-shifting Dudden Sands as much as the eternal Black Combe that towers nearby. He is in the innocent frolicking of children, in the tender, healing kiss of a mother on her baby's feverish cheek, in the hand of a young woman as she slowly brushes her ringlets back from her fair forehead, and in the fire that is kindled between two passionate souls as their bodies arc together as one, in ardent earthly rapture.

It is the face of God that shines out through human genius of all kinds, whether it is Leyland's *Head of Satan* or Liszt's *Mephisto Waltz*. God is in Stephenson's locomotive, in Brunel's bridges and tunnels, and Cook and Wheatstone's telegraph. Most of all, though, he is hidden, concealed until the end of time, or at least until the shadow of death descends, ineluctably, on each of us, one by one. To presume to know His exact shape is a piece of arrogant folly that should, itself, qualify the doctrinaire among us for the flames of Hell – *if* such a place existed! Such creeds are worthless as withered weeds.

In this spirit I have just reworked and submitted an old poem to the venerable *Halifax Guardian*, calling it 'Heaven and Earth', carefully composing it in such a way that the devout will doubtless find in it a confirmation of all that they believe, and so both the hypocritical curate and sanctimonious old dame will nod approvingly at its pious sentiments. Yet it is far less about God than about Man – about *me*, truth to tell, and how my daily cares and pleasures threaten to obscure the greater purpose of my life, and the glories of the world to come, whatever they might be:

On *Earth* we see our own abode,
A smoky town, a dusty road,
A neighbouring hill, or grove;
In *Heaven* a thousand worlds of light
Revolving through the gloom of night
O'er endless pathways rove.

While daylight shows this little *Earth*
It hides that mighty Heaven,
And, but by night, a visible birth
To all its stars is given …

And, may I smile, O God! To see
Their storms of sorrow beat on me,
When I so surely know

That *Thou* the while are shining on;
That *I*, at last, when they are gone,
Shall see the glories of thy throne
Beam brighter far than now.

And so I muddle through, just as I did a year since, hoping that something will bring me to the safe harbour where I can, at last, become whatever it is I am meant to be. Despite my ability to blot out what grieves me most, I do not have the strength of character that led Papa to set aside his literary ambitions – although perhaps he did so *only* under the pressure of a wife and growing family, and so is no more to be congratulated for his virtue than an animal is for caring for its young. While I no longer cherish any hope of hearing from Coleridge, I will continue to write *what* and *when* I can.

In the meantime, Leyland has organised the first meeting of our 'literary society' for three weeks hence, and to ensure that I will find no excuse for absenting myself, the devil has set the meeting place at the Lord Nelson Inn in Luddenden village, just a fifteen-minute walk from my station. If nothing else, this will prove a welcome distraction from the monotony of my work.

V.

A Visit from Grundy

May 18th, 1841 · Luddenden Foot

What is this wild, itching, feverish, incandescent urge to be something we are not? Why is it that we cannot, as Pascal has it (or so says Coleridge, for still I have not read the Frenchman), just sit quietly in a room? Is this simply healthy ambition, or is it a pernicious malady that invades our hearts and souls and, goading us like a demon, will never let us rest? If his life were not so miserable, one would be tempted to envy the simple labourer, for the notion that he might 'rise' to anything beyond his given lot is fantasy, reality crushing any dreams of advancement to a more exalted station in life.

Did Papa, in encouraging us to read widely and indiscriminately – surely believing that he was providing us with a most wholesome nourishment – instead *poison* us with dreams of fame and glory? For as unladylike as it may appear, each of my three sisters, and each in her own way, has an unslakeable thirst for something beyond what she knows, the same insatiable hunger that makes the present unbearable to me. We yearn always for that *next* thing, believing that all will at last be solved, tidily sewn-up like the end of a novel; yet even when our dreams *are* realised, we are not contented, but posit a new utopia that will surely, finally, make us happy, and will at long last liberate us from this feverish ardour that keeps us from real rest.

The successful, it seems, are those who can bend such fervour to their own designs, breaking it like a wild stallion into a docile plough horse, or taming a raging fire into a smithy's glowing embers: men who have as much – if not more – persistence and patience as they do genius and ambition. I, alas, have none of the former qualities, and doubt very much if there remains much of the latter. I envy such men the plodding nature of their progress in life, though surely they do not consider it as such. For them, it is the careful planning and execution of one goal after another, all linked together like railway stations in the undeviating path of their success. Surely they are in the right, at least as far as society is concerned, but my ability to acknowledge this fact hardly means that I can, by sheer force of will, become one of them, any more than a horse can be transmogrified into a steam engine, or a doubter can become a believer.

These thoughts spring to mind in the wake of a recent conversation with the railway engineer Francis Grundy, for he at last kept his promise and stopped at Luddenden Foot for a visit. At the Anchor and Shuttle we came to know each other a bit over drinks, and a banal discussion of his rooming situation in Halifax with Stephenson's nephew led to a discussion of the great man himself. I mentioned how imposing, even aristocratic, a figure he cut.

'Aristocratic indeed!' said Grundy, ordering us both a second brandy. 'Do you know that Stephenson is the son of an illiterate collier, and that he himself did not know his letters until he was eighteen years of age? So much for aristrocracy, my friend.'

'By God, he has a noble heart, then, to have overcome such impediments and attained such renown.'

'I doubt not that he has such an organ beating in his breast, but it is surely the union of intelligence and steady application that made his fame, and he is the very picture of today's self-made, self-improving man. Surely, it is revealing that his first locomotives are called not just *Locomotion* but *Active*, *Hope* and *Diligence*! Besides, a noble mind such as his has led him to a noble life, none of which has anything at all to do with his origins.'

From time to time, we encounter persons to whom we almost immediately confide the whole of our character, our hopes and dreams, our fears and anxieties – often despite our better judgement. Perhaps it was his unassuming manner, or perhaps it is because he, too, is the son of a minister, a yoke we are both seeking, each in his way, to cast off. In any event, I felt instantly at my ease with Grundy, although I am quite certain that the free-flowing brandy, for which he had insisted on paying, assisted in this operation. He is an unassuming, courteous, pleasant fellow, physically average in nearly all respects: in height (middling), colouring (neither swarthy nor fair) and features (pleasant but not truly handsome). An abundance of almost impossibly thick brown curls is his only distinguishing feature.

To the extent I can determine, however, he possesses a penetrating, practical mind – that of an engineer – which focuses on the concrete and seeks solutions to problems, in nearly all situations. His precision of thought and calm temperament together seem to give him the ability to place his finger calmly and adroitly on the essentials of a topic of discussion, while others of a more nervous constitution – such as I – might spin wildly about in circles of fruitless speculation and abstraction.

He speaks like a gentleman of the middle orders, without the haughty air that one sometimes hears from the upper classes or those who would pretend to them, or the roughness of the lower. He is connected, through his Unitarian ties, to the theologian James Martineau and his sister Harriet, the writer, and was even educated by the former for a time.

I told Grundy briefly about my family, from Papa's transformation from humble Irishman to Cambridge gentleman, about the deaths of Mama, Maria and Elizabeth, and, finally, about our nonetheless happy childhood of making plays and scribbling stories in the Parsonage. I confessed to him my fervent dream to be an artist or poet, and told him in the briefest terms about my failure as a painter in Bradford, my six months in Broughton (included: my early success as a tutor, my meeting with Coleridge, and the sanitised version of my 'amicable' dismissal by Mr Postlethwaite; excluded, at least for the present: Agnes Riley), my return to Haworth and my success at working on the railway.

Grundy listened carefully and, after a moment, asked, 'Are you happy, Brontë?'

I had not anticipated such a question, which I felt bordered on the impertinent, particularly from one I had just come to know. 'What do you mean by that? In my position here at Luddenden Foot?'

'Yes, I suppose that is what I mean. Are you content with doing this work while your heart lies elsewhere?'

I shifted uncomfortably in my chair. 'I don't really see that I have much choice, Grundy. It is work that has finally secured my independence from my father, and allows for significant advancement, and increasingly – as today – I can comfortably leave the dreary minutiae to my subordinates, and devote my time to other pursuits. It may appear to you that the station is but a rude wooden hut in the wilds of Yorkshire, and that I have no prospects and wretched pay, and no society congenial to my better tastes, but the reality is more complicated. I have nearly doubled my salary in less than six months, and see no reason why I cannot advance further in the company if I so desire. I can be in Sowerby Bridge in a matter of minutes, then up the hill to Halifax by omnibus or, for that matter, to Leeds or Manchester in under two hours. As for company, there are not only manufacturers and gentlemen farmers in the district with whom I converse quite readily; there is also a circle of artists and writers from Halifax and its environs that will begin meeting regularly in just a few days' time.'

Like the barrel of a hunter's gun, sweeping along with its prey through an autumn sky, Grundy had focused on the key words in my long reply to his simple – and yet at the same time not at all simple – question about my *happiness*.

'You don't have a *choice* you say? Well, it seems to me that you do, though perhaps you just don't care for the choices on offer.'

How much better adapted to this world are such fellows such as Francis Grundy! And how much clearer is the vision of those who do not yet know us, for they do not share the affection – or disdain – of our friends, which invariably distorts all attempts at candid assessment. I felt my back arch into a defensive posture, but I already liked Grundy too much for this to grow into a heated argument, so I simply said, 'Explain what you mean, my Unitarian friend,' for friends we were surely becoming.

Grundy smiled, clearly pleased with this familiarity, and leant forward on his elbows.

'Here are the choices I see: one, you may remain as you are, not terribly happy with your work, continuing to dabble in poetry without the means to consecrate yourself fully at its altar, but at least independent of means; two, you seek another position, though it is likely that anything else, with the possible exception of tutor in the house of a wealthy family, would be far more repugnant to you than the post you currently hold as station-master; three, you may quit the railway and return to Haworth once again to become utterly dependent upon your father, which will make you miserable, I would think, and cause you to despise yourself and annoy others; four, and last, you may quit the railway and Yorkshire altogether, striking out for America or the Antipodes to try your fortune or, closer to home, travel to Edinburgh or London or Paris. But such adventures require great courage – or recklessness – and a willingness to cast one's prior life, family and friends to the four winds, to turn one's back on one's entire world and begin entirely anew, just as your father did when he left Ireland. Unless, like him, you wish to become a clergyman. In fact,' he concluded, 'that might be just the thing, Brontë.'

The brandy had put me in that odd yet warmly comfortable state where I was as much observer as participant in this scene, both within and without, but Grundy's final addendum, about taking holy orders – which I see now had only been meant as a riposte to *my Unitarian friend* – caused me to laugh aloud.

'Alas, as for the Church, I have not one mental quality – except perhaps *hypocrisy* – which would make me cut a figure in its pulpits!'

We ordered a final drink and I grew more serious. 'You speak of *despising myself*; well, one thing that causes me to have such feelings already is that I know I shall never have the courage or strength of character that inspired my father to strike out across the Irish Sea and to brave the inhospitable, and surely humiliating, climate at Cambridge. Such an action is positively heroic in my mind, and so intimidating as to cause me to think I could never equal such a feat.'

Grundy sat only in tactful silence. Wishing to lighten the mood, and spurred on by the golden spirit coursing through my veins, I said, 'Did you not forget some additional paths my life might take?'

'Oh?' said he, sitting up with renewed seriousness. 'What would those be?'

'Why, surely, I could pitch myself headlong off a railway bridge, or lie down on the tracks in the Summit Tunnel, or, more simply, throw a noose about my neck and hang myself from the tallest available tree!'

'Certainly, that is a choice each of us has at all times. I was supposing that you were not so unhappy as all *that*, Brontë,' and he seemed not to know whether to smile or remain in great earnest. I quickly assured him that I had spoken in jest, as he drew his watch out of his pocket to verify the hour, for his train would be along shortly.

'But wait now, what of this?' said I, as we finished our brandy, Joe Leyland's own recurrent phantasm coming to mind: 'what if I should marry a wealthy woman and live happily ever after, with no greater activity required of me than to write poetry?'

'That,' said the practical Grundy, 'is only slightly less desperate than jumping off a railway bridge, old man, and could prove just as painful.'

Back at the station, we shook hands as he climbed aboard his railway carriage, and we promised to see each other soon.

VI.

Success on Two Fronts

June 6th, 1841 · Luddenden Foot

So much has happened in the span of just a few days that I know not where to begin! I had just begun to despair utterly of ever seeing my poems in print, and was a hair's breadth from abandoning any such literary attempts ever again, when the *Halifax Guardian*, on May 22nd – a date I shall never forget – announced that though it regretted the delay in publication of a new poem by Northangerland, it would, in fact, publish 'Heaven and Earth'!

To me it mattered not that this was a 'mere newspaper', for its editors show considerable discrimination in their taste and routinely make it clear that they would rather print no poetry at all than some of the doggerel that graces the pages of its competitors. In any event, the thought of seeing my work in print makes me giddy with anticipation. It matters little that the poem is a revision of something written years ago, for indeed, even the most varied works of our greatest poets so often seem to sprout from a single seed of inspiration, do they not?

Just a day later, Leyland, with mock solemnity, opened the first meeting of our informal literary society at the Lord Nelson in Luddenden. Among the dozen luminaries or so that had gathered that day were Dearden, Nicholson, Crossley and young Heaton, but also Francis Leyland, the perpetually excitable Frobisher, and even my old companion and confident from Haworth, John Brown himself. A long, monastic-looking table was flanked with benches, while at each end stood a large armchair. Leyland had placed himself at one extremity and me at the other.

'Before we formally inaugurate this most *informal* of societies, gentlemen, I wish to raise a glass to His Excellency, Sir Patrick Branwell Brontë, whose work is to be published soon in none other than the esteemed *Halifax Guardian*!' Joe's congratulations were both genuine and sarcastic: as he had long ago told me, and was oft fond of repeating: *It is quite possible to be, in a single phrase, both in earnest and in jest; the two are hardly mutually exclusive, little man!*

John Brown, whose wit – if not his learning – equals that of Leyland, added loudly, 'Surely Branwell failed t' mention 'is connection to *you*, Joe, for 'ad they known of it, your enemies at the *Guardian* would've banned any such publications 'til the Last Judgement!'

Joe laughed good-naturedly. 'Damn you, Brown, you're forever changing the subject. *Now* let us raise our glasses to Mr Brontë, who has at last placed his booted foot on the golden path to poetic glory!'

Despite my habitual timidity, and yes, even despite Leyland's teasing, I was happier than I had been for a very long time. As the applause subsided, Crossley said, 'What is the poem, Brontë? Do you have it with you, by any chance?'

I was prepared to say, out of sheer diffidence, 'No', and such a reply would indeed have been the truth. Leyland, however, knows me too well: 'Before Brontë replies modestly in the negative, I must reveal that not only has he committed the poets of old to memory, but also that he has learnt by heart the words of the present generation – including, quite naturally, himself, ha ha! So yes, Crossley, he has it with him,' tapping his forehead with his index finger, 'he has it right there.'

There were now vociferous calls for me to recite the poem, and so recite it I did, for I remember lines of poetry the way Spence recalls the numbers in a ledger. Our table grew hushed and expectant, as I began to speak from memory:

Of Earth beneath, a little space
Our eyes at once descry;
But Heaven above us meets our gaze
Like an infinity …

When I had finished, Leyland exclaimed, 'The Devil take you, lad, you are forever and ever, world without end, the son of the Reverend Brontë! Did you take this pious turn from sheer desperation to be published, or to please your good papa? Or did you steal it from those devout and upright sisters of yours?'

Once the general mirth had subsided somewhat, Leyland spoke again, for he was the self-appointed founder and chief of this learned tribe. 'Now, from the Brontean sublime to the profoundly ridiculous: I would like to propose a competition to all of the would-be bards and poetasters among us today.'

'Capital idea, Leyland! How I *do* relish a contest!' said Dearden, rubbing his hands excitedly.

'Yes, yes, Dearden, we know, becalm yourself,' replied Leyland. 'Now, where was I, before the Bard of Caldene so churlishly cut me off? Right then, the contest: like the sculptor wresting living beauty from lifeless clay, I propose that you take a most pedestrian, even maudlin image, and attempt to give it as much authentic poetic grandeur as possible.'

At this, Leyland produced an engraving, which he then circulated around the table. 'I suspect that nearly all of you recognise this as an engraving of that modern masterpiece, the celebrated Landseer's painting, *Old Shepherd's Chief Mourner*. The painter is an old friend of mine, you see' – here I believe Leyland applied a most liberal definition to the word friend, for he had met Landseer only once or twice, and was chiefly fascinated by the artist's relationship with the Duchess of Bedford, which was rumoured to be more than one of patronage, so much so that her youngest daughter Rachel was said to be his – 'yes, an old friend, and I mean the great man no disrespect. The painting is not only technically perfect; it is also brilliantly composed, created expressly to wring scalding tears from ageing widows, passionate weeping from pious spinsters, and wrenching sobs from hypocritical curates and beastly little children. Indeed, I think even rough mill workers and village whores would be inclined to shed a tear over this poignant scene of a grieving canine, his sweet head resting on his master's humble casket!'

Joe's train of thought was picking up steam, and there was no stopping him.

'You see, that devil Landseer knows which side his bread is buttered' – here he shot a glance down the table at me, as if to say, as he had on more than one occasion, 'the lucky bugger's got the Duchess of Bedford, he *forded her bed* long ago,' or 'is it his skill with the brush or with some *other* instrument?' or, after far too much to drink, quite simply, 'he's having it off with his patroness, by God: which do you suppose earns him *more*, that or his damnable animal paintings?', etc., but even Leyland knows better than to spread such gossip about the powerful abroad – 'it's all about animals,' he continued in one of his familiar veins, 'for this age is positively *mad* for the lower creation. It is as if, since good Victoria took the throne – God save her! – all human feeling, all passion, all joy and grief, desire and despair, had been driven out of human creation as *in poor taste* – for the only wish of our betters and those striving to be better – and what a century of bedeviled strivers this is! – wait, now where was I ...?'

I have found that two of the first effects of drink work in direct opposition to each other: on the one hand, in the speaker's mind, the connections between and amongst the topics of conversation are multiplied – or perhaps are merely rendered freshly visible – as if he were floating skyward in a Montgolfier balloon, like the one we watched travel over the moors as little children, and thus he can comprehend in a single glance the vast network of ideas resembling the rivers and canals, the highways and railways, all linked together in an ever-increasing web of signification.

On the other hand, this exalted state is, most unfortunately, accompanied by a precipitous loss of memory and a tendency for the enthusiasm of the moment to overwhelm the specifics of the argument itself, like the surge of a hurricane over the orderly streets of an otherwise placid coastal village. Or to return to the image of our aeronaut, he ascends so high that the routes, rivers and rails form a beautiful but abstract image, more striations and variegations of nature than signs of effective human communication.

In short, Joe had lost the thread, with no Ariadne available to help him find his way back.

After a brief pause during which there was much laughter at his expense, Joe quickly enough retraced his rhetorical steps and found where he had left off. 'Ah yes, human feelings are in very, very bad taste these days … what does Parry say in that jolly song about governesses?

Where 'tis hoped that the lady will try to conceal
Any fanciful feelings or flights she may feel.
For this gentleman's family's so very genteel,
    they're so very genteel!

'Yes, gentlemen, crush all genuine feelings; that's the way of this century, by God! Apparently, only beasts are permitted to receive or display affections. Does this not appear to you as truly absurd, that we drive out what is *most* human in us and yet praise it when it appears on the face of mere animals, like Landseer's dog? It calls to mind that passage of Holy Scripture about the demons and the swine, what is it Brontë?'

I, the parson's son, sighed and obliged, suspecting that Leyland could full well recall the scripture in question, even in his current state, and was only using this occasion to have a bit of fun at my expense. 'It's in Matthew, Mark and Luke. If I can recall Matthew's account, it goes something like this: "So the devils besought him, saying, If thou cast us out, suffer us to go away into the herd of swine. And he said unto them, Go. And when they were come out, they went into the herd of swine: and, behold, the whole herd of swine ran violently down a steep place into the sea, and perished in the waters."'

'Are all passions, then, *demonic*, and fit only for swine? Remember, the Jews – and the Mohammedans for that matter – revile pork, my friends.' Turning to the innkeeper, Joe shouted, 'Jem, any chance we might have a platter of cold pork? It would be *just* the thing to give us our passion back, by God!'

More laughter ensued as Jem duly brought forth our luncheon. Like many such a meeting that begins on Mount Olympus, it descended quickly into the River Lethe, for I can't recall much of anything specific that was said thereafter: there was much jocularity, and wordplay, and a great deal of drinking, and clapping of backs, until at last we all began to take our leave, shaking hands, the poets among us promising to work on the poem about Landseer's grieving dog, to be read at the next meeting. Sitting at the end of the table, against a wall, I was the last to rise. Brown and Leyland met me at the door, each of my bearish friends seizing one of my arms to prevent me from leaving, my feet comically moving in the air.

'Not so fast, little man, we have a surprise for you.'

'I don't know what mischief you have in mind, Joe, but I really must return to the station, for the afternoon is waning.'

My friends merely laughed, dismissing my concerns out of hand. 'Tut tut, Brontë,' said Joe, 'the station runs itself by now, you have already seen to that. And are you not the stationmaster? Come come, let's go upstairs for your treat.'

Either man was, on his own, capable of breaking me in half, so the union of the two made any idea of further resistance absurd. They marched me across the room and up the broad staircase, roughly pushing me into a bedchamber and closing the door behind me. 'You are not to leave this room for at least one hour, though you may take two,' shouted Brown, laughing. 'I certainly hope you rise to the occasion!'

As the door closed behind me I turned to find a woman sitting on the edge of a bed. She was surely older than I, but far from matronly, and piled on her head was flaming red hair, far redder even than my own, with girlish freckles on her face, arms and bosom, the last of which was uncovered in the old fashion, before creeping modesty had turned most women into tightly wrapped sweets, whose delicious charms were mostly to be guessed at, but never glimpsed. She had catlike green eyes, very pretty in their way, and when she smiled her lips stretched to cover her teeth, by which I guessed she was none too proud of them. After a moment of confusion, I realised that my friends had purchased me a whore, and I instinctively recoiled, bumping against the door.

'Now now,' came a voice from without, 'I am keeping watch, Brontë, so do not even think of escape!'

At last, the woman spoke. 'Is it yer firs' time, young one?'

'Heavens no,' said I indignantly. 'What I mean to say is that I have been with women, but never … uh … never …'

'Never wit' a *whore*?' said she matter-of-factly, in a pronounced Irish accent.

'Yes, I suppose that is what I meant, but I would never put it quite that way.'

She stood up and walked over to me, took my hand, and drew me to the edge of the bed, where we sat together. 'Ye mightas wail *put it t'at way*, 'cause I knows what I be and amn't ashamed to spake the trut'. Aye, t'ere's plenty o' ladies t'at sell 'emseln and don't see t'ey be every bit t'whore *I* be, so to me t'at's worse still, being a whore and not knowin' it, eh mister?'

I simply nodded. I had always resisted my friends' attempts to throw me together with prostitutes, of which even Haworth had a supply: it was not unusual to come upon them, either alone and waiting, or plying their trade against the squalid wall of a ginnel or in the high grasses growing between the stones of the churchyard. Once I had expressed great disgust after happening upon just such a scene occurring up against the walls of Haworth Church itself, at which John Brown had said, 'Ha ha, lad, at leas' they were *ou'side* the church! In mediaeval times, the great cathedrals, York Minster itself I'm certain, harboured all manner of commerce. There were no boxes or pews, and the people wandered round doin' their business, including *that* most essential of activities. Can you imagine, today, a dainty bishop deliverin' his homily w' people havin' it off in the back corner of the church, up against the wall? Nay, we're so civilised today! How far we've come, eh? No wonder the poor folk were constantly threatened with eternal damnation, so that men like me and Leyland were made to carve the façades with *Last Judgements* designed to terrify them – they deserved frightenin', the mucky animals!'

I also thought of the last time I had seen Maggie, in the Square Chapel, and how, had she permitted, I too would have *had it off with her*, as Brown would say, would have possessed her right there in a place of worship. Such a reform church had no high altar, but if it had, and it was the only place to fornicate, I would not have hesitated to do so.

All of this and more swirled like a maelstrom through my mind in the brief time it took to hear this woman's words.

'I understand,' I responded. 'But I have a rather different notion of love, I'm afraid, and so do not wish to waste your time, uh … Miss … Madame …'

'Just *Maeve* … it means "t'intoxicatin' one" in Irish, in't t'at foonny?'

'Yes, well, Maeve, I'm sure you understand what I mean.'

'Well, aye and nay. First off, t'em friends of your'n an't goin'ta let ya leave t'is room fer a good bit o' time. Second t'ing is, whilst y' may t'ink t'a' love is all about grand passions and pretty words and havin' your heart shot t'rough with an arrow or suchlike, I've yet t'a meet a man who did not, at least in one of da wee corners of his heart, simply wish to feel a woman's body against his, t' drown himself in her flesh t'e way some men drown t'emselves in drink. Do you never feel like doing t'at, mister?'

'I have always held such transactions to be degrading to both parties,' said I, although I felt the solid ground of my argument begin to crumble beneath me.

'Now hare me out, young mister; I was born in a poor quarter o' Dublin, and kin remember goin' t' bed hungry, an me Ma and Da' wit' nut'in' a-tall in t'eir bellies, and as soon as I could get 'way from t'ere I did, crossin' t'e sea to Liverpool, using me young body to pay me very passage. Liverpool's a big, brutish, mucky place wit' sailors from round t'world, and after a few years o' *t'at* special bit of Hell, I bolted, I did – hoofed it all t'way t' Halifax! You may t'ink folks is rough and tumble round here, but t'ey's as gentle as wee lambs when stacked up agin' t'em Liverpudlians, by Jaysus! And some of t'em sailors, 'specially when t'ey be flamin' drunk, would as soon knock ya o'er t'e head or break yer neck, as t'ey would see ya in t'e nip, or grab yer knobs an' fanny!'

'Still –'

'Still, nut'in',' said Maeve. 'Would I wish for ot'er choices for such a one as me? By Sweet Jaysus and the Vayrgin Mary I would, but t'is is all I've go',' and she stood up and waved her hand from head to foot.

She paused for a moment, and her enigmatic, tight-lipped smile and feline eyes – they were, indeed, intoxicating in their way – were enough to dispel the last of my equivocations.

'But never mind all t'a',' she continued, 't'e trut' is, as I say, t'at t'em friends of yers won't le' eit'er off us leave t'is room, or me have me wages, for a' leas' an hour or so.' Taking my spectacles off and setting them on a night table, she turned and bent to kiss me, rather sweetly in fact. Why I found this surprising, I don't know. Had I expected a tigress?

'An' I like you wail enough – you seem a gentleman an' a *gentle man* – so I'd rat'er airn me keep the usu'l way t'an keep blatherin'an' rabbitin' on,' adding with laugh, 'if they'd a-wanted a lecture or a homily they'd o' hired a perfessor or a priest, dancha t'ink?'

'But,' said I weakly, protesting once last time.

'But nuttin' … hush, young one,' said she. 'Joos' lie back and breathe deep … shhhh … aye, t'as it,' and she set expertly about her work. I abandoned all scruples, all resistance, perhaps because I was so desperate for a woman's touch, perhaps because the drink had just reached its maximal effect, or perhaps because I felt that nothing was to be lost and everything to be gained. At last, my mind was swept free of its old obstructions, and I breathed more easily; at last, then, did my body respond fully to her caresses, as we fucked not once but twice, and when Joe at long last knocked on the door two hours later, I was already stiffening again, wanting to fuck her a third time. I use the word intentionally and without shame, because this is what it is was – this and no more.

'Well, love, I reckon i's time fer me to frame off, but I'm sairtain we'll meet again, eh?' said Maeve, running her hand expertly from the underside of my chin to the tip of my now fully erect cock, which she squeezed: *Jaysus*, as she would say, did I want her again! But soon we were dressed and out the door, Joe handing her a few coins – I did not ask him how much, as if not knowing how much she had cost could somehow nullify the transactional nature of our encounter – and slapping me on the back, shouting, in high glee, 'Now that warmed me nicely – this calls for a drink, by God!' Of course, with Joe Leyland, *everything* calls for a drink: boredom or excitement, grief or joy, anticipation or celebration, victory or defeat. Maeve smiled knowingly at us both as she left the inn, and the two of us settled into our chairs at a smaller corner table, for John Brown's duties – or fear of his Mary – had already called him back to Haworth.

'I can tell by the ruddy complexion you display that such a romp was *just* what you wanted. Let me tell you, there is nothing wrong with a gentleman seeking such companionship from time to time. It will put you in a much, *much* better temper, and keep starvation from the door of such creatures as Maeve. We are winners all round, eh? Just think: if we were all as holy as the Reverend Brontë – sorry, little man, but he is always the first to spring to mind when it comes to paragons of virtue – Maeve and her sisterhood would be reduced to begging in the streets.'

'It is certainly true that I felt,' said I in earnest, 'as if a great weight had been lifted, and I hardly know how to explain it.'

'That,' said Joe, folding his hands and assuming a pious air, 'was no doubt your conscience sliding off into the sea, like the swine perishing in the waters of today's Gospel reading.'

Leyland's response was not what I was seeking, for already his mention of Papa had made my brow perspire, in a far less pleasurable sensation than it had upstairs. I bit my lip and looked out the window, wondering: had the Reverend Patrick Brontë ever resorted to this? There was no doubt that he was a man of passion, for he had fathered six children in seven years! Poor Mama! For those last years of her brief life, she was either pregnant or recovering from it. Father must have been waiting like a hungry animal for her to be just well enough to receive his advances.

And yet, *she*! surely she had equal his passion, if not more. And here duty was passion, and passion duty. Perhaps it was she who could not get enough – I blushed at such a thought directed at my long-dead mother – and I remembered her words in my dream: *my heart has always been more ready to attach itself to earth than to heaven*. If only a fraction of such a passion for the pleasures of this earth was passed down to her children, is it any wonder that – in this age in which, as Leyland said, strong feelings are held to be in *very bad taste* – Charlotte, myself, Emily and even little Anne could, if we did not take care to conceal ours, appear to be positively mad? Can there be any doubt that, finding little encouragement without, our precocious little band of mourners twisted its feelings inward, creating veritable empires of passion through our wild and boundless scribbling?

VII.

The Depths of the Human Heart

July 22nd, 1841 · Luddenden Foot

I have said little about my daily life, and so for the sake of my future self – a doddering old fool who will, most likely, have learnt absolutely *nothing* in the elapsed years – reading this some thirty or forty or fifty years hence, I will devote a few lines to my quotidian occupations.

The station has thus far taken the better part of my time and attention, but Spence continues to be invaluable and positively encourages me to take time away when I please. The problem, of course, is that I am always pleased to leave. It is not that I detest my work, or that it is particularly difficult, beyond the constant worry that something might go wrong and I be held responsible. How easy it was to be promoted when I applied myself as I did at Sowerby Bridge! Indeed, I do now see that a man of some breeding, who can read and write – and yes, work out figures – and who is willing to perform this drudgery cheerfully, whatever it may be, day in and day out, will almost surely succeed in the world. Indeed, in some respects, such success is almost laughably easy.

But what of those qualities required for steady advancement? Does the man of intellect have *those* in just as ample supply? Doubt is permitted here, for it is possible that much more important than the power of his mind is his ability to follow orders (i.e., to be *led*), and to be content or at least willing to tread the same ground day after day, like a mill horse eternally grinding grain. Despite Joe's half-serious insistence that I am the *master* of my station, I, too, must follow the strict orders of the railway or jeopardise my very position. Last, but surely not the least of necessary qualities, is the ability to maintain a calm temperament and untroubled brow in the face of anger or dismay, rather than answering it with similar wrath or exasperation or, as I am especially wont to do, fleeing the scene entirely to avoid such conflict.

In short, I neither love nor despise my employment, but in some ways feel that I am singularly unfit, by my very temperament, for such work. It occurs to me that I have succeeded thus far *by pretending to be someone I am not*. How many make their way through life in just this way? Or, to flip the coin, how many have found a vocation that corresponds point by point with their inner nature, so that the trials of their post are not aggravated by even more, and often much costlier, internal battles? For these last struggles sap my strength in far greater measure than anything that might occur at the station itself. Charlotte, I am quite sure, is currently at war with herself as well, as she seeks at once to maintain dominion over her charges and remain sufficiently compliant to her employers. I suspect she would willingly trade places with me.

Beyond the predictable rhythms of the station, I have come, on these warm summer days, to explore the surrounding hills and valleys, which have a diverse kind of beauty far preferable to the monotony of the moors above Haworth. Accompanying me on many of my rambles is one of Papa's fellow clergyman, the young, freshly ordained Reverend Sutcliffe Sowden, who is an avid walker and something of an amateur geologist. Happy are the hours that we have spent exploring, up hill and down dale, in this warm season, and few words pass between us: when we speak, it is of the glorious, varied landscapes, of our families, or, at times, of matters specific to religion. It is curious, is it not, how we can have such a diversity of friends, all of whom play a part in the warp and weft of the fabric of our lives? Sowden could not be more different from Leyland, and yet I esteem them both, each in his own manner.

I have also, through railway business, my rambles, and my occasional halt at the local public houses, come to know a number of the local merchants and manufacturers, good solid men of business, who nevertheless enjoy a puff and a stiffener, and who most of all love to laugh: James and John Titterington, manufacturers of worsted wool; George Thompson, a maltster and corn dealer; John Murgatroyd, a cloth manufacturer; and one George Richardson, who appears to dabble in just about everything.

Some, but not much, time remains for pursuits of the mind, and I frequently borrow books in Halifax, from Francis Leyland's shop in Cornmarket, or at the nearby Old Cock Inn, where there is a library of nearly 2,000 volumes and more than a dozen periodicals. I even mean to take the train to Manchester to buy some second-hand books, when time permits. There is little leisure for poetry, but I make the effort when I can. Joe's challenge to us all has, of course, prompted an effort that I would surely not otherwise have made. My poem is not really about Landseer's dog, but about my own yearnings and strivings, and about my own dead mother and sisters, and begins thus:

All that man chases through his whirl of years
All that his hope seeks, all his caution fears
Dazzle or drown those holy thoughts that cling
Round where the forms he loved lie slumbering …

Unlike Landseer's canine, I have sought to annihilate and bury my sorrows; have I not been right to do so? What is the alternative: to stretch myself over their grave in Haworth Church all my life, like a faithful dog?

On my trips to Halifax I have been tempted, on more than one occasion, to seek out Maeve, but have each time resisted, for there subsists in me a remnant of shame over our encounter, nourished by a youthful pride that chides, 'What, man, can you not possess a woman's affections without paying for them?' And yet, far more powerful than the craving for drink is my desire to be with a woman, and I know not how long I can persevere: I need only call to mind the release I felt in her arms, as I thrilled in the wickedness of the moment, as if I were one of the damned who writhe with full as much ecstasy as pain as the flames of passion consume them.

So I argue with myself each day. Indeed, just writing about the topic causes my heart to beat a bit faster, my brow to flush and my body to stiffen with desire. I readily confess to these pages that my desire is not for Maeve herself, but for what she does; any woman of similar – or superior – attractions who could as expertly perform what she does would be a perfectly suitable substitute. Perhaps there lies the true sinfulness of my desire? I can hardly say.

August 8th, 1841 · Luddenden Foot

My life increasingly assumes the dreary contours of routine, and my free moments are given more to earthly pleasures than poetic composition or contemplation of the divine. At our recent meeting in Halifax I did present, as did we all, the requested poem on Landseer's dog, and by secret vote I was the winner. Perhaps I might even try to publish it someday – who knows? Even these assemblies – with their predictable, if enjoyable, conversations descending quickly into foolish, drunken banter – are not a fixed part of my routine, which alternates from the station to the public house or inn, an occasional visit to one of the local manufacturers' houses for drinks or dinner, or rambles with Sowden.

On the day of my 'triumph' with the canine poem in Halifax, I at last surrendered to my desires and went to see Maeve, whom I paid to spend an entire evening with me. In addition to what one would expect me to do with such a woman, I found myself opening my heart to her, as a Papist would to his confessor. Was it because she, herself, was a Catholic? I surely doubt *that*. No, there was something comforting in her presence, although whether she even listened is hard to say; she might well have been as indifferent a recipient of my spiritual outpourings as she was of my bodily passions, but she nodded charitably and smiled or frowned at the appropriate moments. Late in the evening, as we lay, my head on her breast and our red hair nearly intertwined as one, I told her about the death of Mama, and of Maria and Elizabeth. Maeve then told me that she was, nearly to the day, the same age as Maria.

How can I describe what I felt next? Unexpectedly a great surge of grief broke over me, and I felt both that my heart was in my throat, suffocating me, and that my lungs and stomach were collapsing together into a searing ball of flames. I sobbed like an infant – great, wracking sobs that I thought would never end, as hot tears spilt out onto her pale, freckled breasts, which earlier I had watched sway above me as she brought me to the relief of a sweet instant of paradise.

Now, like a little child, I buried my head in her neck until, at length, as she calmly stroked my hair and whispered, 'Whist now', my weeping subsided. Within just a few moments, she worked what seems to me now a miracle of sorts, for soon the blubbering baby was transmuted back into the hungry man, and I was devouring her lips and breasts and thighs with my mouth, and before long was moving within her until I was cleansed, for the tide of grief that had surged over me moments earlier now flowed back out, as I arched my back and felt every last artery throb, each individual nerve tingle and explode with pleasure.

What did Maeve feel at this time? I confess that I know not; if, in her heart of hearts, she was dreadfully bored and weary from her work, she was far better at masking her true sentiments than I am in my own occupation at the station, for she, too, arched her back and tightened her legs around me with apparent enthusiasm. As I have said, is my indifference to her feelings, my carelessness and cold debauchery the *true* sin – if sin there be – rather than this act itself? At any rate, I have now determined that such a sin is so insignificant that I will make regular visits to her another part of my routine, for having tasted such relief I already thirst for it anew. The world tells us this is *wrong*, but I cannot fathom why, and do not wish to try. How can such pleasure, which has no victim, be a crime? How can such pleasure displease God, if loving and forgiving He truly be, and if He himself created it?

Fools believe that we are simple creatures, that we cannot hold two warring notions in our minds, or conflicting feelings in our breast, but is this not the very nature of *Man*? Are we merely wild beasts led only by instinct? Or automata possessing no feelings, simply carrying out our daily tasks as part of one colossal industrial machine? Are we angels whose every action is in accord with the will of our Creator and His commandments? Of course not. And how simply do we view one another, even our own friends and family, as if they were mere sketches in pen and ink! Truly, the depths of the human heart are unfathomable. Deep within Joe Leyland's comical, irascible, lascivious, debauched and inebriated heart lies also goodness and generosity, and a longing for all that is beautiful, while surely buried within my own chaste and demure sisters are three passionate beings who – blindly and unwittingly, perhaps – are yearning not just to *esteem*, but to *love*, to possess and be possessed, to worship and be worshiped, to become one flesh with another being, as I had just done with Maeve.

Is it any wonder, then, that I alternate between states that are blithe and gay and those that are downcast and sad, sometimes within the same few moments? That I can long for worldly success one day and yet also feel that such yearning is nothing but vain folly the next? That I continue to believe, on occasion – usually where drink has exhilarated me momentarily, it is true – that my great gifts will cause the name of *Brontë* to be remembered down through the ages, while the next I am certain that it will sink into oblivion as soon as the earth rains down on my coffin?

Is it a contradiction that I pursue the pleasures of the present hour with a fanatical zeal despite – or because of – the knowledge that in the blink of an eye my life will draw to a close, and yet I also seek the peace of that final, real rest of the tomb, praying that God – whatever shape He might take – will forgive me for my trespasses? That I have at once the blasphemous desire to supplant God Himself, and yet the annihilating, impious impulse to blot myself out of existence?

And yet, life – our life, my life, all of human life – takes place in that twilight region, those crossroads of contradictory passions and impulses, that swirling maelstrom of words, intentions and deeds, which men – the hypocrites! – sit in judgement upon, tallying as 'good' here and 'evil' there, but which only the Divine One can fully comprehend.

It was in this agitated and contradictory state of mind that I wrote a poem today, which ended thus:

When I look back on former life
I scarcely know what I have been
So swift the change from strife to strife

That passes o'er the wildering scene
I only feel that every power –
And thou hadst given much to me
Was spent upon the present hour
Was never turned My God to thee

That what I did to make me blest
Sooner or later changed to pain
That still I laughed at peace and rest
So neither must behold again

I do find some solace in my recent poetical victory, however. Although the entire 'contest' was something of a bad jest from first to last, it is encouraging that I can still sit and write, when I force myself, and quickly produce verse that is superior to that of published poets, some of whom are nearly twice my age. Surely I should not give up, for if I possess any gift in this world, that is it.

VIII.

A Wrestling Match

August 27th, 1841 · Luddenden Foot

Last night I behaved in a way I hope never to repeat.

I was again at the Lord Nelson, but this time in very different company. After a long hot day at the station, I invited Spence and Killiner to walk with me to Luddenden, where some of my less literary acquaintances were gathering for drinks.

Spence, as usual, declined, citing a need to be at home with his wife, who was ill. Killiner, whose only occupations in the world are railway porter during the first part of the day and prodigious tippler for the remainder, gladly accepted the rare invitation, and together we made the fifteen-minute stroll as afternoon lengthened into evening, and a fine, cooling breeze arose from the north. The bright green leaves of spring were fading into an array of deeper hues, and here and there even a precocious autumnal yellow, as if we needed reminding that such pleasant days were soon to be no more.

In Luddenden we found an illustrious company gathered around a table: George Thompson and John Titterington; Joseph Earnshaw, the local shopkeeper; and Archibald ('call me *Archie*', he insisted) Ingram, in town to visit his cousin, Mr Thompson. Oddly – or perhaps not, given their occupations – these men, all ten to fifteen years older than I, looked somewhat alike: sandy brown hair, ruddy complexion and respectable clothing stretched over prosperous bellies.

Here the conversation was decidedly different from Leyland's company of poets, for even when the latter are well in their cups, they retain a certain – albeit relative – level of decorum, and even the most lascivious remarks are made to impress with their wit, rather than offend with their coarseness. In short, we remain poets and gentlemen, no matter how roaring drunk.

Ah, but this crowd! I found a certain thrill in surrounding myself with such men, whose language was calculated to shock not only the parson's son but also the gentleman in me, although I decided to restrain my own language before my subordinate, Mr Killiner. It would be better for the stationmaster to stand out for his good manners and admirable restraint than for an ability to play the chameleon, bending my character to meet theirs. I confess that had the porter not been there, I might well have joined more lustily into their game, with the same sort of thrill of sinning that has come to characterise my weekly visits to Maeve.

It should be noted that these men are respectable members of society, and that they are not only capable of stringing together sentences of proper English, but can do so in such a way that their speech is entirely devoid of oaths and obscenities, sufficient to converse with all manner of gentle society, just like good Mr Postlethwaite, or for that matter even Mr Tyson at Sunny Bank, and of course my old friend John Brown. To a one – excepting Mr Killiner, that is, who may also be excluded from the above comments about their powers of conversation, although he is happy enough to drink, listen and laugh – they are also in regular attendance at church each Sunday, and all but one are married.

But it is here at the inn that they can show quite another side of themselves, and it is almost as though the effort of behaving like proper gentlemen and upstanding husbands and fathers has so exhausted them that they can only be restored to themselves by concentrating as much bawdiness and profanity, as much drinking and carousing, as possible into a few hours each week. Like a locomotive letting off steam, or a patient being bled, their very existence seems to depend on eliminating an excess that threatens to overwhelm them.

Is it any wonder, then, that their descent into a chaotic, indecorous and sometimes quarrelsome hubbub is rapid indeed! Thus it was that last night we were soon all hurtling downhill towards the basest, most indecent of conversations imaginable. For the briefest of moments, I wondered what the reaction of Papa and my sisters would be, and shuddered. My father would be deeply saddened; Charlotte shocked and outraged; Emily bored and thoroughly unimpressed; Anne dismayed but perhaps quietly resigned. Did they know that similar scenes had already been played out at the Black Bull, just a stone's throw from the Parsonage and mere steps from the church itself?

After two hours or so of such polite conversation, we were all pleasantly intoxicated. Titterington fairly shouted for silence, then proclaimed, 'There are some ladies upstairs for those who know what to do with them.'

Perhaps it was because I had just spent an evening with Maeve in Halifax, or perhaps – strange as it may seem – I wanted to be with *her* alone, as though even with a prostitute I must be monogamous; whatever the case, I consulted my watch and reached for my hat.

'I really must go, Titterington. Morning will come all too soon, I'm afraid, and Killiner and I will need to be at our posts long before the early train arrives at 8:00 o'clock.'

Killiner looked at me in surprise and, I thought, with a hint of dismay. 'Well,' added I, '*he* may certainly stay as long as he likes, for I am only his superior at the station, not here.'

Whether Titterington took my imminent departure as a reproach, or he simply did not wish anyone to miss the fun, he fairly shouted, as though half in jest, 'Now Brontë, what art thou, lad, a miss nancy? Surely thou art ready for a good *pull*, eh? Sod it all, lad, 'appen there's *one* upstairs t' please thee … 'ave a look … we'll even let thee go first, since thou art so bloody ready to depart.'

It was then that I realised what had most impelled me to flee: the thought that Maeve herself could be one of the women waiting upstairs. It was one thing to know, in the abstract, that she sold herself to other men; it was quite another to know that she would spread her legs for one or more of these fellows while I stood idly by, listening. Yet how foolishly absurd to think that somehow this would *sully* her! No, it really had nothing to do with her, and everything to do with me.

In any event, I rose to leave, putting on a brave face and attempting to laugh.

'Now see here, Titterington, I appreciate your kind offer, but I insist.'

This time it was Thompson who spoke up. 'Let 'im go, John. If 'e's too holy for us we can spare him any invitations in future, eh? It's that much more quim for the rest of us to swim in.'

After a few sniggers at this witticism, storm clouds seemed, nevertheless, to gather over our little assembly. At last, Killiner – it may be only to remain in his superior's good stead, I know not and care not, but was grateful nonetheless – also stood and said, 'Mr Brontë's right, I'm afraid, we really mus' be off now', and at that we made for the door. I had almost reached the threshold when I felt two strong arms reach round me from behind and lift me clear off, then slam me back down upon the floorboards. The handful of other patrons in the Lord Nelson looked round and stared, then quickly resumed their conversations, from either indifference or embarrassment.

Titterington knelt above me, laughing with demonic glee. My size had deceived him, however, and he could not know that I was an experienced wrestler and boxer; within seconds, it was I who knelt over him, his arms pinned to the floor and his stomach heaving like a beast at slaughter. The storm of laughter that had accompanied his ambush became a shower of comments: 'Oh ho! Look at Brontë go to it!' or 'It's the Lion and the Mouse!' or 'How are the mighty fallen in the midst of battle!' or 'Hell fire, wha' a brayin' li'l Branwell's givin' big John!', etc. John tried to free himself, but I was far stronger than he had expected, though I panted with the exertion, as ever. His last resort was total surrender, and then laughter, as his thick neck relaxed and his head dropped to the floor.

'All right, all right, I am vanquished! I am vanquished!' said he, as the assembly erupted into gleeful applause. 'Here Brontë, help a dozy bugger up, will you?'

I did as Titterington commanded and walked with him back to the table, shaking hands all around. Even Thompson, who had just moments ago seemed ready to provoke a further quarrel, softened and, finally, grinned, shaking my hand.

'And now, truly, I must ask your leave to depart, gentlemen,' said I, doffing my hat.

'Just a moment, Brontë,' said John. I wondered what he could possibly want *now*. 'Wait for me out in the road – I want a word with you.'

Whether he had decided to speak to the 'ladies' upstairs or wanted a word in private with the remainder of the gathering, I know not, but within two or three minutes he had joined me outside, where I waited alone, Killiner having made his way home – or perhaps to another public house, I know not.

'I shouldn't like to say this in front of those gentlemen,' he said, gesturing over his shoulder towards the Nelson and assuming the softer tones that he surely used with the local gentry, not to mention his wife. 'But permit me to express my apologies for that. I fear debauchery loves company as much as misery does, lad.'

'Well,' I responded, 'I shouldn't like to say *this* in front of them, but will tell you that I already see a certain lady in Halifax, and that is sufficient at present. I know I can hardly compel you to keep silent on the matter, but I'd appreciate it if you would try, old man. Beyond that, I'd really rather not talk about it.'

How marvellously strange that the human heart can harbour such a successive range of emotions, like the colours of the rainbow! For Titterington's beastly conduct melted away, replaced by a pathetic, almost childlike benevolence.

'Of course, of course,' said he, adding his own request. 'Though I can hardly keep *those* blockheads' – again gesturing towards the inn – 'from gleefully reporting it all over God's creation, I would appreciate it if you would avoid recounting our wrestling match to others.'

I assured him that, by all means, I would keep the matter to myself. We shook hands warmly on the bargain, and parted friends, each swearing allegiance to the other. Still, as for rolling on the filthy floor of a country inn, *I will have no more of it*. How much lower can a gentleman go?

IX.

Ambition

September 11th, 1841 · Luddenden Foot

How quickly the true troubles and cares of life can bring us back to earth! Poor Spence! His wife has, in fact, fallen quite ill, and with no one to care for the little boy – for he and Mrs Spence are from Leicestershire and have no family here – the poor man is quite beside himself. Even paying a servant girl to watch over the two whilst he earns his bread with the railway is too dear, and more than that, the devoted husband and father is no good to me here in such a state, for he does nothing but pace the floorboards and wring his hands. Yesterday I finally sent him off, fairly *commanding* him to care for wife and child, and not to return until she was either better or he had found a solution for caring for them that was suitable to him.

'But Mr Brontë,' said he, wiping his brow, for his anxiety combined with this warm September day to bathe him in perspiration, 'I know how you depend on me, especially for the account ledgers.'

'Come come,' said I, assuming an air of calm for his benefit, 'who do you think kept the books at Sowerby Bridge? Why, I did such a marvellous job there for Mr Duncan that I was quickly promoted to stationmaster here, have I not told you that? Think not for a moment upon it; only, tend to your missus and that lad of yours, and all will be well. Of course, you will need to find a solution within a few days, for no company will pay for a worker who does not perform his duties. That's something only a government sinecure – like being the poet laureate – can provide,' I concluded, trying to make him smile. But the poor fellow merely snatched his hat and coat and made his way up the hill towards his ailing wife.

It has been such a long time since I have done any of the work that I had so quickly shifted to Spence that I nearly took pleasure in sitting at my desk with the ledgers, and recalled for a brief moment the initial excitement and energy I had felt in my first days with railway. I knew, too, that surely this rudimentary bookkeeping was something I could resume doing for the brief span of time Spence required to tend to his young family.

Yet how different is this work from what I had pictured for myself in the past! Down the hill, soon arriving from Sowerby Bridge, the next train whistled merrily, and although it was the urgent signal of the present, it somehow seemed to represent the call of all of my ambitions – past, present and future. I thought of those summer afternoons long ago when I lay beneath a glorious sky, some noble page of poetry spread beneath me and luminous white clouds above, whilst sweet winds whispered through the trees, revealing the wondrous future fate intended for me! I recalled other hours spent wandering on the moors beneath an iron-grey sky, with nothing but lake and stream to break the stern monotony of withered heath and windy hill! My books and my rambles, my heedless fancy and boundless imagination suggested a world of wild wonders, bold adventures and divine scenes beyond the gloomy horizon. Even the moon was transformed, as I stood beside Papa'a door gazing through the window after a nightmare, transmuted into a magic vessel gliding towards unknown regions.

Why did this whistle bring such scenes to mind, scenes that time has left so long behind? Is it that old, poetic ambition that cannot be killed, rising once again like Polidori's vampire? For though I may try to crush it, or at least place it neatly into a trunk, like a child's toy, it will not let me rest, and calls out to me that *perhaps* it is not too late. As I sat amidst my work, I hastily began to scribble lines in my station notebook, which I recopy here:

Amid the world's wide din around
I hear from far a solemn sound
That says 'Remember Me!'

I looked out the window to see Killiner preparing for the train's arrival; a handful of people had appeared, either to welcome arriving passengers or board the train themselves. A particularly pretty young lady held a parasol above her head, against the warm late-summer sun, her golden ringlets swaying against her delicate neck and bouncing along her lovely shoulders as she chattered impetuously with her mama. I thought of Maggie, and Maeve, but most of all of my poor, forsaken, Agnes, and dipped my nib again into the inkwell, hurrying to complete one more stanza before the train's arrival. It whistled again, louder, as the locomotive laboured slowly uphill:

What was that sound? T'was not a voice
From ruby lips and sapphire eyes
Nor echoed back from sensual joys
Nor a forsaken fair one's sighs.

I rose and walked out to oversee the unloading and loading of goods and passengers, but as soon as Killiner signalled that he needed no further assistance, I returned to my poem. I looked at the lines above and felt they had been written hours or days or years, rather than just moments before, but I closed my eyes and concentrated myself to the utmost; as the train left the station with yet another whistle, I once again took up my pen:

I, when I heard it, sat amid
The bustle of a town-like room
'Neath skies, with smoke stain'd vapours hid,
By windows, made to show their gloom.
The desk that held my ledger book
Beneath the thundering rattle shook
Of engines passing by

The bustle of the approaching train
Was all I hoped to rouse the brain
Or startle apathy.

I paused, staring into the distance, fixed on nothing in particular, my eyes focused far beyond anything in my field of vision, as the engine's smoke dissolved into the shimmering azure vault above.

Soon quiet descended once again, though a steady westerly breeze carried one last whistle from the train as it laboured uphill to Hebden Bridge. I continued:

And yet as on the soft wind's swell …
And solemn as a funeral knell
I heard that soft voice known so well
Cry – 'Oh Remember me!'

I concluded the poem with remembrances of the dreams and wild imaginings of a childhood filled with books and rambles on the moors I have described above, which I wrestled at last into verse.

I suspect Leyland will read the poem and pass the following judgement, or something quite like it: 'You'll never get *that* published, young Faustus – there is nothing about the Almighty … haha! It's all about *you-you-you*. Besides, no one wants to read a poem with engines rattling through it, pouring smoke on the very windows through which they might wish to glimpse the Divine! And a *ledger book*? Bloody hell, man! Why not write a poem about privies? Ha ha!'

The simple truth is that I have made *Ambition* my god, and it is *Ambition*'s unrelenting voice that forever calls: 'Remember me!'

X.

A Religious Ramble

October 23rd, 1841 · Luddenden Foot

The trains come and go, one after the other, and with them the minutes, hours, days and weeks. Already more than a month has flown by, and I wonder what, if anything, I have accomplished. The *sensible* man would say, 'Why, you have performed your duties well, and each day in which you do so is further proof that you are capable of thriving in your post; such is the way to success in your chosen vocation.' But my ambitions are in a quite different sphere, and far from feeling that I am moving forward, I feel that I am marching in place. How appropriate that I am the *station*master, then, as life seems to pass me by!

These thoughts were on my mind when, a week or so ago, I took a day to ramble about these wild hills with the Reverend Sutcliffe Sowden, who has the living at Hebden Bridge. He may seem to those who do not know him to be a quiet, even timid gentleman – odd for a parson, for most of his tribe adore hearing the sound of their own voices – but once familiar, he warms considerably, and never fails to carry his weight in conversation. Perhaps, indeed, Sutcliffe is more scholar than preacher. He is a great lover of nature, especially geology, and when he has left behind city and town for Mother Earth he is quite transformed. In his presence, the contrast between our brief and insignificant lives and the ancient cliffs and hills is even more acute. As we climbed in the direction of Cragg Vale, my lungs were no match for his, which clearly expanded with delight as he fairly raced ahead of me. He waited for me on the old stone-flagged road, but then dashed up the hill to a large outcropping of rock, not unlike the one on which I had lain all those months ago, just after my arrival at Luddenden Foot.

Sowden leapt onto the rocks and gazed around in every direction, his arms outstretched as if to embrace the universe, or take flight into the vast cerulean sky above, which was punctuated by only a few white wisps of clouds.

'Is God's creation not glorious?' he shouted, his countenance beaming with delight. He sat and pulled his knees up to his chin and wrapped his arms around his legs, hugging them to his chest like a little child – just as I had done, although my view of the creator had been somewhat more ambivalent.

I drew up to him at last, panting and sweating from the effort. When I had caught my breath, I climbed onto the rock next to him. 'It is,' said I, still breathing hard. After a long pause, during which nothing passed between us, I added, 'Though he surely shows His face but rarely.'

Sowden turned to me not with a look of judgement, but of fraternal concern. 'Why, what do you mean, Brontë? He is in every living thing – in you and in me, but also in this rock here, in those moors beyond, in the cascading leaves all around us – even in those rooks circling high above us.'

'Do you mean to say,' said I, smiling and turning to face him directly, 'that you, the right Reverend Sutcliffe Sowden, of the Church of England, subscribe to the heresy of pantheism?'

'Not at all, not at all,' he said calmly. 'But I do believe in humility. Logically, the moment one accepts a position of humility – by that I mean not just that oneself does not and cannot know everything, but that Mankind and his various systems and religions do not and cannot know everything – for who are we to describe in detail a God we have never seen? – well, that is the moment one is liberated from the either/or arguments.'

'What do you mean?'

'Well, you call me – in jest, I am quite certain – a pantheist. I have been called worse things. But in all earnestness, if I am truly humble, and confess that all religions are but man's weak attempt to understand the omnipotence and infinitude of God, the old black-and-white arguments melt away.'

'Ha ha, I can see it now, Sowden! Standing before your homely little congregation, you announce: "See here, ladies and gentlemen, we cannot understand the omnipotence and infinitude of God, and so never mind all of those things we have said were *right* and *wrong*, including that nasty obligation that you be in church each Sunday, for who dares try to sound the depths of the mind of God, whose face we have never seen." Are you daft?'

'You misunderstand me, Brontë, and are creating contradictions where they need not appear. Why can we not say that man can never fully know God, for *He* is God after all, and we are but fallen sinners? Further, why can we not say that God reveals Himself over time, and that we believe that though our Christian tradition has taken shape over the centuries, it is our best understanding of how we are to worship and serve the Creator and his creation?'

'It still smells strongly of heresy to me,' said I. 'And I suspect that you hardly propound such views from the pulpit.'

Sowden coloured up a bit and laughed gently. 'You are right *there*. I'm afraid the good people of Hebden Bridge might be a bit confused. All I am telling *you* – man of intellect that you are – is that I see no contradiction between seeing God everywhere in his creation and yet worshiping him – as, after all, we are instructed by the Church – as its Creator, any more than I see science and religion as mortal enemies, as some would have them be. Each is a pathway to a larger truth, a truth that only God possesses. The rituals of the Church – which, I can confess to you, the son of a clergyman, constitute my least favourite duties – are the simple, imperfect tools we use to try to understand God, and to help our parishioners understand and serve Him, in our daily lives: no more or no less.'

I realised that our friendly 'dispute' could turn endlessly in circles, like the rooks above, but the day was too beautiful and the company too agreeable for that, and I admired my new friend for a breadth of mind and spirit – not to mention a genuine goodness – that far surpassed mine. To my mind, once one let go of the notion that one had access to the *Truth* – be he an Anglican, Presbyterian, Baptist, Congregationalist, Unitarian, Quaker, Wesleyan or any other of the band of Methodists, or for that matter a Papist, Jew or Mohammedan – anything was possible. So, I changed the subject – somewhat.

'What is clear is that we have but a brief moment on this earth, and I feel it slipping away from me before I have even begun to live. I cannot imagine a lifetime of work on the railway, and yet I have thus far succeeded. Is this merely the disillusion that all men face as they grow older?'

'Have you prayed about this?' he asked.

'I have,' I lied – for I have long since abandoned, if not God himself, then at least the childish idea that He is a divine telegraph operator at the far end of a mystical line stretching to heaven, and, still more, that He passes His time waiting for *my* message to come through. The truth is that I have meditated upon it, in an attitude very like prayer, and have dwelt upon it so often in these pages that my understandably exasperated future self – to whom I send my sincere apologies over the years – will likely by now already have cast this notebook into the fire in boredom or disgust.

There was a long pause, and we could hear only the wind lifting sweetly through the woods below, and the occasional cawing of the eternal rooks.

Sowden turned to me and said, 'Do you remember how God spoke to Elijah at Horeb? He came to the prophet in a *still small voice*. Perhaps, if you listen quietly, you will hear such a still small voice within yourself, telling you what you should do – perhaps, with enough prayer, that is how God will speak to you, for he speaks to us all in the ways we are most apt to receive him.'

Was it my own guilt about not praying that caused me to interpret this last phrase as a reproach? At any rate, he paused, scratching his chin thoughtfully. 'There is some truth to your assertion that a bit of reality – I prefer that word to *disillusion* – must in some manner accompany us into our adult lives and that we must clear away some of the illusions of our early youth, for if they were to remain with the same intensity, we would be eternally dissatisfied and perhaps go quite mad.'

Sowden's earnest counsel was honestly and kindly given, but I could not help teasing him for his choice of scripture. 'The *still small voice*, eh? Does that not come only after poor Elijah learns that "the Lord was not in the wind" and "the Lord was not in the earthquake" and "the Lord was not in the fire"? So much for finding God in all things! Even Holy Scripture denies *that*. It's right there in black and white, in the book of Kings.'

'Son of a clergyman!' growled my friend in mock anger as he leapt down from the rock, pronouncing it as if it were a far less polite oath. 'It's always a mistake to quote scripture to such a one as you.'

'And,' said I, delivering the *coup de grâce*, 'what does that voice say when finally it does speak?'

'What doest thou here, Elijah?' answered Sowden.

'Precisely. I suppose that means, at finish, that I am in constant communication with Jehovah, because it seems to be the only thing that still small voice ever says to me: *What are you doing here, Branwell?*'

Sowden had finally had enough of this conversation, particularly as I had turned his heartfelt concern into a jest, though he laughed gamely enough, shouting over his shoulder, 'You're hopeless, Brontë,' as he strode ahead of me, for our rambling was already drawing to a close, the shortening autumn days restricting our movements as they had not in summertime. We were silent, although he quietly gestured towards those natural phenomena that he deemed especially noteworthy as we crossed moorland, traversed woods and fields, and at last arrived in the small town of Hebden Bridge, where I had promised to accompany him.

As we walked along the Calder towards his modest parsonage, I looked at my friend's mild and earnest countenance, his firm and elastic tread along the riverbank, and thought of the general benevolence, even comfort, I always seemed to feel in his presence, which then led me to wonder again at the wide diversity of friendships a single man can have. How different was he from them all, whether Brown and Leyland, Grundy, or Titterington and his friends, and they from one another! If they were all shepherded into a room, we would quickly find, I am quite certain, that they would have little to nothing in common, except for me. I was the centre of that particular universe, but each of them, in turn, was his own sun, of which I remained a mere satellite, and so on. My head grew dizzy at the thought of such a web of human connections, which made the railways and telegraph lines sprouting and spreading throughout the kingdom seem a mere child's toy.

Meantime, Sowden had again grown serious. 'I do believe, Brontë, that the only unpardonable sin is despair, and I will pray that *that* is one that never afflicts you.'

I, however, retained a jocular mood, my favourite armour against such earnest talk. The very thought of anyone – even my thoughtful, intelligent, and yes, *holy*, friend – for if anyone merits that appellation it is he – *praying for me*, as though I were a lost cause, annoyed me seriously – so I continued to jest: 'Now now, Sowden, fear not. I really am not going to lie down in the Summit Tunnel and wait for the Manchester train to roll over me, or drown myself in the Calder, or the Rochedale Canal over yonder, for that matter – I pledge my word! It has not come to that, old man, nor will it ever! I shall board a ship to America or New Zealand, or even throw myself into fervent prayer in a monastery, if ever I feel the icy fingers of *true* despair upon my neck!'

Alas! True, creeping despair does pay me a visit, and far more often that I care to admit.

XI.

Two Wives

November 23rd, 1841 · Luddenden Foot

Ever since the celebrated wrestling incident at the Lord Nelson, I am become a great favourite of Titterington and his merry band, if only because the humourous memory of a small, bespectacled man of gentlemanly appearance and speech capable of pinning a mighty manufacturer to the floor is a novelty that never fails to produce a smile among them. That I am willing to drink right along with them has made me all the more sympathetic, as though I were conferring a gentlemanly status upon them by the very act. Whether it is because they are afraid to wrestle with me, or because Titterington has shared my confidences – I am no longer worried by them to partake in their libertinism, but generally grab my hat and bid them all a hearty adieu when the whoring begins.

Not that these fellows are incapable, as I have before noted, of behaving very much like gentlemen, and it is before their wives – for most are married – that they most diligently strive to conduct themselves in an upright fashion, and I have even had the pleasure of meeting *Mrs* John Titterington of late.

Although I had not wielded a brush in a very long time, I succumbed to her entreaties that I paint a portrait of the happy couple in oils. The fact of the matter is that she is a lovely woman in her early to mid-thirties, a real local beauty, all lovely shoulders and creamy white neck, perfect form and, to crown all, one of the most exquisite, irresistible little faces I have ever beheld. My first thought upon beholding her was, 'Good God in Heaven, Jim, what need have you for commerce with whores when you have this beneficent fairy adorning your hearth!' But surely only those who live *within* a marriage can truly know its hidden truths. We external observers are mere sailors upon the deck of a vessel, only guessing at the murky depths of the sea.

In any event, upon learning that I had once dabbled in portraiture, Mrs Titterington was insistent, even implacable: 'Oh John, we *must* have Mr Brontë paint our portrait in oils, we simply *must*!'

'Well, we cannot *make* him do so, can we?' said my friend, winking at me as if to say, I cannot even *wrestle* it out of him! 'What do you say, Brontë? I'll make it worth your while, eh?'

This is one woman, I quickly realised, looking at Mrs Titterington – fairly bouncing on her toes in anticipation, like a spoiled child – who is accustomed always to having her way, one of those creatures who is a pure delight as long as she encounters neither opposition nor indifference. To take up the maritime image once again, I, like mariners who, after a long and stormy voyage across the turbid Atlantic, reach at last the crystalline waters of the West Indies, suddenly had a penetrating glimpse directly into the heart of this particular instance of matrimonial felicity: my friend Titterington simply has a deep-rooted fear of ruffling his wife's humour, and so it goes without saying that she always gets her way. He is her slave, and her dominion will surely grind him to dust over the years. Is it any wonder that he seeks refuge in the company of his friends and, upon occasion, in the arms of a whore?

Whatever the case, painting the happy couple suited me just fine, for the thought of spending some time in the same room as my friend's beautiful wife – yes, he would be there too, but I had an excuse for gazing at her for several hours on end, since I knew his features far better than hers – and earning a few extra shillings, whilst rendering him service in the bargain, caused me to cast my better judgement to the wind. From all that I can tell, they are pleased with the result. If they are not, their manners have dictated otherwise, for they immediately paid me and thanked me heartily for the portrait, which already has pride of place above their roaring fire.

Did I too hastily abandon my painting career? I think not,

but it often occurs to me that a lack of focus and persistence is woven into the very fibre of my being; I only hope I can find that thing, or that person, or that occupation, to whom I can devote myself utterly, in a bond that will prove my salvation.

December 9th, 1841 · Luddenden Foot

Spence's wife has improved sufficiently so that he has returned to his work, but not so much as to relieve him of all cares. He seems, still, utterly distracted by the very thought of her demise, staring into the distance, pacing the floor and, sometimes, even sobbing quietly at his desk. I do my best to cheer the man, vainly hoping that levity will distract him from his gloom.

'But Sir,' said he yesterday, 'what if she *dies*? I have no one here to care for the lad, no family or friends, and how will I find a wife in these – but the Devil take me for running on so fast, as if she were already dead and buried. Oh, God,' said he, burying his head in his hands, 'I will not be able to bear it!'

'See here, Spence,' I said, 'Did you not say she was much improved? For surely you would not be *here*, at your desk, if she were in grave danger. I think you are seeing hobgoblins where none exist, lad. For just as surely as a train that has passed through the Summit Tunnel and down through Hebden Bridge can *only* be arriving here at Luddenden Foot, so your wife, having come out of great danger and improving, however slightly, each day, is on the road to full recovery!'

'Oh Mr Brontë, if only a person's health were as simple as that, but I hope and pray that you are right.' He sighed again, then returned, distractedly, to his ledgers.

I usually let the poor fellow leave the station early, for by day's end I simply cannot bear to watch him struggle to remain at his post, and when I do, he fairly flies out the door and up the hill to his home. Does this make me a compassionate fellow, an irresponsible stationmaster, or both?

XII.

The Messiah

New Year's Day, 1842 · Luddenden Foot

As I dip my pen in my inkwell, the clock has just chimed midnight, signalling the otherwise unremarkable arrival of *Anno Domini* 1842, unless a January snowstorm is somehow to be considered exceptional.

I wonder what the year will bring. I was unable to go to Haworth this Christmas, for Spence's wife has again taken a turn for the worse, and I thought it best to remain nearby. I would greatly have liked to see them all – yes, even Charlotte. She and Emily, it happens, are to leave England to study in Belgium, for the purpose, I am told, of becoming sufficiently learned, cultivated and polished so that they might open their own school. Charlotte is surely the driving force behind this new adventure, for Emily would happily remain reading, writing, walking the moors and peeling potatoes for the rest of her life. I cannot help but wonder whether this is merely an excuse for Charlotte to abandon her post at the Whites', where she has doubtless felt nothing but grinding injustice, although, most likely, she has been confronted only with the normal expectations of a governess. As she always says, she has always preferred acquiring knowledge to imparting it, and for that, I can hardly blame her – how similar we are in this way! How much more pleasant to imbibe at the font of knowledge than to lead horses there, especially those that do not wish to drink!

Charlotte gave her notice just before Christmas and has surely bullied Emily – for no one on this earth but *she* is capable of bullying Emily – into being her companion, for Papa would hardly permit her to study on the continent alone. He is to accompany them to Brussels next month. Aunt Branwell, meanwhile – sometimes stern but, in the end, ever-indulgent and loving aunt – has agreed to fund the whole enterprise, Charlotte no doubt bringing all of her powers of persuasion to bear, framing the entire thing as what is *most* needed to secure the girls' independence. I am curious to see what comes of this latest scheme. Should I envy them? I do, secretly, though Charlotte would laugh outright at the notion that a man, with so many occupations open to him, should ever envy a woman.

Anne, meanwhile, continues steadily along at Thorp Green. How curious that our baby sister seems to be the only Brontë child who has succeeded in making her way as a grown person. Does she lack the quality of almost permanent dissatisfaction that seems to afflict Charlotte and myself? Is this what fuels ambition, I wonder? Does Anne have a reservoir of patience that allows her to suffer the slings and arrows of outrageous employers and their spoilt children, or has she simply found a superior situation with a superior family, the Robinsons of Thorp Green? I should like to see her at her work, although I confess that the reported beauty of the eldest daughter Lydia intrigues me just as much. Perhaps someday I will pay her a visit, despite the distance.

Winter has truly come in earnest and the snow blows sideways as I write these lines, the gale whistling through the eaves and insinuating itself into the cracks in the casement. I have before me a bottle of brandy, with which I am celebrating the arrival of the New Year. The snow provided a welcome excuse from other engagements, for surely I would otherwise have been swept up into one of Leyland's drinking bouts, if not an actual *fête*. I saw him recently enough, however, at the Choral Society's annual Christmas performance of Handel's Messiah. The Reverend Sowden was too busy with parish matters to accompany me – for I would rather someone of his nature, at once truly pious but lacking all pretence and hypocrisy, at such a performance of sacred music – so I invited Joe, who in turn brought along his brother Frank. The three of us sat near the front, where the event's organiser – our old friend Frobisher, of course – paced back and forth nervously, dancing on the tips of his toes, glancing down constantly at his gold watch and gesticulating for everyone to be in place.

Soon the overture had begun, and the single tenor sang the librettist's first words, taken from Isaiah:

> Comfort ye, comfort ye my people, saith your God.
> Speak ye comfortably to Jerusalem, and cry unto her,
> that her warfare is accomplished, and her inquity
> pardoned. The voice of him that crieth in the wilderness:
> prepare ye the way of the Lord; make straight in
> the desert a highway for our God.

What was it in these words, coupled with Handel's music, which immediately brought tears to my eyes? I had no wish to weep in the presence of Leyland, for there would be no end to his ridicule. Was this the *real* reason I had wanted to come with Sowden? Not so much for the presence of his company, but for the absence of Leyland's derision? Indeed, of late, I have mostly preferred the extremes of the Reverend Sutcliffe Sowden on the one hand, and the Titteringtons and their wild and rollicking band on the other. Was this an echo of my preference – like Charlotte's – in work, for either the purely cerebral or mindless drudgery? Whatever the case, I have of late found myself avoiding Leyland, and even Grundy for that matter.

In the present moment, this meant that I could not give free rein to my emotions, and I did my best to contain them. I remained calm for almost half an hour, but when the chorus sang, in that lovely passage –

> For unto us a child is born, unto us a son is given,
> and the government shall be upon His shoulder;
> and His name shall be called Wonderful, Counsellor,
> the mighty God, the Everlasting Father, the Prince of Peace.

– I felt again my heart rising to my throat and tears welling up; feigning a cough I made my way to the back of the assembly room, where, in a dark corner, I allowed the tears to stream down my face, though wiping them furiously, knowing that soon I would need to return to my seat. I made sure to cough again as I sat down, and apologise to those around me. I held fast until the Hallelujah Chorus – '*He shall reign for ever and ever*' – and was again overcome, again retreating to the back of the room, this time sobbing uncontrollably.

I finally returned to my seat as the soprano sang 'though worms destroy this body, yet in my flesh shall I see God.' *Why* was this affecting me so? I had always felt a swell of emotion, even as a small child, in the presence of sacred music, but this time I was overwhelmed, suffocating with both a kind of nameless grief and yet somehow, at the same time, buoyed by a vague joy of belief in something greater than myself. As, at last, the oratorio ended, I listened attentively to the libretto, more closely than ever I had attended to even scripture itself.

A single voice sang: '*Then shall be brought to pass the saying that is written: "Death is swallowed up in victory"*,' followed by a duet, which sang: '*O death, where is thy sting? O grave, where is thy victory?*' Then, at last, following a bit of theological explanation, come the final words of the chorus, which struck me with the force of a blow in a boxing match, for I felt I *truly* understood – in my flesh and bones, in the depths of my heart – for the first time in my life, the central meaning of Christ's sacrifice:

> Worthy is the Lamb that was slain, and hath redeemed
> us to God by His blood … Blessing and honour, glory
> and power, be unto Him that sitteth upon the throne,
> and unto the Lamb, for ever and ever. Amen.

Not seventy times seven, but seventy *thousand* times seven had I heard this message in my life, and yet here it was as fresh and new as if I were a naked savage emerged from the jungle wilderness, hearing the Gospel for the first time.

The scapegoat, that sacrificial lamb that had existed from earliest times, was here elevated to a universal. Feeling more like a black sheep myself, I was not sure what any of this had to do with *me*, but at last I understood one thing: just as the ancients had slain virgins to propitiate to Gods, and the Jews had sacrificed a lamb to purify themselves before Jehovah, so the Christian God himself offered up his only son as a sacrifice for our sins. He was bringing a cycle of violence to an end.

Man, meanwhile, was largely a spectator in this drama. His task, it seems, was to sin and then to ask for forgiveness, and of course to *believe*. I had always thought that 'whosover liveth and believeth in me shall never die' meant simply believing in the Christian version of the Almighty, but no, I at last saw that it means believing in the *actions of the messiah*, in the sacrificial drama at the centre of the faith. For after all, one can believe in the existence of any number of things; I can truly believe in goodness and yet reject it; I can believe in the ocean but never sail upon it; I can believe it best to renounce a literary career, and yet be unable to do so.

These thoughts revolved through my mind as the final notes sounded, followed by sustained applause. Leyland was clearly impressed by the performance in quite a different way, nearly shouting, 'Did you hear that tenor take liberties with the music, as though he himself were the composer? And the drummer was nearly a beat behind the orchestra throughout! Worst of all, the Hallelujah Chorus was murdered outright! See if I don't have a grand time teasing old Frobisher!' he fairly crowed with delight.

'Really now, Joe,' said I, 'Poor Frobisher is already as tightly strung as one of those violins there; do you really think that's kind?'

'Oh no, of course it's not *kind*. I mean to have some fun, though, and I *will* have it. What's the matter, Brontë, did the music make you tender and kind yourself? Are you ready to trade your full-time post as stationmaster and your part-time employments of poet, drinker, smoker, whoremonger, gossip, scoundrel and accomplice to Joe Leyland's mischief-making for a collar in the Church of England, just like dear Papa?'

Leyland had pronounced *Papa* in an infantile manner, to make certain that I grasped the full weight of his insult. Sometimes I wonder why I am friends with such a man as this. And yet, who has not been drawn to a friend by the warmth and brilliance of his good qualities, which can often overpower and cast into the shadows their corresponding defects? Eager to steer the conversation away from how overcome I had been, I refused to be offended, instead laughing along with him and assuring him, as I had Grundy, that the only quality I had that would allow me to take to the pulpit was hypocrisy.

'Say,' said I, wishing to direct the conversation even further away from myself, 'There's the man himself,' and I nodded over Joe's shoulder at Frobisher, who was mopping his brow with a handkerchief and again pacing to and fro as the orchestra packed up its instruments. Joe took the bait and left me alone, for his efforts to disconcert Frobisher would surely pay off far more readily than his attempts to annoy me.

'There he is,' boomed Joe, 'the impresario himself! Surely you will allow your old friend to buy you a drink after that impressive performance, eh Frobisher?'

Soon the four of us were sitting around a table at the Old Cock, tumblers of whisky in our hands.

'Now,' said Joe, raising his glass, 'Here's to the most interesting performance of *The Messiah* I've yet heard.'

As if on cue, Frobisher knitted his brows. 'What do you mean, interesting?'

'Well surely you know, John, that *interesting* is a polite word employed by men of refinement, like me, to indicate that something is amiss … ha ha.'

'I don't follow you, Leyland.'

'Come now, man, *yes* you do – I'm sure you do! Did you not hear that tenor's libretto! And the drums were at least a beat behind … and the dreadful chorus, mangling the most important bits of the oratorio, you know, the bits even the least cultivated in the audience have come to hear? At least the tenor could carry a tune!'

I thought it might now be Frobisher's turn to cry. He took to heart everything he touched, even in the most indirect manner, as if he were responsible for anything musical that transpired in all of greater Halifax and beyond. He looked like a child whose sugarplum has just fallen in the dust, or whose favourite toy has been crushed beneath the wheel of a passing waggon. Despite my affection for Leyland, I have always detested such instances, when the strong prey upon the weak, and so tried to intervene.

'I have to confess, Frobisher, that I heard no such thing. I let the music wash over me in the most general sort of way, but was entranced as never before by the words – or more specifically, how certain phrases are repeated as the music builds towards its climax.'

Joe glared at me, and so I pacified him through blasphemy. 'And I'd never really appreciated how strange, almost comical, it is that a merciful God offers his only begotten son to be sacrificed for our sins – and why? Because God – yes, yes, the *same* God – is a wrathful, vengeful God who will otherwise send us to Hell. Oh, and by the way, he not only has these two very different sides to his character, he can somehow remain the father and yet become the very son he has offered up as a sacrifice! I'm sure the Holy Spirit is, dovelike, soaring above it all as well. No mean trick, eh?'

Francis, who had spoken but a word or two all evening, said in dry, almost priestly tones, but with just the slightest glint of that familiar Leylandesque twinkle in his eyes: 'That's called the Holy Trinity, Branwell. Has the Reverend Brontë never mentioned it to you?'

My words and those of his brother were sufficient to cheer Joe considerably, as he laughed and slapped Frobisher roughly on the back. 'See here, John, you know I only like to tease you. I meant no harm.' Here he paused, but was unable to help himself. 'But you *must* admit that the chorus was a disaster.'

Frobisher did his best to defend the singers, but a truce was quickly reached by his simple admission that *yes*, they could have used a bit more time to rehearse, and that last year's performance had been far superior. In this way, he could both ease his conscience and avoid calling Leyland a liar. After another whisky or two, we all parted friends.

Outside the snow continues to swirl, tracing lacy patterns on the upper panes and building creeping drifts on the lower reaches of my windows. What will the Year of Our Lord 1842 bring? Will I again be seated here, thinking the same thoughts, a year from now? Will I be no closer to my dreams of childhood, and yet no more able to renounce them than an opium eater can abandon his daily tincture?

XIII.

Quarrel and Reconciliation with Grundy

January 20th, 1842 · Luddenden Foot

I have fallen out with Grundy, but have already set things to right – at least I think so. A few nights ago, on a snowy afternoon, I sat by a roaring fire, drinking with Titterington and company at the Lord Nelson, when none other than Mr Francis Grundy, railway engineer, appeared at my elbow. We were already well into our cups, and I extended my hand heartily, truly glad to see him. After introductions all around and a hearty invitation from Jim Titterington to join us, Grundy said, a look of real concern written on his face, 'May I have a word, Brontë?'

I excused myself and we crossed the room, sitting at a small vacant table, from which I gestured for more to drink.

'Are you all right, Grundy?'

'I am quite all right; it is you who concern me,' he replied, with what struck me as an air of superiority, even sanctimony. I began to feel the blood rise to my face but remained calm.

'And *what*, pray, concerns you so, my friend?'

'Well, three times this month I have asked if you should like to meet for dinner, or for drinks, and three times you have refused, using your Mr Spence's troubles as an excuse. And yet, I happened to be on my way through Luddenden Foot this afternoon and stopped at the station to shake your hand, finding you gone but the supposedly unfortunate Spence sitting tranquilly over his ledgers! He directed me here.'

'Spence's wife has improved again somewhat, although her health is still delicate. It is one thing to walk the fifteen minutes to Luddenden village, and quite another to make the trip to Halifax and back,' I snapped. Was Grundy truly concerned about me, or did he envy my local friendships? It was hard to tell. He spoke quietly, soberly.

'See here, Branwell' – his use of my Christian name serving as a reminder of our intimacy – 'you know that I am quite willing to visit you at your convenience. But my feelings aside, I fear that you are taking a turn for the worse, for these men' – here he gestured towards Titterington ever so slightly with his forehead – 'these men are not congenial to your superior tastes, but are vulgar, hard-headed, half-educated, manufacturers. What could you possibly have to discuss with *them*? I fear for your mind – and your spirit – in such company, truly I do.'

Now I was truly upset, insulted on my own account, of course, but also wounded for my friends – for they *were* friends, and I was certain that they would do anything for me. I was not so sure about Grundy, or Leyland, for that matter.

'I suppose,' I retorted in an ill-humoured tone – for the brandy that had so recently been an amusing ambrosia was now turned to wormwood – 'that sitting with *you*, Grundy, and hearing about your fascinating connections with the great Unitarian intellects, your lessons with Mr Martineau and intimate acquaintance with his even more famous sister, etc., etc., is a worthier pursuit? And lest you forget, my dear sir, the last time you and I were together you nearly fell into the Calder, you'd had such a skinful! If I remember correctly, I fairly dragged you to your quarters in Halifax and tucked you into your little crib, before stumbling back up here to Brearley Hall.'

Grundy's face revealed shock and dismay, which quickly settled into a tightly controlled anger. He pushed his glass of brandy across the table to me, saying, 'Here, Brontë, I think you need this more than I do.' He stood, paid for our drinks, and strode directly out of the inn without another word.

I was furious with him, and even more with myself. How complicated and varied the interpretations of this small event! Had I been avoiding Grundy, and was my mind sinking irremediably into a grovelling carelessness, a permanent depravity, a determination to see how far mind can carry body without both being chucked into hell? I had been unfair to him, true; but had he not also been unfair to me? Spence's wife really had taken another turn for the worse, but then had just seemed to rally, two days later.

How many of our actions stand on this knife's edge? We may think that we are acting in the interests of others when in fact we are shaping arguments for our own benefit. In the happiest of circumstances, we find a world receptive to our deepest desires, and can make that which is purely selfish seem altruistic, like Charlotte's scheme to study in Brussels, which she has so cleverly framed as the last bit of polish needed for her and Emily to open their school.

In any event, I felt that Grundy's concern was, if not misplaced, at least exaggerated. There was enough truth in it, though, that I felt a pang of gratitude to him as my ire began to recede and I joined my friends for a last round of drinks, after which they began their whoring and I made my way to my quarters and a restless sleep, despite the considerable quantity of brandy I had drunk and the snowy silence that enshrouded Brearley Hall.

I awoke more than once, and each time I thought of Grundy: to have him question my *mind* and my *spirit* was what had wounded me most deeply – or should I say, what cut closest to the bone? That my bodily conduct is often cause for reproach I will freely confess, but for my friend to think that my *thought* – which I have always believed would be my salvation – was in danger of decay and extinction was too great an insult.

This is not the first time that my life has come to resemble something that I wrote, in innocence, long ago. How strange it is, that writing should precede experience, as if a biblical prophecy! Should it not be the reverse? Should one's writing not draw on the experiences of one's life? Nevertheless, the dispute with Grundy recalled to me a stanza that I wrote many years since, its lines still inscribed, *verbatim*, in the very mind he believed was in such peril.

I arrived at the station the next morning before everyone else, my senses sharpened as they sometimes are following a night of heavy drinking, the freezing walk through the newly fallen snow more bracing than the strongest dose of coffee. I sat down directly and copied the stanza on a fresh sheet of railway stationery, to make the point to Grundy that I was at my post:

The man who will not know another –
        Whose heart could never sympathise –
Who loves not comrade, friend, or Brother,
        Unhonoured lives – unnoticed dies!
His frozen eye, his bloodless heart,
        Nature, repugnant, bids depart!

Had I somehow, mysteriously, known long ago that I would need these verses? Was this pure chance? Or a third option: was there – as Grundy himself seemed to hint – a deep flaw within my heart and mind that inspired these childish verses but has only now made itself manifest in my life? This last possibility was inadmissible, and I quickly crushed it, dipped my pen into its well, and continued writing, this time new verses to complement the old:

Oh Grundy! born to nobler aim,
Be thine the task to shun such shame;
And, henceforth, never think that he
Who gives his hand in courtesy
To one who kindly smiles to him,
His gentle birth or name can dim.
However mean a man may be,
Know – man is man as well as thee.

I sat, my breast full of the oddest assortment of emotions: pleased with these verses, annoyed with my conduct of the night before, still angry with Grundy, and yet desperately wanting his friendship.

A train announced its arrival from Sowerby Bridge, and I blew on the wet ink and locked the sheet away, only returning to it when the train had continued towards Hebden Bridge:

However high thy gentle line,
Know, He who writes can rank with thine.
And, though his frame be worn and dead,
Some light still glitters round his head:
And though his tottering limbs seem old
His heart and blood are not yet cold.

I paused, guilty of the sin of arrogance, I fear, for I thought: practical Grundy is hardly a literary genius, so if the first lines were not sarcastic enough, these ought to do! I suppose that hitting my friend, the practical railway engineer, over the head with a pickaxe ought to do the trick.

I was still angry, I realised: how dare he impugn my mind – regardless of the company I keep!

Oh Grundy! shun his evil ways,
His restless nights, his troubled days,
But never slight his mind, which flies
Instinct with noble sympathies,
Afar from spleen and treachery,
To thought, to kindness, and to Thee!

P-B-Brontë

My closing words were genuinely felt, thought I, as I posted the poem to Halifax. If I had avoided Grundy, it was not because I did not esteem him, or had done so consciously, but rather for some indescribable reason that I, myself, did not wholly understand; and Spence's wife – who really had been very ill – provided a convenient alibi. I had, in truth, been glad to see Grundy that night, until he had expressed such earnest concern. Was it possible, finally, that what ultimately lay at the root of my wrath was that I shared his concerns?

Three days passed, then four, then five – still no word from Grundy. By this time my doubts had turned to regret, and subsequently from regret to fear, fear of having lost a true friend. As soon as I was able, I took an early train to Sowerby Bridge, and an omnibus to Halifax, where I proceeded directly to Grundy's rooms, which he still shared with Stephenson's nephew. This latter gentleman had clearly just risen, for he wore only a dressing gown and a puzzled, sleepy look as he opened the outer door. I introduced myself and was soon shown into a rather slovenly bedroom, where Grundy slept curled up like an infant, his back to the door, snoring loudly. I decided to make light of the entire matter, in hopes that he would too, and so shook his shoulder with a playful roughness.

'Hello there, Lord Grundy, awake! 'T'is the arch-sinner Brontë, come to beg your forgiveness and offer an invitation to break your fast!'

Grundy rolled over, his eyes squinting from beneath his thick mop of curls. 'I should tell you to go straight to Hell, Brontë, after your shabby treatment of me last week.'

It strikes me now that I was playing a new role, that of jovial, coaxing Joe Leyland. 'Come come, Grundy, I was not in my right mind, and perhaps – just perhaps – you struck a nerve. Perhaps I myself was beginning to wonder whether I should restore a bit of equilibrium to my life. But you should know that – and I say this in the cold, sober light of day – Titterington and his fellow manufacturers are true friends, in their way, and I do believe that if I were ever in trouble they'd be the first I'd call upon for assistance. Do you not know such men, whose rough-hewn exteriors conceal hearts of gold?'

As I recount these matters, I see that it was this apology – wrapped though it was in excuses and admonitions – that finally won Grundy over. He sat up, pulling his knees up to his chin, and said, 'I accept your apology, Brontë.'

I extended my hand, which he shook warmly, smiling at last.

'But what of my poem?' I asked. 'It was meant in earnest.'

'It's not bad for an impromptu, but do you not think friends should speak face to face of their differences, rather than seek reconciliation through poems sent by penny post? Sometimes I think that recent innovation brings out the worst in people. Besides,' he added, darkening somewhat, 'it did not escape me that your poem at once meekly begs forgiveness and yet quite forcefully insults me further! Or did you think I was too dim to grasp your sarcasm?'

I saw that Grundy was right on all counts, and with his usual straightforward manner had not been afraid to upbraid me gently on the poem, despite our reconciliation. How could I remain angry with such an honest and faithful fellow? Only the best of friends will tell us the truth, especially when it is as unpleasant and as unflattering as this. It seemed Grundy would rather take a chance that I would lapse back into moroseness or even anger – indeed, would rather fall out with me – than frame a deliberate lie.

Near his lodgings, hard by Cow Green, stands the King's Head, known for the copious breakfasts that it serves the farmers who bring their livestock to the cattle market. We ordered our meal and settled in with two steaming mugs of coffee.

'I know,' said Grundy, this time mischievously, for now all truly was forgiven, 'that you disparage my talking of the *Martineaus* –'

'I said I was sorry, Grundy …'

'– I know, I know,' Grundy smiled, 'I'm just repaying your kindness a bit. Now, you've made it clear you are sick unto death of the name *Martineau*, but what if I were willing to provide a written introduction for you and your poems – which, by the bye, are really quite good when they do not have a petulant sting in their tail for those unfortunate enough to call you friend.'

'I've nearly given up being published by anything or anyone but the humble *Halifax Guardian*, which will hardly bring me wealth and fame,' I sighed. I reminded Grundy of my innumerable letters to the *Blackwood's* and of my unanswered letters to Wordsworth and others, and of the day that I had spent with Hartley Coleridge, which now seemed a lifetime away.

'In short, I will take all the assistance I can get, my dear sir, and I promise that no more shall I mock the hallowed names of Grundy or Martineau, I swear it!' Grundy laughed as I added, 'Though I cannot promise to be so respectful towards your heretical Unitarian sect in general.'

He, for his part, made the same promise, vowing to spare all Brontës in future, but reserving the right to criticise the Church of England, which in his view was no better than a pale imitation of the Papists in *la Città eterna*, without any of its peculiar benefits.

After breakfast, we shook hands and parted, now better friends than ever.

XIV.

Debauchery and Dismissal

February 25th, 1842 · Luddenden Foot

Although there is a minute more of light with each passing day, how dark it still remains, and how deeply I feel buried in winter! Yet another snowstorm has come and gone, and like life itself, it begins with beauty and wonder, settles into a cold and hard uniformity and then, at last, slowly melts away. I have not much of moment to report, for my days are a monotonous – if pleasant enough – cycle of work and play. By play I mean seeing my various friends – mostly Grundy, Leyland, Sowden and Titterington – and Maeve, who continues to tutor me in the amorous arts and sciences.

A week ago, I expressed surprise at one of the positions that she had placed us in, and she merely laughed and said, 'Listen to me, young one, happen such knowledge will be more useful t'an t'at book-layrnin' o' yours, I'd place a wager on't.'

That the prostitute should be instructing her customer concerning how they should proceed might seem odd, but she is always careful to say things such as, 'We kin do whate'er pleases ye, ye know … I jus' t'ought ye might like to try somet'in' *new*, ye know, to see how't *feels*.' Although each manner has its own pleasures, they *all* feel indescribably good, especially that flash of ecstasy when mounting lust explodes climactically, and then settles into an all-embracing calm, like a ship struck by lightning, which then quietly, gracefully sinks to the bottom of the sea.

My work gives me little trouble, but even less satisfaction. I valiantly struggle to keep up with – which in my case simply means to give the slightest fig about – the ledgers during Spence's absences, which he claims will now become less frequent. Yesterday, still somewhat agitated, he walked over to where I sat and stood before me, arms crossed.

'Mr Brontë, I'd like to thank you for your generosity where I'm concerned. I know I cannot continue in this way: missing work or, when I am here, working with a mind so distracted that t'is almost worse than if I weren't here at all. I remember the joy you evinced almost a year ago upon discovery of my enthusiasm for figures, and I feel that I've especially failed you in that regard, for to keep the ledgers as they must be requires a concentration I simply have not had in sufficient measure.'

I tried to reassure the man, still anguished over his wife's delicate condition, for her recovery seemed to take at least one step, if not two, backwards for every step forwards. She is forever 'getting better' but not long after begins to fail again; if I did not believe him to be a man of integrity, and had not, moreover, visited the sick wife and seen the little lad gamboling about – for they live hard by me – I think I might doubt the veracity of his tales of her vacillating health.

Do hardened men of business enjoy sending their employees to the devil? Did Postlethwaite, despite his eloquently expressed and seemingly genuine regret, as he dismissed me from my duties as tutor, in fact take a kind of morbid pleasure in sacking me? I truly cannot say; I only know that the thought of dismissing Spence – especially when his fragile little family depended so entirely upon his livelihood, for which he had removed them such a great distance, that they had neither family nor friends within a hundred miles – made me feel quite ill, more than any toxic combination of liquor, cigars or spoilt food ever could. I had, in fact, not even permitted the thought to enter my mind until quite recently, when his absences had again increased, and, at last, slowly – for my mind is uniformly unfit for such hard practical considerations – it began to dawn on me that either Spence would need to be fired, or *I* would be charged with incompetence and lose *my* place.

As if he had sensed the coming crisis, Spence thus stood before me, his face an ashen mixture of sadness and desperation. I gestured to a chair nearby. 'Sit down, Spence. See here – you know I have often told you that Mr Duncan had delegated his ledgers to me at Sowerby Bridge, and you know that I am entirely capable of keeping them. That I have made no secret of my lack of relish for such work is simply testament to my confidence in *you*. But –' I paused, groping for the right words.

'But,' said Spence helpfully, 'this cannot go on and on in this fashion. I know, Mr Brontë, I know. Just allow me a month, at which point I'll either find a solution to permit me to return in full vigour to my post, or I'll give over, and leave the railway.'

Having no desire to dismiss the poor fellow and, above all, wishing at all costs to avoid any unpleasantness, I found his solution eminently acceptable. 'Absolutely, my dear Spence: that is a capital plan. Let us revisit the matter a month hence.'

I have utter confidence that Spence will return, and it will be with great relief that I hand the accursed ledgers back to him.

April 6th, 1842 · Haworth, The Parsonage

How much has changed in the six weeks this journal has lain unopened! Only now do I have the force to open it, for I have been lying in a stupour for the past fortnight, incapable of anything but dragging myself out of bed to perform the minimal motions of existence: washing, dressing, eating, visiting the privy, eating again, and going to bed again as soon as these early spring days permit. I wish for once it were Midwinter again, and I could spend most of my hours in bed, the covers drawn over my head!

More to the point, I wish it were Midwinter again so that I could live my last days at Luddenden Foot over again, so numerous and deep are my regrets!

Having secured the promise from Spence that he would be back at his work with renewed diligence by late March – for I could not conceive of the other alternative – it was as if a great weight had been lifted, and rather than redouble my efforts with the accounts, I abandoned them entirely. After all, I reasoned, Spence would fly back through the columns and restore order within hours, so why should I take any more of an effort with them than was absolutely necessary to get from one day to the next? I grasp only now just how burdened I was by Spence's own tribulations, and the effect that they had on the station; for once we had agreed on the plan to resolve the situation by late March I was positively giddy – even childlike – with excitement, in that state of mind where relief breeds a desire to celebrate.

Leyland was only too happy to oblige me in my inclinations – which is to say to accompany me on my infernal descent – and so I began to see him again at least once a week, and I arranged, in my trips to Halifax, to see Maeve whenever possible. Most commonly, I would spend an afternoon and evening drinking with Leyland, taking care not to drink so much that I could not perform with her later. Once, indeed, I had so much to drink that no matter what attempts Maeve made to revive my desire, I failed to respond. This was enough to 'chasten' me, and so I henceforth carefully calibrated my drinking so that I arrived at Maeve's in a state closer to passionate, if drunken, ardour, than to unconsciousness. Indeed, if I was careful – and there was both art and science to this as well – I would arrive hungry for her, but sufficiently benumbed so that our congress lasted far longer than usual, so that I somehow felt that I had satisfied her as much as she had me, though such thoughts, I'm quite sure, were folly.

When I was not drinking with Leyland, I was doing so with Grundy, or Titterington, Thomson and their friends at the Lord Nelson. If I was not imbibing, I was thinking about it, and the same was true of Maeve – I yearned for her with a constant ache that was utterly physical; I burned for her as Dante's Paolo and Francesca did for each other in Hell, and it did not take long after satisfying my urges with her for them to return with redoubled force. As February faded into March, I found that even she – she who had shown me more things than I could ever have conceived of, and had often let me have her twice and, on a few occasions, thrice – was not enough, and I joined Titterington and his merry band in their frequent whoring, utterly abandoning myself to the worst kind of grovelling, careless debauchery imaginable. As long as the women vaguely pretended to be interested, and willingly spread their legs – and of course they did both of these things happily, for such is their business – that was all that was required for my arousal; in fact, despite the constant drinking, I seemed to be aroused permanently. I became brazen, and even managed to seduce a pair of barmaids – one, fittingly enough, at the Old Cock and the other, most imprudently, at the Anchor and Shuttle, where we did it behind the privies, nearly in view of the station itself. My thirst for both drink and women quickly became insatiable, and it could be slaked only briefly; in the receding tide, I was soon alone, adrift and athirst for more.

I stopped visiting the Reverend Sutcliffe Sowden entirely.

A cold, objective – and above all, pious – observer might find this account incredible. And yet, it happened. For who has not, at some point in his life, found that all of those demons he has, for so long, held more or less successfully at bay, have broken through his fortress at its weakest point, overwhelming him body and soul? What breach in a dam or dike does not grow wider with the eroding force of river or sea? Who on this earth has not at least once in his life surrendered to his basest desires – or worse, revelled in them, plunging with relish headlong into wild and reckless abandon?

I now see clearly, from the cold sobriety with which I write these lines, that far worse than this appalling conduct – which, I frequently assured myself at the time, was temporary, just a bit of a spree – was the arrogance that accompanied it: was I not, I reasoned, the stationmaster, as Leyland had long ago pointed out? Was not my word *law*? Could I not direct matters as I saw fit at *my* station? Soon I was revelling in my conduct, not just my debauchery outside the duties of my post, but even the carelessness with which I kept the books, and most of all, that I seemed to be accountable to no one. I even let the taciturn porter Killiner – who spent every evening equally drunk, sometimes even with me, in the company of Titterington and friends – oversee the accounting, for he did know his figures, if not his letters, passably well. On those days I permitted Spence to be absent, I even gave Killiner the key to the cash box, for beneath his rough exterior beat – I was quite certain – an honest, if not golden, heart. We had worked together nearly a year, and I trusted the man entirely. Besides, I continued to convince myself, Spence would soon take over the books again, and set all things to right, would he not?

Alas, the meeting with Spence came too late, for on the afternoon prior to the very day that we were to evaluate his situation, my fellow stationmaster from Hebden Bridge, a certain Woolven, arrived with an inspector from the railway's central offices. I confess that my head still throbbed viciously from a particularly serious bout of drinking the night before; exceptionally, I had stayed up with Titterington *after* the whoring, for his wife was on a visit to her family in Manchester. We thus drank, easily, twice our usual amount, and I had arrived at the station the next morning still feeling the influence of our revels. Now, in the afternoon, nausea had supplanted the numbness of the morning hours. I have no doubt that I still smelled strongly of liquor.

Woolven and the inspector stepped off the 2:10 pm train, each carrying an identical brown leather bag, and each wearing a similar expression, which would, curiously enough, best be called *expressionless*. As we shook hands, I drew in my breath, hoping they would not notice the remnants of the copious amounts of wine, whisky and even gin that I had consumed the night before.

'Good day, Brontë,' said the usually affable Woolven in uncharacteristically brisk and formal tones, 'this is Mr Shaw, the company accountant. We are making our rounds at the stations, routine accounting audits you see, just to make sure things are in order.'

Woolven was my equal at Hebden Bridge, so I was puzzled at his presence. What gave him the right to examine my ledgers? I groped, my head still pounding like a military tattoo, for the proper way to express my puzzlement.

'Are you just accompanying him from Hebden to Luddenden Foot, and am I to take the relay and go with him down to Sowerby Bridge and Mr Duncan?'

'No no,' said Woolven, 'I've been charged with accompanying Mr Shaw on his travels, to provide the point of view of a fellow Clerk-in-Charge.'

Shaw had precious little hair atop a pointed head, which seemed rather too small for his imposing body. Two prominent front teeth, like those of a horse, protruded from his upper lip as he explained.

'You see, Mr Brontë,' said Shaw in an unusually reedy voice, I'm an accountant, not a railway man. The directors of the company believe that it only makes sense to have another stationmaster along on these visits; they think' – I thought it curious that he did not say we think: did this mean that he felt capable of performing his duties alone, and was, in fact, annoyed at having someone else at his side? – '*they* think that it will be of assistance to have the inspections performed in the larger framework of the daily comings and goings of a station … and well, they think that only a stationmaster can really know what *that* is like.'

He agitated his hands in front of him, trying to force himself into something like a smile, although he seemed a singularly mirthless character. 'I don't know, I don't know,' he said, still waving his hands nervously as if imploring a locomotive to stop in its tracks, his shrill voice cleaving my head like an axe, 'I don't know, Mr Brontë, next time we may call on you, and you may be charged with accompanying me in my examination of Mr *Woolven's* ledgers. Ha ha!'

These frail attempts at humour did manage to set me somewhat at ease, as I followed them into the station. Woolven turned to me and said, 'Oh, terribly sorry Brontë, we did not make ourselves clear. The inspection must be done independently. You may wait outside.'

I turned on my heel and walked slowly to where Killiner stood, near a stack of lumber, and promptly sat down. The sun was already declining, but my biliousness had reached its zenith. I was fast approaching that critical moment in the day where I must either fight bravely through to bedtime, after which I would be rewarded with the blissful, sober sleep of exhaustion that comes the night after a bout of drinking or, more likely, take another path by having the first of many drinks that would, in turn, merely postpone my suffering to another day.

'Wha's to do?' asked Killiner, tipping his head in the direction of the station. ''ave we done summat?'

'An inspection,' I replied simply, but seeing that the porter did not grasp my meaning, I explained, 'They're examining the ledgers, the accounts, and so forth.'

My arrogance – or denial of the gravity of the situation – had become so great that I was far more worried about when and where I would procure my next drink than I was the outcome of such a routine matter.

Killiner, however, blanched at these words.

'What is it, man?' I asked, confused.

'It's nowt, really … i's jus' tha'…'

I caught at last his meaning – or thought so. 'It's just that since I have taken over the books from Spence you are not so confident? There there, Killiner, have no fear, if there's just a tiny bit of irregularity here and there we can quickly make amends, I'm sure.'

Finally, though, my confidence – hubris, if you will – was routed by the reality of the situation, and my heart began to sink like a stone, my nausea from the previous eve now multiplied a hundred-fold, so that I thought I would in fact be sick. My forehead was suddenly damp with beads of nervous perspiration, and my blood ran cold.

It was at least another thirty minutes before Shaw and Woolven emerged from the little station house in time to catch the next train, whose arrival moments earlier I had not even noticed as I sat in icy terror. Both men shook my hand and

Shaw said, 'We shall send along our results by official letter, Mr Brontë, within two or three days.'

Neither looked me in the eye.

I lived in such a state of anxiety for the next three days that I thought my nerves would snap: there was no carousing, but each night I swallowed two or three large glasses of brandy just to sleep, and such sleep was intermittent, and riddled with ominous dreams, from which I would awake each morning remembering no specific details, filled only with a sense of murderous threat, of oppressive foreboding.

Meanwhile, the much-awaited meeting with Spence finally occurred, and he happily reported that he would soon return with his full powers of concentration, for his wife's sister had agreed to come and care for the little boy, and to nurse her sister – who, Spence assured me, seemed truly on the mend – back to full health. Only my apprehension about the audit prevented me from expressing the joy that I would naturally have felt, and which I endeavoured to feign, at this good news.

The fourth day after the visit, when I thought I could bear it no longer, I received the following letter, neatly written by an anonymous hand, on the same stationery that I had used for my petulant poem to Grundy. It struck me like a thunderbolt.

> March 30th, 1842
> Mr Patrick Branwell Brontë
> Clerk-in-Charge
> Luddenden Foot Station
>
> Dear Mr Brontë
>
> It is with the deepest regret that we inform you, that after a thorough review of the ledgers of the Luddenden Foot station on March 25th, we have determined that your employment is to end, effective upon receipt of this letter.
>
> The company's accountant discovered that the station's accounts were in a very confused state, and that, upon

closer examination, there existed a shortfall of 1 pound, 1 shilling, 7 pence.

The company has determined that since insufficiently conclusive evidence exists of theft in this matter, the missing amount will simply be deducted from the remainder of your salary.

However, it is expected that you will have fully removed yourself and your belongings from the Luddenden Foot Station by no later than April 1st, at which time Mr William Spence will assume the duties of Clerk-in-Charge.

Most sincerely, etc.

XV.

The Parsonage Again

April 17th, 1842 · The Parsonage

How much more formidable, more God-like, is *mercy* than wrath?

Perhaps the reason I have written so little in these pages about Papa is that his boundless forgiveness, not to say indulgence, of me makes him such a towering figure in my imagination. I returned to Haworth not to a shower of condemnation, but to the warmth of a father's embrace of his prodigal son, a father who forgave and believed – or at least wished to believe – everything. That I presented a somewhat altered version of events, omitting my late debauchery, surely smoothed the path.

My story this time? I had generously delegated to, and fully trusted, both Spence and Killiner, and my only practical fault was not verifying the ledgers. My only true sins – both quite pardonable, in that they arose from the laudable Christian virtues of Faith and Hope – had been to give, quite generously, more responsibility to those in my employ, and to believe – naively it now seemed – that they would fulfil their duties. For what was I to do? Blame my subordinates after the fact, thereby dragging them under with me? Shattering Spence's already fragile existence? Casting Killiner into the streets as a beggar?

Nay, Christ-like, I took their sins upon me: such is the story I told Papa, and have almost come to believe myself. How much do we deceive others, but especially ourselves, just to be able to set one foot in front of the other in this life!

Under Papa's watchful eye, and in the quiet of the Parsonage – for Charlotte and Emily are at school in Brussels, Anne has resumed her post at Thorp Green, and Aunt Branwell leaves me to my own devices – I have returned to my abstemious self. My flesh is at last purged of intoxicants, and my incessant yearning for the flesh of a woman has been replaced with an almost constant desire for slumber. I have at long last had some real rest, as mental depression slowly yields to strength and sanity. As a result, I begin to feel whole and human again, and have taken to long rambles on the moors. Their stark beauty in this season is astonishing, and with an eye no longer jaundiced, I see all anew, feel the winds caressing me as if for the first time, almost as though I had been sent hurtling back in time, and am once again a young boy, half-savage and hardy, and free.

Although I still, after a fashion, love them all – yes, even Charlotte – I find my sisters' absence the most healing balm of all, for in their collective gaze I would surely stand condemned. They would no more believe my version of events at Luddenden Foot than Papa would credit me capable of what truly transpired. Is this because they never wish to think well of me, while he always does? Is this the nature of belief itself? Why has the same reality – viz., my past behaviour – led different members of my family to view me in ways utterly contrary? Do the girls, like the elder son in Christ's parable, forever see the prodigal son, while Papa in his mercy sees only his contrite little lad, come home once more? Does anyone glimpse the person I *truly* am? Do I?

May 10th, 1842 · The Parsonage

I have seen Joe Leyland again, for the first time since my dismissal. The opportunity was provided by the untimely death of Thomas Andrew, our village surgeon of the past quarter century. So great was the outpouring of public grief – for he was a friend of the poor, who charged only what one could pay, which was sometimes nothing at all – that it was determined that a memorial to him should be placed in Haworth Church. Needless to say, I thought of Leyland, for this provided not only work for my friend, who these days seems to be struggling as much as I to secure an income, but vouchsafed an excuse for me to contact him without covering myself with shame. Within two days he had accepted to dine at the Parsonage and to appear before the monument committee. He arrived in Haworth in good humour, his mirth matching his girth, for drink has begun to give him not only a flushed face but a rounded waist. He did his utmost to be appropriately serious and abstemious at dinner, though not wholly succeeding.

Over our roast beef and boiled potatoes, he asked father, 'Well, Mr Brontë, you must be quite pleased to have your son back in the nest, if only for a short while. How quiet it must be here without the chatter of females!'

Papa frowned. Such talk was not to his taste, and he appeared to take such a remark as a slight. 'My daughters do not chatter, Mr Leyland. They've been reared to speak only when they have something of substance to say.' His brow remained furrowed whilst he chewed a particularly stubborn morsel of beef.

'I beg your pardon, Reverend, for that choice of words. But surely it must be quieter than usual here these days,' said Leyland, colouring up and taking a rather too large draught of the wine he had been offered with dinner.

Papa would not be so easily distracted. 'In my experience,' said he, with a steely gaze that, in my guilt, seemed to bore to the very centre of the world of corrupt pleasures I had shared with Joe in Halifax – that aptly named Devil's Cauldron – and its neighbourhood, 'the conversation of a serious woman is far preferable to the banter of frivolous men.'

After an uneasy silence, Joe said simply, as he lifted his glass in tribute to Papa's wisdom, 'Well, let us agree to *that*, sir. Now tell me more about the late Mr Andrew.'

Truth to tell, the entire day was excruciating to me: first, a dinner where I sat between, on the one hand, an all-merciful and forgiving father who knew nothing of the depths of my debauchery at Luddenden Foot, and on the other, my erstwhile companion in said activities, who was surely all too ready to resume them – and from his appearance had not ceased since my departure from the railway.

Second, a meeting with a committee of well-meaning but ignorant townsfolk, wherein I felt heartily ashamed of their bad taste and worse conduct, for the monument they wish is far from what Leyland can, and should, do for the cost. My friend has been to Haworth often enough, I trust, to make allowance for gothic ignorance and ill-breeding. As Joe took his leave, I wanted nothing more than to bend my steps towards the Black Bull with him and John Brown, and to down successive glasses of whisky to kill the pain.

What pain? Why, the weight of Papa's mercy and forgiveness, which pressed down upon me more heavily than a direct condemnation ever could; his near-reprimand of my friend during dinner and my inability to *be myself* before either of them; and finally, the embarrassment elicited by the words and actions of certain members of the monument committee. My throat fairly burned with thirst. But I have made a promise to myself, and – without ever giving words to such a vow – to Papa, who stood at my elbow as my friend took his leave. 'Shall we, Branwell?' said the former, turning his steps towards the Parsonage, upon which the latter doffed his hat, winked, and, drawing me aside, said in a jolly *sotto voce*, affecting the accent of the simple townsfolk who had so much embarrassed me earlier in the day: 'Le's ge' t'gether soon, eh young Faustus, we can 'ave a do – we mun make up for los' time!'

May 22nd, 1842 · The Parsonage

Despite that single day of temptation when Leyland was in Haworth, I remain sober, and gain strength and flesh, filling my less-than-perfect lungs with the pure, bracing winds of late spring as I ramble the moors and hilltops, often up the steep valley of the Sladen. I sometimes pause at what as children we called 'The Meeting of the Waters', the waterfalls on South Dean Beck, before pushing up the arduous hills to the heights of Top Withens. Catching my breath at last, I can gaze for miles in every direction, my face whipped by the atmospheric tumult that usually blasts over the ruins of the old farm, *wuthering* as the common folk call this bracing ventilation. I know the owner, Jonas Sunderland, and he and his wife Mary sometimes offer me a reaming pint of ale to fortify me on my trip home, though the trip downhill is always less onerous than the ascent, is it not? Scenes of childhood throng about me on these walks, sometimes even eclipsing the charming vistas of present day, and yet it is not with bitterness that I welcome the ghosts of the past, but only with a kind of sweet melancholy, so much have my mind and body improved of late.

I have renewed old friendships, especially with Brown, Grundy and, of course, Leyland – which is to say, those who both know me and believe in me, unlike my family, the head of which believes in me without knowing me, the rest of whom fancy they know me without believing in me. Last week, in the company of Brown, and inspired by the debacle over Andrew's monument, on which Leyland has begun work in Halifax, I sat at the Black Bull – my drinking limited to a single, salutary glass of wine – where I happily sketched a half-buried tombstone in which is chiselled *Resurgam* – I will rise again – and dispatched it to Joe; just today I wrote Grundy a letter, enquiring about another possible employment with the railways, perhaps even on the Continent (if my sisters can thrive there, why cannot I?), for the old, cold reality is that now that I am well, I must escape the very walls and walks that have healed me, for I still have a great desire for activity and do not despair of making my independence.

I have assured my friend that I have at length regained health, strength and soundness of mind far superior to anything shown by that miserable wreck he used to know by my name, and that I can now speak cheerfully and enjoy the company of another without the stimulus of six glasses of whisky. What I need, really, is a motive for exertion. I paused for a moment, pen in the air, and thought of Maggie. Surely, she would have given me a reason to exert myself!

And yet – that would have meant abandoning my literary ambitions once and for all, of course, and despite my earnest enquiries to Grundy about practical employment, I am – to my great surprise – finding that one poem after another of mine is now being published. It began on a desperate whim, when I sent along 'On Landseer's Painting', remembering as I did Leyland's discourse on the dismal state of English art and letters. To my utter astonishment, the *Bradford Herald* agreed to publish it, and thus emboldened, I began a veritable poetical campaign, and have published three poems in that esteemed journal, and am preparing three more, for I have at last found someone – its editor – who, *mirabile dictu*, not only publishes my work but asks for more! At the same time, I have appeared in the pages of the *Halifax Guardian* and the *Leeds Intelligencer*, in every case as my alter ego, 'Northangerland'.

This *nom de plume* – which would deceive none of my closest friends, including my sisters, if they were here to read the local papers – is meant only to mask my identity from Papa and his associates, for although I crave fame, I do not wish to reveal my name until and unless I am truly a success in the world of letters, which is to say in London or Edinburgh. Perhaps, truth be told – the *real* truth – is that I do not wish the good Reverend Brontë to know of the despair that runs through my verse, as in this sonnet, which both the *Herald* and the *Guardian* chose to publish a few days ago:

PEACEFUL DEATH AND PAINFUL LIFE

Why dost thou sorrow for the happy dead?
  For if their life be lost their toils are o'er,
  And woe and want can trouble them no more;
Nor ever slept they in an earthly bed
So sound as now they sleep, while dreamless laid
  In the dark chambers of the unknown shore,
  Where Night and Silence guard each sealed door.
So – turn from such as these thy drooping head

And mourn the *dead* alive, whose spirit flies,
    Whose life departs, before his death has come;
Who knows no Heaven beyond his gloomy skies;
    Who sees no Hope to brighten up that gloom:
'Tis *he* who feels the worm that never dies,
    The *real* death and darkness of a tomb!

Could it be that I also wish, cloaked as Northangerland, to convince myself that the *real* Patrick Branwell Brontë does not share such despair?

This afternoon, as I walked to post my letter to Grundy, the sun shone brightly in a rare cloudless sky, of the kind one sees only in this season. As I entered the square at the top of the Main Street, all of a sudden – or so it seemed to me – down from the fields and moors above Haworth, there floated hundreds – nay, thousands – of dandelion seeds, like manna from heaven, like a benediction, a sign from the eternal universe itself. As I stood on the cobblestones between the Black Bull and the steps of the church, I wondered if my recent string of small victories – victory over drink and lust, yes, but also the rapid publication of my poems – would at last be a turning point. I began to think that there was hope yet to brighten my gloom, and that I might even once again appeal to *Blackwood's*: if only I could at last appear in its hallowed pages, then only mighty London would remain unconquered.

I stood still to watch the fleecy white seeds of the dandelion dance in the sun-bathed breeze, and remembered that, as children, we had called the seed heads 'clocks' – for plucking them from the earth and blowing on them as hard as we could, we asserted that the number of breaths required to dislodge every last seed from the plant would *necessarily* represent the time of day. Whether this was because we believed that we – the *genii* of our own little universe – controlled the march of time itself, or whether we thought cruel Father Time was masquerading as an amiable spirit in harmony with the universe, down to the slightest gesture of a child's breath on a single dandelion head, I cannot say.

XVI.

Return to the Devil's Cauldron

June 9th, 1842 · The Parsonage

Today I had a letter from Grundy, informing me that no positions on the railways are available. I suppose I was a fool to entertain, under present circumstances, any very sanguine hopes respecting situations connected with railways, for there is a glut in *that* market. But I had thought that perhaps even something abroad might be attainable, especially given my rudimentary acquaintance with French.

I had carried Grundy's letter out of doors and sat, despite the beauty of this early June day, musing somewhat gloomily on its contents, on a low wall skirting the rear of the Parsonage, when John Brown himself appeared before me.

'There you are! You all right, lad?'

I divulged these same contents to the sexton, to which he responded with his usual joviality. 'Come come, Branwell, 'ave you not begun to have considerable success with your verse? Did you not tell me tha' ambition again stirred in tha' breast of yours? 'ow can *you* still be poorly, with poems published nearly every day and this lovely soft breeze washin' o'er you, and not feel tha' your life is jus' *beginnin'*? For you're 'ardly an ol' man like me' – Brown is one of those men in his early middle years who is still sufficiently confident in his powers of attraction over the fairer sex that calling himself *old* is largely ironical, almost an invitation for others to see him as still, at a mere thirty-eight, handsome, vigorous, and indeed, youthful, for his daily occupations keep him quick and elastic in his movements – 'yes, you're hardly an ol' man like me –

why, you're a mere whelp, a babe of – 'ow old are you, Branwell?'

'I'll be twenty-five later this month, Brown. A quarter of a century. Much more to the point, my years of adulthood have borne no fruit whatsoever: a failure at painting (never my first love, but Papa and I thought it might yield a living); dismissed as a tutor (you may say that my appointment was simply not renewed, but it stings no less for that subtlety); and sacked by the railway. I mentally shake hands with you for your sanguine view of me, but I see nothing but false starts, shipwrecks, derailments and sadly terminated attempts at making my way in the world.'

Despite my recent successes, I had determined to pity myself this day, and was not going to permit Brown to deter me. Indefatigable, he soldiered on in support of the forces of optimism. Drawing a folded sheet from his breast pocket, he said with a grin, 'I've 'ere *jus'* the thing to cheer you up. Our old friend J.B. Leyland 'as asked me to make the great journey to the bustling metropolis of *Ha-LEE-fax*, to examine 'is progress on the monument to Thomas Andrew. In it he says, "And for God's sake, bring poor Branwell. The air will do young Northangerland good, and the Reverend Brontë will surely consent to allow him to serve as the delegate of that august committee with whom I met of late."'

Joe, of course, knew my sonnet on Landseer's dog all too well, and seeing my persistence in using my *nom de plume*, he had appended it to the growing list of sobriquets. Indeed, he had even sent me a brief note of congratulations, with the salutation 'Lord Northangerland'. Brown, however, had been heretofore ignorant of anything and anyone connected to the mythical lands of Glasstown and Angria, including Alexander Percy, Duke of Northangerland. I had only lately confided to the sexton that my verse was appearing in print, and thus had to reveal my pseudonym.

It was with some reluctance that I agreed to travel with Brown to Leyland's studio, for it is with much trepidation that I think back on the scenes there, of my earlier hopes and dreams, of successes and failures, of love and desire, and of genuine heartbreak and coldest debauchery. Will a visit only reopen old wounds? Will I find any joy in Leyland's company there, or only wormwood and gall? In any event, we shall see, for Brown has already dispatched a letter promising a visit from us five days hence; how, he reasoned, could I avoid visiting my old friend, at a distance of only ten miles?

June 16th, 1842 · The Parsonage

Leyland was right: the visit did me good. As Brown and I struck out on the waggon that he uses to transport stones and the other implements of his trade, we could not have had a more brilliant day for the brief journey from Haworth to Denholme, then on to Keelham, and finally to Halifax. With Midsummer a mere week away, the oaks and ash trees are now all fully in leaf, that bright green of spring and early summer that will turn, all too soon, to deeper shades, before the decay and fall of autumn. As we descended, cotton-grass gave way to a riot of summer wildflowers moving rhythmically under the warm breeze, like wave upon ocean wave, while the last blossoms of spring danced merrily in the wind, like rice tossed at a festive wedding.

The becks and rivers, though flowing swift and full, were passing from the rushing rapids of early springtime to the calmer, almost stately motion of Midsummer. They too, however, would soon wither away. I recalled a few lines from my poem called 'An Epicurean's Song', which I'd rewritten just a day or two earlier:

So seize we the present,
And gather its flowers;
For – mournful or pleasant –
Tis all that is ours.
While daylight we're wasting,
The evening is hasting,
And night follows fast on the vanishing hours.

Yes – and we, when that night comes –
Whatever betide,
Must die as our fate dooms,
And sleep by their side;
For change is the only thing
Always continuing;
And it sweeps creation away with its tide!

Or as Joe had said:

Think of the rose, at its most expansive, ravishing beauty
the instant before it begins to brown and wilt away.
Or a fruit, whose sweetest, ripest, tastiest moment
just precedes the beginning of its decline.

Was it this achingly, fleetingly beautiful moment, where spring was – seemingly under our very eyes as Brown's waggon bumped along the Halifax Road – ripening into summer, or was it our imminent arrival *Chez Leyland*, where Maggie had provided the model for Kilmeny under Joe's voracious gaze and I had later, fruitlessly, pursued her myself, that brought to mind my friend's words?

I mused on these things as we made our way into Halifax. The trip had taken a little more than two hours, and it was still before noon, the sun now rising high above us, the pure soft breeze that filled our nostrils quickly yielding to the pungent odours of a bustling manufacturing town. Joe had been watching for us, and as we pulled up to his studio, out he strode in his shirt sleeves, forearms white with marble dust.

'Salutations! Pardon the dust, but *non est pax impiis*, no rest for the weary; in this modern age one must be a veritable machine to make ends meet.'

'I think you mean no rest for the *wicked*, don't you, Joe?'

He surprised me doubly, both in his response and the expression his face wore as he spoke. Although it was as brief as the flickers of shadow and sunshine Brown and I had traversed on our leafy journey from Haworth, a look of great weariness, mingled with sadness and even despair, stole over Joe's usually buoyant eyes and large mouth, the usual attitude of which was a sarcastic smirk.

He answered, seemingly in great earnest, 'Is that not the point, Branwell?' – he generally reserved my Christian name for just such rare moments of gravity – 'Does not our wickedness make us weary? Does not Jeremiah say, as he condemns Babylon for its wickedness, *and they shall be weary?*' Was old Joe simply trying to put one over on the parson's son? Or, more likely, had I placed my own cloak of weariness on his unsuspecting shoulders, attributing to him feelings he did not even have? How often we do this to our fellows, do we not?

Whatever the case, I determined to make light of his words, and parried, 'He does indeed, and Job rejoins that when they die, *the wicked cease from troubling, and the weary are at rest.* I can hardly imagine that great, wicked bearish creature standing before me, Joseph Bentley Leyland, dying anytime soon!'

In the twinkling of an eye, Joe was his old, mirthful self, ushering us into the studio and assuring us that he would be along in a trice, once he had washed and changed. I looked round the cavernous studio, where monuments and tablets far outnumbered anything of a more whimsical, creative, or for that matter happy, aspect. As the balance of his work had increasingly tipped in the direction of church and funerary monuments, so too had the river of scorn he had once poured on my railway career trickled away to a mere stream, and one he revisited only with great sympathy, for as far as he was concerned, we were in precisely the same position in our respective fields. The only difference was that the inexorable march of Death would assure a ready market for *his* products. But *mine*?

Brown silently examined one monument after another, while I tried to imagine a naked Maggie modelling Kilmeny, or Leyland's great *fête* with Listz pounding out his improvisations. I found so doing to be nigh-on impossible, for today all was merely tools, marble and dust. I gazed out the begrimed back windows towards the little shed where I had kissed her that night, and then to the

Square Chapel, where, overcome with desire, I had been prepared to defile God's house – even if it was a mere dissenters' chapel.

Had I been quite mad? No: any man who has been so inflamed with desire that he can think only of becoming one with the object of that most powerful of human yearnings would not scoff at such a notion, for truly *he* has lived moments of great passion, where reason takes flight and his very surroundings fall away, like the flimsy decor of a stage play, or more to the point, like the clothes of a beautiful woman slipping gracefully over each lovely curve of her person, where cascading silk reveals the luminous, shimmering skin of her shoulders, breasts, waist, hips, thighs, calves and feet. Such a man as *this* knows what it is to feel a yearning to consume and be consumed, to run his tongue upon every inch of her frame, to swallow her up and be swallowed up *by* her, to burn together in a growing bonfire of mutual desire.

'A penny for your thoughts, Faustus. Though I'm quite certain they're worth at least a sovereign or two, eh?' Leyland stood at my side, his large hands red from scrubbing, his forearms covered with a proper shirt and coat, and his hat in his hand. His monumental *Head of Satan* gazed ominously across the cluttered room.

I turned to face Joe, answering a question with a question, as in a game of battledore and shuttlecock: 'How are *you*, Mephistopheles? Upon our arrival this morning you seemed, ever so briefly, a bit weary. That's not like you.'

'Nonsense,' said he. But after a moment he waved his hand over the scattered stones, monuments to the recently and future deceased, and smiled. 'Well, truth be told, I am weary of *this* sort of work – but that's surely no surprise to you, Brontë. Have you any idea what a trial it is to find commissions for works of pure imagination, meant to delight the living rather than commemorate the soon-to-be forgotten dead?'

I raised my eyebrows, as if to say, 'Surely you jest, man, do you not?'

A smile of mischief and true brotherly sympathy broke over his face. 'Ha ha, *of course*, my friend, who knows better than clever Northangerland how little use this benighted world of bloody money-grubbing philistines has for a true *artiste*?'

Meanwhile, Brown had found the monument we had ostensibly come to visit and waved us over from the far end of the room.

'Come,' said Joe, 'let's have a quick look and then make our way to the inn – I've already a powerful thirst. I never take a drop before noon, but I heartily welcome a large glass at one minute past. Let's see what Brown has to say about my opus.'

Brown was on one knee, examining the monument, as we approached. ''T'is a wee bit simple, don't y' think, Leyland?' The monument could not have been more austere, and more unlike the sculptor himself. Beneath a triangular tympanum a single dove – the Holy Spirit? – emerged from the stone (this, to be just, was clever), and beneath the bird a single fold of drapery symbolised mourning. On the lower half of the monument lay a monument within a monument, a *tabula rasa* where the dedication to Thomas Andrew was still to be lettered.

As we approached, Leyland looked at me meaningfully and said to Brown, who did *not* serve on the memorial committee, 'Well, Sir John, I could not agree with you more, but see here, the august memorial committee of *Haworthopolis* had very specific ideas about how this simple surgeon, who dedicated his life to serving all people – most particularly the indigent souls of the village – should be remembered. They felt – strongly indeed, would you not agree, Branwell? – that this monument should mirror his very simplicity. And though it pains me to say it, this is a business, and the purchaser has a right to command what he sees fit.'

John ran his hand over the smooth, untouched scroll at the bottom of the monument. 'So, when do you think you'll have it to Haworth, that I might letter the inscription?'

'Hmm … let us say a week or so hence. I've a bit more polishing to do … and see here, at the top of the *tabula rasa*, there is room for a bit of a flourish, for who does not deserve a bit of a flourish in death? The memorial committee be damned! They won't even notice such subtleties … more pearls cast before swine!'

We all laughed as Joe escorted us out of the studio and into the street. 'See here, my good fellows, shall we betake ourselves to the White Swan? I slowed my steps instinctively, for this was, of course, the establishment operated by Maggie's parents. Leyland grabbed my elbow and sped me forward, guessing my thoughts.

'Now now, little man, Maggie is married with a child, and she and her husband are naturally now at the Royal – don't you recall? – and so we will quite intentionally avoid *that* place for your sake.'

I wanted to ask, 'How *is* she? Do you see her? What does she look like? Is she happy?' I desire for her both happiness and misery; or perhaps I should say that those two desires warred within me: the half of me that had loved her wished her a bounty of contentment, while the half she had spurned wished her sufficient misery to regret her choice. Anyone who thinks such battles within us to be rare, or illogical, or absurd, is likely an automaton, for are not such contradictions woven into the very fabric of humanity? I confess that I also hoped to avoid Grundy, for while I did not fault the messenger for delivering his unwelcome news, I had no desire to see him. The same was true of Maeve, for she would only be a reminder of – and quite possibility a temptation to resume – my past behaviour.

As we stepped into the inn, there rose to greet us Messrs Francis Leyland, William Dearden and John Frobisher. After the customary exchange of handshakes and pleasantries, we settled into our table. Is there anything like 'settling into' a table with fast friends, when one feels already almost drunk with pleasure just by being amongst them, when the anticipation of the initial toast and first sip is at least as pleasing as that delicious draught itself?

'Well, gentlemen, are you pleased with my surprise?' He made an effort to include Brown, although the treat of seeing these old friends had been arranged far more for my benefit than the sexton's. Joe's manners were generally impeccable, a sign of good breeding; they were only eroded under the influence of drink, which would be soon enough. I, however, was determined to remain temperate, ordering a glass of wine and taking great pains to take rather small sips, rather than the great throatfuls to which I had become habituated at Luddenden Foot.

'I cannot speak for Squire Brown,' I replied, 'but I am utterly delighted to see my old companions.'

'Hear, hear!' was all Brown said, but his words were genuine, and his eyes betrayed the delight of the married man who has briefly escaped his chains to be welcomed into the company of his fellows, with the prospect of a few drinks – and knowing Brown, quite possibly a brief dalliance – before him. We had told Papa that we planned to dine with the sculptor, and not to expect us before late in the evening.

'Well, then,' said Joe, lifting his glass, 'let us toast the return of our *own* prodigal son and his faithful adviser to the Devil's Cauldron.' I still sipped, but the draughts were quickly becoming more generous. Joe leant back in his chair and added, 'The best surprise of all is still to come. Brontë, our good friend Dearden here, the Bard of Caldene, has a gauntlet to throw down. You see, your poems – quite poorly disguised by that ludicrous *nom de plume*, Northangerland, I might add – have attracted quite the notice of a certain number of cultivated *Halifaxois*' – he pronounced this last word with a French accent, omitting the 'H' – 'and I can assure you that such individuals are rare indeed. Indeed, the frequency of their publication has even elicited just a bit of envy, though in the case of the sonnet inspired by Landseer's painting, it was more akin to laughter, and fond memories of a previous contest.'

Pleased with himself, Joe took a generous dose of whisky, at which point Dearden finally spoke: 'You see, Brontë, reading that sonnet brought me back to our previous joust, and now that we are both being published with regularity, I propose a far more serious match, one where we write a substantial poem – perhaps in epic, perhaps in dramatic form, and then let these fine critics here judge the winner.'

'And what, pray, would you consider a worthy subject? Is it up to us to select?'

'*Naaaaay*,' interjected Joe in his favourite, most appalling Yorkshire tones, as the whisky began to warm him, 'thou wil'st do *nowt* of t'kind, y'dozy bastard!'

Dearden smiled, but it was the only indication that he had heard Leyland's remark.

'No, I think it should be a specific subject, as was the case the last time, do you not concur?'

A supercilious version of that well-spoken gentleman, Joseph Bentley Leyland, had suddenly reappeared at our table, speaking in the softened tones of the 'civilised' southerly regions of the kingdom: 'I can assure all this enlightened assembly that Lord Northangerland is capable of *anything* involving the written word. Have we not seen him write with both hands, simultaneously? Can he not compose verse in Latin or Greek, as if he trod the earth in days of the days of Caesar, or of Homer? Is he not blessed by Zeus above with the gift of poetical genius, *mania*, *furor poeticus*? Give him any topic you can devise and watch his genius soar on eagle's wings!'

How often do our own frustrations prompt our attacks on – or, in this case, our making sport of – others? For does not the path of an arrow speak more of the archer than of his target? In other words: was the bitterness of Joe's life as he left the inspired work of his monumental, magnificent, maleficent *Head of Satan* and his voluptuous, alluring and yet sinless *Kilmeny* for the dusty drudgery of commissioned monuments to the dead that which truly lay beneath his mockery? I merely smiled and responded, not to Leyland, but to Dearden, 'Well then, my friendly foe – for foes we must be in such an *epic* struggle – what do you have in mind?'

'I am certainly willing to consider your own suggestions, but I thought of this: what if we each write a drama or a poem, the principal character in which was to have a real or imaginary existence before the Deluge?'

Leyland, already well along with his third large tumbler of whisky, said loudly, '*Après moi, le déluge!*,' but Dearden continued apace. 'Do you think a month's time would be sufficient? I am more than willing to come to *you*, Brontë, what say you?'

We clasped hands on the bargain, but I requested that we meet *not quite* in Haworth, but just outside the village, at the Crossroads Inn, halfway to Keighley. Meanwhile, Joe had risen to order dinner for the assembled, and when he returned a young woman was at his side, with an infant of about six months on her hip.

It was Maggie.

I felt my face grow hot at her appearance; words failed me. Although she hardly qualified as gentry, her simple, yet ladylike appearance – she might nearly pass for a governess – and the presence of the red-cheeked babe caused everyone at the table to stand. She was as stunning as ever, and in spite of myself I fancied her a Madonna with child, though she had lost some flesh, and the slightest lines of care and fatigue encircled her eyes and had begun to march inexorably across her forehead. Those celestial eyes were unchanged, but her lovely tresses were now pulled back in the simplest, most practical way possible. The little boy on her hip was a true cherub, with flawless alabaster skin, an abundance of curly brown locks, and his mother's eyes.

Those eyes.

She stood uneasily before us, for clearly she would not have sought out our company, especially if she had espied Leyland and me from afar. She managed something between a bow and a curtsy, which reminded me of the first time I had seen her. My chest heaved as I felt warm tears swimming in my eyes: no, not for Maggie, and not for me either, but for us *all* – a sudden grief bordering on despair, an inescapable sadness before the transient nature of life, of all beauty and all joy, relentlessly slipping away into oblivion.

'Evenin' gentlemen, how d'ye do?' said she, as those heavenly orbs travelled around the group, lingering on my face – or did I imagine it? – a bit longer than each of my friends. We each responded according to our character, and there followed an awkward silence. Leyland, with a *horror vacui* as always, came to our rescue.

'Mrs Mortimer happened to arrive just as I stepped to the bar. It seems,' he continued, looking at me meaningfully, as if to apologise, 'that her mother cares for the lad so that she can assist her husband at the Royal.'

'Erm, well, gentlemen, I must indeed deposit this lad on 'is grandmother's knee and move meself along, for 'is da' depends mightily on me. I *do* wish ye a pleasant afternoon and all good things hereafter – truly.'

As she uttered this final word, her eyes again found mine. Were hers shining as well, or was I simply imagining it, my own moist eyes merely reflected in hers? Whatever the case, I felt – foolish as it may seem – like a Papist kneeling before a vision of the Blessed Virgin, her radiance washing over me like a benediction. As I removed my spectacles and furtively wiped my tears, I was filled – if only for an instant – with peace, as if I had, indeed, been forgiven, had indeed been blessed. Of course Maggie was no vision, but a woman of flesh and blood, and after another partial curtsy, she and her little boy were off, back to the struggles of their very real life, at which Leyland sat down, shaking his head.

'Well bugger me, she's still a *fine* specimen of a woman. I daresay, if she's not worn out by having too many children – or, more likely, by toiling beside that lout, her husband – she'll retain that admirably elastic form for many a year to come.'

Meanwhile, that other great connoisseur of feminine charms, John Brown, leant over and whispered, 'By God, lad, she's still a beauty – a splendid creature! Her husband's surely a lucky bastard!'

We dined on roast chicken, and Joe grew louder and a bit more inebriated, whilst his brother Francis looked on with mild disapproval, saying, as always, precious little. Whenever a brief respite in Joe's antics permitted it, Dearden, Frobisher and I discussed all manner of things artistic, as well as the proliferation of the latest marvels of engineering and invention, especially the telegraph – at which point Frank joined our conversation, for it is still a passion of his – and the daguerreotype. As the conversation touched on this last topic, Joe pounded the table with his oversized fist.

'Now *there*, lads, is something worthy of discussion! Branwell, t'is a good thing you abandoned the portrait-painting business, for those French devils have come up with something that will surely turn all but a handful of painters into beggars!'

'What do you mean, Leyland?' said Dearden.

'What I *mean*, my dear Bard of Caldene, is that daguerreotypes will soon become cheap enough – for that is the way of all invention, is it not? – to appeal to the merchant classes, and perhaps even more common folk. The tedious process of dabbing paint on a canvas to represent the world and its inhabitants will become rarer and rarer, and so dearer and dearer, so that only the great and illustrious will sit for a painted portrait.'

Leyland was speaking with surprising coherence. I have witnessed such instances – in myself and others – when one's passion for the subject at hand inspires unwonted clarity of thought and expression, even in the midst of drunkenness, the mind like a castaway plucked briefly from a stormy sea.

'What then,' asked Francis, 'will the painters do? Surely not starve in the streets, as you pretend?'

'Not all will. I predict that the finest will be in great demand, but all others will be scattered on the winds of change. Some will abandon their art altogether, while others will perhaps try to master the daguerrotype itself; some will become *practical* painters and, like yours truly toiling away on damnable funerary monuments, they will be reduced to painting broadsides and sketching handbills or designing advertisements for newspapers and magazines; a final group will, perhaps, finally liberate painting from its shackles.'

'Shackles?' said I.

'Yes, young Faustus: *shackles*. Think on it a bit: has not painting always been enslaved to *something*? In the dark ages, it was the mediaeval church; in the renaissance, it was the corrupt popes and the wealthy bankers of Italy; indeed, in all times the powerful have determined what was to be painted, for it was their munificence that fed and clothed the artist. The final stage of enslavement is reality itself. If the daguerreotype can provide a representation of life more accurately, more cheaply and more quickly, painting must find *something else to do*. In this way, it may finally join poetry, sculpture and music as an independent art devoted only to *itself*, which is to say to the goddess of beauty, Aphrodite.'

Leyland leant back, breathless, but evidently quite satisfied with himself, and he took a deep draught of whisky. I was sufficiently armed with drink (and thus courage), and yet far more sober than he, and that combination placed me in the perfect position to resume our old game of undermining each other's theories.

'My dear sir,' I began, addressing him as if in a letter and lifting my glass in salute, 'I see a great deal of wisdom behind your prognostications, but perhaps – alas – an equal share of error.'

'Let us hear your critiques, Lord Northangerland,' said he, folding his arms, but clearly pleased that I wished to play.

'Well,' said I, drawing a deep breath, 'confusion might be a better word than *error*. Are you not the very man who daily vituperates against the current age, where the *market* controls all, and where you are reduced to grinding out a living – you see, I can be clever too – with gravestones, because your artistry is not sufficiently appreciated? This is the same world where we poets' – here I gestured to my friend Dearden – 'are reduced to being published in the local newspapers, and where sentimental novels written for young ladies are the only saleable items? And is it not paradoxical that you condemn a system of patronage that you, yourself, have admitted is in fact your heart's fervent *desire*? Do you not, in fact, wish yourself to be enslaved and shackled by a wealthy patron (or, preferably, a lovely patro*ness*), rather than be set adrift on the market, one which rewards your memorial tablets more than your sculptures? In short, you appear quite prepared to betray your principles – nay, sell your soul – in exchange for a life of ease.'

Leyland tossed back the remainder of his whisky, gestured for still more, and smiled. Was there a trace of bitterness in his grin?

'Very well, Brontë, you seem to have pierced my argument with a multitude of holes, I confess. I would, however, make just a few comments in response, if you will allow.'

I nodded assent, trying mightily to content myself with this single glass of wine.

The weary, serious expression I had glimpsed earlier that day returned, and Joe seemed to speak in great earnest, with a sobriety that could scarcely be credited.

'It is true that I view patronage as at once enslavement and as eminently desirable. That is to say, I detest it in *principle* as much as I despise the market in *practice*, and yet I confess that I desperately yearn for someone to remove the fear of want that haunts me, so that I might focus what abilities remain to me on works of the *imagination*.'

'I thought,' said Frobisher in quiet, but trembling, tones, 'that such was the role of your brother Francis here?'

The nervous musician's timid demeanour, which so often made him the target of Joe's ridicule, and the innocence with which he had uttered this remark, made it especially humourous, and our entire table burst into laughter.

'Very well,' said Leyland when calm was restored. 'I plead guilty to the charge of self-contradiction. Heaven knows *you* never suffer from that condition, Brontë! Ha! But hark me, I do my fair share of unpleasant work, and have the calloused hands to prove it.'

Francis, long silent and long-suffering, spoke. The rarity and sobriety of his pronouncements lend them gravity, and the party gathered about the table – even his loquacious brother – fell silent. 'It seems to me that *you want to do what you want to do*, and yet how many grown men in this world are afforded such freedom?'

His use of *grown men* could not have been more pointed. It is true that neither Joe nor I are doing especially well with the grand adventure of maturity: again, is it all, finally, as simple as that? Or are we in fact *courageous* for refusing to give up and give over? Courage or folly? Is the *puer aeternus* to be admired, or despised?

On that rather sombre note, we parted company, with Leyland promising to have Andrew's monument to us in July, at which time he would supervise Brown's lettering. As for me, I felt strangely, unexpectedly, at peace. Seeing Maggie had not been what I had feared, but was instead like the gentle closing of a tumultuous chapter of my life. The calm – the *wholeness* – I felt was akin to what one feels upon closing a particularly satisfying book. I had succeeded in not drinking much at all, and had accepted Dearden's challenge, which I would take up as soon as I had revised some other poems for publication. It remains all too true that I can hardly make my living through poetry, but at least I am slowly garnering recognition, and who knows what other opportunities might present themselves?

As our waggon rumbled north towards Haworth, the westering sun flickered through the leaves swaying in the still-warm June breeze. For a moment I had that old feeling that *anything* was possible, that my entire life still lay before me. I was in love with the universe and felt both the comfort of a mother's embrace and the intimacy of lovers as they collapse, spent, in a tangle of warm flesh.

Yes, anything was possible, and I would be all right – a thought I retained even as dark clouds began to mass to the east and, by the time we reached the lower reaches of Haworth, a driving rain had overtaken us and chilled us to the marrow.

XVII.

A Proposition from Anne

Midsummer's Eve, 1842 · The Parsonage

I write on the day that marks the completion of my twenty-fifth year on this earth, with hope again swelling in my heart when I least expected it. The depressed figure of several weeks ago seems but a nightmarish spectre of a man, a barely recognisable wreck as foreign to me as a black African or inhabitant of distant Siam. Once again I have a direction, I have purpose, and can feel the world beginning to open up possibilities that I could scarcely have imagined just days ago – and I have the youngest of the family to thank for it.

I returned that day from Halifax to find that Anne had arrived for her summer holiday, after which she will rejoin her employers and their charges, the Robinsons, in Scarborough. As I entered the Parsonage, soaked to the skin – for it was positively throwing down – she exclaimed, part with mirth and part with true concern, 'Oh, my, dear brother, off with those wet things, or you'll catch your death of cold!' while Emily's mongrel Keeper jumped and barked at the commotion, as the wind sent the door flying against the wall with a *bang*.

Soon I had changed and sat before a fire – fortunately John's daughter Martha had, despite the season, been commanded to lay one – with a cup of tea, looking into the cheerful eyes of my youngest sister, who had wrapped a large woollen blanket about my shoulders. I believe that we shared an unspoken – and unspeakable – thrill at finding ourselves alone, for we had a common bond in our *otherness*: I, the only boy; she, the family's youngest, the *baby*, who was forever treated as such, especially by Charlotte. Indeed, as I reflect upon the matter, it seems to me that our shared delight at that moment might well have been due to the absence of this latter individual in particular. For Emily – whom I respect and somewhat fear even as much as Anne adores – would have proven no especial burden before this fire. Papa, meanwhile, was locked away in his study, while Aunt Branwell was occupied upstairs.

Anne has become a pretty thing, though far from a great, strapping beauty: a well-proportioned, if slight figure, and quite a lovely, delicate face, with those bright, intelligent blue eyes approaching almost a violet colour, over which arch a pair of eyebrows that appear almost to have been artfully pencilled; a more gently curved nose – which I envy her – than mine, and lips just slightly fuller than either of her sisters; glowing skin so fair that it is nearly transparent; and framing this pretty face, brown hair which, now that she is grown, is nearly chestnut-coloured. Although she is already two and twenty, I marvelled for the first time – perhaps because we were alone – at what a graceful young woman she is become.

'You examine me, Branwell,' said Anne, smiling. 'Do you think me ugly?'

'No, dear sister, quite to the contrary. I think you have grown into quite a lovely young lady. Surely you must be breaking hearts for miles round Thorp Green. I suspect talk of you has even reached the ancient city of York itself!'

'Stop teasing me,' she laughed. 'No, brother, this plain governess is very much a cipher surrounded by the elegant ladies and gentlemen of Thorp Green, and indeed, the incandescent beauty of Mrs Robinson and her young daughters utterly eclipses such a small satellite as me. I might well be a table or chair, or at best, a servant – for that, alas, is what I am: a glorified servant. Surely you had such feelings in Broughton, did you not? And yet, I was thinking …'

Anne hesitated, gazing into the grate, the flames transforming her eyes into a violet kaleidoscope.

'You were thinking?'

She turned to me and smiled sweetly. Such sweetness is often mistaken for weakness or folly, but I have long since learned that Anne is not only good, but exceedingly thoughtful: nearly everything she says had been much considered, even debated, in that pretty little head sitting on those narrow, sloping shoulders.

'I was *wondering* is perhaps a better word for it: I was *wondering* if you might consider taking up the sacred mantle of tutor once again. After all, by all accounts' – I did not interrupt her to say that it was merely *my* account of the events at Broughton – 'by all accounts you performed admirably. It was just that Mr Postlethwaite had rather low, utilitarian aims, for which your talents were unsuitable, which is to say superior. I ask because young master Edmund – Ned, as the family calls him – has now reached an age – he is ten – where he requires true instruction in the classics. The Robinsons have begun to speak of engaging a tutor for him, effective January, until he goes off to Oxford in a few years – at least that is the plan.'

'I hope,' said I, 'that you have not yet said anything on my behalf.'

'*Branwell*,' she replied softly, her gaze mingling love and firmness in a way more maternal than fraternal, 'you know that I would not do *that*. But I did secret the information away for consideration' – here she tapped her fair forehead – 'first mine, and now yours. After reflection, I realise, if I am to be entirely candid, that I am quite lonely, and that it would be splendid to have my only brother near me, to see him at least once or twice a day, not only for his own worth, but as a constant reminder of home.'

The chill had at last left me, and I removed the blanket and stirred the fire. I took off my spectacles and looked fixedly at her, though her face was now little more than a blur, which in turn put me entirely at ease: my old trick.

'This is *most* unexpected, little sister. It is now my turn to reflect, as you can well imagine.'

'Well then,' said she, 'I will take up my book whilst you cogitate, big brother.' Her small hand brushed a wayward lock of hair off her forehead as the fire crackled anew. Keeper, much becalmed, had long ago fallen into blissful slumber between us, in which he appeared to be dreaming of some sort of prey, for he briefly shuddered and softly barked before settling into a rhythmic snore, his thick muscular flanks and shoulders rising and falling with each breath.

I did indeed *cogitate*, as Anne said. Who has not at least once in his life experienced the sudden, vertiginous, exhilarating, sometimes joyful and sometimes terrifying prospect of new vistas thrown open when least expected? One is so disorientated that one must breathe deeply, and possibly even lie down. A thousand thoughts thronged into my mind, among them chiefly these: Of course Anne was right: I *had* performed admirably for the Postlethwaites, had I not? There was a difference of educational philosophy, surely, and my master had every right to act upon his beliefs. Any regrets I had about the months in Broughton were personal, and I had remained competent to the end.

From Anne's accounts, the estate at Thorp Green was grand indeed, in a pastoral district between Ripon and York, far from the dirty manufacturing of our neighbourhood. A distinguished family – Mrs Robinson was even a cousin of the celebrated Macaulay – with three girls and a boy: Lydia, named for her mother, was now a great girl of nearly seventeen, her sisters Elizabeth (called 'Bessy') and Mary one and two years behind her, respectively. If nothing else, the pleasing surroundings and the proximity of rich, lovely young girls blooming into womanhood – for more than once has Anne mentioned their beauty, though she is far less laudatory as concerns their *character* – would be a fresh beginning, and perhaps a family such as this would have an appreciation for my talents of which Mr Postlethwaite and his breed are incapable.

I continued to muse. Perhaps, indeed, I am destined to teach, for I increasingly believe I am ill-suited to any other occupation, especially those connected to the dirty, money-grubbing business of commerce. Perhaps the post as tutor – to only one lad, after all, and hardly a baby – would allow me to ramble, to sketch and to write, all the while making my living amongst people of a certain quality, far removed from the oppression of home.

We sat together for what seemed a very long while, but what was likely only a period of five or ten minutes, Anne quietly turning the leaves of a book that we had long ago used to learn to draw, William de la Motte's *Characters of Trees*, and I staring into the fire, this new and sudden and entirely unexpected opportunity rising up before me. From time to time I could feel her gaze flit furtively over to me as she read. All we could hear was Keeper's snoring, the crepitations of the fire, the wind and rain still lashing the windowpanes, and the march of time as Papa's inexorable clock marked our passage into the future. Or was it ushering what *had* been the waiting future into the present and just as hurriedly into the past? I seized an iron and stirred the embers in the grate, then stood, my back to the fire, and faced Anne.

'I am intrigued, I must say. Much good, I think, could result from such a situation, and I might just be well-suited to it. What do *you* think?'

The young woman of hard common sense that lies just beneath my sister's sweet exterior sat upright, closing her book, her finger marking the page; those eyes now seemed to have a quality of steel about them. 'If you think, brother, that I would jeopardise my own position just to find *you* one, you are quite mad. No, no, I have thought and prayed about it, and am certain that if you apply yourself steadily and conduct yourself scrupulously, you will surely prosper, which will only redound to *my* benefit as well, for I will have done the family a great service.'

Anne knows nothing of Broughton beyond my official account, and neither Papa nor I have revealed to anyone the reasons behind my departure from the railway. The worst of my conduct has always been confined to the environs of Bradford and Halifax, and even those few times I have had too much drink at the Black Bull have occurred when my sisters were at school, or in Anne's case, at her employers. In short, that person known by John Brown, but especially by Joe Leyland and his circle, or by

Agnes or Maeve, is an utter stranger to my family.

No, here was the good brother, stirring the fire and sipping his tea, *cogitating*. After all, thought I, I *want* to be good, and if I am happily employed, in a beautiful neighbourhood, with ample leisure to continue my writing, why should I *not* begin to gravitate towards good, and away from evil? Finally – I considered with a pang of regret that felt almost like a betrayal – if I am utterly plain with myself, living at some remove from Leyland and Brown might be a change far more salutary than disadvantageous. As I considered, I could find no reason for not accepting such a position, and began to build castles in the air about my life as a man of letters at such a fine estate, though finally I said to myself, *you are running on too fast, slow down, Branwell, slow down.*

'How much time have I to reach my decision?' I asked.

'I leave in ten days' time to spend six weeks with the family at Scarborough. It is so beautiful there, Branwell – I am certain that you would also love the place, for it is nothing like the west coast of England. She laughed. 'You see, I am already quite swept away by the waves of that place and begin to digress; I beg your pardon. I was going to say that you should make a decision by the end of the family's holiday at the seaside, for they will surely begin advertising for a tutor upon their return to Thorp Green on the twentieth of August or so.'

'I will indeed give it much thought,' said I, but I could not bring myself to be hypocritical enough to add, *and prayer*. I reserve such hypocrisy for Papa alone, and that is merely a question of daily survival.

'Very well,' she replied. 'While you reflect, I shall broach the subject with my employers. Once you have decided, write to me in Scarborough, at Number 15, The Cliff. If your answer is *yes*, I – or perhaps even Mrs Robinson, for she oversees the education of her brood – which is to say that she hires those who *do* educate them – will write you a formal missive requesting a letter of interest from you in return.

I smiled at how thoroughly Anne had worked this all out in her mind. 'Very well, sister, I shall continue to ponder it most assiduously,' said I, twirling the poker and bowing with mock reverence before resuming my seat.

But my mind is, at this hour, already quite made up: to Thorp Green I shall go.

Keeper snored and the fire crackled on. After another long silence, Anne laughed, holding her book for me to see in the firelight. 'Branwell, look. You naughty boy – you made sketches of soldiers and castle ruins throughout poor Mr de la Motte's quite earnest efforts to teach us how to draw trees!'

XVIII.

All's Right with the World!

July 5th, 1842 · The Parsonage

What a difference a fortnight makes! I am now thoroughly reconciled – indeed, giddy with anticipation – at the thought of beginning anew at Thorp Green. For am I not still a youth, with life before me? My conversations with Papa's curate, the Reverend William Weightman, have only confirmed me in my resolve. He appeared on my birthday, just as I was finishing the composition of the lines above, for Anne had decided to surprise me with a special tea for the occasion: there was not just a birthday cake, as is the new fashion, but also nuts, jellies and sweets. A small but agreeable party we made: Weightman, Papa, Aunt, Anne and I. A long morning ramble under clear skies, the prospects of my life to come, and the genial company now seated around me combined to make me feel better than I had in many a month, perhaps even many a year. Not since I embarked on my railway career – or possibly not even since I set out for Broughton – has my heart been so light. What a joy it is, to begin anew!

Anne was not now merely the youngest Brontë daughter and sister; with Charlotte and Emily in Brussels she was the *only* one, and despite her self-effacing manner she clearly relished her role, serving the handsome young curate and laughing at his witticisms – always appropriately calibrated not to offend the ladies or his fellow clergyman, of course, although I privately believe that the son of a brewer must surely know some jokes of a more ribald nature – while her own pretty face glowed with pleasure, just shy of a perpetual blush. I took considerable delight in teasing her once he had departed, at which time he and I promised each other a long ramble on the moors three days hence.

'Well, well, Miss Anne, I see that your organ of veneration has been hard at work in the presence of the handsome and distinguished young curate. You were positively radiant as he spoke!' We returned to the dining room – which only Aunt Branwell insists on calling the parlour – where today's warmth had rendered a fire unnecessary.

'Nonsense,' said she, but after a moment of staring into the cold grate, added, 'It is true that his visits are a source of considerable pleasure, for rare are the instances of proper contact with young gentlemen of his – his learning and manners.'

'Oh ho! You hesitate, which means that it is more than learning and manners that act as a magnet upon you. I think you might just be in love. At least that is what Charlotte has intimated, and now I have seen signs of it myself.'

Anne frowned, her distinctive brows rendering her displeasure so plain that she hardly needed to speak. 'Yes, Charlotte has quite fixed ideas about Mr Weightman, whom as I'm sure you know she was fond of calling Miss Celia Amelia. Has it not occurred to you, brother, that *she* was in love with him? And while I would not claim that it is the sole reason for her escape to Brussels with Emily, could it not be at least partly because she could not bear to see one that she knows will never seek the hand of a girl so plain and penniless as she – or any of us, for that matter?'

'Hmm. It's possible. For all her force and intellect, there is a part of her which, like her childhood heroine Mina Laury, desires to throw herself at the feet of an idol. Perhaps she'll find the proper object of that passion in Brussels.'

Anne ignored this, as she does most of my unkind comments.

'I *wonder*, Branwell, why it is acceptable for men to gaze and gape in shameless admiration of feminine charms – for I regularly witness such performances at Thorp Green, and will surely see it every day at Scarborough, as the young Robinsons are paraded like show-horses, or cattle before the slaughter, choose your beast – but why is it so unbecoming for the softer or weaker sex, as you gentlemen would call us, to show any admiration whatsoever, no matter how innocent, for the *male* of the species? It is absurd.'

I had no proper reply to such an audacious statement, and so simply said, 'Dear, *sweet* Anne' – this was a long-standing jest between us, a reference both to her being treated like a baby and to her temperament, which nevertheless sheathes a will of iron – 'sweet Anne, I am sure you are not questioning the proper order of things, where loveliness is the special prerogative of woman. An ugly *woman* is a blot on the fair face of creation, but *gentlemen* need only strength and valour – and, of course, a fortune in the bargain.'

'That is precisely what I mean,' she replied. 'Does that truly seem fair to you, brother?'

'I don't know. Does *life* seem fair? Is it fair that people of our education and breeding – and yes, I am speaking now of the Brontë offspring as intellectual equals, as we are – must bow and scrape as servants before the rich, whose manners and learning are vastly inferior to ours? Is it fair that the half-illiterate mill owner is richer than a scholar or curate or tutor ever will be?'

Anne bit her lip and again knitted her brows. Keeper, who had wandered in and placed his large, square head on her knee, whimpered. She at last appeared to be resolved to change topics. 'Well, as for Mr Weightman, I can only say that if his greatest sin is that he is sweet and kind to such plain spinsters as the Brontë sisters – and might I add that he is every bit as charming and kind to *everyone* he meets – surely he will have no trouble gaining entrance into Heaven.'

Still, it was clear that she could not yet let go; after another silence, she added, 'Truly, Branwell, I *do* want you to know that I do not cherish a *grande passion* for Papa's curate, for I have never had to mask my esteem for him by giving him a feminine appellation or condemning him as a *thorough male flirt who has scattered his impressions far and wide*, as has Charlotte. I do love him as a brother, though, just as Papa loves him as a son.'

This last comment was uttered with great simplicity – all kindness and no malice – and yet it recalled to me how much better my friend had been than I, Papa's own flesh and blood; I felt no envy of Weightman, but only gratitude to him and shame of myself.

To lighten her mood – and mine – I responded, as we made our way upstairs to bed, 'And see, in any event you will soon be led away from temptation and delivered from evil as you make your way to Scarborough, and next year your happiness will be complete as your brilliant and companionable brother joins you in your work of training the tender Robinson plants, and together we shall watch their buds unfolding day by day!'

I must confess that as I uttered these words I was imagining the blooming of the rosy Robinson girls, for though I would be tutoring Edmund I would surely see his older sisters with great regularity. The thought of being able to – what did Anne say? – *gaze and gape in admiration of their feminine charms* at such close proximity fairly intoxicated me with anticipation. Of course, I must do so discretely, for their mama will surely be on her guard against such a low ruffian as I – ha ha!

The gentleman in question, the Reverend William Weightman, did indeed call upon us again on this bright July day, desiring that I walk out upon the moors with him. Still thinking of Anne's passionate words, I said, 'Why don't we make it a triumvirate? I shall play the role of chaperone, with a fierceness to rival Keeper's,' at which both of them laughed and – or was it my imagination? – both of them blushed.

'A capital idea, Branwell,' said he, bowing ever so slightly. 'Why should not Miss Anne come along? Although I am sure that she, like me, will ignore your incessant teasing.'

'As the day is so lovely, I'll consent to go a small way with you gentlemen, but must bend my steps homeward, ere long. I leave two days hence for Scarborough, remember, and I've a number of arrangements to make this afternoon.'

Soon we were out of doors, with Keeper in the vanguard, walking in silence. A warming southerly breeze caressed our faces, twisting the curls at Anne's temples like kite strings, and playing havoc with both the curate's hair and mine. On the horizon, billowy clouds piled high with startling rapidity, but their dazzlingly white hue foretold no risk of a spoiled perambulation.

As we made our way up towards Penistone Hill, something had attracted Anne's attention as she and I walked arm in arm. Above a heap of abandoned quarry stones there grew three primroses, peeping from between the twisted roots of an old ash tree. She broke from me and skipped forward – a young girl again, with the slight figure to match – where she tried, on the tips of her toes, her best to clutch at them.

'Allow me to gather them for you, Miss Anne,' said the curate, and in an instant the flowers were in her hand. She positively glowed with delight, but seemed unable to speak. 'Thank you,' said she at last, in some confusion, again taking my arm. 'It seems a two-fold miracle that such flowers should grow *here* and that they should grow *now*, in this late season.'

'Oh Heavens,' said Weightman, 'Up in my neighbourhood, in Westmorland, such so-called early spring flowers may be seen blooming as late as August, and we have just passed midsummer, remember. After all, in these rough hills spring comes late, summer is brief, and all too soon we are reminded of the ephemeral nature of beauty – of all earthly things – as autumn is rapidly succeeded by winter.'

As our footsteps carried us further onto the moors, my companions entered upon a banal and therefore *harmless* discussion concerning the flora of the North of England, while my mind wandered in quite another direction. These three flowers, clinging stubbornly to life far later than expected, seemed to me to augur well for the three young people who trod this uneven path: I had made up my mind to go to Thorp Green, if the Robinsons would have me; Anne was highly valued by them and could, seemingly, continue in her capacity until all three girls were quite grown; Weightman, just three years my senior, had an illustrious career before him, for he had made himself indispensable to our father, and beloved throughout the parish, and beyond.

As we reached the foot of a particularly steep incline, Anne – whose breathing is often even more laboured than mine –

slackened her pace, then halted altogether. The midsummer sun had just begun its slow descent to the west, and its rays bathed my sister's glowing forehead and bright, speaking eyes as she turned to face us. 'I believe that *here* is where we must part company. Keeper will prove an able guide and protector, so you need fear nothing on that account, gentlemen.'

'Well then,' said my friend, 'Off you go to Scarborough, eh? So often do you speak of your love of the sea that I must suppose you will be happy there?' His tone was more interrogative than declarative.

'Yes, I suppose so, although the young ladies will have no patience with my "dreary lessons" at such a fashionable resort – believe me, they will only have eyes for the young gentlemen to be met along the sands or upon the Spa Bridge. I have no great hopes of making any progress with my charges until we return to Thorp Green, I fear.'

'I suppose I'll not see you until the Christmas Holidays, then?'

'That's right. But did you not just say that *autumn will be rapidly succeeded by winter*? In that case we shall see each other very soon indeed!' said she, laughing winsomely and clutching her flowers like a treasure, although doing her utmost to appear restrained as they shook hands and she called 'Come, Keeper!' and began the walk home with her faithful companion. As they drew away from us, it occurred to me that not only did Emily's dog take her place at Anne's side; Anne herself played the same role for Keeper!

Weightman and I followed her briefly with our gaze, but I could not possibly guess what my friend was thinking. Even if she were not my sister, I am not sure that I could enter upon a discussion of feminine charms with the right hand and confidante of the Reverend Brontë, any more than I had been able to do with my erstwhile friend, Sugden Sowden.

As we climbed a particularly steep hill, I wondered if Sowden had learnt of the particulars of my dismissal, and had to conclude, grimly, that *of course* he had: for after all, Calderdale was a small place indeed, and was it not my counterpart at Hebden Bridge itself, Woolven, who had participated directly in the audit that resulted in my dismissal? Would not Sowden, hearing nothing from me, have enquired of Woolven as to my mysterious disappearance from the district? Truth to tell, I am more ashamed than ever of my behaviour in those not-so-distant days, from which I nevertheless now seem to be separated by an eternity.

In Weightman, I had found another Sowden-like friendship, but unpolluted by my own appalling conduct and the shame that ensued. Like Sowden, he has an affection for life nearly as strong as his love of God, and in his work with the simple folk of Haworth, he has made that selfsame love of God, rather than any fear of hell, the ruling motive for our obedience. His kindness extends equally to all, and far from making him a *thorough male flirt*, it simply demonstrates a genuine goodness blended with an eagerness to please. This man, who once walked ten miles to post valentines to all three of my sisters – surely because he felt sorry for them – is truly the *opposite* of a heartless Don Juan. Can he help it if he is naturally pleasing to the fairer sex, and should he be condemned for exercising that gift of God? Were he not so affable and good, I would surely envy him his good looks, stature, and most of all the great esteem in which he is held in the district, especially by Papa. But like Leyland – though for entirely different reasons – Weightman is one of the elect of this life who is quite simply nearly impossible to dislike.

We decided to make the climb to Top Withens, and when we at last reached the farm and caught our breath – he quickly and I with considerably more difficulty – he sat quietly on a large stone with his arms folded, the wind whipping his hair as clouds raced to catch the sun, as it bent towards Liverpool and the sea beyond. Jonas and Mary Sunderland were nowhere to be seen, and only a few scattered sheep grazed on the hillside, bleating occasionally to remind us of their presence.

'Now that we are alone,' said he with genuine interest, 'tell me what you are about these days, Branwell. Are you in search of another post on the railways? Contemplating a return to the life of a tutor? Are you writing?' This was very much like him, to ask about *me* and say nothing of himself.

I at last was breathing freely and so spoke evenly. 'I have looked into the matter of the railways, but alas, my friends in the business report that there is a great glut in that market at present.' I paused, contemplating whether I should share the news about my possible employment by the Robinsons of Thorp Green. *No, not yet.* 'As for being a tutor, I have certainly not ruled that out. All would depend upon the suitability of the situation, the nature of the employers, and whether such a post matched my talents and inclinations.'

'And the writing? How goes that?'

I determined not to share my *nom de plume* with Weightman, but instead spoke of my current project, the long poem I am revising for the great challenge with Dearden: 'Azrael, or the Eve of Destruction.' In it, Noah confronts the Azrael, angel of death, over Methuselah's grave, where they argue over the very existence of God. I failed to mention that the clash of these mighty figures represented the doubts within my own soul, or – especially – that I found Azrael's speech far more interesting than Noah's.

'Ah, a sacred subject! Your father will approve.'

'I'm not at all convinced,' I said ruefully, 'that Papa will approve of *any* of my poetry. And I am certain that he is far more concerned that I make my independence with something more reliable than poetry.' Here I felt I could be honest. 'What is sometimes a source of gall is that *he* instilled this passion for letters in us all; *he* encouraged my longing to distinguish myself in the world, whether through painting or writing or some more modest, steady employment; *he* has vaunted my talents, keeping me ever from harm when, perhaps, such harm might well have been most salutary.'

'Are you saying,' said Weightman, 'that you wish you had been set adrift, penniless, in the world? Surely that is not the case.'

'No – no, of course not. But our father infused us with his love of the written word in early childhood and sanctioned it as long as we were young; but now he expects us to crush our passion as he did his, as though such blotting out were as natural as a falling leaf, instead of what it feels like: the plucking of a limb from one's body, if not the extermination of one's very soul!'

Weightman sat quietly for a few moments, pondering. At last, he turned his kindly face to me.

'Perhaps you *have* been too petted in this life, and perhaps the Reverend Brontë has come late to the understanding that the chances of your – indeed, of anyone's – making a living in painting or poetry are remote indeed. I'm sure that you can see that both of these failings – if failings they even be – proceeded from the purest motives, from paternal *love*, from a desire for your happiness.'

This, too, I knew to be true. Papa's love and clemency were unfailing, and yet his goodness only made me, in my heart of hearts, sink further into shame. 'I know, I *know*: he wants only the best for me, and worries incessantly what will become of me – what will become of us all – if he should die.'

More silence. There seemed little more we could say on this topic: it was intractable. The prospect of Thorp Green now rose before me like a golden dream, as I imagined a life of ease, gentility, and the leisure to pursue my writing. Still, I kept this from Weightman, wishing to wait until my appointment was assured.

'Well then,' said he, slapping me genially on the back, 'that's enough grim talk. Tell me about your poem.'

I explained that Azrael denies the existence of God and preaches defiance to the crowds assembled at the burial of Methuselah. It is human pride, says the angel of death, which cannot abide the thought of returning to dust:

> Nature abhors to look at naught
> And frames for ease a world of thought. –
> So – when the Sickman lies to die
> He gasps for Hope in Agony
> And as the Earth yields none to save
> He makes a Hope beyond the grave! –
> Thus Heaven is but an Earthly dream,
> Tis Man makes God – not God makes him!

'Why Branwell,' said Weightman, 'this is very, very good!' Then laughing, he added, 'Of course I sincerely hope that Noah has the final word, and that his argument is even more persuasive, else you will go the way of the great Milton, of making the denizens of Hell more appealing that those of Paradise!'

'Would that I might aspire to such a sin,' I replied, and though I said it with a smile, I wondered how much truth there might be in such an assertion. Would I – Faust-like – trade all for poetic glory? But I hastened to add: 'But fear not, my reverend friend, Noah will obliterate Azrael's argument, and I shall be as orthodox in my theology as I am brilliant in my execution!'

As we hopped down from our perch, Weightman slapped me once more on the back and said, 'I have a good feeling, Branwell, that things are going to turn your way. As for me, someday I will have my own parish, and perhaps even a charming wife and a house full of little ones.'

'It sounds like the happy end to a novel in three volumes, Weightman,' said I, laughing. Despite my jest, though, my mind raced forward: I pictured Papa's death, for surely he would die before any of us; Weightman's appointment as his replacement; and yes, even the latter's marriage to Anne, followed by the inevitably handsome offspring who would grow up happily, as we had, despite our many losses, in the venerable Parsonage. I, the eccentric but celebrated uncle, would be welcomed with great fanfare on my rare visits from London.

Why not? Why not indeed?

The clouds did not overtake the sun until we had reached Haworth, at which point a broad sunbeam, like Jacob's ladder, shone down through the heavens, beyond Weightman's rooms at Cook Gate. He pointed and smiled as he made his way home.

'Branwell, surely that should inspire you to ensure that Noah's argument triumphs over Azrael's! What does Mr Browning say in that little sixpence volume you lent me? *God's in His heaven – All's right with the world!*'

XIX.

Mirth and Mourning

July 15th, 1842 · The Parsonage

Leyland has, at last, brought the Thomas Andrew memorial to Haworth. We have all had our part in it: the sculptor has fashioned it; Brown has lettered it; and I have provided the inscription – with the editorial oversight of the committee, of course. Even Weightman took part, at Papa's request choosing its emplacement and overseeing its installation. The inscription reads thus: *This Tablet was erected by those who knew his worth, & who feel that, while in his death the neighbourhood has lost an honourable and upright man, the poor have lost an able adviser in their calamities, & a generous friend in their need.*

John Brown, as he finished the lettering in the stifling July heat – for summer is now truly upon us – mopped his brow and said, 'Verily, I've never 'ad such an audience … I felt like a soddin' player on a stage, for 'eaven's sake.' But he was grinning in habitual Brownian fashion.

Leyland followed the inscription of each letter with his right forefinger, wiping away the dust as he went. 'You are simply not to be trusted alone, Brown. I am here to ensure that my masterpiece is not destroyed – after all, such script is not like one of Brontë's poems, where an errant word can be scratched out and replaced with another. *Written in stone*: the expression exists for good reason.'

Weightman, ignoring Joe's banter, sighed, for countless were the times that he and the good surgeon had held vigil at the bedside of a dying man, woman or child. He placed his hand on the cool stone, and his eyes shone with tears. 'Such are we all; we go the way of all the earth. God bless you, Thomas.'

Brown, Leyland and I were silent. Soon Weightman took his leave, as did Brown, for he had three graves to dig: a young family struck down by cholera. No doubt, Weightman had also stood with *them* at their suffering, and had sorely missed the presence of his old friend the surgeon. As we set forth on the road to the Crossroads Inn, where we were to meet Dearden, it was clear that Joe had no desire to dwell upon such grim matters. With his business concluded, he looked forward solely to liquid refreshment.

'Great God in his Heaven, Brontë, I have an unspeakable thirst, and this heat and dust do nothing to improve upon it. I feel like a lost soul wandering the Arabian sands, one who has lost all hope of finding an oasis.'

'Recall, my dear sir,' I laughed, 'that the inn is but a little over a mile from here, and hardly a trek across the Sahara! Do try to keep your dipsomania in check, now do.'

'Fair enough, fair enough. But your remark has not made my thirst any less acute. Quite to the contrary, like a lover whose desire flames up at the sight of his beloved, like the prisoner who hears the keys of his freedom rattle in his gaoler's pocket, so doth my thirst increase as we draw nigh!'

'I think,' said I, 'that *you* should be competing with Dearden for poetical laurels, not I.'

'No indeed,' he replied, 'I could hardly enter a contest with so elevated – nay, sacred – a subject as yours. No biblical themes for me, young Faustus; my style is more that of Benjamin Cooke, *fils* – do you remember his *In Vino, Veritas*? Joe began to sing in his deep baritone:

Round, round with the glass, boys, as fast as you can,
Since he who don't drink cannot be a true man.
For if truth is in wine, then 'tis all but a whim
To think a man's true when the wine's not in him.
Drink, drink, then, and hold it a maxim divine
That there's virtue in truth, and there's truth in good wine!

Relieved to be alone with Joe, and to quit the outskirts of Haworth, I entered into the fun, feigning opprobrium: 'For shame, Leyland; don't you think such thoughts do nothing but justify poor conduct?' Though I felt a pang of remorse at making sport of Weightman's genuine sorrow over the loss of Dr Andrew, I added wickedly: 'Do you not fear what will happen when *you* go the way of all the earth?'

He was swift to reply: 'Why, what an idea, coming from the great Northangerland, who published – correct me if I am wrong, please – just a week or so ago, in the illustrious *Halifax Guardian*, 'An Epicurean's Song'. How does it begin? Upon Sorrow's visitation … something … something?'

'No, no, that is not it at all,' I corrected. It begins thus:

The visits of sorrow,
Say, why should we mourn?

'And does not the great Northangerland go on to proclaim: *So seize we the present, / And gather its flowers?*'

'He does indeed.'

'Well then, *petit bonhomme*' – ever since Liszt's visit to Halifax Joe has added this Gallic version of *little man* to his repertoire – 'let us heed his advice and *carpe* ourselves a wee bit of *diem*. Who knows but there might be some rosebuds to gather up yonder,' said Joe, nudging me conspiratorially, as we came into sight of the inn. 'Yea, verily, a few drinks and a romp or two with a wanton wench – some lusty rigmutton or even a passive rompstall – either would suit me just fine today, by God – maybe even one of each – what could be better to clear one's mind and cleanse one's spirit?'

I have of late been so abstemious on all counts that I said nothing, but trembled at the memory of my late debauchery, my blood running cold with a fear that I could again fall into such conduct. *Flowers, rosebuds, primroses.* It was only after we had shaken hands with Dearden and settled at our table, drinks in hand, that I recalled the primroses that Weightman had so recently gathered for Anne: she had placed them in a glass until they were quite withered, and this morning, when Martha threw them out, I noticed that only two of the three remained. What had become of the third?

As we lifted our glasses in our first toast of the afternoon, I remembered reading somewhere that Cooke, whose *In Vino Veritas* Leyland had just sung with such unbridled glee, had ultimately, and quite intentionally, drowned himself – not in wine, but in the mighty River Thames itself.

October 18th, 1842 · The Parsonage

It cannot *be*! The man who so quickly became a good – and true – friend, and might well have become my spiritual guide, young William Weightman, is dead. I have been utterly silenced by the lightning-fast blow of his departure, for what is there to say in such moments? Two months have passed since I visited these pages, for I could not bring myself to open a notebook in which recent happy times were so vividly inscribed. How could I bear it? I just now begin to recover my wits, and following Papa and Aunt's stoical example – and with the memory of Weightman's life and death as another – I have determined that self-pity must ultimately give way to action, and so once again I take up my pen.

A day after the visit to the Crossroads – where I had produced from my pocket not *Azrael* but another sheaf of papers I had mistakenly brought, thus obliging me to recite, as best I could, from memory – I again saw Weightman, sharing with him Noah's response to the Angel of Death. As we sat on a low wall under the cooling shade of a spreading oak, I produced the poem I *should* have carried to the inn the previous day.

'Now,' said my friend, 'let us hear if the eloquence of Noah can surpass that of Azrael!'

'I suppose,' I replied, 'that if it does not, you will ascribe his failings to the literary – or worse, moral – deficiencies of the author himself, eh Weightman?'

'Naturally,' said he, all smiles. It was ever his way to nudge, rather than cudgel, one towards virtue. If I were ever to achieve a pure yet simple, unassuming faith, like his – or Anne's – it would be due to the influence and example of such a one as he, which so reminded me of my old friend Sowden, whose friendship I had so carelessly abandoned during my dark days at Luddenden Foot.

A faint breeze lifted the leaves above us; the only other sounds were a fly buzzing lazily round our heads, and John Brown's shovel – digging yet another grave – in the distance.

'Well then,' said I, 'this is what I have, for what it's worth. Noah stands over the grave of his grandfather, Methuselah.' I cleared my throat and read from the last few lines:

Shall storms from heaven, without the world,
        Find wilder storms from hell, within?
Shall long-stored – late-come wrath be hurled;
        Or – will you – can you turn from sin?

Have patience if too plain I speak,
        For time, my sons, is hastening by:
Forgive me, if my accents break;
        Shall I be saved and Nature die?

Forgive that pause: – One look to heaven
        Too plainly tells me He is gone
Who, long, with me in vain had striven
        For earth, beneath its Maker's throne.

'Very nice,' said Weightman, by way of encouragement. At the same time, he frowned, scratching the handsome, perfectly straight nose that I so envied.

'What is it?' I queried.

'It's just that … that Noah – for all of his sacred *gravitas* – lacks the passion of Azrael.'

'Hold fast there, my reverend friend,' said I, 'I have only just begun.' I read on, intoning the words as dramatically as I could:

He is gone! – My Father! – full of days –
From life which left no joys for him;
Born in creation's earliest blaze;
Dying – himself its latest beam.

But he is gone! And, oh, beyond,
Shewn in his death, God's latest sign!
Than which more plainly never told
An angel's presence, his design

'Ah, *now* we are getting somewhere,' he laughed. 'I can smell fire and brimstone in the air already … or I suppose in this case it is the damp of the coming deluge.'

Like some genuinely pious souls, my friend was able to embrace clear notions of good and evil without indulging in either fanaticism or hypocrisy, and while his theology was surely orthodox, he could – like Sowden – often stand beyond the narrow confines of his own faith, and have just a bit of innocent fun – that same sense of fun that caused him to tease my sisters, or to shower them with attentions that they would surely never find elsewhere.

'Quiet, please!' said I, but fully sharing his mirth. I read on:

By it, the evening beam withdrawn
Before a starless night descend;
By it, the last blest spirit born
From this beginning of an end!

By all the strife of civil war
That brews without yon fated town;
By all the heart's worst passions there,
That call so loud for vengeance down;

By that vast wall of cloudy gloom,
Piled round heaven's boding firmament;
By all its presages of doom,
Children of men – Repent! Repent!

When I had finished, Weightman applauded enthusiastically. 'You have outdone yourself, Branwell! Azrael is vanquished! And to conclude your poem with the words *Repent! Repent!* It is better than a Baptist sermon,' said he, clutching his sides. 'I can still hear your father's old nemesis, the Reverend Winterbotham – may God preserve him in the Canadian wilderness – crying from his low pulpit down there' – here he gestured towards the squat dissenters'chapel at the bottom of the Main Street – '*Children of men – Repent! Repent!*'

It was my turn to tease my friend: 'Am I catching a whiff of the heresy of universal salvation? Tell me, truly, do you hold such heterodox views? Must I denounce you to the religious authorities – viz., to my own Papa?'

To myself, however, I thought, far more seriously: *Ah, here is another place that Anne and my friend are compatible*, for she has let fall more than one hint in my presence that she rejects the traditional notion of Hell; whereas Emily has said, staring at me pointedly, that *we cannot know what lies beyond, but there can surely be a hell on earth, of our own making.*

'This is what I think, Branwell,' said he, with a sudden earnestness suffused with a goodness I could neither mock nor resent. 'I think that a fear of Hell – which, despite your raillery, I believe very much in – will never be the ultimate cause of a person's conversion, but that if one strives always to follow God's example of *love*, surely one will see the Kingdom of Heaven: there is a reason that the Gospel of John tells us that God *is* love, not that God *has* love or *loves us*. The more of *love* we have within us, the nearer we are to Him, and the more of His spirit we possess. One cannot be goaded into real love by the threat of eternal damnation, but real love – yes, even our pale, feeble imitations of Christ's ultimate love and sacrifice for us – will save us from eternal suffering, of that I am certain.'

Weightman paused, looking into the distance, as I myself often do. 'Besides, who are we to sound the depths of God's mercy?'

As I write these lines, it is no exaggeration to say that my heart is full, my throat choked with emotion, my cheeks streaked with tears, for this was to be the last time I would see my friend well. His athletic frame sprang up as he said, 'In that spirit, I have some poor cottagers to visit in the outlying districts, but surely I'll see you again very soon, Branwell.' We parted company with light hearts, as he said over his shoulder, 'So – off the poem goes to the *Herald* or the *Guardian*, eh?'

'The first, I believe,' said I. 'I think such a pious subject befits such a weighty publication, don't you, Reverend? Indeed – and here I do not jest – I am contemplating omitting Azrael's soliloquy altogether and changing the title. After all, what better way to ensure Noah's triumph than killing off his rival? Not unlike your abandonment of Hell in favour of love.'

'Yes,' he shouted over his shoulder, laughing, '*you* are the one insisting on damnation, while I embrace the love that vanquishes it.' He gave a final, hearty wave as he strode out of sight.

It was just three days later, early in the morning, that Mr Ogden of Cook Gate – Weightman's landlord – sent a young servant girl to say that the curate had fallen ill. Walking as fast as our legs could carry us, Papa and I crossed the street, passed the White Lion, and strode down the ginnel. Although the brief walk took only five minutes, it seemed it would never end, so great was our concern. The sun was just rising in the east as we arrived.

Mrs Ogden took our hats and coats and showed us into Weightman's bedroom, where we found a wreck of the man we had known and loved. Papa, though composed without, nevertheless swallowed hard at the sight. He had seen his trusted lieutenant just two nights earlier; he had noticed that the young man did not look well and bade him stay at home a day to rest. Believing it a passing indisposition, Papa had thought nothing of his absence the following day.

Now, however – alas! – we found an ashen figure with sunken eyes, who weakly confided that it was indeed the cholera: a sentence of death, and not a rapid or painless one, either. There was nothing to be done. I stood in utter disbelief at the blow, and like a boxer whose wind has been knocked out of him, I struggled simply to breathe.

Papa stood over him, I at the foot of his bed, and together we recited the 23rd Psalm: *The Lord is my shepherd; I shall not want ...*

I said the words mechanically, thoughtlessly, as I tend to do with all memorised scripture or liturgical language; my mind was elsewhere: like the blood pulsing at my temples, a single thought pounded again and again, like a drum: *this simply cannot be, this simply cannot be.*

We continued: *Yea, though I walk through the valley of the shadow of death, I will fear no evil: for thou art with me; thy rod and thy staff they comfort me.* What a shepherd, this Lord, leading his lamb to slaughter, I thought angrily. The psalm made no sense whatsoever to me; I found no comfort in any of this.

Thou preparest a table before me in the presence of mine enemies: thou anointest my head with oil; my cup runneth over. Enemies? Weightman had no enemies. My anger only increased at these words, so entirely disassociated were they from the reality of a good man dying a pointless death.

Surely goodness and mercy shall follow me all the days of my life: and I will dwell in the house of the LORD for ever. How odd – how foolish, really – that I could at once feel the utter abandonment of God, and yet be prepared to strike a bargain with Him: *Oh God, if you exist, please save my friend, for he, truly, deserves to live. If you save him I will change my ways, I will do your will.* I prayed thus, not even knowing what I meant. I was desperate. As we recited the final words, *I will dwell in the house of the LORD for ever*, I could restrain my sobs no longer.

Weightman, whose voice had been inaudible but whose lips had moved with ours, already had the look of the next world about him. Papa stayed a few moments, but now having the work of two clergymen before him, he bade his curate goodbye with a promise to visit that evening. I stayed on, drawing a chair to my friend's bedside as I brushed my tears away.

'Come now, Branwell,' said he, the old smile returning as he turned his head towards me. 'I have no horror of death. God's will be done.'

'But it is so *unjust*,' said I. 'Of all people ... why?'

'These things pass our understanding, Branwell: *Watch therefore, for ye know neither the day nor the hour wherein the Son of man cometh.* And why should I be protected more than another?'

Now I was irrationally angry with Weightman himself. I gritted my teeth and cried, 'Damn it, Weightman, I am sick unto death of this maddening, passive resignation of the faith! Do you not see the injustice in this? Does your blood not boil with fury? Do you not wish to say, shaking your fist at the heavens, "there exist two possibilities: either there is no God, or He is heartless, cruel, unjust or inept!" Do you not wish to *live*, Weightman?'

He seemed already to have an acceptance of death that I could never imagine for myself, as he calmly surveyed my face and smiled with now unbearable kindness. 'Certainly I wish to live, Branwell. I long to do some good in the world.'

That this good man – so much better a man than I could ever be – could possibly feel that he had *not* done much good in the world was the most heartbreaking thought of all. All of my fury, all of my rancour, melted away in the presence of such humility, and I suddenly shared a small measure of his unshakeable calm, as if it were radiating outwards, enveloping all in its orbit. Did he know that by saying this he had saved me – at least for a few instants – from my wrath and self-pity, since now I was obliged to comfort *him*? Or did he do so instinctively?

In any event, I responded, 'Nonsense, Weightman. You have done more good in your few years here in Haworth than I will ever to do, even if I live to the age of Methusaleh,' and wishing to make him smile in his suffering, I added, 'God knows that *I* will not be walking ten miles to post valentines to the sisters Brontë!'

His sunken eyes somehow managed to brighten perceptibly. 'Thank you, Branwell, for saying so,' said he, stretching his hand weakly towards mine, then squeezing it. 'I will miss our heretical talks, however. Speaking of Methusaleh, did you finish your poem?'

I smiled, but with tears streaming down my cheeks, at his usual thoughtfulness. 'I have indeed, and sent it off to the illustrious *Bradford Herald*, where it is to appear next week.'

'And it is no longer the story of Azrael, but only Noah's warning?'

'Yes, I have simply rewritten the first fifty lines or so and shipped it off as "Noah's Warning over Methusaleh's Grave (From an unpublished poem)".'

'Wait a moment,' said Weightman, 'do you mean to say that Azrael's insistence that God is an invention of man – because of his fear of death – was to come *after* Noah's warning to repent?'

'It was.'

'Well, then, in that case I am glad that you will not be publishing the entire poem, for the only thing worse that naming the entire poem after the angel of death would be giving him the last word.'

I must have looked puzzled. My friend continued: 'Don't you see? Azrael should begin the poem, with his argument then demolished by Noah, not the contrary!'

'But it is God's wrath – the great deluge – that concludes the poem, proving the veracity of Noah's words.'

'Ah, I see,' said my friend, growing serious, 'but remember the power of words. For even the flood eventually subsided, but the Word of God remains. Indeed, is not our Lord Jesus Christ the *Word made flesh*, as John says?'

Even for such a sceptic as me, his comments made a purely rhetorical – in this case poetical – kind of sense: always conclude with the argument that you wish to triumph, else your villain may well seduce your reader into sin. What I could not say to Weightman – and which his imminent demise only strengthened – was how much more appealing and persuasive I found Azrael's words than those of Noah. Is this why I have given him the last word, have named the poem for him, and have failed to complete it, never even *writing* the lines devoted to great flood's destruction of the earth?

'Yes, yes,' I lied, 'you are right, of course. That is surely why I decided to publish it as I have.'

The curate's hand again reached for mine, as he said, 'Friend, I am tired and I think I just might be able to sleep. Will you come again?'

'I shall be here every day, as often and as long as you like.'

Although William Weightman looked, on that day, as if I might see him no more, he suffered on bravely for nearly two weeks, the strength of his young, so recently vigorous constitution refusing to be vanquished by illness, like Jacob wrestling through the long night with the angel of the Lord. His resignation, his willingness to die, was not at all the same as a *will* to die, for he loved the life he believed God had given him. It seemed that I was in attendance at his deathbed for so long, and so acute was his suffering, that I cannot now even bear to bring it mind. At last he died tranquilly – as tranquilly as anyone can quit this world – on the 6th September; we buried him four days later in Haworth Church, where he joined his old friend the surgeon, Thomas Andrew, for one final, everlasting vigil together.

As the days at last turned cool and September gave way to October, Papa prepared to preach a funeral sermon in Weightman's memory. That Sunday afternoon even Joseph Bentley Leyland appeared – at my request, for we were to discuss yet another monument, for a subscription had immediately been raised by the good people of Haworth to memorialise their beloved curate – at the service, sitting with me in our otherwise vacant family pew, as the Reverend Brontë took to the pulpit.

As a sign of the importance of this event – or of just how affected he was by Weightman's sudden passing – Papa had, for the first time in his many years at Haworth, written the sermon, for until now he had always preached extempore. He began with a passage from First Corinthians: *The sting of death is sin, and the strength of sin is the law. But thanks be to God, which giveth us the victory, through our Lord Jesus Christ. Therefore my beloved brethren, be ye steadfast, unmoveable, always abounding in the work of the Lord, for as much as ye know that your labour is not in vain in the Lord.*

Father squinted through his spectacles, his large hands grasping the pulpit to steady himself: *Both in biographical sketches and funeral sermons great care should be taken to consider, full as much the interest of the living as the fame of the dead; and everywhere, and at all times, there should be a due regard to truth, whether it may please or displease, disappoint or satisfy.*

Did this mean that he was not really going to talk about Weightman, but was using his death as a mere pretext for the usual consideration of man's need to repent? It now seemed an age ago that Weightman had sat gamely with me under the oak tree, listening to my recitation of Noah's warning. Papa has forever been kind and patient, and he does have a lively sense of humour, but I am not at all certain that he could have simultaneously viewed Noah both seriously and ironically, as my friend had been able to do. The sermon continued, with little sign that it would include anything about the unfortunate Weightman:

Die we must, whether we will or no, and judged we must be, though we should call on the hills and the mountains to cover and hide us from the face of Him, who will sit on the great white throne of judgement. And should we on the last day of account be found to have been under the law and not under grace, then we shall discover by sad experience that the sting of death is sin, and the strength of sin is the law.

I looked at Leyland, who smelled of liquor. His head nodded forward as he struggled mightily to keep his eyes open. I wondered if he was stale-drunk, or if he merely possessed the remnants of the previous night's tippling. Papa's gaze wandered about the assembly, though I felt it settled all too often on me: was this mere imagination, fuelled by guilt? Each time his eyes met mine I felt it was he, not the law of God, who was the 'stern and inexorable judge' whose sentence of eternal damnation he was describing with considerable gusto. I nudged Leyland's knee with mine.

Yea we must come, continued Papa, *after all our windings and subterfuges, and seek out the strait gate and narrow way, which is Christ, the truth and the life. We must enter in at the one, and walk in the other, if we would escape hell, and get into heaven.*

Was he looking at, or beyond me? His vision has of late deteriorated somewhat, and so it is difficult to say. *This may puzzle, or perplex, and disgust fallen proud man; the infidel may sneer, the scorner may laugh, the philosopher may despise, the lukewarm may disregard, and the sophist cavil; and Satan, and the evil deceitful heart may join the unholy alliance; yet the cause of God must stand.*

I could not help thinking about Weightman on his deathbed, his eyes sunken, his skin almost blue, his thirst unquenchable, his heart racing, and yet his brow clear and untroubled. Before he died, I had shown him 'Noah's Warning' in the *Herald*, and he had asked to hear it again. 'Listen to me, Branwell,' he said with difficulty, 'you have a gift and you must pursue it. A gift from God Himself.'

'You are kind, my friend,' said I, tears again stinging my eyes, 'but I must also eat, and can no longer be a burden to Papa.'

'You'll find a way, I am sure of it. Follow what you love, so long as it is honest, and right, and good, and harms no one. *Love*, remember; not fear.'

I took his counsel to heart, and the very day he died – after I had written to Anne, Charlotte and Emily – I sat and once more addressed *Blackwood's Magazine*, enclosing a revision of 'Sir Henry Tunstall,' hoping against hope that they would at last see fit to publish my work. A month has passed, and *Blackwood's*, alas, has been as silent as my dead friend's tomb.

Papa continued, meanwhile, seemingly repeating the same point in as many different ways as he could conceive: *Our frail bodies must soon perish, and return to the dust; but by the power of Him who has said, 'Let it be,' and the universe was created, they shall be raised in their own proper identity, in a manner far surpassing the comprehension of man, and probably of the highest Archangels, when this mortal shall put on immortality, and shine with unfading splendor for ever and ever.*

At last he turned his attention to poor Weightman, his approach to ministry – rightly saying that his curate *thought it better, and more scriptural, to make love of God, rather than the fear of hell, the ruling motive for obedience* – his origins and education, his agreeable manners, cheerful constitution, and sound and orthodox (I suppose these are synonymous for Papa) religious principles. As the sermon moved from preaching to an appreciation of the deceased, Leyland opened his eyes fully and appeared, at least, to pay attention.

Gazing far into the distance – here it was plain my father was resolutely not looking at me – he said, *We were always like father and son ... giving and taking mutual advice, from the best motives, and in the most friendly spirit; looking on each other, not as rivals, but as fellow labourers in the same glorious cause, and under the superintendence of our common Lord and Master.*

Despite the true attachment that had developed between Weightman and me, I could not but feel a pang of jealousy at such a pronouncement. Like the biblical father's for his prodigal son, Papa's love for me knew no bounds, but I still felt myself to be a resounding disappointment, an abysmal failure in his eyes, and his almost supernatural patience and mercy only heaped further guilt and loathing on my sinking spirit.

Thus, our reverend friend lived – but, it may be asked, how did he die? Father assured the congregation that in his frequent visits to the young man's deathbed he saw him *in tranquility close his eyes on this bustling, vain, selfish world; so that I may truly say, his end was peace, and his hope glory.*

I, too, had seen such tranquility in his eyes, but it alternated with great pain and suffering, and a struggle to cling to *this* life. Of course, who could blame the Reverend Brontë for omitting such details? I certainly could not, and yet I remembered my dream – or was it, finally, a memory? – of Mama's death, dear Mama lying there in the vault just steps away from where Papa calmly read his sermon: *My heart has always been more ready to attach itself to earth than to heaven.* Had he similarly told himself a more uniform, orthodox story, about his own wife's death? Surely this would, in itself, be no sin; it was just another tale to make existence bearable.

The Reverend Brontë at last moved towards his conclusion, looking, I was quite certain, squarely at Joe, if not me. *We may easily comprehend why the wicked have a desire for life, and a dread of death and judgement; but, that the followers of Christ should tremble at the last step of the journey, which will introduce them into His presence and His glory, can only be accounted for by the weakness of their faith, and the remains of sin, what would chain them down, or keep them back from those unspeakable pleasures that he has in reserve for them in the kingdom of their Heavenly Father.*

'*Sitio!*' complained Joe in a blasphemous whisper; his irreverence and thirst had made it impossible for him to attend any longer to Papa's peroration. I am certain his thirst was real; his breath was certainly pestilential.

Brethren, the human heart is weak, wicked and wrong in its reasoning and conclusions; let us, therefore, not trust in it, but in the strength and wisdom of God, let us walk by faith and not by sight, and be always prepared for death and judgement, looking forward to, and long for, a glorious resurrection, and eternal salvation, through Jesus Christ, our Lord and Saviour; to whom, with the Almighty Father, and Holy Spirit, we would ascribe all glory, praise, power and dominion, both now and forever. Amen!

'Amen!' said the packed church in response, and no voice was louder or more enthusiastic than Joe's. Soon we were at Sexton House, availing ourselves of John Brown's hospitality, since the pubs were closed for the Sabbath afternoon.

'Poor Weightman,' said Brown, with none of his usual jocularity. ''e was a good'n; not a mean bone in 'is body. And now – God bless 'im – the Reverend Brontë 'as to go in search of yet another curate, and in the meantime take on all of 'is burthens himself. Branwell, 'ave you written a text for the good man's monument?'

'I have – though I confess that my father had a hand in the final version, for there were certain words he wished to add.' I pulled a folded sheet from my waistcoat pocket, smoothed it on the oaken table, and read:

THIS MONUMENT

WAS ERECTED BY THE INHABITANTS,

IN MEMORY OF THE LATE

WILLIAM WEIGHTMAN, M.A.

WHO DIED SEPTEMBER 6TH 1842, AGED 26 YEARS

AND WAS BURIED IN THIS CHURCH

ON THE 10TH OF THE SAME MONTH.

HE WAS THREE YEARS CURATE OF HAWORTH,
AND BY THE CONGREGATION, AND PARISHIONERS
IN GENERAL, WAS GREATLY RESPECTED,
FOR HIS ORTHODOX PRINCIPLES,
ACTIVE ZEAL, MORAL HABITS, LEARNING,
MILDNESS AND AFFABILITY:
HIS USEFUL LABOURS WILL LONG
BE GRATEFULLY REMEMBERED,
BY THE MEMBERS OF THE CONGREGATION;
AND SUNDAY SCHOOL TEACHERS,
AND SCHOLARS.

Joe seized the sheet as I wiped tears from the corners of my eyes. I still could not believe Weightman was dead. Dead and buried. Or as Papa had just said in his sermon, *the visitation of death, the darkness of the grave, the worm of corruption, the loathsome work of decomposition, eternal separation and oblivion.*

Mephistopheles performed his usual magic; which is to say, he distracted me from such sombre ruminations. Nor did the whisky hurt.

'See here,' he said, holding the sheet at arm's length with great ceremony, 'I detect the hand of Brontë *père* in these words: *orthodox principles, active zeal*, and most of all, *moral habits*, whereas Brontë *fils* is responsible for *learning, mildness* and *affability*. It is almost as if the first three had been inserted by an editor – the editor of the Lord,' he laughed.

'Mind you,' he continued, knowing how fond I – and indeed, the entire family and parish, including Brown – was of Weightman, 'I mean no disrespect to the deceased, for the few times I met him he was always of a right jolly disposition. He had that rare ability – rare, at least, among clergymen – of maintaining a gentle kind of holiness without making you feel as if he was, in his heart of hearts, condemning you to the eternal pit full of fire.'

I thought of Sugden Sowden, who also possessed that rare gift. Did Papa? Perhaps he did, though Joe – pointedly or politely – failed to mention him; perhaps it was my own guilt – the poison corroding my own heart as I slept in his house, wore his clothing and ate his food – that transformed each kind look into an unspoken censure, each gentle word into an implied denunciation. Had my culpability jaundiced my perception of even the simplest, most merciful of his actions?

I have long since determined the necessity of a new beginning at Thorp Green, and just after Weightman's death received confirmation from the Robinsons that they would, indeed, be most pleased to engage me as tutor to their son Edmund after the Christmas vacation. Leyland had found great amusement in my new post, and the solemnity of this day was not about to prevent him from swimming in the waters of his favourite new source of fun.

'Let us speak no more of death; let us toast life!' said he, taking a large draught of Brown's whisky, refilling his glass, and passing the bottle to me. 'Indeed, let us toast your acceptance as tutor to the esteemed Robinson family, far from these besotted and be-sooted districts, in the new Eden of Thorp Green! Three lovely lasses, you say, ripening into adulthood one on the heels of the other!' He smacked his lips. 'And what of the mother?'

'Mrs Robinson? What of her?'

'Well, truly, the apple doesn't fall too far from the tree, in my experience. If the Robinson lasses are as comely as Anne has hinted to you, does it not stand to reason that their good mama is as well? You can't get lovely strapping lasses from a pinched crone any more than you can get blood from a stone, eh Brown?'

John nodded his assent, but gestured for Leyland to lower his voice; this was hardly talk he wished his Mary or the girls to overhear.

Meanwhile, I realised that the appearance of Mrs Robinson had never occurred to me; to my understanding she was easily fifteen years my senior, perhaps more. I said so.

Joe laughed, reverting to his favourite obsession. 'Why little man, have you so soon forgotten about Landseer and his lovely Duchess? Twenty-one years between them, my friend.' He tapped his forehead knowingly. 'Not to mention, a much safer business than seducing one of the young ladies. I suspect their reverend papa would frown even more on catching you in their beds than in his own, ha ha!'

'You are absurd, Leyland. I *am*, however, delighted at the prospect of a lovely, civilised setting; employment that is well matched with my interests and talents, and the leisure to pursue my poetry,' I pronounced with a somewhat lofty air.

Annoyed, no doubt, that I had not risen to take his bait, the sculptor said, 'Oh yes, by all means, tell us, Northangerland, about your writing. By my count you have published eight or nine poems in just the past three months; you have been a veritable whirlwind of activity.'

I laughed. 'See here, my dear sir, it is not as if I had anything else to do in Haworth, and now that at last someone sees fit to publish my work, it is as if a tap has been opened.'

'So, should we expect to see further outpourings of genius, or has the well at last run dry?'

'In truth,' said I, fervently hoping that what I was about to say was not true, 'I think the well ran dry long ago, for most of these poems are reworkings of things I penned long ago.'

'Nonsense,' said my friend – for despite his incessant mockery he truly wished for my success as fervently as he did his own. 'The poem on "Landseer's mongrel", or whatever the bloody hell it was, the little piece on "The Afghan War", and the pious "Noah's Warning" – all new material, and I am quite sure the revisions of earlier poems were so substantial that one could hardly find a resemblance. And don't imagine for a moment that I missed, just the other day, your article on Thomas Bewick, in the *Halifax Guardian*. So, you have even turned your hand to appraisals of the great artists, in prose no less. I shall look forward to a denunciation of Landseer's sentimental animals, followed by a panegyric to the great Leyland and his monumental *Head of Satan*!

'It grieves me to disappoint you, Leyland, but even "Noah's Warning" has its origins in my childhood scribblings,' said I, ignoring his last comment.

'Well, still, I am sure that, like you, it is utterly changed.'

He paused for a moment, then added, 'Though I confess to being profoundly disenchanted upon reading that you had confined Azrael, the Angel of Death, to oblivion – cast out, his wings clipped, poor fellow, like his master Lucifer before him – for he was by far the most engaging part of *that* poem! At any rate, what new works are on the horizon? The reading public – lowly Yorkshire swine that they are – surely awaits your next shower of poetical pearls with bated breath!'

Suddenly, with a rare, serious look – such was the effect of the curate's death on us all, even Joe – he added earnestly, 'Or were you too occupied with poor Weightman?'

'Strange as it may seem, Weightman's illness and death have been a spur of sorts, for each time I saw the poor chap, he encouraged me. He liked "Noah's Warning" and urged me to continue, and while he slept I revised and wrote, even sending a poem to *Blackwood's* the day he died. I am at present revising a long poem called "The Triumph of Mind over Body".'

By now we had drunk enough whisky so that the title of the poem caused both Brown and Leyland to laugh aloud. 'Oh ho, a work of pure fantasy, eh? Ha ha!'

In vain did I try to convince them that it was a rewriting of a long, serious poem about Lord Nelson: they would have none of it – none but the title that is, which, in their current frame of mind, was a seemingly inexhaustible source of mirth. Who has not attempted to speak in earnest to friends who, for whatever reason, have been possessed by such passing madness? In the end, there was nothing to do but capitulate, and to join in their laughter. 'I am vanquished!' said I at last, laughing nearly as heartily as they. When our levity subsided, there was a prolonged moment of silence.

'*Un ange passe*,' remarked at last Leyland, 'as our hereditary foes across the Channel would say.'

I thought not of Azrael, or Saint Michael and All Angels', whose names were given to Haworth Church, but of William Weightman himself, so recently joined the world of spirits, if such a world exists.

Joe was thinking of the young curate as well.

'Mr Weightman was privy to the secret identity of Northangerland, eh? Were you not afraid he would divulge it to the Reverend Brontë?'

'No, not a whit … and at any rate,' I added, suddenly, quite unexpectedly, nearly choking once again with a grief I strove to conceal, 'the secret has gone with him to his tomb.'

Leyland looked at Brown with mock suspicion. 'Well, in that case only your friends in Halifax and a certain worthy Haworthian, yclept Saint-John-in-the-Wilderness, are complicit. Can the latter rascal be at all trusted?'

Brown laughed. 'If y'think I'd introduce any strife or bother twixt the Reverend Brontë and Branwell, y'r' soddin' daft, Leyland. I say so for purely selfish reasons, mind. The more 'armonious things are for the parson, the bett'r for the sexton. And the philanthropist in me' – here he winked –'knows that the more I maintain the Reverend's trust, well, the bett'r for all parties concerned, eh?'

After we shook hands that evening upon parting, I stopped in the churchyard, among the dead, and gazed up at the Parsonage, whose yellowing grey sandstone bricks contrasted sharply with a vivid, almost sapphire sky, punctuated here and there with wisps of pure white clouds, drifting languidly above the moors.

The most harmonious thing of all, I thought at last, will be for me to live far from here, to make a fresh start, to begin anew.

XX.

Another Death

November 2nd, 1842 · The Parsonage

For the longest time – ever since we lost Maria and Elizabeth, in what seems another age – I pretended that *Death* was the stuff of poetry, fantasy or nightmare, and that it affected only others, especially the poor villagers – and that somehow those close to me had a supernatural charm that warded off the Grim Reaper.

Was it that I felt we had already made our human sacrifices, first with Mama, and then with my sisters, so that no other tribute was due? Did I believe that the Parsonage walls had been infused with a homeopathic tincture of death that strangely warded off *Death* himself? Or did I believe that Papa's piety somehow encircled and protected us with a fortress of *Goodness*, of *Virtue*, that would forever bar its return? How, I wonder, could I persist in this fantasy in spite of Papa's own constant attendance upon the dying, and in the face of the perpetual sounds of Brown's chisel on gravestones, or his shovel in the churchyard just beyond the Parsonage wall?

Or is it simply true that a youth – for at twenty-five I am more youth than mature man, although I sometimes feel I have lived more lives than a cat and am wearier than an old draught-horse – is it simply true that a youth is incapable of grasping his own mortality, and that only the constant witness of the deaths of others will, eventually, succeed in penetrating his thick skull with the reality that the Reverend Brontë had been all too willing to recall to us at Weightman's memorial service? *Die we must, whether we will or no.* Would youth fail to strive, and the world thus come to an end, if it knew that all is for naught?

This is a long way of saying that Aunt Branwell is dead, a second blow in almost as many months, and that my mind struggles to comprehend this loss; like an explorer happening upon a foreign land, where all customs and language are unknown, I am paralysed with incomprehension, with disbelief, unable to think or act in any meaningful way: I am incoherent, so much so that it was Papa who wrote to Anne at Thorp Green, and to Charlotte and Emily in Brussels, and all are *en route* to Haworth. I have only now regained sufficient presence of mind to reflect upon what has happened.

It occurs to me that I have written almost nothing concerning Aunt in these pages, and doubtless this is because I have taken her for granted. For how does one write of the air one breathes, the walls that protect one from the frigid blasts of winter, the sun that warms one's body and soul as spring melts into summer? When she came to live with us after Mama, her younger sister, died, Aunt became in some respects the guide and director of all the happy days connected with my childhood. Like Papa, she was firm and yet loving, and had law not forbade it, she might well have married him. How often have I heard him say, once I was a grown man, that Aunt had shared his labours and sorrows, and had behaved as an affectionate mother to his children?

The truth is, however, that she was far more rigid in her discipline with the girls than with me. Although Charlotte has often claimed, resentfully, that Aunt made me her especial pet, is it not natural to assume instead that the latter quite simply always believed that her province was to instill good breeding and a sense of neatness, order, punctuality and, most of all, a *mastery of self* in the girls, and that every aspect of the formation and education of the boy was the responsibility of her brother-in-law? Is there not a reason that tutors teach boys and governesses girls? Just so, the division of labour within a family along such lines is a practice hallowed by time.

Indeed, my sisters would normally have been in attendance at her deathbed, but in their absence, it was I who sat and held her hand, whilst she writhed in agony over five days. At times her screams seemed as though they would rend the heavens, and whether I would or no, I could not but recall, once again, my memory – or vision – or dream – of Mama, crying out ceaselessly: 'Oh God my poor children! – oh God my poor children!'

By the fourth day I was wild with distraction, nearly joining my own cries to Aunt's: 'My God, can't someone *do* something for her?!' I confess that an impious thought crossed my mind, as I tried to arrange the pillows for her comfort: why is it that a lowly horse's suffering is acknowledged with a rifle shot, and why do we even understand – if not fully sanction – the gravely wounded, agonising soldier who implores his fellow – be he friend or foe – to end his existence with a similar gesture, and yet extinguishing the suffering of poor Aunt could not be contemplated?

At last, on 29th October, she expired, and I was flooded with a relief I would be ashamed to avow to anyone but these pages; if nothing else, her suffering made it easier to release her to Death, for in this instance he was our great friend and ally, withdrawing Aunt from a living hell on earth. Just before her last breath, God – or Nature, that great mother – had granted her peace, so that her features regained a measure of her natural calm and reserve. As I beheld this woman, who for twenty years served as my mother, I thought of her peculiarities, which had become as permanent a part of the Parsonage as the stone floors and stairs: the tales of her youth in Penzance, her love of romance and her general disdain of the lower creation, which was a source of constant, if mild, disagreement with my sisters, especially Emily; her overlarge, old-fashioned caps, the pattens in which she clicked about indoors to keep her feet warm, not to mention the sweltering temperature at which she kept her room at all times. As tears ran down my cheeks, I felt at last only gratitude for her life, and a rare instance of peace at her death: she had fulfilled a duty; she had suffered, as if for her few sins, in her final days on earth; and now she had the real rest we all crave.

I have at last responded to Grundy, who at my request sent a fair copy of 'The Triumph of Mind over Body' – let Brown and Leyland mock me as they will – to Leigh Hunt, Miss Martineau and others. Already he has heard back from them, reporting that *all spoke in high terms of it.* So distracted was I by the suffering and deaths of my friends, however, that I did not for some days even open the letters, and when I did, I found myself chastised by Grundy – does he still hold a grudge from our dispute of yore, I wondered … Surely not! – for not responding to his letters quickly, or enthusiastically, or gratefully enough to suit his tastes. He does seem ever ready to assume the worst on my part, and given my past conduct I cannot say I blame him entirely. And yet – even after I sent word that there was no misunderstanding between us, but that Weightman had died and now Aunt was dying – he persisted, adding that his sister, whom I have met but once, implied that I had the same penchant as Aesop's boy who cried wolf, or that I was simply enamoured of the *idea of death.* I have assured him that the suffering was all too real, of a kind I would not wish my worst enemy to endure, and that dear Aunt is dead.

Tomorrow she is to be buried; let us hope that her funeral closes this grim chapter, and that brighter days lie ahead.

November 28th, 1842 · The Parsonage

We are all gathered in Haworth once again, and how strange we have become, one to the other! If we were not united in grief, I should wonder what we would have to discuss. Weightman, Aunt, even Mary Taylor's younger sister Martha, like the unfortunate curate, a victim of the cholera in Brussels: all dead. How dreary and void everything seems, and even if we seek a gay moment, the bleak season reminds us of our grief. Gone are the leaves, the soft breezes of summer, and the bright skies under which I rambled so often with Weightman – all of it a distant dream, now no more real than a fairy tale. Wrapped we are in cold and damp, enshrouded in moor grime, and there are days when one can barely glimpse the church steeple from what was once our little 'schoolroom' above the front door to the Parsonage.

Anne was the only one to arrive in time for Aunt's funeral, and once we had consigned her mortal remains to the earth – according to her wishes 'as near as convenient to the remains of my dear sister' – Anne walked slowly to the new memorial to Weightman, which had been installed and lettered by Brown just days before. Her small hand gently caressed the small image of an open book carved beneath the lettering, and her eyes welled with tears. Were her tears for Aunt, or for Weightman? She answered my question directly.

'He was so *young*, Branwell.'

At first I said nothing, my shining eyes mirroring hers. At last I placed her arm in mine as we walked towards the door. 'I am afraid I was not always calm in the presence of poor Weightman; I raged against God at his unjust fate, until the curate himself had to comfort and calm *me*.'

Anne smiled, wiping her tears, as we emerged from the church. 'Now *that* does not surprise me. Even in the face of stern death, I suppose his angelic smile chased the clouds from that brow of yours, and his musical voice even made you smile, or laugh, before it was silenced at last.'

In complete earnest, with no trace of mockery, I whispered to Anne, 'So you did care for him.'

'Have I not told you,' she responded with a smile as celestrial in its way as the curate's, 'that we all cared for him; we all loved him, each in his way. It was not as if he singled me out. He was not *my* darling, he was *our* darling – and by that I also mean you and Papa, and indeed everyone who had the honour of knowing him.'

'That's true,' I confessed. 'So we did. He was a good man, which makes his death all the more bitter a pill to swallow.'

'How then,' said she, seeking to change the subject slightly, but in a way that would still allow her to discuss Weightman, 'did he turn you from your anger?'

Not wishing to reveal the details of my publications, I told her that we talked – and even joked – about poetry, and that my friend had encouraged me to continue writing, and was happy that I was to be employed at Thorp Green. I turned to Anne.

'I hope you, sister, are pleased that I am going to join you?'

'I've told you, brother,' she said patiently, 'that I would never have recommended you for the post if I did not think it best not only for you, but for me.'

'My greatest wish is to make my independence, and in so doing to make you – and everyone else – proud. What may seem to some a list of failures will then take on quite a different aspect.'

'It is my wish, too, Branwell. I am sure that you will like the Robinsons, and they you. They are of quite a different order from the Postlethwaites – at least from what you have related to me – a somewhat higher and more ancient family, real gentlefolk, not purse-proud tradespeople or arrogant upstarts. Thorp Green is far from our manufacturing districts, where people have nothing to do but make money.'

After a moment, however, she added, biting her lip: 'Though I do think the conduct of the ladies of the house could use some improvement.'

'The *young* ladies, you mean.'

'Well yes, that's especially what I mean … although I'm afraid they are a reflection of their worthy mama, who is raising them solely as superficially attractive, marriageable items, and she is interested not so much in their minds and souls as in their beautiful faces and forms, and ensuring that they acquire the showiest of accomplishments, so that they might attract rich young gentlemen, like moths to a flame. Mrs Robinson's idea of maternal success would be to contract three solid marriages of interest, three 'Smithfield-bargains' as they say, for her girls. The eldest, her namesake Lydia, is a particularly vexing flirt. So you see, brother, that there is good and ill to be encountered at Thorp Green.'

The image of a lovely young woman whose sole desire seemed to be to flirt shamelessly did not dismay me as much as it did my sister; quite to the contrary. Anne paused before the Parsonage, glancing down in the direction of The Black Bull. 'I confess, too – please don't be cross, Branwell – that I think it not at all a bad thing for you to be removed from the orbit of John Brown and your friend Joseph Leyland for a time.'

It flashed upon me now. Had she discussed this with Papa? Was this, in fact, a snare into which I had blithely, blindly, blundered? It was entirely plausible. Angered at the possibility, and wishing to defend my friends as much as myself, I stiffened with resentment.

'See here, Anne, have you seen any unbecoming conduct from me?'

'I have not,' she rejoined, 'but remember what Miss Austen says: *Every man is surrounded by a neighbourhood of voluntary spies*. People gossip, I'm afraid, Branwell.'

'Well,' – I paused, not knowing what to say, for we are often at our most bewildered and angry when we face, in our heart of hearts, the truth, for why should such wrath and confusion be present in the absence of culpability?

'Well,' snapped I at last, 'ignorant tongues may wag as they like, I know that my conduct these many months' – I was careful to confine my statement to my life *after* Luddenden Foot – 'has been beyond reproach. But on one thing we can agree: with my departure in January, the issue will be of no practical relevance.'

More than three weeks have passed since this interview, and today we bade a fond farewell to Anne as she began the journey back to Thorp Green, where she is to remain for the holidays: such is the bargain that the Robinsons struck with her, in permitting her to mourn the loss of Aunt these many weeks. In the interim, Charlotte and Emily arrived from Brussels, so that all of Papa's 'little ones' were reunited at his table for the first time in many a month.

XXI.

Two Sisters, Two Conversations

December 17th, 1842 · The Parsonage

How strange it is that children emerging from the same womb can be in some things so different! Emily has returned from Brussels seemingly unchanged, but Charlotte is another person entirely. The plain, small creature, though unaltered in her appearance, now holds her head high as she speaks of how valued she is by Monsieur and Madame Heger, the directors of the school there. Do I detect a slight blush and *frisson* when she mentions the name of that gentleman? Or am I making the same mistake I made with Anne and Weightman, assuming that my sisters must be as infatuated with the opposite sex as *I* have been. Monsieur Heger even sent a letter to Papa, which he opened and, having perused to his satisfaction, proudly asked Charlotte to read to us all, in French. What follows is the essential:

> I have a profound admiration for you, for in judging the father of a family by his children one cannot be mistaken, and in this respect the education and sentiments that we have found in your daughters can only give us a very high idea of your worth and of your character. You will undoubtedly learn with pleasure that your children have made extra-ordinary progress in all the branches of learning, and that this progress is entirely due to their love of work and their perseverance. With pupils like this we had very little to do; their progress is more your work than ours, etc., etc.

Emily shifted uncomfortably, whilst Charlotte tried, unsuccessfully, not to glow with pride as she read the letter in her vastly improved French. It has been determined that Charlotte will, in the new year, return to Brussels, for the Hegers have offered her a position as teacher, but Emily will stay in Haworth to assume the direction of the household that Anne took over after the death of Aunt Branwell.

At first Papa tried to persuade Emily to return to Belgium, but soon, seeing that she longed to remain at home – for she loves this place as much as I have come to loathe it – and knowing that she would happily throw herself into the household duties that would leave her mind free to wander the wild landscapes of its imagination, he soon relented. Truth to tell, he was all too pleased himself, to kill two birds with a single stone, to have both a daughter at home as a companion, and to be relieved of the troublesome quotidian business of housekeeping, or worse, paying someone else to do it. Here was the perfect balance, then: Anne was independent and valued in her position; Charlotte, now, too would be; I was about to leave his roof again and would no longer be a drain on his purse; and Emily, like Aunt, was a cherished family member who would provide an invaluable service, asking only that she be fed and clothed, with a roof over her head and books to read. So yes: to Brussels Charlotte will return.

In the meantime, her time in the Belgian capital has further exaggerated her unfortunate habit of sprinkling her speech with Gallic spice: rarely does a conversation pass without the listener being treated to a handful of French expressions. To this now has been added the occasional phrase in German, for her study of that language has also been considerable these many months. Of course, Emily has shared the same course of study, but if it were not for the frequency with which she has her nose in a French or German book, one would never know this – indeed, one would never guess that she had sailed beyond fair Albion's shores at all.

I have had numerous occasions since Anne's departure to sit alone with Charlotte, whilst Papa and Emily go about their respective business. I find that I have little to say, for our childhood games, our *scribblemania*, our rivalry, is as dead and buried as Weightman and Aunt. I recall at such moments the words of my Sir Henry Tunstall, returning to England after sixteen years in India, in the poem I revised and sent to *Blackwood's*:

So, Old Affection is an empty name,
When nothing, loved or loving, keeps the same;
But, while we gaze upon the vapour gay,
The light that gave it glory fades away:
And Home affection – where *have* we a home?

As the time of my departure draws nigh, so grows my desire – almost a manic desperation, like Leyland's growing thirst as he approaches a pub – to be gone, to leap forward to the next phase of my life at Thorp Green.

I was turning these thoughts over in my mind as I sat before the fire with Charlotte the day after Anne's departure. She was leafing through one of our childhood favourites, not de la Motte's drawing manual, but Bewick's *History of British Birds*. Little does she know that I – which is to say, Northangerland – published that short essay on the artist in the *Halifax Guardian*, less than a week before Weightman's death.

As she browsed through the well-worn volume – her face, even with thick spectacles, close to the page – I found myself torn between fervently wishing I could tell her of my publications and desperately wanting to keep my secret buried for all time. The latter impulse carried the day, and I said merely, 'Ah, yes, Bewick. Do you remember how we would sit and pore over that volume and copy the drawings?' To share some of the thoughts expressed in my article from the *Guardian*, as if they had only just occurred to me, was a compromise I allowed myself, permitting me to 'read' some of my article to Charlotte, without divulging its actual existence.

'I have lately been thinking quite a lot of him,' I said.

'*Really? Bewick?* He seems a rather old-fashioned subject to be reflecting upon these days.' In a few words Charlotte had –

as she so often does – unintentionally flown directly to the heart of the matter. Indeed, there was something birdlike in the movement of her head, as it moved to consider me.

'*Precisely,*' said I. '*Exactly*. In these days of *modern* art – with its worship of brilliant effects, of imposing masses of light and shade – such a country-loving, nature-worshiping fellow as Bewick does seem like a subject out of antiquity, even though he almost created the modern style of engraving.'

'*Dis donc, mon frère,*' she replied, 'you *have* given this a lot of thought. So, what is it in the artist that has drawn you to these reflections?'

'I was not long ago leafing through that very book you have in your lap, and I thought – it is hard to describe – that there is something peculiarly *English* about Bewick, a particularly English desire to portray the realities of life. His little woodcuts somehow have the power to extract from everyday life scenes and situations of the greatest power or pathos. He somehow knew that to possess control over the mind it is not necessary to carry it beyond the world we live in.'

'So, you are advocating for flat, humdrum reality as the proper subject for art? *Comme c'est banal!*'

I laughed. 'No: what I am saying is this: when you look at his illustrations, you see the bent grass waving, the cold wind whistling, as if you felt with the traveller the length and loneliness of his road.'

'Ah, then it is of the *manner* of depiction of which you speak, not the subject. *Ce n'est pas pareil.*'

Charlotte paused for a moment before continuing. 'After all, do not forget Bewick's castle ruins, his tombstones, his gibbets and, most of all, his fiends brandishing pitchforks.' She moved her little arm comically, stabbing, like a she-devil flourishing the implement of her trade. 'Surely *those* are not images of the *realities of life* as you say.'

As she spoke, her fine, large brown eyes were for a fleeting instant those of my playmate of old. How much has changed since I rode to surprise her at Roe Head School – she just sixteen years old, I not quite fifteen – in those days where hope was not yet tainted with disillusionment! In those days, she would correspond privately with me, saying that it was to *me* that she *had the most to say*. How altered we are!

Charlotte squinted critically as she closed the volume, and the phantom companion of my youth had already vanished. 'Do you think, brother, that the same thing might be said of literature?'

I must have appeared puzzled.

'What I mean is this,' she continued. 'Do you believe literature should touch primarily on the realities of life or go beyond them? What of haunted castles, ghosts roaming the moors, gypsy fortune-tellers, and the voices of faraway lovers conveyed on a breeze across hill and dale and moorland? What of that supernatural black dog, the Gytrash? Is any subject appropriate to literature as long as the manner or *style* can make you – what did you say? – *feel the length and loneliness of his road*? Or must we keep to *the world we live in* as you put it?'

'This world,' said I, 'is so full of wonders that I can scarcely imagine the need for something beyond it.'

'That sounds heretical, brother.' She was not smiling, but I was.

'No, I am not talking about religion, sister dear, though I think we *do* carry our own heavens and hells with us wherever we go … here' – I struck my forehead – 'and here' – I placed my hand over my heart – and the memory of Agnes Riley washed, unexpectedly, over my entire being, and tears sprang to my eyes. I have done my utmost to forget her, to forget everything about Broughton, as I have of late begun to do with Luddenden Foot.

'What *is* it, Branwell?'

'It's Aunt,' I lied. 'It's Weightman, too. It's all still such a blow.'

'But you're happy, are you not, to be joining Anne at Thorp Green?' said she, genuinely trying to cheer me.

'I am indeed,' I responded, briefly feeling my old love for her begin to rise like a skiff on a swelling ocean tide.

'And do you still write?'

'Very little,' I lied again. 'Do you?'

'I haven't the time at the *Pensionnat*.' Those large, luminous eyes stared dreamily beyond me, as if gazing across the Channel, all the way to Brussels. 'But if I did, I have long since bidden farewell to our old friends in the tropical latitudes of Glass Town and Angria, for I wish to paint from *life*.' She paused and laughed gently. 'You see, Branwell, we agree after all! I, too, believe we should confine ourselves to the world we live in.'

'Well, this *is* a change. Was it not I who upbraided you for being a writer who loved more to dwell upon Indian palm groves or genii palaces than on the wooded manors and cloudy skies of England?'

She blushed ever so slightly – or did I imagine it? – and said, '*Eh bien, voilà*, Branwell, I *do* listen to you sometimes. Even the most flawed vessel can carry the truth – is that not something Papa might say in a sermon?' I was not so sure, but I accepted her admission, despite the sting in its tail.

The passing renewal of affection I felt for her in that moment makes me wonder if I have, at times, painted too harsh a portrait of Charlotte in these pages. Or was it merely this momentary *rapprochement* – to use a word she herself might choose – that made me warm to her? In any event, I returned her smile. 'Truly? You? The Queen of the Romance, creatrix of Mina Laury and the Duke of Zamorna? What of your ghosts and gypsies? What of the yearning lover's voice transported across the countryside more swiftly than a telegraph message?'

'You said it yourself, did you not? If we can carry heaven and hell within us, with their legions of angels and demons, surely we are able to produce a ghost or two – or a fierce Gytrash – to haunt *ourselves*. And why could not a gypsy fortuneteller simply be someone in disguise, with an intimate knowledge of those she pretends to amaze? Could not the voice of a distant lover we hear in the wind be the product – a projection – of our own yearning?'

'You do not at all sound,' said I – thinking of my own feverish, if clandestine, writing, revising and publishing since my return to Haworth – 'like someone who has given up on writing.'

'I *think* about it all the time,' she confessed, 'but I have long ago abandoned the silly notion that I could achieve riches or glory with the pen. Papa is hardly getting any younger, and we must all put away such childish things and secure our independence.'

'At least,' said I, frowning, 'Aunt has left each of you girls enough money to keep the wolf from *your* door for a time, should Papa die suddenly.' We had recently learned that Aunt Branwell's testament left nearly 300 pounds respectively to Charlotte, Emily, Anne and our cousin Eliza in Penzance.

'But at least a man is *free*, Branwell, to pursue whatever profession he wishes. That's why Aunt left you no money. And please don't talk so about Papa – he won't die, he is as hale and hearty as ever, despite his failing eyesight.'

'Wait – did you not just say that he is hardly getting any younger? If that blooming girl Martha Taylor and vigorous Willy Weightman can die in the flower of their youth, we have to be prepared for the possibility that our sixty-five-year-old father could succumb, and that when it happens we shall all be homeless.'

'But starting next month you have a post, and it is essential that you retain it, for as you say, Emily, Anne and I have a small provision in case the worst occurs. From Anne's reports, I have no doubt that you will be better suited to the Robinson family than to the Postlethwaites, and I never could see you as a railway man, though I credit you for trying.'

The wise elder sister – who in fact knew nothing of my life in Broughton, Sowerby Bridge or Luddenden Foot – had returned fully, sending the carefree friend of my youth headlong to oblivion. I bristled defensively. 'Do you doubt,' said I, 'of my capacity to retain the post at Thorp Green?'

The directness of my question shattered the remaining shards of the short-lived harmony that we had enjoyed before the fire.

'I believe you have the mind' – here she imitated my earlier gesture in a way that made it impossible to discern whether it was in earnest or in mockery – 'to do anything you want in this life, but whether your heart' – she again mimicked my motion – 'embraces it is another question. I pray that it will, but remember, *der Geist ist willig, aber das Fleisch ist schwach* – which being translated' – she added pedantically – 'means that *the spirit is willing but the flesh is weak.*'

I grimaced and said nothing, wondering why she felt it necessary to quote scripture in German.

At last, Charlotte stood and walked over to kiss me on the forehead. '*Bonne nuit, mon frère. Fais de beaux rêves,*' said she, like a mother wishing her little one sweet dreams, leaving me staring stonily into the fire. She had succeeded in casting clouds of doubt over the hopes I had for my new life at Thorp Green, which heretofore had glittered like a sunrise on a dewy, cloudless morning. I, too, hope that my heart will warm to my new situation, for I can no longer move from post to post: I need safety, security and a measure of stability, no matter how modest.

The next day Charlotte travelled to Brookroyd to see Ellen Nussey, and I was not at all sorry to see her go. My sister loves me, and I her, but as in so many families, this does not signify that we particularly relish each other's company.

December 20th, 1842 · The Parsonage

The days pass with agonising slowness, so much so that I find myself wishing Anne back from Thorp Green, and even Charlotte returned from Brookroyd. Winter has thoroughly closed his icy fingers around the Parsonage, and I find that I have no desire to leave the warmth of the fire. Papa, however, has his duties, as does Emily. There is little chance that she will bring a book to the fire – as long as I am there, at least – and even less that she will engage in any kind of badinage. Such conversations, she has made it plain on innumerable occasions, are no more to her than a peculiar form of hypocrisy sanctioned by society.

Yesterday, however, my desire for company grew so strong that I could bear it no longer, and I found Emily in the kitchen, kneading dough and reading a German book she had propped upon the table. She did not look up when I entered, but only continued her dual activities.

She is the tallest of the three – indeed, taller than I – with dark, liquid grey-blue eyes that seldom look a person in the face, auburn hair, a rather poor complexion like Charlotte's, but with Anne's long, graceful neck. Her lithesome, graceful figure – unlike dumpy Charlotte or delicate Anne – has, despite her efforts to conceal it, ideal proportions, not unlike Leyland's *Kilmeny*. But woe betide the man who dares take notice of her, especially in that way! I would call her a hoyden, if a hoyden could be silent and earnest.

There is room for Keeper – who, since Aunt's reign has now ended, sat with his nose pressed against Emily's knees, in true devotion but also hoping, surely, that a scrap of dough might find its way to the floor – in the mysterious wilderness of her heart, but not for any male suitors, I think. Her height, her physical strength, her quick intelligence, her utter disdain for conversation that does not have a specific *purpose*, her head for logic, but most of all her stubbornness – for she is as confident of her own views as I am uncertain of my own – combine to intimidate anyone who would dare approach her, family or no. Even Charlotte now treats her with gloves of kid: when Emily insisted that she would not return to Brussels, Charlotte's resistance was soon routed, even though this means that she will have to travel alone across the Channel and live in solitude in the *pensionnat*.

'Yes?' she said, still not raising her head as I stood before here. The 'yes' was uttered with closed teeth and seemed to express the sentiment, 'Go to the Devil!' Or was I imagining this?

'What are you doing?'

At last Emily looked up, still kneading the dough, waiting for me to grasp the foolishness of my question. I changed tack: 'What I mean is, how are you?' Knowing that this question alone would be construed as the worst kind of twaddle, I continued, 'Are you truly resolved to stay in Haworth? Will you not miss Brussels, or your pupils, or the Hegers? Haworth is so isolated, for God's sake – it's a perfect misanthropist's Heaven!'

On those rare occasions when her gaze is raised, it beams like a lantern through the darkness, cuts like a knife through tender flesh. As she stared, I chattered on; for who has not experienced such moments, when the stony silence of one's interlocutor only makes one more voluble. Usually, of course, it is Leyland, with his loathing of silence, who fills the void while others pause in thought. To make matters worse, Emily has the rare talent, solely with her gaze, of making one feel foolish, regardless of the gravity of the topic of conversation or the elevation of one's sentiments.

At last she spoke, with her typical intensity. 'In Brussels we were *isolated in the midst of numbers*, as Charlotte has said, and so returning home is quite the opposite, you see. Here I have Papa to care for, and he and Keeper to share my company – and they both love me unreservedly, unconditionally; neither wishes to shape me into something I am not, and can never be.' She paused, gazing fondly at the mongrel, whose ears had perked up and tongue had tumbled out of his mouth at the mention of his name, and she allowed herself the faintest shadow of a smile. 'And *Monsieur le Chien* does not even require conversation. So you see, Branwell, we are a suitable trio to divide the desolation amongst us.'

Clearly she was every bit as eager to see Charlotte return to Brussels and me to take up my new post at Thorp Green, as we were to do so. I sensed that even Anne – from whom, in youth, she had been inseparable, almost as if they were twins – was no more necessary to her happiness than Keeper, and indeed perhaps less so. As Emily spoke, she proved that the dog – who sat like a devouring flame on the kitchen floor – hardly needed to wait desperately for an errant scrap of dough, for she pinched off a generous portion for him as a bit of a treat. Such behaviour was hardly surprising: I have witnessed her giving him the best portion of a leg of mutton on occasion. With Aunt's death, however, she could do so with impunity.

Keeper smacked and slavered and Emily returned to her kneading, so that only the sounds of an occasional *thump* of the dough and the wind whistling round the Parsonage walls joined the dog's rapid mastication of his delicacy. Outside fell the first feathery flakes of a snow shower, as the short day lengthened quickly into evening.

'*Hal*-low! Do you see?' said I. 'The first snow of the season.'

'Does it stick fast, or melt away as it lands?'

I approached the window and looked up towards the moors. The snow clung to the low stone wall, but melted wherever it touched grass or shrub or tree, or any other living thing.

'It depends,' I replied, and I pressed my forehead against the windowpane, the icy glass cooling my brow. I turned to find Emily smiling enigmatically to herself – whether it was in appreciation of the subtly of my response, or because she generally considers me an utter imbecile, would have been impossible to determine – and I found myself wanting to kiss her on the cheek, if such a gesture would not have been ill-received.

With nothing more to say, I performed a slight bow and said, 'Now then, *Mademoiselle*, I will leave you and your trusted assistant, *Monsieur le Chien*, to your labours.'

An almost inaudible grunt of assent was all I received in return, signalling that Emily Jane had finished with me.

XXII.

Thorp Green

February 5th, 1843 · Thorp Green

I arrived here a fortnight ago. The 21st of January was a wild, tempestuous day, with a strong north wind and a continual storm of snow drifting on the ground and whirling through the air. The railway covered only part of the journey, and the incessant snow threw impediments in the way of both horses and steam engines. The Robinsons had sent the coachman, William Allison – Billy, he insisted I call him, with a grin – to collect me in York, and for the final miles of the journey, we progressed at a mere crawl.

At last, however, the coach came to a rest before the stately portico of a grand house, and soon I stood in a well-lighted, spacious gallery. The first person to greet me, apart from the servants, was Anne herself. She looked well and seemed delighted to see me. How different she is from her 'twin' of old, Emily.

'Branwell!' she exclaimed, 'Here you are here at last! We had quite given up on you, believing you to have been stranded at an inn, or heaven forbid, in a snowdrift. But here you are, none the worse for wear, it seems!'

The 'we' in question was Anne and her pupils, who had filed in behind her as she was speaking. Young Edmund or 'Ned', a solidly built young fellow with sandy hair and matching eyes, stepped forward boldly to shake my hand, saying 'Welcome, Mr Brontë', as his three older sisters curtseyed. The youngest of these, Mary, is fifteen, just passing from girlhood to womanhood, but already with a kind of coquetry about her that will likely serve her well. She is the shortest of the three young ladies, and yet has a pleasing roundness to her form, an embonpoint immediately suggesting a kind of voluptuousness to me – I am ashamed to confess. She has bright, darting green eyes, porcelain skin and flaxen ringlets, which she shakes at every opportunity. Elizabeth – whom everyone calls 'Bessy' – is a good-looking girl of sixteen, but a bit of a hoyden in the truest sense of that word. I have since learned that she passes many any hour with the grooms and stable boys, and that she can and does swear as heartily as they. Her complexion is a bit darker, as are her eyes and her hair, but she is a handsome creature nonetheless.

Lydia, the eldest, is everything that Anne has hinted, and more. She is positively beautiful: tall and slender, but not thin, so perfectly formed that a corset would be superfluous, exquisitely fair, but not without a brilliant, healthy bloom; her hair, which she wears in a profusion of long ringlets, is of a very light brown, strongly inclining to yellow, her eyes are pale blue, but so clear and bright that few observers would wish them darker.

As I surveyed the Robinson children, another presence made itself felt, as their mama sailed elegantly into the hall. 'Ah, Mr Brontë, you do exist. I was beginning to think you were a phantom of your sister's overactive imagination. I regret that my husband Edmund is indisposed this evening and has already taken to his bed. His poor health is, I fear, yet another reason to enlist your services, for he *had* considered giving little Edmund lessons in the classics, though I did *tell* him that he hardly need occupy himself with such tedious matters; that is the reason we have tutors such as yourself.'

'I am afraid,' said Anne, 'that it is my own limited knowledge of the classics that is most at fault, for young Edmund has already outstripped all that I can teach him.'

'Nonsense,' said Mrs Robinson peremptorily. '*Primo*, Greek and Latin are the province of men – everybody knows that – and *secondo*, Master Edmund here is no longer a little boy, so a governess will not do. You, Mr Brontë,' said she, bowing her head ever so slightly, 'are to be the *bridge* between the rudimentary childhood lessons he has received thus far, and his university studies. We have high hopes that Ned will follow in his father's footsteps, to Oxford.'

Later, when we were alone, Anne spoke plainly: 'You see, Branwell, there are *poor* clergymen like Papa, whose curacy is their entire life and livelihood, then there are clergymen like the Reverend Edmund Robinson – nominal curates who live by their inheritance. The Reverend Robinson inherited Thorp Green Hall and the manorial rights of Little Ouseburn.'

As for Mrs Robinson's appearance, while she lacks the stunning, youthful beauty of her namesake Lydia, she is a very pretty woman, somewhere between thirty-five and forty years of age, quite diminutive in stature but very well-formed indeed – she requires neither rouge nor padding to add to her charms – and she has olive skin like Bessy's, and bright glancing eyes like Mary's. Anne's only comment about her, beyond her disapproval of the great lady's rearing of her daughters, was that her chief enjoyments seem to be in giving or attending parties, and in dressing at the very top of fashion. It is true that she was – and always is – beautifully dressed. There is a certain *hauteur* in her manner of addressing Anne and me – we are, after all, her paid subordinates – that tells me that I shall have precious little to do with her, and that I shall be kept at arm's length from her lovely daughters as well.

I did not have to wait long to learn just how true this was. She turned to her lady's maid – whose name I have since learned is Ann Marshall – and said, 'Even *I* am not so cruel as to send Mr Brontë back into this snowstorm. Marshall, please see that he has what he needs for tonight, and when the snow has stopped and the servants have quite shovelled us out, we shall have his things moved to the Old Hall.' It was then that I learned – at first, I must confess, to my dismay, for by not literally 'living in' as Anne does, I will have far fewer opportunities to appreciate the young ladies – that I am to be lodged at the former 'Monk's House', which is to say the old timber and stone hall that long predates the main house at Thorp Green, although it lies within its grounds.

I awoke the next morning to the scraping sound of picks, scoops and shovels, and looking out the window beheld a veritable phalanx of domestics clearing paths, walks and drives. A brilliant sun shone fully in a wintry sky so pure that it took my breath away as surely as breathing the glacial air would do if I were one of the unfortunate lads labouring in the snow below. The cold, dry day and the absence of any manufacturing in the district made for an azure vault the likes of which I had not seen since my arrival in Broughton three years since. How much – and how little – has changed since then!

After breakfast, I at last met the master of the house, the Reverend Edmund Robinson. He stands no taller than I, and his illness has left him emaciated. He was most respectful, enquiring after the family, especially Papa, in the wake of the recent loss of his curate and his sister-in-law.

'The only constant in this life is change,' he said in a deep bass voice, sighing, 'and our only hope heaven.' Perhaps he was only a clergyman in name, but his speech seemed authentically pious and orthodox enough. Anne had told us about little three-year-old Georgiana, who died two years since; was this the cause of the Reverend's own melancholy and frail health? Whatever the case, I pity him, for he appears to be a good man.

March 22nd, 1843 · Thorp Green

Man forever wishes to be elsewhere – *ailleurs*, as Charlotte would say. Why cannot he – why cannot I – sit quietly and contentedly without longing for *something more*? What is this endless yearning, this eternal restlessness, this unquenchable thirst? I am no closer to understanding it now than I have ever been. How I envy those who march calmly, coolly through their lives, content with their lot and undesirous of change, agitation, action and *fulfilment*; or those others, though unsatisfied, who can harness their desire to the chariot of a single-minded pursuit.

How often have I pondered just these questions, which appear to have no answers!

Many, no doubt, would call me an eternal malcontent, but I cannot help it, for such agitation is in my very nature. *At least a man is free*, Charlotte would say. For Papa, such disquietude, such yearning, will only cease when *we as Christians look forward to a joyous resurrection*, as he said at Weightman's funeral, *in the hope of being forever reunited above, with those who have been taken from us by death, and whom we have loved here below.* Dear Mama, sweet Maria and Elizabeth! Is it as simple as this?

I can complain of nothing, for I am treated with the utmost respect by the Robinsons, and my quarters in the Old Hall are spacious, almost palatial, so that I can ramble about, can escape myself as it were, writing in one room, drawing in another, reading in yet another. Beyond the few hours each day I devote to Edmund's instruction – he is a dull boy, but like many a dullard he at least he applies himself and does not misbehave, which suggests that he will have no difficulty becoming a cog in the great wheel of society's machine; then again, what am I saying? The lad will inherit this estate, so will do just as he pleases after his papa dies – but I digress – beyond these few hours (sometimes four, sometimes six) I am at liberty to do as I please in this dreary season. Even the vast library of Thorp Green is at my disposal.

The infrequent glimpses I have of my charge's sisters have only confirmed Anne's portrait of their conduct: each, in her own way, appears to be an incorrigible flirt, and the simple fact that I am a young man is sufficient to titillate them – what a profusion of white teeth, what shaking of ringlets, what batting of eyelashes! The middle girl, Betsy, seems somewhat different, and yet even her hoydenish conduct – her *shocking language* as her mama and sisters call it as she strides about acting like one of her papa's grooms, though that lovely form could never be mistaken for such – seems a quite deliberate sort of provocation calculated to impress upon me that she is capable of *anything*. At the very least, the three adorable creatures are endlessly entertaining and forever pleasing to the eye.

In short, here I have what I wanted – time and space to write in genteel surroundings – and yet still I am sick unto death with unhappiness and loneliness. Anne is occupied with her three flighty charges, and besides, too frequent conversation between governess and tutor might rouse suspicion in the family, for surely we would be thought to be talking about *them*! Haworth – lonely, isolated, benighted, insalubrious Haworth – seems now a bustling metropolis to me, and how I miss the company of John Brown and the occasional visit of Leyland! Even watchful Papa, taciturn Emily, lame Tabby and young Martha Brown would be a sight for sore eyes.

Was it my last letter – or perhaps one from Anne, still in league with Papa – that caused him to visit this last week? No, he assured me, he had been summoned to York to bear witness in a trial, and how could he not see his beloved children when that city lay just ten or so miles from Thorp Green? I had managed to find enough strength each day to fulfil my duties, but would immediately retreat to the Old Hall and, more often than not, to my bed. There I lay, gazing at the hard grey sky and bare, lifeless landscape – for though the snow has receded, spring has yet, in this dreariest and my least favourite of seasons, to show the first signs of life – when Anne and Papa entered my room.

'My son,' he said tenderly – for while I have so often felt judged in his eyes, I have never felt unloved – 'you look better than I feared, but worse than I hoped. Are you sure this is the right place for you?' He looked about the room and seemed to approve, though his brow remained furrowed.

'Papa,' said Anne, 'I must go, for the young ladies have their lessons, and their governess surely can't keep them *waiting* – what a climax of horror *that* would be!'

As she turned to leave, there was a soft but rapid knock on the open door, and without awaiting the habitual *Come in*, in glided Mrs Robinson, flushed from her walk across the grounds, followed by a respectable-looking, fortyish gentleman, with large greying whiskers and kindly blue eyes, whom she introduced as Dr John Crosby, the surgeon who attends the Reverend Robinson.

Our 'sweet Anne', guilty of the most cutting sarcasm, turned crimson, but Mrs Robinson had failed to – or in any event had chosen not to – hear her remark.

'Ah, good, Miss Brontë, I am so glad you are here as well, for I wanted to see the whole family – well, those I *know*, of course – together. Mr Brontë, your children are a credit to you. You should know that they are wondrously valued by my husband – poor dear, he is ill again today or would have accompanied me – and myself.' She apparently felt she needed no introduction, and her words fairly tumbled out, she spoke with such vivacity. She is inordinately fond of giving *particular* words a great *deal* of emphasis, a habit her daughters have not failed to adopt.

Papa bowed and spoke in accents far more Cantabrigian than Irish, as if wanting to impress upon Mrs Robinson the superiority of his learning. 'The honour is all mine, Mrs Robinson,' he said deliberately, 'and it is we who are gratified.'

She waved Papa's words away as if they were small, noxious puffs of smoke. 'Nonsense. However,' said she, looking directly at me where I lay, 'we are worried to find that Mr Brontë is not as well as when he arrived here. That is why I have asked Dr Crosby to step over to the Old Hall with me, for I always trust his diagnoses.'

As she spoke I surveyed her face – of which I had scarcely had more than a glimpse since my arrival that snowy January night – and her form. There is something indescribably beguiling about those glancing eyes, that dark skin and hair, her rapid speech and movements, making her almost as exotic to me as would be a Florentine princess or a Persian concubine. Her lips are sensuous, her teeth beautiful, and her mouth turned up into a perpetual smile at its corners. Her nose is large but well-formed, while her substantial, smooth forehead, high red cheeks and lovely white neck do not betray an age much beyond thirty. Nor have the years been unkind to her form and figure, for she is neither too thin nor too stout, and chooses her fashions to accentuate her womanly shape.

I was not cognizant of the extent to which I had been staring until her gaze met mine, but rather than turning away, it held mine steadily for at least two seconds, at which point I looked down at my hands.

'Thank you,' said Papa. 'You are most kind.'

'We shall have young Mr Brontë up and about in no time,' said Mrs Robinson, 'with Dr Crosby's assistance, of course. Well then, Miss Brontë, will you accompany me back to the house? The young ladies must be waiting for you by now, but I will tell them that I have *quite* monopolised you.' Anne followed her mistress through the door, turning to me with wide eyes as she left, as if to say, *Good Heavens, Branwell, I truly hope she did not hear me!*

Off they went, Papa and Anne promising to write each other soon. I wondered what intelligence about me passed between the two, but forced my thoughts into another channel. Our father stood back and allowed Dr Crosby to approach and examine me. After a few moments, he walked to the hearth and turned, warming his back, his arms and his hands, which he rubbed together behind him as he balanced on the tips of his toes.

'Time will tell, of course, but I believe Mr Brontë is depressed in spirit, which may be nothing more than good old-fashioned homesickness. He'll be fit as a fiddle in no time.'

Papa smiled sadly, his large furrowed forehead, shock of receding white hair and enormous white side-whiskers giving him the appearance of an ancient sage. 'I am pleased. Doubly pleased, primarily because his elder sisters died of consumption and it is that which I most fear for my children, but also because we miss him, and it is heartening to know that he misses us.'

'Of course I miss you, Papa,' said I, clutching his large hand, and for once I spoke sincerely, my heart warming to the old man. How long it takes a son to grasp fully the boundless kindness, love, sacrifice and forgiveness of a father!

'As much as I sometimes yearn to quit it when I am there, I miss my home when I am not; and as much as I fervently wish and need to make my independence, I am sometimes lonely here.'

Crosby bounced again on his toes. 'All of this is quite normal,' he assured us. 'Now, what *I* recommend is fresh air, vigorous exercise and new scenes. When I think of the sick and dying that I have attended upon, even of the poor Reverend Robinson,' here his voice dropped as he nodded in the direction of the great house, as if someone else were listening, 'you are a most fortunate young man, and your cure is within your own reach.'

He walked over to my bedside, thrusting his now warmed hands into his pockets. 'See here, springtime is fast upon us, and on the first warm day I invite you to walk over to Great Ouseburn to dine with me and my nephew William, who lives with me. We will show you round the countryside here, which, you will find when springtime comes, is unsurpassed in its beauty. Believe you me, Mr Brontë, the snow and slush of winter, the thaws and mud of early spring, will all be as distant to your memory as the pain of childbirth is to a mother as she runs her fingers through the locks of her laughing babe.' He spoke nearly as rapidly as Mrs Robinson, his voice somewhat reedy and yet somehow agreeable – because lively and jovial – all the same.

'I would be most grateful, Dr Crosby,' said Papa. 'A little wholesome male company would not be amiss, for surely Branwell misses his friends in Haworth and Halifax.' He did not particularly emphasise the word *wholesome*; it was unnecessary.

'And,' said Crosby, 'if you have not yet been to York since your arrival here, we shall plan an excursion there together soon. Have you seen the Minster?'

I said that I had not, and that I had only passed through the city in the snowstorm the day I arrived.

Crosby was astonished, but pleased. 'No? Heavens, surely you must ride with me to York, where I often have business to conduct. In short, that's the only medicine you need for this ailment, Mr Brontë.'

Papa stood and they shook hands, whereupon Crosby rapidly clapped his hat on his head and walked out the door, calling over his shoulder, 'Fresh air, Mr Brontë, exercise, getting out and about, that's the thing!' Soon my father, too, took his leave, for he still had the long journey home before him. His pursed lips seemed to tremble; his eyes shone with tears.

'Papa, what is it?' I asked.

'When I think of your aunt, or poor Mr Weightman, I know how fortunate I am still to be living, but each time I leave you I fear I might never see you again. And when I think of your mother, and your sisters Maria and Elizabeth, I worry about you, Charlotte, Emily and Anne as well.'

'Nonsense!' said I with great authority and rapidity, hoping that my imitation of Mrs Robinson would make him smile, which he did, if only faintly.

'We will all be just fine,' I pursued. 'Indeed, I intend fully to try the good surgeon's "medicine" soon, and I promise to write often, to tell you how I am faring, all right?'

Once Papa left, I did consider Crosby's advice to be sensible indeed, and my heart was grateful for his diagnosis. At last my thoughts turned to Mrs Robinson, to those brilliant glancing eyes and dusky skin, the hair just a shade darker than chestnut, the flushed cheeks and heaving bosom as she arrived from out of doors, and most of all how our eyes met and interlocked. I clutched my pillow in my arms and pulled my knees up to my chest, as through my window I watched the sun emerge from a large cloud, with a promise of spring.

XXIII.

A Journey to York

April 14th, 1843 · Thorp Green

I have at last been to York with Dr Crosby. What a lovely old place it is, with its mediaeval walls, timbered houses, and the great Minster towering over all. My companion and guide gave me a walking tour of the old city, including a detailed history, from the time of the Romans to the arrival of the railway four years since, thanks to George Hudson, the 'Railway King' himself. After three hours of walking, during which he rarely stopped talking – a discourse far from harassing, and doubly pleasant for me, as his explanations were most informative and relieved me of the need to speak much at all – my guide at last took care of his 'business', purchasing a number of remedies at an apothecary's shop in Coney Street, after which he conducted me to a nearby pub, the Ouse Bridge Inn, down Spurriergate.

'Surely,' he said with vigour, for our tour had not seemed to tire him a whit, 'you must be ravenous. I know I am! And a glass of wine would be just the thing, don't you agree Brontë?'

I nodded in assent, trying not to appear too eager, though after the long walk I had an almost Leylandesque thirst. The doctor was well-known in these precincts, and was greeted with gusto by the proprietor, a barrel-chested gentleman whose copious black whiskers put Crosby's own ample specimens to shame. His hair was as dark as jet and thick as wool. As he approached our table the doctor leant over and whispered, winking, 'His parents came to York straight from Italy! Joseph Dimock here is really *Giuseppe D'Amico*.'

One would never have been able to tell his origins from his speech, for he spoke just as one might expect a York publican to speak. After Crosby made his introductions, Joseph said, 'Say, Dr Crosby, 'ave you 'eard o't' passin' o' ol' Dr Beckwith?'

'No, by Heavens,' said my new friend, visibly shaken at the news. 'I had heard that the poor man was ill, but *this* – this is a blow!' He turned to me in explanation. 'Dr Stephen Beckwith was beloved of his patients and a good friend and trusted adviser to many another practitioner, too, by Jove – including your humble servant himself.'

'Aye,' said Dimock, 'he were indeed. There's e'en talk of raisin' a s'scription to se' up an'elegan' memorial or some sooch in t' Minster.'

I filled the silence that ensued by saying, 'I have a dear friend who does just such work.'

'Oh?' asked Joseph, ''ere in York?'

'No, in Halifax.'

''*al*-ee-fax? Why that's nigh on 'alfway t' Liverpool! We've a load o' sculptors right 'ere in York!'

I was embarrassed to have mentioned Leyland. Of course the Minster would be surrounded by masons, stone-carvers and sculptors. Why would anyone pay for a stranger like Leyland to work at such a great distance? I pictured the good doctor's effigy bouncing across Yorkshire on a waggon, just as Kilmeny had. *Maggie Mortimer: was she again with child?* I wondered.

I took a large draught of wine. 'Yes,' I said, with a forced laugh. 'Foolish me! I only meant to make conversation.'

Dimock laughed heartily, his hands on his hips. 'Well I weren't mockin' ye, lad! I's jus' tha' this place is fairly *crawlin'* with sculptors! A man can har'ly walk ten paces wi'out hearin' tha' infernal *tink tink tink* o' t'ammer an' chisel!' He shook hands with us both and retreated to his labours.

Crosby was still shaking his head over the death of his fellow surgeon, Beckwith. 'The last time I saw him was at the very chemist's that you and I just visited. He was a great believer in the healing properties of laudanum. Have you ever taken it, Brontë?'

'Just once,' said I. 'Some years ago – 1839, I think it was – I was in Liverpool and my face began to twitch uncontrollably. The laudanum gave me some relief, and soon the symptoms faded away.'

'Well,' he said, scratching his whiskers thoughtfully, 'Although I hardly shared Beckwith's unbounded enthusiasm for the drug – he subscribed to Young's view, in his *Treatise on Opium*, that it cures just about every ailment known to man – it can be of help. It's all a question of the proper diagnosis, Brontë – and moderation, of course.'

The truth of the matter is that I am frightened by opium; it was only when gripped by the incessant tic that drove me to desperation that my friend Merrall, who was travelling with me to Liverpool, had, not knowing what else to do, led me to the apothecary's for aid. The amount of laudanum had been modest indeed, and had no more effect than a mild and transitory sense of exaltation, at once somewhat quite similar to, and yet strangely different from, the effects of strong drink. I have no wish to 'experiment' further with the drug.

I thought of Hartley Coleridge, whom I had never seen again, he who had never responded to the translations I sent to him after returning to Haworth. What had he said about his great father? *He stunned himself into oblivion.* I reflected, too, on De Quincy – yet another who has never responded to my letters – and his *Confessions of an English Opium-Eater*:

> Oh! Just, subtle, and mighty opium! … to the guilty man, for one night givest back the hopes of his youth, and hands washed pure from blood; and to the proud man, a brief oblivion … thou callest into sunny light the faces of long-buried beauties, and the blessed household countenances, cleansed from the 'dishonours of the grave'. Thou only givest these gifts to man; and thou hast the keys of Paradise, oh just, subtle, and mighty opium!

No, it is quite enough that I have lived through a period of debauchery that consisted primarily of perpetual drunkenness and lechery; the bitterness of Coleridge *fils* and the heretical adoration of De Quincy on the subject of opium are sufficient to terrify me.

All of this flashed through my mind in the time it took to take another draught of wine.

'I fear,' said I, 'that laudanum is not for me.'

Crosby laughed. 'I already know you well enough, Brontë, to guess that you've read too many fanciful poems and tales about opium – "Kubla Kahn" and the like, eh? You think you'll finish your days with incurable methomania, do you? Rubbish!' He leant over and whispered, 'Of course I would never betray any of my specific patients' medical secrets, but I can tell you that people like the Robinsons take laudanum for all manner of ailments, especially those that afflict the softer sex.'

I sat quietly, eating my mutton, not knowing how to respond to such intelligence. From the street came the rattle of coaches, the clip-clop of horses' hooves, the cries of drivers and, on the hour, the tolling of the great bells of York Minster. Within, the pub bustled with activity, as Joseph and his minions sought to assuage his patrons of their thirst and hunger, and to lighten their purses.

At last Crosby spoke again.

'Now tell me, Brontë, you've been at Thorp Green nearly three months. How do you like the place? And what do you think of the family?'

I meant to tread this ground carefully, for as fond as I already was of the good doctor, I am a late arrival at the place, whereas he has long been in the Robinsons' service.

'It has been quite a remarkable change,' said I vaguely. 'The setting, the house – and, I see now, York itself – are lovely, but I am so removed from all that I know that I sometimes feel quite at sea. And yet, it was just such an escape that I desired.'

Without knowing just how accurate were his comments, Crosby said with a laugh, 'Too bad we can never escape ourselves, eh Brontë?! We have to drag *that* along wherever we go, ha ha!' He grew more serious, however, and leaning over conspiratorially, asked again, 'But what do you think of the family?'

'Edmund is a good lad, and he applies himself diligently,' I said, faltering somewhat at the end of my sentence.

'*But* he is a bit of dolt – it's quite all right, you can say it,' he said, smiling.

I was frightened at the prospect of where such talk might lead, so replied only, 'I would not say that so much as that his talents are likely rather in an area of endeavour other than pure scholarship. He does work hard, and he is a well-behaved young fellow.'

Having failed to draw me into a conversation on poor Edmund's shortcomings, he moved on to the young ladies. 'And the three young ladies?'

I took a deep breath, and must have coloured up, for he continued, 'Ah, there, my young friend, you, too, are smitten by the trio! My nephew can scarcely go to church without trembling before the *angelic creatures* as he calls them.'

'They are lovely girls, I will not deny; and they have been kind enough to me, if a little coquettish. But that is to be expected at their ages.'

'Well, finally, what think you of the Reverend and Mrs Robinson?'

'I have scarcely seen the gentleman, poor man, he has been so ill, but he seems a genuinely religious fellow.'

'Hmmm … yes … indeed … indeed …' he appeared to concur, albeit somewhat vaguely. 'And the lady of the manor?'

I had not forgotten her kindness in bringing Crosby to see me, nor that strange communion of gazes we had shared that day, but those images had of late been eclipsed by others, for on the rare occasions that I glimpse her she never lingers to speak, but only tilts her head slightly in recognition and continues on to whatever her destination might be.

'Well, she seems a kind enough lady, that's clear,' said I, not really knowing *what* to say. 'Very elegant, very lively. She appears to care a great deal about her children's education, and what will become of them when they are grown. But you see Crosby' – he has insisted that I call him thus – 'I rarely cross paths with her, even in the house, and when I do, she simply nods her head and sails off.'

The good doctor simply grunted 'hmm' and lapsed into an uncharacteristic silence. For the rest of our meal and for much of the ride home to Thorp Green, he appeared to be musing on something; I should like to know what it is.

XXIV.

Two Ladies

May 13th, 1843 · Thorp Green

I have been frightfully lonely, but today at least I had the distraction of a letter from Brussels, where Charlotte has long since returned. There is nothing extraordinary in this epistle – quite the contrary is true – and yet perhaps for that very reason my eyes welled up as I read, for here was my old playmate, my writing partner and beloved sister. Were these tears of shame? Have I truly been too severe in her regard? In her letter she seems genuinely solicitous of my health:

> Are you in better health and spirits and does Anne continue to be pretty well? I understand Papa has been to see you – did he seem cheerful and well? Mind when you write to me you answer these questions as I wish to know – Also give me a detailed account as to how you get on with your pupil and the rest of the family. I have received general assurance that you do well and are in good odour – but I want to know the particulars.

She then opens her heart – at least some of its chambers – to me, as in the old days, the slant of her hand and the proliferation of dashes betraying the speed and passion of her thought:

> As for me I am very well and wag on as usual, I perceive however that I grow exceedingly misanthropic and sour – you will say this is no news, and that you never knew me

possessed of the contrary qualities, philanthropy and sugariness – *das is wahr* (which being translated means '*that is true*') but the fact is the people here are no go whatsoever – amongst 120 persons, which compose the daily population of this house I can discern only one or two who deserve anything like regard – This is not owing to foolish fastidiousness on my part – but to the absence of decent qualities on theirs – they have not intellect or politeness or good-nature or good-feeling – they are nothing – I don't hate them – hatred would be too warm a feeling – They have no sensations themselves and they excite none – but one wearies from day to day of caring nothing, fearing nothing, liking nothing, hating nothing – being nothing, doing nothing –

I looked up from her missive and out onto the lovely grounds of Thorp Green, trying, in vain, to imagine being employed in a large and bustling city like Brussels, and more to the point, surrounded by over one hundred young ladies. I would surely go mad, too – though not for the same reasons. She continued:

Yes, I teach & sometimes get red-in-the-face with impatience at their stupidity – but don't think I ever scold or fly into a passion – if I spoke warmly, as warmly as I sometimes used to do at Roe Head they would think me mad – nobody ever gets into a passion here – such a thing is not known – the phlegm that thickens their blood is too gluey to boil – they are very false in their relations with each other – but they rarely quarrel & friendship is a folly they are unacquainted with –
The black swan Monsieur Heger is the sole veritable exception to this rule (for Madame, always cool and always reasoning is not quite an exception) but I rarely speak to Monsieur now for not being a pupil I have little or nothing to do with him – from time to time he shows his kind-heartedness by loading me with

> books – so that I am still indebted to him for all the pleasure or amusement I have –

I sat and reflected on her situation, and how it resembled and differed from my own. I, too, felt isolated and lonely, but now I had Crosby as a friend, at least, and have Anne nearby, whereas Charlotte no longer has even fierce, laconic Emily. Yes, I sometimes must suppress my impatience with Edmund's dullwittedness, but he is my only charge, and is a pleasant enough lad, who at least applies himself.

I wonder if Monsieur Heger is truly *the sole veritable exception* or if she has made of him an idol, as I suspect she did of Mr White. Is she playing at being Mina Laury, and is the poor unsuspecting schoolmaster now her Duke of Zamorna? Given how the mind works, it would not at all surprise me, for in her letter she next confesses that she has not – contrary to what she told me in Haworth – utterly abandoned the 'infernal world' – the world below – of Angria we created together. Indeed, she hints, it is *always*, almost *fanatically* present:

> It is a curious metaphysical fact that always in the evening when I am in the great dormitory alone – having no other company than a number of beds with white curtains I always recur as fanatically as ever to the old ideas the old faces & the old scenes in the world below.

As for me, my mind has again returned to thoughts – if not the activity – of writing, following an impromptu interview with Mrs Robinson a few days since. I sat with my pupil in the library – where we often are when Anne and her charges occupy the schoolroom – on a glorious May day, the windows open and a perfect breeze – neither too warm nor too cool, softly agitating the sheer white curtains. Edmund had begun to grow impatient, and glanced with increasing frequency at the verdant paradise that awaited him just beyond, in the park. My concentration, too, was beginning to wane, when the lad's mother, a small parcel in her hands, swept almost silently into the library, only the slight rustle of her garments announcing her arrival. I rose hastily.

I confess that I had thought a great deal about her after my conversation with Crosby in York, if only because of his somewhat mysterious behaviour. She approached Edmund from behind, leant over, and wrapped her arms around his neck, turned his head to the side, and placed her mouth – it truly was lovely, second only to her eyes in beauty – on the boy's forehead. 'My sweet Neddy, still slaving away like a navvy?' She turned to me and, though smiling, said with unwonted gravity, 'Why surely, Mr Brontë, the boy should be allowed to romp a bit before this lovely day is gone, do you not agree?'

'As it happens, ma'am,' said I, bowing slightly, 'the day's lessons were just now drawing to a close.' I do not know what possessed me, but I dared the slightest bit of levity. 'But even if that were not the case, I would obey you in this, as in all things.' Again I bowed.

'Very well, Edmund, run along. I have some things to discuss with Mr Brontë.'

I wondered what she could possibly have to say to me.

'Please, let us sit down, Mr Brontë,' said she, motioning to two of the larger, more comfortable chairs at the other end of the library, mine an armchair and hers a sort of low stool or tabouret, around which she elegantly arranged her ample skirts.

Smiling somewhat sadly, she said, 'As I am sure you know, the man of the house would normally be the one to speak to you about his son's learning – about how young Edmund is progressing under your tuition – but you see' – she paused and sighed – 'you see, there are a *number* of such things that now fall to me, as heterodox as that may appear. My poor Edmund is so sick and emaciated that there is little business he can attend to at present.' She bit her lovely lower lip and added, 'He really is capable of *nothing* but trying to preserve what is left of his health at present.'

Not knowing how to respond, I simply said, 'I see.'

'So that is why *I* am here, to ask how my son gets on in his studies.'

'He is a delightful pupil, ma'am, most diligent and compliant, with a good – a pure – heart.' All of this was quite true, but it was an incomplete truth; I knew that mentioning his mental inferiority would be a death-sentence – a 'no go whatsoever' as Charlotte might say.

'*But?*'

Here was a poser for me. It was my duty to be truthful, but how was it to be done? Too *much* truthfulness could send me packing to Haworth; too *little* might easily be detected and could destroy any trust my mistress might have in me.

I took a deep breath. 'But … uh … some of the subjects are particularly toilsome for Edmund.' I paused. 'After all, Mrs Robinson, do we not all find some things easier to master than others? Surely Edmund is not alone in that.'

Those dewy lips parted in an utterly dazzling smile. 'That is true indeed, Mr Brontë, and it pleases me that you see matters that way. And let us be candid – my son hardly needs the knowledge of a *scholar*, the sort of mastery *you* have, for he will inherit Thorp Green regardless. What he needs are simply a gentleman's acquirements.'

If she had meant this as a compliment, I can hardly say I received it as such. And yet, I found myself not caring in the least, for I had suitably responded to her enquiry, and was now utterly in thrall to her bright eyes and smile – those lips! – her dusky skin, and the fragrance of perfume and powder that arose from her neck and bosom, so close were we now to one another.

She lifted the parcel in her lap, which was a small package wrapped in colourful paper, the string tied with a bow. 'Please open it,' said she, eagerly. I readily complied.

'This,' said she, 'is a signed copy of Macaulay's *Lays of Ancient Rome*. As you may know, he is a somewhat distant relative of mine. I – we – would like to give it to you as a small token of the progress you have made thus far with young Edmund.'

'This is most generous, madam, and most unnecessary. I was only performing my duties.'

'Nonsense,' said she, at which I looked down, trying not to smile. I failed.

'Is there something amusing in all this?' said she directly, but not unkindly.

I looked up to find her examining at me: her gaze enveloped completely, and how much warmer, how much more intoxicating than the strongest liquor it was!

I could not look away as I perhaps should have done, but replied, 'As a tutor and occasional scribbler I am most attentive to language, and – well – I rather like the way you use that word – "Nonsense!" – that's all. I mean no disrespect.'

Mrs Robinson coloured slightly and became more serious, changing the subject. 'Why yes, your sister has told me that the Brontë children are all fond of poetry and the like, *scribbling* as you say. I confess that I have asked her to tell me *all* about you … hence my choice of your gift,' said she, pointing to the *Lays*.

'Yes, well, as you might imagine that was a passion of our youthful, overheated imaginations; now in our maturity we are all become quite serious, I can assure you – three of us pursuing teaching and one managing the Parsonage at home.'

She seemed somewhat disappointed at this news. 'Do you mean to say that you never write poetry? Even for your own amusement?'

Did I imagine it, or was there a sweet solicitude in how she looked at me? I could hardly imagine such a gaze bestowed upon my sister.

Indeed, something in her manner invited an unwonted candour from me. I suddenly yearned to bear my soul to her, to tell her that I was a man of extremes, that I was beginning to think that I must crush all poetic desire if I am to make my independence in the world, since it appeared that the only alternative would be to live – and die of starvation in – the world of my own imagination. I wanted to tell her that the idea of writing poetry as a calm pursuit in one's leisure hours – which is to say a pastime of no pecuniary benefit – was so foreign, nay, anathema to me that I would rather nip it in the bud, amputate it entirely from my being, smother it in the crib, cast it overboard as Jonah's shipmates did him to appease Jehovah. But I said none of this.

'I will occasionally scribble a few lines, just as I sketch a building or tree from time to time.'

'Surely you have the time to do more,' said she, again smiling. 'Certainly we are not working you too hard here at Thorp Green!'

After a pause, as if considering something, she added, 'Indeed, if you have any pieces of which are particularly proud, I would be willing to send them along to Macaulay. Like your father, he is a Cambridge man.' Apparently, Anne has told Mrs Robinson a great deal over the past three years, and Papa's pedigree was surely one of the first things that she revealed.

With this she rose and again thanked me for the 'progress' of my pupil, as I too stood and faced her. The spring sunshine, entering through the open window, caught her bright eyes and dappled her dark hair, just as it might a swiftly running beck and the bright green leaves dancing above it.

She offered her hand as she did so, and when I placed mine in hers, she gave it a squeeze so imperceptible that I scarcely knew whether it was real or imagined.

XXV.

On the Banks of the Ouse

May 18th, 1843 · Thorp Green

Since this last encounter, my mind recurs far more often than is salutary to Mrs Robinson, and I find I cannot think of much else. Had there been something different in her gaze, in her smile, in the squeeze of her soft fingers as we shook hands? No, surely. What a fool I am to think such a lady as *she* would care for a poor, unconnected tutor such as I! When I think of it coolly, rationally, it occurs to me that a greater fool than Patrick Branwell Brontë has never breathed the breath of life: that a more fantastic idiot had never surfeited itself on sweet lies and swallowed poison as if it were nectar.

'*You*,' I say, 'a favourite of Mrs Robinson? *You* of importance to her in any way? Go! Your folly sickens me! How dare you? Poor stupid dupe! Blind puppy!'

All the reproofs in the world, however, are vanquished each time her image rises before me, transformed in my overheated imagination into an angelic form, her glancing eyes turned to flashing beams, her dappled *coiffure* transmuted into a shimmering halo: Hera, Juno, Ceres, oh goddess, oh Queen of Heaven! At such times, I feel giddy – even mad.

I have read through Macaulay's *Lays of Ancient Rome*, and have determined that I should not, in fact, abandon my verse altogether. Why should I not try my hand once again, through the benevolent offices of my mistress? Yesterday afternoon, with these thoughts in mind, I set out across the park with the book in hand, my lungs drinking in the fresh spring air and my eyes the beauty of the landscape, when I came across Anne, who, it so happened, was doing the same thing, a book in her own hand. Her black and white King Charles spaniel Flossy trotted alongside her.

'Hello, Branwell,' said she, 'You look so well!'

'I surely *feel* better,' said I. 'You did not lie, sister – springtime in this neighbourhood is lovely indeed, and how could I remain ill with such life bursting forth all around me?' Though I have never had Anne's – or especially Emily's – wild enthusiasm for the lower creation – yet another trait I share with Charlotte – even *I* could not resist squatting to give Flossy an enthusiastic pat on the head on such a splendid day as this.

Pointing to my book, Anne said, 'What have you there?'

I hesitated, fearing that Anne would impute greater meaning than warranted to the gift of the book, but with feigned nonchalance handed it to her and said, 'Oh, this? It's a copy of Macaulay's *Lays*. The Robinsons made a gift of it to me, in gratitude for my efforts with Edmund.' *Poor lad*, I almost added, but Anne's mind was already flowing along in the same channel.

'Poor lad!' said she, 'he *does* struggle to learn anything at all, doesn't he? If he weren't such a fine, docile boy I would call him a blockhead or a dolt, but that seems far too cruel an appellation for such a sweet young man.'

She handed Macaulay back to me. 'Yes, when I first began at Thorp Green – can you fathom that it has been nearly three years, brother? I think I just might be the family champion of steadfastness – except for Papa, of course.'

I must have looked downcast at these words.

'Now see here, Branwell, I didn't mean it *that* way. You worked on the railway nearly as long, and in the end, I'm sure that just wasn't for you. I simply meant to say that I have been here for what seems an eternity.' Her countenance darkened for a moment. 'If you only knew the number of times that I have wanted to give my notice!'

'But Anne, that is not what you were about to say, is it? What has this to do with the book?'

‘Oh, for Mercy’s sake, yes, forgive me.’ Her forehead was once again smooth and free of care, and her eyes laughed under those thin, arched brows. She playfully locked her arm tightly in mine as we walked the path towards the River Ouse: my baby sister once again.

‘I was going to say that when I first worked here, I was showered with gifts, but like a husband whose ardour for his bride cools after a few months, so too the family began to take me for granted as the subordinate that I am – quite right of them, I might add, for I found such attentions embarrassing – and the presents ceased.’

She smiled and stooped down, fairly throwing her arms around Flossy, adding, ‘But they saved the best for last, didn’t they, boy!’ For the spaniel had, as a puppy, been a gift from the young ladies of the household.

We were within a quarter of a mile of the Ouse by now, and so I asked Anne if she would like to continue on. ‘As long as we do not go too quickly,’ said she, ‘for you know how my shortness of breath can tire me. Needless to say, however, Flossy will make a jubilee of it!’

She took my arm again and we walked together in silence for a few moments. I turned over in my mind what she had said, and I had to confess to myself a certain foolish disappointment that I had not been especially favoured by Mrs Robinson – or *the Robinsons*, as I had quite intentionally said to Anne.

As we approached the Ouse, Anne grew somewhat serious. ‘Mrs Robinson does ask a great many questions about you, Branwell. Unusual questions: where have you worked, what you have studied’ – she blushed – ‘even whether you have ever had admirers.’

I fought back the feelings that now welled up at this unexpected revelation, assuming a stern mask and lying, with uncharacteristic coolness, ‘Well, you know that my only true encounter with the fair sex was the disastrous visit of the unfortunate Mary Taylor, when she revealed her feelings and I shrank from her like a fool and a coward.’

Anne frowned as we walked in silence until a thought occurred to me, a way out, the perfect – indeed, most obvious – distraction from Anne's apparent misgivings about our mistress. 'Don't you see why Mrs Robinson wants to know all about me – especially about *les affaires du coeur?* It's as plain as the nose on Flossy's adorable little face.'

She could not resist smiling at this, and turned to me as we approached the banks of the Ouse.

'No? Why, Heavens, dear little sister,' said I, 'how innocent you are! Have you not seen what shameless flirts your three charges become when I'm in the vicinity? Or, for that matter, when any biped in breeches, including those who throng about them after church, is within shouting distance? Of course you have, for you told me of their conduct before I had ever witnessed it myself. They are naughty little monkeys, don't you think? I can only imagine their good mama's anxiety at their conduct, for if, as you say, she is concerned only that they marry well, she must live in mortal dread that one or more of them will run off and marry a nobody at Gretna Green. And who could be more of a nobody than their brother's tutor, the son of a poor clergyman? Since I have unquestioned access to the house, is it any wonder that she wants to know everything about me, especially if I am a vile seducer, the very Devil amongst them? Ha ha!'

Anne seemed utterly calmed by this speech, on whose cleverness and reason I had to congratulate myself. I confess that I had nearly convinced myself of its veracity; although I hoped I was wrong and feared I was right. Still, would Mrs Robinson not have made such enquiries even before engaging me as tutor?

'Those giddy girls have driven you mad,' said I, changing the subject. I pointed at the small volume she was carrying. 'Now tell me what you are reading.' She passed me an edition of William Cowper's poems.

'Of course, your beloved Cowper. Do you never tire of him?' I handed the volume back to her. Clearly she had not, so I did not give her time to respond. 'Let us test my memory: his last poem, that monument to despair and oblivion, 'The Castaway'.

Fear not, for I'll not recite the whole thing, just the last stanza – will that do, Miss Brontë?'

Her furrowed brow suggested that Anne feared that I was mocking her, Cowper, and even the Almighty himself; and though I could feel her silent consternation, I sallied on:

No voice divine the storm allay'd
No light propitious shone,
When, snatch'd from all effectual aid,
We perish'd each alone;
But I beneath a rougher sea,
And whelm'd in deeper gulfs than he.

To make light of death, of Cowper's own struggles, his belief that he had been abandoned by his God at his life's end, was a source of terror rather than amusement to Anne. We approached an old oak tree that had fallen under the weight of the winter's snow, and its dead roots stretched out imploringly, impotently, towards the westering sun. One of its larger branches now formed, horizontal with the riverbank, a graceful bench, where brother and sister could sit and watch May's swift steam rush southwards towards York. It even gave gently with our weight, like the seat of a gig on its spring, and I could bounce us if I chose with a simple flex of my toes. Flossy, never losing sight of his mistress, carefully, almost daintily, explored the edge of the river, occasionally leaping and barking at a bird that flew too close, or perhaps at other creatures that remained unnoticed by the limited senses of his human companions.

Anne turned to me. 'Do you not think, brother, that there are certain subjects that should remain above ridicule? Must everything be a *jest* to you?'

'Forgive me, Anne. I'm afraid I am overtaken at times by the attitudes of some of my childhood characters. Do you recall old Robert Patrick Sdeath, that red-haired minion of the Duke of Northangerland?'

'Yes, yet another of your *alter egos*, that one in particular having the nasty habit of mocking sacred scripture, among other things.' She shuddered.

'*Whisht*,' said I, trying to pacify her with an imitation of Tabby. 'Do you know that even dear Mr Weightman was known to jest in this way? Truly, he did.'

'Did he mock *scripture itself* or those hypocrites who would use it to justify their own place in heaven, while flinging others into Hell?'

I had to confess to myself that it was only the latter and never the former, and we lapsed into silence. So full was the Ouse that it crept here and there onto its banks, where wildflowers – bluebells and purple orchids, mostly – had begun to dot the bright green grasses, and all waved together in a gentle breeze, like loved ones gathered on the docks of a great port city, bidding their beloved *adieu*.

Meanwhile, Flossy had returned from his investigations, and now pressed his head against his mistress's knee, his eyes full of the purest, simplest love, his tongue lolling about as he caught his breath. Anne returned his affection with tender scratches behind his pendulous ears and sighed as she gazed at the swiftly passing current.

'I find it difficult to conceive that such an innocent lamb as *thou* wouldst ever fear for *thy* soul,' said I at last, bouncing our bench with a single extension of my toes.

She smiled, in spite of herself. 'I must suppose you mock the common folk and not scripture with your employment of *thou* and *thy*.'

Her countenance grew dark again. 'Ever since that fateful day in our childhood, when the earth shook and the bog exploded, and afterwards, when Papa preached his sermon about the end-times, I have lived in mortal fear of dying unshriven and unforgiven. Or worse – as the Calvinists would have it – of being one of those predestined to damnation.'

'Nonsense!' said I, doing my best to imitate Mrs Robinsons herself, and drawing yet another, albeit slight, smile from Anne. 'If there is such a place as Heaven –'

'*Branwell!*' Anne fairly shouted. 'Do not utter such blasphemy!'

'Now, now, baby sister, calm yourself. Do you not believe in your heart that only the wicked among us – wicked not just in their thought but in their deeds – will be damned for all eternity?'

'For by *grace* are ye saved through faith,' said she. 'And that not of yourselves: it is the gift of God: not of works, lest any man should boast."

"So, you are suggesting that it is the presence of the slightest doubt – the blasphemy with which you charge me – that will send one to his perdition? Have you not had a doubt in your life – about God, that is, and the Bible – about Heaven and Hell?'

'I have, Branwell,' said she, her eyes beginning to brim like the Ouse before us. 'Of course I have. That is why I fear death and damnation.'

Poor Weightman, thought I. *Poor Anne*. They really would have made a handsome couple, and pious, too – the kind of genuine piety that makes one *want to be good* rather than ridicule such fervour. Regardless of whether he had had feelings for her, or she for him, I was struck by how much in sympathy their gentle souls would have been. In that moment I felt a surge of love for them both, one living and the other dead.

'We all have doubts,' I assured her. 'Even Papa would agree with that, would he not?'

I had spoken in earnest, although what followed rang false to me: I now became, myself, one of those hypocrites I so abhorred, as I added, 'All we can do is pray for God's grace, his forgiveness.'

This was hypocrisy precisely because when I pray to God I feel more like Cowper's castaway, my prayers themselves cast into an unresponsive void: *No voice divine the storm allay'd, No light propitious shone*. It occurred to me: is not this sort of hypocrisy – the sententious pronouncement of religious beliefs that we, ourselves, do not hold, only for the benefit of others – a sin as bad as blasphemy itself? For if nothing else, the blasphemer says what he honestly feels, and what true believer would ever blaspheme? How could it be that I could feel, at once, a kind of tender, fraternal, almost religious love for Anne, whilst beneath its surface, just as genuine, rose a fury at a God – or Man, who invented God – who would allow such a sweet soul to be tortured with thoughts of eternal damnation?

Anne coughed, and I noticed the air had begun to cool, as the sun descended behind a line of trees to the west. 'Here, sister, give me your arm. Let us wend our way home.'

As we made our way through a patch of woods, past the dairy and stables, and onto the vast lawn at Thorp Green, the grand hall itself rose up before us. Although we walked in shade towards the great house, the setting sun shot above us to illuminate the billowing clouds beyond it. For a boy raised in the crowded parsonage of a squalid village, here was a palace set in a pristine land; I could not have created anything more splendid in Angria itself. As I gripped my copy of Macaulay's *Lays* in my left hand and squeezed Anne's with my right, I felt the last remnants of the gloom that had encircled me since my arrival at last melt fully away, like the final snows of winter.

What I fool, thought I, *to have been depressed here!*

XXVI.

Seduction

May 22nd, 1843 · Thorp Green

Plans are afoot for the summer holidays: Anne will, as usual, return to Haworth for a time next month, after which she will travel to her beloved Scarborough to join the Robinsons. To my surprise, I am to remain at Thorp Green in June, and accompany the family to the seaside in July. I learned of this all only this morning: as I awaited my pupil in the library, perusing the bookshelves, I heard behind me the familiar rustling of Mrs Robinson's garments. Her countenance was flushed, whether from her usual brisk movements or some interior cause, I knew not. In her arms she carried four volumes.

'Good morning, Mr Brontë,' said she. 'I am sorry to inform you that young Edmund is not well this morning. My poor angel has a fever and a bit of a cough, and one can't be too careful with these things.' Indeed, thought I: Maria, Elizabeth, and her own little Georgiana – all taken in childhood.

'Oh, I am so sorry,' said I with genuine concern, for he truly is a pleasant, if dull, little scholar. 'Not too serious, I hope.'

'I am quite certain that with sleep and two or three days' rest, he will mend himself in no time at all,' she responded, smiling. 'While I am here, I would like to discuss another matter,' she added, and without pausing for me to respond, she continued, 'Since you have *just* arrived in January and are making such progress with Edmund, I wonder if you might stay at Thorp Green until we go to Scarborough. I worry that he will forget all that he has learned.'

She paused for a moment, her lips parting slightly, her nostrils widening and bosom rising ever so slightly as she drew in a breath. 'I hope you and I can speak plainly with each other, Mr Brontë.'

'Why yes,' said I, 'of course.'

She ran her hand along her right temple, as if to smooth her hair, but no such adjustment was necessary. Did I imagine it, or did her hand tremble slightly?

'The *truth* is – and you and I can speak of this, even if my husband chooses not to' – here her brow clouded over – 'the *truth* is that Edmund's gifts are not of the intellectual kind, though he is such a good boy. The *truth* is that with enough effort – and especially under your constant tuition – he will know more than enough to succeed his father at Thorp Green, although I am not so convinced that he has a promising future before him at Oxford. What we ask is just two or three hours of lessons a day in the summer; the rest of the time you will be free to ramble, to write or do whatever you are inclined to do.'

Another pause. 'I know how fond you are of your sisters, and your venerable father, so *do* take a day or two to think about it if you wish.'

My mind raced forward so quickly that such a period of reflection was hardly necessary: yes, I had been lonely and miserable at the outset, but the family had embraced me, so much so that I began to feel an especial favourite, and Dr Crosby had grown into a faithful friend, through whom I had begun to meet fellow lovers of music, art and literature in the proximity. Although I was careful to exercise moderation, we even met from time to time at one of the public houses in Little Ouseburn. Thorp Green is beautiful, and so near to York, where I have since returned, both with Crosby and the family itself. Surely Papa will be pleased that I am so valued, and I will not shed any tears over my absence from Haworth, even though being there with my two younger sisters and without Charlotte has its appeal, and I do miss the company of Brown and Leyland, among others. Finally, and of capital importance, the brutal truth is that I might well be sacked – eventually – if I choose not to obey the Robinsons' command.

All of this flashed like lightning through my mind. I looked at Mrs Robinson, and the thought of walking these halls and grounds alone, seeing only her and her three saucy daughters, with her husband confined to his bed and my sister far, far away, gave me an involuntary, irrational *frisson*. I even considered ... but before the thought could fully form itself, I crushed it, saying again: *stupid dupe!* But it did not matter, for just being in the presence of my mistress and her daughters would allow me to *gaze and gape* to my heart's content.

I must have smiled at this thought, for Mrs Robinson grew serious and said, 'Does something amuse you?'

'No, no, not at all,' said I, inventing on the fly. 'I was just thinking, in fact, how pleased my father and sisters will be that I am so valued at Thorp Green. I believe they would gladly be spared the pleasure of my company in return for such assurances!'

'Very well then, Mr Brontë. Does this mean that you have made your decision? No need to reflect?' The blush had faded from her cheeks, but her lovely eyes and teeth were now fully deployed in a beguiling smile.

'No need to reflect at all, madam.'

'I am *so* pleased to hear it.'

I looked down at the four volumes, which she still held in her arms. 'My, but those must be getting heavy. May I disencumber you? I'll be happy to find a place for them on the library shelves.'

She extended the four small volumes to me, still smiling. 'You may take them, but they are for *you*, not for our library. I was in York and saw them at Mr Bellerby's shop in Stonegate last week, and it seemed to me that it was *just* the kind of thing that would please you. Upon perusing them myself – for I confess that I have cut the pages and read a few of them – I am more certain of this than ever.'

Such unwonted familiarity brought forth in me, as it often does, a nervous, slightly jocular response. 'Ah, so this is a thank-you gift for my agreeing to stay, rather than an inducement to do so.' The moment the words had escaped my lips, I desperately wished to call them back; my mistress, however, was happy to be part of the game. Her smile remained, as the years and social distance between us seemed to collapse in an instant, and she responded, 'How could this be payment when you have not yet performed your duties?'

'You are correct in this as all things, ma'am,' said I, bowing.

Still smiling, she paused – did she bite her lip like a young girl, or did I imagine it? – then bowed slightly and swept out of the room.

My daily duties abruptly cancelled, I sat down near an open window, where I could feel the warming breeze on my face and where birdsong drifted in from the park. From time to time came a burst of chatter or laughter from the schoolroom above, where Anne instructed the young ladies, or the occasional shout of a farmhand in the distance, but otherwise all was calm. I opened the first of the four volumes, curious to see what Mrs Robinson was so certain to be *just the sort of thing that would please me*, finding the following on the title page:

THE

POETICAL WORKS

OF

PERCY BYSSHE SHELLEY

EDITED

BY MRS SHELLEY

IN FOUR VOLUMES

LONDON:

EDWARD MOXON, DOVER STREET

MDCCCXXXIX

The frontispiece bears an image of the eternally young poet, along with his signature, while the title page quotes Petrarch. What a lavish gift, though I, as I flipped through the volumes, whose pages had, as Mrs Robinson had candidly reported, been cut.

I noticed a small slip of paper, with only the initials LGR. It smelled strongly of perfume and had been used to mark the page to Shelley's 'Epipsychidion'. I sat with my legs crossed, the book on my knee, and my left hand running the paper beneath my nostrils as I read somewhat distractedly, still thinking about our conversation:

Our breath shall intermix, our bosoms bound,
And our veins beat together; and our lips
With other eloquence than words, eclipse
The soul that burns between them, and the wells
Which boil under our being's inmost cells,
The fountains of our deepest life, shall be
Confus'd in Passion's golden purity,
As mountain-springs under the morning sun.

Distracted no more, I sat bolt upright, filled suddenly with an ardent admixture of desire and apprehension. Surely, this was not intended for *me* – and yet the perfumed paper had not been placed upon this poem by chance. I knew not what to think, and a number of contradictory thoughts crowded upon me: Oh God, could it be? Stranger things have occurred, surely, than a liaison between a tutor and his mistress. But *no*, this could not possibly be true: she is the daughter of a clergyman; the wife of a clergymen, her father an evangelical like Papa, no less. She is the doting mother of four children, one whose conduct is above reproach, or my sister would surely have fled long ago. Certainly there is much that Anne does not sanction about the *manner* in which Mrs Robinson is raising her children – especially her daughters – but never has she hinted at immoral conduct. I read on to the poem's end:

We shall become the same, we shall be one
Spirit within two frames, oh! Wherefore two?
One passion in twin-hearts, which grows and grew,
Till like two meteors of expanding flame,

Those spheres instinct with it become the same,
Touch, mingle, are transfigur'd; ever still
Burning, yet ever inconsumable:
In one another's substance finding food,
Like flames too pure and light and unimbu'd
To nourish their bright lives with baser prey,
Which point to Heaven and cannot pass away:
One hope within two wills, one will beneath
Two overshadowing minds, one life, one death,
One Heaven, one Hell, one immortality,
And one annihilation. Woe is me!
The winged words on which my soul would pierce
Into the height of Love's rare Universe,
Are chains of lead around its flight of fire –
I pant, I sink, I tremble, I expire!

Oh God! It was not solely the choice of this particular poem, but of Shelley himself. Shelley: he who had eloped with a sixteen-year-old girl and later abandoned her, pregnant, for another sixteen-year-old girl, she who would write *Frankenstein; or, the Modern Prometheus*, and who so many years later would edit the very book that I held in my hands. Shelley, whose first wife Harriet had drowned herself and the baby she carried in the Serpentine in Hyde Park. Shelley, who had been expelled from Oxford for refusing to repudiate his pamphlet, *The Necessity of Atheism*. Shelley, who wrote infamously of marriage:

> I conceive that from the abolition of marriage, the fit and natural arrangement of sexual connection would result … In fact, religion and morality, as they now stand, compose a practical code of misery and servitude: the genius of human happiness must tear every leaf from the accursed book of God ere man can read the inscription on his heart. How would morality, dressed up in stiff stays and finery, start from her own disgusting image should she look in the mirror of *nature*! –

This, then, was the book that Mrs Robinson had decided would be *just the sort of thing to please me*. My ears and face hot with desire, my mind aflame with the possibilities, I gathered up the volumes and walked directly to the Old Hall, where I took out a sheet of paper and dashed off a letter to John Brown, that Old Knave of Trumps, the essence of which was to tell him of my situation, and ask if he thinks I should go to extremities with her.

I feel powerless to act, to think, to read or to write. I am on tenterhooks until I know the issue of this situation. I wonder – I wonder if Crosby might provide some insight into all of this. If tomorrow young Edmund is still unwell, I shall do my best to find the good surgeon, if not here at Thorp Green, then at home in Great Ouseburn. But how to ask him without really asking? Aye, there's the rub.

XXVII.

Standing on the Precipice

May 23rd, 1843 · Thorp Green

Good God – what a dream I have had! I sat in the front row as Papa preached from an impossibly high pulpit. For this was not our homely parish church in Haworth but rather the immense interior of York Minster itself. The subject of the sermon was the sanctity of marriage, which I found unbearably tedious; I grew weary and writhed, yawned, nodded, pinched and pricked myself, and rubbed my eyes, at which my father showered several blows on the boards of the pulpit, scowling down at me as if to say *thou art the man of whom I speak, the defiler, the adulterer!*

'Now then,' he resumed more calmly, if no less sternly, 'As Paul says in his Letter to the Hebrews, "Marriage is honourable to all, and the bed undefiled: but whoremongers and adulterers *God* will judge".' Wide awake at last in my shame, I turned to avoid his gaze, finding that the cavernous cathedral held not only a full and attentive congregation, but my employers, Mr and Mrs Robinson, who sat on either side of me in this, the box closest to the pulpit. The first of these sat to my left, hunched in his nightcap and nightgown, swathed in a woollen blanket, his eyes sunken into his pale, wasting face; the second sat to my right in a low frock of silk, something from an earlier era – that of her youth? – her arms, shoulders, neck and bosom splendidly bare as she smiled and squeezed my hand in hers. She seemed no older than I.

'So often,' continued the sermon, 'man believes that adultery is a sin of the flesh, and so it is, so it is. Yet it is not *merely* a sin of the flesh, but far more seriously it is an extension of man's original transgression: to be – to know – to possess – more than God has granted him. It is the sin of the first man and woman. It is wrong to say that Adam and Eve were simply *cast out* of Eden; nay, in disobeying God our first parents *chose* to walk out of the Earthly Paradise that He had wrought for them. Think of the word "transgression" itself: in its Latin origins, it is a *going over* or a *going beyond.* Adam was no more an automaton than we are.

'Yes, and tradition tells us that this was also the sin of Lucifer's fall. Even the *pagans* who could never know our Lord and Saviour Jesus Christ understood – as we learn from the story of Icarus – the danger of human transgression, of overreaching – for is not human yearning just another form of lust, and is not lust the most sinful kind of desire?'

My mistress squeezed my hand again; her husband coughed.

'That is why,' the Reverend Brontë pursued, 'it is natural that Paul should continue directly from a consideration of adultery in verse 4 to this, in verse 5: "Let your conversation be without covetousness; and *be content with such things as ye have*: for he hath said, I will never leave thee, nor forsake thee."'

At this, Mrs Robinson leant over to me and repeated the same words, in a blasphemous whisper, in my ear: 'And I will never leave *thee*, nor forsake *thee*.' She took my face in her hands and turned my mouth to hers, and soon deep, passionate kisses were followed by caresses, for as we kissed she guided my left hand from her right cheek, down along her soft neck and into the warm, dewy cleavage between her breasts. I was wild with desire for her.

Over her shoulder, across the central aisle, I saw Brown and Leyland sitting together; they smiled and nodded enthusiastically, as my hands moved over her neck and shoulders and breasts. Strangely, as the flame of our passion leapt higher, Papa no longer seemed to see us; were we somehow shielded from him; or did he not care what transpired before his pulpit? He simply continued with his sermon. 'Are not, in fact, adultery and theft just the result of man's *acting* upon his covetousness? Do not most sins spring from man's arrogance and pride, and his lack of humility and contentment?'

I heard nothing more, for I was drowning in lust, as deaf to my father's sermon as the castaway who slips beneath the waves is to the shouts of his fellow mariners who seek to save him. At last I was conscious that the congregation had crowded round us, pushing one another to get a better view of our amorous proceedings; and yet, I did not care, and as I slipped Mrs Robinson's silken gown from her shoulders and bent my head to kiss her breasts she cried out in delight, using my Christian name for the first time, 'Oh Branwell! *Branwell*!' She uttered my name repeatedly until I wondered why she would not stop – and at last her form seemed to fade quite away, along with Papa, and everyone else, until at last the very walls of York Minster vanished into air.

Only the voice remained, incessantly calling my name.

'Branwell! *Branwell*!' It was Anne, shaking my shoulder to wake me. She laughed. 'Goodness, brother, you were in the deepest of slumbers, though you were moving about and uttering nonsense. You just brought to mind Flossy, when he is dream-chasing dream-rabbits before the fire!'

'What is it, Anne? Is everything all right?'

'Yes, yes, of course. I just wanted your august opinion on a matter of the utmost importance. I was certain you would be up at this hour.'

Anne sat down upon my bed. I rolled over and sat up, rubbing my eyes.

'Yes?' said I.

'I want to ask the Robinsons a favour, and yet I wonder if it will be poorly received. It's about Flossy.'

I grunted for her to go on, thinking: *my dream was interrupted by a question about a DOG*?

'I think it would be such a lovely surprise for Emily and Papa if I could take him with me to Haworth next month.' She paused, the morning sun making fireworks of her eyes beneath those perpetually lifted brows. 'What do you think?'

I thought about Mrs Robinson – both the real one and she who had just dissipated with my dream: if it was true that she was quite adamant about having Anne take her usual holiday whilst I remained at Thorp Green, surely anything that would ensure the plan would be readily accepted. Besides, was not the dog Anne's anyway? I said so.

'Wasn't Flossy a gift to you, and is he not yours to do with as you see fit? Why, you could regularly thwack him on the skull with a walking stick if you wanted, or tie a large stone around his neck and drown him in the Ouse, for all the Robinsons care.'

I was well aware that such language would shock her; it was small punishment, thought I, for her having prevented me from consummating my adulterous embrace of the phantom Mrs Robinson. My words had the desired effect.

'Branwell! Do not speak so, even in jest. They are sentient creatures, after all. Remember, *a righteous man regardeth the life of his beast*.'

'Yes, yes, I know, Anne. Of course we should not be cruel to any creature. I simply illustrate a larger point, which I hope your pious outrage has not entirely cast into obscurity: *Flossy is yours*. So, by all means, I am sure your request will be granted, if you even think it necessary to ask.'

Her smile had returned, and she ran her hand through my hair. 'I think,' said she, 'that despite your attempts to shock your little sister, you are not in the end such a *mauvais garçon*.'

Long, long ago, when we were children, Emily had found a part of my *History of the Young Men*, read it, and written on the back of its title page, in rudimentary French: 'It was very well written, I thought. No, not really. My goodness you are a naughty boy and you will be a shocking man.' While most such things are quickly and forever forgotten, Emily's name for me – *un mauvais garçon* – had stuck, to become a permanent part of Brontë family lore, by sheer force of repetition.

Anne leant over and placed a gentle kiss on my forehead, and was soon on her feet and out the door, calling 'Goodbye, dearest brother, thank you for your wise counsel, as always!' As so often with Anne, it was difficult to tell whether or not her words concealed just the slightest hint of raillery or sarcasm.

Another free day before me, I dressed, breakfasted and set out in the direction of Great Ouseburn, to find Dr Crosby, turning over in my mind just how to ask about Mrs Robinson. I was at a loss but had close to an hour to consider things while I walked. Unfortunately, I had not even reached Little Ouseburn when who should appear before me but the good surgeon himself.

'Hello!' cried Crosby. 'I must say that from all appearances you have made a full recovery, young man!'

'And that without the aid of your cure-all, laudanum, I would point out.'

'Now now, Brontë,' said he, laughing, 'that was Dr Beckwith – may he rest in peace – not me, remember? I simply stated that it was a substance commonly employed and not nearly so dangerous as some might have you think. *Moderatio*! As with anything else, eh lad?'

'Yes, yes, *moderatio*. Not such an easy proposition as some think, however, is it?'

'Oh, I don't know. With enough will anything is possible.'

As Crosby uttered these words it occurred to me that he was part of that large portion of mankind for whom moderation is as natural as eating and sleeping, and who gaze uncomprehendingly, and thus often in hostile judgement, at the other lot, those who – like me – are forever at risk of plunging headlong into wild license, as I had at Luddenden Foot. I shuddered. My own thoughts, though, were far from censorious, for I could no more dislike the affable Crosby than I could a John Brown or a Joe Leyland.

Seeking to turn our conversation in another direction, and to know his destination, I ask whither he was bound at this early hour.

'Why, to see your young pupil, of course,' said he. 'And pay a regular visit to his father, who as you know is more gravely ill. I might ask you the same question.'

'It so happens that I was on my way to see an illustrious surgeon in Great Ouseburn, but as I conjured him in my mind's eye, he appeared before me, as if by magic, like a little green man!'

'Ha! Well then, let us walk together,' he said, clapping me on the back.

I was silent for quite some time as we walked, not knowing how to broach the subject. Presently, Crosby solved the problem for me, taking my elbow and turning me to face him in the lane. It was another lovely spring day, and leaves of the freshest, sweetest shades of green waltzed on the breeze above us.

'I must ask you something, Brontë.'

'Yes?'

'What do you think of your mistress?'

A chill ran through me, and nervous perspiration sprang to my forehead.

'I'm not sure I know what you mean.'

'Well, then, let me enlighten you, though a part of me feels I should hold my tongue. I have been alone in the presence of Mrs Robinson on numerous occasions since your arrival – to discuss her husband's health of course – and she is increasingly impatient with our usual topics of conversation.'

'I still don't know what you are talking about, Crosby.'

'Can you guess what – or I should say *whom* – she wants to discuss?'

'No,' said I, but my heart rose at the possibility.

'*You*, of course.'

I feigned astonishment, though in fact his words were the final piece of a puzzle and confirmed what I had hoped – or was it what I had feared? I was ecstatic at the possibility of losing myself in her – and here the images of this morning's dream returned – and yet was terrified at the danger of discovery.

'I don't understand,' I lied again.

'She speaks about you incessantly and wants to know if you talk about *her*.'

'And what do you say?' I asked.

'I must confess, Brontë, that it's a rather embarrassing position to be in, so I say very little. I am caring for her sick husband and am paid by *him*. When asked a direct question, such as whether you talk about her, I answer as simply as possible.'

'And what is your response?'

'My response is that you do not speak of her any more than is appropriate for a subordinate, at which intelligence she bites her lip and gazes out the window towards the Old Hall.'

I could bear it no longer, and told Crosby about the gifts, especially *The Poetical Works* of Shelley, and how she had marked 'Epipsychidion' with a perfumed paper bearing her initials. Crosby mused for a moment, then said at last, 'If I had any doubts – though I really did *not* – they have now been removed: Mrs Robinson clearly wishes to have an adulterous liaison with you. Her husband is ill, and yet I suspect that she feels herself to be still "young" and full of passion, if you take my meaning.'

'What makes you think she would betray her husband by going to such extremities?'

'It would not be the first time.'

'How do you know?'

'I just know. I refuse to say more than that.' It was clear that he would speak no more on the topic, and I realised that I did not want to know either, did not even want to think of her with another man, whether her husband or someone else, and sought to blot such images out of existence. I determined that if she loved me now, her past was irrelevant.

'So what,' I asked, 'do you propose I do?'

'That, my young friend, is entirely up to you. If you are asking me if I would object to such a liaison on moral grounds, I can tell you *absolutely not.* We all have animal appetites – some of us greater than others – and I don't believe mere human convention should stand in the way of them. As a doctor I can affirm that a bit of exercise would do both you and your mistress much good,' and here at last the glimmer of a smile appeared on Crosby's face. 'What your master doesn't know won't hurt him, surely.'

He paused and frowned. 'On the other hand,' said he, 'I'm afraid society does not share my heterodox views, which are closer to Mr Shelley's than to the Church of England.'

'What do you suppose Mrs Robinson's views of marriage are, then?'

'I suppose she is a staunch supporter of the institution as it exists today. For is she not rearing her girls to be as *marriageable* as possible? But I suspect she does not utter such words as *love* in the same breath as *marriage*.'

'So, according to you, she is a hypocrite?'

'That might be one way of seeing the matter. However, she might just consider it practical. She might just see marriage as an invaluable instrument to get what one wants, and to do as one pleases: and that is where *love* comes in.' He paused to reflect. 'Of course, if she had a happy marriage she might indeed have a different view of the matter.'

Crosby went on to reveal something entirely unexpected. The lady's husband, it seems, is not at all the grave, pious gentleman that he shows to the world, but is in reality a waspish, splenetic creature who earlier in his married life had, himself, conducted innumerable liaisons. He would leave his wife and young children alone for whole seasons at a time whilst he, perpetually inebriated with his boon companions, whored his way through London. He would return just regularly enough to plague the household with his antics and father another child. It was only when his debauchery began to erode his health that he was at last confined to Thorp Green. When no one is near, he continues, from his very sickbed, to heap unrepentant abuse upon Mrs Robinson. Only Crosby and Ann Marshall – and, increasingly, the older girls, who at last begin to see things as they are – have been honoured with glimpses of the true Mr Robinson, and this only by chance, for if he knows anyone else is near, he immediately dons his pious mask.

I turned this revelation around in my mind; it changed things considerably, for my mistress was now the *victim*. Had she not been buried alive in an infernal marriage? If she had, as Crosby hinted, once taken a lover, surely it was a case of legitimate revenge. She was not the epitome of hypocrisy but instead its lovely martyr. Her showering of gifts, her incessant talk of me – all now seemed plain. She was not a depraved, wicked, insatiable woman, but a sweet damsel in distress, crying out for salvation from her captivity.

We walked on in silence.

'I wonder,' said Crosby, 'whether I've said far too much.'

'You know, my friend,' I said, slapping him on the back, 'that even if I did not cherish your friendship in and of itself, I have quite practical reasons for holding my tongue, for would we not be mutually destroyed if I were to divulge any of this?'

I paused and looked up at the shimmering verdant ceiling high above our heads, the leaves positively making love to the mild spring breeze. 'Does Mr Robinson ever speak of *me*?'

'Interesting question. In fact, your name is no longer mentioned. The mistress was used to talking about you, and once even suggested that she send your poetry to McCauley, but her husband grew so peevish with jealousy – or so it seemed to me, for I was present – that I have never again heard your name uttered between them. If I had to guess, I would say that you are not entirely out of his mind, and so I would take care not to do anything that might be reported back to him.'

As I pondered this additional intelligence, I saw that our brisk walk had already brought us back to Thorp Green Hall. Crosby again took my elbow, bidding me to sit with him on a low wall within sight of the great house.

'Well,' said he at last. 'Do you reciprocate her feelings?'

'I do.'

But dare I betray my master? His choleric nature seems another obstacle to overcome. If we were ever discovered I would surely be dismissed. And yet, if I spurned my mistress, would she not in all likelihood find a pretext for sacking me, since she would henceforth find my appearance repugnant to her? *Hell hath no fury*, after all. Or was I justifying a possible betrayal through mere sophistry? Still, it did appear to me that I was navigating between Scylla and Charybdis, and indeed, Crosby's thoughts were sailing right along beside mine.

'If ever you were discovered you would be dismissed, you know. Then again, if you refuse her you may also be dismissed, though in a more deliberate and amicable fashion, of course.'

'What am I to do?'

'I told you,' said my friend, 'that is up to you. There's nothing I can do … although …'

'What?'

'Well, the one thing I *can* do is to tell her that you mentioned her gift, and that as we talked you finally declared your love for her, but begging that I keep it to myself and tell no one. I will inform her that while I do not believe in breaking confidences, my duty is nevertheless, above all, to *her*. Once she knows how you feel, it will be up to the two of you to decide what to do next.'

If exultation and dread can reside in a single bosom, they shared mine: exultation at the thought that my mistress loved me, dread at what could go awry if ever we were discovered. I stood on the edge of a precipice, feeling I could not only soar like Icarus, but like him fly too close to the sun. Papa's dream-image, leaning over the impossibly high pulpit, flashed before me, but was soon succeeded by that of my mistress, pulling my hand into the marvellously moist area between her ample breasts.

Yes, I stood on the precipice, but not for long: I jumped. 'Yes, Crosby, tell her how I feel.'

'I will indeed,' said he, and soon we were on our feet and crossing the vast park, parting ways before the house.

'Just one thing, Brontë, and it is no small matter. Indeed, it goes to my very livelihood and the welfare of my nephew William, who is like an only son. I wish to know nothing – absolutely nothing – of this matter henceforth, and will speak of it no more.'

I looked at him, puzzled.

'You see,' he continued, 'I cannot fall from the favour of the Reverend Mr Robinson, for if ever he discovers your proceedings, I must be able to say, with honesty, that I was unaware of them.'

I nodded assent and we shook hands in agreement. As I write these words, my nerves are strung as taut as an archer's bow, for I know not what will happen next.

Volume Three

My mistress is DAMNABLY TOO FOND OF ME.

– Branwell Brontë, letter to John Brown, May 1843

Yet then I was at Thorp Green, and now I am
only just escaped from it … during my stay
I have had some very unpleasant and undreamt
of experience of human nature.

– Anne Brontë, Diary Paper, 31st July 1845

My novel is the result of years of thought …
a vivid picture of human feelings for good
and evil – veiled by the cloak of deceit
which must enwrap man and woman …

– Branwell Brontë, letter to J.B. Leyland, 10th September 1845, on the subject of his unfinished novel, *And The Weary Are at Rest*

I.

The Pleasures of the Flesh

June 27th, 1843 · Thorp Green

Oh God, it has happened, as I both hoped and feared it would.

Hoped, because her flashing eyes and pleasing form, her elegant manners and sometimes haughty bearing – yes, even the superiority she so often enjoys placing on display – have provoked in me, if not love, then lust: I desire everything about her, everything she *is*, and everything she *has*. Sometimes I wonder what space there is between these two most powerful attractions. Surely, this is love, is it not? How does one know what is one, and what is the other? When we are together, I wish to *consume* her, body and soul: to inhale her perfumed flesh, to devour and become Thorp Green itself.

Feared, of course, because I feared, and fear still, discovery. For in that case our passion will have destroyed us both. And yet, this fear itself – as long as it does not prove prophetic – provides all the more intense excitement to our union.

My mistress – no longer Mrs Robinson but Lydia, my sweet Lydia – for I shall henceforth call her by that name – is mine, and I am her infatuated slave. Anne and Flossy left for Haworth some ten days ago, but until then I lived in almost unbearable anguish, not knowing what would happen. After Crosby spoke to my mistress on that day, now a month since, I rarely saw her, and when I did, she took great pains never to be alone with me, and to avoid my gaze at all costs. I began to think that the doctor's intelligence had, in fact, wrought a negative effect upon her, and that she thoroughly despised me. As the days and weeks passed, I could bear it no longer, at last seeking him out to discover what could be amiss. He is ever hearty and amiable with me, but his brow grew clouded when I accosted him in the park that day, some two weeks ago.

'Did we not, Brontë, near this very spot, shake hands and promise to speak of this no more? Is your word not to be trusted, lad?' His tone was midway between exasperation and controlled wrath.

'But she appears to wish me forever out of her presence, Crosby! I would rather be cast out of the household than endure this treatment.'

'You promised not to speak of this,' he repeated, 'and I refuse to be drawn in. However, I will utter one word, which you may attach to whatever, or whomever, you see fit: *patience*. Now then. Trouble me no more with this, or our friendship will suffer, if I don't positively knock you down.'

'Very well,' said I, adding, 'I'm sorry, Crosby, it won't happen again.'

Perhaps, thought I, strolling down to the Ouse that afternoon, perhaps her aloofness is not a sign of indifference, but the only way to control herself. Perhaps the French are correct, that love cannot long remain concealed – *l'amour ne peut longtemps se cacher*, as Charlotte might say – and so she has brought down a curtain to shield herself from the gaze of others? Surely, sometimes, lovers take greater pains to avoid each other when they meet in a larger assembly? Whatever the case, I was still not thoroughly comforted by the doctor's uttering of *patience* – though a flame of hope began to flicker once again.

I would soon discover the truth.

On the day Anne left for Haworth, Mrs Robinson – for she was then still known under that name to me – proclaimed a school holiday not just for young Lydia, Bessy and Mary, but for Edmund as well, and the four children set off in high glee for York, accompanied by Ann Marshall, my sister and Flossy. These last two were to take a coach to Leeds, whilst the children and their guardian were to have a day of shopping.

I stood next to Mrs Robinson to bid my sister good-bye, her husband feeling particularly ill that day and unable to rise from his bed. As the family's fashionable clarence, with the eternally grinning Billy Allison sitting atop it, at last rumbled out of sight, my mistress turned to me with the most serious of gazes and said, 'May I see you in the library, Mr Brontë?'

'Of course,' said I, but she had already turned on her heel and was sailing so quickly into the house that I could scarcely keep pace. She stood by the entrance to the library and as I walked in she quickly closed and bolted the door.

A man who has never experienced what I did that day would scarcely credit its reality, would dismiss it as mere rubbish, the stuff of sentimental novels. But he who has loved, and has been loved in return, with a passion that burns so bright that it renders one insensible to all other thought or feeling – the love that Shelley calls *passion's golden purity* – would nod his head in recognition, remembering even in his dotage what it felt like when the entire world fell away, nay, when the universe was eclipsed by a whirling, exploding passion that seemed to know no bounds: when he and a woman made a universe unto themselves.

Lydia fairly threw herself into my arms. There were at first no passionate kisses or caresses, only an embrace more like that of parent comforting a child. Who the child was here, and who the parent, was unclear. Could we each have been both? Could she, overseeing her children, her house and her sickly, embittered husband, have sought for a moment the consolation that a little girl finds on her father's breast? Could I be seeking in a single woman, a mother, a sister, a mistress, a lover?

Such considerations come only now, for in that moment we simply held each other fast, as all rational thoughts fled.

At last she let go of me, and I was surprised to find her eyes – the same stern orbs that had seemed to rest on everything and everyone but me in the past few days – wet with tears.

'You love me, then?' said she, fervently pressing my hand.

'I do,' I responded, wiping her tears from her eyes.

Although no one could possibly see into the library on such a bright June day, she drew the heavy curtains kept closed in winter, and at long last kissed me, and soon we were embracing each other with seemingly boundless hunger, with an unquenchable thirst. She had worn a far simpler frock than usual, and just as she had in my dream, she guided my hand to her breasts. This, however, was no dream. No, she did not vanish into the air, but placed my other hand between her legs, where she was dewy with anticipation. Our mouths and hands were frantic, our breath panted with mounting desire. Soon she had my staff, already hard, in her hand, which she stroked methodically, expertly, until I was wild with expectation, until I thought it would burst the very confines of its own skin. How long it had been since I was with a woman!

The only proper place to recline was a chaise longue, and we lay there, she beneath me. So full was I with desire, so long had been the wait, that after just a few thrusts, I had spent myself entirely. As reason began to return to me, I thought, *what if she is with child from this?* The danger of such an eventuality – for us both – caused me to shudder, but Lydia soon soothed my mind, rubbing the wrinkles from my forehead with her fingers, as if drawing the very thoughts from it.

'You should know that after poor Georgiana was born' – here she became serious, if not sad – 'I learned I could have no more children.' She soon brightened, however, as if to forget past woes, and, though no one was near, whispered into my ear, as her phantom self had in the York Minster of my dream, this time saying, 'but this means that I am *free*.'

I begged forgiveness for how quickly our congress had ended, but she placed her right forefinger on my lips and said, 'Hush. You are young, and I daresay you have not been with a woman for a very long time. And yet I can tell that you are no stranger to our sex. Let us take a walk on this lovely morning and talk things over, for we have plans to make.'

I had no idea what these plans might be; all I cared was that I could again possess her as I just had, and as often as possible.

Our passion momentarily abated, we quickly adjusted our garments, after which she pulled back the bolt on the door and we made our way down the great entry, under the portico, and out into the sunshine, as if nothing had occurred. And yet, what had happened was, to me, as monumental as the earthquake that had struck above Haworth in our childhood, as potentially cataclysmic and perilous as the bog that had exploded in its wake, nearly sweeping us away, whilst Papa, wild with anxiety, feared us all dead.

'I suppose,' she began, as we walked out onto the grounds, in the direction of my lodgings at the Monk's House, 'that by now you have guessed that it was not just little Ned who needs you for his lessons. *I* need you – *I* want you. And now that I have had you, I will want you whenever I can have you.' She paused for several seconds and turned to me.

'Have you ever taken laudanum – opium?'

Strange question.

'Yes,' said I, 'just once. But I fear that any habitual usage might catch me in its grip, and that an irreversible addiction could ensue. It is the same with drink – I must very careful, I have found.'

I paused, looking down at her dark eyes flashing beneath long lashes, her soft, enticing lips parted in a beguiling smile as I continued. 'I am afraid that I might well be among those unfortunate souls who tend towards a mania with all forms of euphoria, and the more I experience of such exaltation, the more I want to annihilate myself in it, so much do I wish it never – ever – to cease.'

She let out a sigh, not of sadness or regret, but more like a moan of rekindled desire. 'That is why I mention opium, for the exaltation of two lovers far surpasses its effects, and can forever be renewed, and yet such ecstasy is restorative and salutary, not debilitating or noxious, is that not so?'

'But what,' I asked, as we reached the Old Hall and she bade me enter, 'if we are discovered? Surely the house is full of spies. Discovery would mean disaster for mistress and tutor alike, would it not?'

'That is precisely what I want to discuss with you. We must be cautious, ever so cautious, and if we are, no one will be the wiser. You have unquestioned access to the house, do you not? And my husband, the poor thing, is wasting away in his bed more often than not. Still, let us vary our assignations, never creating an observable pattern of behaviour. We must never grow careless, never let our guard down. Ours is a delicate bubble, to be protected at all costs.'

'No one else must know,' I said, marvelling at her ability to feign concern for her brute of a husband. I suppose she had practised this most necessary of hypocrisies for most, if not all, of her marriage.

'Of course not' – here she paused, biting her lip in the loveliest, most girlish way – 'though it might be necessary, after all, that Ann Marshall know. You see, she owes me her life and livelihood, and may serve as a lookout if need be. Otherwise, we could be surprised *en flagrant délit*. She may, indeed, have to serve as the conduit through which I send for you, or announce that I am coming to you.'

I thought of her lady's maid herding the children, Anne and Flossy into the large coach that morning.

'She already knows,' said I, 'doesn't she?'

'I have told her nothing directly,' said Lydia, blushing somewhat, 'though she is a perspicacious creature and perhaps has an idea or two on the subject.'

'Ah, like the good surgeon himself,' I laughed, at last beginning to feel at ease. Lydia had turned her back to me and was gazing out the bedroom window that looks onto the rear of my lodgings, where trees have been warped by the north wind and a large stone wall runs along the lane. I approached her from behind and buried my face in the warm, soft flesh of her neck, encircling her waist with my arms, breathing in her lovely scent as though it were life-giving oxygen. She smelled of perfume – the same perfume she had placed on her bookmark of Shelley, a volume of which stood on a night table, next to a bottle of wine.

I left her briefly to pour two large glasses, and raising mine to hers, I recited – feeling that my ability to commit verse so effortlessly to memory had found, at long last, a practical use – these lines:

One passion in twin-hearts, which grows and grew,
Till like two meteors of expanding flame,
Those spheres instinct with it become the same,
Touch, mingle, are transfigur'd; ever still
Burning, yet ever inconsumable:
In one another's substance finding food …

'I thought,' said she, smiling mischievously and swallowing a large portion of wine, for here no decorum was necessary, 'that you said you *must be very careful* with drink.'

I followed her example, responding dismissively, 'Oh, it's all about moderation, of course. Just a glass or perhaps two of this claret can only be good for body and soul,' said I, dismissively. 'Though the only *food* I need to nourish me stands before me.' In a moment we had finished our glasses and were again locked in a tight embrace, the wine freeing us to an even greater extent, if such a thing were possible.

'I want,' said I, whispering in her ear, 'to see and touch every inch of you. Off with those garments! Let us be like Adam and Eve.'

Making her best attempt to appear thoroughly wicked, Lydia said, 'Before the fall, or afterwards?'

'The Devil take theology,' said I, attempting to surpass her heretical words. 'If you promise to forget that you are a clergyman's daughter and a clergyman's wife, I shall do my best to forget that I am a clergyman's son.'

She drew the curtains and coyly began to undress. 'You do understand, my boy, that I am an old woman, one who has given birth to five children. Do not expect to see the smooth perfection you would find under the garments of a young girl.'

I thought inevitably of her daughter, the young Lydia, the breathtaking beauty of her face and form, but neither of us would mention her daughters any more than we would speak of my sister. While it was true that she was no Kilmeny (damn Leyland and his theory of spoiled fruit!), *my* Lydia was beautiful nonetheless: a long, swanlike neck; perfectly, still shapely, round breasts; wide, graceful hips; and lovely thighs, legs, and tiny, flawless feet. She loosened her dark hair, which tumbled luxuriantly onto her shoulders whilst her darksome eyes flashed with renewed desire.

'Now you,' said she, as she hastened to remove my clothing herself, as if I were a little boy. Pushing me down upon the bed, she grasped my prick with her right hand and, kissing me from knees to forehead and back to knees, stopping to take me into her full lips for a moment, and at last sliding down upon me and moving above me with a slow intensity like nothing I had felt since Agnes. Aided by the wine and the relief of our first encounter, our amorous congress was this time slow and languorous, for we found in one another a seemingly inexhaustible supply of sustenance, like an eternal shower of manna from Heaven.

At one point, I whispered in her ear, 'I know about your husband … his true nature … each time we do this, you are repaying him for his conduct, aren't you? Happiness is the best revenge, is it not?'

At these words she moved faster, tightening round me and moaning, drawing me up and out of myself, until at last we collapsed together, panting. At length I smoothed her hair away from her cheek as we lay side by side, and whispered in her ear, 'I pant, I sink, I tremble, I expire!'

Repeating what she had said in the library, she said, 'You love me, then?'

'Yes, darling Lydia, I love you.'

She moaned – or was it a whimper? – with pleasure at these words, and buried herself in my arms, her richly scented hair spread across my breast: now she was the little child seeking solace and protection. I drew my sheet over us both and together we fell into that blissful slumber that lovers have known since time immemorial. When I awoke she had donned my dressing gown and was wandering around my room, examining my sparse furnishings and my few belongings, another glass of wine in her hand. Noticing that I was awake and watching her, propped up on one elbow, she smiled, walked over to kiss me, then proceeded to fill the other glass and hand it to me. I sought to undo the sash of the dressing gown she had expropriated, for already I wished to bury myself again in her flesh, but she withdrew from my reach, slapping my hand in jest.

'No, you naughty boy, *to every thing there is a season, and a time to every purpose under the heaven* – surely the good Reverend Brontë's son should know *that*.'

Some believe that a consummated love is a tarnished love. What idiots – what fools! No, by God, having possessed Lydia – or having possessed each other, I should say – I found that my ardour had only redoubled: *Burning, yet ever inconsumable*. Like the drunkard who takes more, not less, liquor as he descends into intoxication, so too I burned with even greater desire for Lydia.

I laughed. 'Oh ho! The clergyman's daughter has returned. Yes, yes, I know, *Ecclesiastes* 3. Shall I venture to guess that Reverend Gisborne's daughter Lydia has in mind verse 5? *A time to embrace, and a time to refrain from embracing*?' I reached again for the sash, but like a young girl playing a child's game, she skipped backwards, just out of my reach.

'How long must we refrain, then?' said I, pouting in such an exaggerated fashion that she laughed aloud. I leapt from the bed and, naked from head to toe, chased her into a corner of the room where a dressing table stood, both of us laughing. She was trapped, and turned to face me.

'Do you know what, Mr Brontë?'

'*Branwell*. What is it, sweet Lydia?'

'You make me feel like a young girl again.'

'And the best part,' said I, closing in on her, 'is that you can be a girl at heart and yet such a woman … such a wonderful, perfect, woman.'

At this I lifted her small but shapely body onto the table and began kissing her, and as I descended, I slowly opened her – my – dressing gown, showering soft kisses down her long, snowy neck and shoulders, her breasts, her waist, and beyond. Any hesitation Lydia had had now vanished, as she spread her legs, took my head in her hands, and pulled me into the glistening petals of her open tulip.

'I want your tongue inside me,' said she, with what was now an almost desperate urgency.

I seized a chair to sit upon, and after moving in a rhythmic circle I plunged into her, thanking God or Mother Nature or the universe for the gift of an unusually long tongue. At the same time, I felt my unclothed member stiffen yet again with desire as she moaned with increasing pleasure. Lydia pulled my hair – so roughly that it smarted – first towards her, so that my tongue would penetrate her ever more deeply, then, after a few moments, upwards, so that I would be standing, sending the chair falling backwards with a crash. The table was just the right height, and soon it was banging against the wall so noisily that we had to cease, and I carried her, while still hard inside her and both of us again laughing, to the bed, where we finished what we had begun, I on top of her this time, her arms and legs clenching me as desperately as a drowning woman might cling to the plank of a shattered vessel.

At last Lydia rose from the bed and began to dress, but she smiled contentedly. 'Ah!' said she, inhaling and exhaling as if she had just climbed a steep hill. 'I feel *so* much improved! Unfortunately, *now* I really must go, for the children will be back soon, and my husband will be waking, irritably, from his nap. I informed Dr Crosby to tell him that I would be off visiting some poor cottagers, but, unfortunately, my Edmund knows that I rarely spend much time engaged in that particular occupation.'

She arranged her hair and clothing, allowing me to kiss her as she left my quarters, and from my window I watched her glide across the lawn towards the portico, her head held regally high as a servant opened the front door for her.

This all occurred several days ago, and we have continued our liaison, varying our rendezvous as she recommended, always sending word by way of Ann Marshall, who surely already knows enough to hang me, though she also appears to know her place, and is the picture of discretion. Since that day when all the children were away our intimate encounters are less frequent and thus – though I can scarcely believe it possible – all the more passionate, delicious, ecstatic. Our respective woes are kindled into amorous fuel, and our passion knows no bounds; that we must be secretive only adds spice to our lovers' repasts: *In one another's substance finding food.* We have been together again in the library, in my quarters, even in the stables. On Sunday last, when her husband was unusually well enough to attend church with the family, she pretended to be indisposed and sent a note to bid me come to her in her own chamber, just adjacent to his.

Lydia has informed me that I am to continue Edmund's lessons in Scarborough next month, but that in such close quarters – where Anne, too, will have rejoined the family – we must be strong, avoiding all temptations. But will I bear it, to be so close to her, and yet so distant? Can love ever hide its face, or must it blaze forth for all to see, in spite of our best efforts to conceal it?

I shall do my utmost to obey my mistress, and so will seek other occupations. Anne has spoken so often of her beloved Scarborough that at least I look forward with very real anticipation to seeing its stately new houses and gardens, walking across the iron Spa Bridge strung high above Millbeck Ravine, treading the sparkling sands of the bay, visiting the crowded old town on the harbour, and walking up the headland above, to explore – and perhaps even sketch – the castle ruins and old Saint Mary's church. We are all to stay at Wood's Lodgings at The Cliff, and I wonder just how I am to control my nerves when my sweet Lydia sleeps so near at hand, when I can almost hear her breathing, when I can so vividly picture myself knocking on her door in the middle of the night, when I can feel myself in her arms!

God, what joy, what intoxication, what ecstasy!

11.

Scarborough

July 22nd, 1843 · The Cliff, Scarborough

Anne did not exaggerate the beauty of this place, where we have now been for more than two weeks; another ten days and we return to Thorp Green. My sister and I have spent nearly every free moment together, for the Robinsons are much occupied in receiving company or in showing off their daughters along the Promenade: much to the young ladies' dismay, this is the closest they will come to a 'season' in London.

The youngest Brontë arrived from Haworth the day after we came from Thorp Green, and though her presence sometimes strikes both fear and apprehension in my heart – for she is a constant reminder of Papa, the Parsonage, and thus my sins, if sins they be – I am still, most often, grateful for her presence. And indeed, if I were simply left alone for the remainder of each day I should be wild with restless agitation in the absence of Lydia.

Once she had recovered from her voyage, Anne made haste to show me the sights of this place that she has come to adore. Within a day or two we had visited all that she deemed worth seeing. How she loved it all – the broad, bright bay, the deep, clear but contrasting blues of the sky and ocean, the craggy cliffs surmounted by green swelling hills, and above all, the brilliant, sparkling waves and the inexpressible purity and freshness of the air! One morning, as we walked along the shore, our footsteps the first to press the firm, unbroken sands, my delicate little sister turned to me and said, with unwonted force: 'Do you know, Branwell, that when I am here I forget all my cares, and feel as if I had wings on my feet, and could go at least forty miles without fatigue? I experience a sense of exhilaration to which I have been an entire stranger since the days of early youth.'

'Would you stay here forever, if you could?' said I. 'Even in deepest winter?'

'I think I would, brother – the wild commotion of the tempest-tossed waves is to me as charming as the serenity of this placid summer morning.'

'In that case,' I replied, gesturing towards the old church of Saint Mary and the castle ruins jutting from the headland high above us, which separates the North Bay from the South, 'do you think those winged feet can carry you *there*?'

Anne smiled and put her arm through mine. 'If I were not so often short of breath – curse that family curse! – I would challenge you to a race, just as when we were children. But yes, let us make the climb.'

Reaching the old church was not too arduous, and it was not long before we had wound round the hill, up Castlegate and Paradise, to its summit. Soon we had caught our breath and were exploring the churchyard, where now stand the ruins of the original transept and great quire. I leant against the tallest of the ruins and looked out at the South Bay below. A thunderstorm the previous night had laid to rest the dust and cooled and cleared the air, and the prospect was magnificent. Sultry July seemed to have given way, if only for a day, to springtime, or early autumn, so refreshing was the breeze that washed over us from the sea, which shone with the brilliant azure reserved for such days, a blue that sought to rival the beauty of Anne's own eyes as they, too, gazed out upon the waters, her hands catching wisps of her hair as they played in the wind, tucking them here and there into her bonnet. She was so lovely, so vulnerable, and yet somehow ever with that core of iron determination, wherein beats a heart of nearly incredible sincerity and goodness. I loved her then, as only a brother can love a sister, and the purity of such love overwhelmed me. Inexplicably, I felt my eyes fill, and soon hot tears were spilling down my cheek.

'What is it, Branwell?' said my sister, noticing that I was dabbing my eyes with my handkerchief.

'I don't know … it's just so *beautiful* … I wish I could explain … it is too much, the fullness of love and life, almost too full for speech … it overwhelms me, it suffocates me, it crushes me … oh, I don't know,' and I clutched her to my breast, tears now become great, primal sobs of grief, until at last I could cry no more. Anne took both of my hands in hers and held me now at arm's length, far enough to survey me in my entirety; we stood like two dancers frozen in time, or two towers of a bridge, whose span was formed by our arms.

'Even Jesus wept, you know,' she said, pausing earnestly. 'And is not sorrow a form of grace, prerequisite to God's forgiveness? Are not tears like the downpours that bring life to the arid plain?'

My paroxysms of grief – whatever their cause – were soon past, and had brought me great relief; as I so often do, I shunted aside such pious considerations in favour of jest, as I wiped a final tear from my cheek and blew my nose.

'I don't know, sister. I am quite convinced that you are a far better theologian than I. Such matters are beyond *my* ken.'

A smile crept over her earnest features, despite her best efforts to maintain a certain air of gravity.

'Now that is a relief – my heretical brother is alive and well! Or are you playing at Northangerland, or his faithful manservant Sdeath?'

'Why, we three are one and the same, an Infernal Trinity if ever there were! Father, Son and Unholy Ghost!'

'Hush!' said Anne, slapping me playfully, ever so softly on the cheek. 'No more of this impious talk!' Yet I could detect no *true* censure in that little face, as it beamed in the bright sunshine, her eyes a mirror of the sea, her hair still dancing in the delicious breeze. Was it the extraordinary beauty of the day that made her accept my impudence in stride? Whatever the case, she soon was positively laughing, taking me by the hand and fairly dragging me up the hill towards the castle ruins, despite her shortness of breath.

Here the wind met no resistance, and as we stood together facing the sea, my hat was quite blown off my head, whilst Anne's bonnet was nearly swept away, her dress in danger of becoming a giant sail. She threw herself into my arms and laughed, 'I feel as giddy as a young girl again!' But her words sent an odd chill through me, as I remembered Lydia's own recent words to that effect. Over my sister's shoulder, down the Castle Road, lay the old church and churchyard, its headstones bearing quiet witness to the inexorable march of time, its tranquil green grass masking the ferocious maw of death that awaits us all.

'Sometimes,' Anne explained later, as we walked back down into town, 'I feel *so old* – that I could not be *flatter* or older of mind if I lived to the age of eighty! But there are other times – like today – when all seems new again, the old exhilaration returns, and my head is full of so many schemes for the future that even those eighty years would not be sufficient. What strange creatures we are, to have such varied emotions!'

I said nothing, for her heart's oscillation between these two extremes was the very picture of my own daily torment: hope, despair, renewed hope and renewed despair. Added to this spiritual malaise was now the physical thrill of Lydia, who gives me almost daily pleasure, but it is a *troubled pleasure soon chastised by fear*, as Pope renders Homer, for I live in constant terror of discovery.

I was deep in these thoughts as we again reached the sands, where the tide had now gone out and seagulls scoured the beach, at times battling with the occasional curious dog, investigating with its nose or digging with its paws.

'Flossy used to love to come here,' Anne sighed.

'Why did you leave him in Haworth, then?'

'So many reasons, really, but which can be reduced to these: it is quite enough to keep up with the three Misses Robinson, Emily fell quite madly in love with him, and Keeper has found a fast friend. He will be better off in Haworth, and Papa is fond of him too. Besides, Flossy's brothers and sisters are all about Thorp Green, so there is no want of canine companionship there, if I need it!'

As we thus strolled along the sands towards our lodgings, there appeared before us none other than Mrs Robinson, Ann Marshall, Mary and young Edmund. Lydia performed her iciest version of Mrs Robinson, bearing no relation whatever to that passionate woman who embraces me with such desperate fervour.

'Miss Brontë,' said she, tilting her head ever so slightly, 'Mr Brontë. I see brother and sister are reunited once again. I *trust*, Miss Brontë, that your venerable father was not *too* pained at his son's absence for the June holidays.'

'I think, ma'am, that our father is quite pleased that Branwell can be of such service. To be valued in one's position is all we can ask, really.'

'Indeed.' She tousled Ned's hair. 'In point of fact, this lad has made considerable progress under your brother's tuition, and I should like to discuss next steps with him since the opportunity has presented itself today, quite by chance. Would you, Miss Brontë, be kind enough to accompany Miss Mary back to The Cliff? I believe she has had quite enough activity, and fear that her fair skin has been too much exposed to the sun, despite the best efforts of bonnet and parasol. We cannot have her looking like a rough labourer, now can we?'

Anne set off with her charge towards our rooms at The Cliff, whilst I walked silently with my pupil, his mother, and her lady-in-waiting. Soon Lydia turned to Ann Marshall. 'Marshall, would you please take young Edmund down to the water's edge? Let him remove his boots and stockings and roll up his trousers, and bathe his feet in the waves. It will be a treat for him,' she said staidly.

'Hurrah!' shouted Ned, throwing his straw hat into the air and himself into his mother's arms with unrestrained glee. 'Dear me!' she said, suppressing a laugh beneath an otherwise stern brow. 'You needn't strangle me for *that*!'

Once the boy's feet were bared, he hopped and skipped down to the water's edge, his left hand clutched by Mrs Marshall, the other accompanying his gleeful whoops with a circular motion as his sandy hair flapped in the salty breeze. *Oh to be a little boy again! If only to begin anew …*

My reverie was interrupted by Ned's mother, who, having become my Lydia again, leant towards me and said: 'There are so many reasons to love the sea, but one not often discussed is that lovers can speak to each other and yet be assured that the sound of the waves will obliterate their words as thoroughly as the rising tide effaces a child's writing on the sands.'

At these words, all doubts, all fears, all guilt, vanished in an instant, leaving only hot, sharp desire in their wake. 'Good God in his Heaven, Lydia, I miss you. I *want* you.'

Edmund was waving as he kicked the waves, shouting for his mama to take notice. She returned a small, dignified wave, and without changing her expression, she said in my ear, 'I am desperate for *you*. I know that I commanded you to keep off, but I do not think I can wait until we return to Thorp Green.'

'What do you suggest, then?'

'Meet me at the boathouse on the shore beneath The Cliff, at midnight. Marshall will be standing without, and *I* shall wait just within.'

So I did, and so have I done almost every night since.

III.

Leyland in York

September 16th, 1843 · Thorp Green

We have long since returned to Thorp Green, and how much less frequently I see my lady! As it happens, our assignations were more easily achieved in the boathouse at Scarborough than here, and the simple addition of Anne's presence in the house has sufficiently altered matters, so that to be with Lydia has become nearly impossible. Only once, since our return, have I held her in my arms, and that was when she again, on a Sunday, professed to be indisposed whilst even her husband – feeling somewhat better that day – accompanied the womenites to church. Despite the possibility of being observed by her servants, she crossed the dewy grounds in a cloak, beneath which she wore only a simple silk shift. As she entered my quarters she bolted the door, threw off her cloak, and then loosened her gown, which fell slowly, gracefully revealing each soft, lovely curve.

'What if,' said I, coming up for air from our passionate kisses, like a flailing swimmer gasping for air, 'what if you – *we* – are discovered?'

'I am the mistress of Thorp Green,' said she, redoubling her caresses, as if again to repay her husband for his past transgressions. When our passion was spent, she lay with her head on my left shoulder, the fingers of her right hand playing gently over my torso, which she was fond of calling my *taille d'athlète*. Her unfathomable brown eyes opened wide as she kissed my mouth, her hand moving playfully down beneath the sheets.

'No servant will dare speak ill of *me.* Even if they knew all, they know how I have suffered at the hands of that … that … of my *dear angel Edmund*,' she added, sarcastically. 'I *detest* that man,' she said, with almost a snarl. 'In any event, it is no matter. Servants are mere automatons – it's nothing to them what their superiors say or do; they won't dare to repeat it; and as to what they *think* – if they presume to think at all – of course, nobody cares for that. It would be a pretty thing indeed, would it not, if our actions were to be dictated by our servants!'

'Still, we – you – must be careful, for if there is enough talk among the domestics, my own sister and your own daughters may begin to suspect, and where such intelligence would lead any of them, who knows?'

At this my mistress pulled me closer, and before she left we found ecstasy once again, but she thereafter seemed to take matters to heart, for this was the last time we were together.

Mistress of the situation she is indeed, for excepting those times when we are alone in our lovers' bubble, it is *she* who decides all, and *I* who must obey. How different from the arch-seducer of my youthful imagination, Percy, Duke of Northangerland! No, it is I who have been seduced, I who am Lydia's infatuated slave, I who worship at the living, breathing, quivering, throbbing altar of her flesh.

And how much easier, really, to be her slave, than to summon the energy to enslave *her*, even if such a thing were possible for an impoverished tutor. How much more exhausting, after all, to be the puppet master than the puppet? Even such a great artist as Landseer, after all, obeys the wishes of his noble mistress, does he not? Does that make him any less a man, or any less an artist? And if the rumours are true, is the Duchess of Bedford any less his slave in the bedroom for all that?

If I have been musing upon these matters, it is no doubt in large part because Leyland has been to visit York, where I spent a long afternoon in the company of him and Dr Crosby. The memorial committee for the unfortunate Dr Beckwith, it so happens, could not settle upon a local sculptor for his monument, so intent were they upon driving down its cost. Finding itself at an impasse, the committee had shown an interest in Joe, whose name Crosby had recalled from our conversation of last spring. Thus, the eminent Joseph B. Leyland had been summoned before the committee, and he was all too happy to spend an afternoon with us thereafter.

We shook hands briefly before the meeting, during which I was free to wander the vast interior of York Minster. I walked to the oldest part of the church, the north transept, and stood before the massive window – five long gothic windows, in fact – called the 'Five Sisters'. I pondered, turning left and walking towards the window at the western end of the nave: *five sisters had I once too.* Standing beneath the Great Western Window, I tilted my head back to gaze at the pointed arch of the upper window, where the stonework and tracery form an enormous heart. The two panels beneath its point depict the Coronation of the Virgin and Christ in Majesty. *Mary, Marie, Maria: dear Mama, why did you leave me, why did you forsake your only son?*

I soon was benumbed by the sheer size and beauty of the church – was quite simply unable to take it all in. I found myself in the first row, near the altar, gazing up and to the left at the grand pulpit, realising at last that this was just where I had sat in my dream. Here, however, no Reverend Brontë preached on the sin of adultery; here no emaciated Edmund Robinson slumped in his seat; no lascivious Lydia guided my hand into her lovely, dewy cleavage; no Brown or Leyland leered approvingly from across the aisle.

No: only the chill damp void of a temple long ago abandoned by God. And yet – here also was peace, beauty, even some sort of vague mediaeval grace, I thought, and as a shaft of sunlight shot down from above, thousands of particles of dust and the occasional fly were illuminated, like actors in a stage light. Anne, who loves this place, once said to me: *If finite power can do this, how great God's infinite power must be!*

But was not this finite human power enough of a token of God's might, if God there be? Must there be Heaven or Hell?

Were they not perversions of the true God; were they not inventions of man's finite power as well, established to subjugate and control the true spark of divinity, a perverse and savagely feudal law Shelley rightly saw *pretends even to govern the indisciplinable wanderings of passion, to put fetters on the clearest deductions of reason, and, by appeals to the will, to subdue the involuntary affections of our nature*? Did he not admit, with clarity so great that it immediately roused the condemnation that always befalls those martyrs who speak the truth, that *the narrow and unenlightened morality of the Christian religion is an aggravation of these evils*, and that only lately has *the fanatical idea of mortifying the flesh for the love of God been discarded*?

Alas, thought I, such fanatical ideas have hardly been discarded. And yet, on the other side of the ledger, Hartley Coleridge's words, spoken that May Day three years since – what a lifetime ago! – came back to me: *Byron and Shelley cast all decency to the wind, breaking hearts and destroying lives.* I felt tired, overwhelmed, confused, and just wanted my mind to *stop* its ceaseless hurtling for a moment. I leant back to admire the massive ceiling, upheld by a multitude of ribbed vaults, and wondered what it would take for the entire structure to collapse upon me. Would that be such a terrible thing, once the impossibly brief initial shock was past? Not another soul stirred in the church, and at length I dropped into a light slumber, only roused by two birds wheeling high above, through the pillars, just beneath the ceiling. They had found their way into the great church, but now flapped about with increasing desperation, seeking a way back out into the open sky.

A large hand clapped me on the shoulder and I jumped. It was Leyland, who had stolen silently up as I had awakened and watched the birds circle above. Soon we had made our way out of the Minster and to the end of Stonegate, where we turned left into Coney Street, passed the venerable Saint-Martin-le-Grand and Leyland's lodgings at the George, and on into Spurriergate, where Dr Crosby awaited us at the Ouse Bridge Inn.

Joe ordered whiskies for the three of us and was soon interrogating me about Mrs Robinson. After my initial requests for advice, I had written no more, either to him or to Brown, for the matter was rendered irrelevant by subsequent events. The ensuing silence had, it seemed, nearly driven him mad with curiosity.

'*Sooooo*, little man, tell old Joe Leyland what has transpired in these many months since you last wrote to Brown that your pupil's mother was *damnably fond* of you? Did you go to extremities? Is she now your mistress in both senses of the word? If so, I can hardly blame you for your silence, ha ha!'

At this speech, Crosby frowned – nay, glowered – and abruptly stood up, hat in hand. 'See here, gentlemen, I just remembered I have some additional business to conduct at the chemist's, and so will leave you to your own devices,' adding meaningfully as he looked directly at me, 'I shall return in a half-hour's time or so.'

Soon I had revealed to Joe, at great length, all but the most intimate details of my liaison: the gifts, the offer to send my poems to Macaulay, the request that I stay behind when Anne travelled to Haworth, and everything that ensued. In so doing, I also explained Crosby's seemingly odd behaviour.

'Ha! Yes, he's no fool!' said Joe, finishing the surgeon's whisky, which had been left where he had sat, and motioning for two more glasses. 'He knows on which side his bread is buttered!'

When the glasses arrived, he lifted his and proposed a toast: 'Let us toast the Year of Our Lord Eighteen-Hundred-and-Forty-Three, for I feel propitious winds of change for you, Brontë. Think of it, you are valued in your *position*' – here he could not help himself, winking lewdly – 'or should I use that word in the plural? A rich woman loves you and has promised to send your poetry to Macaulay. Eighteen-Hundred-and-Forty-Four could prove even better!'

He grew a shade more serious, leaning towards me and lowering his voice, though his almond eyes were still merry and a smile still played on his full lips. 'Damn you, you lucky devil, you have found your very own Duchess of Bedford! Keep her happy and who knows what might transpire. If that invalid husband of hers quits the stage, you will be there to comfort her, will you not?'

Embarrassed to have already thought of this myself, I pretended that it had not even occurred to me – an assertion met with incredulous laughter.

'Oh, come now, little man! You mean to say that it never crossed your mind that you might replace that bugger as master of Thorp Green? You even signed your letter to Brown – for of course he showed it to *me* – Jacob the Supplanter, Son of Joseph!'

'Good sir, I meant to supplant him in Lydia's affections, that's all. Whoever heard of a lady marrying her son's tutor, or a gentleman taking a governess for his wife? Really, Leyland, you are quite mad!'

'Stranger things have occurred, young Faustus. And even if you are not *legally* married, could you not more easily play that role if the good man were dead and buried?'

I began to imagine that such could be the case, and even smiled to myself at the thought, as our conversation turned to news of people at home. Soon Crosby had returned, and the sculptor, now thoroughly informed of the surgeon's resolute desire to remain ignorant of my proceedings with Lydia, hailed him heartily.

'Ah, Dr Crosby, just in time to help me tell my tale of this morning's meeting with the unfortunate Dr Beckwith's memorial committee. I was just saying that though the good man has been dead and buried for some time, work on the monument has been terribly delayed.'

'Indeed,' said Crosby, smiling. In fairness to him, I must confess that his naturally sunny temperament is at all times prepared to return once passing clouds have vanished, and knowing we had finished discussing Lydia, he was more than happy to rejoin our conversation. He looked down, puzzled. 'But where is my whisky?'

'See here, Dr Crosby, it would have quite evaporated, would it not? *La part des anges*, the French call it: the angel's share. Well, blast it all, I think the angels have quite enough of everything, don't you?'

Crosby laughed, as nearly everyone does in Joe's company, as another whisky was ordered from the bar.

I looked across at my friend. For just an instant, a world-weary version of the sculptor appeared, as he had that day in Halifax. Here, thought I, was no Lucifer, no Azrael. He was not Mephistopheles any more than I was Faustus; no more the demonic Gil-Martin than I was the Robert Wringhim he leads to perdition in Hogg's *Confessions of a Justified Sinner*. No, alas: here was simply a man rapidly passing from his youth towards middle age, and growing weary of existence – so very, very weary.

Just as quickly, however, Leyland was again his jolly self, recounting the story, assisted by Crosby, of the morning's meeting with the committee.

'I am sure that when your friend Brontë here wrote to you about the possibility of a commission,' said the surgeon, 'you scratched your head and wondered why in Heaven's name the committee would seek a sculptor so far from York, where you can't throw a rock – forgive the play on words – without hitting a stone carver.'

'I must confess,' laughed Leyland, running his hand through his ample hair, 'that the old phrase *carrying coals to Newcastle* did spring to mind. Of course, any misunderstanding faded once I met the committee.' He leant towards me conspiratorially, but allowed Crosby to hear him as well. 'I know, Branwell, that just last year you were profoundly embarrassed by Dr Andrew's memorial committee in Haworth, but they were nothing when compared to this band of misers. At least your local folk acted purely out of – what did you call it? – *gothic ignarance and ill breeding*, I believe.'

'With all due respect to your friend Crosby, here,' he continued, nodding towards the surgeon, ' – for he is surely the exception that confirms the rule – the committee for Dr Beckwith is a group of parsimonious hypocrites bent upon treating a noted sculptor like a common mason. They have agreed to pay me only £250, *and* I have to supply my own materials, and am allowed only £50 on account to accomplish a memorial fit for royalty: a full-length recumbent statue of polished black marble, over a white Huddlestone tomb. I may be a genius,' he concluded, laughing, 'but I am not a magician. The task is well-nigh impossible, and my own labour has been valued about as much as that of a bricklayer.'

He drained his glass as if chasing wormwood and gall.

'And yet,' said Crosby, 'you accepted the commission, did you not?'

'I did,' said Joe ruefully, staring down at his empty glass. Soon brightening, however, he added, 'At least I won the dispute over the £50 advance. The niggardly philistines – again, present company excluded, my dear Crosby – tried to begrudge me even *that*. Let us spend a bit of that advance, shall we?'

Crosby and I had dinner and one more drink with Leyland before setting off for Thorp Green. We left him laughing with a pair of buxom women, one flaxen-haired and the other a brunette – *courteous ladies of notable distinction* as the late Hogg himself might say – women who had surely noticed not just Joe's handsome features and fashionable checked suit, but also – and far more to the point – his gold watch and the liberality with which he showered his friends with food and drink. I have no doubt how his evening ended, and merely hope that he awoke with enough cash in his pocket to return to Halifax.

IV.

A Jealous Husband

November 4th, 1843 · Thorp Green

Upon receipt of some of my verses, the celebrated Macaulay has sent me a most complimentary letter, which has occasioned – alas! – more heartache than joy. While Lydia would fain have kept the very existence of her cousin's epistle from her husband, she could not resist telling her eldest daughter of it; I suppose it was necessary that her pride in me should burst forth somehow. Young Lydia, in turn, mentioned it to her *papa*. Was this the innocent chatter of a young girl, or a deliberate attempt to gauge the invalid's response to such intelligence? Did she suspect something about her mother and her brother's tutor? In short, was she merely giddy and mischievous, or something far more dangerous?

I learnt of this all yesterday, when at last I found myself in Lydia's arms. She had proclaimed a school holiday, and had, despite the November chill, bundled her children off to York under the guidance of my sister and Ann Marshall. Her husband, it seemed, was particularly ill; Dr Crosby had given him more than enough laudanum to make him sleep the day away. My lady, meanwhile, claimed to be indisposed.

'Oh God,' she said as our hips moved together, 'oh God, oh God – it has seemed an eternity.' Indeed, it had been weeks, and our ardour knew no bounds, and bears no description: as Sdeath might say, *it passeth all understanding*. Afterwards, she buried her head in my shoulder, eventually tipping her face towards mine. I caressed her gently from her long neck to that magical place where hip meets thigh, finding that she had grown thinner since last we were together.

'I *had* to send them all away,' said she. 'I *had* to have you … and not once, but two or three times before they return. I feel like a great dam holds my passion in abeyance, and that when at last we are together it must flow freely, overwhelming everything else, obliterating every trace of every other living thing but you.'

She paused, a single tear trickling down her right cheek.

'You *do* know that I want you all the time, *don't* you?' she continued earnestly. 'I can scarcely eat, for all I want is *you – in your substance finding food*,' said she, her desire momentarily eclipsing her other thoughts, her kisses causing me – impossibly, I thought – already to harden once again with desire. Soon, however, cold reason returned.

'I am in constant terror of discovery, and Marshall says that the servants have begun to talk. I cannot bear the thought of parting with you.'

'Did you not say that one's actions cannot be dictated by one's servants?'

'I did,' said she, biting her lip – adorably, I thought, in spite of her frustration – as she propped her head upon her elbow, 'but as you said, if the *children* discover us, that is quite another matter. And servants talk to children. *And* children are curious.'

She proceeded to explain how she had made the mistake of telling her eldest about Macaulay's letter of praise, and how within a few hours young Lydia had made sure that her father knew about it as well. As a result, the Reverend Robinson was now more splenetic than ever.

'He cannot abide the mere idea of your being able to write *anything*, and was sick all day yesterday as a result.'

'I wonder why, then, he continues to employ me. Why does he not just send me packing to Haworth?'

'Ah, well you see,' she said, attempting a wicked smile as she guided my hands over her body, though to me her face is forever that of an angel, 'if he knew that *you* were touching *me* here … and here … and here … you *would* be dismissed. But he knows that you are valued by everyone and that Edmund is happy and progressing.'

She paused and frowned. 'The fact is that he is one of those people who wishes no one to be happy. It's not because it's *you*, Patrick Branwell Brontë, in particular, it's because it's not *him*, Edmund Robinson. He is like a little boy who would lick all of his sweets at once, or throw them into the dirty lane, rather than share one morsel with his fellows. He is, in a word, *miserable*. It is not as if he has any poetic proclivities or pretensions himself. He is just such a spiteful creature that he is incapable of suffering anyone else to do well, in any endeavour.'

'Still, I wish he hadn't known.'

'I know, *I know*,' said she, impatiently. 'I should not have told Lydia. Indeed, Lydia is the last person I should have told; I am finding her more and more ungovernable – and meddlesome – these days.'

Hours were as minutes as our bodies became one again … and yet again. The third time she said, laughing, 'Now you may do as you *please*, Mr Brontë.' This expression is a great favourite of hers, which she habitually uses to tell Anne or me that we are free for the day. In this case, however, she had something else in mind. I was grateful to Maeve for her lessons, although none of what she had taught me seemed to surprise Lydia.

As she began to dress, Lydia at last grew serious.

'We *must* be careful. I think we would be wise to take *no* risks between now and the holidays, and it is essential that you return home with your sister, to allay all suspicions.'

'But Lydia, how can I bear it? How can you?'

'It is only for a little while – and is it not better to let all suspicion die quite away? For if we succeed in convincing everyone that we are merely mistress and subordinate, we can then find a way to be together once again, of that I am certain. You *must* obey me in this.'

She paused for a moment, smiling as a thought emerged. 'In this case, you may *not* do as you please, Mr Brontë.'

Standing naked before her, I performed a ridiculous bow, saying 'Of course, I shall obey you as in all things, ma'am. Kiss me once more, then,' said I, 'for minding so well,' and refusing to let her dress, I reached for a pair of scissors on my night table. 'Give me a lock of your hair, so that I might pretend it lies once again on my breast.' Growing serious, I added softly, 'Would to God it could do so *legally*!'

She seemed not to hear this final remark, but quickly snipped a generous lock where it would least be noticed, expertly put her hair up, dressed, and kissed me a final time. I know not when I will see her again, beyond the brief chance encounters that would naturally occur.

November 24th, 1843 · Thorp Green

As I write these lines, the last of autumn's leaves, long since fallen, are swept by the north wind, as the sky threatens a day of chilling rainfall. Over the past three weeks I have seen Lydia only in passing, and each time her gaze avoids mine, as if the danger of our eyes' meeting – how I still remember the first time they locked, when I was ill in bed and Papa was here – were so great that it would result in her dashing forwards and throwing herself in my arms.

Or so I like to imagine.

What a toll it takes on one to conceal a great secret, and how much greater the damage if that secret is one's strongest passion! Every second marked by the clock's swinging pendulum is full of deception, is packed with lies. To conceal such truth is to bury one's beating heart, to entomb one's best, one's noblest self. All because of some ridiculous, mere human law, put in place to *subdue the involuntary affections of our nature.* Shelley was right: it was indeed barbaric. I suspect Mr Robinson, however, would not share my view.

Does Lydia suffer as much as I do? Alas, I cannot ask her. But I seem to detect that she continues to grow thinner every day. How I wish I could feel her silken skin moving against mine, smell her perfumed flesh wrapped about mine, form once again, together, one body in ecstatic union, in an instant containing all of eternity. Although on certain days I would like to drown my sorrows utterly, I cannot compromise my position, which now matters to me only because it keeps me near to Lydia. I take no wine, but only some brandy and water once a day, before breakfast, to enable me to face the sheer agony of each day without her.

I ask again: does she ache for me as much as I do for her? Would she sacrifice all for me? If not, who am I to criticise her? Was *I* not willing to ignore the circumstances of Agnes? Why did Maggie choose *her* mate? Virgil may claim that love conquers all, but does it ever? Each day these worries consume me, and only a visit from Lydia could assuage them. Oh God! I am ravaged from within by deceit, desire and doubt, like the worm that never dies, all the while struggling to appear ever the calm and respectable tutor of young Edmund Robinson.

I cherish one hope, which would bring resolution to all: if only my employer were to die and Lydia make me the master of Thorp Green. And why on earth would she not? Have stranger things not occurred, as Leyland said? Is she not a clergyman's daughter and I a clergyman's son, as well as a scholar and promising poet? What would be amiss? Surely it would not be the first time that a woman of significant means married a gentleman who had none. Such reflections only make my inner world more infernal and the efforts to conceal it more strenuous. But then are we not *all* close and resolute dissemblers, and do we not all don the mask of a placid countenance when our hearts are wild with passion and joy, or filled with anger and bitterness?

Soon the Christmas holidays will be upon us, and it has been nearly a year since last I saw Haworth. Will I be able to dissemble as well *there* as I have here? Will Papa's failing eyesight blind him to my guilt? Or will my very words, my faltering tone of voice, proclaim my iniquity to his ears?

V.

The Three Virgins of Haworth

New Year's Day, 1844 · Haworth, The Parsonage

Anne could not wait to escape Thorp Green, but I felt that I was being torn from the place, like a plant uprooted from all that nourishes it. How much has changed since I arrived last January! What once was *terra incognita* has become my only hope of salvation, my promised land – for what would become of me if Lydia and I were cleft asunder? I am wild with desire for her, and yet frantic to conceal all that is true, all that is noble – which is to say our *love*.

Mere human convention condemns our actions; I am convinced that anyone who has felt such bliss as this would praise, or at the very least understand and accept them. For I firmly believe that not one in a dozen persons has ever felt such exaltation, such delirium, and so it is that the vast majority of society is composed of frigid old maids; embittered, gouty old men whose withered idea of pleasure is to be found solely in the bottle and at the table; and couples who have settled into the slow, joint suicide of a passionless marriage. Aye, misery loves company! What does Milton have the King of Hell say in *Paradise Regained*?

Envy, they say, excites me thus to gain
Companions of my misery and woe!

And yet: what of Papa? Surely his passion was as strong as mine, but he turned it into an appropriate channel, according to society's laws (nay, according to *God*'s Law, he would say): six children in as many years. Did not Aunt used to say that Mama had called him 'my saucy Pat'? What had become of this saucy young man, brimming with poetry and bursting with love, when poor Mama died?

Why, the Reverend Brontë had snuffed him out by sheer force of will, of course, had crushed every last trace of these fleshly joys, had obliterated all that was wild and beautiful, all that lived and breathed. Unable to find a wife to share his joys and burdens, he directed the twin streams of his great intellect and boundless passion into the rearing of his children and his service to the Lord. An amputation, I might say: perhaps one required to save the patient's life, but an amputation all the same. But that bottomless *force of will* of his! I cannot fathom it. What is it to control oneself? I do not know, for I have a moral weakness that impedes such exercise of will, this iron will, which is as foreign to me as the towering Himalayas or the deepest reaches of the Amazon.

What I can confess to these pages alone is this: what Papa has failed to pass on to me, he seems to have succeeded in bestowing upon all three of his daughters. Or is it that they must exercise such control, since the field of their endeavours is so circumscribed? In short, because I am a man, the expectations placed upon me are both significantly greater in the arena of my professional achievements and much, *much* less where my personal conduct is concerned? Expectations! Good God in Heaven, there have always been expectations! The very thing that frees me becomes my prison, whereas my sisters' gaol sets them free. And now, since Aunt's death, they have sufficient means to survive should Papa die, while I am left with nothing. It is all the more imperative that I retain my post at Thorp Green, not only to be near Lydia, but to retain my independence.

Charlotte, we have lately learned, is quitting Brussels once and for all. The reasons for this are shrouded in mystery, as she has been for some time employed as a teacher, thus assuring her own independence, and she seems fond of the Monsieur and

Madame Heger – although, as is always the case with her, she largely has praise for the gentleman and censure for the lady. Is she returning because she wishes, as she claims, to start a school? It is with great difficulty that I imagine her doing so, and though Anne would surely be a valued assistant, I can no more imagine Emily teaching little girls than being a patient, long-suffering governess. And where is this school to be? In the Parsonage? Surely no mother in her right mind would consent to sending her precious little girls to live in such a wilderness as that, where disease is rife, the inhabitants churlish and uncouth, and even the Parsonage itself is ruled over by an ageing and severe, if ultimately kindly, old man; where Keeper and Flossy and other assorted animals run wild and fly free; and where, worst of all, the churchyard seems to contain more of the dead than the town does of the living, as if it threatened at any moment to devour parsonage, church, public houses, mills, hovels, inhabitants and all.

Does she return because, as she has written to Emily, she feels that she *ought not to be away from Papa, that she feels it would be too selfish to leave him so long as Anne and I are absent*? I do not for a moment believe this, for Papa was not so much worse when she last left him, and when she did leave him – travelling in great haste and *alone*, which Aunt would never have permitted – he had lost not only his beloved curate Weightman, but also Aunt, who, though she could not be his wife, was surely his helpmate as he struggled to raise his brood, she who was the closest thing to a mother we ever knew. It was only because Emily was all too happy to remain behind that Charlotte could fly back across the Channel. I do not doubt her love of family and, especially, of Papa; it is a love that extends even to *me*. I do believe, however, that she has a core of selfishness – perhaps indistinguishable from her iron will – that overrules all else.

In short, had she wished to stay in Brussels she would have found ample excuses for doing so: for it was not long ago that she claimed that *with even more proficiency in French and German*

I will be better placed to lead a school for young ladies; by teaching, I am no longer a burden on Papa; it would, in fact, be selfish for me to return when Anne and Branwell are making their way in the world and Emily is caring for him; etc., etc.

Do we not all create such happy stories to fit our desires? She now is, most conveniently, turning each one of these arguments on its head. I imagine that Emily, sphinxlike, understands all of this, and clearly wishes to discuss none of it. Anne strives, as always, to put the best construction on everything. As for Papa, he is happy that his dear Charlotte is returning, and despite his failing eyesight there is a spring in his step since we received the news.

I wonder: where will we all be, and how will we fare, one year – five years – ten years – hence? I cannot but think that Joe Leyland is right: 1844 will be even better, at least for me. The future course of my life races through my mind at the speed of a flash of lightning: at last I am published in *Blackwell's*, after which I become the toast of London itself. Riches soon follow, and just as it becomes clear that Brontë no longer needs his post as tutor to young Edmund Robinson, the boy's unfortunate father shuffles off his mortal coil. Lydia – lovely in mourning – soon marries the poet, whose rising star and full purse make him a more-than-suitable match in the eyes of everyone, even his sisters, although they are privately *shocked* that a woman would take another husband so soon after the death of her own.

But what of the three virgins of Haworth? What fate awaits them? If the school scheme fails, as it surely will, perhaps they will turn back to being governesses; though I cannot see that suiting Charlotte or Emily ever again. How often has the first said that she would *rather be a housemaid or kitchen-girl, than a baited, trampled, desolate, distracted governess!* At such moments, Emily nods vigorously, or says vehemently, 'That's right!'. And indeed, has not Emily herself already chosen to be a sometime housemaid and kitchen-girl rather than ever be a governess again? Only Anne, whose equanimity, sense of duty and adamantine will – her own variation of Papa's – seems to have the constitution necessary to the task of governess, though she would hardly disagree with her sisters on the subject of their ill treatment. My situation is different, for I am paid thrice what Anne is, and have only one dull, but affable pupil, who has already long ago reached the age of reason.

No, the school scheme matters not, for my literary apotheosis and marriage to Lydia will allow me a liberality with the poor creatures, though at present *they* have money and I have none. As I write, the thought of my own magnanimity cheers me. Yes, surely, 1844 will mark a new beginning, for even if such visions of the future are chimerical, what good fortune I already have will surely continue: I have a beautiful lady who loves me, and will do anything to preserve our union; I am wonderfully valued in my situation, and both my pupil's advancements and my mistress's affection for me assure my place at Thorp Green; Macaulay has sent encouraging words, and I will set about more methodically to attain the literary recognition that is long overdue me.

Within a few days we return to Thorp Green, and I to Lydia. How fervently I hope that she has devised a plan to allow us to see each other again! I have spent the entire holiday in Haworth wishing myself there, and trying my best to conceal my feelings, my erratic behaviour at times drawing puzzled looks from Anne and Emily, whilst Papa, as I had hoped, has not noticed – or has chosen not to notice – any change in my manner.

VI.

The Ball

January 20th, 1844 · Thorp Green

At eighteen, Miss Robinson has emerged from the quiet obscurity of the schoolroom into the full blaze of the fashionable world. Whilst we, the paid subordinates, were in Haworth, she had her 'coming out' at a magnificent winter ball, to which her mama invited all the nobility and gentry of the neighbourhood, for twenty miles round.

Anne has informed me that the provoking thing – for she is as vexatious in spirit as she is delightful to behold, one of those young ladies whose character repels nearly as much as their face and form attract – will no longer be under her tuition, and I worry what mischief she will cause when set adrift in this way. What will she do with her days, besides dress elegantly, shake her ringlets and tease the local gentlemen of station high and low? Upon the first opportunity her mother informed Anne that she might *do as she pleased*, my sister wasted no time in seeking me out in my quarters, to regale me with the story of the ball.

Anne told me that she had scarcely removed her outdoor garments from our journey back to Thorp Green when Miss Robinson – young Lydia – had seized upon her, desperate to recount just how brilliantly she had shone, how many hearts she had broken, how many women had been driven mad with envy at her beauty and grace. Meanwhile, her sister Bessy stood by, wishing to tell her governess about her acquisition of a new mare, the very mention of which her sister found *inconceivably shocking*. My sister's own gift for mimicry is truly extraordinary, and I laughed aloud as she assumed the alternately sweet and bitter tones of her eldest pupil and her sister:

'*Really*, Miss Brontë,' said Anne in the young lady's voice, swooping dramatically round my sitting room in the Monk's House, 'I'm so *sorry* you didn't see me! I was *charming*, wasn't I Bessy?'

'Middling,' (in an equally skilled imitation of Bessy's slightly deeper voice).

'No, but I really was – at least Mama … and Marshall … said so. Marshall said she was sure no gentleman could set eyes on me without falling in love that minute; and so I may be allowed to be a little vain. I was so much admired; and I made so *many* conquests in that one night – you'd be astonished to hear –'

Anne pirouetted – laughing, but already short of breath – and settled into a soft chair to resume her narration, this time in her own voice.

'I said to her, speaking quite in earnest, that one conquest would be well enough, at which point she laughed, reminding me that we never agree on such points. It was a double delight to her to see the older gentlemen fall at her feet, while their nasty, cross wives *were ready to perish with spite and vexation*.'

My sister has a sense of fun, but her moral rectitude is unquestionable. I knew that she would not have let such comments pass unchecked. 'And what did the wicked thing say when you upbraided her for such behaviour?' said I, still laughing.

'She admitted that it was *very wrong* and promised to *be good sometimes*!'

At this Anne, for all her disapproval, could not resist resuming her imitation of the young lady, saying in Lydia's voice, 'Only don't preach now, Miss Brontë, there's a good creature – I haven't told you half yet …' Still in character, Anne enumerated the many *unmistakable admirers* of young Lydia: there were innumerable *old codgers, only fit companions for Papa and Mama*, a young gentleman who was *rich and gay, but an ugly beast*; a younger son who was good-looking and a pleasant fellow to flirt with but otherwise *useless* because without fortune, assorted country boobies with money but no family connections, and the good rector of Little Ouseburn and his new curate.

Anne brightened and laughed, adding again in her own voice, 'Miss Robinson accused this last gentleman of being *an insensate, ugly, stupid blockhead* – I can only reason from this that he was the sole member of the stronger sex not to swoon at her feet.'

'Ah,' said I, mischievously, 'the pious clergyman chose not to *gaze and gape* at the feast of feminine charms spread before him, eh? His tongue didn't loll out of his mouth like Keeper's beneath the dinner table? Well, jolly good for him! Perhaps he simply doesn't *care* for the fairer sex – he wouldn't be the first clergyman of *that* sort, would he now?'

'That's a wicked thing to say, Branwell. *I*, for one, am curious to meet this gentleman; he must be a person of considerable rectitude to have been resistant to the attractions of Miss Robinson. You men,' she continued, 'are shameless.'

For a moment the image of *Mrs* Robinson and myself in a sublimely shameless frenzy of fornication flashed before my eyes, and I changed the subject just as abruptly.

'Yes, well, we aren't going to change *that* now, are we? Tell me, then, how the ball ended. What philosophical lessons did young Lydia draw from this grand event? Which of the gentlemen does she like best?'

'Ah yes,' said Anne, unable to resist a dramatic conclusion to her performance. Rising out of her chair, she shook her modest auburn coiffure as if it were young Lydia's profusion of golden curls, once more assuming her erstwhile pupil's voice, with an exaggerated sigh: 'If I could be always young, I would always be single. I should like to coquet with all the world, till I am on the verge of being called an old maid; and then, to escape the infamy of that, after having made ten thousand conquests, to break all their hearts save one, by marrying some high-born, rich, indulgent husband, whom, on the other hand, fifty ladies were dying to have.'

I laughed heartily, though none of this came as a surprise. 'My, she is quite the naughty thing, isn't she? And how did you, *good creature* that you are, respond to that?'

Anne sat back down with a smile that seemed half mirth and half resignation. 'You can well imagine, Branwell. I said something like this: '*Well*, as long as you entertain those views, keep single by all means, and never marry at all, not even to escape the infamy of old-maidenhood.'

We shared a final laugh over this, though it was soon succeeded by a prolonged silence. Where had her mind wandered, as her eyes travelled over the grounds, patched here and there with the remnants of the latest snowstorm, and across the sky, dressed in a shimmering gown of winter blue, reflected in her own brilliant orbs? Back to Haworth? To Scarborough? It has been just three days since her twenty-fourth birthday: was she wondering if *she* would ever marry?

'A penny for your thoughts, Miss Brontë.'

She turned with sad resignation, and sighed. 'Oh, Branwell, just the usual thoughts. Will we be all right? How long will father live? Will the school scheme ever be successful? Will any of us ever marry? Where will we all be in a few years, and what changes will we have seen and known? Will we be much changed ourselves?'

I said nothing, but reflected that among her unspoken questions was very likely this one: *Will Branwell be able to keep his position at Thorp Green, though he has failed at all others?* For my part, despite my love for her – and indeed, my love for Charlotte and Emily as well – I wanted to ask: *Should you worry so much about money when you have been provided an inheritance by Aunt Branwell, whilst I received nothing but a Japanese dressing box whose intricate designs I may have admired as a boy, but which now is utterly useless?*

Instead, I smiled, stood up and kissed her on the forehead. 'All will be well, little sister, all will be well. Fear not.'

As she rose to say goodbye, I did my best to make her smile. '*And*, thank you for the performance of Miss Robinson's coming-out ball. I believe that if all else failed – if acting were not such a disreputable profession, mind – you could rival the greatest performers of domestic melodrama at Covent Garden or Drury Lane! Perhaps, like the famed Eliza O'Neill, you could even marry a baronet and retire to his estate. Ha ha!'

Alas, I did little to raise Anne's spirits, and as she left, I realised that mine were as every bit as depressed as hers. I have no doubt that my self-pity has worsened since Lydia – my Lydia – seems to have severed all ties with me. Does she ever think of me? Did she ever love me? I am beginning to wonder, for I scarcely see her at all.

VII.

Lessons

March 28th, 1844 · Thorp Green

I am wondering no more – Heaven be praised! We have at last been together again, at least once a week. Mere chance provided the solution, and happiness has proceeded most unexpectedly from misery. Would that it could continue forever thus!

By dreary February I was so depressed of spirits that I could scarcely drag myself through my daily duties; I had written almost nothing, and even ignored the pages of this diary. I feared that my gloomy countenance would affect my earnest pupil and that my employers would send me packing. One day in the middle of the month I sent word that I was too ill to teach young Edmund. I settled back into bed and watched a regiment of steely clouds march past my window, from northeast to southwest, towards Haworth. I had just begun to wonder what Papa, Charlotte and Emily were doing at that moment when I heard a sharp knock on the door.

It was my mistress, accompanied by her lady's maid, to whom she said simply, 'Please wait outside, Marshall. You may knock if someone approaches.'

Lydia bolted the door behind her and walked rapidly to my bedside, where she spread out her skirts and sat daintily before me, reaching out for my hand, pressing it tenderly in hers.

'Are you *quite* all right, Branwell?'

Immediately my heart swelled with hope, for she had only ever used my Christian name in our most intimate moments. Tears filled my eyes, mingled tears of misery and suffering, but also relief and gladness.

'My sweet boy,' said she, 'why are you crying?'

'I have been miserable without you. It has been utter torture to have you at once so near and so unattainable. I began to suppose that you had forgotten me.'

Lydia again pressed my hand. 'Foolish boy, you *know* I have not forgotten you. Hush now.' With that she leant over to kiss me gently on the forehead, each cheek, and finally, my mouth. She began to draw away from me, but starved for her caresses, I pulled her back, kissing her hungrily.

'No, we mustn't,' said she, resisting me at first. 'I am afraid of being discovered, truly I am.'

'You cannot do this,' said I. You cannot bring a feast to a starving man and then forbid him to partake.' I drew her to me again and soon my hands and mouth had convinced where words had failed, and all fear of discovery – indeed, all awareness of anything beyond the blissful, rhythmic union of our bodies – fell away like a lover's garment. My sickness, it seems, was only *love*-sickness, for in Lydia's delicious embrace all of my symptoms melted quite away, and as I exploded within her I felt that great Godlike flash of joy and oblivion.

'Oh God, Lydia,' said I, 'I have missed you so, my love. You are all I need to heal me.'

She, however, had quite returned to her senses – it was a good thing, too, for no sooner had she straightened her hair and smoothed her clothes – for she had lifted her skirts but not removed any clothing – than there came a brisk rapping at the door. In all of our assignations, this had never occurred, and we both fairly leapt at the sound, so that I rapidly pulled the bed-covers over my body, whilst she walked calmly, though flushed, to the door.

It was Ann Marshall, come to announce that my sister was waiting downstairs to see me. Rather than try to escape unseen, my mistress chose – wisely, I think – to pretend as though nothing were amiss.

'Ah, Miss Brontë,' she said with great condescension as Marshall showed her into my room, 'I am so glad you came, despite your duties with Bessy and Mary.' This last was meant to convey, in fact: *Why are you not in the schoolroom with your pupils?* 'I am certain that you are worried about your brother's condition, as am I. I've just arrived myself, to enquire as to his health and to see what we might do to help him recover.'

My mistress's body had, of course, already done this noble work, but I now feared that this visit from my sister would seal my fate forever, and that Lydia would never again risk being alone in my company. I looked at Anne, and it was clear from her concerned eyes that she suspected nothing – indeed, that she could not possibly dream of what had just occurred in the bed, still damp from our sweet congress, where I lay. She was here merely to see how I was.

'Yes, ma'am, I was indeed concerned. I told the young ladies that I would be back directly, but I wanted to see my brother for myself.'

'Now, now, little sister,' said I with bravado, as my fear of discovery gave way to a wave of relief. 'I am already feeling better for your visit, and suspect I just need some rest.'

Anne sat precisely where Lydia had just before we began kissing, and examined me closely. 'Hmm. Well, other than being too thin – you *must* eat, Branwell – and a bit flushed with fever' – here she leant forward and placed her palm on my forehead – 'you seem quite all right to me.'

As we spoke, Lydia had wandered over to a table that held my drawing materials, and was examining some of my rough sketches. She now held one aloft. 'This is quite good, Mr Brontë. I see that your sister is not the only artist in the family.'

'Oh, goodness, no,' said Anne, always prepared to undervalue her own accomplishments and exaggerate those of others, a sign of genuine humility, yes, but also, conveniently enough, an attractive quality in a governess. 'Branwell is an *excellent* artist. He gave all of us tuition in painting and drawing, and was even a portraitist in Bradford for a time.'

'Is that *right*?' said Lydia, turning to lock eyes with me. 'My heavens: a tutor, a railway man, a poet, a painter. You truly are a man of diverse talents. Drawing and painting were my favourites when *I* was a girl,' she sighed, at last looking back at my drawing. 'I remember being delightfully lost in creation, with no sense of time or place … and how positively *enraged* I would become when someone interrupted me!' She sighed again, as if mourning something far greater. 'Indeed, they are the *only* accomplishments I wish I still practised.'

'Why ma'am, I'm sure Branwell could give you lessons. *Couldn't* you, Branwell?'

Lydia later told me that she had wished to seize at once upon the opportunity, because the idea came from Anne, and thus would be far less suspicious. However, she said nothing while I protested.

'My sister, I fear, has an unduly grand conception of my artistic talents. I believe she would be every bit as proficient an instructor as I, ma'am. Indeed, you should see the portrait I painted of my sisters and myself. My own likeness was so bad that I obliterated myself by inserting a pillar between Emily and Charlotte. Their likenesses are not much better, I fear.'

Anne's eyes narrowed, as if to say that she had quite enough to do, even though no longer teaching young Lydia, but said, 'Of course I will do as you command, Mrs Robinson, but I would hate to detract in any way from my lessons with the young ladies. And truly, Branwell is far superior to me as an artist. Methinks he doth protest too much.'

My mistress bit her lip pensively. 'Well, hmm. Yes, I suppose your sister *does* have a point, Mr Brontë, for not only does she have two pupils where you have one, she is still very much a companion for my Lydia, even if she *has* graduated from the schoolroom to the ballroom. I need her to accompany that headstrong creature on her walks, for it is not proper for a young lady of her rank and prospects to be wandering about by herself, exposed to the attentions of anyone that presumes to address her, like some poor neglected girl that has no park to walk in, and no friends to take care of her!'

She pondered for a moment, gazing out onto the park in question. At last, turning again to me, she said, 'Assuming, then, Mr Brontë, that you will *have* me, I shall follow your sister's advice and take instruction from you once a week, as soon as you are well enough to resume your duties. If I find you to my satisfaction, I may even ask my daughters to continue under your tuition.'

She had, as I say, already healed me, and the next day I returned to my lessons with Edmund, during which my mistress sent word that she would like to begin *her* lessons the following day. Since then we have pursued them with remarkable vigour.

April 21st, 1844 · Thorp Green

Lydia has repeated her assertion, *en passant*, to both Anne and Ann Marshall, that she will not abide interruptions in her lessons now any more than she did as a girl, and so not only is my sitting room locked, but Mrs Marshall stands guard as we silently and quickly embrace. This we do immediately, so that should anyone knock after a few moments, my mistress is indeed already at work on a painting or drawing.

Yesterday I was the culprit. As she sketched the head of a young girl, biting her lip adorably in concentration – for she had become one again herself – I said, 'What does your husband think of these lessons?'

Lydia looked across at me, her pen in the air, with a look of flinty consternation I had scarcely ever seen. The loveable little girl had quite vanished.

'He thinks nothing at all of my lessons. He is happy, I suppose, that I am occupied.'

'But is he not jealous that we are locked away together?'

'I believe I told you that he has never been jealous of you in *that* fashion. He simply does not wish any other man to be successful. His spite over your letter from Macaulay had nothing to do with you really, and everything to do with him, remember?'

'Yes, but does he not fear that you will seek to avenge his earlier unfaithfulness and cruelty towards you by taking up with the handsome and brilliant young tutor?' said I, trying to brighten her mood with a touch of levity.

She smiled, but not for the reason I supposed.

'*He* afraid that I would take up with *you*?'

'Why should that be so absurd, Lydia?'

'First, he is a selfish, arrogant wretch, who believes that while he can – or once could, I should now say, for he is long past such pursuits – seduce any woman he pleases, no one else, and least of all his own wife, can do so. Do you not see that it is the same as with your poetry?'

She leant back from her work, placed her pen calmly in its stand, folded her arms, and stared at me even more fixedly.

'Second, why would he differ from any other gentleman in thinking that while *he* should be able to dip his nib in any inkwell he chooses, his *wife* should be forever faithful and long-suffering, and, indeed, should be quite cast out if ever she were discovered engaged in such activities?'

Despite an unusually warm April breeze coming through the open window, I shuddered, not liking to consider such a thing.

'Third, and last, I am quite certain, that if he could imagine that I might form an attachment, the last person I would take up with would be young Edmund's tutor, who after all is a poor clergyman's son, one whose rank is not much above his other domestics.'

I kindled up inside but tried to remain calm. I was nettled by this blunt reminder; it was as though she had brought her hand across my face with a smart slap. My countenance surely betrayed me, for Lydia rose and came to me quickly. 'Hush, silly boy,' she whispered, standing behind me and wrapping her arms about my neck, which she kissed repeatedly. 'Do not think that I see you that way. I was simply trying to allay your fears, to make you see why my husband thinks nothing of these lessons. After all, ladies in my station are not accustomed to run off with their sons' tutors. And I could almost be your mother, you know.'

She kissed me sweetly on the forehead.

'No, indeed,' exclaimed I, my vexation subsiding as quickly as it had appeared at the touch of her rosy, impossibly soft lips. 'No one who saw us together would suppose that for an instant. You look as young as some women do at five-and-twenty or thirty.'

Lydia laughed indulgently. 'Which is it, Branwell? Those are two quite different ages.'

'*La beauté n'a pas d'âge, Madame*. When I think of my sister Charlotte – please do not think me a cruel or unloving brother – I find that she, who will be eight-and-twenty tomorrow, is already an old woman, every bit the peevish spinster who might provide a laugh or two to the readers of a three-volume novel. You are far younger than she, in every respect.'

'Can that be so?' she responded. 'Why, your sister Anne – though she *does* insist on playing the prim governess – and I confess I would have it no other way, for it surely would not do to have an elegant, sparkling rival of my daughters in the schoolroom, my heavens!'

Lydia laughed heartily at the unlikely phantom she had called forth: the image of little Anne dressed for a glittering ball. When she had at last caught her breath, she said, 'What was I saying? Oh, yes, your sister Anne – she is quite pretty, really, in her properly plain sort of way of course, and surely looks her age, does she not?'

'Yes, yes, but she and Charlotte could not be more different in appearance and temperament, and I think their inner selves are revealed without.'

'Ah,' was all Lydia said, looking up at the clock on the mantle. 'Goodness, I have to *go*!' she exclaimed.

'Kiss me once more.'

She tousled my hair as if I were her own little boy, but refused. 'No, you bad animal, but you will have far more than that to look forward to next time … I must be off.'

I reminded her that in the coming days she was to begin work on a self-portrait, which we are to discuss next week. It was essential, after all, that the pretext for our rendezvous be evident to all, and the truth of the matter is that she really does take great pleasure in the process.

Today is indeed Charlotte's birthday. I wonder – have I been unfair to her? Whence come my harsh – nay, cruel – words? What has she done to me to merit such opprobrium? Do I merely deplore in her character what I loathe most in my own? Is looking at her in earnest simply holding up a mirror to myself? Or does she represent something greater – the constant threat of censure, of disapproval, of condemnation, a sword of Damocles suspended high above me by a single hair?

What became of the unadulterated joy – perhaps greater even than the transcendent but transient bliss of coition, and far superior to the happy but soon-repented oblivion of strong drink – that joy in which we bathed as children, scribbling our poems and spinning, together as one, our tales of Glass Town or Verdopolis, and then Angria, peopling them with Northangerland, Zamorna, Mina Laury and Caroline Vernon, Henry Hastings and Charles Townsend – yes, even Robert Patrick Sdeath and Benjamin Patrick Wiggins, and legions more – that joy where, together as one, we formed a union more perfect, and bore more fruit, than any physical intercourse could ever engender? Each of our fecund minds anticipated the other's next word, our characters and their speeches almost interchangeable, like lovers who, in the flames of their passion, know not where one body ends and the other begins – so, too, were we united in a creative ardour that seemed to know no bounds. Even in our fraternal innocence, Shelley could also have said of us, that we were *one spirit within two frames, one passion in twin-hearts*. It was as if Charlotte *were* me, and I *were* her.

Whither did this passion go? Was it as simple as growing up? Even so, should not a warm regard for each other be what resides in the wake of our juvenile labours, like the softly glowing embers in a grate long after the consuming flames have quite died away?

Let me try to be just and imagine what she thinks of me: a brother she still loves in a theoretical sort of fashion, and for whom she had the highest hopes, hopes that are dimming with each passing year, with each failed undertaking. She has always been of a penetratingly censorious cast, and so she has determined that I am a lost cause, as much as she might wish otherwise. She would be the first to shower me with praise and affection if I were to triumph in the world, but she has decided that such a thing will never happen – just as she would be delighted to flap her arms and take flight high over the moors, whilst knowing that such a thing is equally impossible. I have become, more often than not, something of an embarrassment; and deep within her, she believes that had I fulfilled my childhood promise, none of my sisters would have to be governesses, or start a school.

Now, then: what do I think of *her*? A woman whose hidden passions know no bounds, but have no object or outlet, so that they constantly remain simmering near a low boil, ever threatening to spill over; an almost impossibly short, dumpy thing with lovely eyes and hair, but poor skin and teeth, who might well be tempted to sell her soul to the Devil to look like the exquisite Lydia Robinson – either mother or daughter, for that matter – even though it is just such women whom she most despises. Is her enmity merely envy disguised? Yes, she is consistently unfair to her own sex, whereas the gentlemen – though from this I fear her brother may be excluded – are judged with a far more indulgent eye: was Monsieur Heger as perfect a model of virtue as she pretends, and his wife the harpy she implies?

Doubt, as the French – and, I assume, the Belgians – say, *is permitted.*

Still, even the stronger sex can on occasion be subject to her condemnation and I suspect her image of me is the most unflattering of all: the brilliant brother whose want of application and pertinacity mean that he will never find steady employment or peace of mind; the brother whom God has given talents equal to hers, and who – far more importantly – has the great good fortune of *being a man*, and who has taken these treasures and cast them to the wind. Worst of all, his utter lack of restraint represents a moral weakness that he will never overcome.

Is this truly what she believes? But did not Blake say that *those who restrain desire do so because theirs is weak enough to be restrained?* Is my will truly less strong than hers, or my desire simply greater?

VIII.

Amor Vincit Omnia

May Day, 1844 · Thorp Green

Yesterday, after we had slaked the thirst of our passion – I confess that as I write this phrase I cannot help but hear the booming voice of Joe Leyland, who, deep in his cups, corrects me, his words winging their way magically, as if by salacious celestial telegraph, across Yorkshire: 'After havin' it off, little man, you mean, after going at it, after *fucking* to your heart's content, ha ha!' – and had sat quietly for some time, my mistress rose and shyly presented me with her self-portrait.

Although her painting displays admirable technical skill, Lydia has failed to capture her own beauty, especially her brilliant, flashing eyes and dazzling smile. Is this mere modesty, or has she herself accurately depicted an inner disquiet or foreboding – or worse, an inner unhappiness? Could she be weary of me? I cannot bear the thought. But surely – surely – the manner in which she threw her arms around me and held me fast as our bodies moved together to a rapturous climax was not that of a jaded lover, but rather a woman clinging to her salvation.

'Your painting,' said I, hesitatingly, standing behind her, 'is *very* good.'

'However?'

I encircled her waist with my arms and plunged my face into her exquisite neck, breathing in her perfume with all the vigour of the inveterate snuff-taker relieving his craving.

'However, my darling Lydia, you do not capture a fraction of your beauty. See here: why do you not smile? Why have you made yourself so downcast?'

I carried her portrait to the window and held it in the light. 'Look, Lydia, your eyes even seem to brim with tears. What is wrong, my love?'

Now all-too-real tears streamed down her cheeks. As she dried her eyes with my handkerchief, she sniffled and said, sighing: 'Oh, my dear boy, it is just that we cannot go on in this fashion.'

My heart throbbed; my brow grew hot and moist.

'What do you mean, Lydia? I cannot live without you.'

She smiled a sweet, melancholy smile as she dried the last of her tears and returned my handkerchief. She was radiant, stunning, a woman who had ripened to perfection (*pace* Joseph Bentley Leyland and his fruit-inspired theories of feminine beauty), her person still lovely, her mind still youthful, if seasoned by experience.

'Silly boy, of course you can. Your entire life stands before you, whereas *I* am a weary old woman with nearly fully grown children and a dying husband that I must nurse.'

I could no longer keep from kissing those full, round lips, and again, her neck. '*These* are not the lips, and this is not the neck, of an old woman. And what of the woman whose caresses, just moments ago, moved me to heavenly ecstasy? Was *she* an old woman?'

'You are merely saying that,' said she, 'because you have become dependent – nay, addicted – to me.'

'If you mean the old sense of that word – that I am *bound* or *devoted* to you – this is true. But let us suppose that the modern sense of the word is also apt: did you not tell me, nearly a year since, that the *ecstasy of two lovers is restorative and salutary, not debilitating or noxious*? You told me this the day you seduced me.'

'*I seduced you*? Surely you confuse the facts, Mr Brontë.' She said this playfully, however, as if the very word *seduce* was enough, with the kisses she had received on her lips and neck, to reignite her passions. By Heaven, how fortunate I am to have a lover of such boundless desire!

'Yes, you seduced me, you beguiling, wicked creature. Was it not *you* who had already enflamed my desire with your gifts, and marking Shelley's poem with your perfumed slip of paper?'

By now she had pressed herself against me, her arms pulling me tight, her lovely head tipped upward, her pulpy lips parted in a smile, just an inch or two from mine.

'And *then* what happened?' she whispered.

'Then we went to the library …'

She raised herself on the tips of her toes to kiss my lips.

'And then?'

Each question was now followed by a kiss, each kiss deeper and more passionate than the last.

'You bolted the door.'

'And then?'

'We kissed.'

'And then?' she asked once again, touching me and guiding my hand to touch her, just as she had that first day.

My mind was now a blank and my tongue had grown heavy. I felt at once like a man on fire, and yet, unaccountably, like one moving underwater. I could barely utter: 'And then we did *this* …'

'Wait,' said Lydia suddenly, stiffening and straightening her garments, and walking abruptly to the window, while I fairly writhed with renewed desire.

'Ah, this is perfect!' said she, fairly skipping across the floor and into my arms like a young girl. 'Your sister is at the far end of the park, walking towards the woods with the three young ladies, and Edmund and his dogs are frolicking about them. Marshall is standing guard below. So we have at least ten minutes to *do as we please*.'

And so we did.

As she prepared to leave, Lydia's countenance was again downcast.

'What is it, Lydia? I won't ask you if you still love me, but what is the matter?'

'I told you, we cannot go on in this manner; we cannot risk discovery.'

'We shall be careful, I promise it,' said I, kissing her again on the forehead. 'Do you think I would ever risk losing that smile, those eyes?'

'Well might you say that, now that you are again become yourself, but just a few moments ago neither of us was capable of a rational thought – for such passion as this is a madness that seizes us both and overthrows reason utterly. It is afterwards that I am wracked with fear of discovery, and the thought of losing you. It is well that you are leaving next month for a holiday, for with such a distance between us tongues will cease to wag.'

'What tongues?'

'Marshall says that the servants have begun their gossip again; worse than this, however, are the comments I have heard from my own daughter Lydia, who has taken to teasing her mama about her *rendezvous* with Mr Brontë. She seems born for mischief, and if she cannot produce it from her own actions, she will seek it in others.'

At this my old enemy, *Fear*, wrapped his long, icy fingers round my frame, and all I could do was repeat my vow to take great care to avoid discovery as she stepped out the door and down the stairs to rejoin Marshall. I pulled a chair to the window and watched them glide down the lane and across the park towards the Great Hall; at the same time, in the distance, Anne and the children approached, returning from their perambulations. Edmund raced to see his dear mama, he and his canine companions circling round and round her and Marshall, whilst the young ladies sailed towards them at a more dignified pace. Did I imagine it, or did young Lydia turned her head in the direction of the Old Hall, her hand shading her eyes, which fell directly on mine even from that great distance? I leant back suddenly into the shadow to avoid her gaze. No, surely she did not see me. But what if she did? Was this not my abode?

I again surveyed Lydia's self-portrait, this time at leisure, and thought of what had just transpired: yes, our amorous congress, but more significant because more troubling, her incessant apprehension and fear of discovery, which she captured in her own downcast likeness, in a manner both so naïve and true.

I took out my notebook and began to write. How little I have written these past weeks and months! At first, I was sick from the absence of my mistress, and now I am either consumed with desperate longing when I am away from her, or plunged into a brief, blessed sea of relief when I am with her.

The first few lines of my poem evoke a renaissance painting of the crucifixion. I scribble, erase, rewrite – why must I always begin with something *not* pertinent, something from long ago and far away? Why am I unable to speak from my heart in my poems as I do in this diary? Must every work repose on a foundation unrelated to my true intentions, like the weighty plinths supporting Leyland's stone creations?

It is only in the third stanza that my true subject, her self-portrait, comes into view:

Her effort shows a picture made
To contradict its meaning
Where should be sunshine painting shade
And smiles with sadness screening
Where God has given a cheerful view
A gloomy vista showing
Where heart and face, are fair and true
A shade of doubt bestowing

Ah lady if to me you give,
The power of your sketch to adorn
How little of it shall I leave
Save smiles that shine like morn
I'd keep the hue of happy light
That shines from summer skies
I'd drive the shades from smiles so bright
And dry such shining eyes

I'd give a calm to one whose heart
has banished calm from mine
I'd brighten up God's work of art
Where thou hast dimmed its shine
And all the wages I should ask

For such a happy toil
I'll name them – far beyond my task –
THY PRESENCE AND THY SMILE

I had at first written 'youth demure' in the second stanza, but crossed it out, replacing it with 'happy light' – for Lydia herself, with her foolish talk of being *an old woman*, would surely scoff at such a phrase.

I have every intention of making a fair copy of this poem, to present to her next week.

May 29th, 1844 · Thorp Green

When Lydia arrived the following week for her lesson, I learned there was to be none. Instead, she stood biting her lip, her eyes alighting everywhere but on me.

'What is it, my darling?' said I, as the old signs of trepidation, a cold sweat and racing heart, made their appearance. I sought to draw her to me, but she resisted. Tears welled in her eyes.

'There can be no more lessons, Mr Brontë,' she replied. 'It has become altogether too perilous … I am sorry, but this *must* stop now.'

'The lessons, I suppose you mean, not –'

'Oh, I don't know, I just don't *know*,' said she, tears now welling up in her eyes. 'Of course I want to continue … you make me feel so … so … *young*. But how can we persevere in running such risks? If we stop now – when there is no proof – then we are both safe, but if we continue, I fear – indeed, I feel – that we shall be quite found out, disgraced and both cast out. That simply cannot happen. I will not allow it.' Her jaw clenched with resolution.

'I don't care: we *must* be together … do you not feel this as powerfully as I do? If I were with you, I would be afraid of nothing. Together we could brave Satan and all his legions!'

At this she laughed ruefully, wiping her eyes, which now narrowed with – what it was I could not quite tell – mirth? Condescension? A touch of scorn, even? All three?

'You foolish boy, and I suppose we will brave them without a shilling?'

'*Amor vincit omnia*: we could sail to Canada, or Australia, or New Zealand, and begin life anew. I would do *anything* for you, truly I would.'

At this she relaxed her arms and allowed me to draw her to my breast and kiss her uplifted forehead and cheeks. She sighed and then laughed again, this time softly, dolefully.

'Love only conquers all in those popular novels you yourself are so fond of disparaging. And as for sailing to the Antipodes – Heavens, what a foolish tale of adventure!'

She permitted me at last to kiss her mouth, after which she added, 'You are quite mad.'

'No, just madly in love. I cannot be separated from you.'

'And yet,' replied Lydia, becoming utterly serious again but no longer resisting my embrace, but rather placing her head on my shoulder, 'we cannot be discovered. We simply *cannot*.'

With a Herculean effort, I resisted making the amorous advances to which I would normally have proceeded, but instead gently withdrew from her arms, asked her to sit, and walked across to my worktable, where I had placed a fair copy of my most recent poem.

'Here,' said I, handing her the folded sheet. 'I have a gift for you. Read it.'

As she read the lines, tears again clouded those dark, luminous eyes. She folded the sheet into a small square, hid it in her garments, and prepared to take her leave. Never had she seemed so beautiful: at once strong and passionate, and yet vulnerable and disconsolate. *Now* I wanted to take her in my arms again, to love her as I am sure only *I* can, but I refrained – why, I know not – and a good thing it was, too, because just then a sharp rapping came at the door, which my mistress hastened to open as I seized one of Lydia's sketches and held it aloft, as if in the midst of an earnest critique of its various virtues and imperfections.

Before us stood eighteen-year-old Lydia, in a shimmering pale-blue summer frock, calculated to draw attention to her every flawless curve, and to complement her own enchanting, mischievous, blue eyes; in short, her whole person seemed deliberately contrived to drive the young *beaux* of the neighbourhood, should they be fortunate – or unfortunate, depending on how one viewed the matter – enough to cross her path, positively mad with distraction. It would not take much for her to shoot an arrow through nearly any man's heart.

She had clearly overruled Mrs Marshall's objections and marched up the stairs on her own. Truly, I thought, she is indeed becoming ungovernable, although such reflections were secondary to the profound relief that I felt that she had not discovered her mother and me in any of various stages of undress, or in the throes of passion.

'Now *Mama*,' said she, shaking her ringlets, 'I know you do not wish to be interrupted when you are thus engaged with Mr Brontë' – was it my own guilt that discerned a look of saucy suspicion in those brilliant eyes, or did she truly suspect our proceedings? – 'but Papa is *asking* for you.'

'Well, *that*,' said Lydia coolly, not seeming to care whether her daughter heard her tone of disdainful dismissal, 'is news. What does he want? Cannot one of the servants assist him?'

'Oh, Mama, really, how should I know? He simply wishes to see you.' Turning to me, she added, 'It certainly is not my concern what transpires between my parents, any more than it is yours, isn't that right, Mr Brontë?' Was she trying to ensnare me with what seemed a trivial comment? I chose the safest course and said nothing.

Whether because of the determination with which she had already come to me that day, or the subsequent shock of having her eldest daughter – whose increasingly inquisitive conduct she already dreaded – appear our very door, Lydia has, indeed, discontinued her lessons. I was, myself, sufficiently frightened to have determined that it is best for us to pretend that there is nothing between us, although I continue to ache for her, and to envision schemes that would once again allow us to be together. Surely we will find a way.

It has been three weeks since this last rendezvous occurred. Has Lydia quite forgotten me? Or can she, with the slightest effort of imagination, remember how it felt to be in my arms, as I recall the bliss of being lost in hers? I console myself with this: if my mistress truly wished never to see me again, she would tell her husband not to engage me for the coming months. Indeed, now, just prior to our summer holiday, would be precisely the time to send me packing with the least amount of controversy, *à la Postlethwaite.*

Instead, I have again been summoned, with Anne, to spend July and August in Scarborough.

IX.

Interlude: A Picnic with the Brontë Sisters

June 19th, 1844 · Haworth, The Parsonage

Here we four children are once again, thrown together at the approach of Midsummer. Charlotte is now twenty-eight; I, just a week shy of twenty-seven; Emily Jane almost twenty-six; Anne twenty-four. How changed we are, how very *old*! What remains of those seemingly endless days and nights of childhood, where words and plays and poems and stories and adventures flowed from us in such prodigious quantities, like molten lava streaming from a volcano? How I remember the innocence of those days, when my toy soldiers were seized upon and transformed into the heroes of our plays, over the years transmogrified by the four godlike genii – Tallii, Branii, Emmii and Annii – into the *dramatis personae* of Glass Town, rechristened Verdopolis, and then Angria.

Charlotte and I were rivals and collaborators, while Emily and Anne broke away and created their own world of Gondal. Yes, our characters – informed by reading that would not have been permitted to the children of most parsons (or *persons*, for that matter), but learning had rescued Papa, so little, if anything, was forbidden – yes, these characters were superhuman heroes, vile seducers, bloodthirsty soldiers, wanton adulterers, women both corrupted and corrupt, obsequious courtiers and submissive courtesans, illegitimate offspring, facetious chroniclers, bold blasphemers, cunning hypocrites, cynical charlatans and artful conspirators.

Yes, by God Almighty, did we read! We read as if it were mother's milk, for it was the vital artery that nourished us when all around us lay only death and desolation. I remember when, as a youth, I discovered that it was *Papa* who had written the little tale we had oft read, *The Maid of Killarney*, which he had published anonymously the year after my birth. What a discovery to make, that Papa was not two persons – the tall, gentle, softly spoken, sweet Papa who loved us with all his heart in the warm confines of the Parsonage, and the serious, earnest parson who stood before us on Sundays and preached on Man's fall and Christ's redemption (for is not every sermon a variation on this?) – but three persons: he was a *writer*! Upon interrogation, he confessed that he had also written several volumes of poetry, all meant to be both 'profitable and agreeable', *dulce et utile* he said, and ultimately shared them with us. So thrilled were we that our very own Papa was a published author, that we read and reread his works until we had fairly committed them to memory.

Although I no longer share his views – did I ever, I wonder? – that poetry should have as its aim the salvation of its reader, I wonder if my disdain for novels comes ultimately from him, a prejudice so deeply rooted that it stands firm all these years later, though the entire landscape of literature has been altered, as if by an earthquake, a conflagration, or a hurricane of the West Indies. I still recall what he wrote in the fourth chapter of *The Maid of Killarney*:

> The generality of novels are so many poisonous boluses, sufficiently encrusted with honey to make them palatable, but in no degree adequate to counteract their pernicious effects on the constitution. Our libraries want to pass through such another fiery ordeal as the library of the renowned Don Quixote did, when it was scrutinised by the Priest and the Barber.

Did my father thus cultivate in me, so long ago, a profound distaste for the genre, as some mothers are said to sicken their young boys with draughts of bitter wine, to prevent them from being drunkards like their fathers? Perhaps he should have done the latter, not the former.

A far more interesting question, however, is how the same man who appears to recommend – or at least consider – the burning of novels for their potentially *pernicious effects* on the innocent, could allow his children nearly unfettered access to the most scandalous of writings? Far more 'dangerous' than the silly novels of the age, after all, were the works of Lord Byron, of Shelley, of de Quincy, not to mention the satirical writings of *Blackwood's*, like the *Noctes Ambosianae*. Did he, like so many humble men who claw their way to respectability through sheer force of will and higher learning, trust that reading and writing – especially poetry – were inherently *good*, and that his very presence would shelter his little flock from any possible evils that might proceed from their reading? Did he believe that those benighted souls who did not have a clergyman for a father needed guidance that his own children did not? Was this a form of arrogance, finally?

Or did Mama's death – and then that of Maria and Elizabeth – simply exhaust him, so that it was enough that his children were in good health, happily engaged with their games, their reading, and their scribbling? Yes, perhaps it was as simple as that. How many errors of education must proceed from the simple truth that parents grow tired, and how much more tired poor Papa, with all of his duties, and his young brood! It is only just now that I begin to realise what he has lived, poor man, what he has loved, and most of all, what he has lost. Only now do I start to recognise his sacrifices for us all, and especially for me. Our saviour, he has emptied himself of his own desires so that we might live with a certain dignity, a certain ambition, a certain *hope*. He is ever indulgent, ever merciful, ever forgiving. To think that I have rebelled against him in my heart and soul, in my thoughts and in my deeds! I do not know which sentiment is stronger, my gratitude to him, or my shame and disgust with myself.

But for all this, I do not feel any more inclined to ask God's forgiveness, if such a being exists. As far as I am concerned, *He* quite abandoned us when *He* took Mama and our sisters: there is no forgiving *Him* for that. Nor do I wish to alter, in any way, my conduct, and my only fear when I am with Lydia is identical to hers: *discovery.* We must not be found out; we must be careful; and if we are fortunate, her 'angel' will be dead and buried by this time next year.

Such wishes do not to me seem evil, but merely natural. Am I wrong to think so? After all, does not one fate await us all, and inevitable death mock our transient happiness? Why should we not seize what is ours today, then?

It is late, and the flame of my candle gutters in the soft breeze, as it blows through the churchyard, making phantoms of the curtains of my open window. I must be off to bed, for tomorrow the four of us are to make a picnic at the ruins of Bolton Abbey, along the River Wharfe.

June 21st, 1844 · The Parsonage

Yesterday we departed Haworth before six, in a hired phaeton, to travel the fifteen miles to Bolton Abbey, Emily holding the basket of provisions for our collation. We left the carriage at the Devonshire Arms, just as we had on our first trip here, with Charlotte's friend Ellen, eleven years ago. How little changed is the inn, and even less the ancient walls of the priory, but again, how much altered are we! Mere children we were then, whose fond hopes have, in the interim, begun to slip away. As I write this, I think of my sixteen-year-old self, racing feverishly around our large party – for the Nussey family had met us at the inn, where, if I recall correctly, Charlotte was ashamed of our pony-cart – in a near-frenzy, entertaining all who would listen with a host of facts about the priory and the geography of the area, and quoting poetry wherever appropriate. What an impetuous lad I was, and perhaps even brilliant in my manic way! Had my mind adhered to Leyland's theory of decay? This would certainly explain why I rarely write anything *new*, but instead rework bits and pieces of old.

Together we walked half a mile to the priory, whose long decline began with Henry VIII's closing of the monasteries: the roofs, I have read, were stripped of their lead, exposing the delicate stonework to the elements. As the walls decayed and collapsed, local builders salvaged the stones and employed them anew in all manner of structures along the Wharfe Valley. Such it is with all things – all are born to decay, all are made of the detritus of the past. Food for worms. Bits and pieces of old.

As we walked around the ruins, the naked arches reaching into heaven, I thought how much more fitting is a church such as this than those where man comfortably worships a remote, carefully walled-off God of abstraction. Here man's creation unites with his Maker's, thrusting up into the sky, in sun or wind, in rain or snow, drawing heaven towards our earth again – here, God descends and surrounds every stone – here, He is not walled off from his pitiful, cringing creatures, whilst He looms over them with the threat of damnation – no, here, like a gentle summer rain, He washes lovingly over them in a benediction, a baptism, an amorous embrace.

Or could it be, instead, a great flood, a slow and methodical extermination? The priory church still functions, but it too will someday collapse, will it not? Does not everything eventually meet this fate? Will even York Minster, even Ripon Cathedral, collapse at last? Surely they will. My mind travelled over the Dales, to a recent ramble with Dr Crosby and his nephew Will. We had walked up Grafton Hill where, on that perfect spring day following hard upon a period of rain, we could gaze from Ripon Cathedral to York Minster, taking in, in a single panoramic sweep, all that lay between the towering structures, from the peak of Great Whernside to Fountains Abbey. How exalted I had felt that day – for an instant born anew in the brilliant sky and balmy wind, embraced all round by the serenely waving grasses and vivid, fluttering leaves of spring. Upon returning to Thorp Green, I had immediately set to work on a poem – a rare *new* poem:

O'er Grafton Hill the blue heaven smiled serene
On Grafton Hill the grass waved bright and green
Round Grafton Hill Old England's noblest vale
Opened to summer's sun and balmy gale …

The poem is a paean to Yorkshire, to England, to beauty, to life; yet why does it end thus, with the ruins and woods of Fountains Abbey, with death and oblivion?

Still nearer Grafton – Ripon's holy fane
Like York's drew heaven toward our earth again
And girt by Studley's woods the walls that now
Like sunbeams shining upon winter snow
Mark with their ruin splendours long since gone
And say ONE FATE AWAITS ON FLESH AND STONE

These were my thoughts as we grown Brontë children circled the priory, though I said nothing. Charlotte strode with short but rapid steps ahead of Emily and Anne, who walked arm in arm, whispering occasionally – conspiratorially, no doubt, thought I – whilst I brought up the rear. It was another splendid day, billowing white clouds piled high to the east, but sharp cerulean sky overhead and a lovely warm breeze, on which flitted the occasional bird or bee. At last, we found a place to rest, in view of both the ruins and the river. Emily and Anne set the picnic out on a low, wide wall, sheltered from the sun by overhanging trees.

Charlotte led us in a prayer, after which we ate with considerable gusto, our conversation focused entirely on the meal before us. Finally, as we began to be sated, I spoke.

'Pray tell me, sisters, where do things stand with the school for young ladies?'

Charlotte appeared at once agitated and reluctant to respond, and so for once it was Emily who, following an awkward silence, spoke at last, in her usual direct manner.

'It seems that we'll be advertising soon for our establishment. With you and Anne at Thorp Green, we propose to establish the school at the Parsonage, and have Papa's blessing.'

Papa had already informed me of this scheme, but I was curious to hear it from the lips of my sisters themselves.

'How ever will you *do*, Emily, with strange creatures in the house?' I asked, laughing softly. 'You can scarcely tolerate having your own brother there. Moreover, do you not dislike teaching altogether?'

Emily smiled but hesitated to speak. Charlotte, unamused, spoke for her, as she often does. 'Emily, it is true, does not like teaching much, but she would occupy herself with the housekeeping; I would take responsibility for the instruction as well as the order, economy and organisation essential in a boarding school.'

'Poor Papa,' I responded. 'Sharing his roof with a gaggle of chattering little blockheads in his dotage. And where are Anne and I to sleep when we are home on holiday? In a chair before the fire with our feet up on the fender, next to Keeper and Flossy? In the back kitchen? In the privy? Well, in that case, at least I'll not have far to go when nature calls!'

Charlotte's little face grew red, as she responded sharply, '*You* have hardly concerned yourself with *poor Papa* all these years, have you?' What was this frustration, this controlled fury, simmering just beneath the surface of her every waking minute? It has become far worse since her return from Brussels. What happened there?

Doing my utmost to remain calm, I said, 'I do not know what you mean, sister. I have endeavoured to make my way in the world for more than five years now, and have been afforded neither schooling nor travel.' I paused, then added: 'Nor, for that matter, any inheritance.' These last words were calculated to elicit shame on her part, and perhaps even to silence her, but she would have none of it.

'*Everything* I have done,' said she, eyes now flashing and face a full crimson, 'has been for Papa.' At this, Anne looked down at her hands, whilst Emily watched a pair of linnets hop along a low hedge that lay between us and the Wharfe, as the little birds trilled and twittered with unrestrained joy.

Charlotte soldiered on: 'I left him after Aunt's death, it is true, but I did so because I wanted more instruction in French and German, to be in a superior position to start the school. If it were only to gratify my own desires, I should still be in Brussels.'

She bit her lip and paused, seemingly lost for a moment in reverie, but then continued, looking at each one of us in turn. 'I have not told anyone this yet, but I have just been offered a position as first mistress in a large boarding-school in Manchester, with a salary of 100 pounds.'

Emily started with surprise, while I tried to use this new intelligence to turn the conversation into a more pleasant channel. 'Why Charlotte, that is wonderful news! Surely you will accept, for then all will be gainfully employed' – here Emily glared at me, at which I smiled – 'Yes, yes, *especially* you, Emily, for what you do for Papa is *truly* priceless; what you bring to the household exceeds what you take by a hundredfold!'

Charlotte scowled. 'No, I cannot accept the offer, for in so doing I would have to leave Papa, and that I cannot do. Besides, my weakness of sight makes it nearly impossible to read and write. No … no … it is out of the question. Papa needs me.'

'I see,' said I; there was no point in continuing the conversation, for when Charlotte has made up her mind, there is no gainsaying her. Anne again seemed to be examining something in her lap – perhaps a loose thread in the fabric of her dress, or the lines in the palms of her hands – whilst Emily now gazed at the bank of clouds massing in the eastern sky, for the linnets had flown away.

What all three of us knew, I am quite sure, was this: what Charlotte had just said made no sense whatsover. If Papa needed her *now*, surely he had needed her when she rushed back to Brussels after Aunt's death; if Emily could care for him *then*, she could do so *now*; if her eyesight was *so poor* (I see no evidence of this in her handwriting or her continued daily reading – was she 'going blind' in sympathy with Papa, was she a simple hypochondriac, or worse, an outright liar?), how could the very affliction that prevented her from being first mistress in Manchester permit her to operate and teach in and administer her own school in Haworth?

Anne, ever the conciliator, spoke at last. 'Well, I for one wish you well, for if the school is a great success and you have many young ladies, perhaps I can return home to teach with you, for I am grown weary of Thorp Green and my charges, who – though they have surely become attached to me in their condescending way – do not improve much in their conduct, but instead become more and more impudent and ungovernable. I thank God that young Lydia is no longer under my tuition, though I am still required to follow her about on her rambles, for her mama is so worried she will be accosted by gentlemen beneath her station.'

Charlotte and Emily laughed, for they are ever ready to hear tales of the spoilt Robinson girls, which Anne narrates with all the ease and elegance of a well-written novel, providing her usual mimicry and causing her sisters to laugh until they are short of breath.

I, meanwhile, sat quietly, thinking of *my* Lydia, wondering if I would again be summoned to the boathouse in Scarborough, would again taste ecstasy in her arms, our sighs covered over by the waves crashing upon the midnight sands.

I thought, too, of her young namesake, doubly dangerous as a spy and a flirt, for I had to confess to myself that despite my love for her mother, I did not know if I could resist those pale blue eyes and perfect face and form, those golden ringlets, if she were to make a target of me, to try to shoot *me* through the heart. Already I thought too often of her; how much worse would it be if she tried to beguile me with her charms?

But what madness was this? Why would she try to seduce *me*? Then again, it was the same question I had once asked about her mother – and which was more absurd, that a young lady or her mother would find herself in the arms of a twenty-seven-year-old tutor? Finally, how odd was it, really, that I sat thinking such thoughts, imagining myself alternately in the arms of mother and daughter, while close by my three virgin sisters laughed at their expense. Could a more vivid example be given of the vast chasm that separates our most secret thoughts from our external expression? Or, for that matter, the interior lives of men and women in this century of hypocrites?

'Branwell. *Branwell!*' said Anne, who had finished her anecdote and, with Charlotte and Emily, had gathered up the fragments, knives, dishes, etc., and restored them to our basket. My mind, as I ate, had winged its way fifty miles away, to Thorp Green. What was Lydia doing? Did she think of me? What would happen in Scarborough?

'Branwell,' said Anne, 'shall we walk over to Bolton Bridge? Do you remember what a beautiful spot it is?'

I nodded in assent and turned to speak in a near-whisper to my eldest sister. 'Listen to me, Charlotte: I did not mean to grieve you just now. I know you love Papa and mean to do only good.' I lifted my hat, scratched my head and adjusted my spectacles. 'But you must know that I, too, mean to succeed, to continue to be valued in my position at Thorp Green, to do all that I am able to avoid being a burden upon the family.'

Inexplicably, I felt my eyes begin to fill with tears.

'You must know that I am doing the best that I can, and like a baited animal I lash out when I feel attacked. I never wish to harm you.'

'Come, then, brother,' said Charlotte, her mask of stony indifference cracking slightly under a residue of fraternal love, the collective weight of all of those happy years we spent together as children. 'Let us be friends. Or,' said she, her jaw tightening once again as she regained full control, 'at least let us call a truce until you leave for Scarborough.'

'Yes,' said I, feeling that this was the best I could hope from her, 'let's do just that.'

We walked the half a mile back to the inn and onto the old stone bridge that spans the Wharfe. The water was still high at Midsummer, due to the heavy spring rains, so high that only the great arches rose above its swift but untroubled stream. We stood, we four, at the precise centre of the bridge, silently suspended for a few moments between sky and water, between past and future, the unbearably sweet and transient beauty of life once again urging me to believe fervently in a Creator but also to rise up immediately against Him in rebellion. And why? For withdrawing its delights from us, for making us mortal, for casting us out of Eden – and most of all for taking Mama, Maria and Elizabeth from us.

As I revolved these thoughts through my mind came the words of the Reverend Brontë of my dream: *It is wrong to say that Adam and Eve were simply cast out of Eden; nay, in disobeying God our first parents chose to walk out of the Earthly Paradise he had wrought for them.* I wondered: how would it feel if I were to fall into the water? Would I struggle to remain afloat? Or would I be all too happy to give up the fight, to sink once and for all, like a stone, into the cold, deep currents? Leaning over the rapid stream, I recalled that moment in Hogg's *Confessions,* where Wringham writes of his *insatiable longing for utter oblivion*: 'I desired to sleep; but it was for a deeper and longer sleep, than that in which the senses were nightly steeped. I longed to be at rest and quiet, and close my eyes on the past and the future alike, as far as this frail life was concerned.'

No: it had not come to that, but I knew this feeling, the pull towards nothingness, the desire to blot out everyone and everything – above all my own embittered consciousness. Anne, ever sensitive to the moods of others, drew me out of these lugubrious musings by leaning her head on my shoulder and squeezing my hand.

'Isn't it beautiful here?' said she.

'It is indeed, though are you not eager to regain your beloved Scarborough?'

'I am. But they are entirely different things, are they not? I cherish them both, for one hardly excludes the other. Here nature is in constant transformation: the foliage of the woods and the ebb and flow of the river following the seasons; there, even though the colours of the sea and sky and sands are forever shifting like those of a kaleidoscope, the waves and the cliffs upon which they break sing to me of God's eternal, immutable majesty.'

What could I respond to that? I merely squeezed her hand in return and replied, 'I see what you mean.'

No sooner had I uttered these words than we heard the impact of something striking the water. A young lad had escaped his mother's grasp, clambered onto the bridge, and promptly fallen into the swift current. She shrieked with horror at the sight of her little one's hat floating quickly away, his own head sinking beneath the water. Without a thought, I was out of my coat and hat, and had leapt into the water after him. I was able to reach the boy and drag him unceremoniously to the grassy riverbank, where his mother and my sisters soon joined us. I restored the lad, who was now sobbing unrestrainedly, to his mama, whose cries of terror were changed to tears of joy, alternating with bouts of vigorous scolding for her son's naughty behaviour. His straw hat floated away into the distance.

Rarely have I been thankful to sit in the sun at the hottest hour of a summer day, but yesterday I was delighted, for my clothes were nearly dry by the time we reached Haworth. My boots, however, are quite likely ruined.

Nearly half an hour has elapsed since I wrote the previous line; all this while, I have been seeking the right words to describe how I felt as I leapt from the bridge, into the water, and swam to clutch the young boy and tug him to the shore. I can find no words, except to say that only an animal instinct caused me to do so, divorced from all prior knowledge or the workings of reason, from all consideration of the advantages and disadvantages of doing so – or indeed, of not doing so. Afterwards what I felt was not great joy at the lad's salvation (though I am truly glad he did not meet a watery demise), nor exultation at my own heroism (though the mother and my own sisters, including Charlotte, showered me with praise), but a strange serenity unlike anything I have ever felt.

Peace, true peace. That is all. I do not comprehend it.

July 29th, 1844 · Scarborough

Before arriving here, Anne and I 'enjoyed' the visit of Ellen Nussey at the Parsonage in our final week at Haworth. Charlotte somehow felt it important that her *dearest Nell* see all of us, as if we cared as much to see Ellen as she did; or as if Ellen cared as much to see us as she did Charlotte. With each day, as the moment of our departure grew closer, I became more impatient to *be gone*. Sitting with the young ladies, or accompanying them on their rambles on the moors, to Ponden Hall, Oxenhope and Bradford, I struggled – in vain, I fear – to keep my own mounting passions, my yearning to be gone, my desire both to be with Lydia and yet to avoid discovery, concealed beneath a mask of gaiety. I fear that my conduct has been erratic – *sometimes in the highest spirits*, laughing and talking rapidly, quoting poetry as in days of yore, entertaining Ellen and my sisters; sometimes in the deepest depression, fearing that Lydia has abandoned me, or that we will be discovered. Sometimes, indeed, I even accuse myself of the blackest treachery and guilt, though such thoughts of culpability are rapidly crushed. Has not Lydia suffered at her husband's hands? Is not our love divine, and the narrow notion of adultery a mere conventional impediment?

Whether 'guilty' in man's eyes or not, who has not at least once in his life been driven to near madness by the necessity of concealing a dark secret? In such a situation, what requires more effort than simply to comport oneself as if all were normal? As Anne and I waved farewell to our friends as our coach departed Keighley, I felt mingled relief and apprehension. At least I was now withdrawn from the ever-watchful, ever-critical gaze of Charlotte, and from the fading eyesight of Papa, whom I can scarcely now bare to confront. Is it that I feel true guilt, or is it my knowledge of what he would think if he knew of my proceedings that discomfits me so?

None of this matters, I confess, when I am in Lydia's arms. She has again summoned me to the boathouse beneath Woods' Lodgings at The Cliff; how sweet is love after such an absence! 'You still love me, then?' I said on the first night we met, Mrs Marshall standing guard outside the bolted door. 'It has been a lifetime since we have been together.'

'Foolish puppy,' said she, 'it has been just two short months, and a good portion of that *you* left *me* to enjoy the good and pious people of home. I'm sure you gave me precious little thought amidst such moral rectitude.'

So overwrought had I been at the twin thoughts of at last seeing her and yet being discovered, that I had drunk two large glasses of whisky in short succession not long before arriving: just enough to loosen my tongue and to remove all fear of man and God. The spirits had further inflamed my desire, and I drew her close, my entire being, within and without, hardening with lust.

'I don't give a *damn* about the good people of home. They would not understand this, my love.'

Our practised hands found and caressed each other's bodies, and soon we were moving together in perfect rhythm: at first with an almost unbearably delicious languor, she above me, the motion of her hips bringing me to near-ecstasy as she bent down to whisper, 'No, the good people of home would not understand this … or this … or this …' – each *this* corresponding to the moment at which she took my full length entirely into herself – 'no, they would say that I am an *utterly wicked* woman, I'm quite sure of that.'

'I don't care what they would say,' was all I could manage. 'I don't care what *anyone* would say. I love you!'

Lydia answered only with her body, and as the moments passed, time marked only by the crashing waves, we moved with increasing rapidity, until at last we expired in each other's arms.

This was the night we arrived, and I have seen her several times since.

X.

Enter Mr Roxby

August 4th, 1844 · Scarborough

Two days ago, Anne and I were offered the rare treat of accompanying the young ladies to the Theatre Royal, just a short walk from our lodgings, to see Shakespeare's *Richard II*. I sat just behind my sister, who was next to Miss Robinson and her younger sisters. My pupil Edmund had been spared the performance, which would doubtless have bored him senseless. How different are we all, one from another! I would have walked ten miles to attend such a performance at his age. As for his parents, they were nowhere to be seen; Anne was to be the young ladies' chaperone for the evening, as she so often is. Two weeks ago, we attended a concert at the Town Hall, whose quality far surpassed anything poor Frobisher can seem to arrange in Halifax – except for the famous Liszt, of course. Ah, what the seaside and the rich together are able to draw in their wake, even in such a small place as this!

The theatre is owned and operated by the famous acting family, the Roxbys. Before the play began it was announced that this Saturday there will be what they call a 'fashionable night', with a performance by the celebrated comedian, Robert Roxby himself. I thought it unlikely that we would attend, for the Robinsons are giving a party of sorts that very night, a sort of summer echo of Lydia's coming-out ball the previous January, another chance to show her off – to market her wares, as it were – but to a larger, more diverse crowd. The spacious rooms at The Cliff would more than accommodate a small but well-chosen portion of the *beau monde* spending the summer at

Scarborough, and yet the family can use the excuse of not being at Thorp Green to exclude whomsoever they choose. The essential, of course, will be to invite the largest possible number of wealthy, unattached men.

But as the curtain rose and the King began to speak, all such considerations melted away, the magical incantation of Shakespeare's language more powerful than any sorcerer's spell. For cannot everyone find in his characters not just a mirror of the world, but of himself? In the presence of such genius, how can the aspiring poet be anything but overwhelmed, nay, defeated – routed before he even bends to scratch his first word on the page?

I leant back in my chair, closed my eyes, and throughout the performance let the waves of the bard's genius tumble over me. As always, I seized particularly on those verses that most closely shadowed my own thoughts:

> Woe, destruction, ruin, and decay; the worst is death
> and death will have his day.

Or:

> Let's talk of graves, of worms, and epitaphs;
> Make dust our paper and with rainy eyes
> Write sorrow on the bosom of the earth

Clearly none of these sorrowful subjects occupied the minds of the Misses Robinson, and I was roused from my dreary thoughts by incongruous whispers and giggles. Anne had leant over to silence her charges but was having difficulty persuading them to hold their tongues. Lydia, it seems, was particularly taken with the appearance, in the second scene of Act III, of one of the young actors – a tall, well-built young gentleman with hair as black as hers was fair, eyes as dark as hers were pale, but sharing her fair skin and brilliant smile. Though he merely played the role of Sir Stephen Scroop, he seemed to have captured more than one young lady's heart in the audience.

On the short walk home, I could hear Lydia chattering to Anne and her sisters about the young actor, who appeared to have shot her through the heart.

This Sunday afternoon, I was on holiday from my duties. A steady rain fell without respite and, other than to attend to my corporeal needs, I had yet to quit my room at Wood's Lodgings: there would be no divine offices for me. From my windows I could gaze out beyond the sands, where the low clouds, persistent rain, and steely sea shaded imperceptibly into one another, as in a sketch of charcoal. To the right, no one traversed the Spa Bridge; to the left, scarcely visible beyond the South Sands and harbour, rose the old church – Saint Mary's – and above it the Castle, high on its headland. I was just beginning to doze over a volume of verse when I heard a gentle tapping at the door.

It was Anne, a wet umbrella in her hand, a few stray drops of rain clinging to her bonnet and shoulders. The family had just been to services at Christ Church, and Mrs Robinson had released her for the day, to *do as she pleased.* Once she had made herself comfortable opposite me, she said, 'Oh Branwell, I cannot possibly share this with anyone but you. Indeed, I almost feel as though I am guilty of gossiping. But is it gossip to confide the truth to one's own brother? I promise not to slander, but I *must* share this with someone – and I should like your advice on how to proceed.'

My curiosity was instantly aroused. At first I suffered an instant of dread, fearful that Anne had somehow discovered my proceedings with our mistress, but quickly realised that I would be the last person from whom she would seek counsel if that were the case.

'Of course, Anne, of course. And *no,* it is not gossip to confide in me – would you not do the same if Emily were here in my place? Yes, I thought so. And if you speak only truth, and wish to know my thoughts, how can this be wrong? Finally, even if I were a lying rogue, and wished to tell the world this secret, whatever it is, I am no fool: why would I risk my position, or yours?'

I spoke calmly, though I was impatient to know what she had come to tell me. 'Tell me your story,' said I, leaning back comfortably into my chair, hands locked behind my head, as if to be entertained.

'Well,' she began, 'I am sure the young ladies' fascination with a certain actor on Thursday night did not escape you.' I nodded. 'Imagine that the very next day, in my discreet, matronly role as chaperone, I was accompanying Miss Lydia across the bridge. What a lovely day Friday was, Branwell! What spectacular views, what quickening sea breezes that day!'

'I know you love this place, Anne,' I laughed, 'but what of your tale?'

'Oh, yes, forgive me. Now then, as we glided across the footbridge, whom should we meet but this very young man, the fascinating actor from the Theatre Royal!'

'Well, that's hardly a marvellous coincidence,' said I, laughing again. 'Scarborough is so small, and if you exclude all the servants and merchants and other common folk, as well as all those not wishing to pay to cross that fashionable bridge, you will see that only a handful of people could be crossing it.'

'Still, his appearance there was seen as marvellous by Miss Robinson. Though I cannot prove it, and she heatedly denies it, I am quite certain that she feigned stumbling just as the young man arrived, fairly falling into his arms. She apologised profusely, but had gained her two goals, his attention and his name: Henry Roxby.'

'Well now, this is interesting. Do you mean to say that he owns the Theatre Royal?'

'It's a family concern.'

'And the celebrated comedian who was to perform last night? *Robert* Roxby?'

The Robinsons had been occupied with their grand soirée, so did not attend the 'Fashionable Night' advertised, and I was not about to devote any of my own meagre funds to this purpose.

'The young man's uncle, I believe.'

'Ah yes. They are very much the thespian dynasty, or so I have read in the newspapers. But on with your tale, if you please, Miss Brontë.'

'Well, there we stood on the bridge, frozen for an instant, as the two young people seemed to play the lovers in a melodrama or a popular novel, struck by a *coup de foudre*. I must confess that there was something gratifying in seeing Miss Robinson – who always takes great pleasure in ensnaring men's affections at will, while she remains coldly aloof, torturing them for her pleasure, like a little boy roasting birds alive for sport – in seeing her at the other end of Cupid's arrow. Do you know that she has claimed on more than one occasion that she would never be so foolish as to fall in *love*, pronouncing the very word with disgust? So yes, I confess that I even smiled to myself to see her fall helplessly under the spell of *Eros*.'

'I fear you draw perilously near the Cliffs of Calumny,' said I, smiling, 'or the Sands of Censure … say, why did not the great Bunyan include these in his *Pilgrim's Progress*? What a shame! In any event, I believe you wished to adhere strictly to the facts, did you not?'

Anne laughed softly, no doubt amused by the thought of her Godless brother, lecturing her on morality. If possible, she sat even more erect, as if obeying a command.

'Yes, sir. So, there we found ourselves suspended between earth and sky, cliff and sands, the sparkling waves of the sea stretching as far as the eye could see, Miss Robinson's flaxen ringlets and the flaps of her bonnet tossed merrily by the sea breeze, her dazzling eyes fascinated by the black orbs of the tall and dashing Mr Roxby. The young people introduced themselves whilst I – great nobody that I am – stood awkwardly by.'

Here Anne paused for a moment, gazing out at the various shades of grey.

'You know, brother, that I believe it is foolish to wish for beauty, and that sensible people never either desire it for themselves or care about it in others. So Papa has wisely taught us, I know, but I must confess that the two made an extraordinarily handsome pair. After the requisite introductions, it was discovered that Mr Roxby and his family were also staying at The Cliff …'

'Ah, you see,' I interjected, 'the orbit of the *beau monde* in this town is so circumscribed that even that is hardly a coincidence.'

Anne continued, only slightly irritated by my impertinence.

'Patience, Branwell, I'm just getting to the crucial part of the story. The two elegant young people stood facing each other, suspended above all the world, transfixed each by the other; Miss Robinson was speechless, it seemed, and blushed a lovely rose colour, two phenomena I had hitherto never experienced in her presence.'

'What a lovely picture you paint, Anne.'

Now my sister *was* beginning to be more than a trifle annoyed.

'Very well, I shall hold my tongue for the rest of your tale,' I said, still smiling and leaning back once again in my armchair.

My sister is an excellent narrator, and so I shall record the remainder of the tale in her own voice. As she is wont to do at home in Haworth, Anne leant back and put her feet up on the fender, folded her hands in her lap, and continued.

XI.

Anne's Tale

At last, Mr Roxby, who, I would suspect, is quite accustomed to having this effect on the weaker sex, spoke.

'Miss Robinson,' said he, in a deep baritone. 'I wonder if you and your family would care to be my guests at tomorrow night's performance at the Royal?'

'Why yes – *yes*!'

I stepped forward to speak in her ear, which gesture drew a look of confusion – though, I must say, it was not an unkind expression – from the young gentleman.

'Miss, have you forgotten the soirée your mama has planned for you?' I whispered urgently.

Had we been alone, I believe she would have stamped her elegantly booted little foot with dismay. Instead, she bit down hard on her lower lip and knitted her brows. It was, however, no more than two or three seconds before she had formed a plan.

'Mr Roxby, I regret that we cannot attend. You see, Mama has arranged for something of a soirée tomorrow – like the ball we gave in January on our estate, but of course much smaller – to introduce me to society.' She bit her lip again, this time not in anger, but coyly, smiling in triumph.

'The question then becomes,' said she, 'whether you might be able to attend *our* soirée – after the performance, of course. Surely you might honour us with your presence for a few brief moments? Even if you and your esteemed uncle are fatigued, you are lodged at The Cliff after all, so you will be just steps from bed.'

No sooner had she said this last word than she grasped her error, and blushed a bright crimson. The handsome young actor's face broadened into a smile that I found altogether too direct. He bowed.

'I may only be,' said he, still grinning, 'a humble thespian, but I know not to present myself at such an event without a proper invitation from your parents. I might well be dragged out and shot, or cast headfirst from this bridge, or from yonder headland,' said he, nodding in the direction of the castle high on its jutting promontory.

'Sir,' said my charge, parting her lips in an inviting smile, her bright teeth brilliant in the midday sun, her laughing eyes catching and magnifying the sea and sky, 'I will see to it that you receive a proper, *written* invitation, have no fear.'

At this, the young man bowed deeply and continued on his way. It was only with great effort that I refrained from clutching at Lydia's sleeve, so agitated was I at what had just transpired.

'Surely, Miss, you do not think that your mother will approve of your taking it upon yourself to issue such an invitation to a complete stranger … and an *actor* no less. You know how she feels about keeping clear of anyone whom she has not, herself, approved!'

I can confess to you, Branwell, a far less noble reason for my apprehension: I was – am still, sometimes – worried that her dear mama will fix the blame wholly on me, and will tell me that if I cannot control her daughters then I must seek another situation. Although I have often chafed under the yoke of this position, I would prefer to leave of my own volition, and amicably. But let me continue.

Lydia turned to me, spinning her parasol defiantly, the eyes that had just made love to young Roxby now flashing defiantly, as hard and brilliant as sapphires. 'Oh, Mama's so tiresome! As if I couldn't take care of myself! Besides, I never forget my rank and station. All she thinks about is grubbing after money. But see here, Miss Brontë, did you not remark how elegantly he was dressed? Does his family not *own* the Royal, as well as theatres in Manchester and elsewhere? Are not his father and uncle amongst the most celebrated actors of the London stage? He must be *fabulously* rich.'

'I see, Miss, that there will be no arguing with you on this matter.'

Nor was there, either, with her mama or her papa, for they did not even hear of this until it was too late. Upon our return to our lodgings, she contrived – how, I know not – to have Mrs Marshall dispatch an invitation to Mr Roxby and his celebrated uncle, quite without her parents' knowledge. Why Marshall would agree to this, and put herself at risk of dismissal, is a profound mystery to me. All I could observe, from my distance, was an unusually animated conversation that seemed to end with the faithful servant's acquiescence.

The next evening was the grand soirée. I had no intention of appearing at such a gathering, but Mr Robinson was insistent that the younger girls come, accompanied by their governess. He put a brave face on his illness, dressed handsomely for the occasion, and did his best to move about the company, though he soon enough betook himself to bed.

The drawing room was full of distinguished ladies and gentlemen, chosen either for their relation to the Robinsons, or their potential to become relations. Our mistress was in her glory, arrayed in a dazzling blue silk gown with wide flounces to her elbows, a sheer shawl and long gloves, and gliding about to ensure that everyone had refreshments. From time to time I could hear her loud, vague, affected sigh of recognition – 'Ahhhh!' However, once she had made her rounds, she spent the largest part of her time with her cousin, Lady Catherine Scott, who is quite frail and ill, and that lady's wealthy husband, Sir Edward, a lively older gentleman, quite tall and handsome, with the broad shoulders and erect carriage of a military man, though I later learned that he is no such thing. He was dressed in a dark tailcoat and trousers of rich fabric, and his large side whiskers and sweptback hair were remarkably dark for his age – so dark that I wondered whether he had dyed them! From where I sat with the young ladies, I could overhear some of their conversation, and – yes, I know I am wicked, Branwell – could not keep myself from listening. What was I to do, after all, clap my hands over my ears?

Lady Scott squeezed her cousin's hand and said, 'Lydia, I *do* hope that you will come to us at Great Barr Hall soon. My Edward and I would like nothing better.'

That distinguished gentleman simply bowed his head slightly and said, 'It would be our pleasure, ma'am.'

Mrs Robinson looked up at her cousin's handsome husband with – was I imagining it? – the same inviting smile, the same full, parted lips and bright eyes that her namesake had revealed to Roxby the day before on the footbridge. Is it any wonder, thought I, that her girls are such giddy, incorrigible flirts? With such an example as this in their own *mother*, they hardly need novels to corrupt them!

It was about this time that the doors opened, and the Messrs Roxby – uncle and nephew – were introduced. I heard several muffled gasps from the ladies in attendance, as Mrs Robinson rose to greet the gentlemen, concealing her confusion with a veneer of exquisite grace and the full powers of her charms. It certainly helped that the name of 'Roxby' is known throughout the land, and that these two were impeccably dressed, handsome and genteel-looking specimens of the stronger sex.

Soon her daughter had glided across the room to greet the visitors she had invited, and it was immediately clear to all that Henry Roxby was already acquainted with her. I trembled, fearing that the blame for the initial encounter, as well as the invitation, would be laid squarely upon *me*, for how often has our mistress shifted it from where it belongs – viz., her daughters, or herself – to me, as if a governess could govern all things. Besides, she is *out* in society, so should her conduct really be my responsibility?

But yes, Branwell, I am aware that I digress. There followed a great deal of murmuring, after which the musicians struck up a waltz and some of the party began to dance. In the far corner of the vast salon I could see a red-faced Mrs Robinson, now free to speak her mind, interrogating Lydia. The young lady later revealed to me what was said.

'Yes, Miss Brontë,' said she, after the Roxbys had departed, 'I suppose you may gloat all you please. You were quite right in your estimation, that Mama would not take kindly to my issuing an invitation to a stranger – and an actor no less.' Then her pretty face grew mischievous, as she added, 'But I knew Mama would never make a scene in such a situation, and, was not Roxby simply *divine*? Besides,' she concluded, setting her jaw with determination, 'I *will* have my way.'

She did indeed have her way, for she had danced with Roxby not once, not twice, but three times, and I confess that no author or painter ever conceived a lovelier young couple. Meanwhile, her mama returned to her conversation with Sir Edward and Lady Catherine. As the evening drew to a close and the guests began to take their leave, I felt my time had come to slip away, with the pretext of escorting Bessy and Mary off to bed. Instead, I was arrested near the door by Mrs Robinson, who, liberated of all of her guests, now glowered unrestrainedly.

'Miss Brontë,' said she, her voice quavering with controlled fury, 'I would like a word, please. Such great girls as Bessy and Mary hardly need you as a nursemaid. Run along, girls.' She turned to me, her eyes flashing now with indignation.

'Miss Brontë, I do not know *how* these people came to be invited, but I understand that you and Lydia saw him on the bridge yesterday, is that true?'

'Yes, ma'am.' Was I to say, Branwell, that her daughter had fairly thrown herself into young Roxby's arms?

'And you did *nothing* to prevent her from inviting him, without my knowledge?'

You know, brother, that I swallow my pride a great deal, but that I cannot abide an unjust accusation; I *must* speak out in my own defence. I could feel that my cheeks burned and my hands trembled with emotion, while I protested that I had, indeed, used all means at my disposal to try and dissuade Miss Robinson from inviting the Roxbys, and that my opposition had been routed at every turn.

At last, the good lady relented a bit, for if there is one thing she knows, I do not lie. Indeed, I think she might well like me far better if I were not so truthful. Of course, this is the eternal dilemma of the governess, is it not, Branwell? I am told to *gently remind* the young ladies of this, that or the other thing, which of course has no effect on such giddy, headstrong things. On the other hand, if I were to be firmer with them, I would be treated as a waspish tyrant, a modern-day harpy, and sent packing back to Haworth directly.

In any event, Mrs Robinson softened just a bit, from wrath to mere dismay.

'Do, pray, Miss Brontë,' said she, 'try not to be so touchy! There's no speaking to you. The truth of the matter is that I do not know how I can possibly keep this from her papa, who would be extremely angry if he knew of her treating this young *actor*' – she seemed to shudder at the word itself – 'in such a familiar manner. But I will endeavour to conceal it, for it is often better to conceal what would grieve him in his state. *I* shall deal with Lydia, for I can no longer leave such things to *you*. Oh! – if you – if *any* governess had but half a mother's watchfulness – half a mother's anxious care, I should be saved this trouble.'

Anne paused in her narration to sneeze, whereupon I asked, 'Is that the entire tale?'

'No, not quite,' she responded. 'Once our mistress had finished admonishing me, I went off to bed. No sooner had I lain down than I heard a soft rapping at my door. It was Miss Robinson.'

'Now Miss Brontë,' said she, 'you must tell me everything Mama said. I spied you two deep in conversation just now.'

'I'm dreadfully tired,' said I, 'and do you not think you should ask your *mama* yourself? I don't see how it is my duty to serve as an ambassador between the two of you.'

Lydia, despite her difference in her height and colouring, was now the very picture of her mother, as she responded, 'Goodness, Miss Brontë, do try not to be so sensitive. You *know* I can't speak to her as I can to *you*.'

Because I am closer in age, thought I, or because I am a glorified domestic? But I said nothing. Not that she paused long enough for me to speak, mind you.

'What did she think of Mr Roxby and his illustrious uncle?'

'Again, I would suggest that you speak to her about such concerns.'

'Oh! You exasperate me so! Surely you can tell me *something*?'

'Your mama,' said I, weighing my words carefully, for I had no desire to see them turned against me in future, 'said nothing about the gentlemen, except that she feels that I should have prevented you from inviting Mr Roxby and his celebrated relative.'

'I hope,' replied Miss Robinson, 'that you did not mention Marshall.'

'No, but if she had asked me, I would have told her, for I refuse to traffic in such deception.'

As I said, Branwell, Marshall's role in all this was – and partly remains – a mystery to me. Why did she agree to send the invitations, knowing all too well that by so doing she would anger her employer? Further, why does the daughter wish to keep the mother ignorant of all this?

Lydia continued chattering, seemingly indifferent to my comment. 'Well, in all events, Marshall is one of those domestic creatures who can *do no wrong*. She began as our nurse, you know, and is more family than servant at this point. Mama would find a way to forgive her, I know that.' She paused and said, ominously, 'And who *knows* what she has witnessed? She would not be the first lady's maid to have a lifetime of secrets locked away in her breast.'

At last, she rose from the edge of my bed and skipped away to the door, where she turned to whisper, 'I *will* have my way, Miss Brontë, I *will*. Listen: we *must* go to the divine office tomorrow morning – rain or shine – for Roxby has promised to be there! And you cannot tell Mama.'

And so he was, Branwell. Mr Robinson was ill, and his wife too exhausted from last night's proceedings to attend, and thus Mrs Marshall and I escorted the children to Christ Church beneath umbrellas. We were there early, and when Mr Roxby arrived he positioned himself directly opposite us. Throughout the service Lydia's eyes locked with his, and every few moments she sighed. I am quite certain that neither she nor Roxby heard a word the parson spoke, from the acclamation to the final blessing.

Anne removed her feet from the fender and, now sitting erect and smoothing her dress, concluded, 'That, dear brother, is the entire tale, from start to finish. Who knows what will come of Lydia's mischief? I would never have believed it possible, but this year I am positively *thrilled* to be leaving Scarborough in a few days, if only to remove that young lady from temptation.'

'You asked,' said I, 'for my counsel. What is it you want to know?'

'What I wish to know is quite simple: do I reveal all, including Marshall's role in the events, to my employers, or only answer when questioned? You know I will not lie, but is it right – as Mrs Robinson herself claims – to *conceal certain things*, things that might only grieve others?'

Anne's narrative had elicited, in rapid succession, so many emotions in me that I knew not what to think: trepidation, suspense, amusement and dread. Dread because, despite the lack of any evidence thereof, I had a vague suspicion that Marshall's inexplicable conduct was somehow, at least in part, connected to *me*. I breathed deeply and sought to perform a kind of disinterested calm.

'I say follow your heart, Anne, for it seems always to know what is just. But if I were in your place, I think I would keep entirely out of these affairs, unless of course you see something truly shocking, truly immoral, at which point you will be between the proverbial rock and hard place, for you will likely have to hand in your notice at the same moment you denounce the miscreants.'

Anne frowned. 'Do you know, Branwell, that I have wished myself gone from Thorp Green almost from the beginning – that's more than four years ago! Each time I prepared to leave, Mrs Robinson convinced me that I was *so valued* in my position, and the young ladies *so attached* to me, that it was out of the question. And yet, as you see, when her humour or circumstances dictate it, she is perfectly comfortable treating me with all the respect she would give to a kitchen-girl or farm hand.'

'Well, as you say, such is the plight of the governess – or the tutor, for that matter.'

My sister merely sighed and looked out to sea, where the dark skies grew blacker still in the gloaming, where the rain fell even harder upon the sands and the waves beyond. At length she coughed, and rose to collect her outer-garments, bonnet and umbrella.

'Good-night, brother,' she said, kissing me on the cheek.

Whence, I wondered as I watched her move down the great corridor towards her room, does such strength come? And such goodness! Why do I feel that any traces of those two qualities are, and forever will be, utterly alien to *me*?

XII.

Love and Treachery at Scarborough Castle

August 14th, 1844 · Scarborough

Tomorrow we leave for Thorp Green, and like Anne, I am eager to depart Scarborough. So much has unsettled me here that I can only hope that a period of calm and regularity will resume once the family has returned to its home and we all assume our customary routine. Since the advent of Miss Robinson's *grande passion* for Mr Roxby, I have been thoroughly cut off from her mother, and after hearing Anne's alarming tale I can do nothing but fulfil my duties instructing Edmund; though I ache to be in Lydia's arms, I am almost relieved to be severed from her, so much do I tremble at the thought of some kind of discovery. As I discovered several days after Anne told me her story, such worries were not unwarranted.

One glorious afternoon, after Edmund had finished his lessons, I determined upon a walk to the old church and the castle. Anne was feeling poorly and so I struck out alone, knowing how much she would have enjoyed the lovely breezes, the sun glancing across the waves, the quiet little churchyard perched high above the harbour, the boundless main beyond, and high above it all, the melancholy castle ruins, overgrown with a green riot of vegetation.

I paused to walk the churchyard and said a godless prayer for the unknown sleepers in that quiet earth. Within me arose that old, inexpressible emotion I have so often felt: joy and wonder at being alive, mingled with the deepest sadness, a *mourning*, really, for the brevity of this life.

I followed the familiar Castle Road up to the ruins, and there climbed a wall for a view of both the South and North Bays, and to the east, the vast expanse of the sea, while to the west the ancient town lay at my feet, and far beyond it, mile upon mile of rugged hill and forest, of occasional valleys, across the breadth of England. It occurred to me that at almost precisely this latitude, on the far side of our island kingdom, lay Broughton-in-Furness. How long since I had thought of Broughton, of my six months there, of the joy I found in the arms of Agnes Riley. Agnes! What has become of you? Do you still think of me? Are you quite real? Was it all merely a dream? I thought of our first time together, thrown together, of how she made me feel. Had I given her half the ecstasy she had bestowed upon me? If I had the power of flight, I thought, stretching the front panels of my coat out into the constant ocean breeze, would I wing my way across the country to ask her? Or was I afraid to know the answer? She had called me a *good man*: a sign of her ignorance of the world, no doubt.

As these musings coursed through my mind, I fell into a trance-like state as deep as any dream, and was soon barely conscious of the wind whipping through my hair or the sun warming my brow as I clutched my hat in my hand and gazed to the west.

I was finally roused from my reverie by a laugh from below, where an elegant young couple strolled about, whilst a more matronly figure appeared to survey them from a distance. As the young man and woman walked in my direction, along the base of the ramparts, I heard sweet ringing tones come from beneath the twirling parasol, and a deep, mirthful voice respond from under a broad straw hat: they had halted just beneath me and turned towards each other. The parasol's gyrations had ceased, and I could scarcely see the young man's hat, for he seemed to lean under the lady's protection from the sun, which now served to shield them both from my gaze. I could hear them speak, but the wind and sea prevented me from grasping anything more than an occasional word.

Soon they were once again moving along the base of the wall, as I matched their steps high above. Why did I follow them? I wish I knew – and wish I had not done so. When they paused again to talk, I also stopped and, for a mere instant, set down my hat so that I could sit comfortably, in hopes of overhearing them, for the height of the ruined wall on which I stood had decreased, and I was now much closer to them. At precisely this moment – alas! – a great gust of wind seized my hat and carried it far over the heads of the young couple in question, landing and then rolling on its brim towards the cliff. My reaction was as involuntary as it was instantaneous: I cried out, stretching my hands towards the lost item. I immediately sensed my error, and stooped down to avoid being detected, but it was too late.

My blood ran cold as I fully heard, and recognised, the voice of the young woman, whose dulcet tones were promptly replaced by the shrill cries of a termagant. It was none other than Miss Lydia Mary Robinson. The gentleman, who had already beaten a hasty retreat, was of course Mr Henry Roxby.

'Come down here, *this instant*, I say. Mr Brontë, I insist that you come down *directly*!'

Soon I had clambered down, and stood before the young lady, who, still a picture of perfect beauty despite her wrath, was rapidly spinning her parasol in great agitation, her eyes flashing with indignation.

'Have you been listening all this while, Mr Brontë – spying on me? What cause would you possibly have to do so? Do you not have enough of your own mischief to occupy you?'

At first at a loss for words, I finally stammered, 'I … I … was just out for a stroll, you see. I could not have known that you would be here … with … that gentleman.'

At this moment, Mrs Marshall – for she, of course, was the woman I had glimpsed from afar – walked up, my hat in her hand. Passing it to me, she dared to intervene.

'Now Miss, I'm sure it's merely by chance that Mr Brontë is here – 'e and 'is sister, you know, are quite fond of such rambles.' She looked at me meaningfully, adding, 'I'm quite certain that 'e's the soul o' discretion, and that your secret's safe with 'im.'

This speech only vexed Lydia more, and she stamped her right foot like a little girl.

'Hush! Don't take his part, Marshall. And even if what you say is true, and he is merely an involuntary spy, what's done is done, and I must make certain that he will never speak of it to Mama and Papa. Now wait for me at the top of the road, for I wish to speak to Mr Brontë *alone*.'

Mrs Marshall bowed stiffly and retreated, whilst the young lady turned and gazed out to sea, saying nothing. Once we were quite alone – now with heightened suspicion, she turned and surveyed even the castle ruins to be sure of it – Miss Robinson gazed directly at me, her visage such a curious amalgam of beauty and fury that I knew not whether I could even respond to what she was about to say.

'I don't know what your sister has told you – for though she is a faithful confidant and as pious as a nun, blood is forever thicker than water, no matter what people claim – but that gentleman was Mr Henry Roxby. You may remember him from the Theatre Royal?'

'Yes, he did seem familiar.'

'See here, Mr Brontë, all proper ladies and gentlemen know more than they reveal. This is called *discretion*, the mortar that holds society together. I, for example – though I have no unassailable proof – believe that you and Mama have carried on an illicit *affaire de coeur* – no, don't interrupt me – almost since you arrived at Thorp Green. How do I know, you ask? First, I can see it in your faces, how you positively glow with pleasure when you are brought into each other's proximity – though Mama has become much better of late – perhaps it is over and finished? – although that matters not to *me*. Second, I am no fool – when Marshall has shepherded us all to York for the day, or stood guard at the door of your lodgings, or accompanied Mama down to the boathouse at midnight –'

I felt the blood drain from my face.

'Ah ha! Your face again tells me the truth! You see, I am just as capable a spy as you, Mr Brontë.'

At last, knowing I could speak the truth – almost – and defend myself on at least one point, I responded, 'You should know that I was not spying on you, Miss Robinson. I was merely rambling about, and enjoying the view from high above, on the ramparts, as I always do.'

Perhaps because she believed that my countenance had revealed what she had long suspected, Lydia's face, and indeed her entire being, seemed to become less anxious, her muscles relaxing like those of a predator who has successfully seized and killed his prey, and now can tranquilly enjoy the feast. At last she smiled, a Fury transformed into cunning vixen. The revolutions of the parasol, which had slowed and stopped as she spoke, now began again, but this time with a jaunty, almost flirtatious movement – an artful accompaniment to her glancing eyes and flawless smile.

'Yes, so you say – and even Marshall there' – here she tossed her head disdainfully in the direction of the Castle Road – 'has sprung to your defence. Curious, don't you think, that Marshall would appear to risk her very employment and future prospects by so bluntly disputing the statements of her young mistress? Don't you wonder why?'

I said nothing but assumed that an explanation was forthcoming.

'I am aware,' she continued, 'that now that I am *out* in society, my orbit is more controlled than ever, my every movement observed. Mama wishes me to marry some wealthy booby or disgusting old man for money, and to be as miserable as she has been. Indeed, society dictates that I should not even be seen speaking alone to *you*, Mr Brontë, unless to give you orders in your capacity as a domestic.'

She surveyed me from head to toe, and exhaled rapidly through her nostrils, snorting like her sister Bessy's prize mare. She was thoroughly unimpressed – I was no Henry Roxby, that was for certain.

Lydia's eyes narrowed as she put her arm unexpectedly through mine and directed us towards the cliff, the ocean looming beyond the sands of the North Bay. At the foot of the escarpment, a flock of noisy seagulls battled over something that had washed ashore.

'I can see,' said she, glancing slyly at me as we walked along the edge, 'that you might be suitable for a desperate, love-starved older woman like Mama. Like your sister, you are not *unpleasant* to look at, though you certainly have no particularly laudable attributes, either. I suppose what I mean to say is this: no one would suspect *me* of making love to you, and should anyone observe us in this unusual and never-to-be repeated situation, we will say that I grew faint, and that you did what any gentleman – yes, even a lowly *tutor* – would do, and conveyed me back to Mrs Marshall.'

The young lady could not have contrived to rouse in me a more frustrated, bitter form of indignation if she had tried, her mocking, if bewitching, eyes and sarcastic, curled lip surpassed only in eliciting my irritation by her infuriating insistence on the word *tutor*. My thoughts continued, it seemed, to be written plainly across my face.

'Now, now, Mr Brontë, don't be so touchy! This is simply the way of the world, you know.' She paused for a moment, now biting her lip, and adding, 'It's that same order of things that would keep *me* from seeing Mr Roxby, which brings us back to my subject. Let me lay things out before you, and let us see if you perceive matters as I do, shall we?'

I said nothing, feeling once again the mingled emotions of fear, anger and confusion – and most of all a powerful desire to remove myself from Lydia's presence. I tried to remove my arm from hers, but she would have none of it. 'No no, Mr Brontë, absolutely not, you *will* hear me out,' said she, tugging my arm and fairly gritting her teeth. 'This is how I view the current state of affairs: I wish to continue to see Mr Roxby if I can contrive to do so, and he has vowed to write to me at Thorp Green – and Marshall has promised to help us.'

As we neared the cliff, she at last released me and turned so that we faced each other. I must again have revealed my thoughts, this time puzzlement – perhaps I was too much in shock to have tried to conceal them – for Lydia paused and examined my face briefly, and finally added, 'I see that further explanation is needed. Marshall, understand, is the key that unlocks the entire mystery; you may think her an obedient cipher, but in her quiet way she sees and controls all. Surely she is not the first lady's maid to hold such power, hmm? She knows enough about Papa's conduct of yore – don't seem shocked, Mr Brontë, I am sure Mama has told you, and I have put together the pieces of *that* unseemly puzzle over the years – enough to sow discord in the family and sully his reputation; she has witnessed Mama's proceedings with you sufficiently that if she were to divulge them, Papa would cast off his wife without a shilling; and now I, too, am in Marshall's thrall, for she could likewise destroy *me*. In short, we are *all* dependent upon her discretion, and could all be damaged if the good woman so desired.'

'But,' I said at last, 'why do you permit this to continue? Why have your parents not given Marshall her notice long ago? Surely she would need letters of introduction, would she not? Do you thus not have something to hold over *her* head?'

Lydia smiled, somewhat ruefully I thought. 'Do you think that Mama and Papa want to take such a chance? Do I? How can one be sure? Marshall is clever, if not downright cunning, and she could wreak her revenge through other parties, while holding herself blameless. More to the point, Marshall has proven her allegiance to the family time and again, and has no interest in disrupting the calm in which she thrives. She holds secrets that she could use against each one of us, and so we must all trust her completely. Only the present state of affairs prevents our mutual destruction.'

My head throbbed over the complexity of the matter, and Scott's *Marmion* – one of Charlotte's favourites – came to mind: *Oh what a tangled web we weave / When first we practise to deceive*! I began to understand why young Lydia had used

Marshall to invite Roxby to the soirée, and why her mother had directed her ire at Anne, rather than her lady's maid.

'But what if your parents enquire of Marshall, directly, whither you walked today, and with whom? What if they ask: did she see Mr Roxby?'

'She will say that we saw no one, just as she has averred that Mama was taking tuition from you in drawing and painting, and has – *with* Mama – ridiculed you in Papa's presence. Not too much, mind, for that, too, would raise suspicions – you know, ladies protesting too much and all that.'

'*What?*' I could not help from crying out with dismay, which only provoked laughter from my young companion. Would a just God, thought I, have united such an angelic face with such devilish cruelty?

'Hush, Mr Brontë, I am sure Mama is quite fond of you. Don't you see that such conduct is necessary dissimulation?'

Despite her efforts to calm me, my face burned with indignation at the thought of the sickly old man joining his wife and her lady's maid in mocking laughter at my expense. I felt, for a moment, the fool's craving to hear evil of self that haunts some people like a demon, wondering exactly what had been said in each of these instances.

'So, what would happen,' said I, my anger triumphing over good sense, 'if *I* were to say that you were with Mr Roxby? And I should tell you, Miss, that had you been accompanied by my sister today, and she were asked, *she* would tell the truth, for she would sooner quit Thorp Green without a letter of recommendation than utter a single untruth.'

She waved her hand in the air dismissively. 'Yes, yes, my heavens, I know full well Miss Brontë's saintly character – she is utterly ignorant of all of this, of course, as she is of so much of true human nature – and such honesty has its place, of course; but it also has its limits. This is precisely why I seized upon her being indisposed today to arrange a meeting with Roxby, don't you see? As for you, sir, I am quite certain that you would withhold the truth – for you have daily practise in the arts of deception, don't you? – if you were asked, so I prefer to view your question about yourself as conjectural rather than threatening.'

'What causes you to be so certain?' said I, still angry.

'*Because*,' she whispered seductively, her perfumed, oval cheeks fresh and smooth, her stunning eyes opening wide with mock-desire. '*Because*, dearest Mr Brontë, if you were to say such a thing, I would not only *deny* it, but would say that it was you I saw at the Castle ruins today, that you contrived to lose your hat, and when Marshall ran after it, you took me roughly by the arm and fairly dragged me out of her sight, behind the ramparts, and began kissing me passionately and attempting to proceed to further extremities, as I struggled to get away. It was only when you heard Marshall's footsteps that you released me! Everyone sees the way men look at me – yes, even *you*, despite your infatuation with Mama – and everyone would credit such a tale.'

I gazed at her in wonderment, realising that for each objection I might summon forth (*Why would I lie about Roxby? Why did she wait to report my indecent advances?*), she would have a ready answer (*Mr Brontë had heard about Mr Roxby and has invented a rendezvous to cover his own villainous behaviour; she did not wish to report my conduct until we had left Scarborough, to avoid a scandal*). More to the point, whom would her good Papa believe, his own daughter or his son's tutor?

I felt at once thunderstruck and rooted to this spot, near the cliff's edge; I was speechless as I gazed out on the expanse of the sea, whose incessant, rolling waves seemed to join in Lydia's scorn.

'Look at me, Mr Brontë.'

I turned and saw that if any young lady's eyes were capable of shooting, in the same moment, both the amorous arrows of Cupid and the poisonous darts of Hercules, it was she who stood before me. As if reading my thoughts, she continued, 'Yes, I am quite certain that you will say nothing. Surely you wish to continue at Thorp Green … yes, yes, I see that you do. Why leave, indeed, such a position, as long as it suits you and Papa – and, more importantly, dear Mama?'

She at last turned and walked towards the Castle Road, where

Ann Marshall, leaning against a low wall, waited patiently.

'Oh,' Lydia added, stopping after just a few steps, before Marshall could make out her words, and facing me once more. 'You might be wondering why I choose not to have you dismissed directly.'

In reality, I had not allowed myself even to consider the possibility, but I was, for all my trepidation, curious to hear her reasoning.

'Let us look at the two possibilities: in the first, you are sent packing. Papa is enraged, and it is most likely that he also decides to dismiss poor, innocent *Miss* Brontë' – though I believe she has some true affection for Anne, she said this last with something of a sneer – 'for no other crime than being your unfortunate sister, and so my sisters are without a governess, just when everyone has become used to one another, and Papa and Mama must again advertise, and who *knows* what sort of wretched creature they'll find? I'll confess that I despise them all, though your sister, in comparison to others I have known, is the best one could ever expect from that peculiar tribe. Meanwhile, Mama is so sad – *tellement triste* – without her young Mr Brontë to pay her court –'

I must have scowled, for she laughed and added, 'Now now, sir, please keep that Irish temper at bay ... ha ha! What was I saying? Oh yes, Mama is so sad, and so cross, and thus wishes to deny to her daughter the happiness *she* once had in arms of her son's young tutor – no, don't be shocked, Mr Brontë, the truth is out, but we both have an interest in keeping each other's secrets ... I hope, at least, to have convinced you of *that*.'

I could not refrain from grinding – for want of openly gnashing – my teeth. 'You said there were two possibilities.'

'Ah, yes, just so. As I was saying, we have a mutual interest in discretion, do we not? For the second possibility is this: all continues as it has been, and should you hear of anything concerning Mr Roxby – indeed, should I need you to do anything concerning that gentleman – you will be my humble servant. Is that quite clear?'

Miss Lydia Mary Robinson *would* have the last word, just as she would have her own way, and so spun on her heel and descended the steep road into town, joining Mrs Marshall without a single backward glance.

XIII.

A Letter for Mr Roxby

August 25th, 1844 · Thorp Green

We have at last returned to the quiet daily life of Thorp Green. I have seen little of Mrs Robinson – *my* Lydia – and then only in our proper *rôles* as mistress and tutor. When reason holds sway, I feel a kind of peaceful relief, for so long as we are apart there can be no discovery; but when, more often, passion gains dominion over me, I crave and ache and yearn for her, to feel our bodies together again as one, and I am driven almost mad with desire. To be so near and yet so torn asunder! I would rather, I sometimes think, be across the Channel or beyond, than just a few steps away from her chamber, where her soft curves, enveloped in silk, embrace her bed as once they clung to me. Does she think or feel any of this?

This afternoon, at liberty to do as I pleased, I carried my drawing materials outside, for Charlotte has asked for a sketch of my lodgings. It was one of those splendid days of late summer when banks of white clouds render by their contrast the sky an even more brilliant hue, when a gentle breeze occasionally hints of the shorter days and cooler seasons to come. I sat behind the Old Hall, on the stump of a tree felled long ago, and began to sketch: the trees bent to the left by years of wintry northern blasts; the little lane, skirted by an old stone wall, leading up to the 'Monk's House' (I thought of my distinctly 'un-monklike' behaviour there, with Lydia), the old seventeenth-century building with its steeply pitched roof and tall chimney; the newer addition to the right and the outbuildings to the left; and finally, the brilliant sky and billowing clouds beyond.

I was lost in that blissful inner world of creation – so common in childhood and now so rare – where one loses all sense of time and place, and cannot say how long I worked in silence, a silence broken only by the occasional notes of a songbird and the rustling of leaves that were sere, but not yet ready to fall. It was not until a shadow fell across my sketch that I became aware of the presence of someone standing behind me.

It was Miss Robinson. Her gaze had not met mine directly since that fateful day high above the sea at Scarborough, nor had she addressed a word to me; but now here she was, still dressed in her riding habit from an afternoon outing, a tall beribboned hat cocked jauntily to one side and her eyes full of blue mischief, as confounding and bewitching as ever. She held what appeared to be a small novel in her hands.

I had started when her shadow fell over my sketch, nearly spilling my ink.

'Ha ha, Mr Brontë, you see, did I not tell you? – you are not the only person capable of sneaking about!'

I knew not how to respond, so held my tongue.

'*Mais alors, monsieur, il ne faut pas bouder!* Ha ha! You see, your sister has not broken her head – *elle ne s'est pas cassé la tête* – and heart for naught – she has managed to get *some* French into my own pate over the years. I am not such a great blockhead as she thinks.' She speaks with great rapidity, and, increasingly, like her mother.

I laid down my pen and stoppered my ink. 'Forgive me, Miss, I was not sulking. My mind was still on my drawing, I'm afraid. And of *course* my sister does not think you a blockhead.'

She gazed at me in such a way as to suggest that, regardless of how little esteem she has for me, she was incapable of resisting even this brief opportunity for flirtation.

'Ahhhhh,' she sighed. 'Well, perhaps not a *blockhead*, but I am certain that our austere governess feels that I rarely make inclination bow to duty, that I am incapable of moderating my desires or sacrificing my own will for the good of others, and that I favour all those things that produce the greatest show with the smallest labour.'

What should I say in response to this? Had not she herself told me that *discretion is the mortar that holds society together*? But she had paused only briefly for a response, for she seemed far more interested in hearing herself chatter on than in anything I might have to say. I again held my tongue.

'I see that you are intent upon being reticent with me today, Mr Brontë. But see here, I was setting no trap for you. I readily agree to all such criticisms, but simply choose to view them in quite a different light. Why should I sacrifice my will for the good of others? Would they do so for me? And why should I not seek my pleasure, and wish to dazzle others, rather than pass my days in the deadly dull perusal of dusty tomes? Such pursuits might suit the professor or the monk – or governess or tutor, for that matter – but they are hardly fitting pursuits for a young lady in society, don't you agree?'

'I am sure,' I responded carefully, 'that you have given these things a great deal of thought, and that you will surely do what you think is right.'

'Ha ha!' she laughed heartily, and genuinely. 'Mr Brontë, what casuistry! You are every bit the clever diplomat, a veritable Jesuit! I suppose I am *not* a blockhead, for I am hardly fooled by such cant, which *seems* to say something, but means nothing. Or rather, I would translate it as this: *You are my mistress's daughter, and you will do what you choose to do, and far be it from me to correct you*. Now then, how's that?'

I could not but smile at this. She is a clever girl, despite her years of uneven application in her studies; above all, she knows how the world works. I wondered, for a brief instant, if her desires transcend those machinations at which she seems so adept. Is there more to her than that lovely face and gracious figure, than that keenly scheming mind she has of late revealed to me? Are there great, unspoken, and perhaps indescribable yearnings, or silent stretches of sadness, buried beneath that perfectly fitted riding habit? Surely, if she has not yet felt true sorrow, she will someday – for who can escape *that* in this life?

She would hardly confide such feelings, if such feelings she had, to me. After all, was not the ability of those of her station to mask their true feelings – to *conceal any fanciful feelings or flights they may feel* – one of the talents that ultimately made for their continued success in the world? Thus, still under constant threat of dismissal at her hands, I said only, 'It is indeed true that it would hardly be my place to correct you. For that matter, you are no longer in the schoolroom, so I suppose my sister's views are no longer of much import either.'

'Hmm … well,' said she, passing her small volume, which seemed to be marked with a folded sheet of paper, daintily from one soft white hand to the other, 'while that may be *strictly* true, Mama is always sending her along with me on my rambles, so that I can *never* be alone, and even when she does not speak, I can read it in her eyes whenever she disapproves of my conduct, which is quite often. Remember, I was her pupil for nearly four years, so I know her every mood and gesture, as if she were my own sister. And it is certainly true that she has some tiresome opinions, always thinking of what is right and what is wrong, and has a strange reverence for matters connected with religion. I trust this comes from being raised in your pious papa's quiet little parsonage in the wilderness.'

She paused for a moment, her eyes narrowing. 'And yet, *you* hardly seem to share those proclivities. I've seen you in church perhaps only half a dozen times in all the while you've lived here, and even then, your face seems always to match my own feelings – *when will this interminable service be done!* – ha ha! Though I *do* love the comings and goings on Sundays, for it's one of the rare occasions I am allowed to see other people, and don't feel buried alive here at Thorp Green. I am especially fond of seeing the young gentlemen of the country, who come to worship me, of course, as much as the Almighty! Perhaps more, ha ha!'

She was delighted with herself.

Squinting in the bright sunlight, I could now see, behind Miss Robinson, the unmistakable form of my sister, making its way across the park. The former's sudden, unwonted – unless she had simply become so desperate to coquette with a young man, any man, that even her brother's tutor would suffice – familiarity with me permitted my response, which I whispered conspiratorially: 'I would counsel you to cease such blasphemy, for your erstwhile governess herself approaches. You would not want to hear any more of her tiresome *opinions*, would you?'

'Good Heavens,' said she, for she had remembered the true reason for seeking me out. She drew the paper, which was, in fact, a letter, from the pages of her novel, and tossed it in my lap. 'Now then, you are to send this to Mr Roxby … it's already addressed and sealed … Mama has taken to watching my every movement, and after the incident of the invitation in Scarborough, she is keeping even Marshall under close *surveillance* as well. Quickly now, hide it!'

I slid the letter into my waistcoat pocket and picked up my sketch as Anne approached. Lydia feigned surprise at her arrival. 'Oh! Miss Brontë! I was just admiring your brother's sketch of the Monk's House. It reminds me of the pencil drawing you made of the church at Little Ouseburn.'

Anne reached down and lifted my sketch, which was nearly complete, and held it before her, comparing my rendering to the buildings themselves. 'This is vastly superior to my work, I'm afraid. Just think,' she continued, teasing me gently as she placed her left hand on my right arm, 'what he could do if he really applied himself.'

Miss Robinson, now standing behind Anne, smiled maliciously at me and said, 'Well, I don't know – Ned appears to be making progress – no small feat, for he is a bit of a simpleton, poor lad – under the guidance of Mr Brontë, who is *marvellously* valued by Mama … and Papa, of course.'

'Speaking of your good parents, they have sent me in search of you,' said Anne, oblivious to the *double entendre*.

Having delivered Roxby's epistle to me, the young lady was all too happy to decamp. '*Bon courage!*' she cried over her shoulder as she and Anne made their way back to the house. I am quite certain that this phrase was meant to apply to my delivery of the letter, and not my sketch.

Tonight, as I finished the drawing, adding final shades and shadows, I considered what to do with the missive in question, which I have in my pocket still. Denouncing Miss Robinson to her parents would not do, for she would surely make good on her threat and claim that I had tried to ravish her – and who knows how she might embellish? If desperate enough, she might even denounce her own mother, though I considered that unlikely.

I, on the other hand, may move about as I please, so nothing could be simpler than posting the letter from a nearby village; but I would then have aided and abetted the young lady in her intrigue with Roxby, against the express wishes of her parents. If it came to light that I had participated in these clandestine proceedings, I would surely be dismissed.

As I added P.B. Brontë to the lower left corner of the drawing and today's date to the right, a third possibility arose before me: what if I were simply to *feign* mailing the letter? In that case, I could either destroy it, or keep it as evidence. But to what end? I wrote, in a firm and even hand, the year in the middle of the page, just beneath my sketch – 1844 – and at the bottom of the sheet a note to Charlotte: 'This is only a rough pen-and-ink sketch of the back of my lodgings – the "*Old* Hall", built about 1680 – or 85.'

Why had I written this? Charlotte is far too accomplished an artist not to observe how much time and effort I had put into the drawing – the careful detail, the minute hatching and cross-hatching – it was hardly *only a rough sketch*. Was this true modesty or something else? In denominating it thus, was I already, contemptibly, seeking praise from my sister?

And Roxby's letter? Tomorrow, when I post my sketch to Haworth, will be soon enough to make my decision, so I will sleep on it. Or as Miss Robinson might say: *la nuit porte conseil.*

October 17th, 1844 · Thorp Green

I sent the letter to Roxby – and many more after it. How he communicates to her, I know not. Perhaps he does not, and the love is all on one side? No, no: her pride is far too strong for that. Who knows but that she has contrived to have a labourer or dairymaid deliver them! Despite an initial temptation, I have opened none of Miss Robinson's letters, though I have no doubt that together with her hero's replies they would make a fine bundle of trash, good enough to be printed as a novel. It is, alas, now far too late for anything but absolute submission to the young lady, for any other alternative would lead to my ruin. And yet, I wonder, where will this all end?

Charlotte has finally written, to thank me for my sketch and to admit at last that the scheme to create the *Misses Brontës' Establishment* in the Parsonage has perished in the womb. There are, it seems, no pupils to be had; even Ellen Nussey, with all of her family's connections, has failed to secure a single one. I must say, my sister is quite likely correct when she says that if a mother brought her little girl to Haworth *the aspect of the place would frighten her so much that she would take the dear thing back instantly.* Indeed, she seems almost to be relieved on the subject, and I have no doubt that Papa and Emily are as well. Ever in search of a moral, she writes: *We have no present intention however of breaking our hearts on the subject – still less of feeling mortified at defeat – The effort must be beneficial whatever the result may be – because it teaches us experience and an additional knowledge of the world.*

More to the point, however, what will Charlotte do? She has declined the teaching post in Manchester, and will never again, says she, be 'trampled upon' as a governess (Anne, of course, winces each time Charlotte thoughtlessly utters such comments in her presence). Will she simply live at Papa's expense? What of marriage? No, each time her hand was requested, she refused, and that was many years ago. It is surely too late; who would have her now?

As I watch the leaves fall, I wonder: will I ever again drown myself in Lydia's warm embrace? The ache is so great at times that I think only death would cure it.

XIV.

Worldly Wisdom

November 10th, 1844 · Thorp Green

At last! Oh God, how true it is that absence makes the heart grow fonder, and the flames of passion leap higher. Early today, a Sunday, came a knock at my door. It was Ann Marshall, a letter in her hand. I wondered if it was yet another epistle for Mr Roxby, but no – it was from Mrs Robinson herself. As the lady's maid handed me the letter, I surveyed her from head to toe. As quiet and plain as a Quakeress, she no more looked the part of intriguer, oracle, sphinx or *éminence grise* than my sister. Surely, thought I, this plays a part in her success. And certainly, the Robinson ladies relish being accompanied by such a cipher, who detracts even less than my sister from their own loveliness.

As Marshall turned and left, I opened the letter, or note, really, which simply read: *Come to me in my bedchamber, when everyone has gone to church. The house will be empty.* I watched from my window and saw that all of the children, Anne, Marshall and even Mr Robinson – who has been somewhat better of late – crowded into the family's coach. Once I was quite certain that they were well along to the church at Little Ouseburn, I flew across the lawn and up the steps under the portico, down the great corridor to Lydia's chamber. The door was open enough for me to see her sitting up in bed, dressed only in a silk gown, her dark curls loosely arranged on her snowy shoulders, her bewitching eyes and flashing smile seemingly delighted to see me.

And yet, after so many months, I was tentative, even fearful. Why had she at long last summoned me to her side?

'Are you quite all right?' I asked, trembling with mingled trepidation and desire.

'I am *now*,' said she. 'For the official record, I am indisposed, but that is, I confess, a brazen falsehood. Sometimes such small untruths are necessary for the greater good. The fact is that I am quite the contrary of indisposed. I am *altogether disposed* to have you near me again.'

'You have missed me, then? You love me still?'

'Of course I have missed you, silly boy.' So great was her passion, so swiftly and hungrily did her sensuous lips and creamy neck, her silken bosom and shoulders, her elastic arms and hips and thighs enfold me, that I was soon speechless, as my mind dissipated utterly into a warm, ecstatic glow of pure sensation. Her mouth tasted of brandy, even at this early hour, which only added to my intoxication. If I could think at all, it was only a vague notion that I wanted to be her servant, her slave, to prostrate myself at the altar of fleshly passion, a knight eager to ride to his death for his queen.

As she took me into herself, all she could say was, 'Oh, yes, yes, I want you all the time. All – the – time …' – she repeated the three words rhythmically as they became mere moans, until we reached the climax, an almost electric shock, after which the waves of madness that had submerged us began to recede, leaving cold reason in their wake.

'Yes, dear boy – you see? I *have* missed you.'

'Why,' I was now emboldened to ask, 'have you kept me away so long, then?'

'It was necessary – you know that. We cannot risk discovery, and even this is dangerous, though everyone is at church and I have even liberated the remaining servants for the day, saying I simply wished to be left alone.'

'Why do you deem it dangerous, then?'

'My namesake has let fall sufficient sly innuendos in recent months that I have dared not see you at all.'

It is true that she had not so much as appeared briefly to confirm young Edmund's progress, as she was wont to do in earlier days.

'Ah,' was all I could say in response, afraid of any conversation that would lead even remotely near to *that* young lady, and my part as her clandestine messenger.

'Have some brandy,' said she, pouring us each a rather large glass, and adding no water.

I must have shown surprise, for she laughed and said, '*This* is how I now survive without you, you see. If I had you by my side each day' – here she pulled me close for a kiss – 'I would imbibe less, but this helps me manage, you see.'

She paused for a moment, before returning to the subject of her eldest daughter. 'Lydia is a worry. You see, there exists an apple of discord between us, and time has only deepened the rift. I'm sure your sister has told you at least *something* about her infatuation with that Scarborough actor, Mr Roxby.'

I again said nothing, worried that this conversation might lead into dangerous territory. Lydia only laughed.

'Oh, come now, I would worry if Miss Brontë had not said something to you about the matter. Such unnatural reserve would be suspicious, I think – don't you? It's enough to have that sphinx Marshall lurking about the place; two such creatures would be far too much to bear!'

'Yes, well, my sister did tell me that Mr Roxby had come to your soirée, and that Miss Robinson seemed quite smitten with him.'

'And so she was – and perhaps still is, for all I know. I tried to keep it from her papa, but Bessy – bad animal that she is – made sure he knew all immediately, *sur-le-champ*. He has made his disapproval quite plain, and pronounced that should she be so imprudent as to run off with Roxby or anyone else of so low a station, he would rewrite his will and she would forfeit every fraction of her inheritance.'

'But is he not of a famous family of actors and theatre owners; are they not rich?'

'Whether he is rich or not, I have no idea, but I understand that his fortune depends on the whims of the theatre-going public, he has no estates and no inheritance to speak of, and no family name beyond what appears on the broadsides posted to advertise his performances.'

'What if she *loves* him? Would you prefer to force her into a marriage of interest that will make her miserable for the rest of her days?'

Lydia laughed, unhesitatingly, with a level of scorn so profound that it troubled me. 'I hope she will not be such a fool as to fall in *love*. If I have taught them anything, my daughters should know that it is quite beneath the dignity of a woman to do such a thing. Love! Ha!'

'But did you not,' said I with considerable warmth, 'with tears in your eyes, once ask *me* if I loved you?'

She laughed again, but drew me close to her, speaking softly, smoothing the wrinkles from my brow. 'Of course I did. But that's quite different. We are discussing marriage, here, and I firmly believe that emotion and marriage should have as little to do with each other as possible. One must be clear-eyed as one leaps off of *that* particular cliff.'

'How can you say such a thing?' I replied. 'Has not such a model of matrimony been the source of your own misery? Do you not wish better for your daughter? What if Roxby could make her happy?'

'Nonsense. By my reckoning, there are at least three reasons why she should not consider such a thing. The first is that even if the young couple were "in love" as you call it, such passion fades quickly enough, and I fear that he, in particular, travelling in his circles (surely you have heard the tales of actresses, who are no better than harlots), would soon grow weary of being chained for life to the giddy thing, for her charms will surely fade far more rapidly than his. In short, he might *keep* her, but I doubt not that he would find other women, if he is like any other man I have met, that is. So, logic would dictate that if she is ultimately going to be *kept*, why not be kept in true style, rather than rambling about the kingdom like a gypsy?

'The second reason is that her papa will cut her off without a shilling, and quite rightly, I might add. The third – one about which she likely gives not a fig, for she is a *selfish* girl – she would bring disgrace on the entire family, which would surely affect her younger sisters' own marriage prospects.'

As she spoke, I saw that Dr Crosby was quite right in his estimation of my mistress: she had long ago determined, through bitter experience, that marriage and love were better off remaining utter strangers. And, after all, as the lover usurping her husband's place, how could I argue against such an arrangement? In the end, what truly troubled me was not so much her separation of the two, but what seemed to be a denial of the very existence of true and deep and eternal love altogether.

After a long pause, during which we could hear only the ticking of the enormous clock outside her door, the bare branches scraping along her window in the wind, and our own breathing, I dared say, 'Would you not marry a poor clergyman's son if things were otherwise? Or would you tire of me – or have the folly to believe that I would ever tire of you?'

'Things would have to be *very* much otherwise, would they not?' replied she, gazing out the window, her eyes betraying the flight of her thoughts to some distant place, like the swallows who were just now migrating over France and Spain to Africa. At last, she pulled me close again and said, 'Let's not talk of such castles in the air when our two very real persons are so warm and close, and so perfectly matched, one to another. There is no one like you.'

I tried to speak, but Lydia placed a finger on my lips. 'Hush, my young poet, there is only one thing I want before the family returns from church, and it requires no more words.'

What she wanted was simple: for me to worship her body with mine, and so I did. Would that I could do so every day, and forever, legally!

Christmas, 1844 · Haworth

We are home again, and how changed are we all! – well, all but Emily. Papa's vision grows dimmer still, the school scheme is dead, Charlotte is more irritable and agitated than ever, and even patient Anne has grown so tired of her employment at Thorp Green that I know she would seize any opportunity to leave. Emily is Emily: happily engaged in her household duties or immersed in her reading and writing, with scant concern for, and little patience with, the rest of us.

As for me, I have written nothing, not even a few words in this diary, for many weeks. I can think of only two things, which seem forever at war with each other: keeping my position and seeing Lydia whenever I can. My mistress contrived, twice in November and once in early December, to arrange for us to meet, and each time she met me with hot, seemingly boundless desire, quickly followed by a sudden brooding and nervous talk of her fears of discovery. Was she, at last, feeling remorse for having betrayed her *angel Edmund*, despite so many years of suffering at his hands? Did she fear that she was breaking not only man's law, but God's? Had something terrified her into a newfound piety? Or was it as simple as that she had heard new innuendos from the servants, or her daughters? She did not say, and I dared not ask. Whatever the case, these twin concerns – retaining my place and being with Lydia – are so closely linked as to form a veritable monomania.

Despite the most vigorous efforts, a single solution always rises up before me, like a mirage: if only the Reverend Edmund Robinson would *die*, all would be well. Is this absurd? No, not at all, though only a man who has at once felt a delirium of desire such as mine and stood before such an impediment as this, with his happiness beckoning to him just beyond it, can understand why some men have murdered in the name of love. I am convinced that the great mass of men have *not* felt such things, for their veins are full of ice water, while mine are boiling; alas, these are the automatons who make and enforce society's laws.

I pondered all of this as the Robinson's carriage – for they had kindly arranged for Billy Allison to take us home – conveyed Anne and me on the long holiday journey to Haworth. The rocking of the coach had lulled her to sleep, leaving me to my own thoughts, and from time to time, to survey her delicate features. She looked like a pretty young girl of no more than twelve or thirteen, grown thin from illness and yet blissfully asleep in recovery, for there was a healthy bloom on her cheeks.

As we passed over a particularly tortuous and uneven stretch of the road her eyes fluttered open and she laughed softly. 'Well, *I* for one shall be delighted when the railways have covered our fair isle like lacework, despite the infernal smoke that pours from those dreadful locomotives.'

'I believe your wish will come true in our very lifetime. Did you read in Mr Bellerby's *Gazette* that a line will arrive in your beloved Scarborough within months, and that the city fathers are hard at work on a station? We could well be arriving there by railway carriage as soon as next summer. But tell me, would you prefer to choke and cough on the smoke of a locomotive, so long as you can do so gliding along behind it on smooth rails?'

Anne smiled. 'I fear I shall cough no matter what the means of locomotion, brother.'

'But Thorp Green, at least – and Scarborough, of course – have surely provided you with more salubrious air to breath than Haworth?'

'True, true' – she paused, frowning – 'and yet … I don't know how much longer I can go on.'

'Doing what?'

'Working for the Robinsons. When I return I will be teaching Mary alone, for Bessy is following her sister Lydia out of the schoolroom and into society. Will the Robinsons continue with the same remuneration when my charges have gone from three to only one? Will accompanying the young ladies – to keep off the unwanted advances of low ruffians and country clowns – become my chief employment?'

I could not help teasing my sister, ever so gently. 'I must confess, you have a remarkable talent for protecting the young ladies, especially from actors.'

Anne groaned and rolled her eyes skywards. 'Mercy, yes, Lydia – she is more ungovernable than ever. If I were her mother, I would ransack her things to make sure she is not in correspondence with Mr Roxby, but it is not my place to do so. Can you imagine a subordinate going through her pupil's possessions? Such behaviour belongs only in a novel. No, I would be sent packing in a trice. And then, what if I were to discover something? I would then be in the impossible situation of denouncing Miss Robinson or tolerating a deception that could lead to the downfall of her – and perhaps the entire family's – reputation.'

I shivered. I was chilled not by the frigid December draft insinuating itself into the Robinson's elegant carriage, but by my own participation in young Lydia's all-too-real correspondence with Roxby.

'What would you do,' I asked, 'if you discovered a letter or other proof of a forbidden correspondence or other improper proceedings? Would you confront Lydia? Would you take the intelligence directly to her parents?'

Anne bit her lip thoughtfully. 'I don't know, Branwell. I cannot lie, but I might simply take my leave at last and give no reason other than my feeling – and it is, as I've just said, genuine – that I am no longer as much needed at Thorp Green as I once was, and more needed than ever at home. This last is also true, though with the collapse of the school scheme I know not *what* we'll do.'

Something was missing, and I suspected Anne had left something unsaid.

'I don't know, Anne, I find it difficult to believe that you would not inform the Robinsons of their daughter's conduct, even if you only did so for their – and her – own good. Wouldn't they wish to know?'

She bit her lip again, and her eyes – did water now stand in them? – met mine. 'The truth of the matter, Branwell, is this: I would leave quietly for your sake.'

'But what have I to do with this?' I asked, half-nettled and half-afraid that Anne knew something she had not yet revealed. Again I shivered.

She wiped a tear from her cheek. 'It's just that you have done so well at Thorp Green, you are so valued, and' – she hesitated, as if afraid to continue – 'and this is the longest you have ever held a post.'

Although on another day I might have kindled up at this – my *amour propre* resenting this insinuation that I could not keep steady employment, and that I needed my baby sister to look out for my interests – now I simply breathed a sigh of relief that she did not know anything else, and leant over and kissed her cheek.

'You are a sweet girl, Anne. But fear not, I shall be just fine.'

'Don't you see,' she continued ruefully, 'I am afraid that if I were to find fault with any of the children, or worse, to cast aspersions on anyone's conduct – excluding my own, of course, because *that* is always permitted before one's masters – you would be swept up in the bargain, so that even if I left of my own accord, you would be forever tainted by my animadversions.'

Still relieved, I said, 'Ah, yes, hoist by my sister's petard!'

She summoned a weak smile. 'Hold your tongue, you *mauvais garçon*, I speak quite in earnest. It may not be my idea of the most moral of all solutions, but I would have the satisfaction of knowing that you could continue as young Ned's tutor, and I will not have lied. It may be a sin of omission, but that I can abide, knowing that the Almighty will forgive far greater sins than that.'

'You sound like a good papist, Anne,' said I. 'Shall I worry that you will soon be going off to daily confession and mass?' The very thought made me begin to shake with laughter. 'I promise not to tell Papa or Charlotte, though Emily would, I'm sure, be thoroughly amused.

Anne had grown serious, and I tried to follow suit.

'Yes, I know, you think I make a jest of everything,' said I. 'But now I speak in earnest. Truly, dear sister, I am grateful for all that you have done for me. It was you who recommended me to the Robinsons, and now it is you who would sacrifice yourself for me.'

Anne sighed and responded, 'Well, let us end by saying that it may not come to that, and if it does, it will be God's will, and it will not be so great a sacrifice as you might think – for remember how weary I am of Thorp Green, and how ready I am for change.'

As the coach made its way slowly towards home, I thought: how does a return to Haworth constitute a change? But I said nothing, and soon I, myself, had dozed off, awakened only by what I thought was a little girl's delighted squeal. It was Anne, however – a grown woman, sufficiently on in years even to be considered by some an old maid – who had shouted in childlike glee at the sight of the first glittering snowflakes of winter.

January 3rd, 1845 · Haworth, The Parsonage

Has it truly been a full five years since I began this diary, and two since I began my employment at Thorp Green? So much has happened, and yet am I at all changed? What does *Anno Domini* 1845 hold in store for me? Things may change, but the questions always remain the same.

At times I feel a great transformation is coming, but at others that the train of my life will continue with little perceptible change, except a gradual narrowing, like iron rails that appear to converge in the distance. And what strange tricks time plays upon us! For if I sit on the bank of a river in Midsummer, can I perceive its surface rise or fall, or its current grow swift or slow? Do the bright leaves dancing above me turn sere, or the wild grasses along the water spring up before my very eyes? No, of course not. But remain absent a week, or a month, or a season, and change is unmistakable everywhere.

How much more is this true with people! I witness no change in Anne, and relatively little in my sisters or even Papa, despite his stooped frame and dimming vision. But what a transformation has been wrought in Charlotte's friend Mary Taylor, who has come for a holiday visit. Yes, that lively, lovely girl I treated so shabbily, just five years ago; but *that* Mary Taylor seems as dead and buried as her unfortunate sister Martha, lying in the protestant cemetery in Brussels. In her place has arrived a somewhat stout, resolute young woman, severely dressed and coiffed, who has *definite ideas* about everything and everyone – a quality she shares with Charlotte – and though she has seen Europe, living and teaching in Belgium and Germany, that is not enough, for she has determined to follow her brother to New Zealand in the new year.

I have been a model of discretion and good manners, as has Mary; it is as if the unfortunate episode of years ago had never occurred. How often do we bury the memory of past actions and old feelings, whether warm and profound, or cold and cowardly, enwrapped by a cloak of deceit, simply to get on with the daily business of life? Is this what we are fated to do as we grow old, as Charlotte has so often lamented, destined by the pressures of worldly interests to lose one faculty and feeling after another until they go dead altogether? To become what the world believes to be *wise*, must one's feelings go through a process of petrification which prevents them from ever warring against one's financial wellbeing?

The rest of us left Mary and Charlotte alone as much as possible, though I must confess that I was once guilty of listening to them through a half-open door. A few days ago, upon descending the stairs, I was intrigued by the juxtaposition of the words 'money' and 'heaven' in the same sentence. Papa was from home, whilst Emily and Anne were occupied in the back kitchen.

I crept closer to the door to listen.

'Yes,' repeated Mary, 'you ought to care as much for earning money as you do for going to Heaven. To do so you should look for success in writing, if you cannot bear to teach, and refuse to go begging anyone at all to marry you.'

'But Polly' – for by this name Charlotte, like her friend's own family, has forever called Mary – 'I feel in my heart that a career in letters is utterly closed to me. My youth is leaving me; I can never do better than I have done, and I have done nothing yet.'

'You do see,' said Mary in gentle but firm tones, 'that *logically*, unless you give attention to earning money, you will forever be a prisoner of it. To no one would money bring more happiness, and no one would use it better than you would.'

From their voices, I could tell that Mary stood at the window, while Charlotte paced before the fire.

'Of course what you say is *logical*,' replied my sister, 'but my heart rebels at the very thought of being at all absorbed in petty money matters. I would rather be dead than walking about so, stripped of all of my noblest faculties and feelings.'

'And yet, you say that you long to travel, that you would like to visit all the great capitals of Europe, see all the sights, and know all the celebrities, would you not? If you truly believe success in the world of letters is beyond your grasp, and have abandoned the Parsonage school, surely you must consider leaving home, as Anne and Branwell have. Did you not tell me that you already felt buried in Haworth? Think of what you'll be five years hence if you stay here!'

There was a brief silence, then a muffled choking, a repressed sob.

'Don't cry, Charlotte!' said her friend, which was followed only by the sound of my sister's footsteps up and down the room.

At length she replied, calmly, 'I know it is not logical, but I intend to stay, Polly.'

My heart, I confess, melted, and it was with great difficulty that I was able to stifle my own unexpected and involuntary sorrow. Poor Charlotte! Yes, we had changed, and grown apart, and now such candour was reserved for the sympathetic ears of Mary or Ellen alone – for even Anne and Emily, contributing each in her own way to the family's wellbeing, have grown weary of their elder sister's 'desponding' lamentations on the subject.

And yet, how much are Charlotte and I still so alike in the core of our being, at least in this crucial regard! We both know that it is absurd, that it is illogical, that it is selfish, and most of all, *childlike*, to despise the business of 'money-grubbing', especially since we desire all of those things that money can procure. But understanding this absurdity does not make it something one can, by sheer force of will, tear up by its roots, for it is as much a part of each of us as the colour of our eyes or hair, or the pigmentation of our skin.

At this moment I was discovered, not by the young ladies, but by a pair of canine interlopers, Keeper and Flossy, who had escaped the kitchen and now frisked and wriggled like puppies at my feet. Hearing the commotion, Mary and Charlotte emerged from the parlour, the first wearing a polite but cool expression, the second a look of profound dismay.

'Have you been listening at the door, Branwell?' said my sister.

Deception, like other vices, is perfected with practice; I did not hesitate in responding, in the most natural of voices, 'Of course not, ladies! Heaven forfend! Nay, these two inquisitive quadrupeds heard my footfalls on the stairs and thus came racing from the kitchen to investigate.'

I bowed to the ladies and walked towards that room, calling the dogs to follow me. As I breakfasted, I thought about Charlotte's dilemma, which was common to us all. Anne and I had taken up the yoke of servitude, though we have chafed under it almost as much as Charlotte had. Emily has found her place as housekeeper, which suits her temperament well enough. But the hard truth of the matter is this: Papa had raised us *all* to think far too highly of ourselves, and we have formed ambitions that are quite likely as unrealistic as they are grand.

What indeed, as Mary has asked of Charlotte, will have become of us five years hence?

XV.

The Valentine

February 13th, 1845 · Thorp Green

The snow we had witnessed that December day from our carriage window was the first and last of the winter thus far, for since then it has been a season of frigid rain, the sort that splatters down in large, hard, cold drops, as they fall through air so glacial that one cannot countenance that it is still above freezing. Such rain always makes one wish for the hard dry purity of snow.

Today Crosby and I set off for York, he with a list of remedies to procure, this time at Mr Palmer's, and I with a list of books to borrow – some for me and some for Anne and the Robinsons – from Mr Henry Bellerby's bookshop. Both of these august institutions lie in Stonegate, and we had agreed that once our commissions were fulfilled we would dine hard by, at the venerable Punch Bowl.

As I walked past the large display windows and into 3 Stonegate, I drew the list of books – written first in my lady's hand and then, beneath hers, in my own – from my pocket. More often than not we send such requests by the post, but when Crosby invited me to accompany him, how could I resist coming in person? For the writer, only the embrace of his beloved is more thrilling than the intoxicating smells of paper, ink and leather; to the worshipper of print, what is more inspiring that the sight of tomes of all shapes and sizes, from sixpence volumes to towering collections of the greatest poets, bound in leather and printed on gilded vellum pages, with elegant engravings scattered throughout? And finally, for the man who dreams of being crowned by laurels of poetic glory, what place is more responsible for both his inspiration and – alas! – his despondency?

Mr Bellerby had met me two or three times before today, and has a merchant's memory for faces and names, despite his thick spectacles and, surely, hundreds of patrons' names to remember. Although he has a stammer – certain initial letters giving him particular difficulty – it should perhaps not be called an *impediment*, for it does not prevent him from speaking quickly. Quite to the contrary: it is as if he seeks to make up for the time lost by his defect of speech. Once he has launched into a sentence, it tumbles out more fluently than one expects, as though each thought begins behind a dam which, once collapsed, permits a powerful stream to flow unchecked, as though his mind is forever far in advance of what his lips are capable of uttering.

As I examined some of the newest titles, he walked up behind me, a somewhat portly man of about my height, but without a single hair or whisker on his head, except for two lively, copious dark eyebrows moving above his spectacles.

'W-w-well … now, Mr Brontë it is, isn't it … a m-m-most unusual name, that … y-y-you've come in person this time, have you?'

'I have indeed, Mr Bellerby. As you can see' – I handed him my list of titles – 'I have been charged by my employer, Mrs Robinson, with borrowing some books from your lending library.'

'V-v-very well,' said he, 'b-b-but do you not wish to consider purchasing something?'

'No, not for me this time – but it is not for want of desire. As for the Robinsons, I am certain they will continue to add to their personal library, will they not? But I'm afraid that far surpasses my authority as the young master's humble tutor. It's their account, you see, not mine.'

Bellerby would not be denied a sale, however, and not taking the hint that I had little money of my own, he held up a small volume with gold lettering across its red cover. 'N-n-not even Mr Dickens's *Christmas Carol*? It's a g-g-gospel for our age!'

I had not the heart to tell him that he could not have recommended more strongly against buying the book, by yoking together in a single sentence the words 'Dickens' and 'gospel'.

'No thank you, Mr Bellerby. Christmas is long past, after all.'

To myself I said, *it may have been all the fashion a year ago, but I hardly think anyone will want to read that sentimental trash in future.*

'B-b-but I c-c-could offer it to you at a reduced price … p-p-perhaps a gift to your employers, the g-g-good reverend and his pious lady?'

Was there sarcasm in this last sentence? Or had I become so thoroughly impregnated with Lydia's fear of discovery that I now heard, in every word uttered about her, suspicion and menace that were not, in fact, there? I would certainly not be purchasing anything by such a hack as Mr Dickens, but I felt I should buy something.

Bellerby did it all, and had it all: not only did he publish the *Yorkshire Gazette*, sell books and operate two public lending libraries from his shop; he was also a stationer on a grand scale. I approached, in one corner, a shelf that held printed valentines. I can never see a valentine without thinking of Weightman, and of his kindness to my sisters – and to me, for that matter. Surely they still cherish their valentines, whilst he, poor fellow, is no more. And yet, I still see him springing eternally from his rocky perch on the windswept moor that day, shouting his encouragements: *I have a good feeling, Branwell. I believe things are going to turn your way.*

I was lost in these thoughts when I felt Bellerby looming at my side.

'Ah, y-y-you have a s-s-sweetheart!'

'No, alas,' said I, though in fact I was tempted to purchase a card for Lydia. 'I was thinking of my sisters. Or rather, my sister Anne – you know, you have met her, she is the governess at Thorp Green. I was thinking of playing a bit of a gentle trick on her.'

'Ah, y-y-yes, a p-p-pretty little thing – so quiet. W-w-well then, y-y-you must get her one!'

I chose a valentine, more to put an end to Bellerby's unrelenting efforts than anything else. As he happily assembled the books that

I was to carry back to Thorp Green – perhaps because he had succeeded in selling me something, no matter how small, that I had not expected to purchase – it did not escape him that I examined several volumes of poetry.

'Y-y-you f-f-fond of p-p-poetry, Mr Brontë?'

'I am.' Despite the vaguely encouraging words I had received from Coleridge, the Martineaus and Macaulay, I felt a failure, and so it must have been pride that made me add, 'I even *wrote* some poetry when I was younger. Still do on rare occasions. I've published in the papers, over in the West Riding, in Halifax and Bradford.'

As he placed my parcel in my arms and walked me to the door, he said, 'W-w-well … w-w-why don't you send me some? Even if they've b-b-been p-p-published before, all right? I'm always looking for good p-p-poetry for the Gazette.'

'I'll consider it, Mr Bellerby,' said I, slipping the valentine into my pocket and nodding my head as I exited the shop. 'Always a pleasure, sir. Goodbye.'

Crosby was waiting for me when I arrived at the Punch Bowl, smoking a meditative pipe, a bottle of wine and two glasses on the table before him.

'Well now, Brontë, have you fulfilled your duties? Free to take your ease and share a drink with old Crosby, even at this Whig establishment!'

As he poured, my friend asked if I had news from Leyland. Was the artist making progress on the Beckwith monument, he wanted to know? I had to plead ignorance, as I was unable to offer any intelligence on the subject whatsoever. I had written two letters, both unanswered, so I had at last given up. These last details I chose not to reveal with Crosby, for it hardly boded well for completion of the memorial.

Since discussing Lydia was forbidden, I asked instead after her husband's health. What could be more natural than to show concern for one's employer, after all?

'Oh, Mr Robinson's health wavers, you know. One day I think he's giving us the slip and will soon be following his little

Georgiana to the grave, but the next he is up and about and riding with the family to church. This week coming, for example, he and the lady of the house are playing host to their relations, Sir Edward Scott and his wife Lady Catherine.'

These names had merely a vaguely unpleasant association in my mind until I recalled to whom they belonged. This was Lydia's cousin, and her husband, the rich Sir Edward of Great Barr Hall, near Birmingham. Trying to maintain my calm before Crosby, I took a long draught of port, though I could not avoid clenching my teeth at the thought of Anne's words last summer: *Is it any wonder that her girls are such giddy, incorrigible flirts? With such an example as this in their own mother, they hardly need novels to corrupt them!*

I was not terribly successful, it seems, in concealing my feelings.

'What is it, Brontë? Are you acquainted with Sir Edward or Lady Catherine?'

'No, not at all, though my sister saw them in Scarborough, I believe.'

'Ah indeed, that would not surprise me at all. He is exceedingly rich, you know, and is inordinately fond of the sea. Mrs Robinson says he even has a yacht in Marseilles. You should have seen her eyes flash with envy at her cousin's good fortune, ha ha! One can never be rich enough for the ladies, I suppose.'

While Crosby found all of this quite amusing, I was wrestling with my own envy, coupled with a jealousy that I could no more crush than reveal. Indeed, thought I, was it possible that my friend, the affable Dr Crosby, knew exactly what he was doing? Had he taken into account that, because I am forbidden from discussing my relationship with Lydia with him, he is free to say such things, knowing that I would be at once writhing with emotion and struck dumb by our agreement? I wanted to cry out, but resolved to be calm; there was no other alternative.

'How long are they to remain at Thorp Green?'

'A fortnight, to be precise. Normally, the Robinsons would not feel it necessary to confide such details to such a humble servitor as I; but Lady Catherine, you see, is in quite delicate health, and so the Robinsons have asked that I come round each day to visit her.'

'If she is so ill, why do they travel?' I asked.

Crosby eyed me slyly, and there was now no doubt that he was toying with me, as a cat would dally with a mouse. 'Heavens, Brontë, one would think that you wished to bar Sir Edward and his wife from Thorp Green. Are you certain that you don't know them?'

I took another generous draught of port, the very act of pouring making me feel immediately much better.

'No, Crosby, I have never laid eyes upon Sir Edward and Lady Catherine. Mine is purely idle curiosity. And like you,' I added after a pause, 'I have heard nothing but *good* spoken about them.'

Crosby laughed. 'I never said that, Brontë. But you have guessed correctly. The Reverend Robinson has jested that *misery loves company*, and that Lady Scott will keep him company in his infirmity. Meantime, Mrs Robinson and Sir Edward get on exceedingly, I am told.'

'By whom?'

Crosby seemed puzzled, or feigned puzzlement.

'By whom were you told this?' I repeated.

'Oh, by Mrs Marshall. I'm sure she meant nothing by it.' He paused to take a sip of his port. 'Surely you wouldn't suspect anything untoward where your mistress is concerned, would you?'

'No, of course not,' said I, staring down at the table. The conversation had reached an impasse: there was no way forward that did not involve incriminating myself or Lydia, or making unfounded claims about her and her guest, Sir Edward. And besides – what business was it of the family tutor to be concerned about any of it?

I was happy when our cottage pie arrived, and when the conversation turned to books. I showed Crosby the volumes I had received from Bellerby, and that gentleman's request that I send some poems for possible publication in the *Yorkshire Gazette*.

'By all means,' he said enthusiastically, his mouth full, 'you should! See here, you are still a young man, and the young master will be off to university – well, or somewhere on his own – in a few years. It's far from too late for you to build a career in letters, I'm sure of it! You just want persistence, Brontë. Persistence, that's what matters.'

Now that the subject did not concern Lydia, I felt I could speak to Crosby as candidly as if he were one of my old friends, Leyland or Weightman – or Grundy, at least. 'Surely persistence matters, but what of talent?'

'You've greater gifts than most, I'd wager. But no, believe me, it's persistence that counts. One can be a success – of some kind – with persistence alone, if the effort is great enough; but try climbing Parnassus or any other mountain with no effort or persistence at all, and genius alone! Genuis alone won't buy you a thing, not even dinner at The Punch Bowl!'

I said nothing, feeling defeated and dispirited, believing that I had precious little genius and even less persistence. Oh persistence, single-minded *persistence*! What would it be like to have this quality? Was it not the same attribute that had ensured the success of the Postlethwaites and the Stephensons among us, grinding away tirelessly until, little by little, the world slowly gives way, like the last of the stone yielding at the piercing of the Summit Tunnel? My character is no more capable of such efforts than it is of holding up, Atlas-like, the celestial spheres. Even my sisters have, I am certain, far more of it than I.

After dinner, Crosby suggested a short stroll to the lower end of Stonegate, and then back up to the Minster; he knew I could never refuse it, even on such a chill winter day as this, where a mist midway between fog and rain obscured the upper reaches of the great cathedral's towers. As we arrived at Saint Helen's Square at the bottom of Stonegate, and I turned to gaze at the church of that name and the far greater Minster, barely visible beyond it, I heard my companion snigger.

'What is it, Crosby?'

'Did you know, Brontë,' he said with typical rapidity, that Francis Drake reports, in *Eboracum* – that's his venerable history of York – that this respectable square, with its lovely church, grand houses, and now those new offices of the Yorkshire Fire and Life Insurance Company going up – if it's ever to be completed, that is, for they've been at it for nearly five years, by God – in any event, did you know that this square was once called *Cuckolds-Corner*? Do you think it was named for one *particular* cuckold, or several? Ha ha!'

Was Crosby still playing with me?

As we turned and retraced our steps, I thought: *would I even be successful at persisting in cuckolding the Reverend Robinson?* For this adulterous feat seems, to date, by far the greatest accomplishment of my life.

XVI.

Fury and Deception

March 3rd, 1845 · Thorp Green

Sir Edward and Lady Catherine have come and gone, and I have not seen my mistress since the day of their arrival. On that day she burst, without a knock, into the library, where my pupil was struggling through a page of Latin. Her dark eyes flashed and her fair cheeks burned with displeasure as she indicated to her son that she wished to speak to me alone. The lad was happy enough to lay down his arms in his losing battle with Aeneas, and beat a hasty retreat to his bedchamber.

As the door closed, Lydia spoke to me with controlled fury.

'Are you quite *mad*, or just a fool? What in heaven's name made you think that sending me a *valentine* through Marshall was either proper or wise? Do you know how easily such a thing might be discovered? Do you wish to bring about my *ruin*, and yours with it?'

I sprang up and attempted to draw her into my arms. 'I don't care anymore, Lydia, I *love* you! That is the only madness that possesses me.'

'Don't,' said she, pushing me violently away. 'What if someone were to walk in upon us, you fool?'

I stepped to the door and drew the bolt.

'There now,' said I, seeking again to pull her towards me.

Again she repelled my advances, the arms which had so often embraced me now stiffening in defiance. I fell to my knees, throwing my arms about hers and pressing my head against her, as she struggled to remove herself from me. Like a madman I clung all the tighter, saying only, 'Oh Lydia, Lydia!' At last, in utter desperation, she took hold of a shock of my hair and tugged smartly, as one might do to a child with whom all reasonable exhortations had failed, and I fell back in pain.

'*Now then*,' she said, '*Sit down*.' She indicated a chair with a trembling finger, and I obeyed her command, whilst she herself remained standing, still panting from her exertions. She was, despite the look of mingled fury and loathing that she directed at me, still lovely. How much mother and daughter resembled each other in that uncommon ability!

'Do not speak,' she said, in tones even more clipped than usual. 'I myself shall be quite brief. If you wish to retain your post here – for I have no desire to dismiss you, despite all – you are *never* to do such a thing again. You are to send me no notes, no sketches, no poems, and for Heaven's sake' – here she seemed to kindle up again – 'no valentines. *Nothing*, do you understand?'

Perhaps she saw that tears stood in my eyes, for her tone softened. 'This is the *only* way, Mr Brontë. You are not to approach me, seek me out or speak to me – unless I speak to you first.'

'Will you never come to me again?' I asked, in tones that were half-whisper, half-sob. I removed my spectacles and wiped my eyes. 'Will I never hold you again?'

'I really cannot say,' said she. Did she, too, have water in her eyes?

'Now,' she continued, 'I must prepare for the arrival of Lady Catherine and Sir Edward. Their journey is long and they will require my every attention.'

With that, she spun on her heel, unlocked the door and sailed rapidly out of sight.

Since that day – Saint Valentine's Day – I have felt ill: a constant fluttering in my stomach, a permanent feverish anxiety, a feeling of impending doom. I know not whether it is simply that I fear I will never clasp Lydia to my breast, or whether it is simply a vague unease left in the wake of our last interview. My fond hope is that all of this is groundless, but quite natural, anxiety, which will soon fade away.

Meanwhile, young Lydia continues to make use of me. Two days after the arrival of the guests, she brazenly appeared at my door in the Monk's House, unaccompanied by anyone. When I expressed surprise and concern, she only laughed, waving a dismissive hand.

'Oh, pooh, Mr Brontë, everyone is *far* too occupied to care what I am about. Mama and Papa and the servants are absolutely *engrossed* in playing host for Sir Edward and Lady Catherine. I believe I could absent myself for a day or two and not even be missed, ha ha!'

'Now, Miss Robinson, you exaggerate, I'm quite certain. Not even my sister could be spared as your chaperone?'

'No, of course not, she is slaving away, good creature, in the schoolroom with Mary. That is why I have slipped out to see you now, don't you see? I am here to ask a favour – I so much prefer to call it such, rather than make an order or command, it's so much more pleasant, giving you the appearance of a choice, don't you think?' She laughed gleefully at her own cruel wit.

I said nothing, for what purpose would it serve in the face of this torrent of words, streaming from lips that were forever used to getting their way, and to whom I was bound for all eternity by extortion? I must also have frowned, despite myself.

'Don't be so touchy,' Mr Brontë. 'Goodness, you and your sister are so alike in that regard, always the sullen, injured party, no matter what!'

I tried not to seem further insulted, and simply replied, 'Your wish is my command, Miss.'

'Ah, well, that's better. I'd rather have you tease me just a bit, as long as you also mean it *au sens propre*.'

I nodded my assent.

'Very well. Here is what I wish: you will post this letter to Mr Henry Roxby …'

'As always, Miss Robinson.'

'You interrupt, Mr Brontë – I have not finished. I wish you to read this letter before it is sealed and delivered.'

My surprise at this unusual confidence, as she extended her

letter to me, must have been plain, for she added, 'Go ahead, Mr Brontë, it's all right, read it.'

The letter was brief:

> My Dearest Henry
>
> Yes, now you may at last come to me at Thorp Green, Saturday next. Arrive by foot, after dark, as close to nine o'clock as possible. Proceed directly to the Old Hall (the Monk's House), a tall, antiquated structure that stands across the park from the house itself. You would be well advised to skirt the woods to avoid being seen; do not fear when the dogs bark, for they do so all of the time, and will cease as soon as you enter the building.
>
> Papa and Mama have planned a grand soirée – a ball of sorts, as Bessy's début – during which I am quite certain to be *indisposed.* Little Ned's tutor, Mr Brontë, will stand lookout for us. Even if for but a few moments, I *must* see you!
>
> Your Adored and Adoring Idol, Lydia

I was unable to restrain myself. 'Are you quite mad? This will not do!'

Lydia laughed disdainfully. 'First of all, I'll ignore that insult this once. But do you mean to say, Mr Brontë, that you find it more *moral* for you to carry on for two years with my own mother – no, no, again, please don't try to lie to me – under my own father's very nose, on *his* property and in *his* employ – so that he pays *you* to cuckold him – quite a feat, really, so *bravo,* well done you – you find it, I say, more moral to do that than to assist me in arranging a brief, innocent, rendezvous with Mr Roxby?'

'I'm sorry, Miss, but I don't believe I can do it,' I found myself saying, to my own surprise.

She sighed with mock resignation. 'Oh, well, I did not realise that you had grown so tired of Thorp Green. Mama will be grieved, I'm sure, though she *has* taken quite a fancy to Sir

Edward,' said she, eyeing me slyly. 'What a shame, really, that I must reveal your ignoble conduct towards *me* in Scarborough as well, for – alas! – the whole nasty business will surely taint your good sister's reputation in the end.'

She paused for a moment, rubbing her pretty little dimpled chin as if in deep reflection, though her eyes still shone with amusement.

'On the other hand, the scenes of indignation followed by your own ignominy *would* take my worthy parents' minds off Mr Roxby, and I can surely find someone else to post the letter to Scarborough – that's no great impediment. I'll just postpone his visit for a bit, until you and your things have been quite cleared out of the Monk's House once and for all.'

'Very well,' said I, trying my utmost not to sound angry, for that would not do, either. 'But do you not fear discovery?'

'*Ah ha! Voilà, Monsieur Brontë, c'est simplement que vous avez peur!* It is really only fear that speaks in you, so let us hear no more of what you believe is right, for your hypocrisy doesn't deceive me one whit. I daresay, if I could assure you impunity for life, I think you'd do just about *anything* for me, just to keep your post and all that it entails. You might even kill a man.'

She moved closer to me, bending her face almost as if to snatch a kiss and whispering, while I inhaled the intoxicating odour of her sweet perfume, her glowing, flawless cheeks just inches from mine, 'I daresay you would happily deceive Mama with *me* if I asked, and no extortion would be required in that case, would it, Mr Brontë?'

I stepped back disapprovingly, at which she fairly skipped away, laughing, 'Ah, Mr Brontë, the good parson's son! You don't fool me – I see how you worship me, like all the rest, hard as you might try to mask your feelings! I could make you my slave *sur-le-champ* – if I cared to, ha ha!'

The provoking thing had vanquished me again, so I returned to the true subject of her visit.

'You may consider the letter delivered,' I said simply, looking away to avoid her gaze.

Her mission accomplished, she was soon out the door and walking back to the great house, taking care to skirt the woods so as not to reveal where she had been. As for me, what have I done? Where will this all end?

XVII.

Anne's Discovery

I could scarcely sleep in the days leading up to that fateful Saturday, but all passed without incident – or perhaps I should say almost without incident. The profusion of carriages and coachmen present that evening, as a lovely, powder-like snow began to fall, meant that an additional gentleman walking about the property would likely go unremarked. Indeed, it might almost have suited for him to arrive in his own gig as if he were attending the *fête* itself. How Lydia could escape from the house and find her way to my lodgings unseen, however, was a far greater question. But she was cleverer than even I had expected, and as she crossed the lawn I did not at first recognise her, for she had wrapped herself in Mrs Marshall's plain outer garments, putting up a great cowl to hide her face entirely, and moving naturally, like one of the many ladies' maids, through the crowd of horses and servants, without so much as a single glace or comment directed her way.

As she climbed the stairs, she threw back the hood, revealing cheeks pink equally from the frosty air and from her excitement, her fair ringlets tumbling onto her shoulders, her brilliant white teeth laughing almost deliriously. For all her cunning, love had made her reckless. I could compassionate with her in this, for who – lest he be made of chiselled stone – has not been made foolhardy by love? Only those who have never truly loved at all, I am certain.

'Off ye lendings!' she cried gleefully as she dropped Marshall's cloak on a chair near the fire to dry. 'Ha ha, Mr Roxby would like that, wouldn't he – it's Shakespeare, eh Mr Brontë? *Hamlet*?'

'*King Lear*,' said I, smiling nervously and still watching for Roxby from the window.

'Ah well, both tragedies, *n'est-ce pas*?'

'Yes, that's correct, Miss Robinson.'

After a few moments of standing before the fire, she sat down, uncharacteristically at a loss for words. At last she said, 'You may wait outside for Mr Roxby, Mr Brontë, and show him in when he arrives. I shall wait here alone and turn over a few pages of your books if you don't mind.'

Despite my best efforts to conceal it, I must have shown some concern, and ever quick to read another's countenance, Lydia said sharply, 'Now don't worry, Mr Brontë, I haven't the slightest interest in rifling through your things, reading your scribblings or perusing your sketches over there. I mean *these* and these alone,' she concluded, pointing to two bound volumes sitting on a small table near her chair.

I bowed and took my leave, descended the stairs, and stood sentry just within the outer door of my lodgings. Soon enough a tall, erect figure appeared before me, bowing slightly and saying, in dignified, gentlemanly tones, as he removed his snow-flaked hat, 'Mr Brontë, I presume?'

I nodded in the affirmative and gestured to him to enter and precede me up the stairs. However, he first turned to me, removed his gloves, and said, 'Let me shake hands with you properly, sir. This is a far preferable meeting than our last encounter, in Scarborough,' and laughing gently, 'when I scurried away like a low ruffian and you, poor chap, were unhatted by that ocean gale and also, so I am given to understand, were quite berated by the lovely lady I abandoned. Most of all, thank you for your assistance this evening; I'm quite certain Miss Robinson is as grateful as I.'

Roxby's demeanour was as pleasing as his manner of address was polite, and so I could hardly wish him ill. My only fear was, as always, discovery. I showed him into my rooms without even glancing within, and could hear only the bolt drawn and Lydia's cries of delight at the advent of her hero. There followed only silence.

Once a full hour had passed, I began to worry. Surely we would all be discovered, and what then would transpire? I was considering whether I should climb the stairs to alert them – for if they were truly in love all sense of time would surely have abandoned them – when I was given no choice. Another hooded female figure now traversed the fast-thickening snow, heading directly for my door. Oh God, thought I, who is it?

It was my sister. As she entered, she pushed back her own head-covering and paused to catch her breath.

'Goodness, Branwell,' said she, 'what are you doing out here? You should be dozing before a warm fire with a book.'

My heart raced, and I knew not what to say; surely the blood drained from my face. At last I replied, as calmly as I could: 'I could say the same of you, Anne. What brings you out in this weather?'

'Mrs Robinson, who insisted that I attend the soirée with Mary – and as you might imagine, Bessy, too, was quite adamant that I be there, at least long enough to see the rooms decked out and hear the music, and above all see her in her splendid new dress, after which I might take myself off soon enough – asked that I look in on Lydia, who is indisposed this evening. Imagine my surprise at not finding her in her room. I have looked everywhere but the stables and cannot find her, and have quite given up. Thorp Green Hall is a grand house, but not so grand as that.'

She was becoming increasingly agitated, but at the very moment she spoke these last words, laughter – unmistakably that of young Lydia – rang out from above. Only the face of an innocent lamb such as Anne – so shielded has she been from the baser realities of human nature – could have expressed such a look of astonishment and then, in rapid succession, horror and righteous indignation. Her eyes narrowed in disgust.

'Surely that was Miss Robinson,' said she. 'What is she about in your lodgings?'

At least, thought I, I am not myself with her – though the very thought of my body pressed against that delightful creature gave me a *frisson* of desire, despite myself. I stammered like the bookseller Bellerby. 'W-w-well …'

'Never mind,' said Anne, pushing angrily past me and rapidly climbing the stairs, then rapping impatiently on my door as I followed sheepishly behind.

There followed hushed voices, and after a moment the door opened upon an annoyed Lydia, who began to say, 'What *is* it Mr B –'

She was, if only for a moment, struck dumb by the appearance of her former governess in my place. I followed Anne into the room and could see from the state of my bed and the look of the young couple's hair and clothing that they had been engaged in activities far more compelling than sitting quietly before the fire. I wondered if Anne, in her innocence, could see all of this as well. Yes, *alas*, was my thought: even she would see it.

Ere long Miss Robinson regained at least some of her composure, as she smoothed her hair.

'Good Heavens, Miss Brontë! *You*, sweet, delicate creature, out here in the snow? Surely you will catch your death of cold!'

Anne bit her lower lip with what I am certain was mingled fear and rage: fear of being dismissed for insubordination, and rage at being thunderstruck by such a multitude of hitherto hidden transgressions, chief among them lust and deception. Her face, too, regained its composure, and I marvelled at the air of courage it now projected: my baby sister, transformed into a soldier steeling herself for battle.

'I might ask you the same, Miss Robinson. You have said you were indisposed, and your mother sent me to look in upon you. I found your bed empty, but artfully arranged so as to appear that you were asleep, the covers pulled over your head.'

'Damn it,' the little lady said bitterly, almost *sotto voce*, between clenched teeth. 'I *knew* I should have bolted the door from within and crept out a window, and yet that just wouldn't *do*, I would have fallen and broken a bone, I'm quite sure of it.'

I looked over at her Adonis, wondering if he would be shocked by the use of such language – habitually heard only from Bessy – by his lovely Aphrodite, but he seemed all the more enthralled with her. It was true that there was a powerful energy, an athletic and arousing beauty, in her angry defiance. She was irresistible, and she knew it.

At last her mind appeared to turn into a more practical channel, and she said, much more calmly, 'Well, see here, Miss Brontë, Mr Roxby was just about to take his leave, for he is returning at least as far as York in this snow and so must be on his merry way.'

The actor took his cue and had soon donned his hat and cloak, exiting the stage with only a curt bow to us all, after which we heard the rapid clatter of his boots down the stairs and the loud, swift *bang* of the outer door. Lydia walked to the window to watch him stride across the snowy park; reassured, she sighed with relief and returned to the fire. I can only assume that Mr Roxby found his way to his waiting horse and shivering servant without incident, for we heard nothing of his visit from anyone else at Thorp Green the following day.

'Now then, Miss Brontë' said Lydia calmly, 'stand before the fire and warm yourself. Yes, that's right. We must not further impose upon your brother here, for he has been *most* accommodating, but let us take just a moment to speak of this matter in earnest.'

Anne obeyed, though her face still glowed with indignation. Lydia examined her as if she were an exotic species, carried here from some obscure corner of the globe by one of Her Majesty's vessels.

'Yes,' she continued, 'let us take just a moment to discuss this.'

Anne opened her mouth to speak, but Lydia raised her hand before she could begin.

'No, no, *you* need say nothing just yet, Miss Brontë. I want to thank you – profusely – for coming in search of me. You see – as I will not fail to tell my worthy parents – I became so feverish that I was quite overcome, and, unable to breathe, I foolishly sprang up from my bed and, enveloping myself in Mrs Marshall's cloak, ran outside to cool my brow and breathe in deeply the cold dry air. Clearly the fever made me nearly mad, for what folly to run out into the snow in my satin slippers!

Thank Heavens for Miss Brontë, I shall say! *I* may have left her schoolroom, but *she* refuses to abandon me, for she stands forever as my valued guardian and companion! Yes, yes, truly, God bless dear Miss Brontë!'

Lydia had seated herself by the fire, and now gazed up at us both with a look of defiance, her superior rank all the more evident for our physical position above her.

Anne spoke at last, her soft voice quavering with scarcely controlled rage, while her delicate frame seemed to tremble in every limb. 'And so you would add further deceit to your depraved actions? You would make not just my brother, but me as well, join in your iniquitous proceedings?'

Lydia rose indignantly – whether such consternation was genuine or manufactured was unclear – from her chair. '*Depravity*? An innocent *tête-à-tête*' – here she smoothed another wayward ringlet, then the folds of her dress – 'with a gentleman who happened to be travelling nearby? That is your notion of depravity?' She snorted disdainfully. 'You really do not know the world, Miss Brontë. Peace, peace now; please don't put yourself in such a passion.'

'If such wickedness is what you call the world, Miss Robinson, I am happy to be as little acquainted with it as possible. If this is what it is to have *seen life*, I would rather be buried in ignorance.'

Anne paused for an instant and drew herself up, looking now directly at Lydia. If Truth could have a human face, it was my sister's in that moment: I loved, I admired, I feared her. She continued her address as serenely as she could.

'Here, however, Miss Robinson, is what I *do* know, and these are all quite practical worldly matters, mind; let us deal only with incontrovertible, worldly evidence, shall we? I promise that you'll hear no pious opinions or overwrought emotions from your ill-tempered erstwhile governess. First, your mama and papa have forbidden you from seeing Mr Roxby, and yet you have seen him. Second, you have said you were indisposed when you were not and have already devised the further untruths you intend to tell your parents. Third, you have involved my brother – though he himself must answer for his own deceitful conduct, the extent of which I shudder to imagine – and now me, asking that we join not only in allowing Mr Roxby to visit you undetected, but repeating deliberate falsehoods to conceal it. These are all simple facts, as the barristers say.'

Some particularly loquacious women – those who have seemingly inexhaustible organs of speech and cannot bear for a moment of silence to pass unfilled – fall, in moments of supreme indignation, utterly silent; so it was with young Lydia Robinson, though her flashing eyes and glowing face fully betrayed her fury. For what seemed an hour, but was surely a mere two or three minutes, we heard only the crackling of the fire in the grate, the ticking of the mantel clock and the howling of the wind. Even the horses, groomsmen and coachmen in the nearby stables were silent, as if the world waited for her to speak, while she paced between the window and the fire.

At last, calmly and determinedly, Lydia said, 'Well, we three young people – for you are still young, Miss Brontë, though some might call you an old maid – we three young people need to decide what is the best course for us, individually and collectively.'

As she had with me on the headland high above Scarborough that fateful summer day, she methodically laid before us the different possibilities.

'As I view matters, if either of you – oh goodness, what *am* I saying, I already know that Mr Brontë can keep a secret as well as I can' – here she looked at me and smiled, somewhat wickedly I thought – 'if you insist upon revealing anything about Mr Roxby's visit this evening, we shall all suffer greatly, if not equally.'

'Indeed?' said Anne. 'How so?'

'Why,' she said, gazing into the fire, 'I will surely be lectured yet again – and I hate to be lectured, by Papa or Mama or you, for that matter, Miss Brontë – on the dangers of associating myself with such a man – how it could damage my reputation and the family's, and how marrying such a low creature as an actor is simply out of the question. There will be threats as well:

how Papa will cut me off without a shilling, etc., etc. I've heard them all before.'

She turned then to face us both.

'But you see, those are surely empty threats, and besides, even *if* Papa speaks in earnest, we don't need his money – Roxby has his own. He says his family is quite rich, you know.'

She sat back down, again smoothing her dress and leaning forward with mock-concern. 'No, my esteemed Brontës, *frère et soeur*, what truly worries me is not my situation, but yours. I can weather the storm of shrewish harangues from Mama and the shower of pious sermons from good reverend Papa; I can even support his idle threats of destitution. But *you*, dear friends – for we are almost friends, are we not? – you will surely find yourselves without employment, poor things, for even if you are believed, Mama and Papa will not want you about the place, will they? You, Miss Brontë, will be a constant reminder of my erring ways and, indeed, of your ultimate failure to correct them, whereas you, Mr Brontë, will have been guilty of posting letters to Roxby all these months, and arranging and hosting our *rendezvous* this evening.'

Anne looked at me with shock and dismay, but I was simply relieved that Miss Robinson had said nothing more, particularly about her mother. I turned my gaze to the floorboards, which changed hues by the flickering flames of the fire, now burning low in the grate.

'You see, Miss Brontë, even your beloved brother is of this world. And in this world, a bit of helpful omission here and there, of looking the other way, of telling a harmless white lie now and then – well, that is how one gets *on* in this world. Think what chaos would ensue if everyone were to see the truth in such absolute terms as you!'

Anne sat for a moment in stony silence, then said, 'I must tell you now, Miss Robinson, that if I am asked anything directly by your mama and papa I shall refuse to tell a lie, and the truth will out. If this means I lose my position – as it surely will – I will suffer that blow when it happens …'

Anne's voice trailed off. I knew, from our earlier discussions, that she was thinking of how to preserve my position, far more than her own.

'But …?' said Lydia in honeyed tones, with a sidelong glance, her lovely eyes somehow conveying at once supplication and malicious threat.

'But I am willing to keep silent so long as it is you who speak, and so long as you keep as close as you can to a simple truth: that you left the house, and that I went in search of you, found you, and brought you back. I would beg you to keep any embellishment of this tale to a minimum, and preferably out of my hearing.'

'Well then,' said our young lady, with a deep breath, 'that's much, *much* better. Not one of us has *any* inducement to break this agreement – for let's call it an agreement, an *alliance*, shall we? Ha ha! What our elders don't know' – here she again looked at me meaningfully – 'can't hurt them. Ignorance is bliss. After all, Miss Brontë, were you not so much happier when you were ignorant of these things?'

'But what,' Anne replied, choosing not to acknowledge this last cruel, superfluous remark, which Lydia had delivered like a *coup de grâce*, 'what if your good mama and papa don't believe you?'

'Ah,' laughed Lydia, who had fully regained her usual good cheer, 'but they will, they *will*. For you see, my worthy parents know, as we all do, that Miss Brontë may be a queer creature, but she *always* speaks the truth, ha ha!'

The two young ladies were soon fully enveloped in their cloaks and on their way. As they began to descend the stairs, my sister, who followed her former pupil, turned and looked at me with such an expression as to break my heart. Her indignation had given way to a weary blend of sadness and disgust.

XVIII.

Rendezvous en plein air

June 3rd, 1845 · Thorp Green

Anne has at last given her notice, and will not return after our holiday, for which we depart in less than a fortnight. She has scarcely spoken to me since her fatal discovery of Lydia and Roxby, and she does her utmost to avoid my eyes. She is like one fallen into the sea, who holds her breath until she can at last break through the surface and fill her lungs. This, it is clear, will only happen when she leaves Thorp Green once and for all. For my sake alone she has remained silent, and kept the *vile secret*, as she calls it, though it requires every atom of her will.

Yet, why is it that I feel no shame, but only fear discovery? At least Anne has not discovered me with Mrs Robinson, of that I am quite certain. Just when I began to despair of feeling her again in my arms, especially after the unfortunate valentine incident, this latter – *my* Lydia – as imperceptibly but inevitably as bleak winter fades into hopeful spring, has warmed again to me, in recent weeks favouring me with glowing cheeks and tender smiles, and most of all, those bright eyes rekindled with desire.

Yesterday, as I neared the end of my lessons with the young master, she appeared at the library door, glided directly in, and kissed her boy on the forehead, running her small soft hands through his mass of chestnut curls.

'It is far too beautiful a day, my little Ned …'

'Ma-*ma*!' exclaimed he, 'I'm nearly grown! I'm fourteen years old!'

'Yes, yes, my dear, but you will forever be my little Neddy. In any event, it is far too beautiful a day for you to spend any more time imprisoned in the house, so run along. I have some matters to discuss with Mr Brontë. Stay away from the riverbank, though; the Ouse is running swift and high!'

I thought of the little boy I had rescued from the Wharfe.

'Hurrah!' was all he said, as he threw his arms around his mama's sublime neck, kissed her and ran off to gambol, no doubt, with the dogs, inspect the horses in the stables, and even walk into the woods, where the first bright leaves have at last emerged under a brilliant, cloudless sky. At his age, he will not long be content with such simple pleasures, my own experience tells me. And yet, is there anything as sweet as that feeling in youth, of limitless possibilities against the backdrop of a spring day whose beauty is so overwhelming that one's heart could fairly burst?

Lydia smiled and sighed as young Edmund raced down the hall and out into the sunshine. I expected her to leave me to do as I pleased, but instead she closed and locked the door, saying simply, 'Come to me, Branwell.'

Suddenly, unexpectedly, my every muscle, my every nerve, for so long slack with despair, felt as if they were drawn as taught as an archer's bow, and I could feel and almost hear the blood beating in my veins. I rose and walked to her, and she drew me to her, placing her head on my shoulder.

'I am sorry,' said she, 'for my *froideur* all these months. The chill, you must know, was mostly for show, and it was only because I feared discovery. I still do.'

'Oh God,' said I, 'So you still love me? You still wish to be with me?'

'Of course I wish to be with you, foolish boy.'

I pulled her closer, feeling, for the first time in months, the physical counterpart of the desire that had never ceased to glow in my heart.

'Not *now*,' she said, but there was far more pleasure than displeasure in her voice, as she freely allowed me to embrace her, before standing on the tips of her toes and whispering in my ear. 'Let us meet in the planting of shrubbery to the east of the house, tonight, at nine o'clock. I shall say I wish to take some air and be alone with my own thoughts. Bring a cloak or mantle, as protection against the dew.'

Now she pushed me away, to arm's length, unlocked the door and bade me sit down across from her. Again she whispered, 'Let us not raise suspicions' – then in a more normal voice, so that anyone passing by might hear – 'sit down, Mr Brontë, my husband and I have a proposition for you.'

I could not imagine what such a proposition could be.

'Your sister, as you know, is *determined* to leave us, even though Mary is not quite prepared to come out into society. If only we had one more year, she, too, would be *finished.*' She sighed. 'Ah, well, as much as Miss Brontë will be missed, we hope that you will stay, for little Ned is only fourteen and is far from ready for university, I'm sure you will agree.'

'Indeed,' said I, but I knew not whither Mrs Robinson was heading.

'Very good,' said she, 'I am so glad that we can count on you. I had, of course, *assumed* you would want to stay at Thorp Green' – here she smiled sweetly and leant towards me – 'but I wanted to be certain.'

'Of course,' said I, returning her smile.

'So, then, you will accompany your sister to Haworth? How long do you wish to holiday there?'

'I would not go at all if I could be with you always,' said I in a low, urgent whisper.

'Hush,' she whispered in return, 'hush, naughty boy,' but again she was smiling.

'Usually we spend a fortnight or so at home in June, as you know, ma'am,' I replied in the steadiest tones I could summon.

'Well, that's just the thing I wish to discuss with you, Mr Brontë. Would it be *too* much a sacrifice if you were to return to us after only a week?'

The ire of Saint Valentine's Day was no more, and her voice was sweet, her cheek glowing softly, her glancing eyes searching my face.

'Of course not,' said I, hoping against hope that this June would be an exact replica of that of two years ago. My every limb quivered with desire reawakened.

'Ah, *lovely*, Mr Brontë, I am so glad. You see, the girls will be with their grandmama for the fortnight before we go to Scarborough, and with my duties managing the household, and my husband's failing health, my poor little boy will be quite abandoned without his tutor. He might *like* to run wild, but I fancy he would tire of that quickly enough, and besides, it would be better that he continue his lessons – they need not be too strenuous, mind, for it *will* be Midsummer after all – just to lend a small portion of order to his days. When you are not trying to cram some Horace or Virgil into his head, perhaps you can accompany him on his rambles – you know, as a playmate of sorts.'

'Of course, of course, ma'am, I'd be honoured.'

Lydia leant forward, took my hands in hers, and pressed them affectionately. She had never been lovelier, as she whispered, her lust seemingly risen at last to a pitch equal to mine, 'I wish you to be *my* playmate as well.'

Now my skin was tingling, and every limb and organ was hot and stiff with desire, and I tried to pull her towards me. She laughed again and withdrew her hands, remembering that she had unlocked the door.

'There's one more thing, Mr Brontë. Since you were once a railway man, surely you have been following the progress of the York-Scarborough railway in Mr Bellerby's newspaper, have you not?'

'I have.'

'Then you know that after some delay the first train is now set to arrive at the new station in Scarborough on the seventh of next month. Well, young Ned has been quite taken with this great event and has the mania of today's youth for novelty of any kind: he insists that he *will* be the first of all his acquaintance to take the train, and will brook no argument on the matter.'

Well, in at least one respect, thought I, the young master is just like the womenites of his tribe.

'Yes,' his mother continued, 'I know some hardened souls – usually those who have not undergone the trials of raising a son, I might add – who would say: *Simply tell him 'No!'*, but I cannot bring myself to deprive him of such a treat. He's nearly grown, and surely if he is accompanied by his tutor no harm will come to him. I've discussed it with his papa, and so it is all settled – if you accept.'

'Why of course,' said I, smiling broadly at the thought. 'It will be a jubilee for the lad – and for his venerable old tutor, late of the Manchester and Leeds Railway, for that matter.'

'Just as I had hoped,' said she, standing. 'I will see to it that my husband, when he pays your sister her final wages, also advances your next quarter's salary to aid with your travels home and back. Of course, we shall pay for Ned's and your train fare, when the time comes.'

She extended her hand, which I squeezed again with anticipation, while she leant forward, whispering, '*À ce soir, alors.*'

How impossibly long was the wait, how entirely distracted was I, as the sun crept across the sky! No book, no stroll, no scribbling of letters could speed the passage of time. What a mad, impossible, unreasonable creature is man! We wish our childhoods away and then pine for them until our death; we urge Chronos to hurry us towards anticipated joys, which, once attained, we then desire frozen for all eternity. Is it any wonder that Jehovah sent his flood?

Although I could not make the minutes pass more quickly, I at last settled into some practical employments, those which require not the peace of mind necessary to nurture creativity, but which can be accomplished mechanically, thoughtlessly, step by step, like the laying of bricks, one after the other – if only I could do so with *all* of my life!

I had, indeed, sent Mr Bellerby some verse, the old sonnets on Black Combe and on Landseer's painting, which he published some three weeks ago in his *Gazette*. Encouraged, I sent another pair of sonnets, inspired by Mary Taylor's voyage to New Zealand, and in today's correspondence there arrived a letter from Bellerby, announcing their publication for the seventh of this month. Perhaps there is still hope for my poetic self, for old Northangerland. If only I had the leisure to devote all my time to my craft, I thought, as I gazed out the window towards the house – indeed, if only I were the master of Thorp Green!

I replied to Mr Bellerby immediately, with thanks and a request for some books to read during the holiday, including a French volume, Freycinet's *Voyage autour du monde*. Should I not practise my French when I am surpassed in that language by the ladies, both here and at the Parsonage? How long it has been since I felt, as I did in childhood, the master of all, the quickest of wit and the first to learn a new subject, absorbing words and languages like a sponge drinks in water.

At last, towards nine o'clock, the interminable day began to draw to a close, the sun still shining at that late hour, but now casting long shadows through the woods to the west of Thorp Green. The family had taken its final repast, the workers had retired to their dwellings to rest, and quiet had descended on the estate. As I made my way to our appointed assignation, the cloak under my arm, only a pleasant breeze stirred the shrubs and, beyond them, the sweet young green of the trees above. What a lovely music, that soft rustling of branches and leaves in the wind, somewhere between the patter of a soft but steady rain and the exquisite sound of a beautiful woman's garments falling from her shoulders, hips and thighs.

I was revolving just such thoughts in my mind when Lydia appeared before me, a veritable goddess, *my* goddess. How I had missed her! How long had it been? A lifetime, or so it seemed. My breath shortened with desire. As I took her in my arms, I asked, 'Are you not afraid of discovery, so near the house?'

'No,' said she, 'that is the very thing that makes it so unthinkable. Besides, everyone is occupied, I made sure of *that*. But we cannot stay long.'

I laid down the cloak and we, too, were soon occupied, joined at last again, moving together, at first desperately, then steadily, rhythmically, until we moaned softly in unison, as past, present and future collapsed in an instant of electric joy – like all others but, with the fecundity of this season filling our dilated nostrils, in this warm crepuscular glow, with a quality entirely its own. The wind had ceased, and I could hear only the beating of my own pulse in my temples and a flight of swifts as it swooped round and round in circles, in search of twilight sustenance.

Soon we had returned to our rational selves, our garments in order and the useful cloak again tucked under my arm, for we were both of the opinion that it would be folly to linger.

'Wait,' said I, as she prepared to turn away.

'Yes?' said she, sweetly, but with a faint look of worry imprinted on her lovely brow.

'Will I see you in Scarborough? I mean, will it be as it once was – in the boathouse?'

She sighed, and placed her hand on my arm, looking earnestly in my face.

'What is it, Lydia?' said I. 'What's wrong?'

'I intended to tell you this when you returned from Haworth. But you cannot stay in Scarborough once you have delivered Ned to us. My husband has determined that, since *Miss* Brontë will not be there to instruct Mary, it makes no sense to have *Mr* Brontë there – by so doing he will economise not only on your salary, but also on your rooms, says he. So you must return to Haworth the following day, to complete your holiday, I'm sorry to say.'

I could feel the colour mounting to my forehead. Was this a punishment of sorts, for Anne's departure? Did the Reverend Robinson suspect something?

'Hush now,' said she, before I could even speak. 'Do you not see that I was clever enough to encourage Ned in his designs to travel on the first train to Scarborough precisely so that I could justify your early return to Thorp Green, and so that I could see you one last time in Scarborough before the holiday? – for that, Branwell, shall be your reward.'

She drew me to her, and lifted her head for a kiss, then continued, 'And do you now see that I have sent the girls away to their grandmama's precisely so that we might be together for a fortnight, with only the two Edmunds – both of whom sleep so soundly that we could romp in either's bed without waking them, if we chose?'

I at last relaxed, and drew her to me again, kissing her on the forehead, the cheeks and the mouth. The bushes moved again in the breeze, which appeared to have returned with the final setting of the sun. Lydia tried to separate herself from me, but I pulled her close.

'Tell me, don't you love your husband still – a *little*?'

The moon now shone full upon us, and as Lydia laughed her teeth caught and reflected its beams.

'Not *one bit*, by all that's sacred!' she replied, kissing my cheek. 'You *know* what I think of that creature: once a tyrant, he is now an embittered, mean, sickly old man, who would deprive the pleasure of all the world if he could.'

'Well, then,' said I, emboldened by the passion of her response, 'what if the unfortunate fellow's illness should get the best of him? What then? Would you be free to love the man who offers you a life of *true* happiness?'

'Hush,' said she, not with anger but with fear. She looked about and then, whispering, she added, 'What was that? Did you hear something moving among the shrubbery?'

'No, my love,' I laughed softly, 'it is nothing but the soft summer wind, or better still, the God of Wind, Aeolus, come to bless our union.'

Lydia still smiled while I snatched a final kiss, but her clouded brow betrayed her disquietude, as she broke from me and flew to the house, unobserved.

XIX.

Mankind's Disgusting Ways

June 15th, 1845 · Haworth

Unobserved – or so I thought. For Anne had seen – or at least heard – enough to hang me. Lydia had heard her, not the wind, moving in the shrubbery. My sister did not accost me that night, as my mistress dashed to the great house, and perhaps might never even have mentioned it, had I not pushed her to do so with my usual impetuosity.

Yesterday dawned bright and clear – perfect for our long journey home. Alone again, but this time in a hired coach – for the family needed theirs that day – we were free to talk, but Anne sat in stony silence, her eyes refusing to meet mine, her eyebrows arched even more than usual by a wrinkled forehead, her gaze directed only at the passing scenery.

At last I spoke, making a weak attempt at jocularity.

'Well then, Miss Brontë, you have at last laid down your yoke of servitude at Thorp Green. Whatever will you do?'

No response.

'Anne, I *said* …'

'I heard you, Branwell.'

'Why do you not answer, then?' I queried.

Her face was one of immense and weary sadness, not of wrath.

'Here,' said she, drawing her prayer book from her bag and turning to the back cover. She held the book close to my spectacles.

'I don't see anything,' said I.

'Look more closely.'

I took the book in my own hands and squinted hard, my spectacles nearly touching the page. In the minutest script possible, as we had in childhood, Anne had written, 'Sick of mankind and their disgusting ways.'

As I handed it back, a dried primrose fell to the floor between us: touchingly, she had kept one of Weightman's flowers, and pressed its petals between the pages of her prayer book. Her cheeks flushed as she bent to rescue the precious relic, while I gazed away, pretending not to notice.

When she had composed herself, I said, in reference to her condemnation of the human race, 'Ah, yes, I know how upsetting it must have been to discover the truth about Miss Robinson and Mr Roxby.' I paused and bit my lip, doing my best to manufacture a mien of sorrowful contrition. 'And I know you must be profoundly disappointed in my role in the intrigue. I'm sorry about that.'

Anne's eyes were suddenly wet with tears, which began to spill down her cheeks. My factitious remorse now gave way to genuine concern, for I cannot ever bear to see my sisters cry. Did it forever recall that scene – real or dreamt – when we all wept uncontrollably at the foot of our dying mother's bed? I now felt a violent tug of sympathy, as if there existed an eternal, inner cord of communion between their hearts and mine, no matter how far apart we have drifted in the outer world.

I felt an explanation was in order.

'Wipe your tears, sister. See here, I will tell all: the truth is that nearly a year ago, by sheer chance, I happened upon Lydia and Roxby at the castle ruins in Scarborough, and the former threatened to have me dismissed, and even intimated that she would claim that I – *I*, can you imagine such an absurdity? – that I had tried to force myself upon her.'

I removed my spectacles, so that I could no longer see the heart-rending look on her face, and continued.

'I know it was wrong to aid her in her *liaison*, Anne, but what choice had I? She made it quite plain that I would lose my place, and that you, too, would be dismissed. After what you have done to procure and help me retain my post, how could I let such a thing happen?'

'Well,' said Anne ruefully, 'no one can claim that you are incapable of learning. In two years among such artful, deceitful, hypocritical, wicked beings as the Robinsons you have *fully* become one of them.'

I started to kindle up, but before I could speak she continued.

'Do you not *hear* yourself? Not only do you defend the part you have played in Lydia and Roxby's intrigue – as if practical ends could ever justify immoral means – but you turn the matter artfully on its head, as if all that you have done was for *my* benefit alone.'

It was my turn to sit in silence. At last I responded, 'I acted out of fear, I confess. But truly, I am so afraid to fail again, for a literary career is closed to me, I'm sure, and I don't know what else I can do.'

Anne drew another item from her reticule. It was a part of a page torn from the *Yorkshire Gazette*.

'It seems to me,' said she, 'that you are a published author. That's more than any of your sisters can say.'

For a moment I considered denying it. But how often had Charlotte and I, so long ago, shared the characters of our Angrian saga with Emily and Anne – chief among them Alexander Percy, Duke of Northangerland? No words presented themselves.

'Surely,' said Anne – spitefully now, for though she is filled with goodness, she is human, after all – this time holding the paper close enough for me to read, 'surely you did not think I would fail to recognise such an unusual *nom de plume*? And who but my morbid brother would write such lines as these? She read from one of the sonnets on 'The Emigrants':

Thus, when the sick man lies, resigned to die,
A well-loved voice, a well-remembered strain,
Lets time break harshly in upon eternity.

'Is this your first publication?'

I confessed that there were many, beginning at Luddenden Foot, and published, until just now, in the papers of the West Riding.

'Were they, too, attributed to Northangerland? How could no one in the family know of this, for all of their devotion to newspaper reading?'

'Yes, they were signed "Northangerland", and yes, I assume that you are the first to learn of this. You were at Thorp Green, and Charlotte and Emily were abroad, when nearly all the poems appeared. Papa has never heard of Northangerland, of course. Mr Weightman knew, but I swore him to secrecy – and soon he took the secret to the grave, poor fellow.'

Here a shadow passed over Anne's countenance, clutching her prayer book, the precious flower hidden within.

'In any event,' I continued, 'it never occurred to me that anyone would recognise the name.'

'That is because you think only of *yourself*, Branwell, and not how others might think or feel, whether they have minds and hearts of their own, as if they were machines without feelings, constructed solely to do your bidding. I'm sorry to speak so bluntly, but it's true.'

She bit her lip and looked out the window at the bright June sky, where only an occasional cottony cloud drifted by. At some length she continued.

'I cannot blame you, really, for Papa has always, quite naturally, thought more of his only *son* than of his daughters, and so you have never been asked to think of others, as we ladies must think of you gentlemen. I cannot say that in this you are much different from most of the other men I have met in my short life. After all, it is a very convenient doctrine for the stronger sex, don't you think?'

I began to seethe with resentment, imagining now that this was the most common subject of conversation when my three sisters were together and I absent. Was it because, deep in my heart, I could only agree with her – and with them?

'Well,' I retorted, seeking to keep my own hot, angry tears at bay, 'now that you three girls will be at home with Papa, and *I* the only one profitably employed, I shall be no burden upon anyone. *You* shall have his undivided attention, and only have to suffer my presence on the rare holiday, for I am sure that I will spend as precious little time in Haworth as possible. I cannot wait to return to Thorp Green, and only wish I could stay there all summer!'

At this – inexplicably it seemed to me – water stood in Anne's eyes, and soon tears again began to stream down her wan cheeks.

I took out a kerchief and sought to dry them, but she turned away.

'I'm sorry,' said I, 'Anne – I'm sorry I spoke in anger. I *am* trying to do the right thing.'

Tears had become audible weeping, great heaving sobs, which ended at last in a fit of coughing. I moved next to her and took her in my arms. She struggled briefly but then stopped, at last nestling her slight frame against mine, as when we were little.

When she had finished crying, she turned her face to mine and said, 'Oh Branwell, I *know*. I know *everything*.'

'What do you mean?' I queried, my blood suddenly running cold.

'Mrs Robinson.'

'What of her?'

'Long have I ignored the innuendoes, the rumours from the servants and even from the giddy Robinson girls – that the mistress of the house had an unusually strong devotion to her son's tutor. Long did I believe that tongues would always wag at the first opportunity, and when there is nothing for such people to gossip about – especially those buried in the countryside as they are at Thorp Green – they will invent something. Indeed, I even believed that, should the good lady attempt to seduce you, your pious unbringing would shield you from her unwelcome advances.'

'You did right.'

'Branwell, spare yourself the trouble of foreswearing yourself and racking your brains to stifle truth with falsehood,' she responded, her face that odd mixture of sadness and disgust I had glimpsed only once or twice before. 'I was in the shrubbery that evening and saw and heard for myself. I saw you kiss her there, I heard her say that she did not love her husband, and that she had arranged for you to return while the girls are sent to their grandmama's, so that you could – no I can't say it, can't even *think* it. She is an abominable woman, and she has clearly, utterly, bewitched you. She has corrupted you and deceived her husband. I will not ask how long this has gone on, for I wish to know no more, and detest the very sound of her name.'

Anne paused to wipe the last of her tears, sighing as deeply as her lungs would permit.

'At Thorp Green I have had such unpleasant and undreamt-of experiences of human nature as to sicken me truly,' she continued, 'and I wish only to shake its dust off my feet and think no more of the place or its inmates. I shall say nothing of any of this to anyone, but shall only pray for your deliverance, and for your forgiveness. Only *you* can choose good or evil, and if you choose to make a beast of yourself with … with … *that woman*, God alone will judge. Do you not see that what you do is wrong, Branwell?'

I clenched my teeth and considered defending Lydia – considered revealing my true part in the proceedings; I even considered telling Anne about Agnes, about Maggie – though not about Maeve or the other whores – but was silent. How often does the attempt to protect oneself lead to such craven acts, such cowardice! Very well, thought I: let her think that the innocent tutor had been beguiled by a mature, wicked woman. As young Lydia had said, such sins of omission are *how one gets on in this world*.

At great length I spoke. 'Why do you stay in my arms, and why do you lean your little head on my shoulder, if I am so wicked?'

Anne looked up at me, her wet, pretty eyes betraying both bitter disappointment and unconditional love, so much love that I had to look away, at the passing scenery, itself painfully beautiful on this midsummer day. 'You are my brother,' said she, 'and if I hate the sin, I love the sinner.' And with that, like twin infants, we dozed off together in the warmth of the afternoon, as the coach – our cradle – gently swayed as it made its way home.

July 4th, 1845 · Thorp Green

My week in Haworth was unremarkable, surely because my mind was focused entirely on returning to Thorp Green and my mistress's arms, unfettered by fears of discovery by the young misses Robinson or their governess, who is now never to return. Anne has *escaped*, as she put it to Charlotte and Emily, and since neither of them has ever been able to endure the life of a governess – or for that matter anything close to responsible employment in the world – half so long as their baby sister, they can only welcome her home with open arms, with hearts devoid of reproach.

My sisters' delight in their reunion pales in comparison to the hot pleasure, the wild abandon, the utter exaltation I have experienced in the past fortnight. It is as if Lydia had heard Anne's condemnation in the coach that day, and sought not only to prove it true, but render it but a pale representation of reality. Freed from the shackles of fear – for she dreaded discovery by her daughters and Anne more than anything, and I have determined *not* to tell her what Anne knows – for what purpose would it serve? – she gave herself over to a brief season of mad lust, and I was all too pleased to oblige.

It was, indeed, a honeymoon of sorts, for the warmth of summer allowed us to lie in bed, unclothed, while the soft breeze caressed our skin and reawakened our desire almost as quickly as it was sated. Mr Robinson, intentionally stupefied more than usual, slept, while his young namesake slumbered more innocently. The ever-vigilant Marshall stood guard, a faithful sentry, deep into the night. What did she think of all this? Could she hear our poorly stifled moans, or the sound of the bedposts tapping rhythmically against the wall? Was this still more information that she would lock away for future use?

On several occasions, Lydia sent Edmund happily away to amuse himself outdoors, while she did the same with me indoors. She would bolt the library door, roughly pull down my breeches, seize my already rigid prick, push me onto the settee, lift her skirts, and, already wet with desire, take me into herself, with the inevitable, explosive result. The first time she did this, she said, 'I quite simply *had* to have you – I could not wait, for the more I have you, the more I want you – *l'appétit vient en mangeant, tu sais.*'

Unlike our languorous nocturnal sessions – which resembled an exquisite banquet of many courses, in which we were drunk not only on fine wine and spirits, but especially on each other's flesh, and where we slowly savoured each inch, each taste and odour of the other's body – these brief midday encounters were but a rapid yet necessary slaking of our appetites, like the greedy draughts of water or hastily bolted luncheon of a labourer in the midst of a long day of toil in the fields. If we were not in each other's arms, we were yearning to be so, every warm breeze as arousing as our fingertips, as they wandered softly up and down each other's skin.

As I think on it, it seems to me that if this were recounted in a novel – well, if such truths could ever be printed – how most readers would find such things preposterous! But as I have written before, I am thoroughly convinced that only the man whose body and soul have not been licked by the flames of such desire – at least once in his life – only such an unfortunate man would fail to give it the credence it deserves.

All of this came to an end two days since, when the young ladies returned from their visit to see their grandmama, and this morning the family – less young master Edmund and his tutor – set off in high spirits for Scarborough. Mr Robinson, whom I always try to avoid, seemed tolerably well, and even condescended to nod in my direction as I stood by the coach with my charge, who assisted Billy Allison in helping the ladies to their seats.

Young Lydia positively beamed with pleasure, and I was certain that she had somehow managed to arrange an assignation with Roxby. Her younger sisters chattered, while her mother, the last to mount the steps of the carriage, turned to us, the rising sun catching and magnifying her bewitching brown eyes and flashing smile. Her back was to the others.

'I know you will conduct yourself properly with Mr Brontë and the servants, my sweet angel' – here she glanced at me briefly – 'I shall be on the platform, at the new station, when the train arrives in Scarborough on Monday.'

'*Ma-MA*,' protested the young man, 'I am no child! I could make the entire journey quite alone. I can also find my way to our lodgings – it is only a ten minutes' walk. There is no cause for you to be there.'

'Oh, Heavens, Neddy, that simply would not *do*. It is anticipated that there will be *thousands* awaiting the train's arrival – imagine what sort of persons will be there! All manner of rabble – not to mention the usual persons preying upon the crowd – filthy vagrants, scurrilous pick-pockets, women of ill repute – I can see – and smell – them all now! Ugh!'

'In that case, Mr Brontë can see me to The Cliff!' said the lad, who was just reaching the age where he no longer wished to be tied – or at least *seen* to be tied – to his mama's apron string, or worse, to be considered a miss nancy. Fittingly enough, however, his voice cracked as he said *cliff*, illustrating just how much, in fact, he was still half-man and half-boy.

'It's true, ma'am,' said I, bowing slightly, seeking to cover his confusion. 'I should be happy to accompany Master Robinson to your lodgings.'

A shrill voice came from within the carriage.

'*Ned*!' said Bessy, 'do you not think there are others who wish to watch – and to *be seen watching* – the first train as it arrives in Scarborough? After all, the town's been waiting a thousand years for it, ha ha!'

Her elder sister, never silent for long, added impatiently, as if she had already fixed a rendezvous with her beau, 'Come now,

Ned, give over! We shall all be there when you arrive – perhaps even Papa will appear on the platform if he is up to the occasion – but *do* let us be on our way! At this rate,' she muttered, 'it will be *midnight* before we arrive.'

'Whom have *you* to meet?' responded Bessy. An observer would be forgiven for thinking that one of the elegant young ladies had severely pinched the other, for soon they were quarreling loudly, whilst young Mary laughed gaily at the spectacle and Mr Robinson tried, wearily, to intervene.

Ned, defeated, consented to remain a little boy a while longer, and embraced his mother, after which he and I waved as the coach at last bounced out of sight.

Lucky boy, to have had your mama for so many years, and to embrace her still on the threshold of manhood!

XX.

A Railway Journey to Scarborough

July 10th, 1845 · Haworth, The Parsonage

I am returned again to the Parsonage but shall soon be back in the embraces of Thorp Green and, I trust, its mistress. How long it has been since I have felt such great hope in the future! Three days ago I bade Lydia goodbye in the dark shadows of the boathouse, as the waves crashed just beyond. She came alone, saying that she did not even want Marshall to know. Our brief reunion was the perfect end to a long and memorable day.

That morning in York, Ned and I had climbed into our coach at about half past ten, and within moments, we were on our way to Scarborough, a three-and-a-half-hour voyage. How quickly the railways are changing, and have changed, since I sat in my lonely little station at Luddenden Foot! Here was a mighty train, with two new locomotives and nearly forty first-class coaches, bound for one of England's most fashionable resorts. As it happens, George Hudson – the 'Railway King' himself – was on board, and nearly all the first-class passengers were invited to luncheon in Scarborough before returning to York that evening, to attend a dinner at the Guildhall, hosted by the Lord Mayor himself. Although my charge and I would not be attending either repast, the Robinsons had used their considerable influence in York to secure our tickets.

The young master quickly lost his inner battle to remain a sedate little gentleman, and his utter glee was fully on display as the train picked up speed and we made our way to our first stop at Castle Howard, a palace fit for royalty. Then it was on to

Malton, Ganton and, finally, Scarborough. I wondered if Anne would ever go there again. Would her fond memories and warm feelings for its natural beauty now be blighted by the conduct of those very persons with whom, in her mind, it must forever be associated? After all, she and Emily have just made a trip to York – Emily's first – and Anne had used the delay of the Scarborough railway branch as the reason they did not travel to the coast. Surely that was mere pretext, however; after all, had she ever had a problem arriving at the sea before the advent of the railway?

Finally, we drew alongside a familiar lake, the one Scarborians call 'the Mere', and then, at last, although we could not see the nearby ocean, we were engulfed by a human sea that surrounded the train as it finally slowed and stopped at the new station at precisely one thirty-five in the afternoon, according to the station clock. The entire town seemed to be present, for there were thousands of people of both sexes, and of every age and social order, just as Lydia had predicted. An orchestra played *God Save the Queen* – a very different, very serious and patriotic version compared to Herr Liszt's playful variations – beneath great swathes of colourful bunting. There were two tracks, two platforms and a turntable at each end of the station for each track.

And the station itself! No humble wooden outpost in the Calder Valley was this immense, elegant structure, with its wrought iron and glazed roof. No wonder that it was so imposing: a recent item in the *Gazette* had spoken of its multitude of offices, separate waiting rooms for first and second-class passengers – *and* one for ladies – as well as indoor water closets, storerooms and a refreshment room.

It was Ned's youngest sister who spotted us as we stepped down from our coach, and she broke from the party and dashed to meet us first. Little Mary, it must be said, is now quite a grown young lady, her girlish *embonpoint* of just two years ago transformed into the sensual hips and bosom of a woman, but topped by the same perpetually bobbing golden ringlets, and laughing green eyes, which resemble the colour of the sea on certain warm summer days, when shafts of sunlight pierce an otherwise cloudy sky.

'Ned, Ned!' she cried breathlessly, in a most *un*ladylike way, her excitement knowing no bounds. 'Look at this mass of humanity! Sir Edward says that there must be at least ten thousand people here – they have closed all of the shops in town to make a holiday for everyone!'

'Except for *you*, dear sister,' teased her brother. 'For how *can* you live even a single day in Scarborough without shops to visit, and little gifts to cajole out of Mama and Papa? Whatever will you do?'

Like Emily and Anne, these two younger children seem to have been, from earliest infancy, allies, and Mary only laughed the harder, merely giving Ned a playful pinch before taking the arm he had gallantly offered her and leading him to his elder sisters, mother, and a tall, distinguished older gentleman who was, indeed, the aforementioned Sir Edward Scott. He had, it seems, generously accompanied my mistress to the station in her husband's and his wife's absence.

'Ah,' cried Mrs Robinson, 'my little man is safely arrived!' Then, bowing her head slightly towards me, she added, 'Thank you, Mr Brontë, for delivering our precious goods.'

Sir Edward looked at me curiously, with a regard that was neither wholly contemptuous nor particularly amiable. He, too, nodded his head slightly, just enough to acknowledge my existence, before we turned towards our lodgings at the The Cliff. The Robinsons had procured a room for me for a single night, after which I was to return to Haworth. I walked behind them all, the chattering girls and their younger brother, whose sister Mary still clutched his arm, and I wistfully recalled the outings with my own sisters in days past – how happy we were too, and how long ago that seems!

From my position I could spy them all, to my heart's content. As we walked, young Lydia turned her bonneted head from side to side, and I could not help but assume that she was on the lookout for her beloved Scarborough play-actor. I examined the erect carriage of Sir Edward, who with his hat upon his head seemed impossibly tall – perhaps taller still than the dashing Mr

Roxby himself. Although he is nearly Papa's age, he has the healthy glow of those of his rank who are fortunate enough to have inherited a vigorous constitution and both the means and the temperament to enjoy it. Mrs Robinson had taken his arm, and I found myself battling a rising tide of jealousy. Or was it envy? Of course I wished to be where Sir Edward stood, with Lydia's arm through mine; but did I also wish to *be* him, and to possess both his physical and social stature? Truth be told, it was both, though even with all that, Lydia would never risk everything to leave her ailing husband. And *he* – if only he would die! *Why does he linger so?*, I found myself inevitably, shamelessly, thinking.

I recalled Crosby's comment, now, about how my mistress and Sir Edward had *got on exceedingly*, and young Lydia's words about her mother: *she has taken quite a fancy to Sir Edward.* I had dismissed these thoughts, however, as mere attempts to provoke me. And the truth was that all of them – yes, my own Lydia herself, who had taught her daughters to emulate her – were incorrigible flirts. The very appearance of a creature in breeches sufficed to draw forth a multitude of sighs, witty utterings (preferably *en français*, of course), fluttering eyelashes, glowing cheeks, sparkling teeth and flashing eyes from this tribe of – one had to confess – remarkably exquisite specimens of the softer sex. And yet, I was certain – and, in the case of the two Lydias, had myself witnessed – that each of them could turn tigress towards any man who ruffled her humour.

That night, in the boathouse, as Lydia – her mouth tasting of the brandy she had taken for courage – took my body into hers, and we were again one ecstatic flesh; as we tightly clasped hands and hungrily joined lips; as we arched our backs and I felt her squeeze me deep within her as the waves tumbled softly outside the door; as we did all this, I could have no doubt where her heart lay, and that one day this would be our daily life. She drew me out of myself, and when, together, as Shelley says, we *panted and expired*, I felt again the blessed relief of oblivion, like Cowper's castaway slipping beneath the waves, but unlike him, I did so joyfully, for a brief instant relieved of all cares, in a flash of ecstatic, simultaneous being and nothingness, where worrying thought is banished with lightning speed to the remotest ends of the universe.

When it was over, my Lydia gave me a last kiss before escaping to her quarters.

'I wish,' said I, 'that I could stay.'

'Now now, silly boy,' said she as she took her leave, 'we have discussed this, and it is quite out of the question. But we shall see each other again soon, at Thorp Green, and *there*' – this she said placing her hand playfully between my thighs – 'we shall have quite the joyful reunion, I promise you.'

I waited a few minutes before emerging into a beautiful early morning, where the stars shone as they do only at the sea-coast, far from the factory chimneys of the West Riding. As I walked along the front of the boathouse, my face tilted up to the heavens, I nearly ran into a man, whom I was surprised to find I knew. It was Robert Pottage, the Robinsons' gardener, unusually far from home for a man of his humble station. He seemed as confused to see me as I was to see him.

'Why Bob,' said I, slapping him jocularly on the back, 'what brings you to Scarborough? Surely you and Mrs Pottage are not on holiday? Who is tending the garden at Thorp Green, my good man?'

He seemed particularly embarrassed, and though he does not share Mr Bellerby's condition any more than I do, he stammered, 'I – I – I … erm … w-w-why, Maister Rob'nson asked me to come 'long behine Billy, t'help wi't' horses and luggage.'

'But was that not two days ago?' said I. 'I'm surprised that you're still here, then.'

Pottage looked at me sheepishly, and toed the sand nervously, as if he were a boy caught stealing sugarplums. 'Ah, well, t'maister tol' me that happen I could stay on t' see t' train arrive today, an' after all, I ain't never seen the sea, Mr Brontë. I'll be on me way home t'morro'.'

'By Heavens, man, then walk with me up to the castle ruins yonder! Have you been *there*? My hand to God, there is nothing like the stars shimmering over the sea on such a night as this!'

I still felt the tingling exaltation of a man whose body has just been with the woman he loves, who has just tasted the earthly rapture that surpasses all others.

Pottage reported that he had already been up to the castle, and so declined my offer, citing the need to sleep a few hours before an early departure. We shook hands and said our good-byes.

'Very well, Bob. But you see, I can now travel home almost entirely by railway, and so there will be time enough for sleep then, despite the bumps along the way, ha ha! In all events, I will see you soon at Thorp Green,' I said exultantly, feeling as though I were already master of the estate.

'Yes, yes,' said he, and it seemed he could not escape quickly enough, which I thought odd, for Bob Pottage is always a hale fellow well met, with a ready smile and a kind word, if not a bawdy jest and mischievous wink when there are no ladies within earshot.

Ah well, thought I, *I shall go it alone*, and so climbed up to the promontory, where, standing on a cliff, I stretched my arms out to the sea as if to embrace it in its entirety, then lay on my back on a wall, extending my hands once again, this time upwards, where thousands of stars glimmered so brightly that I felt I could reach out and pluck them from the heavens at will.

At length I sat up and pulled my knees close to my chest, circling them with my arms, and inhaled the cooling, incessant breeze. *All will be well*, I thought. *Yes, yes: all will be well.* I am not yet thirty, and my lady loves me, I am valued in my position, and my poems continue to be published. And just possibly, I will soon be the master of Thorp Green itself, at which point all of my time – well, when not obeying my lady's orders, that is – will be spent on poetry. *If I could pray, thought I, such would be my idolatrous prayer.*

The next morning, I rose at seven o'clock and, saying only a cool and formal goodbye to Mrs Marshall – for the family were still in bed – I made my way to the station to begin the long journey from Scarborough to York, from York to Leeds, Leeds to

Bradford, and finally, onwards to yet another new rail line, from Bradford all the way to Keighley. I would only have to walk the four miles home from there. In just over ten years, I mused, the tentacles of the railway had reached nearly every corner of Great Britain. Who knows but that the whistle of a train may someday soon reach the lonely hills of Haworth itself?

Scarborough, so perfectly clear and windswept the night before, now lay shrouded in a blanket of summer fog. As I gazed from the coach window, I saw that, though we were moving through the mist, one could scarcely tell that the train had left the station.

XXI.

Torn Asunder

July 31st, 1845 · Liverpool

Oh God, what a blow have I received! I feel as though my life were ending – that I am suffocating, a man buried alive. I am better only when my mind is sufficiently drowned or stunned, but such relief is transitory, leaving only bitterness and gall, regret and shame, and the stale taste of the previous night's intemperance on my lips. For a fortnight, I have ended nearly each day in a state of torpor, since the fateful day I received word of dismissal from Mr Robinson. I am never to return to Thorp Green, and, if he has his way, never to see my darling Lydia again.

The letter arrived on July 17th, and in it my employer, without entering into details, claims to have *discovered my proceedings*, which he characterises as *bad beyond expression*. I am warned *on pain of exposure to break off instantly and forever all communication with every member of his family*.

Once I had received the full force of the initial blow, I spent my hours and days – both in sobriety and inebriation – musing about what might have happened. How could I not? Had someone seen Lydia and me together? Perhaps it was no coincidence that Pottage was outside the boathouse that night. Had he been sent to spy? Or perhaps he had merely wandered by, and hearing our muffled moans, peeped through a crack to discover us *in flagrante delicto*. I recreated the scene in my mind, but this time from the perspective of Pottage, peering through a keyhole or a knothole, watching his employer's wife astride me, her pendulous breasts, which I had freed from her gown, swinging within reach of my thirsty lips and eager hands. I was within and without, and despite my suffering grew stiff with desire and remembrance as I gazed over the imaginary gardener's shoulder at the phantom lovers.

If he had witnessed such a scene as this, the gardener could scarcely be expected to comport himself normally with me just a few moments later; that would certainly explain his strange manner.

And yet, thought I: *No, that could not be what happened.*

The wording of the letter, I thought, was curious: *pain of exposure*? Surely Mr Robinson could not expose *me* without exposing his wife. This, therefore, seemed little more than an idle threat. *Every member of his family?* What did *that* signify? Finally, after several days of such reflections, the truth flashed upon me with the clarity of a cliff emerging from the darkness of night into the light of day, as the sun shoots brilliantly from behind a neighbouring mountain: something had transpired between the two Lydias, mother and daughter, and the elaborate and fragile edifice of deceit that they had constructed had come tumbling down. Yes, that must be it. Might Roxby be involved? Perhaps Marshall? Yes, surely Marshall had something to do with it.

A second, far more complicated, story begins to take shape in my mind. In this tale, young Lydia is again discovered with her beloved thespian, and her mama threatens to reveal all to her dear papa. I can see it all develop, like the scene of a wretched novel that one might read to pass one's time in a railway coach: mother and eldest daughter – alone but for the faithful Marshall, the mortar holding this edifice together – are locked in battle. Perhaps they are walking together on the Spa Bridge, high above the sands, with the lady's maid following a pace or two behind them.

'Ma-*ma*,' cries the daughter, 'you must *not* tell Papa.' Seagulls circle and scold, contesting each other for a dead fish that has washed ashore. The sun is brilliant on this cloudless day, and the two Lydias wield elegant parasols rather than gladiators' swords, and are protected by bonnets rather than helmets. The younger bites her lip, takes a deep breath, and turns to face her mama.

'Indeed, if you do, *I* shall tell him all about you and Mr Brontë.'

'And *what*, pray tell, will you tell him?'

'I will say that you are lovers and have been almost since his arrival at Thorp Green more than two years since.' Her passion grows as she speaks, and in my imagination she stamps her pretty little foot, just as I have seen her do in life. 'You will be *quite* cast out!'

The elder Lydia's cheeks are flushed, but she laughs. She is more beautiful, in my mind's eye, than ever. Would that I could capture that imagined instant for all eternity, as in a daguerreotype!

'Pray, tell, my angel, what evidence do you have of such perfidious conduct on the part of your esteemed mama?'

'I am *certain* that you are paramours!' she cries, hoping – like so many of us, so often – that the passion of her words will compensate for their lack of sense. 'I have seen for myself the poem he wrote for you, and the valentine he gave you.'

Now it is the mother's turn to fly into a rage. 'You – you – you cunning vixen, you have rifled through *my* possessions? How dare you!'

Her daughter, finding this chink in her mother's armour, attacks. '*And*, I am certain that Marshall here has seen enough to banish you from Thorp Green and, indeed, from all of society.' She stares defiantly, exultantly. 'Now then!'

Ah, young lady, *grosse erreur*! Mrs Marshall, witnessing all, now steps forward and says, 'Why Miss Robinson, I haven't the slightest idea what you could possibly mean.' Her voice has a practised innocence to it, and her gaze the cold steeliness of a sabre.

Like a wrestler who, at the last moment, flips his opponent and snatches an unexpected victory from the jaws of defeat, Lydia the elder laughs triumphantly.

'Ha ha, you wicked creature, did you *really* think you could set Marshall against me, that she would ever take your part?

Who pays her salary? *You*?'

Here an unanticipated fog rolls in from the sea, obscuring my vision. What happens next? Does the mother keep the upper hand, with the silenced daughter still desperate for her Roxby, and yet forbidden from seeing him? Does Bob Pottage report what he has seen, if indeed he has seen anything, the two tales merging? If so, do mother and daughter, reinforced by the omnipresent Marshall, join forces to preserve their good names, in an uneasy alliance? Perhaps Pottage only saw Mrs Robinson *leave* the boathouse, followed a few moments later by me, which permitted her to concoct a story that only a sickly old fool like Edmund Robinson would believe, his vanity even in his weakened state not permitting him ever to imagine himself a cuckold: she knew I was leaving the next day and had asked to see me in private, to tell me *not* to address the younger Lydia, who had reported that I had made inappropriate advances to her. *Yes, yes,* says the young lady, now standing in fear of her mother and quite possibly still hoping to win a belated approval of Roxby – for after all, how much more suitable was a rich actor than a destitute tutor! – *yes, Papa, Mr Brontë laid hands on me and positively attempted to ravish me.* Despite his weakness, Robinson is furious, his deep bass thundering like that of Zeus from Olympus, *By Heaven, why was I not told of this?!* Mrs Robinson explains that they had every intention of telling him once they returned to Thorp Green, but wished to spare him such grief during his convalescence in Scarborough, which seemed to be going so well.

Do I forgive my Lydia? Of course I do, for she has no choice. Yes, I tell myself, she is planning for the future – for *our* future – of course that's it, sending me away only to call me back when the old man dies. Summoning all of her courage, she even feigns approval of his letter of dismissal, though her heart breaks and yearns for me, and when she at last retires to her chamber that night, her eyes shine with tears.

Yes, that must be it.

The vague outlines of a third story occasionally rise up before me like a spectre, one that I blot out the instant it appears: in this vision, Lydia smiles broadly at Sir Edward, as together they step aboard his yacht in Marseilles, the warm sun glinting on the gentling undulating Mediterranean, reflected in her inviting brown eyes and sensual mouth, her teeth brilliant as Mallorcan pearls. As I stare out, today, at the cold grey Mersey, I know nothing could be more absurd, and that my mistress waits only for me.

Yes, I have been packed off to Liverpool and the coast with John Brown, for after several days of finding me slumped and unresponsive at the Black Bull, Papa determined that a change of scene was in order. We have taken a steamer along the Welsh coast and seen Penmaenmawr, and I have even written some verses, bad as they are, to sum up my state of mind:

Cannot my soul depart?
Where will it fly?
Asks my tormented heart,
Willing to die.
When will this restlessness
Tossing in sleeplessness –
Stranger to happiness –
Slumbering lie.

Trash – I wrote better as a mere child. Has it all been for naught? What will become of me now?

Brown and I are to meet soon to lift a glass – *many* glasses, it is safe to say – and so before we do, I must write to Charlotte, who surely will be unable to conceal her cold and silent rage at my conduct. Her *genuine concern* for my wellbeing is so obviously false that her eyes can scarcely mask her condemnation of my every word and act.

I duly assure Charlotte of my contrition, of my regret for my frantic folly, and promise amendment when I return, knowing that she will share my letter with Papa. Indeed, she will share it with anyone who will listen, including Emily, Anne and especially

Ellen Nussey, framing her letters, to 'Dear Nell,' I doubt not, with her own wise commentary.

As I seal the letter, my own hypocrisy leaves a bitter taste, but I know an evening of heavy drinking with John Brown, that faithful Old Knave of Trumps, will put matters to right: the first thing to disappear will be the hammering within my skull, and soon a gentle warmth will spread from my throat down my chest, and from my trunk through my arms and legs, until I can feel only a vague and pleasant shimmering where once my body was, like a man submerged, from the neck down, in a warm bath.

Since our return from a pleasure-steamer tour of the Welsh coast, Brown has tried his utmost each night to send me upstairs with a woman – *to ease your body and mind, lad* – and each night ends the same: I stumble off to bed and to a drunken, solitary slumber, while he shrugs and throws his arm about a whore's waist – and on at least one occasion there were two, one for each arm – and slurs some sort of heretical 'moral' about my failure to avail myself of the feminine bounty that Liverpool has to offer.

Tonight, it was, in the broadest possible Yorkshire accent he could muster, 'Why, then, man, we mun no' le' such riches as these go t' waste, eh? What would t' parson Brontë say? Summat like how we should no' bury our riches, buh use 'em for they are gifts of God hi'self, eh? If we fail to use 'em, they'll jus' be takin' away like' – and here his Yorkshire accent vanished, replaced by a quite remarkable imitation of my father, in the Cambridgian tones he usually reserves for the pulpit – 'for would not the good reverend say, quoting Matthew: *For unto every one that hath shall be given, and he shall have abundance: but from him that hath not shall be taken even that which he hath.*'

Slapping his chosen partner on her buttocks as he followed her up the stairs of the inn, he added, now in his own laughing voice, 'Y'don' reckon I want to be cast into t'dark, where there be weepin' and gnashin' o' teeth and all manner o' bother, do ya? 'cause that's what became of the dozy bugger who buried his talent.' He winked and nodded towards his partner, a buxom woman whose skin was so dark, whose hair was so raven-black, as to lead one to believe that she was a gypsy, or perhaps a mulattress, probably orphaned on the streets of Liverpool, like so many other unfortunates too numerous to count. I thought of Maeve and wondered if ever I would see her again.

Contemplating Brown, whose mind was clearly set on matters of a purely fleshly variety, I asked myself why Papa allows – indeed, encourages – him to be my guardian, this same John Brown who blasphemes with delight, mocking sacred scripture, whoring and drinking as much as possible whenever he is from home. But here is no great mystery, in the end, for like most men – like Titterington and his band in Luddenden, for example – John dexterously shows one face to polite society and quite another to his trusted confidants. Indeed, his conduct abroad, strange though it may seem, has never affected his faithful service to Papa and the parish, his paternal duty to his six daughters, or – as unfaithful as he is – his apparently genuine esteem for his Mary.

Is this hypocrisy, or simply survival? Is it an abberation or, in reality, the very thing that allows for the smooth functioning of society's great machine in this utilitarian age? I recall young Lydia Robinson's admonishment to Anne in my lodgings on that snowy evening, which now seems so distant: *Think what chaos would ensue if everyone were to see the truth in such absolute terms as you!*

But what of her mother, of my darling Lydia? Does she yearn for me as I do for her? Does she ache to have me in her arms, to feel my hands and mouth move over her like a summer breeze, to lose herself with me as I with her, with the same sharp longing that tortures *me*? Writing this, I feel myself begin to harden with desire, and addressing my letter to Charlotte, I wonder if tonight I might just be tempted to join Brown in his pursuit of the softer sex, for surely I could close my eyes and transport myself, through the power of imagination, back to Thorp Green, or to the boathouse at Scarborough, where the swelling and crashing surf without was as nothing compared to the surging, heaving tide of passion within.

Does she think of me as ceaselessly as I do of her? How could she not? If only I had a word from her, a mere crumb from my mistress's table! Perhaps a letter awaits me at the Parsonage. Yes, surely there will be some communication from Thorp Green when I return.

August 4th, 1845 · Haworth, The Parsonage

Home again. *Home.* The poem I began in Liverpool concludes:

Home it is not with me …
My home has ta'en its rest
In an afflicted breast
That I have often pressed
But may *no more*

Meanwhile, I have succeeded in procuring some work for my old friend Leyland: the carving of a memorial for one Joseph Midgeley of Oldfield, which John Brown will be charged with lettering and mounting in Haworth Church. I've written Joe today, to bid him visit Haworth soon, and to tell him that a woman robed in black and calling herself MISERY followed me, in my journey with Brown, wherever I went.

XXII.

Love and Duty

August 17th, 1845 · The Parsonage

No letter has arrived from Thorp Green since I returned a fortnight ago, alas. I found only Papa and my sisters, in various attitudes of quiet sorrow (Anne), cold indifference (Emily) or simmering reproach (Charlotte, of course). The trip has done my sisters more far more good than it has done me, surely, for it removed me from their sight and allowed them to resume their feminine communion unhindered, while with Brown as Mentor, my journey has hardly instilled in me a newfound rectitude or different proclivities: nay, quite the contrary is the case.

But at least I have seen new sights, breathed in the fresh breezes of the Irish Sea, and gazed up at the stony brow of Penmaenmawr from the steamer. I even tried at last to join Brown in his whoring, with no success. It seems that despite my occasional phantasms of being in the soft embraces of her lovely daughters, Lydia is now the only woman for me, the only one who can arouse the longing and desire which, in the debauched days and nights of Luddenden Foot, burned so hotly that no number of women could quench it. Now, only a soft ember glows in my heart, and it glows only for my Lydia, my angel, my idol. All hopes of salvation are in her, for only *she* holds the key to unlock my future happiness, both in love and in the world. While some might call this a monomania, I cannot think but that it is quite simply *true*: without her love I am bereft, for her body's absence turns mine to lifeless stone; I am certain that she longs for me, and that if only Robinson, that eunuch-like fellow, that bloodless mock-husband, would quit the stage, which is to say get seriously down to the business of *expiring*, I would at last have his lady – whom I can only consider *My Wife* – and his estate, and all of my worries would at last and forever be removed.

Such were the thoughts – which God and man would both condemn as shocking and sinful, I am well aware – that moved slowly through my clouded mind this morning, after a particularly serious bout of drinking at the Black Bull. I sat on the sofa stroking Flossy, not out of any affection, but absently, to give my idle hand something to do. I gazed not out the window, but into the folds of my breeches, my chin nearly reposing on my breast as if in an attitude of slumber, for even lifting my head required a great effort. Quick, impatient footsteps entered the room, and Charlotte's voice, in which I forever hear condemnation, struck my suffering senses like the sound of fingernails dragged across a schoolboy's slate. Each hair on my head seemed to ache as she spoke.

'Well, Branwell?' said she.

'What is the question, dear sister?' I queried, irritably, my eyes now raised to meet hers. She stood wearing an apron, one hand on her hip and the other holding a piece of paper aloft.

'I was wondering when you might consider seeking employment?'

'Really, now?' said I, rallying to my own defence. 'Why, I *have* been employed, you will recall, for longer than anyone but Anne. I might ask the same question of you. With the scheme for the Misses Brontës' School for Girls blasted to atoms before it ever began, surely you are sufficiently liberated to seek a position as a governess – or seek a husband, if that is more to your liking.'

Knowing that she had refused at least two offers of marriage but was now ageing and increasingly desperate, I added this last comment with deliberate cruelty, as if running her through with a sword.

Water rose to her eyes, but she quickly mastered herself. 'Do you think, Branwell, that because I am poor, obscure, plain and little, I will betray my own heart and soul to marry a man I do not love, for mere convenience or comfort – for *money*?'

Flossy whimpered slightly at the vehemence with which Charlotte said this, pressing his velvety muzzle against my right knee, at the same time looking up at her with his soft brown eyes, unsure of whether to fear or pity her, I'm sure. I shared his sentiments.

'I beg your pardon, Charlotte, I meant no offence,' said I with feigned concern. 'Of course, you are quite right. I, too, worship Cupid, and have felt the full sting of his arrow.'

The boy in me – her childhood playmate – wished to go on, to confide in Charlotte, to tell her that I was still wracked with uncontrollable desire for my mistress, and that once Robinson died I would have both love and livelihood, united in my goddess Lydia. Instead, I bit my lip and looked down at Flossy, who now gazed up at me with the stupid but irresistible love of a dog for the humans in his life, even though he was Anne's, not mine. Flossy – our last living and breathing link to Thorp Green.

But Charlotte had guessed my thoughts, at least in part.

'I hope that you refer to some unnamed and suitably unattainable young lady, and not' – here she paused, uncertain as to whether she should proceed.

'And not to *whom*?' asked I, goading her onward.

'Not – not a *married* woman, a diabolical temptress from all I can determine. Anne refuses to speak of her, and I can hardly fault her for not wishing to revisit the disgusting ways of anyone in that wicked family, least of all the horrible mother.'

'I don't wish to speak of them either, but I will not hear such calumny of Lydia – of Mrs Robinson.'

'So you believe that what I say is false, is defamatory? Did she *not* seduce you?'

I considered. In fiction Alexander Percy – viz., Northangerland – was always the effortless seducer, but here in cold reality it was clearly to my advantage to allow Charlotte and the others to think me the victim, the innocent young tutor tempted into iniquity by the rich and corrupt older woman, who, after all, held his future in her pretty, immoral hands. Besides, it was close enough to the truth, was it not? And yet, I burned with indignation; I yearned to spring to Lydia's defence. For what my father and sisters would condemn as lust was merely their narrow, conventional view of the matter – why was the perfect, passionate union of two beings a sin, after all? How could something that made us feel like Gods be evil? What was it Shelley had written? *Religion and morality compose a practical code of misery and servitude.*

I tried – but failed – to hold my tongue, and turned the conversation away from *who* seduced *whom*, and into another channel.

'We love each other, Charlotte, and this is hardly something I expect *you* to understand.'

'But what of *duty*, Branwell? Surely you are concerned about God's law, if not man's: rectitude of conduct and resignation point out the straightest road from this world to the next.'

I scoffed, emboldened and reckless. Reckless after a fashion, of course, for I knew Papa was visiting parishioners, and that no one else was listening.

'If there *is* a God, I hardly think *He* is much concerned with affairs such as this, and am quite convinced that if I have transgressed anything, it is a mere human law. More to the point, if you had ever felt the true love of a *grande passion*, which like a hurricane sweeps away all, whether erected by God or Man, that stands in its way; if you had ever felt such love – yes, sister, even for a *married* man – you would, I am convinced, trample every last thing in your path, brave Satan and all his legions, and like that Great Deceiver himself you would raise your fist and defy your very Maker.'

She flushed at this slight but chose not to respond.

I paused here, wishing to add: *If you had ever felt the transports procured by the ecstacy of two bodies fused into one, kindling in pure, powerful flame* – but such a remark was not only beyond the pale, it would simply confirm her opinion of my depravity, so I simply said, 'If never before have your veins been on fire, if never once has your heart beaten faster than you can count the throbs, you cannot possibly know what you would do, and you certainly are not equipped to sit in judgement upon *me*.'

As I spoke, Flossy buried his muzzle even further into my leg, as if to hide, and Charlotte's face grew scarlet with wrath. She trembled so greatly that she had to reach out to a table to steady herself, as if shaken by something unseen, something far beyond my own transgressions.

'Do you think,' said she, eyes flashing and fists clenched, 'so little of me? That I would cast away all that I have learnt, and all that has sustained me? That in a moment of temptation, when body and soul rise in mutiny, every law and principle would melt away into nothingness?'

'*Nay*,' said I, in a Yorkshire drawl, hoping to moderate, if not annihilate entirely, her wrath with a bit of levity, '*nay*, Sister, it is because I think so *much* of you, for clearly you are a woman of great passion, like all of the Brontës before you.'

Here there came neither laughter nor anger, however, but great tears spilling down her cheeks, as if from a hidden source.

'Truly, sister, I meant no offence. Let us speak no more of this. You were asking me about seeking employment, and I fear you touched a nerve. You are right, of course, but I know not where to begin, and in my sorrow I find no will to recommence.'

Now I was simply prattling on like a fool, trying to fill the void, to distract Charlotte from her own hidden sorrow, whatever it was. Could it be that she still harboured esteem and affection for me, which leapt as high as a bonfire in our youth, but which the intervening years had seemed so utterly to have extinguished?

She wiped her eyes with her apron and tendered the piece of paper. 'Here,' she said simply, and turned and walked from the room. I squinted at the scrap of paper, which had been torn from the *Leeds Intelligencer*, announcing the proposal of a new railway line from Hebden Bridge to Oakworth, via Oxenhope, Keighley and Haworth. Yes, the railway seemed to be coming to us even sooner than we had expected.

In the meantime, I am swallowing my old aversion and reworking a childhood story as a novel, to be called *And the Weary Are at Rest*. Perhaps there is hope for me yet, in at least one of these two directions.

August 29th, 1845 · The Parsonage

Hope indeed, but of a third kind, one I was beginning to think impossible! Dr Crosby has written to me and wishes to meet with me at Harrogate on the 3rd of September. I am fit to burst through my very skin with elation, anticipation and dread. What news will the good doctor bring from Thorp Green, from my Lydia?

XXIII.

Crosby in Harrogate

September 4th, 1845 · The Parsonage

I have seen Dr Crosby. The flames of hope leap no higher, but neither have they been fully extinguished. Yesterday I hired a gig and arrived at the Crown Hotel in Harrogate at half past ten, where Crosby already sat at an oak table, a large breakfast before him.

'Hello!' said he in his usual hearty manner, waving me to a chair across the table from him. 'So sorry, Brontë, but I was positively ravenous after my ride, and was not sure when you would arrive. Here, let me order you something to eat.' He proceeded to order a rasher of bacon, eggs and potatoes, along with a pitcher of strong coffee and a pint of ale for each of us.

I removed my cloak and hat and vigorously clasped the doctor's hand, showering him with questions about Lydia: How was she? How did she look? Did that brute of a husband – still an ogre, for all of his sickliness – make her life a hell? Did she ask after me? Had she sent him to see me? What were her instructions?

'Now now, lad,' he began soothingly, 'Becalm yourself, and most of all,' he added, looking around the room, 'lower your voice. We will have ample time to discuss all these things, to the extent that I am allowed to do so. First tell me, how are you, and what do you do with your time?'

'I have lost my love and my livelihood. How do you think I am?' I replied somewhat testily.

'Peace, Brontë, peace. I know you must have suffered greatly, but surely you are not angry with *me*?'

'Let us not place such suffering in the past tense, Crosby. Do you think I could forget one that I cannot help loving, and not regret losing the single post in which I performed with such success in my life?'

Softening, I added: 'And surely you must know that I yearn to return to the neighbourhood and its inhabitants – yes, you among them, Crosby – I had come to view with a fondness even greater than that which I hold for my childhood home?'

'Now that's better, Brontë,' he said, smiling once again. 'I promise I come with news, but we must eat and drink, and you must calmly tell me what you are about these days, and then we shall see about it.'

I breathed deeply, determining that after nearly two months of silence I could wait a few moments longer. It would be foolish to damage my friendship with Crosby – both because he was a genuine friend, and because he could surely be of service, for he quite possibly had influence over Lydia herself, in the odd way that subordinates – especially medical men who hold life and death in their hands – sometimes do.

Over breakfast I recounted the trip to Liverpool and the coast of Wales, explained that I was considering making an application for the post of secretary to the proposed railway line to be constructed through Haworth, whilst writing the odd poem here and there, but that I had devoted most of my hours of time snatched from downright illness – an 'illness' that mingled lovesickness and the results of drowning my sorrows – to the composition of a three-volume novel, one volume of which was nearly completed.

Crosby laughed. 'Have you not told me on more than one occasion that you would never stoop so low as to write a novel?'

'True,' I replied. 'But, finally, I felt that I must rouse myself to attempt something while roasting daily and nightly over a slow fire – to while away my torment awaiting word from Thorp Green. Several years ago, Hartley Coleridge told me that in the present state of the publishing and reading world a novel is the most saleable article; I knew he was right then, but I hated that he was: I have always disdained today's fiction as the production of money-grubbers like Mr Dickens, written for the delight of empty-headed, mostly female readers without a single original notion rattling about in their heads. A good *story* is all readers want today!'

'And what,' said Crosby, 'is wrong with that?'

'But what of *ideas*, and what of *feelings*? What of *art*?'

'But cannot a novel have all those things? What of Defoe, or Smollet, or Fielding? What of Walter Scott, or Miss Austen, for that matter?'

'Yes, of course, you are right, but such novels are as rare as an April snowshower. What enrages me is that where ten pounds would be offered for a work of poetry or translation from the classics, the production of which would require the utmost stretch of a man's intellect, two *hundred* pounds would be turned down by the proud author of a three-volume novel – a *triple-decker* as people are calling it now – whose composition would require no more effort that the smoking of a cigar and the humming of a tune, for Heaven's sake.'

'So, you *know* this state of affairs to be true,' said Crosby, stroking his thick side-whiskers thoughtfully, 'and yet you simply wish it to be otherwise.'

'Yes,' I laughed bitterly, 'I'm afraid *that* is the story of my life. My sisters aren't that much different, I'm afraid. We seem especially – nay, spectacularly – ill suited to what people call the *World* or *Society*. Perhaps if we had significant fortunes to our names, it would be quite another matter, but alas ...'

I suddenly felt a desire for strong drink: my mouth was parched and my head throbbed, and having little money, I ordered a gin and water. Indeed, since losing my post at Thorp Green, I have utterly abandoned my earlier aversion to gin – which has now become an old friend, one who does me a great deal of good at very little expense.

Crosby cleared his throat, perhaps uncomfortable with talk of money, given my recent dismissal. 'Tell me, then – now that you are prepared to abandon all poetic scruples and launch your career as a novelist – what is the subject of your novel?'

'Ah, well, it is the result of years of thought. If it gives a vivid picture of human feelings for good and evil – veiled by the cloak of deceit which must enwrap man and woman – and if it reveals man's heart, as well as the conflicting feelings and clashing pursuits we meet on our uncertain path through life, I shall be gratified enough. Who knows but that I might at last see some income in exchange for my efforts?'

I had again come around to the topic of money. Does it not *always* come back to that? My sisters and I could rage all we want, shake our fists at the world, but we could no more change it than King Canute could halt the tide from rising.

I sighed and emptied my glass. 'And that, Crosby,' said I after a long pause, 'is all I have to relate.'

Another pause.

'Will you, my friend, now tell me why I have been summoned more than half-way to Thorp Green for this interview? Do you have word from Lydia? From Mrs Robinson? What happened? Does she suffer?'

Crosby himself sighed, as though he had suffered as much as anyone else. At last he began, slowly and, it seemed to me, carefully. 'I wish I could say exactly what transpired, but I know little more than you, Brontë. I can say with certitude that the conduct of young Lydia – Miss Robinson – has become increasingly outrageous, and that she has so harassed and worried her parents as to fairly tear the fabric of the family to shreds. I sometimes wish that she would simply run off with her Mr Roxby and leave the family in peace. If she does not do so quickly, I'm quite certain that her parents will arrange a marriage of interest with some rich old gentleman of the neighbourhood, or worse yet, some young rake who needs reforming. I'm fairly certainly neither of those possibilities would end any happier than an elopement with Roxby, though of course in the last case she would quite likely be cut out of her papa's will.'

'Enough of Miss Robinson, Crosby – do you bring word from her mother? Can you tell me why I was dismissed? For the good reverend simply barred me from all contact with every member of his family. It is a mystery to me, though I've some notions of what might have happened.'

'I must say, Brontë, you look positively ashen. You could use another drink, I'm quite sure – something proper, this time.' Crosby called for a bottle of whisky to be brought to our table, jesting, to introduce a bit of levity, about our common Irish origins.

'Ah,' said he, 'now *that's* some good medicine!' Leaning forward and wrinkling his forehead as if to focus his attention, he continued: 'Now then, Branwell – we are still friends and so I may call you Branwell once we both have a drink in hand, eh? – yes? Very well, Branwell, here is all I know: *something* occurred after you left the young master in his parents' care in Scarborough. I have asked my friend Mrs Marshall, but I'm afraid her loyalty to her employers trumps all, and she has only alluded to the great breach in the family over Miss Robinson's infatuation with the young actor. That is precisely why I spoke of her, because I somehow feel that the naughty girl is involved in *everything* that has gone awry at Thorp Green. But perhaps that's unfair.'

'I don't believe it's unfair at all, Crosby' – I could not bring myself to call him by his first name – 'Do you know that the little vixen threatened to tell her mama and papa that I had made improper advances towards her, if I failed to keep her conduct with Roxby a secret? And I know you have sworn me to silence concerning my connection with her mother, but now –'

'But now,' Crosby interrupted, 'there is no such connection, and while I still wish to hear no particulars that could implicate anyone criminally, it will do no harm for us to admit, here and now, that your former mistress was inordinately fond of you, and is much aggrieved at what has befallen you. Of course, she cannot write to you *herself*, for her husband has given Mrs Marshall strict orders that all of the correspondence of the household is to pass through his hands, and has made it plain that even the slightest hesitation from his wife's lady-in-waiting will result in immediate dismissal, without so much as a fare-thee-well or a letter of reference. All the more reason, I'm afraid, that Marshall refuses to divulge what occurred in Scarborough, other than Miss Robinson's mad pursuit of Roxby, of course.'

'Does Mr Robinson treat his wife poorly? I cannot bear to think of her suffering at his hands.'

'He seems to have forgiven her,' said Crosby, adding with a wink, 'if, that is, there is anything *to* forgive. No, he calls for her all of the time, and she is forever at his side, or following me out of his room, questioning me about the health of her "Angel Edmund".'

At first I ground my teeth at this, but the gin and whisky were having their effect, loosening my clenched jaws, and I soon reasoned that Lydia was doing this for *me*, for *us*. Regardless of what Robinson had or had not discovered – or, more likely, had or had not suspected – my sweet Lydia had made it her mission to dissipate his wrath or dispel his suspicions. She would remain his devoted helpmate to the bitter end, for the sake of her children and so that she could then, at long last, be united with her *true* love. Perhaps, as I had imagined, she and her namesake had reached an uneasy truce, but one that was forever in danger of being broken.

How could I not but hope that this was true, and how much more so did it seem likely when Crosby reached into his pocket and drew out two gold sovereigns, which he slid across the table to me.

'What's this?' said I.

'Why, don't tell me you are such a poet that you don't recognise cold, hard cash when you see it!' laughed Crosby.

'But this does not make sense … the Reverend Robinson had already advanced my salary and paid my travel expenses.'

'Ah, but this is from *Mrs* Robinson,' said Crosby. 'She managed to arrange matters so that we had a few moments alone, and it was her idea that I meet you here, and that I give you some money, for she feels' – here I am recapitulating, Brontë – 'wretched about your departure, and the manner in which you learnt of it. She devised a story to explain my absence, and the expenditure of the two pounds in Harrogate, and I confess that I, too, have been part of the deception.'

Here Crosby's eyes filled; his esteem for me, aided by a generous infusion of whisky, was plain. 'You see, Branwell, I am also saddened by your departure, and feel the absence of your friendship keenly.' He wiped his tears from his cheeks and smiled: 'Just look at me, a sentimental old fool!'

Although touched by my friend's demonstrations of genuine affection, I could not help thinking how quickly and gladly I would exchange the sovereigns, which I carefully placed in my own pocket, for the mere sound of Lydia's voice, her tender words in my ear, her soft, full lips so close that I could turn and press them to my own!

Later, as we took leave of each other, Crosby clapped his begloved hands on my shoulders. 'By Jove, Brontë, I almost forgot: you are under *no circumstances* to contact Mrs Robinson, or anyone connected to Thorp Green, including me, unless you hear from me first, do you understand? While it has far more to do with Mr Roxby and Miss Robinson than anything else, your former employer has a veritable army on the lookout for communications from either you *or* the young actor, and I fear he has even placed spies among the postmen for miles round, including in my own little village.

Although I burned with vexation, flames of hope mixed with those of despair; the two sovereigns in my pocket and the whisky now fully and warmly in possession of me, I shook my friend's hand enthusiastically, and promised to follow my lady's commands faithfully.

'Did she say anything else, Crosby?' said I. 'Can you not remember one thing to report to me verbatim?'

Crosby rubbed his chin thoughtfully and at last remarked, 'Ah, yes, there was one thing: I believe she said, "Tell him to be patient, and that all will be well." Yes, I believe that was it.'

So, I am cast down but not cast away! Surely, surely her plan is to marry me when at last Robinson quits this world for the next! So it is that I am no longer suffering the torments of Hell, but instead dwell in a Limbo or a Purgatory, a twilight region where hope and fear share dominion.

September 10th, 1845 · The Parsonage

Poor Leyland! He put off a planned visit to Haworth when a bust that had been commissioned cracked irreparably just as he was giving it his final touches. Surely there is a lesson here, but I am far too indolent to seek it. To distract the poor fellow, I repeated to him what I'd said to Crosby about my novel, though in truth I have already begun to lose interest in it; to cheer him I added a couple of my customary sketches, including one picturing a bust of myself that has been cast down to earth – we return to the clay, after all – with, in the distance, the silhouette of my Lydia as sculptress. The caption below reads: *A Cast – cast down but not castaway.*

Although it occupies my mind and helps pass the hours and days, there are moments when I'd like to cast away this wretched novel. Yes, I call it *And the Weary Are at Rest*; it is a retelling of the story of Alexander Percy's seduction of the married Maria Thurston, with my Lydia both seducer and seduced, and I a mere spectator – for would not Percy, Lord Northangerland, do something? I have no heart for it, and the thought of trying to make it *saleable* is almost as loathesome as the thought of becoming a bank clerk. Then again, I'm not sure what I have the heart for until Lydia is restored to me. I suffer from constant mental exhaustion, which arises from brooding on matters useless at present to think of.

Meanwhile, I will continue to urge Phidias – for such has Leyland jocularly begun to call himself, comparing his cracked bust to the Greek scuptor's lost *Zeus at Olympia* – to come hoist a glass in Haworth, for of what other use are the two sovereigns in my wallet?

October 25th, 1845 · The Parsonage

I've at long last heard again from Crosby, but not on the subject I expected. At the same time, his news was hardly a surprise: on October 20th, Miss Lydia Mary Robinson at last made good on her threat, and eloped with Mr Henry Roxby of Scarborough, marrying him that evening at Gretna Green. Her father, it seems, has channelled what little strength he retains into further wrath, and threatens to make good on his own threat, to have her written entirely out of his will.

I can picture the smartly dressed couple – truly, as handsome as any described in the latest novel – kissing at their first opportunity, then driving all day to reach Gretna Green, passing through Thirsk and Bowes, Penrith and Calthwaite, and at last, as night approached, the final stretch through Carlisle and into Scotland. Or perhaps the runaways took the railway for part of their journey, by the less direct route, *via* Newcastle? In any event, I hope the weather was kind to them, that the sun shone brightly on their escape, and that all went as planned. I strongly suspect that Roxby will have no easy time of it with his young bride in the long run, but I envy him the honeymoon.

I did not share the news with Anne, for on those rare occasions when we converse at all, we never speak of Thorp Green and its inhabitants, and young Lydia's decampment would only confirm her severest opinions of the young lady – and, for that matter, of her mother. Besides, she will likely hear about this matter from some other source, and soon enough.

As for me, I have proposed myself as secretary to the new railway. And so I wait. I wait for word from Lydia; I wait to hear from the railway; I wait to see what other opportunities might come my way. It is hard to say, on any given day, whether, in my breast, hope or despair prevails. These were the thoughts dominating my mind as I rode this morning, with Papa, to a meeting in

Keighley. His eyesight is dimming, and so I often accompany him on such short journeys; I am sure that it has the further advantage, from my sisters' point of view, of ridding the Parsonage of my presence – or so I imagine. They have been behaving of late in mysterious ways: they are together even more often than usual, and there is a great deal of whispering and shuffling of papers, of falling silent at the approach of my footsteps.

As our gig bounced along the road to Keighley, the rays of the shortening day's sun struck and ignited the last flaming foliage of autumn, and against a cloudless sky the trees seemed, for an instant, to concentrate in their beauty not only life's boundless hopes and limitless joys, but also its bottomless depths of despair – and not just of my own life, but that of every human who has lived since the creation of the universe. My heart so brimmed with this fullness – with the unspeakable pleasure of the moment and the equal measure of regret – nay, it was more akin to the sharp pain of mourning – at its passing, for pass it must – that tears started to my eyes. God Almighty, if Thou art in Thy Heaven, thanks be to Thee for this Thy creation, whose beauty surpasses all words – but why oh why oh why must such beauty be so fleeting as to disappear whenever we draw nigh to contemplate its sublime plenitude?

Beautiful moment, thought I, do not pass away – *Verweile doch, du bist so schön!* But as quickly as it had come, it was gone, and the world was as flat and colourless as before.

November 23rd, 1845 · The Parsonage

Rarely do Papa and I speak, and seldom does he appear in these pages. I wonder, again, why that is? When I was a young boy, he united in his erect carriage and quizzical brow, his seemingly inexhaustible erudition (at lessons) and fearsome holiness (at church), everything I thought worth admiring – nay, worshipping. In short, he was a god. Or, at the very least, God's great prophet.

There was no specific moment of shock or crisis that caused me to view him differently, which is to say *as mortal*, no humiliating or shameful episode of drunkenness or passing impiety – though he was certainly entitled to drown his sorrow or curse his Maker when he lost Mama, then Maria and Elizabeth. No, it was more a gradual, imperceptible wearing away, like the erosion of the cliffs at Scarborough, or the ancient fort on Penmaenmawr, or the smooth recesses on the stone steps of York Minster, worn by the feet of six centuries of pilgrims.

Quite simply, I retained my affection and respect – akin to awe – for the old man, and those feelings are, curiously enough, the very reason I have nothing to say to him. What I mean is this: I simply disagree on matters religious – which is to say the very centre of his existence – and have too much affection for him to wish to break his heart with my own apostasy, too much respect for his strength of character and force – in short, his *goodness* – to contradict what I consider to be his ridiculous, fanatical adherence to primitive superstition. In short, I hold my tongue, for that is the surest way to avoid injuring him, insulting his beliefs or displaying my hypocrisy to the world.

I confess to these pages alone, however, that it is difficult to sit still and not cry out 'Bollocks!' when I hear *thank the Lord* for this, or *thanks be to God* for that. Whence the silence to which I am bound: I can no more join in such foolish pieties than I can denounce them as such. Does Papa know all of this? If so, he has surely determined that silent prayer for my eternal soul is his sole recourse. So much the better for us both, then. Or does he feel that my failings are somehow *his*, has he blamed the peculiar education he gave me – keeping me from school precisely to *protect* me from the very things that have, to use language he might employ, *ensnared* me? Could it be that he is driven by despair to a silence not so dissimilar from my own?

Practical business matters, at least, escape this contradiction of character, and so it was with no great ceremony – albeit with a heavy heart, I am certain – that he informed me, this morning, that he had learnt through a fellow clergyman that the secretaryship of the railway committee had been awarded to someone else. The sweet man – for he *is* that – placed his large hand awkwardly, tentatively, on my arm, saying: 'Well now, Branwell, it was not meant to be. The Lord must have other plans for you.'

He patted my arm and walked out of the room, relieving me of the obligation to respond.

XXIV.

Publications

November 8th, 1845 · The Parsonage

Today the *Halifax Guardian* has again published my work, this time the poem 'Real Rest'. The poet-narrator – Branwell/ Northangerland, of course – addresses a bloated corpse that floats upon the waves, and considers what it would be to exchange places:

> Thou hast what all men covet, REAL REST.
> I have an outward frame unlike to thine,
> Warm with young life – not cold in death's decline;
> An eye that sees the sunny light of heaven –
> A heart by pleasure thrilled – by anguish riven –
> But in exchange for thy untroubled calm,
> Thy gift of cold oblivion's healing balm,
> I'd give my youth – my health – my life to come,
> And share thy slumbers in thy ocean tomb.

How typical, that my one glimmer of success is in that field of endeavour where I find the most pleasure, but which brings no financial gain! For this reason, I am again plaguing poor Grundy, in hopes that he might be of assistance in finding a post somewhere in the ever-expanding world of the railway. I have little hope, however, and in all probability have neither the will nor the force to retain such a post – in the unlikely event that I were to obtain one.

November 25th, 1845 · The Black Bull, Haworth

Chill winter approaches with a vengeance, chasing the last of autumn's leaves, which cling to the trees as last bits of matted hair and dried flesh cleave to a corpse. Cadavers below ground, cadavers above, and Brontës in the church vault. How long it has been! Mama a quarter of a century ago; Maria and Elizabeth four years later. And yet, how the sobs – yes, ours and Papa's, but also Mama's – still din in my ears!

Meanwhile, encouraged by the success of 'Real Rest', I have written another poem, 'Penmaenmawr', inspired by my trip with Brown – but intended for Lydia's eyes. How well I remember sailing under the Welsh mountain, when the band on board the steamer struck up *Ye Banks and Braes*. The sorrowful Scottish tune only added to my bitterness, and I trembled as I heard the final lines of the song:

And may fause Luver staw my rose,
But ah! She left the thorn wi' me.

Surely, surely, though, Lydia is no false lover, and she is not the thief in question; I may be abandoned, pricked by the bitter thorns of desertion, but only for a time: cast off by the Reverend Robinson, but not cast away by my sweet Lydia. Like one who keeps a talisman in his pocket, rubbing it whenever he needs to call forth hope or courage, so I kept in my breast her words, reported by Crosby: *Tell him to be patient, and all will be well.* No, she is not false, for how could one love with such passion one day and coldly turn from her lover the next? Surely, such a thing cannot be possible.

'Penmaenmawr' is the only way I can imagine communicating with Lydia, since I have been forbidden all contact with her. I even took back, almost immediately, the one letter of comfort I had intended to send her through the private channel of Dr Crosby, dreading not only the consequences of discovery but the good doctor's reprimands. I know that printed lines with my usual signature 'Northangerland' will excite no suspicion, as my late employer shrank from the bare idea of my being able to write *anything*, so *he* won't know the name.

I have informed Joe how much I could use an hour sitting with him – by which, of course, I mean many hours of drinking and conversing about all manner of things – and that I would promise not to be gloomy. It was my hope that my friend would find the time to come to Haworth, though I fear, as I did not hesitate to tell him, that his *e're long* has become *ne'er*, so I have informed him that I will do my best to accost him soon in that latter-day Gomorrah, Halifax itself. We shall see whether he delivers my poem to the *Halifax Guardian* and whether it is published. If it is, will Lydia see it? If I wanted to be certain I would submit it to Bellerby in York, though that gentleman has likely also been instructed to ignore all communications from me. After all, would he rather publish an unknown poet, or lose a wealthy client?

I tremble, half with hope, half with fear, that she will see these lines:

I had an ear which could on accents dwell …
An eye which saw, far off, a tender form
Beaten, unsheltered, by affliction's storm –
An arm – a lip – that trembled to embrace
An Angel's gentle breast and sorrowing face –
A mind that clung to Ouse's fertile side …

Am I mad? What if Anne sees this? Or, for that matter, what if Charlotte does? The truth is this: I do not much care. Is now the time for timidity, for caution? For fear of my three unemployed, unpublished, unwed, virgin sisters? No: like the great Welsh mountain, let me:

… arise o'er mortal care;
All evils bear, yet never know despair;
Unshrinking face the griefs I now deplore,
And stand, through storm and shine, like moveless

PENMAENMAWR.

Midwinter, 1845 · The Parsonage

'Penmaenmawr' was indeed published in the illustrious *Halifax Guardian*, two days ago. More may come of this than I reckon on, but I care not a whit. Yesterday, I contrived to accompany Brown to Halifax, where at long last I was able to settle in for a long conversation with Mr J.B. Leyland, the eminent sculptor himself.

The first thing I noticed upon entering his studio was a life-sized effigy of a man lying recumbent, his right arm extended straight along his right flank, his large left hand folded over his heart. His aquiline nose, a larger version of my own, stands out from a drawn, almost scowling visage.

'Who is *this* unfortunate gentleman, my dear sir?' said I. 'By all that's holy, rarely have I seen a beak more hooked than my own – and to think that *his* is cast in stone for all eternity!'

Mine, I thought to myself, will be food for worms all too soon. How strange that such despair can flow just under the bright surface of life, like a dark and vast subterranean river beneath the joyous green riot of spring.

'And my word upon it,' I continued without a pause, as this Stygian stream coursed through my mind, 'he seems unhappy to be there – I hope his countenance is more joyful in the afterlife, at least.'

Leyland laughed, clapping me on the shoulder with hands still dusty from the chisel. A beam of ephemeral midwinter sun slanted down through windows set high in the studio's south wall, giving shape to the white dust that hung in the air from his morning's work. Or, perhaps more accurately, the dust gave shape to the shafts of sunlight, just as a sail or stand of trees allows us to catch, for a fleeting instant, a glimpse of the otherwise invisible wind.

'Ho ho! So, the calumny begins before you grant me not so much as a meagre salutation, eh Brontë?' Before a roaring fire he removed his smock, washed his massive forearms and hands, and then warmed himself for a moment.

'The unfortunate gentleman,' he at length replied, nodding over his shoulder, 'is none other than your friend Dr Crosby's late acquaintance, Dr Stephen Beckwith of York.'

I remained silent, remembering that he had received the commission – and advance – for this work more than two years earlier.

'Yes, *yes*,' he continued gruffly at last, 'I know very well: it has taken me altogether too long, but at last it's nearly complete. I can only hope it brings me, through its placement in the great York Minster, more commissions, because the Devil take me if I've made a bloody farthing on the damned thing.'

'Heavens, Leyland, you don't habitually begin using such shocking language until you've a drink or two in you.'

'What makes you think, little man,' said he, pulling on coat, gloves and hat with a wink, 'that I don't already have a drink or two in me? But come, let's go.'

Brown, who had some business to conduct with Leyland's assistant, was to remain behind at the studio, whilst we walked uphill to the Old Cock, which had the advantage of being less than ten minutes away, and nowhere close to Maggie and her husband's establishment near the new railway station at Shaw Syke. Seeing her would only be a reminder of dashed hopes, youthful aspirations and ambitions unfulfilled. Who knows but that she has another child – or two – by now? I would not ask Leyland about such matters, though he could surely answer, since his own studio is a mere stone's throw from there.

Our walk to the Old Cock was just long enough to chill us thoroughly, and so it was with heightened pleasure that we entered Mr Nicholson's establishment. The good man himself was there behind the bar as we entered, standing well over six feet, his powerful arms wiping a glass dry as one of his boys stirred the fire crackling in the grate and his wife bustled about taking and delivering orders. Nicholson has jet-black eyes and hair, including wide side-whiskers. One would guess him a gypsy or a Sicilian, like Dimick in York, if it were not for his fair skin and merry blue eyes. He encourages levity, for it is good for business, but he brooks no nonsense or violence, and has been known to lift, one in each hand, two skirmishing drunks, and fling them out into the snow. Like Maggie's own father, I would not wish to cross the man, that much is certain.

It is unlikely that any such thoughts have ever occurred to Leyland.

'Hello, Tom!' he cried as we shed our outer-garments. 'How are you, old man?'

'Greetings, ma'am,' Joe added, bowing ceremoniously to Mrs Nicholson, a dumpy little thing with a pretty heart-shaped face, whose form still hints at a voluptuousness of days gone by, and whose coquetry is just sufficient to please the patrons without angering her husband. Quite to the contrary: Tom seems to know that such flirtation, like a moderate amount of levity, is good for business.

'Please, oh *please*, ma'am, bring us two of your smoking tumblers of brandy and water, for we are as chilled as Captain Parry on one of his celebrated voyages to the Arctic Circle!'

Mrs Nicholson laughed, her ample bosom shaking. When she turned to go, and Joe was certain that her husband was otherwise occupied, he leant over and whispered in my ear. 'Laugh if you wish, Brontë, but I'd give *her* a tumble. There's *something* there – you can just see it in her eyes when a woman truly *revels* in it, can you not?'

I thought of Lydia and shuddered – whether from the chill or other half-formed reflections that I would not permit to fully flower, I know not. Soon, thought I, it won't matter: both cold and depression will melt away in the warmth of my beverage.

'You could certainly *attempt* it,' said I, nodding in Nicholson's direction, 'if you wished to be killed.'

Joe merely winked at the good lady as she returned bearing our steaming cups and, taking a first mouthful, said simply: 'Aahh!'

I felt the same, for the effect of the warming liquid was well-nigh miraculous. It was not long before all doubts, all sadness, all inhibitions began to lift, like the summer fogs in Scarborough, which, more often than not, burn away in the midday sun, to reveal white sands, glimmering waves and brilliant skies.

'Well, young Faustus, I suppose you wish to know what I've been doing these two years that I have failed to complete the good, yet no less dead, Dr Beckwith, eh? The truth is that I took the advance from the committee in York and spent it on the pleasures of the flesh, I'm afraid. I had to borrow money from Francis just to complete the stern old fellow.'

'My dear sir, I've had my own troubles, as you know.'

'Yes, yes, you've not been reticent about *your* tribulations.'

I frowned: the fog had not fully lifted. Despite my repeated insistence that I am *no whiner*, I fear Joe may always think that I am. Nevertheless, perhaps for friendship's sake, he gamely pretended otherwise.

'Come come, cheer up lad! Above all,' he added, lifting his glass, 'drink up! All will be well, I'm sure of it. Your Dr Crosby is a good man – I've seen it for myself – let him guide you through the labyrinth to come. Either the lady will be yours, and all's well that ends well, or she will prove false, and so she is not worth a second thought.'

I frowned again, feeling the chill begin to return.

'See here, that was said only in jest, Branwell.'

'And your debt to your brother?' said I, somewhat testily, not at all convinced that my friend was jesting.

It was Leyland's opportunity to glower. He sighed, drained his cup, and signalled for another round, though my glass was still more than half-full.

'What happened is this, and you will see why I have no wish

to dwell upon it: I spent my advance from the committee in York and then had nothing to show for it. Francis – dear old Frank, God bless him – once again rode to the rescue. He gave me enough money to complete the other commission, as well as pay off my other debts.'

He gazed now in the direction of Francis's bookshop, just a street away, at 15 Cornmarket.

'He did it on one condition,' he continued, nodding his head in just that direction, as if Francis himself sat at our table, 'that I never again ask for such assistance, with the understanding that if I did make such a request, he would be obliged to refuse. "Not even," said my brother, in great earnest, but also with a tear trembling in his eye, "if it means you are carried off to debtors' prison, for I must now think of my wife, and soon, a family".'

He confided that Francis had converted to Catholicism to marry his new wife, Ann. This seemed not to be the time for jesting about the evils of Popery, so I merely followed his gaze out into the street, where the first dry snowflakes of winter had just begun to fall. After a protracted silence, Leyland at last summoned his forces, fairly slamming his glass to the table and gesturing to Mrs Nicholson for more.

'By God, let us drink to forget, Brontë: we both have our sorrows, but nothing that can withstand the tides of the River Lethe, so let us plunge in together: *Round, round with the glass, boys, as fast as you can!*'

There is little I recall from the rest of the evening. Who paid Nicholson? Do I remember seeing Francis, or do I only imagine it? There was certainly singing – was there not? How did I find my way to Brown, or he to me, and when did we return to Haworth? At what hour did we arrive, and did I disturb anyone at the Parsonage?

Such questions would discomfit a typical man, but I fear that my utter loathing of self has, like an overflowing glass, reached such a height that no further increase is possible, so that all fresh indignities simply splash away as excess. I am too numb, too stunned, too drowned even to remark – let alone worry – about such matters. Am I humiliated that Brown most likely carried me to bed like an infant? I should be, of course, but I simply blot it from my mind and think no more upon it. And I cannot change this any more than I can prevent the sun from rising.

When I awoke this morning, it took what seemed – and what may have been – hours to determine whether I was awake, and where I lay. Familiar feminine laughter answered both questions. At length I sat up, safe in my own bed, and it occurred to me that at least one of the drums beating a tattoo in my skull would cease if I could overcome my biliousness sufficiently to swallow a bit of coffee. As I descended the staircase I heard renewed laughter, and so drew quietly near enough to the dining room, which Aunt Branwell had forever insisted upon calling the parlour – to overhear the proceedings within, for its door was just sufficiently ajar.

From their soft, rhythmic footsteps, I could discern that the three of them were walking in a circle around the table. In childhood I, too, would have been of their number – nay, I would have been the leader. Out floated Emily's strong voice, reading a poem whose beginning I did not hear, but containing such heretical lines that I could have written.

Or perhaps, more accurately, they might have been written about me:

I've watched and sought my life-time long;
Sought him in heaven, hell, earth, and air –
An endless search, and always wrong!
Had I but seen his glorious eye
Once light the clouds that wilder me
I ne'er had raised this coward cry
To cease to think, and cease to be;
I ne'er had called oblivion blest –

A low canine whimper prevented me from hearing what followed; faithful to his name, Keeper had quitted his post in the kitchen to carry out a reconaissance mission, and had taken up the position of sentry between me and the door, ignoring my instructions to *hush* – or *whisht*, as Tabby would say. The beast was not, however, unhappy to see me; on the contrary, his tail made its own drumbeat on the door while he gladly submitted to my caresses, as I rubbed his massive head and scratched behind his little petal-shaped ears. The door flew suddenly open, and Charlotte stood before me, her cheeks flushed with anger or embarrassment – if it is not one it is generally the other – as she uttered her customary accusation: 'Really now, Brawell – were you listening at the door?'

My tongue seemed quite stuck to the roof of my mouth, my hair wild from the night's sleep and the evening that preceded it. She leant over the threshold and sniffed.

'*Pouah!*' said she, expressing even her disgust in French as she smelled, no doubt, the odours redolent of last night's spree. Stepping out and nearly, but not completely, closing the door, she spoke in an urgent whisper, like an actor on a stage. I had no doubt that she wanted her sisters to hear her, but at the same time wished all three of us to think that she did not.

'Branwell, can we have no peace in this house? Have you no self-government, no desire to avoid dissipation?'

'Well, good morning to you too, dear sister,' said I, my tongue at last sufficiency freed to speak, although the pounding between my temples had only increased. 'You should know that I was not listening at the door,' I lied. 'No indeed, I just came to administer a pat on the head to old Keeper here. And it's not at all clear to me how my troubles impede you from doing anything, if it means I'm either away from home or fast asleep when I'm here.'

I reached for her arm, but she pulled away.

'See here, Charlotte, each day from Midwinter's dark gloom will grow longer, and I'll wager that *Anno Domini* 1846 will bring happier times to us all.'

'This is no jest, Branwell,' she said with deadly earnest. 'We *do* love you, but –'

'Yes, yes, I know: *you hate the sin but love the sinner*. I've heard that one before.'

She at last closed the door fully behind her, speaking in a low voice clearly not meant, now, to be overheard.

'That is true, but what I was going to say is that I shudder to think that you have hidden most of your misdeeds from your father's and sisters' eyes, but that all the same it is clear that you make no effort to improve your circumstances, but instead slide further into intemperance and dissipation, and appear to be either stupefied with self-indulgence or – as is the case this morning – recovering from its effects.'

'Come now, I was not meant to be a saint, but it's hardly as bad as all that.'

'Every faculty, both good and bad, strengthens by exercise; therefore, if you choose to use the bad – or those which tend to evil till they become your masters – and neglect the good till they dwindle away, you have only yourself to blame.'

'You speak like an oracle, Charlotte, and all that you say is indisputably true. What would you have me do?'

'Fortify yourself against temptation.'

'Ah, well – if *that's* all,' said I with a laugh. 'I shall henceforth endeavour not to yield to temptation,' adding internally: *or at least make a greater effort to conceal my conduct from you, dear sister.*

'Come, Keeper, let's see what temptations can be found in the kitchen,' this final word – *kitchen!* – clearly summoned immediately to the beast's mind images of Emily's generous bounty, for he leapt up excitedly and was all too happy to abandon his post at such a prospect.

Charlotte was amused by none of this, and sighing slightly once more, she passed into the dining room and closed the door behind her. I walked audibly away, but then crept back on the tips of my toes and pressed an ear against the door. Within, Charlotte spoke to her sisters, as was often the case, in a tone slightly redolent of a schoolmistress.

'It's decided, then,' said she, 'each of us will contribute a score or so of poems to the volume.'

'Are you quite certain,' Anne asked, so softly that I could scarcely discern the words, 'that you do not wish to ask Branwell to contribute some of *his* poetry?'

'Absolutely certain,' replied Charlotte. 'Did you not say that he had published poems in York under his ridiculous *nom de plume*, Northangerland? And see here' – she must have had before her a copy of the *Halifax Guardian*, turned to the very page where 'Penmaenmawr' had appeared – 'he's just done it again, under our noses, without saying a word about it. Does he think we are blind to this, any more than we are to his degrading conduct? God only knows what he did in Halifax yesterday! Let him have his secrets, and we shall have ours.'

Yes, let them have their secrets. *Moreover, thought I, good luck and Godspeed being published, ladies*. At least I have succeeded at that, by heavens, far more times than you three ever will.

March 3rd, 1846 · The Parsonage

The days, weeks and months pass with no word from Thorp Green, not even from Crosby. Will I never hear from Lydia? Will Robinson never expire? That alone will be my salvation, I am certain of it.

Meanwhile, I have no prospect of employment – or perhaps more to the point, no interest in pursuing it. All desire, all ambition have fled. What strange creatures we are, to be capable, at one moment of our lives, of almost superhuman striving – even such irregular striving as mine has been – to make our way in the world, and yet at another to look back at oneself coldly, as if upon a stranger, to find our erstwhile ambition pure vanity, even a kind of white-hot madness! How can two such different beings reside in the selfsame breast? When does the arc of our lives begin to curve downward, the fruit begin to rot? Surely it is different with everyone, but should it already be so with me?

So, whenever I can, I drink. Yesterday, I borrowed a sovereign from Papa to 'pay a debt' – he need not know that it was a debt I had not yet incurred, I reasoned – and to organise a shooting match, and instead spent the afternoon seeking oblivion. I found my tongue could scarcely move when Charlotte returned from Brookroyd, where she'd been on a visit to Ellen. My door was slightly ajar, and so she entered without knocking. The effects of the day's drink had begun to dissipate – surely that is the only reason I can even recall our interview.

'Good evening, Branwell,' said she. 'How have you been?'

I rose unsteadily from my chair to embrace her and nearly fell.

'The same old steady body, as you can see, sister.'

'That's all you have to say?'

'Hmm,' I grunted more than spoke. 'How was the journey? And how was dear Miss Nussey?'

'What did you say?' she responded. What I had said seemed perfectly intelligible to me, but was not, apparently, to her.

'Never mind,' said I, first sitting on the edge of my bed, then stretching myself out as if to sleep. 'Never mind,' I repeated.

'Branwell, I know you seek relief from your sorrow, but you should not seek it in drink. In your weakness and depression, you have made it your medicine and support, your comforter, your recreation, your friend. Do you not see that you risk absolute bondage to that detestable propensity, so insidious in its advances, so inexorable in its tyranny, so disastrous in its effects?'

I was sufficiently conscious for this sermon to anger me, so I sat back up and said, raising my voice and fixing her eyes with mine, 'If I could, I would ring a bell and order six bottles of wine – and by Heaven, I'd drink them dry before your eyes, just to spite you!'

Charlotte began to go without a word but could not resist a parting shot.

'Emily said you were a "hopeless being" and I now see that it is all too true. I cannot stay in the room while you are in this state.' She turned promptly and walked out, closing the door with bang.

God damn you! You and Emily can go to straight to the bloody Devil, is the last thought I recall before falling into a troubled sleep.

March 28th, 1846 · Haworth, The Black Bull

After that last unpleasant interview with Charlotte, I determined to improve my conduct, and at the very least to lift my head above the swift stream of my dissipation. Alas, just two days had passed when a most unexpected occurrence cast me down yet again: yesterday all the family were occupied but I, when a parcel arrived, intended for *C. Brontë, Esq*. Surely, thought I, this is a mistake – and indeed, the letter 'C' seemed rather to resemble a 'P' to my eyes. Since anything destined for Papa would have included 'Reverend', continued my logic, this could only be intended for me. Who had sent it? Was it a gift from Lydia? Another book, perhaps this time sent directly from a publisher, so that her kind gesture could not be detected by her jealous husband? Was it a signal to me that we would soon be reunited?

Alas, how often do we know full well, in the deepest recesses of our hearts, the truth of such matters, though every atom of our waking selves labours mightily to silence it! I now believe I knew all too well that this was indeed a 'C' and not a 'P' – for even the most ignorant schoolboy would not mistake one for the other – and that I tore into the parcel not despite its intended recipient, but because of her.

What I discovered were the page proofs of a volume called, quite simply, *Poems* by Currer, Ellis and Acton Bell. So, they had finally done it, although it was clear from the enclosed correspondence that they had paid for the publication themselves. So, what then? A publishing house would issue the scratchings of an ape, if said primate had enough money to pay for it! Had I Aunt Branwell's inheritance to fling to the wind, I, too, could put a volume of Northangerland's verse into print. After all, I had written as much publishable verse as the three of them combined, and published no small amount of it already.

Nevertheless, as I flipped feverishly through the stack of proofs,

I saw some good, even brilliant things, especially from the vigorous pen of Ellis Bell. In 'The Philosopher', I found the poem that I had heard Emily reciting, and could at last know its ending:

> … I ne'er had called oblivion blest
> Nor stretching eager hands to Death
> Implored to change for lifeless rest
> This sentient soul, this living breath –
> Oh, let me die – that power and will
> Their cruel strife may close;
> And conquered good, and conquering ill
> Be lost in one repose!

Sphynx-like sister of mine, though you may call it cowardly, you, too, understand my yearning for *real rest.* And you, sweet Acton Bell, have written some lovely verse as well; you too see that 'In all we do, and hear, and see, / Is restless Toil and Vanity,' and that 'Pleasure but doubles future pain, / And joy brings sorrow in her train,' but your solution is to 'Trust God, and keep His statutes still, / Upright and firm, through good and ill.' Do you not see, Anne, that without your fairytale God, who obstinately refuses to speak a word or show his face, all is indeed vanity, *vanitas vanitatum, et omnia vanitas.*

Omnia.

As I turned at last to Currer Bell's poems – and it occurs to me now that it is as significant that Charlotte placed hers first in the volume, as it is that I perused them last – I heard voices and footsteps in the Parsonage, and tried in haste to wrap up the parcel of proofs so that they appeard untouched, but my trembling hands were unable to perform the task. I determined to tell a partial truth, though I now see that there was no veracity to it whatsoever. I wrapped the proofs as best as I was able and strode into the entryway, whence I could see Charlotte warming her tiny self before the parlour fire.

I walked over and held the package out to her and said, apologetically, 'I regret to say, Charlotte … that … that I thought this was for me and opened it in error. You will see that it is addressed to a so-and-so Brontë, Esq., so I could not *help* but think, through simple process of elimination, that it was intended neither for our good reverend Papa nor for any of the Misses Brontë.'

Two days without drink, along with what embarrassment I was capable of summoning up, united to cause the proofs to tremble almost violently in my hand, so that at last I set them firmly upon the table.

Charlotte was uncharacteristically quiet, her great watery eyes gazing out from beneath her broad forehead. For a moment, all was quiet but the ticking of the clock on the stairs. Was her brow flushed from her walk, did it glow from its proximity to the fire, or did it betray some unspoken emotion? She appeared to be weighing how best to respond, but at last said simply, 'Thank you, Branwell. I will henceforth take care to instruct my correspondents to address me as "*Miss* Brontë", to avoid any further confusion.'

I stood mute – and apparently dumb – before her, steadying my trembling hand on the back of a chair, and for such a length of time that she was finally required to say, 'It that all, Branwell?'

As with so many other things since we had grown up and apart, we were now, apparently, to feign that I had not seen the proofs, and that my sisters had not written them. How wrong we are to believe that *make-believe* is solely the province of childhood! No, alas, it is not that pretending ends as we age, but that we fashion it carefully into an instrument of practical deceit. Even the world of imagination must submit to the inexorable logic of the utilitarian.

These thoughts occupied me as I stared past Charlotte and into the fire; so lost in contemplation of the vanity of all things – yes, truly, Acton Bell had put her finger on the question, but unfortunately had retreated to an easy answer, to *the* easy answer – was I, that she was obliged to repeat herself.

'Will that be *all*, Branwell?'

This she said not with scorn or anger, but what was far worse, with what seemed to be an infinite reserve of pity.

'Yes,' was all I could reply, and I turned and walked out.

All of this – the arrival of the parcel and my perusal of its contents, interrupted by Charlotte's appearance and our brief interview – took less than a quarter of an hour, and yet, as I write about it the following day, I must confide that it was a far greater blow than I had at first believed; that to see my sisters' poems, if not their actual names, in print, was a stinging rebuke, for their contempt was – is – so, so great that they could not – would not – ask me to contribute my verse, even though I alone – as they are now all too aware – have been published. I blame Charlotte for this, as for most things. Yet it is hardly anger that I feel, for such an emotion demands a reserve of energy of which I am no longer capable.

I now write with a steady hand, from my customary seat in the Bull, where the new owner, Enoch Thomas, has just brought me another – and my last, for my reserve of funds has also run dry – gin and water. One thing is clear: I must escape Haworth, this accursed village in the wilderness, where I feel increasingly buried alive, as if Mama's, and Maria's and Elizabeth's graves, indeed, as if all the flagstones of the church and all the scattered slabs of the entire churchyard were thrown open as at the Last Judgement, a maw gaping obscenely to consume me, to consume us all.

I am determined not to be the object of my sisters' pity, and so must find employment, even if it takes me abroad. I have written to Leyland, and will make the trip to Halifax in less than a week hence. If a solution does not arise from that, I will at least have vouchsafed a few hours of levity, of escape, with a kindred spirit or spirits, for I have written Frobisher as well with a proposition, to set a poem on the recent events in India to Gluck's *Mater divinae gratiae*. Above all, I must have pleasure, and I will get it where I can, for in truth, when I fall back on myself I suffer so much wretchedness that I cannot withstand any temptation *to get out of myself.*

XXV.

Mother and Child

April 29th, 1846 · The Parsonage

A full month has elapsed since my last entry in this catalogue of woes. I did meet with Frobisher at the old parish church in Halifax, and I did indeed drink myself into a stupor with Leyland – not once, but thrice – but neither of these events was especially remarkable. No, something else occurred of a quite unexpected nature, and which shook my being, wretched as it is, to its core.

As I walked Upper Kirkgate towards the Square, a cheerful voice rang out in surprise, with an accent I vaguely recalled, as if from a previous life – nay, almost as if from a dream.

'*Hal*-low! By Jove, if it isn't young Mr Brontë himself! I wondered if our paths would ever cross again! Did I not tell you I find myself in Yorkshire from time to time? Yes, even here in the Devil's Cauldron, ha ha!'

It was Moses Tyson, the master of Sunny Bank, and thus employer of Agnes Riley herself. Could it really be that six years had passed since I had seen her walking, for the last time, towards her parents' cottage that spring day?

'I will never forget you, my sweet, beautiful girl.'
'Nor I you, Mr Brontë.'

As is so often the case when suddenly presented with strong and unexpected emotions, I was entirely at a loss for words, and indeed scarcely even knew where I was. At last, I mustered a question.

'And how do you do at Sunny Bank, and in Broughton?'

'Come, come, Mr Brontë, let's not be so formal. Let me offer you a glass – or two, eh? – and I'll bring you thoroughly up to date on the comings and goings round about Broughton, for I've at least an hour until my lad returns from the Piece Hall up yonder. Let's walk together and see if we might find a public house on our ramble, eh?'

When has a thirsty boozer – especially such an impoverished one such as I – ever refused such an offer? Indeed, my confusion at seeing Tyson had only inflamed my thirst, and I knew Leyland was occupied at that hour. After a stroll of a few moments, we found what appeared to be a relatively new establishment, and soon were seated, a reaming pint of ale – for such was the farmer's preference – before each of us.

'Now then, young Brontë, first let us hear what has become of *you*.'

I gave him the shortest possible account of my life since leaving Broughton, artfully omitting, of course, my dismissals from the railway and from Thorp Green, allowing him to infer that I had left each post of my own accord, for the *next best thing*. My shame was too great: that my friends had knowledge of my failures was already too much to bear; why tear open these wounds before a mere acquaintance?

Yes, I explained, I had indeed found some success in writing – I was published, after all, and was not that in some small way a success? Indeed, I was in Halifax to enquire about a new position, which promised even more leisure to write, said I. If only, I added inwardly, I *had* such leisure, without being pestered by the small but countless botherments, which like mosquitoes sting us in the world of workday toil. Oh Lydia, if only we could be joined at last, such a life would no longer be a dream! Of course, such a man as Tyson, whose understanding – or at least whose interest – was limited to just such workday toil, would find such language at best, incomprehensible, and at worst, offensive. Having satisfied my interlocutor, I again turned the conversation to Sunny Bank, doing my utmost – though apparently failing – to feign nonchalance.

'Ah *ha*,' said Tyson quickly, winking and nudging me sharply with his elbow. 'I always knew you fancied our little farm – as much for its human residents as for its lower creation, I daresay!'

I pretended not to understand.

'Oh, come now, Brontë, I am talking about that lusty young woman, Agnes Riley. I saw how she looked at you that day, and heard the rumours that circulated about the two of you, though I supposed you'd be the last to know *that*, wouldn't you, since you fled the area after only a few months, eh?'

Six years. Agnes would now be thirty-one – an old maid.

'Ah yes, I think I remember her, said I. 'Is she still in your employ?'

'No indeed … erm …' Tyson hesitated, as if unsure of what to disclose. 'She seems to have flitted off … God knows where.'

'Oh, I see,' was all I could say.

We may have been seated in a smoky Halifax pub, but these actual surroundings fell away as wave upon ideal wave of memories burst upon me: Agnes's skin against mine, my mouth upon hers, her entire person tightening around me with a quickening rhythm until our ecstasy joined and eclipsed that of nature's itself, so that the bright green leaves of early spring seem to shudder in faint response to our own supernatural *frisson*. Most of all, however, I saw her as she was at our final interview, her impossibly dazzling eyes brimming with tears as her feverish hands touched my forehead and my heart, and she claimed that what we had felt that spring would last forever.

I wondered: could Moses Tyson read all of this in my own eyes? In any event, he was trying his utmost to call me back to the present, here, in *Anno Domini* 1846.

'Brontë, are you listening to me? What would you say if I told you that, just this very moment, I glimpsed in your own features the same expression I saw on Agnes Riley's countenance the day you came to Sunny Bank? Ha! Indeed man, if didn't know better, I'd suspect *you* as the father of her child!'

Now, as if by a magnetic force, I was drawn hurtling back to the present, and suddenly hung on his every word. 'What did you say? A child? What child?'

'Why, Agnes Riley's child, of course,' Tyson again paused, as if uncertain of how much he should say. 'She died,' he at last said hastily, 'the poor bairn, wee Mary. A sickly little thing, I'm afraid, but never peevish, never cried, or so they say, as if she had already made her peace with this life and the next. She lived only a year or so.' Tyson sighed, resorting to the pious sentiment reserved for such occasions: 'Ah, well, she was spared this vale of tears, poor little thing.'

Tyson chose not to dwell on this subject but returned instead to his earlier insinuations.

'Yes indeed, Brontë, there were *three* young women of the neighbourhood who became in a family way around that time. Not that such a thing is so very miraculous, mind you, but in such a small market town as Broughton it surely set tongues wagging that three unmarried girls gave birth, and that all three refused to name the father! And you, skipping off just in time to avoid being considered in any of the cases! Or, rather, perhaps, being considered all the more strongly for your rather sudden departure, ha ha!'

'I knew of Eleanor Nelson,' said I, remaining quite serious in the face of his mirth. 'She was dismissed by the Postlethwaites while I was still at Broughton. Who was the third?'

'Why,' said Tyson, again with a wink and an elbow, none other than that bonny lass Frances Atkinson, who was employed by your old landlord, Dr Fish. Surely you remember *her*? Though I am happy with my lovely Abigail, I must say she was a natural beauty, that one – the kind to prompt a married man to do foolish things.'

Lust flashed over Tyson's embrowned features, like a brief moment of sunshine on an otherwise cloudy day. I myself could hardly forget Frances's saucy manner with me, but I knew I could only be the parent of the dead child.

And so he talked, on and on – after ordering a second pint – about this and about that, including the Postlethwaites – the boys were now nearly grown, of course, though I was astounded to imagine this to be the case – and the Fishes, but I lent only half an ear to his account. Surely far more pious and upright personages than I have sinned as I did that day, meeting their interlocutors' eyes and nodding meaningfully at just the right moments, and yet without listening to much, if any, of what is being said. Had Tyson said, at any moment, 'Brontë, what did I just say?', I am not at all certain that I could have answered.

Such was not the case, however, and he chattered volubly on, between rapid, appreciative swallows of the ale ('Ah, just the thing!' he said nearly each time). At length it occurred to him to send a little lad to fetch his servant ('There's no mistaking my lad,' said he. 'He's nearly a foot taller than just about anyone else you'll meet!') and when at last the said hireling appeared, it was none other than my erstwhile nemesis, John Nelson, whom I could thank both for introducing me to Agnes and for tearing us asunder. Now, however, the hardy youth had grown a broad-chested, towering young man, who looked as though he could lift me from the ground and crush my throat with a single, swift movement of his arm.

'Ah, John, you remember Mr Postlethwaite's tutor, Mr Brontë, surely? Now then, be a good lad and shake hands.' The young man frowned and uttered a syllable that more closely resembled 'hmmph' than 'yes', but his massive right hand obediently shook my considerably more slender, and thoroughly uncalloused, one. John drew off, and turning to me, Tyson explained, 'Since his sister was dismissed, young John there has found it harder and harder – *wor'* and *wor'* as he himself might say – to work for the master, so he jumps at any chance to get away from Broughton and Postlethwaite, who is happy enough to lend him out to me. I do wonder how long the lad will last there. Not that his master is bad – far from it, as you yourself know – but you understand, I'm sure, how relations might be strained once a member of one's own family is sent packing from a situation.'

I did understand, and once again reflected how glad I was that Anne had already left Thorp Green when I received my letter of dismissal. It had been quite bad enough for her to learn of my conduct there. I wondered, again, whether she had witnessed

Lydia and me *in flagrante*, or had simply heard us, in the shrubbery that night. The thought of her seeing me with her mistress in the throes of amorous congress was unbearable, and so I blotted it out, like so many other thoughts, so many memories, so many regrets.

Yet as soon as this image was crushed, one even less pleasant to consider recommended itself to me. What if John Nelson – he who had witnessed Agnes and me in the clearing – had, in his own occasional employment at Sunny Bank, tried to force himself upon her? Worse yet, what if she had welcomed his advances? No, no. Although they were of the same social order, I could not bear to imagine the boorish fellow with her, with my Agnes: more images to blot out, to cast to oblivion.

Whether from my downcast look, from the liberality inspired by his two pints – for who does not spend more generously after drink? – or from the length of time that had elapsed since last we had seen each other, Tyson, as he took his leave, insisted upon buying me the drink of my choice. I ordered a tumbler of whisky, and once the good farmer had made a valedictory salute from his waggon, whose horses were directed by the ever-grimacing John Nelson, I sat back down and drew out one of the sheets of the paper I keep folded in my coat pocket, for the germ of an idea had been planted in our conversation.

I could not at first write, but instead gazed out the window at the busy passers-by, many headed to and from the new railway station, which had already become inadequate to the needs of the bustling city: Frobisher had told me that discussions were already underway concerning a larger building still, an elegant structure of stone to reflect properly the importance of Halifax and its industry.

My thoughts wandered from this to my days on the railway, but I was soon called back to the present when a baby cried audibly, perhaps even from one of the rooms of the inn. I thought about baby Mary – *my* baby Mary, Agnes's baby Mary: *our* baby. Dead, and long since. Poor angel! And yet, how much happier than I, how free from every care! At last, I began to write, titling my poem 'Letter from a Father on Earth to His Child in Her Grave'.

Yes, thought I, smiling ruefully in response to Acton Bell, the child is *in her grave*, not *in heaven*. No namby-pamby, no sentimental, religious twaddle here.

Was it the drink, or the shock, that strangely made me feel at once shaken, and yet quietly, almost coldly, outside of myself, like a distant observer? I felt a conventional kind of sadness for the poor little thing – not unlike, in the end, Tyson's own sentiment, it occurred to me – but this was wrapped in an outer numbness, an *absence* of real grief, beyond which my mind could only reflect upon how fortunate my daughter was never to have known this world's woes and wiles, to have been freed from care. I began to write, and found that, as seems always to be the case, this poem was far more concerned with myself than with poor little Mary, or anything else. The real grief was for me, for my lost youth; the poem had, in the end, the same subject as 'Real Rest', and I had simply substituted the dead infant for the floating corpse:

> If seen, men's eyes would, loathing, shrink from thee,
> And turn, perchance, with no disgust from me;
> Yet thou had'st beauty, innocence, and smiles,
> And now hast rest from this world's woes and wiles,
> While I have restlessness and worrying care,
> So, sure thy lot is brighter – happier – far!

I added a few more lines, concluding with 'THOU are freed from care!', and signed the poem, not to hide my identity from my sisters, should they come across this particular edition of the *Halifax Guardian*, but to announce it spitefully – angrily – proudly – to them in upper-case letters: NORTHANGERLAND.

I sighed, realising that there now remained in all likelihood no other subject for my pen. I am turning round upon myself, descending into a private inferno where the only demon I meet at each turn of the downward spiral is myself, whom I encounter each time with more shame and disgust, and yet on whom I also feed for what little poetic nourishment remains. Indeed, had it not been for the chance meeting with Tyson and the news he imparted, I would certainly not have been stirred to such activity, pitiful as it was.

And yet, at present I am hardly disposed to blow my brains out, or leap from a tree with a noose dangling about my neck. The *marital* noose, however – ah, that would be quite another matter! Again I thought of Lydia, the possibility of a rope so sweet that it would rest as gently as her own soft white arms round my neck. As the whisky took full effect, I lost myself in pleasant thoughts of being the master of Thorp Green, where no practical worries would assail me, when the large head of Joseph B. Leyland – the sculptor himself now become, with his increasing girth, something of a monument of a man – appeared at the window of the pub, his features contorting into laughter when he identified me.

'Why the Devil take me, in all my life, little man, I never thought I'd find you *here*!' he exclaimed upon entering the pub and shaking my hand.

As if emerging from dark shadows into bright day, I squinted, uncomprehending, at my friend. He simply nodded in the direction of the bar and winked. 'Don't you remember our friend Maggie, the beautiful Kilmeny?'

There, indeed, stood none other than Maggie, a child on her hip and another *en route*, for her skirts showed ample evidence of the advent of yet another blessed event. My gaze of wonderment came as much from astonishment that I had been drawn into her husband's new establishment – always scrupulously avoided – as it did from the vision before me. The appearance of Tyson in Halifax had so surprised me that the particulars of the physical world had dropped quite away, and so it was only now that I finally knew where I was.

Maggie handed her little girl to an older woman and walked towards our table, at which point Leyland whispered, 'See here, Faustus, now that I've found you out at last, I must make my way to the privy. Fear not, however, I shall return!'

Whether the needs of nature had truly called him away or he had left to afford the two of us a few moments of intimacy, Leyland nodded and left me face-to-face with Maggie. I stood and bowed awkwardly but knew not what to say. She, on the other hand, had her usual simple confidence.

'How fare you, Mr Brontë? What has it been, four or five years?'

I responded as best – which is to say as vaguely – as I could, providing the same neatly edited account of my activities I had just shared with Tyson. As quickly as possible, however, I turned the conversation back upon her and her family. The coming child would be the third, for the crying I had heard moments ago was her second. So many children, so quickly! Well, yes, thought I: poor Mama, with her six children in as many years. Maggie was only half-way along the road my own mother had travelled. I genuinely hoped her end would be happier.

Surveying her features, I could see why her fortunate husband, like my own Papa, would hardly be dissuaded by an infant's cry from being drawn irresistibly to her sweet embrace, for despite the lines that had begun to form with the passing of the years and the growing cares of motherhood, she remained a charming woman, her maternity only adding to her considerable gifts. Although the comparison might seem ridiculous to some, she glowed like one of those Italian Madonnas who somehow radiate at once both holiness and a sort of languid voluptuousness, the Mother of God made sweet flesh.

'I see that your mind,' said Maggie, now smiling broadly from the safety of marriage and motherhood, 'still floats away, just as it used to do. Do you know that I was studying you for some time as you wrote and gazed out into the street? – or far beyond, for all I know!' As she had that night in the Square Chapel, she made an effort to speak in softened, more genteel tones – along with money, one of the keys to social advancement. No doubt with the encouragement of her ambitious husband, Mortimer.

Not knowing what to say, I simply replied, 'Ah, well, that must have been quite a sight,' adding, in a weak attempt at mirth, 'Yes, it could be the subject of an engraving or painting: "The Poet

Seeks his Inspiration in the Smoky Streets of Halifax", ha ha!'

Whether Maggie could tell that my laughter was forced and the attempt at humour *manqué*, I could not tell. 'Well,' said she, 'I don't know how you do it, sitting there all day and just *thinking* and *writing*. I don't have a moment's rest, which reminds me that I must rescue little Mary from my mother-in-law – or rather rescue my mother-in-law from *her*!'

Another Mary.

At this moment, Joe returned from his own important business, and said briskly, 'Well then, Mrs Mortimer, we are off to an engagement across town – we are late, in fact – so we will allow you to resume your duties.' We bowed and were on our way.

'What engagement?' I asked as we rambled uphill, to Cornmarket and the Old Cock.

'Well, we certainly have an engagement with the bottle. But I thought you wanted deliverance from an awkward situation. How could you not remember that this establishment belonged to Maggie's husband?'

Although I could simply have said that I had been to Halifax precious few times in the past several years, I was already sufficiently in my cups to reveal all to Leyland – for to whom else could I confess such things? – how surprised I had been to see Tyson, and to hear the story of Agnes's baby, its death and her disappearance. As I spoke, I remembered the farmer's curious hesitancy; what might he have distorted, or even invented, to protect me – or more to the point, to prevent me from returning to Broughton? How likely was it that Agnes – who was born at Eccle Riggs, a stone's throw from Broughton, and had spent her entire life in the neighbourhood – would simply vanish? She *had* said that she'd 'fairly like to run off someday', had she not? – but still, it was scarcely credible. And what if little Mary had in fact lived, or had never existed at all? I suppose I shall never know.

Joe, however, had predictably enough fastened onto the three simultaneously pregnant young women in the tale – the *Holy Trinity*, he called them. I found this too blasphemous even for *my* taste, and told him that if he must mock the poor things –

and me in the bargain, of course – he might wish to call them *The Three Graces*.

'Very well then, the Three Graces. But the heart of the matter, you devil, is that *you* really were a very naughty lad once you'd escaped the petticoat tyranny of Haworth! Ha! Are you absolutely *certain* that you did not plant your seed in all three of the girls, *seriatim*? I suppose you had to make up for some lost time, eh little man?'

Leyland paused and seemed to reflect. Whether he was gazing into the remote distance or at the ample bosom of Mrs Nicholson nearby, he did not reveal, but at length he sighed and said, 'Ah, how delicious to be a Sheik, with a harem at one's beck and call! No need for a cigar after a hearty repast, when one has *that* at one's disposal. I can't think of a better life, unless, of course, one could have Landseer's situation, with a beautiful and wealthy mistress!'

Seeing me scowl, he said, 'Oh, so sorry little man, I forgot about your Mrs Robinson.'

I could in fact see that Leyland was truly sorry he had spoken thus. For deep within his corrupt and jaded breast, there beats, in the end, a heart not utterly devoid of human kindness. Indeed, I sometimes wonder if my corresponding organ harbours any such noble sentiments, or if bitter gall has consumed all else.

The next day, with a splitting headache that my morning coffee had no power to dispel, I took my poem from my pocket and found that it was not at all so bad as I had thought. It is often the case that we condemn what we have written in a white heat when we remain still bathed in inspiration's afterglow; is it because we still feel the ardour of its source, and so can see how poorly our real work conforms to our ideal? And yet, at a distance, when our passions have fully cooled, we have the impression that such work was written by another, often better, self. Indeed, we sometimes find that it is nearly impossible to imagine that we should have authored it at all.

After making a few corrections here and there in the cold and sober light of day, I submitted it personally to the offices of the

Halifax Guardian, in which august periodical it was published on April 18th of this Year of our Lord, 1846. Did anyone in the Parsonage see it, since we do not have a regular subscription to the newspaper in question? In the end, I find that I am quite indifferent on the point, and that is perhaps not such a bad thing, even though I fear it is part of a more general indifference towards life itself.

XXVI.

Boundless Hope, Eternal Despair

June 1st, 1846 · The Parsonage

The days, weeks and months pass, and no solution presents itself. All employment is either barred to me or so distasteful that I would rather suffer the humiliation of remaining under the Parsonage roof with Papa and my sisters. *Everything* is equally intolerable. I cannot help but think how different life was just a year ago! Indeed, only now can I fully appreciate just how ideal my situation was: though in constant fear of discovery, I was able to roam the park at Thorp Green for hours, and when the occasion presented itself, lose myself thoroughly in the hills and valleys of Lydia's warm embrace. Ah, my nostrils hungrily drinking in the smell of her perfumed flesh, my hands beneath her long, alabaster neck, clutching at her thick auburn hair as her back arched and her breasts heaved upwards, her hips moving against mine! Her mouth, her mouth – oh God, her mouth – tasting wonderfully of French brandy as it pressed against mine! Oh, our summer idyll of a year ago, the two Edmunds fast asleep in their rooms whilst we two feasted on the seemingly unending pleasures of each other's flesh made one, forever and ever, Amen!

I remember, too, when just over a year ago – Whitsuntide I think it was – I sat on the grassy banks of the Ouse and, with a commingling of fear and pleasure in my soul, I thought of a future still possible. I recall gazing at the great hall of Thorp Green, musing on how like a puzzle, or a Russian doll, or a Chinese box, it all was: that my heart should be imprisoned in

Lydia's, and yet she herself was a prisoner of that house, of that man. I took out pen and paper and wrote her maiden name – Lydia Gisborne – in Greek letters, and put these thoughts to verse, but adding the sad truth of how changed things now are:

> The sky though blue was soon to change to grey –
> I, on that day, next year must own no smile –
> … My Hopes, they too, to woe's far deeper sea,
> Rolled past the shores of Joy's now dim and distant isle.

I sketched myself gazing across a river and towards the setting sun, with two stones, one marked MEMORIA and the other, a gravestone, inscribed with the Greek for *Alas!* Like a schoolboy, I even wrote 'Lydia B –', for I dared not write Lydia *Brontë*, though I do it now – just to see how it would appear. Lydia Gisborne, Lydia Robinson, Lydia Brontë. If only that sequence told the tale of her life!

Surely I am now gone fully mad, for I *still* cherish the hope that Lydia will be mine. All of my problems would vanish, like a nightmare at waking – how easy all would become, if only Robinson were at last to shuffle off his mortal coil! But even I, in my heretical state, can no longer *pray* for his death – at least not under the roof of the Parsonage and in sight of the church and the teeming churchyard, whose appetite even entire families cannot sate.

Still, does it really matter? For either You are there, God, listening intently, and already know what is in my heart, and have therefore damned me for all eternity, or You are *not*, and my prayer would have been uttered in vain. Two rather unhappy alternatives – the first cause for terror, the second for desolation. Best not to think on either.

June 13th, 1846 · The Parsonage

Heavens – or God – or the Gods – or the Universe – be praised, for as I wrote the lines above Robinson was already dead and buried! I am beside myself – *outside* of myself – but now in the best possible fashion. I wrote to Mrs Marshall immediately, to have her ask her mistress precisely *how* and *when* I am to join her. Lydia and I will be united, and this period of lethargy, this long winter of discontent, will at last draw to a close. My sufferings will be redeemed, and with enough time they will collapse into the past as a brief episode – surely I shall laugh at my present self as much as a grown man does at the recollection of his schoolboy antics! How –

I have placed a dash there, for my Lydia has exceeded even my fondest hopes: my letter to Mrs Marshall has prompted her to dispatch none other than her coachman Billy Allison to Haworth, and he awaits me at the Black Bull! This is beyond even my wildest hopes and dreams, and surely the next time I write in this journal – if ever I bother to do so again – will be from Thorp Green itself, as its *master*!

August 19th, 1846 · The Parsonage

Charlotte has taken Papa to Manchester to have the new surgery performed upon his cataracts, so that at last I am at my leisure to breathe and to think, for Anne and Emily are thoroughly occupied with the house and, as always, with each other; when we *do* speak, their few words lack their elder sister's sharp, sarcastic edge of condemnation. Although it will mean that he will finally see how miserable I am with his own eyes, I genuinely hope that the old man can at least see *something* when he recovers, for the poor fellow has gone thoroughly blind in the course of this past year.

More than two months have passed since I wrote the last entry, and with what bitterness I read it again. *Schoolboy antics* indeed – little did I know how close to the truth I was, and what castles in the air I had erected upon hearing of Robinson's death! And as much as I ache to blot out the words *from Thorp Green, as its master*, I leave them there as a testament to my foolishness. Yes, I am a fool. Charlotte has called me so on more than one occasion, and I begin to believe she is correct. Even Lydia did, that once, when I dared to send her a valentine: *are you quite mad, or just a fool?*

Perhaps I am mad, for despite all, I still preserve the hope that somehow Lydia – and Thorp Green – will be mine. How can it not? Do I not *deserve* it as much as any man who simply inherits his wealth? Nay, for my sufferings, do I not deserve it *more*?

And yet what faculties of reason I have remaining tell me quite clearly that I have received the worst possible blow, my finishing stroke at last, and am utterly lost. The events of the past two months point in only one direction: perdition.

Upon hearing that Allison awaited me at the Black Bull, I raced out of the house and down Parsonage Lane, nearly knocking John Brown over – no small feat, that – as he emerged from his house.

'It's happened at last, John!' I cried out, shaking his hand vigorously. 'God's in his heaven and all's right with the world, it's happened at last!'

I left the sexton scratching his head in the lane, a bemused smile on his face. Although I arrived at the Bull within seconds, I now recall those instants with unwonted clarity, as if gazing at a daguerreotype and examining each detail of my surroundings: the sun shone broadly, and at the approach of Midsummer even the churchyard hummed with life, from May midges buzzing about, to a young couple walking hand-in-hand amongst the graves, whilst a dog chased a cat uphill towards the moors.

I fairly bounded down the lane, turned right, and raced past the church to the Black Bull. I stopped just outside the threshold to catch my breath. Betty Hardacre, the chemist, saluted me with her broom from across Main Street, whilst Martha Brown carried a brown-paper parcel in the direction of the post office; I had not even seen her in my dash to the Bull. I thought of the book of *Poems* once more, and how I cared not a *fig*, now that my dreams were about to be realised. Just think what Northangerland – no, no, it will be Patrick Branwell Brontë henceforth – just think what P.B. Brontë will do when he is not harassed by the incessant, grinding need for money-grubbing!

As we shook hands, the usually cheerful Allison wore a grave expression on his face to match his black attire – *no doubt,* said I internally, *for the sake of appearances, given his master's recent demise*. He had arranged for us to meet in one of the rooms at back of the inn, and soon we were seated, a bottle of whisky and two glasses between us. The coachman poured me a large dose before giving himself half as much.

I could contain myself no longer, and I saw no need for discretion. Even if he were not one of the domestics who positively *knew*, he surely had heard the rumours about his mistress and the tutor. Besides, his master was – at long last! – dead anyway.

'Tell me Billy,' I said eagerly, 'how does my lady fare? Am I to go with you to Thorp Green, or must I wait a few days?'

Allison shifted uncomfortably in his chair.

'Have a bit more whisky, Mr Brontë. I'm so sorry to bring bad news; you know that I am fond of you, and hope you will not blame the messenger.'

The accuracy of the expression *my blood ran cold* was never less in doubt than at that moment, for my veins truly seemed to turn to ice, and a cold sweat spread instantly from my forehead down to my neck and shoulders. I shivered more than one does in the depths of a terrible bout of illness.

'Good God, man,' said I, 'What on earth is it? Please tell me that your mistress is not herself unwell!'

Allison seemed to gather a bit more confidence at this, though he sighed and knitted his brows in concern, as he leant back in his chair, crossing his arms over his waist.

'Well, sir, that is just wha' I've come to tell you. I regret to report tha' Mrs Robinson is in a dreadful state o' health, and her sufferings are enough to break one's heart. She is' – here the coachman looked at me meaningfully – 'agonised by guilt for her prior conduct, and in the master's final hours she was repentant, wearing herself out in attendance on him, though I know not if 'e ever forgave her, which seemed to distress her doubly. She spends 'er days on 'er knees, cryin' bitter tears and prayin' for forgiveness.'

'You *witnessed* her in such a state? I find it difficult to believe – no disrespect intended, Bill, I merely say this as one subordinate to another – that your mistress would conduct herself in such a manner before her coachman.'

I was beginning to grow impatient. No, in fact it was now anger that was dawning: how could *she* cry for forgiveness from Robinson after his years of abuse? And if such repentance were real, did it mean she truly regretted all that she and I had done together?

A gentle *man*, if not a gentleman, Allison permitted himself a soft smile. 'No, o' course not, Mr Brontë. T'was Mrs Marshall confided in me, she did, and I've no reason t' doubt the truth o' t' matter.'

'But surely she has a thought for me, Bill?' The ice in my veins had thawed, and began to boil. 'Why have you come all the way to Haworth to tell me this? Does she not wish to see me?'

Allison did not answer this last question directly but told me simply that he had been charged with informing me that his late master had, before passing into the next world, altered his will, not only cutting young Lydia off without a shilling as punishment for her elopement with Roxby, but also leaving her mother powerless to do anything but rely upon the executing trustees. Mr Robinson, he added, had so clearly communicated his dislike of his son's tutor to said gentlemen, that they now detested him – me – with a vengeance.

'Surely,' said I, as my heart continued to sink, and shock gave way to desperation, 'this is exaggeration, Bill. Surely her wish to see me is greater than theirs to prevent it?'

My eyes, at last, filled with tears, as the coachman assured me that further communication was quite impossible, and that I was above all to stay away from Thorp Green.

'I regret to say it, Mr Brontë, but at least one of the trustrees 'as declared that if he sees you 'e'll shoot you. That might be nothing but bluff and bluster, but I wouldn't test it if I were you.'

It was now I who poured myself a large glass of whisky, before offering some to Allison, as an afterthought.

'No, Sir, thank you,' said he, rising to take his leave and seeking to make small talk. 'I've a long road ahead and on these steep hills I must have me wits about me at all times. I imagine you've had more than one 'orse break a leg right 'ere in this devilish Main Street, eh?'

Every horse in Yorkshire could be shot in the head, and the streets and storefronts of Haworth painted with their blood, for all I cared.

'But will you not allow me to send a message to my –, to L –, to your mistress?' I said desperately.

Allison hesitated, biting his lip thoughtfully.

'I don't think tha'd be wise,' said he at last, smiling weakly as we shook hands farewell. 'The only thing I'd like less than seeing *you* shot by a trustee of the estate is seeing *me* shot by one. They've made it clear to Mrs Robinson that she is not to communicate with you, or there'll be bother, so that, the fact o' the matter is, e'en my presence here today is already a risk o' sorts, and could turn 'em against 'er.'

The coachman paused and shifted somewhat uncomfortably, as he added, 'Indeed Mr Brontë, I 'ave no doubt that it's the mistress's natural goodness that induced 'er to send me 'ere to give you the statement of 'er case.' His usual sunny disposition had clouded for only a brief moment, for now he mustered a hearty 'Farewell, Mr Brontë!' as he gestured for me to keep the bottle of whisky, closing the door behind him.

I drank the rest of the bottle as quickly as I could, then sat as I fell deeper and deeper into the well of my own despair, when at last there erupted from its depths a great volcano of loss, not just of Lydia, but the loss of far more, of everyone and everything: of childhood, and hope, and ambition; of my talents – if any talents there were – and my prospects; and finally, of my self-respect, if ever I had it. Nothing but loss, and grief at the loss, and shame at the inability to turn it all somehow to account, to make a triumph of failure as some artists do. Even *that* I could not manage. I wept like a child, until at last my sobs drew two kindly souls from the next room, who walked me up the lane to Sexton House, whence Brown himself in turn half-dragged me and half-carried me to the Parsonage.

I was thus already dead when the nails in my coffin arrived within two or three days of Allison's visit, in the form of a letter from Dr Crosby, whose hand I immediately recognised. It would be untrue to assert that I did not feel the slightest bit of hope kindle up at the arrival of his letter. Perhaps the coachman's visit was mere theatre, something Lydia had orchestrated from Thorp Green for the benefit of the servants and trustees – for I had no doubt that Mrs Marshall was capable of being not only a double agent, but also an informant of the latter gentlemen against her own mistress. Perhaps Crosby, from the independence and safety of Great Ouseburn, would be able to communicate the *true* state of affairs, and even bring news from Lydia herself!

Charlotte, Emily and Anne, were occupied – I could hear them reading, through the closed parlour door, their voices moving as the Three Graces circled the table in their habitual dance. Papa was closeted in his study with his curate, Mr Bell Nicholls, whilst Tabby and Martha Brown bustled from the inner to the outer kitchen and back. I know that the poor villagers believe that the Parsonage, sitting above the rest of the town, higher indeed than all but the steeple of the church itself, is as grand as a manor house, but I was suffocating within its narrow walls.

As the weather was fine, I crushed the letter into my pocket and strode out of doors and to the end of the lane, where village gives way to pasture, and pasture to moorland. To the left, Penistone Hill lay high above the town, while to the right rose even higher the Pennines, where as children we had so often hiked to Top Withens and even beyond. What dreams we had concocted up there, where the bracing wind has slanted the few firs and thorns that cling to the rocky soil!

I found a large stone to make an ample seat and, as a bank of clouds massed above the hills, rolling in from the direction of Halifax, I drew the letter from my pocket and held it for a moment, closing my eyes and bowing my head in an attitude of prayer: *Let it be the news I most fervently wish to hear, that my Lydia still loves me, and will endeavour to be with me in one fashion or another.*

I exhaled, opened my eyes, adjusted my spectacles, and opened the letter with trembling hands.

Alas! Though it was, like the good doctor himself, kind and faithful, full of pity for both me and Lydia, it bore no good news. 'Though I am used to the rough vicissitudes of this weary world,' Crosby wrote, 'I shed tears from my heart when I saw the state of that lady and when I knew how *you* must feel.' His letter continued:

> When I mentioned your name, dear friend, she stared at me and fainted. When she recovered, she in turns dwelt on her inextinguishable love for you – her horror at having deluded you into wretchedness – and her agony at having been the cause of the death of her husband, who, in his last hours, bitterly repented of his own treatment of her.

The good doctor goes on to describe her state of mind, which he says is *totally wrecked*, fairly debarring me from any hope in the future. In short, he sent me a mere complement to, rather than a contradiction of, the message that Allison had brought in person. I even wonder if the latter, worried that I might appear at Thorp Green with a brace of pistols, had himself urged the good doctor to write.

Crosby concludes his letter with vague words about how, though I *must not write to her*, Lydia knows how much I must suffer and that she seeks to make amends. What this means I know not. Make amends to God? To the memory of her late husband, whom she so ardently claimed *not* to love after we lay together on the cloak at Thorp Green, within just a few yards of the bed where he would eventually breathe his last? To me, even though she has sent word, through both coachman and doctor, that I am forever banished from her presence?

Here is what I do know: my hopes are thoroughly and definitively dashed, and I cannot even bring myself to eat. My nights are dreadful and I cannot sleep, and having nothing to do merely makes me dwell on past scenes – of Lydia, her thoughts, her voice, her body against mine – till I would be glad if God would take me. No matter what the next world – if world beyond the work of worms there be – I could not be worse than I am in this one. I am too hard to die and too wretched to live. And my wretchedness is no longer about castles in the air, but about stern realities. My hardiness lies in my bodily vigour. My mind sees only a dreary future, which I wish to enter upon as much as a martyr wishes to be bound to the stake.

At least the martyr answers a higher calling and looks forward to a well-earned paradise. I do neither.

XXVII.

The Woeful Impotence of Weak Resolve

December 7th, 1846 · The Parsonage

How long since I have opened this diary! Perhaps it is because so little has happened, for I am no closer to any meaningful change in my existence, despite my efforts at obtaining work. At least I was spared the presence of my family for several weeks, for I 'screwed money out of Papa,' as Charlotte said scornfully, with the promise that I would use it to seek employment in and around Halifax, and so I fully intended to do, stating aloud my intentions to my sisters and Papa as I put on my coat and hat to take my leave – as if making the promise audibly would oblige me to obey it. I did not add, however, that I was to sit for Leyland, who agreed to sculpt a medallion of me in return for a poem I was to write about his ancestors: a project – like my novel – I have left unfinished, though I've not had the courage to tell Leyland himself just yet.

It was a lovely, breezy morning in mid-September, with massive, billowing clouds sailing slowly, calmly, towards the west. Charlotte accompanied me out the front door, standing at the threshold whilst I stood in the garden below, the church at my back. Only in this way could the diminutive thing look down upon me.

'So, you're off to Halifax, to seek a post, you say?' she said, doubtfully.

'I am indeed, sister dear.'

'I am convinced that if only you would behave more steadily you could do almost anything you set your mind to, Branwell.'

'I am not certain *that* is possible,' I laughed. 'Better to ask the zebra to change his stripes, or the mountain to come to Mahomet! But fear not, I'll no longer be a drain on the family's resources, or an impediment to anyone's happiness. I'm far too hearty to die just yet, Charlotte, so we shall see what path I find forward, for like yonder sun, forward I must go, eh?'

I turned to leave, but my sister could no longer restrain her natural tendency to pontificate.

'The *right* path,' she intoned, 'is that which necessitates the greatest sacrifice of self-interest and leads to the greatest good of others.'

I wished to be gone, and yet could no more resist the opportunity to speak than she had.

'I see,' said I, climbing back up the steps and reaching round her to close the door behind her, so that now I stood above her and we could not be overheard. 'I see,' I repeated, snorting bitterly, my blood beginning to simmer with resentment. 'Let's see now, how have *you* sacrificed your own self-interest? Was it leaving your position with the Whites, and refusing further offers of employment as a teacher or governess, to return home at Papa's expense? Or perhaps it was screwing money out of Aunt to study in Brussels, ostensibly to be equipped to start a school for girls, one only half-heartedly attempted and never realised?'

Or, I said inwardly, my blood now at full boil, *to spend your inheritance from Aunt Branwell – which I would remind you I did not receive – on that meagre little book of poems, which appears to have sunk into oblivion without a trace?*

But I preferred not to reveal the extent of my knowledge of my sisters' paltry literary efforts, and besides, I had kept the best arrow in my quiver for last.

'Oh no, *now* I see all. It must have been refusing Henry Nussey's perfectly respectable offer of marriage. Was *that* your greatest sacrifice of self-interest?'

I looked at her triumphantly as if to say, *Now then!*

Charlotte had stood silent, her uplifted face reddening as I pronounced the litany of her sins. She chose, for whatever reason, to answer only the last of these charges.

'As I have told you on more than one occasion, Branwell, I could never marry a man I cannot love, no matter what material gain it might procure.'

'What do *you* know of love, dear sister? Have you ever felt a passion for another so overwhelming that you were ready to give up everything, even life itself?' My mind flashed to an image of myself, arriving at Thorp Green on horseback, a cocked pistol in each hand. 'Now *that* would be the greatest sacrifice of self-interest, would it not?'

Here she bit her lip, and her great eyes filled with tears, until they spilt down her cheek, but she said nothing in response.

'I'm sorry,' I said, embracing her awkwardly as a wave of rare, genuine remorse washed over me. 'Charlotte, I'm sorry, I meant no harm. Wish me luck, or Godspeed, or what have you!'

With this I at last took my leave, glancing back just once to see the tiny thing still standing on the porch, wiping away her tears.

Alas for good intentions and resistance to temptation's wiles! Although I have made my own half-hearted attempts at discovering employment – compared to mine these past days, Charlotte's efforts to open a school were Herculean – my mornings were largely spent sitting for the medallion or working on the poem I promised to Leyland in return, and the remainder of the day at the Old Cock with Leyland and associates. I resided at Mr Walton's inn at Ovenden Cross, close enough to walk into the Devil's Cauldron each day, but along the steeply rising Keighley Road, where the air is refreshed by a near-constant breeze blowing in from the moors, and there I left a few poems and sketches in lovely young Mary Walton's commonplace book, though before I could get to know her – an utterly charming, green-eyed, freckle-nosed, pious beauty – I ran short of funds, and had to return to Haworth, devoid of both cash and employment prospects.

It was early in the morning when I arrived at the Parsonage, which I entered through the back kitchen, where Tabby and Martha were already fully engaged in the day's domestic duties.

'Why, Mr Brontë!' cried dear old Tabby, 'You coom back ag'in, are you? How you keeping? What news then, eh?'

I begged a bit of bread and indicated that I needed to sleep, then made my way quietly upstairs and into the little room at the front of the house, which we had once used for our 'school', but more often for play and writing, and stretched out on the camp bed placed there for me since my return from Thorp Green. I was surprised to find that Charlotte had not yet seen fit to remove all traces of me. *That is because she knew*, said an unwelcome voice rising from within me, *that you would soon be back*.

To crown all, there arrived yesterday in Haworth a constable, one who very politely invited me either to pay my debts or enjoy a journey to the debtor's prison in York. Of course, Papa rescued me, as he always does. I do not know which is worse: the humiliation of such an event itself, or the detestation of myself that springs from, but long outlasts, the initial shabbiness of my behaviour on such occasions.

What I *do* know for certain is just how loathesome my presence has become to Charlotte. As for Emily, she is, as ever, splendidly indifferent, as if it made no more sense to complain about me than to bay at the moon, or as if I were a new piece of furniture that Papa had decided to add to the dining room. Anne avoids me as much as she is able in this small house; more significantly, she avoids my gaze. How all of this will end, I hardly know, but it surely cannot endure for long.

I used to believe that each New Year offered the possibility of a new beginning, of redoubled efforts, of opportunities for strengthened resolve. What folly! *Anno Domini* 1847, I fear, is unlikely to bring anything good.

XXVIII.

Death, Departure, Despair

January 25th, 1847 · The Parsonage

I am indeed a fool, although about one thing I was correct: the year has dawned inauspiciously. A fool, because I flew in the face of prohibition and wrote a letter to Lydia, one last desperate attempt to communicate with her; inauspiciously, because the letter has been returned, unopened, and accompanied by renewed threats from the executors of Robinson's estate. As if to underscore my misery, the weather has been dreadfully cold: the sky looks like ice, the earth is frozen and the wind is as keen as a two-edged blade. Papa has developed an influenza, and Anne coughs so much that she can at times scarcely breathe, though each suffers stoically in his or her own way.

Honest, kindly Dr Crosby was charged by Mr Evans, M.P., to return my letter, which Lydia was not even permitted to see. He relates that she is in a state of perpetual religious melancholy; even if that were not the case, she is surrounded by powerful people, who hate me like Hell. Crosby exhorts me once again to abandon all hope of seeing her again. She believes, he says, that her sorrow is God's punishment, and has resigned herself to her doom. Is she playacting or sincere? Does it matter?

Any HOPE we held for the future is now crushed, and what is the result of our love? UTTER WRECK. At the moment I venerate her most, I must give up the dream of being the husband of the lady I loved best in the world, and with whom I might have lived at leisure, to try to make myself a name in the world of posterity rather than in the workday drudgery for which I am singularly unfitted, and am in any event unwilling, to bear.

The hard truth of matter is that I have been too much spoilt and petted through life – as Weightman observed long ago – and at Thorp Green I was at last so much my own master, and gave myself so much up to enjoyment, that now when the cloud of adversity has come upon me it will be a disheartening job to work myself up again for life's next battle. I am thrown back to where I was when I was dismissed by the railway; alas, though my army stands now where it did then, my youth, health, hope and both mental and physical elasticity – on which I once built my hopes of rising in the world – have all been slaughtered.

Where great and noble works of art and literature used to rouse my imagination, they now cause only a whirlwind of blighting sorrow that sweeps over my mind with unspeakable dreariness. If I sit down and try to write the ideas that once came clothed in sunlight, they now press round me in funeral black, for nearly every pleasurable excitement that I used to know is either insipid or painful. My idea of paradise used to be having free range of the British Museum and Library for a week, but I now believe I would roam over its most exquisite marbles and treasured volumes with no more interest than would the eyes of a dead codfish. I can scarcely even bring myself to write in this diary.

Most painful of all is that I shall never be able to realise the all-too-sanguine hopes of my family, for at twenty-eight I truly am a thoroughly *old* man – mentally and bodily. And finally, worst of all, is not the most painful reality that there is no one to blame for any of this but myself? For at some point in one's existence, one must cease laying the fault for one's own failings at the feet of others.

John Brown and my other rough acquaintances at the Black Bull seem to think that my unhappiness springs solely from my lack of employment, or my want of ready cash. I do not resent them for it, but they cannot possibly grasp how I would rather lack a shirt on my back than a springy mind, and that my total lack of happiness, even if I were to step again into the glorious light of York Minster, would be far worse than their lack of a hundred pounds when they might happen to need it. Indeed, if a dozen glasses or a bottle of wine suffices to drive off their cares, such cures only make me *outwardly* passable in company, but *never* drive off mine.

Such were the reflections I was in the midst of sharing in a letter to Leyland, when another missive arrived at the Parsonage, this one from Ann Marshall. She repeats Dr Crosby's injunction never to write again, and claims that Lydia is now terrified by vows she was forced to swear to at her husband's deathbed, that she would sever all ties with me, in whom nevertheless lay her whole heart's feelings. Her husband was scarcely cold in his grave when her relations, controlling the whole of her property, overwhelmed her, forcing her to succumb in terror to her previous vows and, more to the point, to *their* wishes.

She concludes by saying that her mistress is grieved knowing that not only will we never see each other again, but that I am left without employment and fully dependent upon my ageing father, and hinting broadly that she will try to assist me. So that is what Mrs Marshall meant by 'making amends' in her previous letter! If ready cash cannot procure happiness, I will nevertheless put it to good use. Leyland has indicated that his medallion of my likeness is complete, and so I will make the journey to Halifax next week to collect it and to celebrate. If I am forever barred from happiness, I will try and get *pleasure* where I can find it, by God.

February 18th, 1847 · The Parsonage

Ah yes, the ensnaring 'pleasures' of Halifax. I did indeed receive five pounds from Dr Crosby, and was determined to use it to greatest possible effect, and as quickly as possible. Well into a second day of steady drinking, I sat, exhausted in body and mind, with Leyland at the Talbot. The depressed geographical situation of Halifax is such that the already brief days of winter are even more deprived of sunshine than in the scattered villages of the surrounding hilltops, and though it was only mid-afternoon, the last rays of sunshine shone through the smoky air as I removed my spectacles, rubbed my eyes, and looked across at my old friend.

'There is a still, small voice of rationality within me yet, Joe, and that voice says that more drinking will only deepen, rather than heal, my wounds; that I drink now not to drive away my cares – for it no longer does – but as a matter of course, by force of habit, and that I now can no more picture myself stopping than I can imagine myself being joined with Lydia in holy matrimony before the High Altar of York Minster.'

Leyland was only half-listening. He must, thought I, be weary of my talk of Lydia, of my self-pity, of my self-flagellation. Although all of this may have been true, I soon discovered by following his gaze that his attention had been diverted for another reason: at my back stood two women – one with reddish hair and the other a brunette – who had just come in from the street.

'Beautiful ladies!' said Joe as he leapt to his feet and bowed, before dragging two chairs over to our table. As the women settled onto their seats, Joe looked from the redhead to me and back, and at last could no longer contain himself.

'Why, little man!' – I did not appreciate this appellation in front of the 'ladies' – 'Don't you recognise your friend Maeve?'

She, it was clear, had recognised me, for she was already smiling knowingly, shaking my hand and saying, with an Irish brogue far stronger than I recalled, 'Mr Brontë'. On her lips, Brontë was once again *Brunty*.

It hardly required a genius to conclude that Leyland had arranged this meeting, for reasons both philanthropic and utterly selfish: the first, because he doubtless believed it would do me good; the second, because he, himself, is short of ready cash nearly as often as I, and felt he could help lighten my purse while procuring a few moments of ecstacy for himself.

I now examined Maeve closely, and noticed that her fair skin had taken on an almost ghostly, translucent pallor, that her voluptuous charms had given way to an emaciated frame. She still retained a fragile beauty, and the body that had given so much pleasure – how much, I wondered, had it ever received in turn? – now stirred in me a welter of memories, a hundred images of her *lessons*, as she had called them. How strange it is to so unexpectedly encounter a woman with whom one has lain, with whom one's own body has been joined, after so many years! Do all such men feel as I did then? Surely she did not share such sentiments, for the coupling in question was nothing more than her trade.

Every few moments Maeve brought a handkerchief to her mouth and coughed. That she was recovering from an illness explained the thinness of her frame. It was no wonder, given the winter we have had thus far.

'Now then, Miss Maeve,' said Joe, 'I thoroughly recommend a flaming whisky punch for any ailments of the throat. You will feel better *immediately*, I swear it!'

It was not long – a few more drinks – before Joe and Isabella (for such was the name of the brunette, who also shared accommodations with Maeve) had excused themselves to a room upstairs, for which it was understood I would pay. After all, Leyland had done the same for me at Luddenden when first I met Maeve, had he not? How long ago that now seems! I thought I was miserable then, but how much happier I was – how much potential I still had!

Maeve coughed again and nodded her head towards the stairs. By the time we reached our room, she was already short of breath, and as I closed and bolted the door behind us and she began immediately, mechanically, to undress, she was wracked by a wave of deep, shattering coughs, her handkerchief now spotted with blood.

Consumption. Poor little Maria and Elizabeth! How the rest of us have escaped it, I know not, but now that we have all lived to nearly thirty, surely we are fully out of its clutches, thank God at least for that. Indeed, my constitution is so hard I cannot die, unless I finally have the courage to decide, for once and for all, to put a rope around my neck and end it it all. *'Tis a consummation devoutly to be wished* – or is it? Courage or cowardice?

Maeve pretended that there was no blood, and I that I hadn't seen it. Her fit of coughing subsided, she continued to disrobe. Although her form still retained an attenuated beauty and grace where once a wonderland of soft, seemingly endless curves beckoned, her ribs now protruded from beneath a bosom reduced by her disease to a drooping remnant its former self. I, who so rarely feel pity for anyone but myself, was suddenly lifted up and carried away by one of those rare, overwhelming waves of sorrow and grief, and – if ever I was capable of such – of genuine compassion.

What I did not feel was amorous desire, not so much because Maeve was unable, in a way, to provoke such a feeling, but because my overwhelming impulse was simply to draw her towards me, one fellow sufferer embracing another. I directed her to put her garments back on, but she resisted, a look of desperation on her wan features.

'But I *need* the money, Mr Brontë,' said she, coughing again.

'And you shall have it,' I responded. 'Though I cannot even take care of myself, let alone another, tonight I shall take care of you, and you me.'

Thus, fully clothed, we slept in each other's arms like little children. Or rather, each of us was both child *and* parent, both cradled and cradling, cared for and caring. I know not the feeling of holding one's own daughter as she drifts off to sleep, but I still remember Mama's arms around me – what security, what love, what paradise!

No dreams troubled my slumber, and I scarcely heard Maeve's occasional coughing. She was surely more exhausted than I, and it was well on into the next morning when Leyland rapped impatiently on the door with his ubiquitous cane.

'Time to settle accounts, young Faustus,' he shouted from without.

'Here,' said I, drawing a sovereign out of my pocket as I hastily bid her goodbye.

'Why 'tis *fair* too mooch, sir!' she exclaimed, rubbing her gaunt fingers over the young queen's portrait on the golden coin. Her face seemed to colour with newfound, almost girlish life after her long night's rest. Perhaps, thought I, she will be quite all right, and we might even see each other again – as we once had.

'Rubbish,' said I. 'You have given me more peace of mind and rest from care in one night than I have had in many years. That is worth far more than I could possibly pay you.'

Having expended the last of my funds I'd received from Crosby on drink, the rooms and Maeve – as well as Joe's tumble with Isabella, which he took great pains to describe to me in the minutest detail – I returned to Haworth, penniless again.

A week later, Leyland wrote to say that Isabella had awakened that day to find her roommate dead, her pillow dyed scarlet with blood, her green eyes gazing coldly into the distance.

Oh God, if I *could* pray, I would ask Thee to send me a sign that my sovereign vouchsafed for her a few moments of dignity and real repose before her final rest!

Midsummer, 1847 · The Parsonage

Dr Crosby has written to say that the Robinsons have, some two months since, departed Thorp Green for Great Barr Hall in the neighbourhood of Birmingham, where they are to live with Sir Edward Scott. Lydia is to help care for her cousin Catherine, Lady Scott, whose illness has only grown worse. 'Thus occupied with service to another,' Crosby writes, 'she may wish to escape her own sufferings.' He concluded his letter with an intimation that additional funds might be forthcoming: 'Mrs Robinson wishes, I am sure, that she could also lessen your suffering, and will endeavour to contrive a way to do so.'

Does any of it matter? Where I used to long only for financial security, now all the ready cash in the world cannot fill the void I feel, were Lydia to send me two hundred pounds a week. Nor would it blot from my mind a flood of images that haunts me continually since reading Crosby's letter: Sir Edward and Lydia, embracing in the room next to Lady Scott's (why would Lydia not? – for had she not done precisely this with me as her husband lay dying?); the two of them walking arm-in-arm together in the vast park that Great Barr Hall surely possesses; Sir Edward buying Lydia her every heart's desire on shopping excursions to Birmingham and London; the two of them clinging to each other as his yacht slips away from the dock at Marseilles; and other, more intimate scenes, which I cannot bring myself to consider, let alone describe.

Most unbearable of all is the thought that, despite good Dr Crosby's protestations to the contrary, she has betrayed her own heart and cast my image to oblivion, blotted me out of her existence, knowing all too well that it would degrade her to marry me. As I write this, chills run up and down my spine, and I recall Leyland's words about Maggie, and about the world at large: *The only people who do not compromise themselves in one manner or another generally finish in Bedlam, or in the debtor's prison.*

Although I fight to crush these thoughts, does even this matter in the end? For I shall never see her again.

June 13th, 1847 · The Parsonage

Last week I published another poem in the *Halifax Guardian*, 'The End of All'. It is a poem I wrote ten years ago, in which Northangerland reflects on the death of his wife Mary. How strange that such juvenile work now gains acceptance, and yet I cannot create anything new – and I am convinced that if I could, it would be rejected out of hand. My novel lies unfinished, as does the poem 'Morley Hall', which I promised to Leyland in exchange for the medallion. Fragments, scraps, shards of broken dreams.

At least I can still publish without paying for it, which is far more than I can say for the 'Bell Brothers' and their shabby little book of poems. Our collective youth may be gone like a dream, but what have *they* to show for it? At least I have lived – lived more in my time at Thorp Green alone than they have in the whole course of their existence, or will to the end of their days, if they numbered a hundred years! They have neither lived, nor made a *living*, with the exception of little Anne. It must be true that misery loves company, for our shared failure is my only consolation. How mean, how pathetic, how bitter – in short, what an ungenerous ass – I have become!

Meanwhile, Papa's vision is wholly restored, and he again writes letters to the papers and reads to his heart's content. I daresay we have not seen him so lighthearted in years. I shall try to do my best not to swamp his spirits; I only wish that mine had half the buoyancy of his.

July 25th, 1847 · The Parsonage

I have, at long last, started drinking less, which at first was attended by a violent palpitation of the heart – an attack of *delirium tremens*, or so says Dr Wheelwright, our eminent local physician. He has told me that despite my hearty constitution I *must* stop the excessive drinking, and has prescribed a daily dose of laudanum in its place, to allay my irritation and produce sleep.

Thus far, at least, I take care of myself bodily, but to what good and for what purpose? The best health will not kill *mental* agony. Leyland has been to Haworth and is the picture of hearty health, despite his corpulence; he claims to see the same in me, but Mephistopheles is never to be trusted. We sat with Brown at the White Lion, behaving with nearly as much temperance as the three spinsters up the lane. As I told my friends, cheerful company does me good till some bitter truth blazes through my brain, at which point I would gladly receive the gift of a bullet to the temple.

I wish I could flee to writing as a refuge, as in days past, but I cannot. As to slumber, my mind, whether awake or asleep, has been in incessant action for eight weeks, ever since receiving Crosby's letter: nothing I do can remove the images of Sir Edward and Lydia in each other's arms, which haunt me like phantoms day and night.

September 15th, 1847 · The Parsonage

Charlotte has left us to visit her dear Nell, and good riddance to her! She is taking the new railway line from Keighley to Bradford, the very same on which Grundy and his brilliant friend Daniel Gooch are employed at present. I only wish I had a telegraph operator at hand, and a willing accomplice at the other end! I would instruct him to apply some blasting powder to one of the bridges over the River Aire, to send her tumbling into the water, from which I would not be there to pluck her, as I did the young lad from the Wharfe.

It now seems that we only speak to quarrel, and such was the case as she prepared to leave yesterday. Her trunk sat corded by the front door as she tied her bonnet and drew on her tiny gloves. My recent abstemious habits accorded me an unusual degree of clarity.

'Well now, Charlotte, you are off at last to see your beloved Miss Nussey, are you? I do hope you will send her my affectionate greetings. I know you have been desirous that she come *here*, or so you say. Are you sure you did not tender the invitation with one hand and fling it away with the other, by an insinuation of how intolerable it would be for any proper person to be within a mile of your reprobate brother?'

This unwarranted, almost arbitrary provocation – yes, I was seeking to provoke her merely for the *fun* of it, to use an odd little word that has gained much currency of late – prompted only a calm and deadly rejoinder.

'On the contrary,' said she, gazing at me with the steadiness of a hunter taking aim at his prey. 'I told her you had been *thoroughly* humbled, and that you were behaving yourself with the greatest civility now that you'd got to the end of a considerable sum of money, whose provenance we could all too easily guess. In fact, I told her you look the complete rake, and would be as smooth as oil if she came to stay. *Now then.*'

She uttered these last words with the same emphasis as, or so I imagine, a soldier in battle who delivers his finishing stroke, running his sword with delight through his enemy's neck or chest. She seemed to relish the battle, glowing with triumph before I could even respond, and appearing no more capable of tears now than the Emperor Nero.

It was the confidence of her utterance rather than the words themselves that most unnerved me, and I stepped backwards as if her blow had been a physical, rather than verbal, attack. I nearly fell over Keeper, who had followed Emily and Anne from the kitchen to say goodbye to Charlotte. I merely scowled and turned on my heel, my blood boiling.

Yes, thought I, *I hope that one of the new bridges over the Aire collapses, or that your train runs into a horse or cow, and that you go straight to Hell, damn you, Charlotte! How dare you look at me with such condescension, such smug self-satisfaction! What have YOU done, but been a parasite on your father and aunt? Have you even published something that you have not had to pay for with Aunt's inheritance? Have you felt love? Do you know the white-hot blast of ecstasy in another's arms?*

Such were the thoughts I angrily turned round in my mind, grinding my teeth until my jaws hurt, so desperate was I for drink. I had that cast of mind that one has when he is so thoroughly lost in thought that he scarcely perceives the physical world around about him, and it is a wonder that he is even capable of walking without falling off a cliff, or being crushed to death by a passing coach in a busy street. And such was still my state a few moments later, as I made my way down the lane towards Main Street, and so it was that I was nearly knocked down by two much larger persons who, it so happened, were come in search of me.

'What ho there, little man,' cried Leyland, laughing and clutching my arm to prevent me from falling. He had sent no word that he would be coming back to Haworth, but here he was, in the company of his frequent associate, the sexton.

'I wanted it to be a surprise of sorts,' he explained, still somewhat short of breath from his uphill walk. 'Besides, it was not certain until today, but I've good news; Brown here and I have just come up the hill from lowly Oxenhope, where we've secured a commission to carve some decorations in the chapel.'

Joe drew out some cash and winked. '*Celebremus*, my dear friends, *celebremus*!'

Any concern for my own health, of what was right, of what my sisters would think, and any other resistance to temptation, weak though it might be, fled at the sculptor's invitation. As we crossed in front of the church *en route* to the Black Bull, I said, far louder than I had intended, laughing like a madman – no doubt because my desperation for drink was matched only by my jubilation that it was so near: 'Thanks be to God for you, Leyland, for I feel as if I had an infernal fire in my veins, that all the waters of the ocean cannot quench!'

I turned to clap Leyland on the shoulder as we entered the Bull, and behind him, walking quickly towards the post office, was Anne, her bonneted head staring down at the cobblestones. Had she heard me? More to the point: do I give a toss if she did?

The remainder of the evening passed in the usual manner, in a kind of joyless mirth – if such a paradoxical expression may be permitted – a great, raucous and communal cascading towards numbness, rapidly spilling over into the still black waters of nothingness.

XXVIX.

Three Novels

January 15th, 1848 · Haworth, The Black Bull

I know not how much longer I can bring myself to write in this journal. What I do know is that I cannot continue to live in this dissipated manner, the fruits of which are now made all too manifest. I am become a burden on friends and acquaintances alike, trailing embarrassment and the need for apology in my wake, wherever I go. Today I wrote to Leyland, asking that he tell Mrs Sugden of the Talbot that I considered her conduct towards me during my 'illness' as most kind and motherly, and that if I did anything to offend her, I deeply regret it and beg her to take my regret as an apology until I see her again. In point of fact, I don't remember her behaviour at all, but John Brown, who brought me home, has assured me of her kindness when I was most in need of it.

What precipitated this most recent 'attack' was an incident that has robbed me of any last feelings of superiority over my sisters; indeed, of any remnants of esteem or respect I had for myself. Now all is bitter wormwood and gall. No, more accurately, that was all I had; now I have nothing.

I accompanied Brown, who had business with Leyland, to Halifax last week. The two had work to do in the studio, and so I determined to spend the time in Francis Leyland's bookshop and lending library in Cornmarket, where I browsed amongst the volumes of poetry. There were new works by Rossetti and the Southeys, by Tennyson, by the American authors Emerson and Longfellow, and even the long-dead Shelley. Moxon has reprinted his edition of 1839 – the same that Lydia gave me – and I picked up the volume containing 'Epipsychidion', my eyes feeling as if hot needles were being driven into them as they moved along the verses, the jumble of words interspersed with flickering images: Lydia's sensuous mouth, those impossibly wicked brown eyes, that voluptuous and yet still-elastic body, as much a slave to my desires as I was to hers. How many times had we melted into each other in the incandescent flames of passion?

Lydia: gone to Great Barr Hall to minister to Lady Scott and, quite possibly – no, I could not bear to consider it, I thought as I read the poem's final words – 'I tremble, I expire!' – and slammed the volume shut in an effort to blot out another set of images, where Sir Edward had replaced me in Lydia's fevered embrace.

As I looked around the shop, I cast about in my mind for some kind of consolation, no matter how petty or childish. Scanning the titles of poetry ranged neatly on the shelves, I sniggered with a bitter, complacent glee at the thought that the 'Bell Brothers' – squandering their inheritance just as they had on the pointless adventure in Brussels – had been published only through the offices of a mercenary bookseller, whilst for six or seven years now Northangerland's poems had appeared in newspapers across Yorkshire. *Ha ha, now then!* I could not help laughing at their foolishness – indeed, at their *vanity* – for seeking publication at such a cost, and how quickly their stillborn efforts had disappeared without a trace.

But alas, even this smallest crumb of sustenance was about to be withdrawn!

If the event I am about to recount were to appear in a novel, even the most benevolent of gentle readers would scarcely find it credible, and would surely place it in the same category as spirits of the dead returning to haunt their erstwhile lovers, or disembodied voices of a loved ones winging their way implausibly along great distances, as if transported through a telegraph wire. The wondrous nature of the occurrence, however, was due not to any supernatural circumstances, but simply to an unlikely coincidence: for just as I was savouring the oblivion into which my sisters' pitiful attempt at literary fame had sunk, the name 'Bell' rang out within the all-too-real confines of the bookshop. I immediately turned towards the speaker.

'Have you heard,' said a small, well-dressed gentleman whose soft tones immediately indicated that he was likely not of Yorkshire, but of the *soi-disant* 'civilised' regions to the south. 'I say, have you heard of the book *Jane Eyre*, by one Currer Bell? It is the *talk* of London – of the novel-reading public, I mean, of course. The critics are falling all over themselves to see who can praise it more. One calls it "extraordinary", and claims that "all serious novel writers of the day *lose* in comparison to Currer Bell". Do you know,' he continued, apparently with a fondness for interrogations of the rhetorical sort, 'do you know that I have recently read that this person has not one but *two* brothers, whose names I cannot recall, who have published tales of their own, just some weeks ago? Imagine, three brothers, all writing novels. Who has ever heard tell of such a thing? Usually it is considered enough of a curse to have *one* artist in a family, ha ha! Be that as it may, I have just purchased *Jane Eyre*, and mean to read it on my return to London,' he concluded, waving one of the three volumes in the air to his travelling companion, 'and I think it will be *just* the thing to help pass the time!'

Unable to master my feelings, I leapt up and snatched it from his hand.

'I *beg* your pardon, sir,' said he with more astonishment than anger.

I examined the book's cover briefly and returned it to him, stuttering, Bellerby-like, in my embarrassment. 'N-n-no, sir, it is I who must ask your pardon.' I pointed at the cover of his book and said, with uncontrolled candour, 'I believe I know the author, and so was simply astonished to discover that … erm … he had published a novel. Please, do accept my apologies.'

I instantly regretted having spoken thus, for the little gentleman immediately pressed one question after another upon me. Where did Currer Bell live? Here in Halifax? Were there *really* three brothers? etc., etc.

In the face of this flurry of questions I simply muttered that I must have been mistaken, doffed my hat and made my way out of the shop and into the smoky streets of the town. I wandered aimlessly about, in a motion as much resembling an infernal spiral as the largely rectilinear streets of Halifax would permit.

Meanwhile, the words I had just heard roared round and round in my mind, incessantly, like a tempest showing no signs of abating: *Currer Bell, the talk of London, 'extraordinary', not one but two brothers, three brothers, all writing novels, a curse to have one artist per family, ha ha … ha ha ha ha ha ha ha ha ha ha ha ha ha!* I was in equal measure attracted and repelled at the thought of reading these books; or rather, to put the matter more plainly and far more accurately, I felt equal measures of repulsion and dread at the thought of reading them as I did at the thought of not reading them.

I had little sense of the time that had passed – minutes, or hours – before I found myself back in front of Francis's shop, where the good man himself stood, alongside his wife – they must have been at luncheon earlier – whom I had never before encountered. He whispered in her ear as I entered. *Papists*, I thought – and Frank a newly-minted one. And yet he looked no different to me than he had when I first met him at Sowerby Bridge. Surely, none of it mattered. What had Ellis Bell written?

Vain are the thousand creeds
That move men's hearts, unutterably vain
Worthless as withered weeds

I could certainly espouse *that* creed.

I looked from Francis to his wife, who returned my gaze with a cordial, though somewhat guarded, smile, as if already alerted by her husband to my conduct towards married women – or at least to one particular married woman. Or perhaps simply being the intimate of her brother-in-law was sufficient to cast suspicion upon me. Whatever the case, Ann Brierley Leyland was a pert, if not remarkably beautiful young woman, with a lively intelligence and a youthful spring in her step. I at once envied, and yet could not begrudge, good Mr Frank his happiness with such a pleasant young lady. They seemed perfectly matched.

'Why Branwell,' said Frank, shaking my hand with genuine kindness, 'what brings you to Halifax? Surely not to see me, a poor uninteresting businessman of quiet, steady temperament and no imagination.' He winked at Ann, drawing her to him affectionately. 'Let's see – is it to exchange the bracing moorland air of the wilderness for the smoky atmosphere we are so adept at producing and retaining down here under the lid of the Devil's Cauldron?'

'I'm sure it will not surprise you in the least that I am here with old John Brown, who has work to do with none other than the esteemed Joseph Bentley Leyland, alias Phidias, so I determined it would do me good to have a change of scenery, to *changer d'air* as the French say, be the air in Halifax ever so noxious,' said I, feigning a mirth I did not, and could not, feel.

'Whatever the reason,' said Frank, waving a hand through the air as if the chimneys of Halifax had discharged their smoke directly into his shop, 'it is always good to see you. Can we be of service, or are you here for no other reason than to bring greetings?'

I asked whether he might have, in his lending library, *Jane Eyre* by Currer Bell, and quite possibly even two more novels, one by Acton and the other by Ellis Bell.

'By Jove, *Jane Eyre*! Why, that book is a sensation! Do you know that its first edition has already quite sold out – We just sold a gentleman from London our final new copy – and a second is being printed? You are in luck, old boy, for the two copies I already possess are forever on loan, but one was just returned this morning.'

It was the same three-volume novel that I had earlier seen in the little fellow's hands, but now I could examine it at leisure. The publisher was Smith, Elder, and the firm had produced a handsome work bound in fine-ribbed brown cloth and gilt-lettered spines.

I turned to the first page and read the first sentence, as flat and pedestrian – indeed quite literally so – as a pavement: *There was no possibility of taking a walk that day*. I realised that I would need peace, quiet, time and, above all, solitude to read every word, as I now felt irresistably drawn to do. I would say that my blood ran cold, but such a description would be inaccurate; more precisely, a series of shudders, at first imperceptible, but gradually gaining in magnitude, wracked my frame.

'And what of Acton and Ellis Bell?' said I, trying my utmost to retain an outward calm.

'Fortunate again!'

This time it was Frank's bride who, believing she was performing a kind act rather than driving another dagger into my heart, turned and snatched a second 'triple-decker' from a large stack of newly arrived books. 'This just arrived yesterday, Mr Brontë. I have seen no reviews of it, so cannot recommend for or against it.'

It – they – were the two-volume *Wuthering Heights*, signed by Ellis Bell, and a third, shorter novel, *Agnes Grey*, by Acton Bell, published together in the usual three-volume fashion.

I looked at the books before me, breathing deeply: and so it was true.

I wondered, and wonder still, had they spent the portion of Aunt's inheritance that was intended to fund the *Misses Brontës' School for Girls* – as fantastical a project as it might have been, at least it had a respectability about it – to try their hand at novel-writing? Was there no end to their vanity? Moving in a mist, and nearly deaf to the Leylands' adieux, I carried the books past the Old Cock and through the Piece Hall. Before me stood the Square Chapel, hard by Leyland's studio, the very chapel I had yearned to desecrate with Maggie that snowy evening so long ago, when Listz made his memorable visit to Halifax. Downhill I continued, the six volumes shifting under my two arms, to Church Street and towards the old parish church, which I entered for no discernible reason.

I was quite alone, except for the windows and sculptures, which included the wooden figure of Old Tristram the beggar and his alms box, standing sentinel near the entrance (*Sorry, old friend, said I, patting his head, I have no money to share with you*), and Leyland's own recent memorial to Bishop Ferrar, the last prior of Nostell Priory, on the western wall of the south aisle. Burnt at the stake, poor fellow! Well, there's at least one area where we've made a bit of progress, I suppose: Frank Leyland won't suffer such a fate for *his* beliefs.

At length I knelt and tried to pray, but nothing came, not even *Lord* … and soon I left the church and crossed Lower Kirkgate and the new rail line along Hebble Brook, and made my way up the path that cuts through the woods at Bailey Hall Bank, at last joining Southowram Bank high above the town. I was short of breath by the time I reached the place where the path meets the main road, and turned to recover from my steep climb through the frigid January air.

Indeed, a bitterly cold wind had begun to blow from the east, and the first flakes of snow with it as I turned to survey Halifax, whose usual clouds of smoke had, if only for the duration of the coming storm, been swept away. A hundred scenes of my life in this town flashed before me, as did the ghosts of Maggie, Leyland, Maeve, Grundy, Listz, Frobisher and many others. The wind flayed my face like an icy whip, and my teeth chattered, as a great shiver wracked me from head to toe.

Under my coat were the novels, which I could no more read up here than I could before the Leylands themselves; but read them I must. In the meantime, however, my trembling grew worse, and it was clear that I needed, above all, warmth. God Almighty! – what madness had driven me to the top of this towering hill on such an arctic day as this?

I returned with haste whence I had come, taking care not to slip on the snow that had begun to accumulate on the stone path. Soon I was at the Talbot, where Brown, Leyland and a young fellow I had never met, one James Drake, sat around a large oak pedestal table. The proprietor, Dan Sugden, stood by, laughing cheerfully, a cloth over his shoulder.

'*Hal*-low!' cried Leyland, who was already well in his cups, 'By God, if it isn't Saint Patrick! Or Lord Peter, or Young Faustus, or whatever your confounded name is, little man – here you are at last! Here now, Sugden Sugdiensis, have that saintly wife of yours bring us another flaming bowl of punch, will you? Yes, that's a good man.'

Joe's manners had already fled, and so I began to introduce myself to the young stranger.

'Oh, pardon me!' said the sculptor hastily. 'This is Mr James Drake of York. He has come to collect old Dr Beckwith's likeness at last, and drag him back to the celebrated Minster. He's as finished as he'll ever be, I'm afraid!'

The young Drake, who could not have been above twenty years old, had clearly been drinking right along with my friend. He introduced himself as a sculptor charged with the transportation of Leyland's monument of Dr Beckwith, and cousin of Leyland's friend Joe Drake, himself a carver and gilder.

'Ah,' said my friend, patting the youth, who sat to his right, on the shoulder. 'Young Jim here is far too modest. We have uncovered that he is of humble origins, the son of a blacksmith. Ambitious, just like you, young Faustus, and your father before you. I've already christened him "Draco the Firedrake", poor lad, for one cannot join this table without at least one such *nom de guerre*, ha ha!'

Turning to me, Joe squinted and said, 'Say, little man, what's that you've under your coat, eh?'

I muttered something about borrowing some novels from Francis and his wife.

'Oh, that's all,' said he, a cloud passing over his otherwise glowing brow. 'If that's the case you've seen the charming couple more than I have of late. Though I shake hands with my brother mentally for his taste, I cannot *stand* to be in their presence, where every word and glance, or for that matter, every silence, is a reproach. Argh!'

I knew exactly what he meant.

It took only the appearance of another bowl of hot punch for Joe to brighten, however.

'Ah, now *that's* the thing,' he cried, thumping the table with both hands, like an infant whose favourite dainty has just been produced from the kitchen, his voice booming with rapid excitement. '*Yes*, that is *just* the thing. Poor Faustus is shivering here, *tremens*, but happily sans *delirium*, it appears … now then, Branwell, put your coat and that insipid trash away – did you say they were novels? By Heavens, how the mighty have fallen! Sanctus Patricius Braneullius Brontëio brought down to the level of reading novels for entertainment! Well, put the confounded things away and let us lift a flaming toast to my completion of both Dr Beckwith and the Oxenhope monument.'

Ah, thought I, as Joe bowed his head in mock reverence to the dead Dr Beckwith. This explains Joe's ready cash, and his eagerness – even greater than usual – for a regular jollification. John Brown – 'Saint John in the Wilderness' as Leyland is fond of calling him – sat smiling silently, even benevolently, though Joe had given him no credit for his own work on the Oxenhope monument. He rarely speaks at such times, though he listens intently; his kind of wit is not in the telling of tales, but of following the line of discussion carefully and, at just the right moment, inserting a mere word or phrase, always unexpected, which generally produces great laughter all round. Along with his general good nature, this quite specific talent – which has the further benefit of allowing such august personages as Joseph Bentley Leyland and Patrick Branwell Brontë to do most of the conversing – makes for a welcome addition to any group of revellers.

And yet, how different is John Brown from me! He is one of those steady bodies in this world who simply carry on with their work, regardless of whether they are praised for it. Fame is the last thing he would ever seek; the gnawing desire to be *known* to the world, to leave one's name to posterity, to avoid somehow the terrifying fate of slipping beneath the waves of this brief life and into lasting oblivion, all of this appears to be utterly foreign to him. Fortunate man! Of course, he does have his human weaknesses: for drink, yes, and especially for the ladies. In short, beneath his workday respectability lies a bit of a rogue. But where's the harm in *that*? Is he not simply a man like any other?

'Brontë!' shouted Leyland, slamming his right fist on the table as I mused thus. 'Are you listening to what Drake is saying about your countryman, Patrick Reid? You seem to have left us, little man! Can you not give over day-dreaming, even for a few moments?'

The table, including Drake, laughed good-naturedly. Dan Sugden, having heard Drake speak of a recent execution, had also drawn up a chair, and listened intently.

'Are you Irish, then, Mr Brontë?' asked our young visitor.

'My father is, yes, but my mother was from Penzance. I have never been to either place, I'm afraid.'

'Well,' continued Drake, whose accent and grammar did not betray his humble origins, a sign that he was intent upon rising in society, 'I was saying that two days since, at York, I witnessed the hanging of the Mirfield murderer himself. Do you know he insisted on wearing his cap to the bitter end, right up onto the Drop? The Devil confessed that he alone had robbed and murdered that old couple and their servant girl – his supposed accomplice McCabe had nothing to do with it, said he – but be that as it may, I'd not be surprised if he'd raped the poor thing in front of them before he slashed all three of their throats!'

'Is it any wonder that some people loathe and fear the Irish?' said I, running my hand casually through my reddish hair, but feeling like the disciple Peter, the moment the cock crowed a second time.

My comment seemed at first to be taken as not worthy of comment, and certainly not worthy of dispute, but Brown – as loyal to Papa in his way as Keeper is to Emily – bravely spoke up.

'Now see here, Branwell, I'd normally keep me mouth shu' and say nowt, bu' yer father's the fines' man I know, and Mr Bell Nicholls, the present curate, is no' far behin' him in goodness, if not quite in learnin'.'

'*Yes*,' said Joe, laughing, 'but that is because they have been *transplanted* to the fair soil of Albion, and because in their overweening ambition they have striven to efface all aspects of their savage, superstitious upbringing. Why, the Reverend Brontë has now no trace of his Irish origin remaining in his speech! He has scrubbed himself as clean as the Parsonage floors! As for Mr Bell Nicholls, he is a much inferior specimen of which Mr Brontë is the perfect exemplum, but he is a specimen all the same.'

Brown's usual deference to his friend Leyland was here sorely tested, and I could see his jaws working as he silently ground his teeth. If the latter did not notice this, he certainly perceived the sexton's furrowed brow and sullen silence.

'Come now, Saint John!' shouted Joe, 'We'll have none of your wild Haworth fierceness here in the polished metropolis!' He banged on the table once again, but this time with such force that it tipped towards the two of us, nearly knocking us over and – far more serious – spilling the contents of our punch bowl and nearly sending it to the floor, where it would surely have been shattered into a thousand pieces.

Brown leapt to the rescue, spilling his own glass but ultimately steadying the table and catching the bowl before it could fall. As he did so, the table rocked back, almost pushing Sugden and Drake out of their respective chairs as well. His good nature could not prevent him from laughing at the sight, and Leyland himself was quick to say that it had all been in jest, and hastened to order another bowl of punch from Mrs Sugden as she wiped the table clean.

The following bowl of punch did its noble, intended work, for I remember little of the evening thereafter. All of this happened two days ago, but I am just now able to summon the strength to read the books that sit before me, here in the security of the Black Bull, where I am quite certain no one from the Parsonage will seek me, unless of course I am too dead-drunk to move and a lad is sent to fetch someone. I shall take care not to let that happen. *Moderatio!* Indeed, when it is time to sleep, I shall leave the books in the capable hands of Mr Thomas himself, for I cannot risk a discovery all too possible in the narrow confines of the Parsonage, especially with Charlotte forever nosing about, as she is wont.

I am overwhelmed with a sensation, which has gone from a transient to, now, almost a relentless feeling, of utter despair and futility, of a yearning for the end; where once I envied the *peace* of a corpse that I imagined floating obliviously upon the waves, I now find myself wishing to *be* him – it – to be dead, to quit at last the pain of existence itself. I folded the large sheet of paper on which I wrote my letter to Leyland, and drew my head and shoulders hanging from a noose, with the caption: 'Patrick Reid "turned off", without his cap. 1848.' I drew a line beneath *Patrick* so that there would be no mistaking my meaning.

I sat sipping my whisky for a very long while. At last, when its welcome warmth began to steal over me and my mood began to shift, I sketched a comical depiction of Brown's rescue of the punch bowl at the Talbot. *There*, thought I, *that ought to entertain Leyland for a moment or two.*

Only now do I lift the first volume of *Jane Eyre* from the table before me, lean back in my chair, stretch out my legs, and begin to read:

JANE EYRE.

An Autobiography

EDITED BY

CURRER BELL

IN THREE VOLUMES

VOL I.

LONDON:

SMITH, ELDER, AND CO, CORNHILL

1847.

XXX.

The Three Genii

January 17th, 1848 · Haworth, The Black Bull

When I was a boy, I could imagine no greater joy than to sit reading before a roaring fire, as a January snowstorm swept across the moors, the feathery flakes piling high on the window ledges, unless it was that of creating my own – our own – worlds in stories, plays and poems, all written in the minutest of script on scraps of old sugar bags and tied together with string, in our own publications, such as *Branwell's Blackwood Magazine*.

Now, as I read the final words of *Agnes Grey* – 'And now I think I have said sufficient' – and close the last of the Bell brothers' novels and take up my own pen, I find myself utterly at a loss for words. In my desolation, such childish joys seem as distant and as fantastical to me as the construction of ancient York Minster does to a century of factories and railways. The past two days have been far from joyful, not because the novels of the Bells are the 'trash' which Joe Leyland, not knowing who had authored them, believed them to be, but – alas! – to the contrary, because they are far superior to anything I could possibly have imagined.

Little, plain, Jane Eyre, all simmering anger and bottled-up passion, begging for release in her *va-et-vient* with her 'master' Rochester, which my virgin sister instinctively writes to resemble two passionate, yearning bodies coming closer and closer together until she saves him from burning in his bed – no coincidence, this. They are thrown apart as he leaves Thornfield abruptly the next day, just as her longing is most acutely awakened; but when he returns with Blanche Ingram, the waltz continues, the two bodies moving with increasing rapidity through a series of events in which her hero masks his passion and manipulates poor Jane, until the ill-fated wedding, at which point they are seemingly torn asunder for all time, until at last the heroine, mystically hearing his voice from afar, runs back to him crying, *I am coming!*

Here, too, are so many details of our common life distilled into fiction: the school at Cowan Bridge and the deaths of Mary and Elizabeth, merged into one; Anne's vivid, satirical accounts of the Robinsons, whose words are placed into the mouths of Blanche Ingram and her crowd; even the Haworth fortune-teller of so long ago, made into a disguise for her hero Rochester! Henry Nussey and his cold, pragmatical proposal of marriage makes an appearance as St John Rivers, whose sisters Diana and Mary are none other than Emily and Anne, with the Parsonage itself transformed into Moor House, and Tabby into their servant Hannah!

The mysterious Mr Rochester is as much my Percy, Lord Northangerland as he is her own Duke of Zamorna. She has given him some of my turns of phrase, and made my vices his, though confining them to a passing, understandable escape from the mad wife to whom he has been shackled till death do them part, because of a *mere human convention*. St John Rivers, too, is an inverted Branwell Brontë, for his noblest qualities – and there are many – are all those I lack. Did he not once burn for 'the more active life of the world – for the more exciting toils of a literary career'? But like good Papa, he had succeeded in crushing these desires, for he had 'heard a call from Heaven' to be a missionary. *His* delusions, at least, are far less destructive than mine.

Ah, but the moral of the story, that's the thing. Jane summons the strength to flee Rochester when she learns that the madwoman living just above her is his wife Bertha, even though, as he points out, he and Jane could live together and no one would be the wiser. *She* would know, says she – and *God* would know.

Is this not an insult, and do I not stand accused, in my conduct with Lydia, by inference? It is as if Charlotte has proclaimed to the world, *Do you not see that DUTY to oneself and one's God must triumph over all things, and will ultimately be rewarded?* And indeed, this being a novel, there must needs be a happy ending, and a marriage. Charlotte has Jane claim herself and Rochester to be equals – 'as indeed we are' – so why must she disfigure the poor fellow and give herself an unlikely fortune? To make this marriage acceptable to today's reader?

Although I may take issue with its pious ending, Currer Bell has done it, she has written a novel, and this is the bitterest medicine of all to swallow. Hers is a long, engrossing, satisfying tale, which has captured the attention of the entire reading public here and, I have no doubt, wherever English is spoken and read. By contrast, my sole, risible attempt at a novel lies unfinished, stillborn, like so much else. Like *everything* else. In the shadow of her accomplishment, of her growing fame, I now see Northangerland's publication in the local papers for what they are: the desperate attempts of a mediocre scribbler to be published at all costs. What I thought of the *Poems* of the Brothers Bell is now a more fitting a description of *mine*: sad, pitiful, pathetic.

Meanwhile, Ellis Bell's *Wuthering Heights* is a wild and wonderful monster of a book. And blowing through it are the violent storms of passion and intellect that one occasionally sees flashing behind Emily's own eyes when she is incautious enough to let down her guard, as when something rouses her indignation. Still, for all of this sound and fury, hardly one word is out of place, and nary a phrase can be imagined other than it is, or *where* it is.

Good Heavens what a story, and with what genius constructed! We ride up to this strange, almost otherworldly place with the outsider Lockwood, for Ellis Bell knew instinctively that her gentle readers would never credit such ruffianly characters and strange scenes, such violent acts and shocking language, without a fellow traveller by their side to share their confusion, dismay and disgust. There is much of Branwell Brontë in the fastidious, supercilious Lockwood, I am afraid; the author scarcely waits three pages to attribute to him an episode at the seashore that all too closely resembles my unfortunate experience with young Mary Taylor. I am also Heathcliff, however, for is not his monomaniacal passion for Catherine Earnshaw but a purer, unalloyed version of mine for Lydia Robinson?

The snowstorm that confines Lockwood to Wuthering Heights turns the land to 'one billowing, white ocean', concealing its features – pits and mounds, the refuse of quarries just like those behind the Parsonage – beneath, just as the welter of bewildering descriptions, events, mistaken identities and dreams precipitate our narrator's subsequent missteps, as when he cannot determine the relationships among and between Heathcliff, Hareton and Cathy.

With what cleverness she has given a single detail, the writing scratched in the paint long ago, '*Catherine Earnshaw*, here and there varied to *Catherine Heathliff*, and then again to *Catherine Linton*,' to foreshadow the conflict at the heart of the entire tale! And as we read on, we find that each chapter is a small story – almost a miniature novel – within itself, nearly every word, phrase and act appearing as inevitable and eternal as if chiselled in stone, like the *Hareton Earnshaw, 1500* carved above the entrance to Wuthering Heights. Each chapter is utterly *necessary* – to us Cathy's word for Heathcliff – like the stones of an arch, though they are placed in such a way to propel the reader forward, as if he were bounding down the rocky path from Top Withens to the valleys below.

Like Lockwood, we will only begin to unravel the mysteries of this place – which is none other than a nightmarish depiction of our own neighbourhood, from Haworth up to Penistone Hill, and from thence across to Top Withens and back down to Ponden Hall – when, with him, we allow Nelly Dean, that curious blend of Tabby Ayckroyd (in manner, though much softened) and John Brown (in learning and speech, when he makes an effort), to tell us the tale. With Lockwood, we feel chilled, and yet our head burns; with him we are excited in our nerves and our brains – as he says, 'almost to a pitch of foolishness'. With him we sit at last before a warming fire, a steaming basin of gruel before us, when Nelly Dean, a basket of sewing in her lap, begins her tale – the *true* tale of *Wuthering Heights*.

What a story it is! And yet, it could not be more different from *Jane Eyre* in every respect, as satisfying as that novel might be. There is no simple moral here, and Nelly does her best – though she often falls short – not to tell us what to think, or whom to judge. Indeed, Catherine Earnshaw and Heathcliff seem to have no God other than each other; if Jane's great fear is that she is in danger of loving God's creature, Rochester, more than the Creator Himself, the lovers of *Wuthering Heights* fear only losing each other: 'If all else perished, and *he* remained, *I* should still continue to be; and if all else remained, and he were annihilated, the universe would turn to a mighty stranger: I should not seem a part of it.' Where is Jane's God – the one Leyland called a pale Zeus – in all of this? No, love itself is the true religion of *Wuthering Heights*, and those who most zealously profess their Christianity – the old servant Joseph and, in Lockwood's dream, the Reverend Jabes Branderham – are nothing more than 'wearisome self-righteous Pharisees who ransack the Bible to rake the promises to themselves and fling the curses to their neighbours'.

Yes, it is true that Nelly tells Heathcliff, just before he dies, that he has 'lived a selfish, unchristian life', and reading these lines I could not help but think that Ellis Bell had *me* in mind. Had I not once responded just as he does: 'I believe you think me a fiend, something too horrible to live under a decent roof?'

If not a religious one, then, what moral lies within this strange tale? It is difficult to tell. Here, certainly, is the great 'crime' of betraying one's heart for money and position: '*Why* did you betray your own heart, Cathy?' But there is so much more, some almost defying description. Does old Mr Earnshaw bring a curse upon his entire family through his goodness, by saving the orphan Heathcliff from the streets of Liverpool? If so, what sort of moral is *that*?

Could the lesson, after all, be that an overweening passion will destroy everything in its path, like the Car of Juggernaut? For not only does Mr Earnshaw's affection for Heathcliff set loose a chain of resentment and revenge, and Catherine and Heathcliff's passion consume them entirely, but both Edgar and Isabella Linton's infatuation for each of them, respectively, adds only oil to the fire. Even Hindley – yes, that poor fellow is *also* me – sets out on his self-destructive path of gambling and drinking only in a state of abject grief, after the death of his wife Frances. It is no great leap to conclude that he, too, has loved too much.

The rejected Heathcliff – 'where did he come from, the little dark thing, harboured by a good man to his bane?' – is the cornerstone of the story, both scapegoat and sacrificial lamb, for he must finally abandon his plans of revenge and die for order to be restored, as the young Catherine and Hareton, possessing the best qualities of the two families (just as the peevish young Linton possesses the worst), are able to join them together at last in harmony. Lockwood might say that the young couple fears nothing, and 'would brave Satan and all his legions', but must we not read this with *some* irony, since our narrator 'grumbles' at his missed opportunity of wooing the handsome young Catherine Heathcliff?

Nay, though they may restore domestic harmony, these two young people will hardly 'labour for their race' like St John Rivers. While Charlotte concludes her story with a quotation from Revelations, placed in the mouth of (to my mind) a fanatical missionary of the Church resigned to dying in a distant land (and concluding her book, to ensure that even the most dull-witted reader will comprehend, with the words *Jesus Christ*), Emily gives us an abandoned church, the old kirk of Lockwood's nightmare, its windows broken and roof bereft of its slates.

As I read the novel's final paragraph –

> I lingered round them, under that benign sky:
> watched the moths fluttering among the heath and
> harebells, listened to the soft wind breathing through

the grass, and wondered how anyone could ever imagine unquiet slumbers for the sleepers in that quiet earth.

– I was suddenly overcome with emotion. My chest heaved, my throat closed, and hot tears soon spilt down my cheeks. How different, one from the other, were *Wuthering Heights* and *Jane Eyre*, and yet how brilliant both! One could scarcely credit that two sisters – two sisters who had lived nearly their entire lives together in four small walls – had written these novels; that anyone could believe that *one* person was masquerading as *all three* Bells showed a breathtaking imperviousness to the intricies of literary style, for not even the Bard himself could have created works both so brilliant and dissimilar. No, it was more likely that complete strangers of different sexes, living on different continents, had written the two tales.

I was weeping, then, not with sadness or with joy, but from that strange sensation one has when confronted by the majesty of human genius, just as I had upon hearing Handel's *Messiah*, reading Shakespeare or Wordsworth, or standing within York Minster. I remembered again entering that great structure with Anne, who clutched my arm and said, her voice trembling with reverential awe: 'Oh Branwell, if man's finite power can do *this*, what must be the power of the Almighty?!'

What, then, of Acton Bell's slim volume, *Agnes Grey*? How like Anne herself it is: a nearly perfect, little gem of a novel, as unlike both of her sisters' books as *frost is from fire*, as Catherine Earnshaw would say. The reader of those two novels, once finished, might feel that he has been to Hell and back, but not here. Although there are gloomy days, dark showers and even great snowstorms in the book, Agnes's voice is so warm, engaging and utterly rational that we come away feeling as if, in her world, the sun is always shining and a gentle breeze is forever whispering, whether rustling through the trees at Horton Lodge or sweeping along the glittering sands at A –, as she has called the seaside resort; how faithfully she has reproduced Thorp Green and her beloved Scarborough!

Still, just as the confectioner sometimes places an unusual tartness at the centre of his sweets, so this novel possesses not only Anne's typical humour but a devastating, scarcely disguised portrayal of her employers, both the Inghams and the Robinsons, the worlds they inhabit, and their guiding 'principles'. Many a time did I laugh aloud, in spite of myself, from the accounts of the horrible Bloomfield children, especially Tom, to her depiction of the Murray sisters, Rosalie and Matilda, who together are a nearly inexhaustible source of amusement, the first so perfect a picture of young Lydia Robinson, all coquetry and vanity, that the author seems somehow to have plucked her from life and dropped her into a book, including entire phrases I myself have heard her utter, the second a swearing, whip-cracking hoyden with the worst qualities of the two younger Robinson girls together, and none of their charming attributes, and whose 'No – damn it, no!' and 'you ass!' directed at her elegant elder sister made me laugh until my sides nearly hurt.

What a marvel that our baby sister was able to *get out of herself* and inhabit the minds and souls of beings who could not be more alien, but whom she had observed with such great care for so many years. How amusing, and how clever, that she has her heroine quote her own pupils, as if listening at *their* door or perhaps even somehow entering into their very minds, in a manner which describes her, of course, but far more revealingly, them:

> Miss Grey was a queer creature: she never flattered,
> and did not praise them half enough; but whenever
> she did speak favourably of them, or anything belonging
> to them, they could be quite sure her approbation was
> sincere ... She had her own opinions on every subject,
> and kept steadily to them – very tiresome opinions
> they often were; as she was always thinking of what
> was right and what was wrong, and had a strange
> reverence for matters connected with religion,
> and an unaccountable liking to good people.

Despite the subtitle of *Jane Eyre – an autobiography, edited by Currer Bell* – Anne's is the most autobiographical of the books, though she has brought dear Mama back to life in Mrs Grey, merged her sisters into one, created a far more flawed version of Papa, and blotted her reprobate brother – as if too painful to recall – entirely out of existence, just as I long ago painted myself into oblivion, in that dreadful portrait I made of the four of us so many years ago. I could have appeared as a young tutor, but he, too, is sent packing to the Devil in this fictional version of events, though my friend Weightman has surely been brought back from the dead, poor fellow, and given not only his own sterling qualities, but some of Papa's, in her beloved Mr Weston. Even his tender gift of the primroses has not been forgotten.

But how much more do I recognise young Lydia in Rosalie's flirtatious torturing – like the slow roasting alive that Tom Bloomfield has planned for a nest of baby birds earlier in the book – of the unfortunate Mr Hatfield! I am quite certain that she would have done the same to *me*, merely for sport, had she not fallen so desperately in love with the dashing Mr Roxby. Perhaps, consciously or not, Acton Bell has created Mr Hatfield to show just how foolish I was to believe that Lydia *mère* would ever marry an impoverished suitor such as myself: 'To think that I could be such a fool as to fall in *love*! … A preference I *might* acknowledge; but never for one like poor Mr Hatfield, who has not several hundred a year to bless himself with. I like to talk to him, because he's so clever and amusing.'

Upon reading this passage, I thought: did Lydia *ever* profess her love for me, or was it only fleshly desire? I could never recall those words – *I love you* – on her lips. Was *my* love for her ever anything more than a coupling – like our two bodies made one flesh – of my ambition and my lust? Have I ever truly loved anyone, least of all myself?

If the audacious Hatfield is a most oblique reference to my own folly, Acton Bell has taken no such pains to conceal her dislike of Mrs Robinson, who under the name of Murray has all of Lydia's flaws and none of her good qualities, except for her beauty. Still, her description of Lydia's view of her governess's goal in educating her girls – to 'strive to amuse and oblige, instruct, refine, and polish, with the least possible exertion on their part' – is, I have to confess to myself, all too true.

The moral of *Agnes Grey* – unlike that of *Wuthering Heights*, if Ellis Bell's monstrous tale even has one – is all too clear, from its first page to its last: only true love, unadulterated by worldly interests, unsullied by ambition for position or riches, can bring happiness. The novel describes a perfect circle, moving from her mother's preferring to live 'in a cottage with Richard Grey than in a palace with any other man in world' to, at precisely its midpoint, Rosalie's insistence that she '*must* have Ashby Park, whoever shares it' with her, and concluding with Agnes and Edward Weston standing high above the sea on a 'glorious summer evening,' watching 'the splendid sunset mirrored in the restless world of waters' at their feet, with 'hearts filled with gratitude to heaven, and happiness, and love – almost too full for speech.'

This seems at once so idyllic and yet so true that I cannot even mock the piety of the novel's subsequent paragraphs, where the Westons 'endeavour to live to the glory of Him who has scattered so many blessings' in their path, and 'keep in mind the glorious heaven beyond, where both may meet again, and sin and sorrow are unknown.' No, no mockery is possible, and the purity of the sweet young couple's love seems not just possible, but in its own way inevitable, so perfectly has Anne constructed her little tale, so great is the contrast with Rosalie's bitter end as mistress of Ashby Park. Even if such love is but an ideal, the reader surely, and most ardently, wishes it to be real.

As I left the Black Bull and walked past the silent church and the scattered slabs of the churchyard, I stopped and turned to face the west, where the sun had just set behind the row of shops along the Main Street, and where, in an otherwise perfectly clear winter sky, two thin wisps of cloud fanned upwards from the horizon to the highest vault of heaven, like the cottony wings of an immense angel, or like the far smaller, icy seraphs we children made just over the wall, in our garden, one winter's day long ago, by lying and moving our arms and legs in the fresh, powdery snow. Tabby had discovered us thus engaged, and shouted, 'Y' childer wail soon enou' *be* angels if ye catch yer death o' cold!'

I could almost see us there again, the snow so dry and light in the cold bright sunshine that it flew from us like puffs of smoke as we played, and there came upon me such wracking convulsions of grief, which no earthly remedy could cure, and for which no heavenly succour was offered, as the celestial pinions above broke silently into a thousand fragments upon the bitter east wind, which had suddenly risen as the sun slipped beneath the horizon.

XXXI.

A Pit Full of Fire

February 5th, 1848 · The Parsonage

How do I begin to recount what has happened in the past few days? I have truly been to *Hell* and back, have seen it with my own eyes, and nearly brought the entire Parsonage and its inhabitants down into the burning pit with me.

Upon returning the novels of the Brothers Bell to Francis Leyland, I promptly set out to drown myself with drink, with the able assistance of that good man's brother, who stood all too ready to assist me. I can recall little of what occurred, so quickly did I seek to blot my consciousness out of existence. There was no time for witty banter, no time for whoring: I wished only for respite, and the bottle was my noose.

When I arrived in Haworth the following day, I went to bed directly, awaking a full day later with a terrible cold and cough, feverish and chilled to the bone. My sisters and Papa have all had the influenza in the past two weeks, so I suppose it was at last my turn. Indeed, I found myself so ill that I had no desire for liquor, and was unable to stop coughing, though I could scarcely lift my head from the pillow.

Good Dr Wheelhouse was sent for. The portly gentleman, whose double chin is so considerable that his overlarge head seems placed directly upon his shoulders, gazed down sadly as he gave me a generous dose of laudanum.

'Here now, young man,' said he, 'this will stop your coughing, and help you sleep. It will also help you get over your dependency on spirits, which you must once and for all *crush*, if you wish to recover fully.'

Feeling I could not possibly sleep more than I already had, I lit a candle and began to read; what book it was I cannot now even recall, for I had repeatedly tried making sense of no more than the first two or three lines, nodding drowsily over the page, and had the sensation of falling – falling fast asleep, yes, but also falling bodily through space, as if into the deepest recesses of the earth.

But *no*, I was very much awake, and walking along ocean sands, every sound and sensation magnified a thousand times over, each object bursting with significance, as if all of human history and knowledge were contained in this plenitude. The moon, three times its usual size, shone with unwonted brightness, and each breaking wave seemed to unlock the mysteries of the universe, things hidden since the beginning of time. This was no ordinary beach, however, but a phantom replica of the sands at Scarborough, and soon I found myself across from the boathouse beneath The Cliff. *Perhaps Lydia is there!*, thought I, and I raced across the moonlit shore and flung open the door.

What I found, instead, was Anne, resisting a man who was attempting to defile her.

'Oh Branwell!' she cried out, as I advanced in a rage, flinging her attacker to the floor. I kicked and trampled on him, and dashed his head repeatedly against the large stones that served as the boathouse floor. Oh God! What a cold creeping horror I felt, as he rose up weakly on his elbows, so that the moonlight spilling through the open door revealed his identity. For the would-be rapist's bloody face was none other than my own.

I turned to Anne, who now stood perfectly composed, as if nothing had occurred. She gave no appearance of having been touched, let alone attacked; her garments were perfectly smooth and crisp, as if Tabby had just starched and ironed them. She smiled, but with just a *soupçon* of mischief in those winsome violet eyes, which shone out from beneath raised brows.

'Brother,' she said in what seemed, most unexpectedly, to be a teasing manner, 'why must you always be at war with yourself?'

I looked down where my other self had lain, and where now

was to be seen only a coil of old rope.

'Come,' said she, 'let's run all the way up to the castle ruins, shall we?'

Just as we had on the moors as children, we raced up the ghostly, empty streets of Scarborough, winding past the old church and further up the hill to the castle gates. This dream-Anne was hale and hearty, and as we arrived past the great ruined castle keep and dashed onto the grassy, windswept headland, she showed no signs of being in the least breathless.

The moon had grown even larger, so impossibly enormous that it filled the sky above the sea below, in which its vast and shimmering pendant was reflected. Anne turned and placed her small soft hands in mine.

'Oh Mr Weston – Edward – you love me, then?' said she, the moon surrounding her face like a nimbus.

'Yes, Agnes, I do,' said I, drawing her to me for a tender kiss.

'*Branwell*!' cried Anne in alarm, pushing me from her, 'What are you doing? Who is Agnes?'

Before I could confess my knowledge of *Agnes Grey*, its author – or the dream-spectre who resembled her – had vanished, and I was alone on the cliffs of the promontory, high above the sea. The moon now began to move towards me, growing ever larger by the second, as the roar of the waves reached a deafening pitch. But this was no natural moon approaching, for clouds seemed to billow from above it; nor was this sound the rush of the ocean's swells, for its quickening, rhythmic pace was not of God's creation, but of man's.

Onto the headland rushed a fantastical locomotive, stopping more abruptly than its real counterpart could ever do. Joseph Bentley Leyland, of all people, leant out a window and called, 'Come now, young Faustus, why dost thou tarry? We've an appointment at Luddenden, damn it!'

Soon I had climbed aboard, and within what seemed only moments we had made the journey across Yorkshire, flying through the night sky. I could scarcely formulate a question to ask my friend before we alighted from our carriage at the Lord Nelson, where I had first met Maeve: *the intoxicating one*, now also dead, poor woman. But no, here she was, as buxom and rosy-cheeked as that first night together in 1841, she who later taught me just how many ways there are to savour the pleasure of the body purely for itself, stripped of all accompanying emotion but animal desire.

Soon we were within each other's embrace, our lust seemingly boundless, in a night that seemed without end; she, despite her occupation, appeared to thirst as much for me as I did for her, but at last we collapsed in each other's arms and slept, a long healing slumber, just as we had that final night in Halifax. When I awoke, the sun had risen well into what appeared to be a summer sky, and as she lay with her head propped up, carefully surveying my features, I was nearly blinded by the bright sunshine pouring through the window behind her, surrounding her face like a halo. She seemed altered, transformed; I squinted and frowned, but I could not make out *how*, until slowly, with a shudder of recognition, I knew.

'Why Branwell,' said she, 'how very black and cross you look! And how – how funny and grim!'

The words were not Maeve's, but Catherine Earnshaw's, for the intoxicating one had vanished with the dawn, and the graceful, lithesome figure stretched out beside me was now that of my own sister Emily. She did not touch me, and I dared not touch her, and as she in turn saw that I had recognised her, her brow grew clouded. It was again Catherine Earnshaw who spoke, though the being through whose lips issued these words remained Emily Jane Brontë: 'You are like the rocks beneath, Branwell: a source of little visible delight, but necessary.'

At this moment came a loud rapping on the door; just as he had so often done in the real world, so now did Joe Leyland with his infernal walking stick, in the ideal realm of my dream. As eager as I was to leave Emily, I found that she had already stolen a march on me, for as I turned my head towards her she had vanished into the ether, like a ghost.

'Put your trousers on, little man!' cried Joe, laughing at the sight of my thin legs poking from beneath my nightshirt. 'Time to settle accounts!'

I did as my friend commanded, and followed him out of the Lord Nelson and up a steep rise, much like the path from our beloved waterfalls above South Dean Beck to Top Withens. In the distance rose an old stone edifice, and as we approached, I could hear the distinctive sound of a chisel on stone: *chink, chink, chink*. It was John Brown, high on a ladder, finishing the lettering of a carving over the principal entrance. Here, surrounded by a riot of naked and convulsing bodies so true to nature that this orgy seemed to heave and shudder like fornicating flesh and blood, was the name *Patrick Branwell Brontë*, and the dates *1817–*. The sexton, his hammer and chisel suspended above the second, as-yet-uncarved date, merely tipped his hat respectfully, as if he knew neither me nor his collaborator Leyland.

Joe laughed jovially at my bewilderment and clapped me on the back, lowering his voice with feigned piety, 'Did ye never read in the scriptures: *The stone which the builders rejected, the same is become the cornerstone?*' I followed him through what appeared to be an endless labyrinth of corridors; past old rooms filled with lumber and spiderwebs, and down stairs whose bannisters had quite rotted away. All seemed as if undisturbed from time immemorial, for a thick blanket of dust lay heavy upon all that we saw and touched. The only movement to be glimpsed was a door creaking gently to and fro on its hinges; as it opened an outline of bright light surrounded it, just as it had Emily's head in the Lord Nelson, the luminous rectangle growing and fading each time it opened and closed.

'I know this place,' said I, but my companion simply smiled and nodded his assent. It fell on me like a thunderclap: *I was walking through Wuthering Heights*, at least as it took shape in my own troubled faculties. For here was the very spot where a drunken Hindley had dropped baby Hareton to a certain death on the flags below, the lad only rescued by an unexpectant Heathcliff; there was the ladder to Joseph's garret; here was the landing where a young Nelly Dean had placed the gypsy brat Heathcliff himself, hoping *it* would be gone by the morning, and where later, Isabella Linton had wept and slept. And so the room before me must be –

'Go ahead,' said my friend. 'Go in.'

The room was just as Lockwood describes it, with a chair, a clothes-press, and a large oak case with the squares cut out near the top, resembling coach windows. As I slid back the panels of the old-fashioned couch, the light of a candle left burning within showed plainly, in the paint of the window ledge, four scratched names. I picked up the candle and examined the names before me, but there were no Catherines here: only Lydias. Each of the first two names – *Lydia Gisborne* and *Lydia Robinson* – was struck through with a single, elegant stroke, while the third – *Lydia Brontë* – had been furiously attacked, seemingly with a variety of implements, including flames, so that it was scarcely legible. A final, elegantly-written name – *Lady Lydia Scott* – stood unblemished.

No longer did my body shudder with fear or horror but with rage, so much so that the candle fell from my hand and onto the bed, whose curtains caught fire immediately, and which I strove to extinguish by any means possible – my cloak, a ewer of icy water, even the flaming bedcurtains themselves or those hanging above the open window and moving slowly back and forth in the breeze, gently fanning the growing flames. I raced into the corridor to seek Leyland's assistance, but he was nowhere to be seen, and so I dashed back into the room to find – with the same horror I had felt upon viewing myself in the boathouse with Anne – my own reclining form on the bed, surrounded by flames; in the midst of this blaze and vapour, I lay in deep, seemingly impregnable sleep.

'Wake! Wake!' I cried, shaking myself, but to no avail, for the smoke appeared to have stupefied me. At last, I heard a hissing and the breakage of a pitcher, and felt a rush of water over my face and shoulders.

'Charlotte?' said I, for that was the little figure who now stood – surrounded by a cloud of smoke that encircled her face like a dingy aura – where I myself had just been an instant ago, upon entering the room to find myself unconscious on the bed. How had she become *me*, or I *her*? I looked round, finding the room somewhat altered.

'Charlotte, where are we?' I said, sitting up in the bed.

'Why, in the children's study, of course. Can you not see the garden below and the churchyard beyond?'

And so, as the phantom smoke vanished, I could. It was here in this little room that we had transformed our grief into a vast outpouring of poems, stories, plays and little magazines, several lifetimes of writing before our own lives – our *real* lives – could begin. Here the four Chief Genii – Genius Brannii, Genius Tallii, Genius Emmii and Genius Annii – created, like four infernal evangelists, entire worlds from their feverish, precocious minds: Charlotte and I devising Verdopolis and Angria, and Emily and Charlotte eventually sailing off to their own mysterious land of Gondal.

'I suppose,' said I, drying my hair and face with an untouched portion of curtain, 'I owe you a debt of gratitude.' I held out my hand; she gave me hers: I took it first in one, then in both of my own. I felt, in a sudden wave, that old – and, so I thought, long dead and buried – emotion of fraternal love, of delight in *my* Charlotte. *My Genius Tallii*. I lifted her hand to my lips and kissed it.

'But I – or rather we' she replied, 'owe *you* so much more.'

These mysterious words were lost on me, for I found that however much I sought to dry myself, it was of no avail.

'Charlotte, why do I perspire in this manner?'

'You have a fever, Branwell; do you not remember how ill you are? Here, let us make a clean and dry place for you. You must lie back down.'

'Oh God,' said I, suddenly in agony, repeating what I had said to Leyland as we walked into the Black Bull so many months since, but this time in dreadful earnest, rather than jest: 'I feel as if I had an infernal fire in my veins, that all the waters of the ocean cannot quench!'

Eyes shut, I trembled uncontrollably, as an excruciating pain shot through my body like an electrical current, my fever fairly consuming me in a conflagration. Then all was dark, and for a brief instant, quiet, except for the pulse of blood throbbing through my boiling brain.

When I opened my eyes, the walls of the little room had fallen away, and I stood, my hands shackled and a noose about my neck, in the vast nave of York Minster. High above me, the famous Jabes Branderham of Lockwood's dream – who bore more than a passing resemblance to the Reverend Patrick Brontë, but as he looked when I was a child – leant forward and stretched out his arm, levelling an impossibly long finger at my chest: 'Thou art the Man!' cried Branderham. 'What sin hast thou *not* committed?'

I was devoured by a scorching shame, for everyone I had ever known, living or dead, was ranged behind me: now near me stood not just Charlotte, but all five of my sisters and Mama – dear Mama! – weeping and tearing at their garments. My blood boiled through my veins, my brow searing so that I felt I could not stand another moment without exploding utterly in flames.

But Jabes Branderham had only begun his litany of my sins.

'Verily, verily, I say unto thee, thou hast broken *every one* of God's commandments, in spirit if not in deed!

He proceeded through each of the Ten Commandments, detailing with fiendish relish how all of my various sins related to each – even those I had not, in reality, committed, or even contemplated.

Still my body grew hotter, as if I were now roasting on a spit.

'Doth not the Lord thy God also say, in Leviticus 18, verse 9, that "the nakedness of thy sister thou shalt not uncover"?'

This was too much. Enraged, I found my voice at last: 'God confound you sir,' I thundered, 'I have endured your outrageous discourse long enough! Yes, I am a sinner, and doubtless worse than most. But never – *never*, I say – have I lain with my sisters, and both the Lord above and Satan below know this to be true! *You*, sir, are the deceiver, not I!'

At this Branderham no longer resembled Papa, but began turning a vivid scarlet, as great wings grew from his back, and horns sprouted from his temples; his feet became cloven hooves, and his hands razor-sharp talons.

'So,' he snarled, 'you have seen! Yes, I *am* the deceiver, the

Great Deceiver!' He flew down from the high pulpit and began advancing towards me, flames now issuing from his nostrils. The great cathedral of York Minster and its occupants fell away into the void, except for my three living sisters – Charlotte, Emily and Anne – who wrestled with the demon as he sought to drag me down into the unfathomably vast pit full of fire that had opened up beneath us, to the opening strains of Liszt's *Totentanz.* But they were losing the battle, and slowly, slowly, I felt myself descending with him to that great, eternal inferno, whose billowing smoke rose to frame the desperate, anguished faces of my sisters high above me.

I could stand no more, and wished only for an end – not a poetical, metaphorical annihilation, but true oblivion, true relief, true peace. I thought: would that I had never been born!

But – *mirabile dictu!* – as the last remnants of hope, of life, ebbed out of my body – without, unfortunately, any cessation of the perpetual incineration of my soul – the dark heavens above opened, and a miraculous rain poured forth, so great a deluge as to destroy the demon Branderham and extinguish the very fires of hell, for all eternity. My sisters' faces again loomed above me, as the depleted clouds that ringed each of their faces whitened, fading softly back to form their white – immaculately white – ethereal wings. My genii, my angels of salvation, my Tallii, my Emmii, my Annii!

I felt, for an instant, as safe as I had in dear Mama's warm lap, and so I was – am – now *there*, on a night so long ago, as she reads to me by the lambent firelight. She draws me closely to her breast and points at a Bible. 'See, Branny, my little angel: Paul says that *though I speak with the tongues of men and angels, and have not love, I am become as sounding brass, or a tinkling cymbal.*'

Oh, dearest, most cherished Mama, you have returned! Would that I might prolong this instant for all eternity! But no, my angels are moving now, in great agitation, and though they communicate with one another with force and urgency, I understand nothing they say, as if they were speaking in tongues. I smile, still basking in the warmth of my mother's love. *Love*, true love.

'Branwell!' cried Emily, 'Branwell! Wake! Wake!' My very real middle sister now proceeded to utter a string of curses generally heard only amongst the stronger sex, took hold of me under the arms and dragged me out of bed, pouring still more water on the last of the flames. It had all happened within moments: Anne had discovered the fire, been unable to wake me, and gone to fetch Emily, who had pulled me from the bed and extinguished the fire.

Poor Papa – I do love the old man, for he does, and always has done, his best for me – knew nothing of the event until morning, but has determined that we are now to sleep together in his room. And yet, except to prevent me from lighting a candle, I know not what mischief this can prevent, for he forever sleeps soundly, whilst I, as is the case at present, lie awake, gazing at the churchyard, whose graves seem almost to tumble down the gently sloping hillside, in places seeming no more orderly than a child's collapsed house of cards. Above the scattered dead rises the eternally accusing church steeple, and beyond it, high in the indifferent, glacial heavens, hangs a serene, dispassionate moon, an icy halo cast about its neck.

XXXII.

The End of All

April 18th, 1848 · The Parsonage

With the warmer weather, I feel tolerably better, and for the first time in months. Most of my time is spent sleeping or imagining that Death will soon come calling for me – I have even sketched him, as a skeleton, reaching to snatch me as I slumber. I cannot confide this to my sisters, for they would just say that I am like the little boy crying wolf. Leyland has been to Haworth and urged me in person to meet him and his merry band in Halifax next week, at the Old Cock. Why not? For I have abandoned Dr Wheelhouse's counsel, and since the harrowing dream I recounted above, have refused that poisoning doctor's laudanum whenever he tries to press it upon me. What else could have made me conjure up such terrible visions, worthy of De Quincey himself?

On the other hand, I drink as often, and as much, as I can afford – or have advanced to me on credit. The cheap gin I once disdained is now the only thing that does me good.

June 18th, 1848 · The Parsonage

Nicholson has sent Papa a demand for settlement of my bill owed to him, immediately, under penalty of a court summons. I have written to inform him that I shall soon be able to pay him the balance in full – for that I will write to Dr Crosby, and request an advance through his hands, which I am sure to obtain. I also have an unpaid bill at the Talbot.

I have asked my friends to help me: I have given John Brown ten shillings, to place in Mr Nicholson's hands on Wednesday next, and begged Leyland to see both him and Mrs Sugden at the Talbot, to tell them that my receipt of money from Dr Crosby is morally certain.

If Nicholson refuses my offer and presses me with law, I am RUINED. Since reading my sisters' novels, I have had five months of such utter sleeplessness, violent cough and frightful agony of mind, and I know that gaol would destroy me forever. I cannot admit to them that I have read their work, any more than they will admit to its existence – no doubt, they believe that they are sparing my feelings, but their pity only deepens *mine* – for myself. I cannot hate them, though, for they are good. Yes, even Charlotte – even my Genius Tallii, for all her faults – is good, through and through.

I can only despise myself.

July 8th, 1848 · The Parsonage

Yesterday Charlotte and Anne departed Haworth in haste, but Emily did not divulge their destination, or the reason for their journey. The author of *Wuthering Heights* is not one to be asked anything twice, particularly when the first interrogation prompts a scowl every bit as black and fierce as Heathcliff's first welcome of his tenant Lockwood.

It is only in the ferocity of her gaze that she differs from her sisters, however, for all three have ceased to speak to me unless absolutely compelled to do so. Any last ties of sympathy have been severed, seemingly for all time. How long, I wonder, can we continue in such a state?

August 3rd, 1848 · The Parsonage

Crosby has sent the money, and I am saved – at least from gaol, and at least for the time being. Where Lydia Robinson gets her money, and why she continues to send it to me, are questions on which I prefer not to dwell. Even the feeling of her body against mine is now but a distant memory, and the very bitterness of her loss has begun to ebb away into weary indifference.

My mental wretchedness and corporeal weakness utterly prevent me from doing anything. I only think that, had I the strength and the will, I might still make a fresh start, begin anew, far from Haworth.

When I was a lad, I was fond of saying: *You have only to WILL a thing in order to get it.* But what WILL do I have now? Indeed, what *will* have I ever had? Desire, yes: *desire.*

The End

Afterword

What follows is basic biographical information about the primary and secondary characters of *Oblivion: The Lost Diaries of Branwell Brontë*. They are given in alphabetical order, apart from Branwell, who is placed first. Readers interested in more detail about fact and fiction, the style in which the book is written, or where I have intentionally borrowed words from the Brontës and others, are invited to read 'History and Fiction', 'The Language of *Oblivion*' and 'Notes to *Oblivion*'.

Brontë, (Patrick) Branwell (1817–1848), the narrator and main character of *Oblivion*. Painter, poet, tutor, railway employee and leader in the creation of the Brontë siblings' imaginary childhood worlds. Published numerous poems in the Yorkshire newspapers. Commonly held to be an alcoholic and an opium addict, although concrete evidence about the latter habit is scant. Died in Haworth of tuberculosis, aggravated by addiction and, possibly, *delirium tremens*, although Dr Wheelhouse gave the cause of death as 'chronic bronchitis-marasmus'.

Brontë, Anne (1820–1849). Youngest of the Brontë siblings. Novelist and poet, after serving several years as a governess to two families. Author of *Agnes Grey* (1847) and *The Tenant of Wildfell Hall* (1848), the latter of which is considered one of the first feminist novels in the English language. Its reprinting was suppressed by Charlotte after Anne's death, a decision that affected Anne's popularity and remains controversial to this day. She died in Scarborough of tuberculosis and is buried at Saint Mary's.

Brontë, Charlotte (1816–1855). Eldest of the siblings to survive into adulthood, and the only one to become known and celebrated under the name Brontë. Novelist and poet, author of *Jane Eyre* (1847), *Shirley* (1849), *Villette* (1853) and *The Professor* (her first novel, but published posthumously in 1857). The only Brontë to marry, she may have died from dehydration due to morning sickness, although her death certificate gives tuberculosis as the cause.

Brontë, Emily (1818–1848). Second of the Brontë sisters, and third of the siblings to survive childhood. Novelist and poet, whose novel *Wuthering Heights* (1847) is now considered one of the greatest works in the English language. Information about her life is almost entirely second-hand, as her poems and novel, along with a handful of diary papers and letters, are all that remain.

There is some evidence that she may have written a second novel, perhaps destroyed after her death by Charlotte. Died in Haworth of tuberculosis.

Brontë, Reverend Patrick (1777–1861), born Patrick Brunty. Irishman educated for the clergy (Church of England) at Cambridge, and father of the famous Brontë siblings. Married Maria Branwell (1783–1821), daughter of a successful merchant from Penzance, in 1812. She died of ovarian cancer when Anne, the youngest, was only twenty months old; her death and, later, that of the two eldest siblings, Maria and Elizabeth, had a lasting impact on the surviving children and the content of their literary works.

Brown, John (1804–1855). Haworth sexton and stonemason, and Branwell's confidant and mentor in 'worldly' things. He was believed to be quite well read but seems to have shared and encouraged many of Branwell's worst habits.

Coleridge, Hartley (1796–1849). Eldest son of the great romantic poet Samuel Taylor Coleridge. He did, indeed, receive Branwell Brontë at Nab Cottage on May Day, 1840.

Crosby, Dr John (1797–1859). Trusted physician of the Robinson family of Thorp Green, and friend of Branwell Brontë. Remained in contact after the latter's dismissal and may have been used as a conduit for information and funds from Lydia Robinson.

Grundy, Francis Henry (1821–1899). Engineer and surveyor on the Manchester and Leeds Railway, 1841–1842, where he met Branwell in Halifax and Luddenden Foot. In 1879, he published *Pictures of the Past*, where he provides a lively but sometimes inaccurate portrait of Branwell.

Liszt, Franz (1811–1886). Hungarian pianist and composer, one of the great musicians of the nineteenth century. The date, location and detailed programme of his concert in Halifax in January 1841 are exactly rendered in *Oblivion*, but whether any Brontës attended is unknown – although it is unlikely that Branwell would have missed it. The soirée afterwards, at Leyland's studio, is pure invention (see 'History and Fiction' for more information).

Leyland, Joseph Bentley (1811–1851). Halifax sculptor and friend of Branwell Brontë. Like John Brown, he was not always the best influence on his younger friend, often encouraging his excessive drinking. Although the fictional version of 'Joe' in *Oblivion* is perhaps larger than life, it may not be too far off the mark: a relative called the actual Leyland 'self-opinionated, sarcastic, and unreliable, scornful of religion and of anyone who disagreed with him, only working when the spirit moved him'. All the Leyland sculptures mentioned in *Oblivion* were real, although few have survived. One prominent exception is the monument to Dr Beckwith, which may still be seen in York Minster. Leyland was arrested and imprisoned for debt in 1850, and died early the following year, in the Manor Gaol, Halifax.

Leyland, Francis A. (1813–1894). Antiquarian who ran a bookshop and circulating library in Halifax. Became a Roman Catholic and married Anne Brierley in 1845. Later in life he would defend Branwell's reputation, publishing *The Brontë Family: With Special Reference to Patrick Branwell Brontë* (1886).

Maeve (c. 1812–1847). Irish prostitute residing in Halifax. With Maggie (Heaton) Mortimer, one of two entirely fictional characters to play a significant role in the novel.

Mortimer, Margaret, *née* Heaton (c. 1820–?), also known as 'the Sinless Kilmeny'. Along with Maeve, one of only two important characters in *Oblivion* who did not exist in reality. Her married name and employment, however, are inspired by a real publican, one Benjamin Mortimer of the Royal Hotel, who was convicted in 1860 of 'Adulteration of Beer' by the use of grains of paradise.

Although Leyland's sculpture, inspired by Hogg's poem 'Kilmeny', has been destroyed, photographs may be seen online.

Postlethwaite, Robert (1786–1859) of Broughton House in Broughton-in-Furness, Branwell's employer from January to June 1840. The elder of his sons, John, would later study at Trinity College, Cambridge, and become an Anglican priest. The younger, William, became a magistrate in Cumberland, before emigrating to New Zealand and then, in the early twentieth century, to California, before returning to England at the end of his life.

Riley, Agnes (1814–1909). Like Eleanor Nelson and Frances Atkinson, Agnes Riley was a real person. All three were unwed mothers in the months following Branwell Brontë's six-month tenure with the Postlethwaites. Agnes did indeed give birth to a child named Mary, although recent research suggests that the child did not die in infancy but lived to the age of twenty-seven, when she died at the Ulverston Union Workhouse (which would mean that Moses Tyson, in *Oblivion*, lies to Branwell when he sees him again in Halifax). Thanks to these new archival investigations, we now believe that Agnes spent her life within eight miles of her birthplace and lived to the advanced age of ninety-four (earlier scholarship had suggested that she emigrated to Australia, but that Agnes Riley seems to have been her first cousin).

Robinson, Lydia, née Gisborne (1799–1859). Mistress of Thorp Green near York, and wife of the Reverend Edmund Robinson, employer of both Anne and Branwell. The likely inspiration for Mrs Murray in *Agnes Grey*, and believed by many to have had an affair with the much younger Branwell, the discovery of which likely led to his dismissal. Just as Branwell himself, in *Oblivion*, imagines several different scenarios leading to his dismissal, so too have scholars. Lydia Robinson married Sir Edward Scott on 8th November 1848, just weeks after the death of Branwell and three months after that of Sir Edward's first wife. Died of liver disease in 1859.

Robinson, Lydia Mary (1825–1901). Eldest daughter of the Robinson family of Thorp Green, and the likely inspiration for Rosalie Murray in *Agnes Grey*. She eloped to Gretna Green with the actor Henry Roxby of Scarborough in October 1845, prompting a change in her father's will. A son, named Edmund after her father and brother, was born in 1853. After Roxby's death, she married Henry Lincoln Simpson and lived in Hastings until her death.

Sowden, Reverend Sutcliffe (1816–1861). Branwell's young clergyman friend from his days at Luddenden Foot, who would go on to become friends with Patrick Brontë's curate and Charlotte's eventual husband, Arthur Bell Nicholls, at whose marriage he officiated. He tragically drowned in the canal at Hebden Bridge on a stormy night in 1861, perhaps as the result of a fit or stroke. His future demise provides the rather dark inspiration for the fictional Branwell's comment twenty years earlier: 'I really am not going to … drown myself in the Calder, or the Rochedale Canal over yonder.'

Weightman, Reverend William (1814–1842). The Reverend Brontë's second curate, of whom the Brontës were exceedingly fond. The girls all seem to have been somewhat in love with him, Branwell called him 'one of my dearest friends', and Patrick said that the two clergymen had been 'always like father and son' (the memorial sermon for Weightman in *Oblivion* is reproduced word for word, and almost in its entirety). It is likely that he inspired, at least in part, Edward Weston in Anne's *Agnes Grey*. He died of cholera at the age of twenty-eight; the monument correctly quoted by Branwell and still visible in St Michael and All Angels' Church, Haworth, erroneously gives his age as twenty-six.

Oblivion is above all a work of fiction, as much as it is based on the life of a real person. I will leave it to others to decide whether the book has any merit, but it is very ambitious in its aims: it attempts to be a tribute to the works of the Brontë sisters (see the 'The Language of *Oblivion*' that follows); it tries to understand the inner workings of a troubled individual who also happened to be the only male sibling in the most famous literary family in history; it recreates a society in radical transition; it wrestles with some of the 'big questions' of human existence; and finally, to an extent, it offers itself as a bit of a 'romp' – a 'big read' that encompasses humour, sadness, intrigue, love, lust, sex, addiction, class and gender differences, and the resentments that they can fuel, among other things.

The reader who wishes to know more about the facts of the historical Brontës should consult the many fine works of scholarship on the family, especially Juliet Barker's *The Brontës: Wild Genius on the Moors: The Story of a Literary Family*, or such references as *The Oxford Companion to the Brontës* (see the 'Acknowledgements' below).

At present, I would like to assure those readers who are not Brontë experts or enthusiasts that the general chronology of Branwell's and his sisters' lives has been rigorously respected, while leaving room for invention and imagination. Thus, all of the major phases of the fictional Brontës' lives as portrayed in *Oblivion* precisely mirror those of the real Brontës – from Branwell's different employments and residences from 1840 to 1845, to his sisters' time in Brussels; and from most of his visits to Halifax and Haworth, to something as specific as the siblings' picnic at Bolton Abbey on 20th June 1844. Indeed, the Bolton Abbey passage provides a perfect illustration of my approach to the creation of Branwell's story. Rather than planning everything in advance – for I do not care for spreadsheets any more than Branwell did his railway ledgers – I worked my way through the chronology of his life, and so this particular episode is informed in an organic way by multiple factors: the characters as they have developed in the course of the book; the school scheme and the offer of a job in Manchester to Charlotte; Branwell's preoccupation with Lydia Robinson and his simultaneous attraction to and fear of young Lydia; the antipathy between him and Charlotte; and the physical setting of the Abbey ruins, juxtaposed with a recent poem ('O'er Grafton Hill the blue heaven smiled serene'). Nearly every section of *Oblivion* was composed in this multifaceted manner, informed by multiple historical sources and primary texts, but with an attempt to weave the different elements together as seamlessly as possible.

It is worth noting in passing what an important and often serendipitous role the rapid research afforded by the Internet at times played in rendering the details of the narrative. For example, the long section at the end of Volume I that prominently features Franz Liszt grew out of an initial wish simply to feature such an illustrious person in the novel, since Barker notes that Branwell would have been highly unlikely to miss the virtuoso's appearance in Halifax. As I researched the concert, however, I was able to find not only the entire programme for the evening, but also the complete lyrics to John Orlando Parry's popular song, 'Wanted, A Governess'. It was then obvious that I would need to have Charlotte Brontë herself present at the performance, to reinforce the expectations, humiliations and poor remuneration of that occupation, which is so central to the Brontë sisters' lives and works. Whether the historical Charlotte was there – and it may be quite possible to prove that she was *not* – mattered far less to me than the larger thematic point made by having her suffer through Parry's 'jolly song', as Leyland later calls it. This is a typical instance of the minor 'liberties' that I have taken in this work of fiction, privileging central themes over what I consider insignificant details. However, had she been employed at the time, or already abroad in Brussels, I would not have contradicted such important, well-known facts of her biography.

Once I had decided to extend Liszt's stay in Halifax to a soirée hosted by Leyland, himself the creator of a massive *Head of Satan*, how could I not have the great virtuoso – known for improvising variations on themes many years before they became formal compositions – perform an early improvisation of his *First Mephisto Waltz*, especially since he developed sketches of this work throughout the 1840s? Similarly, his *Totentanz* or *Danse macabre* was planned as early as 1838, so could he not have improvised it in 1841? Finally, by then the Branwell-as-Faust and Leyland-as-Mephistopheles relationship had already begun to develop, and so the final touch was simply to rename the fictional young woman Margaret (her initial name was, I believe, Sally) to make the Faust-in-Halifax story complete. This section and, later, the complex intrigue involving young Lydia Robinson and Roxby in Scarborough and at Thorp Green, are the most fanciful and least historically grounded parts of the novel but, in my opinion, are two of the liveliest. They were certainly among the most enjoyable to write.

Other slight liberties with the known facts were simply inadvertent, and discovered only later. For example, long after writing the passage where Anne returns to Haworth for Aunt Branwell's funeral, and where she and Branwell read the words of the new memorial to William Weightman in the church, I discovered that it was not in fact placed there until several months later. I decided to leave the passage alone, as it captures the spirit of what I was seeking to convey. Some purists of historical fiction may find this highly objectionable, but for me, it is merely the sacrifice of a minor fact to a larger truth.

Similarly, I did not take great pains to research secondary and minor characters, although I worked, as noted, almost entirely within the existing known framework of the Brontë story and respected the major events and extent texts by, and concerning, the family. Besides the characters of Maggie and Maeve – created in an attempt to explain Branwell's otherwise somewhat mysterious depression and descent into debauchery when he should have been revelling in his professional advancement – there are relatively few purely invented characters, such as the engine driver Matthews; the York publican Dimock (D'Amico); the railway accountant Shaw; and the young James Drake (whose older cousin Joseph did, however, exist, and was indeed a friend and associate of Leyland). In each case, these characters serve an important, if minor, role in the plot, providing connective tissue between the known facts and texts.

Nearly everyone else in *Oblivion* is based on historical figures from the Brontë story, although I generally used them as 'empty vessels' to build my story as I saw fit. A particularly striking example of this is the Reverend Robinson, for whom I have no evidence at all of the reprehensible behaviour towards his wife earlier in their marriage, although such a detail makes Mrs Robinson slightly more sympathetic, and also foreshadows the abusive Arthur Huntingdon character in Anne's second novel, *The Tenant of Wildfell Hall*. The great majority of the minor characters come directly and accurately (in terms of their dates) from historical background materials, whether in Broughton (Moses Tyson, the Postlethwaites, the Fishes, the Rileys, the Nelsons, Hartley Coleridge); in Halifax and Luddenden Foot (Leyland, Titterington and his merry band, Frobisher and the other poets, Grundy, Sowden, the other employees of the railway); in Haworth (the successive owners of the Black Bull and, of course, John and Martha Brown, as well as Tabby); and finally, at Thorp Green and in York and Scarborough (the younger Robinson children, Roxby, the lady's maid Ann Marshall, the coachman William Allison, and even the gardener Robert Pottage, who may well have seen Branwell and Lydia in the boathouse in Scarborough – one of many theories of the events leading to his dismissal).

When the documents or even paraphrases of a character's words existed (Grundy, Crosby, Francis Leyland, etc.), I did my best to incorporate those into the dialogue; if not, I invented (the stammering but otherwise quite real Bellerby, Tyson, Postlethwaite, Dr Fish, Weightman, Sowden). In some cases, I moved the language of correspondence into actual dialogue (Hartley Coleridge, Mary Taylor, the Brontës in general); on rare occasions, I even transposed words from one character to another, if I felt that it was part of an overall zeitgeist within the family at the time, although I usually have characters attribute the words ('as Charlotte often says' or 'Emily says you are a "hopeless being"'). For more on this, see 'The Language of *Oblivion*' and the detailed 'Notes to *Oblivion*' below.

In all, I have done my best to be true to the *personalities* of the Brontës themselves, by using their own letters, poems and novels. We see everything, of course, through Branwell's jaundiced eyes, and I constructed his psychological state at each stage of the novel by immersing myself in the facts of his life, the poems and letters that he was producing, and what others wrote to and about him, both at that time and (less reliably, of course, as with Grundy and Francis Leyland) later. My primary goal was to make Branwell in particular, if not likeable, at least more human – someone in whom, for all his faults, most readers could glimpse just a bit of themselves. A related goal was to explore just how much, indeed, he and his sisters had in common, and to ask why, despite the advantages of being a man in a patriarchal society, he failed where his sisters ultimately succeeded. That they died so soon after he did makes the question perhaps more, rathan than less, poignant.

*

Let me conclude this brief note with a few words about the historical Branwell's final days, and the fate of his sisters and their work, for those who are not already aware of these facts.

Branwell's last extent poem is an obscene, ironic poem about Dr Wheelhouse ('While holy Wheelhouse far above'), while the final letter we possess, a note scrawled to John Brown, reads as follows, including the misspellings and other errors (two redundancies are eliminated here, however):

Sunday. Noon.

Dear John,

I shall feel very much obliged to you if [you] can contrive to get me Five pence worth of Gin in a proper measure.

Should it be speedily got I could perhaps take it from you or Billy at the lane top or what would be quite as well, sent out for, to you.

I anxiously ask the favour because I know the good it will do me.

Punctualy at Half-past Nine in the morning you will be paid the 5d out of a shilling given me then.

Yours, P.B.B.

Branwell's old friend from his railway days, Francis Grundy, came to visit him in Haworth in September 1848, reserving a private room at the Black Bull and ordering dinner and drinks for the two of them. As Grundy reported many decades later (and so considerable caution as to the exactitude of his account is warranted), the Reverend Brontë came first to see him, warning him of the great change in his son.

His friend describes Branwell's appearance as: 'a mass of red, unkempt, uncut hair, wildly floating round a great, gaunt forehead; the cheeks yellow and hollow, the mouth fallen, the thin white lips not trembling but shaking, the sunken eyes, once small, now glaring with the light of madness, – all told the sad tale but too surely.' Grundy strove to cheer his old friend, pressing two stiff glasses of hot brandy upon him, which seemed, for a few brief moments, to revive 'something like the Brontë of old'. Branwell claimed that he was longing for death, 'and happy, in his sane moments, to think that it was so near'. Grundy reports that as he left, Branwell took a carving knife from his sleeve, claiming that when he had received the message that an old friend was awaiting him at the Black Bull, it must really have been from Satan in disguise. 'I left him,' concludes

Grundy, 'standing bare-headed in the road, with bowed form and dropping tears.'

Juliet Barker, in her biography of the Brontës, summarises the accounts of his final hours. On Saturday, 23rd September 1848, Branwell was unable to get out of bed. Dr Wheelhouse was sent for, and he promptly reported to the family that the young man was near death. The Reverend Brontë had 'knelt in prayer by his bedside and wrestled for his soul', but Branwell had long ago abandoned religion and at first refused to repent of his many sins. However, his sister Charlotte claimed in a letter to her publisher and friend William Smith Williams that their father brought Branwell to a recognition of his vices and the repentance of them. She reported that Branwell spent much of his last night talking of his 'misspent life, his wasted youth, and his shame', and that she herself, 'with painful, mournful joy, heard him praying softly in his dying moments, and to the last prayer which my father offered up at his bedside, he added "amen"'. She would later add that she believed that 'a most propitious change marked the last few days of poor Branwell's life ... his demeanour, his language, his sentiments were all singularly altered and softened ... a return to natural affection marked his last moments'.

All of this may be quite true, but the reader should keep in mind that Charlotte Brontë was, herself, singularly gifted at rewriting the history of her siblings after their deaths. There is a recognisable, almost patent Victorian piety about her statements, a neat and orderly narrative sequence of events that reminds one more of fiction than of reality. As Branwell's fictional counterpart himself says in *Oblivion*, 'do we not all create such happy stories to fit our desires?'

One anecdote that certainly rings true, but can no more be proven than any other, is Francis Leyland's report that near the end of his last night, as his old friend John Brown kept him company, Branwell recognised at last that had never 'loved any but the members of his family, for the depth and tenderness of which affection he could find no language to express'. At one point he clutched at Brown's hand and said simply, 'Oh, John, I am dying!' adding, *sotto voce*, 'In all my past life I have done nothing either great or good'. Interestingly, Charlotte had expressed similar feelings about herself early in 1847, just before the sisters' novels were published, and the ever-modest Anne famously claimed, in a moving letter written a few days before her death and well after the publication of both of her brilliant novels, that she 'longed to do some good in the world', and that she feared dying having 'lived to so little purpose'.

The family gathered around his bed at nine o'clock on the morning of Sunday, 24th September. After a struggle of twenty minutes or so, Branwell, just thirty-one years old, died in his father's arms. Mrs Gaskell claimed to have it upon good authority that he had insisted on standing up at his death, while others report that he merely started, involuntarily, in such a way that he nearly rose to his feet. We will never know; but given his consistent lack of resolve throughout his life, the latter seems more likely.

On Thursday, 28th September, Patrick Branwell Brontë was at last reunited with his mother Maria and his sisters Maria and Elizabeth, in the vault of the parish church. Dr Wheelhouse recorded the cause as 'chronic bronchitis-marasmus', although it is now believed that he was quite likely suffering from the same consumption that took his two eldest sisters and would soon claim Emily and Anne. If John Brown chiselled his young friend's name into the family monument on the church wall, one would have to have a heart of stone to believe that the poor sexton did not do so with tears in his own, usually mischievous, eyes.

Charlotte took to her bed for a week at her brother's death, leaving the practical work of bereavement to her sisters. Her letters in the days following her brother's death reveal a telling blend of resentment towards, and yet ultimate forgiveness of, her beloved childhood playmate.

Within just a few weeks it became clear that Emily Jane Brontë, the enigmatic young woman behind the author Ellis Bell, was herself extremely ill. The received wisdom has always been that she 'caught a chill' at Branwell's funeral, but it is far more likely that the tuberculosis that killed her siblings was already silently, and for a time unnoticeably, eating away at her as well. Like her character in *Wuthering Heights*, Catherine Earnshaw, who claims she would be 'miserable in heaven', Emily was 'torn from life in its prime', with even the pious Charlotte confessing that her sister had turned 'her dying eyes reluctantly from the pleasant sun'. Refusing all medical intervention until it was too late, she died on 19th December 1848. This time Charlotte rallied and become the great support of both her father and remaining sister Anne.

Anne Brontë's *Tenant of Wildfell Hall*, considered one of the first feminist novels, had been published in June 1848. Given Branwell's state of mind by that time, it is unlikely that he ever saw this novel, but its disturbing scenes of drunken debauchery, vulgar language and unabashed adultery – not to mention the fairly constant, flippant blasphemy – of Arthur Huntingdon surely owe a great deal to her brother's behaviour. This second novel caused a sensation every bit as great – if not greater than – *Wuthering Heights*, and its reputation suffered for more than a century at the hands of her surviving sister, Charlotte, who refused to permit its reprinting at the height of its popularity. There is no denying, however, the elder sister's anxious, loving care for her younger sister, who upon Emily's death began, in turn, to show serious signs of tuberculosis. After lingering in delicate health for several months, Anne was at last granted her fervent wish to return to her beloved Scarborough, where she died, serenely, on 28th May 1849, in the company of Charlotte and her friend Ellen Nussey. She is buried high above the sea, at Saint Mary's – the inspiration for 'the venerable old church' of *Agnes Grey* – near the very spot where, in *Oblivion*, she and Branwell will forever stand together on that windswept day in 1843, and where the view on glorious summer evenings recalls just what her heroine Agnes saw at the moment of Edward Weston's proposal, when her heart was 'filled with gratitude to heaven, and happiness, and love – almost too full for speech'.

Charlotte Brontë would go on to publish two more novels, *Shirley* and *Villette*, the second of which is considered by many critics to be her masterpiece, although it will be forever eclipsed in popularity by the groundbreaking *Jane Eyre*. She was the only Brontë to be known by her true name in her lifetime, and to enjoy the literary and social fame that she and her brother had craved all their lives. After much resistance – initially her own, but especially her father's – she married his Irish curate, Arthur Bell Nicholls, in 1854. She claimed to be 'so happy' in marriage that writing ceased to be the overwhelming compulsion that it had been for as long as she could remember. On 31st March of the following year, however, she was dead. A number of theories concerning her death have been advanced, but it seems clear that she was pregnant, and that constant vomiting and subsequent dehydration were determining factors in her early demise.

In 1857, Smith Elder published Charlotte's rejected first novel, *The Professor*, with a brief preface by her widower Bell Nicholls, as well as the first edition of Mrs Gaskell's *Life of Charlotte Brontë*. The Brontë legend had begun.

The Reverend Patrick Brontë famously outlived all of his children, dying in 1861, at the age of eighty-four. He had transmitted his passion, his erudition, his wit and sense of humour to all of his children, but they – and particularly his son, who seemed simultaneously to venerate and reject his father – had far more difficulty making the difficult transition to adulthood, and exercising duty and self-control over passion and self-indulgence.

The early claims that Branwell was the true author of *Wuthering Heights* have long ago been dismissed. Anyone reading Emily's novel next to his own fragment, *And the Weary Are at Rest*, written at roughly the same time, can see this: the first is almost impossible to put down, while the second is nearly as difficult to soldier through to its conclusion, despite its brevity. Indeed, it becomes even clearer with the passage of time that little of what Branwell wrote has great literary merit. Despite Matthew Arnold's (surely sexist) supposition in his famous poem, he does indeed seem to have been 'the least gifted' of the four Brontës to survive childhood. Or, if as talented, he certainly was, by far, the least disciplined and persistent of the siblings – a theme that runs throughout *Oblivion*.

Branwell remains a fascinating character in his own right, however, for what is also increasingly evident with the passing of the decades is that his early, frenetic, brilliant, even visionary enthusiasm and leadership in the siblings' collective experiment in childhood writing, which was surely a kind of 'grief therapy' *avant la lettre* – the feverish creation of thousands upon thousands of pages of juvenilia, an activity the Brontës called *scribblemania* – was a critical apprenticeship for the three women who would go on to write some of the most treasured novels in the English language. It is certainly also true that besides their somewhat austere, if loving, father, their brother was one of the only men in the world that they knew well, so that their male characters – more often at their realistic worst than at their idealised best – are enormously indebted to this deeply flawed and troubled young man.

Long after Grundy and Leyland tried to do him justice, others would come to share their early fascination with Branwell, notably Daphne du Maurier and Winifred Gérin, who published biographies in 1960 and 1961, respectively. Many other treatments have followed, with Barker's magisterial biography (1994; revised 2010) giving him his rightful place in the family dynamic and history.

Branwell has become increasingly prominent in films – some more strictly biographical than others – concerning the Brontës, from André Téchiné's *Les soeurs Brontë* (1979) to Sally Wainright's *To Walk Invisible* (2016). In the past decade or two, writers and artists have also progressively focused on his role in the family, in works including, among others, plays by Lee Bollinger and Blake Morrison, a short story by Michael Yates, and novels by Glyn Hughes, Douglas A. Martin and Robert Edric. Recent years have even witnessed a rock opera (*Wasted*, 2018) and a graphic novel (Isabel Greenberg's *Glass Town*, 2020), both focused on the siblings' relationship throughout their short lives. The year 2020 also saw the appearance of Finola Austin's *Brontë's Mistress*, which tells the Thorp Green saga from the perspective of Lydia Robinson, *mère*. Clearly, our collective fascination with the Brontës only continues to grow.

Two centuries have passed since the Reverend Patrick Brontë and his wife Maria welcomed their fourth child and only son into the world, on 26th June 1817. When he died thirty-one years later, his sister Charlotte wrote:

> My poor Father naturally thought more of his only Son than of his daughters, and much and long has he had suffered on his account – he cried out for his loss like David for that of Absalom – My Son! My Son! And refused at first to be comforted.

The great hope and joy of the family in his youth, he brought them only shame and heartache later in life.

Unfit for the realities of a rapidly changing society, Patrick Branwell Brontë longed first for eternal literary fame, and later for oblivion, in every sense of that word. As fate would have it, he seems, at last, paradoxically to have achieved something of both, for it has become increasingly evident that the works of the brilliant Brontë sisters would be considerably different without their experiences – many of them unpleasant, tinged with what they, themselves, might call 'wormwood and bitter gall' – with their only, once-cherished brother.

As in his 'Pillar Portrait' of the siblings in the National Portrait Gallery, in which he famously blotted himself out, Branwell's image is slowly emerging from oblivion, although surely not for reasons that he or his family would have preferred.

I conceived the idea for this novel a quarter of a century ago when I read the first edition of Juliet Barker's *The Brontës* in preparation for a class that I was developing as a young academic in North Carolina. From the beginning, I knew the book would be called *Oblivion*, and that I wanted both its language and structure to be a tribute to the works of the Brontës themselves. Most historical fiction tends to be written in a somewhat neutral, modern style, with hints of the period in question, to provide 'local colour'. That the historical figures of this novel – the Brontës – were themselves writers, presented both a challenge and an opportunity, which was how to incorporate their own words into the text where appropriate and use their language patterns to shape the remainder of it. *Oblivion* thus attempts to echo the cadences and vocabulary of the letters, poems and novels of the family, but in a style more accessible to the modern reader. It is unapologetically earnest, romantic and often even melodramatic, as are the works of the Brontës themselves. Indeed, it unabashedly flies in the face of the modernist maxim, *show, don't tell.* For example, like the historical Brontës, Branwell does not hesitate to use italics for occasional emphasis.

Aside from a few archaic expressions to provide a flavour of the time and place, the book attempts to straddle the 1840s and present day. What developed as a guiding principle was this: I strove to create, as much as possible, a seamless fabric both entirely understandable to an educated reader of the twenty-first century and yet which, if it were picked up by the Brontës themselves, would be immediately comprehensible (if perhaps occasionally a little strange, and certainly extremely shocking). For this reason, as I composed, I frequently consulted the 'use over time' function of Google Chrome to assure that words that seem contemporary today were nevertheless already in current usage in 1840. This led to the occasional surprise, such as words of Greek or Latin origin that I had assumed to be quite old, but which entered the language long after the death of the Brontës, through scientific or technological developments in the late nineteenth or early twentieth centuries. While I am sure that I have missed an anachronism here or there, I can assure the reader that the bulk of *Oblivion* would be entirely understandable and even ring as quite typical in the Brontës' ears, if, again, it might seem a bit odd here and there.

Beyond this 'pastiche' quality, Branwell's diaries also have an important element of what the French would call '*bricolage*', or what we might today consider a 'mash-up', although both of those expressions imply a postmodern use of disparate elements to create something new and even strange, whereas what I mean here is the incorporation of the exact language of the Brontës both to provide a flavour of the time and to serve as a wink and a nudge to those who love their work. Some of these are more famous than others, and they are listed in the 'Notes' that follow. They include a number of passages from *Agnes Grey* (especially where Agnes and Rosalie, through a process of double-mirroring, are both inspired by the historical Anne and Lydia and, in turn, shape their fictional versions in my own novel); a handful of phrases from *Wuthering Heights* ('Satan and all his legions'), *Jane Eyre* ('because I am poor, obscure, plain and little') and *The Tenant of Wildfell Hall* ('an infernal fire in my veins, that all the waters of the ocean cannot quench'); as well as a great deal of language from the Brontës' correspondence, especially Branwell's and Charlotte's.

Thus, while the overwhelming majority of the words of *Oblivion* are my own, the novel is sprinkled throughout with the leaven of the language of the Brontës themselves. To take another example, at times Branwell's real letters to Leyland, Brown or his sisters invade his fictional journal, and he often notes that he had just been sharing such thoughts with his correspondent. On a handful of occasions, I have even borrowed language from other writers (e.g., Baudelaire and Flaubert – in translation) or, in one case, from Charlotte's later work, *Villette* (young Margaret Fish is presented as 'a dripping roast' by her mother, in Broughton).

With only three exceptions, all letters and poems are real, and all are accurately dated and incorporated into the story, with only minor changes of punctuation or capitalisation. The exceptions are Postlethwaite's note accompanying his letter of reference, the letter of dismissal from the railway, and Lydia's note requesting that Roxby come to Thorp Green for a rendezvous. Indeed, as noted above, the historical letters and poems largely provide the architecture of the plot of *Oblivion*.

Scholars and lovers of the Brontës may find, at times, that I am providing far too much exposition about certain events of their lives. Hard as it may be for them (and me) to believe, I would ask my fellow enthasiasts to remember that not everyone shares (or even understands) our devotion to the family and their works. I thus felt it necessary to create a narrative that all readers could enjoy, no matter how fleeting or even non-existent their knowledge of this most famous of literary families.

A brief word should probably be said about the explicit sex scenes, which of course would never have appeared in a proper Victorian novel. My justification for these is two-fold: first, Branwell was known, particularly in his written correspondence with John Brown, to use graphic sexual language. For example, from Broughton, he asks for news of Brown and his other drinking companions: '... you say something about having got a cock and hens – I know you have got a cock & a jolly good one too by Jupiter ... And that bow-legged fellow who was always asking me – does your prick stand? – how is his going on or has he lost it altogether? Beelzebub means to make a walking stick of yours, etc.' Second, and far more relevant, is the use of sex to underscore Branwell's addictive nature, his constant search for something between the sublime and oblivion, his attempt to 'get out of himself' (*ekstasis*) through the orgasmic ecstasy or 'earthly rapture' of sexual intercourse. In making this central point in a novel made up of Branwell's private diaries and written well into the twenty-first century, I saw no reason to treat sexuality as it would appear in either a Victorian romance or a family-friendly film.

Indeed, perhaps more disturbing to a twenty-first century reader than these explicit scenes is the frequent objectification of women by Branwell and the other male characters. I would say three things in the novel's defence here. First, this attitude was of course highly prevalent and profoundly normalised in the Victorian era (as, alas, it remains to a certain extent in our own) and is thus a realistic depiction of society. To give just one example of this from the Brontës' own work, readers will recall that Anne cleverly has Hattersley, in *The Tenant of Wildfell Hall*, praise Huntingdon's 'fine stud' and Lord Lowborough's wife Isabella (and Huntingdon's lover) as a 'splendid creature' in the same breath. Second, I am careful to have my own characters condemn (perhaps somewhat anachronistically, it is true) this double standard, as when Anne says:

> I *wonder*, Branwell, why it is acceptable for men to gaze and gape in shameless admiration of feminine charms – for I regularly witness such performances at Thorp Green, and will surely see it every day at Scarborough, as the young Robinsons are paraded like show-horses, or cattle before the slaughter, choose your beast – but why it is so unbecoming for the softer or weaker sex, as you gentlemen would call us, to show any admiration whatsoever, no matter how innocent, for the *male* of the species? It is absurd.

Finally, Branwell's particular obsession with the female body provided me with yet another way to underscore not only his addictive behaviour, but also his tendency to objectify and thus *use* others – women in particular – as, once again, his sister Anne cannot at last refrain from pointing out: 'you think only of *yourself*, Branwell, and not how others might think or feel, whether they have minds and hearts of their own, as if they were machines without feelings, constructed solely to do your bidding.'

There remain some minor, but I think interesting, issues of language. Spelling and even vocabulary were far more fluid and unstandardised in the 1840s. To take a single example, the words 'railway' and 'railroad' were interchangeable, and both may be found in the letters of the Brontës. Over the decades, however, 'railway' became the chiefly British word and 'railroad' the North American term, even though this usage was not yet fixed in the early days of rail. In such cases, I have opted, to avoid confusion, for the term that is today recognised as British. In the same way, words ending in -ize were common on both sides of the Atlantic in the Brontës' time, but are now almost wholly confined to North America, so I have opted for current British use: *recognise.* Certain variants, like 'burnt'/'burned' and 'learnt'/'learned', are both used, as they were in the 1840s and are still today. Such are the minutiae of writing historical fiction.

All works of the imagination demand what Hartley Coleridge's father famously called a *willing suspension of disbelief*, and so it is worth noting here that Branwell's diaries, were they authentic, would be strewn with misspellings (in *Oblivion* he points out what poor spellers he and his sisters are), inconsistencies and incoherent or drunken ramblings. Moreover, the dates and places introducing his journal entries would be written in several different ways (I have chosen a format typical of the nineteenth century) or omitted altogether. I, however, have tried my best to eliminate such distractions, even correcting some of the historical Branwell's texts as I wove them into the novel. The purpose was to eliminate as much interference as possible as we accompany Branwell on his adventures. Similarly, I would ask the reader to (make) believe that a journal could be written as a coherent narrative, just as we do with Emily's *Wuthering Heights* and Anne's *The Tenant of Wildfell Hall.*

The rendering of the language of working people in Lancashire and Yorkshire was no small challenge for a Californian raised in the 1960s and 1970s. I have done my best, using as my model characters in the works of the Brontës themselves and even the Yorkshire accents and expressions of today as depicted in such television dramas as Sally Wainwright's own *Happy Valley* and *Last Tango in Halifax.*

The use of French by Charlotte, Franz Liszt, the Robinsons and others has support both from history and from the works of the Brontës (see Blanche Ingram and her set in *Jane Eyre*, not to mention Jane's use of it with her French pupil Adèle), but its frequency is doubtless greater (for example, when Hartley Coleridge quotes Pascal, or when Joe Leyland uses an expression such as '*un ange passe*') because the author of *Oblivion* is himself a Francophile and, among other things, a professor of French. For that and so many other *faux pas*, dear Reader, I beg your pardon.

As a work of fiction, *Oblivion* is primarily the fruit of its author's imagination. However, it also relies heavily on historians, literary scholars and, more than anything, the works and correspondence of the Brontës themselves. As noted in the 'Acknowledgements' that follow, the works of Juliet Barker, Winifred Gérin, Daphne du Maurier, and long before them (and much less reliably), Francis Leyland and Francis Grundy – these last two appearing as characters in *Oblivion* as well – have provided most of the chronological framework for the novel, although other references such as *The Oxford Companion to the Brontës* (and, of course, the Internet) were invaluable.

My novel is somewhat unusual in its direct (or often slightly modified) use of the exact words of the Brontës themselves, beginning with their correspondence, which one can find cited in a number of different texts, including most prominently *The Letters of Charlotte Brontë* (three volumes, edited by Margaret Smith), Barker's own *The Brontës: A Life in Letters*, and scattered throughout various works devoted to Branwell and his sisters. The same is true of letters by Southey, Hartley Coleridge and others. In no case have I used the exact words of these scholars, although I am enormously indebted to them for many of the details of my narrative.

Far more frequent, if generally less extensive, is the appearance of brief quotations – some quite famous, and at times just a few words – from the published works of the Brontës themselves. Although these have long been in the public domain, I felt it only right to indicate where I have used their words, in a process of 'reinscription' intended both as a tribute to the Brontës and a nod to their readers, and an attempt to provide an authentic feel to the language of Branwell's narrative. I have also noted instances where my chapter titles – the style of which is inspired by those of Anne Brontë's two novels – are taken directly from the works or correspondence of the family or elsewhere. For more on this process, see 'The Language of *Oblivion*', above.

Since this is not a work of scholarship, I have simply given dates (for correspondence) and chapters or titles (for novels and poems), rather than specific editions of the works or correspondence of the Brontës. Where appropriate, chapters refer to the original two or three-volume format of some of the novels, not to modern numbering. This traditional format may still be found in many scholarly editions, such as the Oxford World's Classics series, which is itself based on the authoritative Oxford Clarendon texts. Unlike the notes in such editions, those below do not include references that are clearly spelt out in the text: if Branwell quotes his own poem and gives its title, or cites someone else (Wordsworth, Shelley, Hogg, Scott, or for that matter his sisters and his father), I saw no reason to include in my notes what any reader could easily find through a rapid online search.

My novel is decidedly not intended primarily for an academic audience – far from it! Thus, to avoid distraction to the general reader, I do not use notes or asterisks in the text of *Oblivion* itself, but simply list my borrowings in order below, by chapter.

Finally, it is important to note that instances of language inspired by the Brontës but wholly my own – and one could say this of the majority of the novel – are not listed here. In those rare cases where I may have used their exact words unwittingly, I would ask the forgiveness of my readers and, especially, of the Brontës themselves who, I hope, sleep on peacefully in the quiet earth of Haworth and Scarborough.

–Dd

¶ II. *The Fairer Sex*

A number of phrases in Chapter II appear verbatim in Branwell's letter of 13th March 1840 to John Brown, which, in fact, he mentions that he is writing in his diary entry for that day.

¶ V. *Letters, Poems and Invitations*

… a dripping roast – Lucy Snowe describes herself this way in Charlotte's *Villette* (1853), as she attempts to book a passage to the continent in Volume I: Chapter VI; future entries from multi-volume editions will simply give the volume number followed by the chapter number, both in Roman numerals (e.g., I:VI).

I wrote to Hartley Coleridge – the quotations are from an actual letter of 20th April 1840, which spills over into Branwell's fictional journal entry of that day.

¶ VI. *An Ecstasy Most Unexpected*

… the clouds, the marvellous clouds – I could not resist (anachronistically) using this phrase from Charles Baudelaire's 'L'étranger', the first poem to appear in his posthumous *Petits poèmes en prose* (or *Spleen de Paris*) of 1869. In the context of *Oblivion*, the final lines of the prose poem, in which the 'enigmatic stranger' is asked what he truly loves after having declared that he hates gold the way some people hate God, could not be more fitting:

> Well then, what do you love, extraordinary stranger?
> I love the clouds … the passing clouds … over there …
> over there … the marvellous clouds!

Clearly there is a kinship between Branwell and Baudelaire (as there was between Poe and Baudelaire, whom the latter famously translated). All three are, in one sense or another, *poètes maudits*, and this similarity is particularly true in the next note. Poe, Branwell and Baudelaire were born in 1809, 1817 and 1821, respectively, and all were influenced deeply by romanticism and its various offshoots; all, indeed, may be considered late romantics, and all were addicted to both beauty and chemical substances, which Baudelaire aptly named *les paradis artificiels.*

If this is blasphemy, what is an eternity of damnation compared to such moments of ecstasy? – in another of Baudelaire's prose poems, 'Le Mauvais Vitrier' ('The Bad Glazer), the final line is: 'Mais qu'importe l'éternité de la damnation à qui a trouvé dans une seconde l'infini de la jouissance?' ('What is eternal damnation to one who has found in the space of a single second an infinitude of ecstasy'). In French *jouissance* means both 'enjoyment' and 'orgasm'.

¶ VIII. *Nab Cottage*

… *the woeful impotence of weak resolve* – Hartley Coleridge, cited by his brother Derwent in his 'Memoir of Hartley Coleridge' (1851). Also the title of Volume III, Chapter XXVI of *Oblivion.*

… *her bright, speaking eyes* – in a discussion on beauty, Agnes compares the 'bright, speaking eyes' of a lovely bird to a toad, noting that both are helpless and harmless, but treated differently purely on the basis of appearance, in Agnes Grey, XVII.

… *you are by no means the first or the only person who has applied to me for judgement of his writings* – the fictional Coleridge's words here and in the paragraphs that follow are a mingling of language taken from a letter he would later draft but probably not send to Branwell, dated 30th November–December 1840, and from the famous letter that his uncle, the Poet Laureate Robert Southey, wrote to Charlotte in March 1837, where he suggests that '[l]iterature cannot be the business of a woman's life'.

… *in the present state of the publishing and reading world a novel is the most saleable article that exists* – these are Branwell's words, from his letter of 10th September 1845, to his friend Joseph B. Leyland. Much later in *Oblivion*, he will expand on this in a conversation with Dr John Crosby, with more material taken from the actual letter (see Volume III, Chapter XXIII – Crosby in Harrogate), and will refer to this earlier fictional conversation: 'Several years ago Hartley Coleridge told me that in the present state of the publishing and reading world a novel is the most saleable article; I knew he was right then, but I hated that he was.'

In short, my advice to you is the same old Southey gave your sister – again, this passage draws from both Coleridge's and Southey's letters, mentioned above.

¶ IX. *Love and Treachery at Sunny Bank*

… still burning in my gullet … crush my ribs like a rotten hazelnut – upon being struck by Edgar Linton in a pivotal scene in *Wuthering Heights*, Heathcliff exclaims: 'Do you suppose I am going to go with that blow burning in my gullet? … By Hell, no! I'll crush his ribs like a rotten hazelnut before I cross the threshold!' (I:XI).

¶ X. *Dismissal*

Is not everyone, at some moment of his life, before putting away such childish dreams? – although I have not used his exact words, I must pay homage to Gustave Flaubert for his brilliant formulation of the difficult transition from youthful idealism to mature pragmatism (one of the central themes of *Oblivion* as a whole is Branwell's inability to effect this change), in a famous passage from *Madame Bovary*, III:VI (1857) that ends with this phase: 'chaque notaire porte en soi les débris d'un poète' ('every clerk carries within himself the remains of a poet').

I awoke conscious of no sensation but a parching thirst and a sickly loathing – Branwell uses this language in 'Angria and the Angrians' (1838), for his character Henry Hastings, who has just awakened 'from the sleep of a Debauchee'.

¶ XI. *Farewell*

… the eternal rocks beneath the changing seasons – in Catherine Earnshaw's famous speech in I:IX of Emily Brontë's *Wuthering Heights*, she constrasts her feelings for Edgar ('the foliage in the woods … [t]ime will change it … as winter changes the trees') with her love for Heathcliff ('the eternal rocks beneath – a source of little visible delight, but necessary'). Earlier in this same passage,

she violently strikes her head and heart, in answer to Nelly Dean's question about what is preventing her from a 'smooth and easy' marriage to Edgar: '*Here!* and *here!* … in whichever place the soul lives – in my soul, and in my heart, I'm convinced I'm wrong!' Agnes Riley, by contrast, is quietly resigned to her fate, and her gestures are meant as a benediction of sorts to the departing Branwell.

¶ XII. *The Parsonage*

The Parsonage – this chapter's title is the same as Chapter I of Anne Brontë's *Agnes Grey*.

Our young poet sets off to seek his fortune, in the wild, wandering, adventurous, romantic, knight-errant-like capacity of clerk on the Manchester and Leeds Railway! – adapted from a letter, Charlotte Brontë to Ellen Nussey, September 1840. Much of what follows in these notes, particularly in the case of Charlotte's spoken conversation, documents a similar pattern of direct or slightly adapted transposition from the Brontës' historical correspondence to my fictional dialogue.

… she is also a noble, warm and generous creature: I doubt not that she would die willingly for one she loved, and her intellect and her attainments are of the very highest standard – Branwell's thoughts about Mary Taylor are in fact Charlotte's, from a letter of 20th November 1840, again to Ellen Nussey.

… as a real goddess, as long as she took no notice of me – several phrases here are taken directly from Lockwood's anecdote about breaking the heart of a young woman 'at the sea-coast', in the opening pages of *Wuthering Heights*, I:I.

¶ XIII. *The Dead and the Living*

… I feel that my heart is more ready to attach itself to earth than heaven – Branwell's dream here owes a great deal to Juliet Barker's account of the death of his mother. I have, however, added the words above, written by a much younger Maria Branwell to her fiancé Patrick Brontë in 1812. Meanwhile, Patrick's grief is expressed in words and emotions similar to Heathcliff's at the end of Catherine's life, in *Wuthering Heights* II:I: 'oh my love, my life, how can I

bear it?'; at the end of his dream, Branwell echoes Heathcliff as well: 'How ever will I bear it?'

Papa watched over his little bereaved flock with truly paternal solicitude and affection – for he was our constant guardian and instructor and he took a lively interest in all our innocent amusements – William Dearden, later quoting Branwell in the *Bradford Observer*, 27th June 1861.

... and that velvet pall descended – and descended – slowly – slowly – into the horrid clay, etc. – Branwell quoted these and the lines that follow them as examples of his work, in his December 1835 letter to *Blackwood's Magazine*, in which he proposed himself (at eighteen years of age!) as a replacement for the recently deceased James Hogg, 'the Ettrick Shepherd', who had frequently contributed to the magazine. Some of Hogg's works play an important role in *Oblivion*, from 'The Sinless Kilmeny' (the inspiration for J.B. Leyland's statue and the subsequent intrigue between its physical model, the entirely fictional Margaret Heaton, and Branwell) to *The Private Memoirs and Confessions of a Justified Sinner* (1824).

They reckon to be very grand folks indeed – Charlotte's words in this scene are taken nearly verbatim from a letter to Ellen Nussey, written in mid-August 1840, which is to say contemporaneous with Branwell's journal entry here.

... her head seems too large for her body – unlike Charlotte's, some of Branwell's words and thoughts here come from a much later source, the recollections of her publisher George Smith in *A Memoir, with Some Pages of Autobiography* (1902).

¶ XIV. *The Sculptor and the Railway Clerk*

... spinning about the world – these words come from the novelist Elizabeth Gaskell, Charlotte's first and most famous biographer, in her posthumously published *Wives and Daughters* (1866): 'if these new-fangled railways spread, as they say they will, we shall all be spinning about the world' (Chapter LII).

... a nature as restless and variable as mine! – as Branwell set out for Broughton-in-Furness, Charlotte described Branwell to Ellen:

'I who know his variable nature, and his strong turn for active life, dare not be too sanguine' (letter of 28th December 1839).

¶ XVII. *A Magic Carpet Ride*

married, buried, devilled and damned – Leyland's expression here is in fact the historical Branwell's, which I have lifted from an earlier letter to John Brown, sent from Broughton on 13th March 1840.

¶ XVIII. *A Promotion*

Let us hope that his removal to another station will turn out for the best. It looks like getting on at any rate – taken nearly verbatim from Charlotte's letter to Emily of 2nd April 1841.

… the imagination should be pruned and trimmed and judgement cultivated in its place. It is time to clear away the countless illusions of our youth – letter from Charlotte to Henry Nussey, 11th January 1841.

¶ XXI. *The Mephisto Waltz*

… was die Welt im Innersten zusammenhält – from Goethe's *Faust*, Part I (1808), Scene 4, lines 382–383. Listz goes on here to utter perhaps the play's most famous line ('Verweile doch! du bist so schön!') in Scene 7, line 1699. It also serves as the title of the following chapter.

¶ XXII. *Verweile doch! du bist so schön!*

… soulless an' heartless – from one of the most celebrated quotations from *Jane Eyre*, II:VIII. Later in *Oblivion* Charlotte herself will use it at greater length.

Why do you betray your own heart, Maggie? – in another famous quotation, this time from Emily's *Wuthering Heights*, Heathcliff memorably says, '*Why* did you betray your own heart, Cathy?' (II:I).

¶ I. *A Letter from Charlotte*

... stripped and bereaved – Charlotte will use this phrase many years later in her moving letter of 13th June 1849, to William Smith Williams, in the wake of Anne's death: 'It is over. Branwell – Emily – Anne are gone like dreams – gone as Maria and Elizabeth were twenty years ago.'

... to repel the rude familiarity of children – letter of 3rd March 1841, to Ellen Nussey. The accompanying sentiment, of preferring pure physical labour to the dual mental and physical strain of instructing children (or teaching *tout court*) runs throughout the correspondence and works of the Brontës, and indeed the narrative of *Oblivion* itself, as Branwell demonstrates in the following paragraph.

¶ III. *The Leylands in the Wilderness*

Halifax Marble Works – the wording here is exact and appears thanks to Daphne du Maurier's *The Infernal World of Branwell Brontë* (1960).

¶ IV. *Who, Then, is My God?*

If we love God and wish to serve Him – these are the words of the Reverend Edward Weston, in Anne's *Agnes Grey*, XI.

[W]orthless as withered weeds – from Emily Brontë's 'No Coward Soul is Mine', perhaps her most famous poem.

¶ V. *A Visit from Grundy*

... a rude wooden hut – the fictional Branwell is here using language the historical Grundy himself will employ nearly forty years later, in *Pictures of the Past* (1879).

... as for the Church, I have not one mental quality – except perhaps hypocrisy – which would make me cut a figure in its pulpits! – Branwell in a letter to Grundy, 9th June 1842.

¶ VI. *Success on Two Fronts*

… that warmed me nicely – so says Hindley Earnshaw, after administering a flogging to Heathcliff in *Wuthering Heights*, I:VII.

¶ VII. *The Depths of the Human Heart*

… stretch myself … like a faithful dog – Isabella uses these words in a very different context, to Heathcliff, in *Wuthering Heights*, II:III.

… blithe and gay … downcast and sad – the words are William Heaton's, from a letter quoted by Francis Leyland in *The Brontë Family: With Special Reference to Patrick Branwell Brontë* (1886).

When I look back on former life – these are the final quatrains of a forty-line untitled poem addressed to God, which begins 'Oh Thou, whose beams were most withdrawn / When should have risen my morning sun' and is dated 8th August 1841, in Branwell's so-called 'Luddenden Foot Notebook'. All poems attributed to the fictional Branwell in *Oblivion* were written by his historical counterpart; I have reproduced them faithfully and done my utmost to place them as exactly as possible in the chronology of his story.

¶ VIII. *A Wrestling Match*

I am vanquished! I am vanquished! – 'We are vanquished! We are vanquished!' cries Catherine during the altercation between Heathcliff and Edgar, in *Wuthering Heights*, I:XI.

I will have no more of it – in his 'Luddenden Foot Notebook' Branwell wrote: 'quarrelled with JT about going but after a wrestle met him on the road and became friends … Will have no more of it.'

¶ IX. *Ambition*

I thought of those summer afternoons long ago – the remainder of this paragraph is a prose rendering of lines 31–61 of the poem that follows in his entry of 11th September, which begins 'Amid the world's wide din around', in the 'Luddenden Foot Notebook'.

¶ X. *A Religious Ramble*

… we must clear away some of the illusions of our early youth – on

11th January 1841 Charlotte wrote to Henry Nussey, already referenced once above: 'At this age it is time that the imagination should be pruned and trimmed – that the judgement should be cultivated – and a few at least, of the countless illusions of early youth should be cleared away. I have not written poetry in a long while.'

… his firm and elastic tread – Agnes describes Edward Weston's 'firm, elastic tread' in *Agnes Grey*, XIII.

¶ XI. *Two Wives*

… one of the most exquisite, irresistible little faces I have ever beheld – this is a slight adaptation of Lockwood's description of young Catherine Heathcliff in *Wuthering Heights*, I:II.

… as long as she encounters neither opposition nor indifference … a deep-rooted fear of ruffling his wife's humour – thus Nelly Dean describes the early days of Catherine's marriage to Edgar Linton in *Wuthering Heights*, I:X.

¶ XII. *The Messiah*

He was bringing a cycle of violence to an end – this passage resembles far too closely the work of the twentieth-century French thinker René Girard (*Deceit, Desire and the Novel*; *Violence and the Sacred*; *The Scapegoat*; etc.) not to acknowledge him here.

Did you hear the tenor take liberties … the Hallelujah Chorus was murdered outright! – Leyland's critique comes nearly verbatim from the *Halifax Guardian* of 1st January 1841, as quoted by Barker in an endnote.

¶ XIII. *Quarrel and Reconciliation with Grundy*

… vulgar, hard-headed, half-educated, manufacturers – these are indeed Grundy's words, but from his much later *Pictures of the Past*.

… a grovelling carelessness … a determination to see how far mind can carry body without both being chucked into hell? – from Branwell's letter to Grundy of 22nd May 1845 and one of the epigraphs of Volume II of *Oblivion*.

T'is the arch-sinner Brontë – the 'arch-sinner' comes from Branwell's juvenilia, and has even been used by the Oxford University

Press as the title of a publication of two of his tales, *The Hand of the Arch-Sinner: Two Angrian Chronicles of Branwell Brontë* (1993).

It's not bad for an impromptu – Grundy estimates that the poem was 'necessarily an impromptu' in *Pictures of the Past*, perhaps because it was written on railway company stationery, as noted in *Oblivion*. It was truly a thrill to see the poem in person – along with Branwell's wallet and notebook – at the Brontë Parsonage Museum in 2016.

¶ XIV. *Debauchery and Dismissal*

… plunging with relish headlong into wild and reckless abandon – from *Jane Eyre*, III:I.

¶ XVI. *The Parsonage Again*

The Parsonage Again – this is the title of Chapter VI of *Agnes Grey*.

… once again a young boy, half-savage and hardy, and free – 'I wish I were a girl again, half savage and hardy, and free' (*Wuthering Heights*, I:XII).

… gothic ignorance and ill-breeding – Branwell, letter to J.B. Leyland, 29th June 1842.

… the atmospheric tumult that usually blasts over the ruins of the old farm – reminiscent of Lockwood's words in *Wuthering Heights*, I:I. Top Withens is said by some to have inspired the setting, if not the architecture, of *Wuthering Heights*.

I have at length regained health, strength and soundness of mind … a motive for exertion – passage taken directly from the above-cited letter to Grundy, 22 May 1842.

¶ XVI. *Return to the Devil's Cauldron*

… a fool to entertain, under present circumstances, any very sanguine hopes respecting situations connected with railways, for there is a glut in that market – Branwell to Grundy, 9th June 1842.

I mentally shake hands with you – 'I mentally shake hands with you for your answer, despite its inaccuracy'; Rochester to Jane, in *Jane Eyre*, I:XVI.

¶ XVII. *A Proposition from Anne*

Anne has become a pretty thing – this description is a slightly idealised version of Ellen Nussey's recollections in *Reminiscences*, as quoted by Juliet Barker in *The Brontës*.

You examine me, Branwell … do you think me ugly? – an inversion of Rochester's famous question in *Jane Eyre*: 'You examine me, Miss Eyre,' said he: 'do you think me handsome?' (I:XIV).

William de la Motte's Characters of Trees – no relation to the author of *Oblivion*, although the Brontës did own his book, complete with Branwell's scribblings, as noted in Christine Alexander's and Jane Sellar's *The Art of the Brontës* (1995).

¶ XVIII. *All's Right with the World!*

All's Right with the World! – The title is from Robert Browning, 'Pippa Passes' (1841), to which Weightman alludes at the end of this chapter.

An ugly woman is a blot on the fair face of creation, but gentlemen need only strength and valour – a near-exact transcription of Blanche Ingram's comments on 'the young men of the present day' in *Jane Eyre*, II:II.

A thorough male flirt – Charlotte to Ellen Nussey, letter of 14th July 1840.

… watch their buds unfolding day by day – from Agnes Grey, I.

'Allow me to gather them for you, Miss Anne', said the curate, and in an instant the flowers were in her hand – Anne will later recreate this scene in her own *Agnes Grey*, XIII.

… too petted in this life – Branwell will famously say this of himself years later, in a letter to Joseph Leyland, written 24th January 1847.

¶ XIX. *Mirth and Mourning*

Mirth and Mourning – the title of Chapter XVIII of Anne's *Agnes Grey*, as well as one of her poems.

I had produced from my pocket not Azrael but another sheaf of papers I had mistakenly brought – although Dearden would many years later write that it was at this very meeting at the Crossroads

Inn that Branwell would read from an early draft of *Wuthering Heights*, both the spuriousness of his claims and the needs of my own narrative have led me intentionally to ignore him; instead, I simply have Branwell recite his poem from memory.

The more of love we have within us, the nearer we are to Him, and the more of His spirit we possess – from *Agnes Grey*, XI.

I long to do some good in the world – Anne will famously write this heartbreakingly self-effacing phrase in one of her final letters, to Ellen Nussey on 5th April 1848.

The sting of death is sin – much of Patrick's actual sermon, which was published in Halifax that year (1842), is reproduced here nearly verbatim.

¶ xx. *Another Death*

… *pit full of fire* – when young Jane is asked by the Reverend Brocklehurst what hell is, she replies, 'A pit full of fire' (*Jane Eyre*, I:IV). Also used as the title of Volume III, Chapter XXXI of *Oblivion*.

… *the guide and director of all the happy days connected with my childhood* – Branwell to Francis Grundy, 29th October 1842; the general thrust of this entry and a few other precise expressions come from this letter, as well as one dated 25th October, also to Grundy.

… *a somewhat higher and more ancient family* … *not purse-proud tradespeople or arrogant upstarts* – from *Agnes Grey*, VI.

… *superficially attractive* – although not an exact reproduction, Anne's speech here owe's a great deal to Agnes's description of the Murrays in *Agnes Grey*, VII.

¶ xxi. *Two Sisters, Two Conversations*

I have a profound admiration for you – letter from Constantin Heger to Patrick Brontë, 5th November 1842.

Bewick's History of British Birds – this is the book young Jane is reading in the opening pages of *Jane Eyre*; Branwell's thoughts and at times exact wording in this conversation with Charlotte come from an article he published on 1st October 1841 in the *Halifax Guardian* under his pseudonym Northangerland.

… a writer who loved more to dwell upon Indian palm groves or genii palaces than on the wooded manors and cloudy skies of England – Branwell, in 'Angria and the Angrians', December 1837.

But at least a man is free – 'un homme au moins est libre', from Flaubert's *Madame Bovary* (1857), II:III.

The 'yes' was uttered with closed teeth and seemed to express the sentiment, 'Go to the Devil!' – this is how Heathcliff welcomes Lockwood in the opening chapter of *Wuthering Heights*: 'The "walk in" was uttered with closed teeth and expressed the sentiment, "Go to the Deuce!"' (I:I).

… a perfect misanthropist's Heaven! – this is again Lockwood, in the opening lines of *Wuthering Heights*, I:I.

In Brussels we were isolated in the midst of numbers – Charlotte to Ellen Nussey, May 1842.

… divide the desolation amongst us – Lockwood once more, in *Wuthering Heights*, I:I.

… like a devouring flame on the kitchen floor – Charlotte to Emily, letter of 1st October 1843.

¶ XXII. *Thorp Green*

… was a wild, tempestuous day, with a strong north wind and a continual storm of snow drifting on the ground and whirling through the air … impediments in the way of both horses and steam engines – from *Agnes Grey*, VII.

She is positively beautiful – Branwell's description of young Lydia comes directly from Anne's fictional Rosalie Murray, in *Agnes Grey*, VII.

… she requires neither rouge nor padding to add to her charms – Branwell's description of the elder Lydia is a blending of Mrs Murray from Chapter VII of *Agnes Grey* and Branwell's lost letter of May 1843, to John Brown (as quoted via extracts made by Lord Houghton in 1859, per Barker).

… climax of horror – from *Agnes Grey*, XII: 'Climax of horror! actually waiting for their governess!!'

¶ XXIV. *Two Ladies*

Are you in better health and spirits and does Anne continue to be pretty well? – Charlotte's letter to Branwell of 1st May 1843 is given here with only a few alternations of punctuation.

¶ XXV. *On the Banks of the Ouse*

'You,' I say, 'a favourite of Mrs Robinson? You of importance to her in any way? Go! Your folly sickens me! How dare you? Poor stupid dupe! Blind puppy!' – a transposition of Jane's thoughts about Mr Rochester, in *Jane Eyre*, II:II.

… those hypocrites who would use it to justify their own place in heaven, while flinging others into Hell – in *Wuthering Heights*, I:V, Nelly describes Joseph as 'the wearisomest, self-righteous pharisee that ever ransacked a Bible to rake the promises to himself and fling the curses on his neighbours'.

¶ XVIII. *Standing on the Precipice*

I grew weary and writhed, yawned, nodded, pinched and pricked myself, and rubbed my eyes – Branwell's words here are inspired by Lockwood's dream of the Reverend Jabes Branderham's sermon in *Wuthering Heights*, I:III.

As Paul says in his Letter to the Hebrews – unlike Patrick's funeral sermon for Weightman, this 'dream sermon' is pure invention.

… a righteous man regardeth the life of his beast – Agnes slightly misquotes Proverbs 12:10 to Mrs Bloomfield in *Agnes Grey*, V: 'The merciful man shows mercy to his beast.'

… plunging headlong into wild license – Rochester's words in *Jane Eyre*, III:I.

¶ I. *The Pleasures of the Flesh*

'You love me, then?' said she, fervently pressing my hand – Lydia uses the same words as Edward Weston, in the final pages of *Agnes Grey*, XXV. Clearly there is not a little irony here, since Lydia will never tell Branwell that she loves *him*, and their relationship is above all else one of mutual sexual gratification.

Ann Marshall, who surely already knows enough to hang me – from the missing letter to John Brown referenced above, quoted in Lord Houghton's Commonplace Book, per Barker.

¶ II. *Scarborough*

... the broad, bright bay ... wings on my feet – much of the description of Scarborough, as well as Anne and Branwell's own reflections, come directly from the final two chapters of *Agnes Grey*, XXIV–XXV.

'I feel so old – that I could not be flatter or older of mind if I lived to the age of eighty! – towards the end of her diary paper of 31st July 1845, Anne will use this phrase: 'I for my part cannot well be flatter or older in mind than I am now.'

... troubled pleasure soon chastised by fear – Branwell will use this Homeric phrase in a letter to Grundy in October 1845.

You needn't strangle me for that! – Edgar says to Catherine, of her unrestrained glee at Heathcliff's return, 'don't strangle me for that!' in *Wuthering Heights*, I:X.

¶ III. *Leyland in York*

... taille d'athlète – French for 'athletic build', as in *Jane Eyre*, I:XIV.

I detest that man – a disillusioned Lady Ashby (née Rosalie Murry) says this of her husband in *Agnes Grey*, XXIII.

Servants are mere automatons ... It would be a pretty thing indeed, would it not, if our actions were to be dictated by our servants! – slightly modified version of comments made by Lady Ashby in *Agnes Grey*, XXII.

If finite power can do this, how great God's infinite power must be! – Ellen Nussey reports that the historical Anne said something quite similar in her final visit to York Minster – although shortness of breath prevented her from completing the sentence – just days before her death in Scarborough in late May 1849 (*Reminiscences*, 1871).

¶ IV. *A Jealous Husband*

'Kiss me once more, then,' said I, 'for minding so well' – near the end of *Wuthering Heights*, in II:XVIII, Lockwood overhears Hareton say something quite similar to young Catherine, as she gives him his lessons in reading and proper diction.

Would to God it could do so legally! – this and some wording that follows comes from the now missing May 1843 letter to John Brown, previously referenced.

... close and resolute dissemblers – a phrase from *Agnes Grey*, XVII.

¶ V. *The Three Virgins of Haworth*

Surely no mother in her right mind would consent to sending her precious little girls to live in such a wilderness as that – the historical Charlotte will echo her fictional brother's words in a letter to Ellen Nussey, in August 1844, but this passage also recalls Nelly Dean's comment to Heathcliff, about failing to take care of his new bride Isabella ('in such a wilderness as this', i.e., Wuthering Heights), in *Wuthering Heights*, I:XIV.

... rather be a housemaid or kitchen-girl, than a baited, trampled, desolate, distracted governess! – Charlotte to William Smith Williams, letter of 12th May 1848.

¶ VI. *The Ball*

The Ball – title of Chapter IX of *Agnes Grey*.

At eighteen, Miss Robinson has emerged from the quiet obscurity of the schoolroom into the full blaze of the fashionable world – this chapter of *Oblivion* is by far the most extensive verbatim, or slightly adapted, use of a Brontë text, including a few lines from Chapter VIII – The 'Coming Out' and a great deal from Chapter

IX – The Ball. Here the names have been changed and the entire story is narrated by Anne, for Branwell's entertainment.

Where will we all be in a few years, and what changes will we have seen and known? – these words echo the style of Anne's diary papers, for example that of 31st July 1845: 'I wonder how we shall all be and where and how situated on the thirtieth of July 1848 when if we are all alive Emily will be just "30" I shall be in my 29th year Charlotte in her 33rd and Branwell in his 32nd and what changes shall we have seen and known and shall we be much changed ourselves?'

¶ VII. *Lessons*

Lessons – Chapters II and III of *Agnes Grey* are called 'First Lessons in the Art of Instruction' and 'A Few More Lessons', respectively.

... it is not proper... no friends to take care of her – from *Agnes Grey*, XIV.

bad animal – John Reed memorably refers to Jane as a 'bad animal' in *Jane Eyre*, I:I.

... as if Charlotte were me, and I were her – this clearly recalls Catherine's famous 'Nelly, I am Heathcliff!' in *Wuthering Heights*, I:IX.

¶ VIII. *Amor Vincit Omnia*

I would be afraid of nothing. Together we could brave Satan and all his legions – such is the Miltonic comment Lockwood, grumbling, makes upon seeing Hareton and young Catherine together in the final chapter of *Wuthering Heights* (II:XX): 'They are afraid of nothing ... Together they would brave Satan and all his legions.'

¶ IX. *Interlude: A Picnic with the Brontë Sisters*

Emily, it is true, does not like teaching much – several of Charlotte's comments throughout this passage are adapted from her letter of 24th July 1844, to Constantin Heger.

... had gathered up the fragments, knives, dishes, etc., and restored

them to our basket – from Anne Brontë's *The Tenant of Wildfell Hall* (hereafter, *Tenant*), I:VII.

... *sometimes in the highest spirits* – the fictional Branwell's description of his conduct here is based on a passage in the first edition (1857) of Elizabeth Gaskell's *Life of Charlotte Brontë*, I:XIII.

¶ x. *Enter Mr Roxby*

... *my discreet, matronly role* – 'Well, your mama thinks you ought not to go beyond the park or garden without some discreet, matronly person like me to accompany you, and keep off all intruders', from *Agnes Grey*, XIV.

... *she would never be so foolish as to fall in love* – Rosalie Murray says famously, 'Oh! It prokes me so – To think that I could be such a fool as to fall in *Love*! I detest the word!' (*Agnes Grey*, XIV). The comparison of her to a cruel little boy is inspired by Tom Bloomfield's sadistic antics earlier in the same novel.

... *it is foolish to wish for beauty, and that sensible people never either desire it for themselves or care about it in others* – from *Agnes Grey*, XVII.

Oh, Mama's so tiresome! As if I couldn't take care of myself! – this is again Rosalie Murray, from *Agnes Grey*, XIV.

'Do, pray, Miss Brontë,' said she, 'try not to be so touchy! There's no speaking to you else' – this remark, as well as the comment about 'half a mother's watchfulness – half a mother's anxious care' are from Mrs Murray in *Agnes Grey*, XIV.

¶ xii. *Love and Treachery at Scarborough Castle*

... *sleepers in that quiet earth* – the final words of Emily's *Wuthering Heights* (II:XX).

... *the fool's craving to hear evil of self that haunts some people like a demon* – the elder Catherine (Earnshaw) Linton in *Wuthering Heights*, I:XI.

¶ xiii. *A Letter for Mr Roxby*

... *make inclination bow to duty* – these and some of the words that follow are from *Agnes Grey*, VII.

... she has some tiresome opinions, always thinking of what is right and what is wrong, and has a strange reverence for matters connected with religion – from *Agnes Grey*, VII.

... a fine bundle of trash, good enough to be printed as a novel – Nelly says this of young Catherine and Linton Heathcliff's 'love letters' in *Wuthering Heights*, II:VII.

... the aspect of the place would frighten her ... We have no present intention however of breaking our hearts on the subject ... an additional knowledge of the world – Charlotte's words, which Branwell gives in italics here, are taken directly from her letters to Ellen Nussey of 2nd October and 14th November 1844.

¶ XIV. *Worldly Wisdom*

... forfeit every fraction of her inheritance – slightly adapted from *Agnes Grey*, I.

... such a fool as to fall in love – again, *Agnes Grey*, XIV.

... enwrapped by a cloak of deceit – Branwell to Joseph Leyland, 10th September 1845. Also one of the epigraphs to Volume III.

... destined by the pressures of worldly interests – this dialogue, including a number of sentences transcribed verbatim, merges language from a letter of Mary Taylor to Charlotte of 5th April 1850 with a later recollection of the friends' discussion of this same topic, provided by Mary to Charlotte's first biographer, Elizabeth Gaskell, in a letter of 18th January 1856.

Have you been listening at the door, Branwell? – Catherine says to Edgar Linton, 'Have you been listening at the door, Edgar?' in *Wuthering Heights*, I:XI.

¶ XV. *The Valentine*

It's a g-g-gospel for our age – I have anachronistically placed the Scottish novelist Margaret Oliphant's words into Bellerby's mouth here. After the death of Dickens, she recalled that the book had been viewed as a 'new gospel' upon its publication in 1843. For all his disdain of the author of *A Christmas Carol*, Branwell unwittingly echoes the narrator's final comments about Ebenezer Scrooge who 'did it all, and infinitely more', when he goes on to say, 'Bellerby did it all, and had it all'.

... *smoking a meditative pipe* – when Lockwood returns to Thrushcross Grange at the end of *Wuthering Heights*, he discovers that Nelly Dean is gone, replaced by 'an old woman ... smoking a meditative pipe' (II:XVIII).

¶ XVII. *Anne's Discovery*

Off ye lendings! – Rochester famously makes this allusion to King Lear as he steps out of his disguise as a gypsy fortune teller in *Jane Eyre*, II:IV.

... *at least long enough to see the rooms decked out and hear the music, and above all see her in her splendid new dress* – from Rosalie Murray's 'coming out' in *Agnes Grey*, VIII.

Peace, peace now – in her Preface to the second edition of *Tenant*, Anne Brontë writes that 'if there were less of this delicate concealment of facts – this whispering of "Peace, peace," when there is no peace, there would be less of sin and misery to the young of both sexes who are left to wring their bitter knowledge from experience.'

... *seen life* – 'and as for my son – if I thought he would grow up to be what you call a man of the world – one that has "*seen life*," and glories in his experience ... I would rather that he die to-morrow! – rather a thousand times!' So says Helen in *Tenant*, I:III.

... *inexhaustible organs of speech* – the expression is Anne's, in *Tenant*, I:IV.

I hate to be lectured – so does Gilbert Markham, as he tells his mother in *Tenant*, I:IV.

Miss Brontë may be a queer creature – 'Miss Grey was a queer creature ... she was always thinking of what was right and what was wrong,' says Agnes, at once assuming and lampooning the perspective of her pupils, the Murray sisters, in *Agnes Grey*, VII.

¶ XVIII. *Rendezvous en plein air*

... *the Ouse is running swift and high* – the historical young Edmund (Ned) Robinson drowned in the River Ure in 1869.

Tell me, don't you love your husband still – a little? – this scandalous outdoor scene, and some of its most shocking language, are taken directly or slightly adapted from *Tenant*, II:XXXIII.

¶ XIX. *Mankind's Disgusting Ways*

Mankind's Disgusting Ways – as we learn in this chapter, Anne Brontë wrote the words 'sick of mankind and their disgusting ways' in miniature handwriting in the back cover of her prayer book.

I now felt a violent tug of sympathy, as if there existed an eternal, inner cord of communion between their hearts and mine – Rochester uses these words in *Jane Eyre*, II:VIII.

… *as if they were machines without feelings* – from Jane's famous speech in *Jane Eyre*, II:VIII.

… *thought more of his only son than of his daughters* – from Charlotte's letter of 2nd October 1848, written to William Smith Williams in the wake of Branwell's death.

… *a very convenient doctrine for the stronger sex, don't you think?* – Gilbert Markham makes a similar comment to his mother, in a humorous vein, in *Tenant*, I:VI.

… *spare yourself the trouble of foreswearing yourself and racking your brains to stifle truth with falsehood* – this paragraph owes a great deal to *Tenant*, II:XXXIII, where Helen discovers and confronts Arthur's infidelity.

At Thorp Green I have had such unpleasant and undreamt-of experiences of human nature – Anne's diary paper of 31st July 1845, quoted as another epigraph to Volume III.

… *if you choose to make a beast of yourself* – in *Tenant*, II:XXIII.

… *if I hate the sin, I love the sinner* – young Helen Graham, in the context of her infatuation with Arthur Huntingdon, makes a similar declaration to her sceptical aunt in *Tenant*, II:XVII. This Christian commonplace is usually credited to Saint Augustine: *Cum dilectione hominum et odio vitiorum* (Letter 211, c. 424). Gandhi would later use it in his 1929 autobiography.

¶ XX. *A Railway Journey to Scarborough*

… *any man who ruffled her humour* – as noted previously, this expression comes from *Wuthering Heights*, I:X.

¶ XXI. *Torn Asunder*

… *discovered my proceedings* … *to break off instantly and forever all communication with every member of his family* – paraphrase from Gaskell's *Life of Charlotte Brontë*, XIII.

¶ XXII. *Love and Duty*

… *that eunuch-like fellow, that bloodless mock-husband* – Branwell, in his letter to Francis Grundy, October 1845.

… *rectitude of conduct and resignation point out the straightest road from this world to the next* – ironically, these words come from Maria Thurston, in the Angrian tale Branwell revised as his unfinished novel, *And the Weary Are at Rest*, when she is tempted to betray her marriage vows.

… *brave Satan and all his legions* – as in the previous example, this Miltonic expression is taken from the concluding chapter of *Wuthering Heights*.

… *two bodies fused into one, kindling in pure, powerful flame* – compare with Charlotte's own words, reminiscent of Shelley, and spoken by Rochester, in *Jane Eyre*, III:I: 'a solemn passion is conceived in my heart … and, kindling in pure, powerful flame, fuses you and me in one.'

… *when body and soul rise in mutiny* – *Jane Eyre*, III:I.

… *because I am poor, obscure, plain and little* – Jane's celebrated speech in *Jane Eyre*, II:VIII.

¶ XXIII. *Crosby in Harrogate*

… *while roasting daily and nightly over a slow fire* – a number of Branwell's comments here and in the paragraphs that follow, concerning both his own work-in-progress and the genre in general, come from his oft-quoted letter to Leyland, 10th September 1845.

… *constant mental exhaustion, which arises from brooding on matters useless at present to think of* – letter to Leyland, 25th November 1845.

¶ XXIV. *Publications*

… *my late employer shrank from the bare idea of my being able to write anything* – the content, including some precise wording, of much of this entry is taken from the same letter to Leyland, 25th November 1845.

… you hate the sin but love the sinner – as above, from *Tenant*, II:XVII.

Every faculty, both good and bad, strengthens by exercise – this dialogue between Charlotte and Branwell owes much, including some literal transciption, to the conversation between Helen and Arthur Huntingdon in Anne's *Tenant*, II:XXIII.

In your weakness and depression you have made it your medicine and support, your comforter, your recreation, your friend – this passage owes a great deal to *Tenant*, II:XXX.

Emily said you were a 'hopeless being' – Charlotte quotes Emily thus in a letter to Ellen Nussey, written 3rd March 1846, the precise date of Branwell's diary entry here.

I must have pleasure … I cannot withstand any temptation to get out of myself – this sentence combines Rochester's sentiments in *Jane Eyre*, I:XIV ('I have a right to get pleasure out of life: and I *will* get it, cost what it may') and Branwell's own letter to Leyland of 28th April 1846.

¶ XXV. *Mother and Child*

… pestered by the small but countless botherments, which like mosquitoes sting us in the world of workday toil – Branwell to Leyland, 24th January 1847. Given the centrality of this theme to *Oblivion*, it is worth quoting the passage in question here at slightly greater length: 'I had reason to hope that ere very long I should be the husband of a Lady whom I loved best in the world and with whom, in more than competence, I might live at leisure to make myself a name in the world of posterity, without being pestered by the small but countless botherments, which like mosquitoes sting us in the world of workday toil. That hope, and herself are gone …'

No namby-pamby, no sentimental, religious twaddle here – similar language was used in a positive review of the Brontë sisters' own *Poems* (*The Critic*, 4th July 1846, cited in Barker).

¶ XXVI. *Boundless Hope, Eternal Despair*

...the streets and storefronts of Haworth painted with their blood – an echo of the teenage Heathcliff, who imagines having 'the privilege of flinging Joseph off the highest gable, and painting the house-front with Hindley's blood' in *Wuthering Heights*, I:VI.

When I mentioned your name ... she stared at me and fainted – the historical Branwell paraphrased the actual communication he had received from Crosby in a letter to Joseph Leyland, written in the summer of 1846.

I am too hard to die and too wretched to live ... a martyr wishes to be bound to the stake – Branwell to Leyland, June 1846.

¶ XXVII. *The Woeful Impotence of Weak Resolve*

The Woeful Impotence of Weak Resolve – the fictional Hartley Coleridge's description of himself in *Oblivion* (see note above).

... the mountain to come to Mahomet – Francis Bacon's phrase is used in both Charlotte's *Jane Eyre* (I:XII) and Anne's *Tenant* (I:II).

The right path ... is that which necessitates the greatest sacrifice of self-interest and leads to the greatest good of others – Charlotte to Ellen Nussey, 10th July 1846.

... the initial shabbiness of my behaviour on such occasions – these words about Branwell are in fact Charlotte's, in a letter to Ellen Nussey of 13th December 1846.

¶ XVIII. *Death, Departure, Despair*

... the sky looks like ice – the description of the weather and the state of Patrick and Anne's health comes from Charlotte's same letter of 13th December 1846.

... to return my letter – several of the paragraphs that follow come directly, at times verbatim, from Branwell's letter to Leyland of 24th January 1847.

If I am forever barred from happiness, I will try and get pleasure where I can find it – as above, these words are inspired by Rochester, from *Jane Eyre*, I:XIV.

... betrayed her own heart ... it would degrade her to marry me – two key phrases from *Wuthering Heights*, of course, in II:I and

I:IX, respectively.

… *gone like a dream* – a phrase used more than once by Charlotte Brontë, including references to her own youth, but perhaps most memorably to speak of her siblings, in her moving letter to William Smith Williams of 13th June 1849, written two weeks after Anne's death.

… *lived more in my time at Thorp Green alone than they have in the whole course of their existence, or will to the end of their days, if they numbered a hundred years!* – slightly adapted from Arthur Huntingdon's remarks to Helen in *Tenant*, III:XXX.

… *cheerful company does me good till some bitter truth blazes through my brain, at which point I would gladly receive the gift of a bullet to the temple* – letter to Leyland, 16th July 1846.

… *an infernal fire in my veins, that all the waters of the ocean cannot quench* – Arthur Huntingdon's words, in *Tenant*, II:XXX.

¶ XXIX. *Three Novels*

… *tell Mrs Sugden of the Talbot that I considered her conduct towards me during my 'illness' as most kind and motherly, and that if I did anything to offend her, I deeply regret it* – Branwell's letter to Leyland, 9th January 1848.

… *as flat and pedestrian … as a pavement* – Flaubert memorably calls Charles Bovary's conversation 'plate comme un trottoir de rue' in I:VII of *Madame Bovary* (1857).

¶ XXX. *The Three Genii*

The Three Genii – this alludes to the four Brontë children as the presiding creative spirits or 'Chief Genii' of their early juvenilia: Brannii, Tallii, Emmii and Annii. The genii here are, of course, limited to Charlotte, Emily and Anne.

¶ XXXI. *A Pit Full of Fire*

A Pit Full of Fire – as noted earlier, this phrase is from *Jane Eyre*, I:IV. Since Branwell's recent reading of his sisters' novels has inspired his entire dream, the notes that follow indicate only where I have used exact wording without a clear reference to those texts.

I kicked and trampled on him, and dashed his head repeatedly – from *Wuthering Heights*, II:III.

... how very black and cross you look! And how – how funny and grim! – so says Cathy to Heathcliff, when she returns from Thrushcross Grange transformed into 'a very dignified person' in *Wuthering Heights*, I:VII.

... like the rocks beneath ... a source of little visible delight, but necessary – in *Wuthering Heights*, I:IX.

'Wake! Wake!' I cried – this passage owes a great deal, including some exact language, to Jane's dramatic rescue of Rochester in *Jane Eyre*, I:XV.

Thou art the man! cried Jabes – Lockwood's dream in *Wuthering Heights*, I:III.

I do love the old man, for he does, and always has done, his best for me – paraphrased from Elizabeth Gaskell's third-hand report, in her *Life of Charlotte Brontë*.

¶ XXXII. *The End of All*

The End of All – as mentioned in Chapter XVIII of *Oblivion*, Branwell published a poem – a revision of a much older work – with this title, in the *Halifax Guardian* in June 1847.

Nicholson has sent Papa a demand for settlement ... I am RUINED – much of this brief entry in Branwell's diary, including some verbatim language, comes from his letter to Leyland, 22nd June 1848.

My mental wretchedness and corporeal weakness utterly prevent me from doing anything – from the same letter of 22nd June 1848.

When I was a lad, I was fond of saying: you have only to WILL a thing in order to get it – paraphrased from Ellen Nussey's *Reminiscences* of 1871.

ACKNOWLEDGEMENTS

Writers do not exist in isolation and their works do not emerge *ex nihilo*, and *Oblivion: The Lost Diaries of Branwell Brontë* is no exception. It is my great pleasure here to thank those who have had, in one way or another, a hand in helping to bring the novel into being. A colleague once told me that in thanking large numbers of people one will inevitably forget – and in so doing possibly anger or hurt – someone else. Still, I do not think that such danger should prevent one from making the effort, any more than the knowledge that one can never fully realise one's artistic vision should keep one from trying to do so. I sincerely hope that anyone who is not specifically named in the paragraphs that follow will still accept my general thanks if she or he had anything, directly or indirectly, to do with the creation of this book.

Oblivion has scholarly underpinnings, and although I do not feel the need to create a formal bibliography here, I must note that Juliet Barker's authoritative study *The Brontës* first introduced me to Branwell's story; it remains the single greatest influence on the shape and structure of my novel, and my copies of both the first and second editions of her work, not to mention a Kindle version, are the most highlighted, dog-eared and bookmarked texts in my library. All these years later, I remain grateful for her inspiration, as well as for her initial, encouraging correspondence in 1999. A year later I entered university administration and shelved my project for nearly fifteen years, but I continued to read works both by and about the Brontë family whenever time permitted, with the intention that I would one day write the novel you have before you.

While this is not an exhaustive list of all of the sources I have consulted, other works of particular importance in the creation of Branwell's universe were Barker's own *The Brontës: A Life in Letters*; Margaret Smith's three-volume edition of *The Letters of Charlotte Brontë*; *The Leyland Manuscripts* (from the Brotherton Collection, Leeds); Daphne du Maurier's *The Infernal World of*

Branwell Brontë; Francis Leyland's *The Brontë Family, with Special Reference to Patrick Branwell Brontë*; and Francis Grundy's *Pictures of the Past*. These last two authors, who appear as minor characters in *Oblivion*, wrote many decades after Branwell's death, and their accounts are to be treated with caution, despite their great interest. Similarly, Elizabeth Gaskell's *Life of Charlotte Brontë* is both highly engaging and frequently unreliable. I am grateful to Barker (once again) and to Lucasta Miller (in *The Brontë Myth*) for providing critical perspective on Mrs Gaskell's complex legacy. In a completely different vein, Raymond Bellour's 'Vivre à deux', which appears as a 'postface' in a French edition of *Wuthering Heights* (*Hurlevent*, Folio 2015), is a metafictional (and, indeed, metacritical) essay ostensibly 'written' (posthumously, in French no less!) by Branwell; it is an especially suggestive meditation on the theme of incest flowing just beneath the surface of *Oblivion* and only bursting fully into view in the climactic 'A Pit Full of Fire' chapter, as part of Branwell's opium dream.

As should be clear from the 'Notes to *Oblivion*', equally or perhaps even more important are the many primary texts inspiring and at times woven directly into the fabric of the novel. These include the poems of the Brontës, especially Branwell's, where I relied heavily on Victor A. Neufeldt's indispensable three-volume *Works of Patrick Branwell Brontë*. The other texts that loom large are the novels of the *annus mirabilis* of 1847 (Anne's *Agnes Grey*, Charlotte's *Jane Eyre* and Emily's *Wuthering Heights*), as well as Anne's second novel, *The Tenant of Wildfell Hall*, published the following year. These and other primary texts are, when silently transposed or adapted in the narrative of *Oblivion*, dutifully credited in the 'Notes', though it is possible that a brief phrase or two escaped my attempt to create an exhaustive list.

Many reference works were of service, perhaps none more than *The Oxford Companion to the Brontës*, edited by Christine Alexander and Margaret Smith. Finally, it is important to acknowledge that the Internet offered a breathtaking wealth of information, as it does to all writers today. Innumerable details of the novel (to give just two examples, the detailed programme of the concert in Halifax and the spread of the railways across Yorkshire in the early 1840s) were the result of my online research, which was at times rapid and focused; at others, though leisurely and even random, it led serendipitously to the unexpected incorporation of what would become important, even essential, components of my tale (e.g., the words to John Orlando Parry's 'Wanted, A Governess' or Franz Liszt's improvisations).

In something akin to the proverbial message in a bottle, I decided quite late in the editing process to see if I might find more accurate information about Sunny Bank, the farm near Broughton-in-Furness where Agnes Riley and her parents were employed as agricultural labourers. Graham Brooks of the Cumbria Local History Federation replied almost immediately, collating members' responses to my enquiry. I am grateful to all the individuals who took the time to look into this matter, but none more so than Colin Robertshaw of Broughton-in-Furness itself and a member of the Duddon Valley Local History Group. Colin not only discovered the name of the farmer at Sunny Bank, Moses Tyson; he spent countless hours researching the fate of the 'real' Agnes Riley and her family; walked the roads, lanes and paths in and about Broughton and beyond, taking notes and photographs; created, compiled and forwarded maps and satellite images, as well as birth, death and census records; and finally, kindly read the 'Broughton section' as well as the much later chapter featuring Tyson in Halifax and provided advice of a historical, linguistic and logical (i.e., plot-related) nature. He was even able to inform me that the osprey would have disappeared from Hartley Coleridge's neighbourhood by 1840 (though it would later be reintroduced), and so at his suggestion it was replaced by the grey heron. Another of Colin's remarks in our many email exchanges further inspired me to add a few words from Wordsworth's *The River Duddon*, sonnet XXXII ('peace of heart' and 'calm of mind and soul'), to the end of Volume I, Chapter III of *Oblivion*. I would also like to thank Liz Kerrey of the Cumbria Local History Federation, who originally circulated the request whose replies were compiled by Graham Brooks, and who later carried out an independent check on the records of the Riley family. The specificity and historical accuracy of the early chapters of the novel owe a great deal to these good people, while any errors clearly remain my own.

As it is for so many scholars and writers, the Brontë Parsonage Museum was a priceless resource. The years of my novel's composition and revisions corresponded precisely to the period in which the museum was planning and executing its *Brontë 200* celebrations, and yet its team never failed to respond quickly and graciously to even the most minute or arcane questions about Branwell and his family. My thanks go to the entire institution, but certain individuals – some no longer there – deserve special recognition: Lynne Howell and Amy Rowbottom, for their general kindness and responsiveness; Linda Pierson, for her detailed responses on everything from midges to dandelions, from modes of transport to the prevalence of cattle and sheep on the moors in the Brontës' day; Linda Ling, who posted a link to the earlier 'online pandemic version' of *Oblivion* in the members' area of the museum's website; Sarah Laycock, for her many kindnesses, including a memorable hour we spent together in Haworth in late May 2016, looking at, among other treasures, Branwell's wallet, his 'Luddenden Foot' notebook and the poem he wrote to Grundy on railway stationery; and finally, the incomparable and indefatigable Ann Dinsdale, who despite her overwhelming responsibilities – which of late have included keeping the museum going in the midst of a global pandemic – has always found time to answer the questions of an unknown first-time novelist with patience, grace, speed and scholarly rigour, including one about the history of Haworth street names as recently as mid-2021, as this book was going through its final edits.

Certain colleagues past and present at Salve Regina University in Newport, Rhode Island, deserve special thanks, including former president Jane Gerety; director of library services Dawn Emsellem-Wichowski and her entire staff, especially Genna Duplisea, who provided detailed information on the work of archivists for a modern-day 'prologue' to the novel (though it was ultimately eliminated from the manuscript, I remain grateful to her); and Ryan Tillett of the copy centre, who came to the rescue at a critical moment, when my own printer would not function.

Much of this book was written in France, and I have a number of friends there to thank for their generosity, hospitality and support: in Poitiers, Mme Odile Collas and the extended Collas-Griffiths clan; in Saint-Georges-lès-Baillargeaux, François Martin, Claudine Maës and their families; and finally, Bernard and Mauricette Passedroit, who made available as a writer's retreat not one but two homes in 2016, the first in Saint-Nazaire-sur-Charente and the second in Savennières, in the Loire Valley. The daily experience of living and speaking entirely in French and yet *writing* in English – and a very peculiar English at that – is one I will never forget. Many thanks as well to Terry Jacome, subletter extraordinaire, who for several consecutive summers permitted me the peace of mind to leave behind my life in Newport and wholeheartedly pursue my writing and editing in France, and to my delightful flatmate in Poitiers, Chérine Fouad, who kept me company and helped me celebrate the completion of the book's first draft.

In 2019, my former classmate Fiona Doloughan graciously invited me to give a talk and reading from *Oblivion* in London, as part of the Open University's seminar series on 'Life Stories'. I am grateful to her and her colleagues for the opportunity, and to her and her partner Regine Hampel for their boundless hospitality at their homes in both Newnham and Westward Ho! I cherish our renewed friendship and appreciate their enthusiastic support of my efforts to be published in the United Kingdom.

Several people read the novel in its entirety before its publication. I am grateful to them all: Melissa Davis, for her detailed feedback and genuine enthusiasm; Andrew Snook, who gamely took a first crack at rooting out Americanisms and made many other helpful comments; and Simon Donoghue, who convinced me that the book had the potential to reach a wider audience. When the COVID-19 pandemic struck early in 2020, I resolved to do yet another close edit of the novel and post it for friends to read, which I did from March to June of that year. Heartfelt thanks to those who read the entire book online – no small feat – and who thereafter strongly encouraged me to pursue traditional publication: in California, my dear friends Kimberly Severson and Matt and Teri Rowan; in Rhode Island, my *cher ami* Peter Baylor; in North Carolina, my former colleague and *lieber Freund* Dave Limburg.

Others who have read portions of *Oblivion* or are familiar with the project and have been consistently supportive include (in no particular order and with apologies to anyone who may be unintentionally omitted here): Oriana Federico, Alex Evans and Kitty Guptill, Lenny and Christine Mendonca, Dave and Karen Goldstein, Art and Candy Frankel, Matt Ramsey, Roxanne Snook, Deb Curtis, Jen McClanaghan, Andy Padlo, Merna Chance, Laura Limburg, Scott Severson, Debbie Donoghue, Liz Fields, Gretchen Van Dyke, Sarah Rock, Marion Gayraud, Emmanuel Sanséau, Julie Leriche, Melanie Walton and Elena Soini, Esther Alarcón-Arana and Norman Rusin, Claire and Emmanuel Dary, Aida and Tim Neary, Rosie and Craig Condella, Mike and Bobbi Warren, James Mitchell, Emily Colbert Cairns, Deb Cherubini, Mike Grandchamp, Taten Shirley, Mary-Gail Smith, Erin Fitzgerald, Jeff Stone, Sarah Marlien, Patricia García, Michael Budd, Cheryl Morgan, Mariann Maida, Jackie Brooks and Heather Axen.

A very special word of thanks is due to Mathilde Tollet, fellow lover of the nineteenth century, not only for her constant encouragement as I was editing the novel and seeking a publisher, but for sharing with me a memorable, almost weekly, bilingual 'pandemic bubble', filled with a great deal of food, drink, laughter, and the occasional serious discussion, during the first COVID-19 lockdown. If I retained a shred of sanity after the collective planetary ordeal that was 2020, it was partly thanks to her friendship.

Each spring I teach a first-year writing-intensive course on the Brontës, *Scribblemania: The Brontës and the Passion of Writing*. I am grateful to my students for their enthusiasm, which annually reminds me that the Brontës' works, written in the 1840s and 1850s, continue to speak directly and urgently to our most vital human emotions and societal concerns, well into the twenty-first century. Three former students in particular must be thanked by name: Effie Gianitsos, whose paper on love as religion in *Wuthering Heights* may well, I realise now, have subconsciously influenced Branwell's remark that 'love itself is the true religion' of that novel; Meg Parham for her enduring friendship, warm encouragement and a memorable photo shoot in Seattle in June 2021; and Casey Donahue for her infectious enthusiasm, delightful madness, genuine kindness and much-needed assistance with the intricacies of social media.

I am doubly fortunate to have an editor who is a student of Victorian literature and lives on 'the tops' near Haworth itself. Sarah Meaney has helped transform *Oblivion* into a text suitable for publication in the United Kingdom, and in so doing has taught me a great deal about everything from the difference between 'em' and 'en' dashes to British spelling, and from the finer points of authentic Yorkshire and Irish idioms to the proper colour of the Parsonage's bricks. More important than any of those specific minutiae, has been her general, sustained attention to detail as we worked together to make the final version of the novel the best it could be. Perhaps most impressive, however, has been her almost superhuman patience and constant good humour in the face of my all-too-frequent, compulsive bursts of perfectionism. Through my partnership with Sarah, I have not only realised a dream; I have gained a friend.

I could not be more grateful to Jamie McGarry and his team at Valley Press, especially book designer Peter Barnfather, for this work would not be in your hands, dear Reader, without their willingness to take a chance on such an audacious project – an ambitious, sprawling novel that tries to be many things to many audiences. I am delighted that *Oblivion* is appearing in Scarborough, where several of its important scenes take place, and where my favourite Brontë sister, Anne, is buried high above the sands she walked so long ago as the governess to the Robinsons.

Although I met her late in the process, the marvellous Mathilde Mauguière has become perhaps *Oblivion*'s greatest champion. I will do my best to see the book into French translation someday, Mathilde – *je te promets*.

Finally, I will be forever grateful to my parents, Glenn and Myrna de la Motte, for the gift of their work ethic and the example of their love of family, as well as their boundless support throughout my life, regardless of what they themselves might have thought or done in my place. Thanks also to my siblings and their spouses: Mark and Laura de la Motte, Daren and Bob Schadt, and Matt and Susie de la Motte, for their unconditional love for, and unwavering support of, the 'baby' of the family.

Branwell learns all too late that 'though I speak with the tongues of men and angels, and have not love, I am become as sounding brass, or a tinkling cymbal'. I give final thanks to my own children, Maria Johanna de la Motte and William Paul de la Motte, for teaching me, in their childhood, this and a multitude of other lessons. As adults and friends, they continue to delight, astonish and inspire me. This book is dedicated to them.